The Outsiders

The Outsiders

by Robert Carson

Little, Brown and Company · Boston · Toronto

Published simultaneously in Canada
by Little, Brown & Company (Canada) Limited

PRINTED IN THE UNITED STATES OF AMERICA

To Harry Sions, with gratitude and affection

PART ONE
Queen of the Cow Counties

one

CASS BRENNAN walked up to his uncle's house, a little sweaty from hurrying.

It was a September morning. Quiet lay in the air. There was a smell of gathering heat, of dust, of prickly dry vegetation floating on a whisper of wind, of horse droppings; of cesspools, water on lawns and flowers, hot irons pressed to starched linen, leather, wood fires, cooking, and cologne.

The two-story wooden house of Lucius Brennan on a corner of Sixth Street lay considerably westward of the main body of Los Angeles, just where the hills were beginning to rise. There were few neighboring dwellings. It was a comfortable sprawling place, surrounded by lawns and small orange trees. A pair of towers with conical roofs set off the front exposure on either side. Scroll-saw decorations embellished the entrance and tried to relieve the bluff squareness of design.

Stopping a moment inside the picket fence, Cass caught his breath. He was a homesick native returned, for he had spent the last three years at Punahoa School in the Sandwich Islands, exiled by his mother under strict orders not to return even on vacations.

Cass had been seasick as well as homesick, going and coming from the Islands. He did not like unfamiliar places, and the ocean repelled him. Seeing again the smelly tide flats and bare brown hills of San Pedro, the waist-high brush and sandy wagon tracks, the silvery cottonwood trees and peeling trunks of the eucalyptus, the boulders and gravel of the meandering Los Angeles River, the swirls of dust and sleepy Mexicans in the Plaza, his mother's old adobe town house—seeing all that had brought shamed tears to his eyes. An honest pride stirred in him. It was a wonderful city. Honolulu didn't compare, nor San Francisco.

There were twelve thousand citizens, horsecars, amusement parks, a cultivated society, gas lights, railroads to the north and to San Pedro and Santa Monica. This very year of 1881 the President of the United States, Rutherford B. Hayes, had come visiting briefly. Not long ago a convention participated in by Cass's uncle had voted to split the state of California into northern and southern halves to end domination by the richer, more thickly settled upper part with its capital in faraway Sacramento, and only approval of Congress was needed for a new state in the south having Los Angeles as the seat of government.

Lucius Brennan was a mover and shaker in local affairs, a prominent man, a booster—the author of a widely circulated book entitled *A Glimpse of Paradise* which extolled the benefits of Southern California and was helping to bring more residents. It was Lucius who had gone to the Centennial Exhibition at Philadelphia in 1876 with pamphlets, Los Angeles newspapers, and hundreds of views of the town on lantern slides for stereopticon showing. His brother Cassius had married into the old Villanueva family, thereby making Cass a descendant of the first white people in the country; his mother was owner of Rancho de San Cristobal, sixteen thousand acres of which remained north and west of the San Fernando Valley.

To Cass, Lucius was a second father, an enduring image from his earliest childhood. That Doña Maria was no friend to his uncle didn't matter; he felt sure he loved him more than his exasperating, mysterious, bewildering, tenacious mother.

He knocked on Lucius's door. It was opened by Fidelia, the elderly woman who cared for the house in an erratic fashion. She was a mountain of flesh, black and slatternly, and spoke only Spanish. In response to her question, Cass replied a trifle haltingly, without the soft and melodious accents she gave to the language, admitting he was hungry, and followed her back along the hallway to the kitchen. He had not talked in the first language he had learned for several years, and before that Doña Maria had restricted its use at home (he had to grow up in a Yankee world, she said coldly); anyway, now his head was full of Latin and Greek and all the stupefying parts of English grammar, and a bit of the exquisite simplicity of Hawaiian.

From Fidelia, Cass received two tortillas wrapped around chunks of beef dripping with hot sauce and a cup of strong coffee heavily sugared. It was a *californio*'s breakfast of the sort favored at the San Cristobal and had the taste of homecoming to him. He saw the woman watching him. Her expression was quizzical. Fidelia had small respect for anyone, and he knew the sight of his blue serge suit and plug hat with a string attached for hooking in his lapel had roused the sense of the ridiculous

10

strong in her kind. But she was only a *mestizo,* Mexican-Indian, a half-breed. To his annoyance, though, he was aware that his eyes were nearly as dark as hers. Uncle Lucius's eyes were bright blue and his father's had been the same, they said. He hated the color of blue, therefore, and secretly detested the fate that had given him the dark eyes of the Villanuevas.

"Qué vas hacer?" Fidelia asked ironically.

"You know what I am going to do," he replied.

"No, no. Qué vas hacer, niño?"

"Don't call me a baby, Fidelia, or I'll pour hot coffee on you."

She laughed. "As you say, *caballero.* So you are going to march today? Why?"

"Because Los Angeles has a hundred years."

"That is not long. Yang-na was here before Los Angeles—no man remembers how long. Why don't the gringos march for Yang-na?"

"Nobody marches for Indian villages," Cass said. "They are of no importance."

"As you say, Don Cassio," Fidelia said. "But you should wait, no? In a little while will be Mexican Independence Day. You are not all gringo. Why don't you march then instead? What does Doña Maria say?"

"Nothing."

"There will be better marching. The day has more spirit. It is all yellow and red and a *gran baile* afterward and everybody drunk. The bands play louder, too."

"That day should be forgotten. Los Angeles is an American town."

"You consider so?" Fidelia shrugged. "Los Angeles is shit. From a burro, not a horse."

"Bastante!" Cass said, and flushed in his anger. "I wish to see my uncle. Is he ready?"

"Quién sabe?" Fidelia said. "I took him hot water and he bathed naked in his tub. Then I took him a piece of meat and a cup of coffee. Who knows?"

Leaving her abruptly and ascending the broad staircase, Cass knocked on the door of a front bedroom. Lucius called for him to enter. Cass stopped where the tin tub still rested, half full of soapy water and surrounded by an area of stained carpet disfigured by previous baths. His uncle's furniture was old and crudely made. The carved bed had an enormous bulk surmounted by a canopy, but the draw curtains had been removed. There was a tall bureau of surprising delicacy that looked out of place, obviously of English origin, which had probably traveled around the Horn long ago. Cologne scented the air; Lucius always used it in abundance despite the repressed criticism of his associates, who even considered such additions as hair oil and bay rum unmanly. On the rumpled covers of the bed one of Lucius's numerous cats, a particolored creature of orange and white and gray, observed Cass with pale yellow eyes. A bachelor, a man of mystery with few close friends, Lucius seemed to save his deepest affection for his favorite animals.

By a window was a plain deal table littered with papers, pamphlets, books, stationery, sealing wax, ink well, pens, an almanac, a ledger of prodigious size, and a bottle of whiskey and two glasses. It was here that Lucius worked, read and thought when he wasn't in his real estate office near Second and Main streets. *A Glimpse of Paradise* had been inscribed on the table, and presently a pile of scribbled, blotted sheets were being held down by a small, short-barreled revolver; these Cass assumed to be the speech his uncle was scheduled to deliver upon the conclusion of the parade today. Glancing beyond the handsome cat, he noticed a pillow dented by Lucius's head and displaced sufficiently to reveal the curving butt of a heavy Colt's pistol beneath.

Lucius stood in the little circular tower room he used for dressing, which had a doorway but no door. He was a big man, over six feet in height, tending to heaviness, looking older than his forty-two years because of a recent affectation of clothing, his broad face dark with a close-cropped, stubbly black beard. His coarse hair was worn long at the back, and he was attired in a black broadcloth suit, brocaded vest cut low to reveal a ruffled shirt with pearl buttons, and an old-fashioned high stock encircled by a black cravat. On his head sat a plug hat tilted at a rakish angle, and affixed to his lapel was a large scarlet rosette that identified him as one of the occupants of the reviewing stand for the parade. When he smiled at Cass, his teeth gleamed brightly in the darkness of his face and beard.

"You look elegant and very grown up, Cassius," he said.

"Just Cass, sir, please."

"Of course. But why?"

"Oh, Cassius sounds out of date. They make jokes about it."

"Really? I'm getting out of date. You had a grandfather who memorized whole sections of Gibbon's *Decline and Fall* and admired the Romans above everybody else. That was the reason for the given names of your father and me."

"I know," Cass said, "but that's all over now."

Emerging from the tower room, Lucius paused to stroke the cat on the bed; it arched its back and purred. "A remarkable people, those early Latins. They took what they needed and never failed to make their appropriations legal—according to their codes. They remind me of Americans. You weren't unduly impressed by them?"

"I haven't thought much about it."

"Well, no matter." Lucius went to the bureau and removed a hand-kerchief from a drawer and scented it with cologne and put it in his pocket, picked up a cased repeater watch and wound it with a key and dropped it in his vest pocket after ascertaining the time, and stretched the thick golden watch guard hung with seals across his middle. "I've arranged for you to march with the Odd Fellows. They're in the second division, and form on Front Street at Third. Don't forget to join me when I'm through orating—I want you properly introduced now you're home."

"Yes, sir."

From the bureau to the table was a few steps: Lucius moved slowly over, thinking of other matters. The revolver was put in his right hip pocket. Lifting his eyes to Cass, he grimaced. "Force of habit, my boy. I don't think I'll ever need one again."

Cass waited silently, for his uncle had picked up the manuscript of his speech. He read rapidly, frowning a little and pulling his black brows together, putting the pages one behind the other as he finished them. When he came to the end, he doubled the sheaf and stuck it carelessly in a coat pocket and sighed. "One of these days," he said, "I must try the effect of the truth. Just for the novelty. But not in a public gathering, I suppose."

They went downstairs together, Lucius explaining that Kirby Jennison and Moses Smiley, two of his closest associates, were coming for them in a carriage. In the musty parlor where the curtains were closed, he sat down and lit a cigar and gazed reflectively at Cass.

"What are you going to do now?" he asked suddenly.

"I don't know, sir."

"More schooling? I imagine you need it."

"I hate more learning," Cass said, "unless it's for some purpose."

"Well, do you have some purpose in mind?"

"No, I guess not."

"What does your mother say?"

"She's willing for me to go up to Santa Clara College and then study law afterwards and become a lawyer like my father—to help keep the San Cristobal."

Lucius fingered his beard. "Why can't you attend school here?"

"Well—"

"Because I'm here, eh?"

"I guess so," Cass said unhappily.

"A hell of a note . . . What if I found you a place in a lawyer's office and you read the law at your leisure? You could pass the bar examination in due course and fulfill Doña Maria's hopes."

"That sounds wonderful, sir," Cass said.

There was a short silence. "The trouble is," Lucius said, "Doña Maria would never agree, if only on the grounds that it was my idea."

Cass's heart sank. Lucius was right. His mother would certainly not consent to such a handy and pleasant arrangement. To his bewilderment and sorrow, she had an unbending aversion to Lucius and all of his works, so deep and long standing that she would not even discuss matters in which he was involved. Something had happened in the past—a past beyond Cass's earliest memories—that made her unalterably opposed to him. Cass had tried to find out what caused the enmity from both of them, but Doña Maria had declined to entertain his questions and Lucius had pretended, not too convincingly, that he was mystified by her attitude.

Lucius was staring at Cass through a puff of cigar smoke, his lips faintly twisted by disappointment. "I wish you were mine, Goddamn it," he said. "You'd have a chance to travel and gamble and play the fool, to get out of town and see the world, to reach manhood the way a boy should—there wouldn't be this pulling and hauling and tea-table discussion." Then he shook his head disgustedly. "Or would there? I haven't got the means to set you up properly, and your mother has. I'm talking through my hat, Cass. I was in the wrong bank in the crash of '75 and nothing has gone as well as I wanted since."

"I'm not asking for anything, sir. If I could just be with you—"

Cutting him off, Lucius got up, apparently detected a deposit of tobacco ash on one of his shining boots, and took an antimacassar from a chair; the small disfigurement vanished as he bent and twitched the cloth. His boots were as much a part of his ambience as the odor of cologne, the pistols, the elaborate linen, a certain good-humored courtesy extended to everybody. In the old days *hacendados* and men of quality had never worn shoes, and Lucius persisted in a vanishing custom.

The door knocker sounded. Lucius motioned for Cass to come along. Fidelia was ahead of them in the hall, admitting two callers: Kirby Jennison, a tall, leathery, long-faced engineer and contractor, and Moses Smiley, round and small and rosy-cheeked, a former Methodist minister turned land-dealer and auctioneer. When Cass was introduced by his uncle, they greeted him with flattering unction. The natty Moses, attired in a striped suit, wash leather gloves and high collar with a narrow string tie, commented fulsomely on the changes in Cass since he had last seen him—his additional height, weight, new maturity, and obvious growth in intellect. None of these praises pleased Cass. He was well aware that he had not inherited the height and bulk of the Brennans,

14

which he wanted; he was far more a Villanueva, thinner, slighter, dark-eyed and aquiline-faced. However, courtesy compelled him to inquire on the well-being of Moses's family, of whose existence he knew through his uncle; Kirby was a widower, having married a Mexican woman of considerable wealth, and had two stepdaughters he regarded with ill-concealed dislike and never mentioned.

"You are kind to ask, young man," Moses said, "and I did not know you were aware that I had a family. The fact is, their condition is to be deprecated. My youngest, the baby, recently contracted a rash which puzzles the medical profession. It has been unfortunately communicated to the others in my brood, and now my poor Bessie is applying lotions to six little sufferers."

"According to rumor," Lucius said, "you have again put Mrs. Smiley in an interesting condition. Is that true, Moses?"

"I have every reason to believe we are going to be blessed by another increase, yes, sir," Moses said.

"By God," Kirby said. "You ought to keep your underwear sewed up winter and summer. Can't you leave the lady alone or make the rounds with Lucius once in a while and cool yourself off in another bed? How many mouths do you expect you can feed?"

Glancing at Cass, Moses said, "This is not a subject I think we can pursue in the presence of Master Cass . . . Lucius, you look to be in good form. I hope we are going to partake of your wisdom and best flights of fancy today."

"Wisdom I won't guarantee," Lucius said, "but in dealing with the Queen past and present you may count upon some delirious flights of fancy."

"How shall I address you in the presence of the multitude, sir?" Moses said. "As 'Judge' or 'Colonel'?"

Lucius smiled. "Why, that's a moot point. I was a magistrate only briefly. On the other hand, my military rank dates from back in the 60's when the Mounted City Guards were formed. I bought drinks for the house at our first meeting and was elected lieutenant colonel by acclamation. Probably you'd better call me 'Colonel,' Moses."

"In my estimation, Colonel," Moses said, "you are merely exercising the traditional modesty of men devoted to the god Mars."

"No, he's telling the truth," Kirby said. "I was a Guard myself, and we'd scatter at the sound of a bung being knocked out of a beer keg. The only engagements we ever fought were with each other in whorehouses."

Moses eyed Cass again, cleared his throat, and suggested that they go.

Cass followed his elders to the barouche Kirby had provided, complete with top-hatted Negro driver and a pair of spanking bays. At

Kirby's suggestion, he sat beside Moses in the rear-facing seat and settled his hard hat firmly on his head.

They set off at a smart pace, raising eddies of dust. Kirby told the driver to make a sweep to the north so they could observe the preparations and put down Cass at his appointed spot.

"And exhibit me in triumphal array," Lucius commented.

"Why not?" Kirby said. "You're one of the local sights, Colonel."

In five minutes they were at the center of Los Angeles. A cheer went up, and Cass craned his head around. The barouche was skirting the desolate, trampled Plaza, the heart of the old town where stood the church and the adobe houses that marked the beginning of the settlement. Toward the river, on sloping ground, lay Doña Maria Brennan's home and gardens, the shutters closed and the high wooden gate barred. Off to the left was Chinatown and a narrow thoroughfare called Nigger Alley, until lately an unbroken double row of gambling houses, saloons and bagnios; once the miserable Indians, dispossessed of their Yang-na, had caroused and fought there and been herded into a nearby corral for safekeeping at the height of their drunkenness, until disease and malnutrition and alcohol had finished them off. Beyond could be seen the remains of Sonoratown, formerly a malodorous collection of shacks, the habitat of bewildered immigrants from Mexico come to a strange town and a strange language and little better fitted to cope with the fair-skinned invaders than the Indians had been. The beginnings of a curious village as destined to be a crossroads of contending races as any of its Mesopotamian predecessors in the dawn of men were embalmed in the Plaza, but Cass was indifferent to them. His uncle said it was an eyesore and had to be cleaned up, and had headed a committee taking steps in that direction; if the Queen was to become a modern city, and as sure as hell and high water it was, then these reminders of the aborigines and mission priests and Spanish soldiers in leather jerkins and mountain men and trappers and gamblers and gold-hunters and prostitutes and teamsters hauling out of Salt Lake and Santa Fe and Mexicans dreaming in solitude until the arrival of ships from Boston woke them up and lordly *rancheros* counting their cattle and acres in the thousands had to go. Cass believed in this with all his heart. The past was dead, and its vestiges a dusty note of derision that merited annihilation.

From thirty or forty throats came hoarse cries: "Don Luis, Don Luis! *Arriba! Qué hombre!*" "Luis" was as close as they could come to "Lucius," and they were only *sonorenses,* poor whites, *mestizos,* blacks, laborers, vagabonds and jailbirds, already a little drunk; but they were saluting Cass's uncle, and his chest swelled in a yeasty pride. Don Luis

16

acknowledged the reception with an outstretched arm and vertical palm, like a Roman imperator.

"That's a hell of a following you've got, Colonel," Kirby said.

"They represent votes," Lucius replied. "When the situation calls for it, they even represent four or five votes per man. Are you opposed to the democratic processes?"

Centennial Day was a great success. Although the main avenues were cleared for the parade, every side street was jammed with carriages, wagons, carts, sulkies, even a few ancient two-wheeled *carretas* driven by rustics, and innumerable restive riding horses; sidewalks and vacant lots overflowed with men, women, children, babies, dogs, and several pigs and little parties of panicked chickens which had escaped their pens. People came from throughout the county—especially the newer towns of San Gabriel, Newport, Santa Ana, Los Nietos, Tustin City, Richland, Spadra and San Fernando—there were in excess of twenty thousand gathered, counting the local citizenry. The Southern Pacific Railroad Company depot was gaily done up in bunting, and when the Wilmington train pulled in carrying several hundred passengers the locomotive and cars were found to be decked out in flowers and banners. So also were the engines of the Colton and Anaheim trains, and the equipment of the Los Angeles and Independence Railroad from Santa Monica. The weather was intensely clear and hot, and a man's eyes could roam into the distance for thirty miles, across the plain, up on the mountains, and atop Fort Hill catch a glimpse of the aquamarine sea.

Every window and balcony along the route of the march was crowded, and some roofs, and the wooden sidewalks creaked under the weight of people packed shoulder to shoulder, many holding their young. Men of substance had on swallowtails and claw-hammer coats and elegant neckwear, and their women wore dresses of silks and satins and lacy hats and carried fancy parasols.

From one end of Main Street to the other, the buildings were transformed by bunting, arches of evergreens, and twin displays of the national colors and the Bear Flag Republic. Pico House, the Oriental Buildings, the Fashion Stables, Colonel Wood's Opera House, Abbott's Theater, the Grand Central and St. Charles hotels, the Farmers and Merchants Bank, the City of Paris Dry Goods Store, Pete Eggar's Saloon Bar, the Lanfranco Block, the Court House, the Post Office, the Daily Intelligencer building—everything was brightened by holiday decorations. Over the doorway of the home of the French consular agent were intertwined the Bear Flag, the *Tricoleur,* and the Stars and Stripes. On Spring Street was a triumphal arch of wood and plaster, imposing in

17

size, enriched with wreaths, streamers and flags, and bearing the legend: "1781—NOW 1881—PREPARE FOR 1981!"

The parade reflected a stylish precision. General Morgan Griswold, who had fought under Grant in the West in '62, served as Grand Marshal, and with his aides headed the column in an open carriage. In a blue frock coat of military cut, wearing a yellow sash and a large silver star on his left breast, plus carrying a baton, the general radiated dignity and an air of command. Other prominent figures were scattered through the divisions, afoot and on horseback. Several bands furnished martial music.

Among the marchers were the Veterans of the Mexican War, a stalwart group now in their vigorous sunset years; Civil War soldiers wearing both the blue and the gray in perfect amity; the Los Angeles County Patrol shouldering ceremonial muskets with nickel-plated barrels; the Los Angeles Mounted Pistoleros, every member on a spirited black horse and carrying sidearms; the Sonora Vaqueros in picturesque sombreros, embroidered vests and velvet pantaloons split down the sides, their saddles and bridles heavy with silver ornamentation; the French Benevolent Society pulling a decorated cart containing three young ladies who depicted Faith, Hope and Charity; a gilded car that embowered Miss Rachel Shapiro, in a filmy white dress and the crown of a goddess, representing the Spirit of Los Angeles; the Forty-Niner Engine Company No. One, sixty men in blue shirts and red caps, tugging their hose cart on long ropes; Assurance Engine Company No. Two, whose equipment was drawn by white horses, with the boys in red shirts, silver capes and black hats; the Wilmington Hook-and-Ladder Company; the Junta Patriotica de Guadalajara; and such diverse groups as the Knights of Pythias, Improved Order of Red Men, Ancient Order of Hibernians, Irish Literary Society, Irish Temperance Society, and Independent Order of Odd Fellows, not to mention the drivers and riders on the floats mounted atop wagons from the Pennsylvania Brewery, the Boyle Heights Soap Factory, and the Southern California Steam Coffee Company.

The route of the parade covered Main, Aliso, Commercial, Los Angeles and Arcadia streets, and then swung around the Plaza and went down Spring Street to the arch; after which the participants disbanded and joined the spectators before a flag-draped reviewing stand on the north side of the Plaza containing dignitaries, where the literary exercises of the day were to be conducted. Restaurants and funeral parlors contributed chairs, and those unable to find accommodation sat on the sidewalks, filled windows and doorways, and perched on ledges and rooftops.

18

Cass discovered walking in the ranks was no easy interlude. He stepped out bravely when the band in front of the Odd Fellows played "Yankee Doodle" and the "Battle Hymn of the Republic," but soon dust coated him and the heat in the lines of men was stifling. If he trod on the heels of the Odd Fellow in front of him, he was apt to be cursed. His toes stuck together and blistered. He was tired and thirsty. The rim of his plug hat became a band of iron and seemed to tighten steadily on his aching head; each vagrant puff of air blew the string attached to it behind his ear and tickled him. His collar grew limp and soaked and sweat stung his eyes and dripped from his armpits and groin. Unruly bystanders taunted the civilians with cries of "Hay-foot-straw-foot" and "Pick up your flat feet" and "Stop holding up the parade."

At dispersal he sat down promptly on the edge of the sidewalk, removed his torturing headgear, and employed a handkerchief to mop his streaming face.

Lucius sought him out. "Come along," he said. "I have a place for you on the stand. How was it?"

"All right," Cass said. "How did it look?"

"Splendid. There'll never be another one like it—not in a hundred years."

"My feet are killing me."

"No matter," Lucius said. "Stand up straight and walk as if they didn't hurt."

Cass matched his uncle's masterful long strides with an effort, squaring his shoulders and putting an imaginary ramrod in his back. He wished he had a revolver in his pocket and a speech ready and six feet of height and black whiskers and still looked immaculate and cool and smelled of cologne. Not in a hundred years would there be another man like him.

They ascended the steps at the rear of the reviewing stand, and Cass was engulfed in a flurry of introductions. He met O. F. Gordner, President of the Day, the mayor, councilmen, the sheriff, the lieutenant governor of California, several members of families as rooted in tradition as the Villanuevas, shaking the hands of people he had not met since childhood, for Doña Maria had little to do with anybody these days.

"Your mother didn't come, eh?" Kirby asked.

"I don't think so," Cass said, and watched his uncle go forward.

"Well, she missed rubbing elbows with a lot of stinkers," Kirby said.

The crowd below was restless and irritable. Directly overhead, the sun blazed down. Many of them had had nothing to eat since an early breakfast. Some of the men had been patronizing the saloons and were talking loudly. Hawkers peddled lemonade, beer, pretzels, sandwiches, sticky candy and cold water. A baby wailed, a man stumbled and almost fell and evoked vast laughter, and musical instruments being tuned set up discordant sounds. Behind the rostrum the notables moved, waved to friends, whispered in ears, and shuffled papers.

The band was mustered by the leader and rendered "Hail Columbia." The audience settled down. A scuffling among youths was hissed into silence. President Gordner introduced the Chaplain of the Day, Reverend Moses Smiley. Rubicund and benevolent, he called upon Almighty God to bless and uphold Los Angeles in the present and future, shed His grace on those gathered here and their issue and others who would presently join them in the work of building a great city.

Although Moses was a crony of his uncle's, Cass felt annoyance. Why should a Protestant clergyman—and one without even a church, incidentally, and now in an unhallowed profession, for Moses's small congregation had failed to support him and his large family, and he had renounced them—be allowed to call on heaven this particular day? The town had been settled and nurtured by Catholics. The true faith had tolerated and even welcomed these other men when it didn't have to. Many a Catholic was in the audience and would have been flattered and honored to have a priest address them in the celebration of a place named for the Blessed Mother. It was typical of the Americans to use one of their own kind to invite divine help; they had intended to own the country from the first, and to exclude in every possible fashion the people who had preceded them. But then Cass realized he was being unfaithful to Lucius.

President Gordner, a banker and landowner, succeeded and thanked Reverend Smiley, produced a manuscript, put on his glasses, and haltingly read a tribute to a city fairest of the fair, bathed in constant sunshine, cooled by gentle zephyrs, abounding in all the fruits and cereals of the earth, overlooked by snowcapped mountains, protected from the effete east by countless leagues of inhospitable deserts, caressed on a near shore by the mighty Pacific Ocean, inhabited by a sturdy and upright folk devoted to the Lord, good works, hard labor, innocent diversions and economic progression.

His auditors tired of him and coughed and spat and shuffled their feet. Laughter was heard on the outskirts of the assembly, and bumpkins wrestled with one another. Individuals drifted off to home or saloon or a spot of shade. Gordner concluded in garbled haste. He took profound pleasure, he said, in introducing Professor Gadson E. Briggs, the noted elocutionist.

Professor Briggs had a squat body, a high forehead partially veiled

20

by a shock of dark hair, and fancied himself on his resemblance to the bygone Little Giant of Illinois, Stephen E. Douglas. The title of his address, announced in rich accents, was "Los Angeles: A Vision."

"More than fivescore years ago," he said, "not far from where we are gathered in solemn yet festive conclave dedicated to the hundredth anniversary of a magnificent city we are determined shall not perish from the earth, a party of weary Spanish soldiers led by a worn and emaciated officer with the mein of a seer and a prophet ascended to the highest point and, in the ethereal glow of a golden sunset, gazed out on a scene of beauty that beggars the powers of description. These men, honed to the sharpness and strength of Toledo blades by the rigors of travel and battle, descried the brooding immutable mountains above the San Gabriel Valley, the plains of sylvan green, the illimitable rolling hills in the garb of autumn, the lakes like perfect mirrors reflecting a scarlet wrath of a declining Phoebus, the forests fit for Diana's hunting, the deep valleys where an army might hide, and to the west the crescent puissance of an unknown sea. At their feet, so to speak, were the tumbling waters of the Rio Porciuncula, which we know as the Los Angeles River, nourishing umbrageous trees and verdant greensward on which gamboled herds of deer and antelope beyond the numbering of man. Far in the dissolving distance stood great islands, Santa Catalina and the San Clementes, tall sentinels protecting the gates of Paradise.

"Gazing upon this scene, a light not of this world in his hollowed and fiery orbs, our officer struck his breast. 'My vision!' cried he. 'My vision incarnate! The vision I saw in my native Granada before ever I came to New Spain! All my life I have sought it, through every hazard and in every clime!' Wherewith he knelt and gave fervent thanks to that Blessed Lady, the Queen of the Angels. His companions eagerly besought him to tell of the vision, and he duly related how, high on a hill above the stream called Guadalquiver, a mysterious sleep came on him and he dreamed of a fabled land so beautiful his heart was nigh riven. Into the dream appeared Our Lady, bathed in a wondrous radiance, and indicated the exact spot they now saw, with only the Rio Porciuncula substituted for the Guadalquiver. 'In due time, after many a vicissitude,' said the Queen, 'you will, Captain Tomas, found a city in my name that shall eclipse in grandeur, magnitude and fame your own Granada.' Trailing an immense train of pure light, she then ascended to Heaven.

"'Comrades,' cried Captain Tomas, rising in triumph from his prayers, 'our way is clear. Will you join me in the founding of a city here for Our Lady—a city to be named Nuestra Señora la Reina de Los Angeles—an eternal shrine in honor of the Queen of the Angels?' 'We join with you gladly and in holy reverence, bold captain!' cried the others . . ."

Kirby's elbow was jabbing into the ribs of Cass. He blinked and tottered. "I don't mind your eyes being closed," Kirby whispered, "but you were starting to snore, boy. Brace up."

"I'm sorry," Cass whispered back. "I'm so tired—"

The professor's buncombe had a certain appeal, and in better spirits, Gordner presented the Poet of the Day, Virgil Hoch, editor of the *Intelligencer*. He was a pale young man with a reedy voice, and his poetasting often occupied columns in the back pages of the newspaper. Prepared for the occasion, he opened up at once:

> *Bestir thyself, dear Muse! environ me with fire*
> *To indite a paean to my city's name;*
> *Bring lofty fancies to my earthly mire*
> *And lift me to the level of her heav'nly fame.*
> *The years in their unending round have rolled in*
> *A hundredth memorial of our city's life;*
> *And now with soaring aspirations we begin*
> *To contemplate another century of joy and strife . . .*

The elbow dug into Cass once more. "The colonel's next," Kirby said. "You don't want to miss that, do you?"

"No, sir. But I just can't seem to help—"

"Listen to the beautiful poetry, boy."

Virgil Hoch was concluding:

> *In each Angeleno's breast is raised a shrine*
> *Where within burns the Queen's quenchless flame;*
> *Beyond all else she dominates this heart of mine*
> *And carries us forward every one—to deathless fame!*

Decent applause rose out of the assemblage, perhaps in relief that it was ended. Unfortunately there were also shrill catcalls and lip-farting noises made by rowdies. Gordner quickly brought Lucius to the podium and announced Colonel Brennan as the Orator of the Day. Lucius stood calmly watching the crowd. His manuscript was out, as yet unfolded. He crumpled the manuscript with one hand and rubbed his chin with the other, evidently collecting his thoughts.

"A hundred years isn't much [Lucius said]. The Indians were here for thousands of years, without the written word, praying to heathen gods, eating snakes and lizards and furry varmints and ground-up acorns and going around naked—waiting for the white man to come and kill them off.

22

"Then Hernán Cortés landed in Mexico in 1519 and took what he needed—and like us he needed everything. A few years later he was writing the king back in Spain and describing California, which was an island according to him, populated solely by women and very rich in pearls and precious stones. That idea originated at the start of the sixteenth century when a writer named García Ordóñez de Montalvo published a romance called *Las Sergas de Esplandian* that dealt with a black queen, Califia, and her black female subjects; she lived somewhere near India, Ordóñez wrote. After the story had been repeated enough, the fiction became fact. Cortés sent an expedition to find the island. His men, and others following their trails, got no farther than Baja California, but they did discover a few pearl fisheries. Califia wasn't about, though, nor any black women that were not just squaws.

"Three hundred and fifty years ago Juan Rodriguez Cabrillo, who was a brave sailor, beat up the coast against fierce headwinds and landed at San Pedro before he died. It's possible that he saw Yang-na, the Indian village here. A couple of other navigators came in time—Sir Francis Drake in the Golden Hind, and Vizcaíno for the Spaniards. Then everything stopped for a century and a half. Meanwhile, the Thirteen Colonies formed on the east end of the continent, Charles the First had his head cut off in England, and Frederick the Great won historic victories. The world changed completely, knowledge increased, revolutionary new ideas took hold—and Yang-na remained the same, a bunch of brush huts beside a river.

"During the first half of the eighteenth century the Jesuits built missions and tamed the Indians in Lower California. Before they could move up north the Spanish king put them out of business for their politicking and replaced them with Dominicans and Franciscans. The gray friars were given Upper California and a great man to lead them, Padre Junípero Serra. In 1769 he arrived in San Diego.

"In August of the same year the Spaniards went through Yang-na en route to Monterey and were bothered by earthquakes. The land looked barren and the natives were unfriendly, so the newcomers didn't linger. But they never failed to give new names to wherever they were, and Yang-na was rechristened after the feast day on which they camped, *Nuestra Señora la Reina de Los Angeles*. When they had missions established at San Diego and Monterey, and another sixty miles from Monterey, a fourth was founded at San Gabriel in 1771. The soldiers liked the Indian women and the male Indians objected and some of them were slaughtered and then everybody was ready to accept salvation.

"Now, you must understand that the missions in Alta California, all twenty-one of them built a day's march apart from San Diego to Sonoma, as well as those in Baja California, were a commercial proposition. The savages had to be saved, but they were also to be used. Being serfs, they had no part in any discussions and their complaints remained unheard. Much use was made by the authorities of the Franciscans and their well-financed Pious Fund. Without them and their money and their laboring Indians, the rickety Spanish government, whose main object was to colonize and defend and profit by its overseas holdings, could not have afforded to develop this howling wilderness. Although it sounded better to say the missions were only intended to bring Christianity and civilization to the unenlightened natives, the politicians planned for the church to operate for a maximum of ten years, after which its properties would be converted to secular use and the support of settlers.

"The Franciscans naturally opposed that solution. Their organization was excellent and their wealth grew enormously, and they managed to stay almost intact until 1835; in the meantime Mexico had revolted against Spain and become independent, and the revolutionaries had to have the money they could come by in dissolving the mission system. The Fathers had a sour answer for the laymen, though—they simply destroyed or gave away everything portable before the government administrators could close in on them.

"Los Angeles was part of an over-all plan, one of the pueblos meant to furnish supplies for the army. Governor Felípe de Neve had his troubles in recruiting settlers, because nobody was eager to move to a new and miserable village at the end of the earth. He had a Captain Rivera scouring Mexico for him, offering money, clothing, tools, guns and domestic animals, but the best the captain could produce were twenty-two men and women and twenty-two children—*mestizos,* mulattoes, Negroes, Indians, and a pair of lonely Spaniards.

"De Neve was our first booster. He laid out the Plaza and plotted the town, and a hundred years ago today had a little parade of his own when he marched in his motley crew. The mission padres and their Indians were on hand from San Gabriel, and in front of the procession a man carried a banner with a picture of Our Lady painted on it. The governor made a speech. No one took down or remembered what he said, but probably he told his audience what every speaker has since, including me—that this is going to be a great city, given time.

"For fifty years there was no noticeable improvement in the pueblo. The houses were of adobe and melted in heavy rains, the roofs were of thatched tules and leaked, the colonists were lazy and got drunk and fought each other and some of them had to be run out of town by the soldiers. Padres sent over from the mission kept complaining of the bad behavior of the Angelenos. They cut down all the trees for firewood, butchered in their front yards and left the offal for the dogs and buzzards to clean up, fouled their irrigation ditches with excrement and refuse, and wouldn't pay taxes. They raised horses, cattle and sheep, wheat and corn, and later on grapes that were converted into wine and brandy, most of which they drank themselves.

"The old order vanished quickly, as it has ever since in Los Angeles. Thirty-five years after the founding only one name among the original settlers was still on the rolls, and just a couple of descendants. This town has always belonged primarily to outsiders. We're a fraternity of strangers.

"The revolution in Mexico and the exit of the Spaniards meant the substitution of one bad government for another. Unresisting, the Angelenos allowed the gringos to grab the land, control the finances, expand the smuggling, and command better local revolts against the governors in Monterey. The wars the United States fought in Texas and Mexico were distant echoes in this sleepy town. Finally, as the tide of conquest reached here, some resistance was offered to the seizure of California, but that was largely because the young men enjoyed a little riding and light fighting. If the Americans hadn't been careless and led by quarrelsome, egotistical fools like John Charles Frémont, they could have had Los Angeles for the asking. When it was surrendered they had a fine parade and a grand ball that everybody enjoyed.

"As a dumping ground for the dregs of humanity, the Queen has had few equals. She had those miserable colonists to start with, and then soldiers who had served their terms and married Indian women, misfits driven from Spain and the Spanish possessions, runaway sailors from nearly every nation on earth, renegades from the States and murderers from Canada, gunfighters out of Texas and Sonora, importations from Mexico consisting of crooked politicians and shipments of criminals, ladies of ill repute, and the outpourings of orphanages. During the gold rush days she offered a haven for gamblers, thieves, road agents, rustlers, confidence men and fallen women. This overflow from the Mother Lode country contributed to a busy scene, for between 1850 and 1870 Los Angeles was the widest open town on the North American continent—it had more booze, saloons, gambling, bagnios, murders, gunfights, knifings, horse thieves, bandits, jail wreckers, lynch mobs, preachers of new religions, bullfights, dead Indians, secret societies, dishonest office seekers, fighting chickens, holdups, dogs and drunkards than you could find anywhere else under creation.

"Perhaps the geographical location of Los Angeles has contributed to a unique character. We are at the true crossroads of the Southwest, Latin America and the far Pacific, thirty-four degrees three feet north, one hundred eighteen degrees fourteen feet west, in the most temperate of zones, off the main track of the storms that rage on the northern reaches of the ocean. It is rarely too hot or too cold, and snow almost never falls.

"Still, this is not the terrestrial paradise Ordóñez invented for Queen Califia and her black women. The river that sustained Yang-na is feeble, and droughts frequent. During my own time, in the rainless years of '62 and '63, I saw our largest industry, cattle raising, destroyed entirely and the ranges littered by dead and dying beasts. Water must be brought in, or wells dug. Irrigation is a necessity. Our harbor is twenty miles away, a nearly open roadstead unsuitable for anchorage except in windless weather. We totally lack the mineral deposits, the manufacturing and navigable rivers that have made other cities grow and prosper.

"This is a *made* town. Made by men, and still in the process of creation. The Spaniards had to bring everything with them, and would have perished but for the supplies forwarded from Baja California. Nothing indigenous was of much value. The clear, beaming skies were danger signals rather than a blessing. Happily, the mission Fathers were from Spain, another arid land, and knew how to irrigate and enrich the ground. What you see around you—groves, vineyards, flowers, domestic animals, vegetables, the very moisture that permits these things to live— all have been introduced into an empty expanse of wild grass and scrubby trees and the dry washes of forgotten floods by the hands of devoted emigrants.

"It cannot be claimed that fortune has favored Los Angeles especially. In the state capital at Sacramento she is called 'Queen of the Cow Counties.' Discovery of gold in the north in '49 took care of throwing the balance of power to San Francisco. Treasure, prestige, importance, size, self-approbation, shipping, culture, political influence, resources—they're all up there—and the terminus of the transcontinental railroad to boot. We had to sell our souls to get the Southern Pacific to build a branch line down here, and now the S.P. would like to foreclose on such hopes as we have of immortality. For years we have without avail been trying to break the power of the trusts and to persuade Congress to disburse the funds to build us a decent harbor at San Pedro. To provide for the future in the matter of sufficient water we will have to go into the mountains and maybe even to the Colorado River, but arguing the muttonheads among our voters into voting a bond issue for that seems close to impossible. And few of us appear interested in the vital necessity of getting the Santa Fe Railroad into Los Angeles from the south and providing competitive freight and passenger rates—some-

26

thing we've got to have if we don't want to wither on the end of a long vine.

"My friends, we must go on *making* this city. It is a phenomenon, possibly without sufficient reasons for ever being more than an overgrown village, and it won't come of age of itself. The inexorable laws of nature have always prevailed here in their awful simplicity. Lacking the Indians to condemn to forced labor, the Franciscans would have failed. The Spanish preyed off the religious and the Mexicans off both. Mexicans were fair game for the energetic Americans.

"Certain benefits accrue in return for the sacrifices. Consider the steps of the Queen from infancy; brush huts and savages eating uncooked reptiles to mud houses and unlettered brawlers and dogs devouring tripes in the Plaza and open *zanjas* carrying contaminated river water to gun battles and abortive revolutions and saloons and fancy houses and grand balls and herds of thousands of cattle to grapes and oranges and olives and three-story buildings and sidewalks and horsecars and buried water pipes and opera houses and railroads and no more epidemics of typhoid and measles and lots on Main Street selling for twenty dollars a front foot. To see order and comfort rise out of a wilderness, to proliferate in numbers and strength, to come by the material things that enable man to turn to the spiritual things—surely that is enough for a lifetime. Take comfort in saying goodbye to a difficult century. The new one can be no worse, and it ought to be much better. If I had the gift of prophecy, I would assure you it'll be far more interesting.

Lucius was silent for a moment, regarding his audience sardonically. "Thus ends our lesson in history and philosophy for the day. I hope the truth has not discommoded or unsettled you. Thank you for your kind attention."

They were interested and held by his talk, but puzzled by it. Moses Smiley replaced Lucius to pronounce a benediction. Amen having been said, the meeting dissolved in haste.

His brows drawn and his lips pursed, Kirby said, "What do you think?"

"About what he said? It was very fine. I didn't know he knew so much about Los Angeles." Troubled and muddled, Cass saw no reason to tell Kirby that he was astonished by his uncle's boldness and cynicism and hurt at his allusions to the Spanish and Mexicans. The Queen seemed scarcely respectable in his recital. To speak of the mission Fathers in that fashion was not good policy when one had been, at least, a Catholic once. And the current practice was to mention the Indians with sorrow and remorse in public. Dwelling on the lurid 60's and 70's in Los Angeles just wasn't done these days. Cass found his uncle the most bewildering yet, possibly deserving of his mother's cold reservations—and still fascinating.

"He's a damned fool," Kirby said flatly. "He had to hold them, but he didn't have to do that. I wonder if he was drinking this morning—"

Lucius caught Cass's eyes and summoned him with an uplifted finger. Momentarily, Cass experienced an impulse to flee. But he went straight to his uncle and told him he was better than Daniel Webster.

In Pete Eggar's saloon, where Lucius took Cass, began another episode in that strange and protracted day. Moses did not accompany them, on the plea that his temperance principles wouldn't permit, and Kirby came only long enough to drink a single whiskey, saying he had to go to his office and study urgent papers.

The long, cool, dark room was crowded and noisy, and more customers kept coming in. It was hard to get up to the bar or the free lunch tables. Lucius seemed to know everybody, and at his call to the bartender of "the usual, please," willing hands forwarded to him a shot glass of liquor and a chaser of soda water. Cass was presented to innumerable men. Talking indiscriminately of orange crops, growing mulberry trees for the cultivation of silkworms (the current craze), drilling artesian wells, local and state politics, and the price of land, Lucius had a joke or consolatory words for each listener.

Insinuating himself into the crowd at the food display, Cass ate rye bread and boiled eggs and liver sausage and ham and cheese and slices of cold beef until he was bursting. His uncle came to rescue a now torpid nephew.

"I'm proud of you, you know," he said. "You've been complimented to me highly. You make a good impression, Cass, and I want to be sure you meet all the people who count."

"I appreciate that, sir."

"Unless you decide to go away when you're older, this town should more or less belong to you—and you to it. Caesar said it was better to be king of a village dunghill than an ordinary citizen in Rome. Do you understand me?"

"Yes, sir," Cass replied.

"You should have a glass in your hand. Conviviality is part of belonging, eh? Does your mother allow you anything alcoholic?"

"Well, she lets me drink a small glass of wine once in a while at supper since I've been home."

"Excellent," Lucius said. "Then beer would not be amiss."

28

The beer was chill and full-bodied. Cass downed it thirstily and felt a circle of warmth in the middle of his belly. Somebody handed him a second schooner. Following his uncle, he listened with a new pleasure to the talk.

Cass lost track of the time. He had meant to go home early, but his head took to whirling in an agreeable fashion and he forgot Doña Maria. After a long while in Pete Eggar's, he and his uncle repaired to a bar in a hotel with a band of convivial wanderers who were in a mood for more jollity. There always seemed to be a schooner of beer in his grip.

During a moment aside, Lucius said confidentially in Cass's ear, "This is good for you, you know. I've worried about you occasionally. Of course going away to school was different, but otherwise it's appeared to me that you were too much in the company of women. A man needs the society of men to develop."

"Yes, sir. I know. I would have been glad to go to Punahoa, but— but I was so lonesome. I missed you most of all, sir."

Lucius put a hand on Cass's shoulder and his fingers dug in. "Those are the kindest words you could say to me, Cass. I deeply appreciate them. Believe me, I was aware of your absence. If I didn't write you too often it was because I hadn't much of anything to say and was afraid your mother might not take too kindly to my solicitude."

A small gleam of insight saddened Cass. He doubted that his uncle was being entirely truthful. Ashamed of the disloyalty, he nevertheless suspected Lucius had pretty well forgotten him in the course of those three years; something Doña Maria had unquestionably counted on. Lucius was a man of action and of the moment and could forget easily. Perhaps she knew him better than Cass thought.

Sunset came and the Welsbach burners were lighted in the bar. The revelers started going home. Lucius proposed they eat, and took Cass into the hotel dining room. They sat at a table for two, conscious of their intimacy, affection and rapport. They leaned toward each other in mutual enthusiasm, the difference in their ages washed away by animated revelation; Cass was suddenly aware of his uncle's youthful spirit and the absence in him of the reserve that other adults unfailingly displayed to the young. The old love and understanding between them had been completely reestablished in the course of a few hours. Ordering a bottle of wine, Lucius told the waiter to pour a glass for Cass.

"A toast," he said. "Good luck to our reunion." They clinked glasses. "Let there be no more interruptions of our lives together. I'm going to treat you as my best friend and a grown man from now on, Cass, and you shall have to act both parts perfectly." He chuckled. "When you go home tonight and try to explain to Doña Maria, don't tell her we drank together and swore eternal amity."

"She wouldn't object."

"I'm sure she would."

"In that case," Cass said, "I won't offer any explanation."

Lucius rubbed his chin. "No, don't take that attitude. She deserves better. This is no contest between us for possession of you. But I've got to make a man of you somehow."

It occurred to Cass that his uncle was under the influence. Remarks made at one time or another by Doña Maria had hinted this was not an unusual event. His forehead was flushed and beaded by drops of perspiration, his eyes bloodshot, his speech burring with an unusual sentimentality. His heart ached at this evidence of a flaw in his hero. He was startled by Lucius's next words; it was as if the thought processes going on inside his head had been accurately read.

"Among other things, Cass, you'll have to toughen your tender heart in coming to manhood, and the sooner the better. Toughen it toward me and Doña Maria as well as toward the generality of mankind. That mostly involves being able to distinguish between fact and fancy, and discarding illusions. And then having the nerve to accept the facts. And to know what you want. What do you want?"

"I don't know."

Lucius hesitated. "To resemble me? It'd be a natural reaction, considering the circumstances."

"Yes, sir."

Smiling, Lucius rapped the table with a finger for emphasis. "Wrong. That's an illusion. I'm an illusion. So is the Queen I attempted to explain today, to my disservice." He laughed. "But don't worry. We will not read my speech in the newspapers tomorrow. Virgil Hoch and the others are sure to take care of the lapse."

"Maybe that would be better," Cass said.

"Of course it would! But try to remember the truth I rashly uttered. It's supposed to be immortal, you know."

"I don't want to make you disgusted with me, but I like the illusions better."

"Certainly. Everybody does. Give lip service to 'em, but take care to be guided by the facts. They represent power and money, and you have my solemn assurance no man is happy without both. The truth need not prevail, and usually doesn't—it's just there to be acknowledged in private and used when necessary."

"I guess I don't understand—"

"I can tell that by your expression," Lucius said. "I'm going too fast,

I suppose. Listen to me. God didn't intend for you to grow up a pantywaist, a milksop, the instrument of a determined mother, the enfeebled inheritor of a false tradition, a slave of the San Cristobal, an obedient servant. There is no need for you to believe implicitly that weak lungs brought me to California, and my brother because he felt a duty to take care of me. I left New York to avoid serving in the army—I didn't give a damn about Abe Lincoln's war or who won or whether the blacks were freed. Neither did Cassius. He got a girl in trouble and had to follow me. The reason we settled in Los Angeles happened to be that it was an easier place for two penniless fellows to make their way than anywhere else. Has Doña Maria told you any of this?"

"No, sir."

"Well, you should know. We were a couple of stalwart orphans, descended directly from the kings of ancient Ireland like all of our kind, and our fortunes were under our hats. I became a clerk in a store, a miner in a silver strike in the Owens Valley which didn't pan out, a gambler, and a runner for a whorehouse. Cassius had a more distinguished career—he kept books for a merchant, changed to being a bailiff at the courthouse, and read Blackstone's *Commentaries* and rose to be a bobtailed lawyer. Every other unmarried male in town under the age of sixty was courting Maria Elena Concepcion Villanueva, and we joined the mob. She was seventeen and beautiful, and it didn't hurt that she was the sole heir of Don Ygnacio Villanueva, who had eight Spanish leagues or so of land and lived in a high style. My brother won the prize. I'll be damned if I know how, except that he had a way with women that finally got him three bullets in the belly and made you a posthumous child."

"Is that true, sir?" Cass asked.

"Then you've heard of it?"

"Oh, people talk. Fidelia was sore at me once, and said—"

"She would," Lucius said, and laughed. "Yes, it's true. The drought was on when Cassius got married and it didn't lessen, and pretty soon he and his father-in-law were in difficulties. I think the struggle bored him, and since he was something of an orator, he decided to run for office. In those days Los Angeles was rather evenly divided between northern and southern supporters—the Federals never could trust the California levies they raised and only used them for home guard duties—but you had to be on one side or the other if you wanted to be elected. Cassius chose the black Republicans because they were winning. Unfortunately, he didn't receive enough votes to mount the bench, and defeat appeared to make him lose his sense of proportion. He took to drinking more than was necessary and formed a close acquaintance with a light lady named Susie Figueres. She already had a lover, Chawed-Nose Bob Holgate, a ruffian who had lost some of his face in a rough and tumble fight. One night Bob surprised Cassius in Susie's boudoir and didn't bother to play fair—my brother sat up in bed and held a pillow in front of him, but it wouldn't stop .45 slugs . . . Is my recital upsetting you, Cass?"

"No, sir. It's just that I've had too much to eat and drink."

"Let me finish and we'll get some fresh air. Don Ygnacio and Doña Maria were determined to protect the Villanueva reputation and I was willing to help, so we paid off whoever had a hand out and cooked up a story to the effect that Cassius was a victim of the bitterness left by the war and political rivalries—"

"Did my mother know about Susie?"

"Yes. How could we keep it from her? Well, the story—which was repeated so often people began to believe it—backfired on us. Bob went into hiding after the shooting, discovered he was a hero, and returned and surrendered. He was a Texan, and the seceshers supported him, the damned fools. He was admitted to bail, got a continuance of his trial, and swanked around town suborning witnesses. Susie decided to improve our fiction by saying that it was a fair fight following a north-south argument between her lover and Cassius. Getting a fair-minded jury able to convict the murderer looked impossible. I couldn't stand that, so I borrowed a sawed-off shotgun from a Wells-Fargo messenger I knew, loaded both barrels with buckshot and split the wads, and went hunting for Bob. I found him entertaining in the bar of the Bella Union Hotel. He was carrying a derringer, but his hand was still in his pocket when he got blown all apart. The trouble is, I fired two barrels at once and winged several bystanders. There was a lot of indignation, and talk of hanging me in an impromptu fashion. I stayed in jail until Don Ygnacio and the aroused Republicans got me out. Then somehow the grand jury never could get around to bringing in a true bill on me. Nobody really liked Bob, and as soon as his pieces were picked up and buried they forgot him."

Lucius summoned the waiter and requested his bill. He paid with a gold piece, waving away the suggestion of change. The waiter retired bowing. Cass sat watching his uncle with a full heart.

"It was a foolish thing to do, I suppose," Lucius said, a note of apology in his voice. "The idiotic political implications lingered on and threats were made against me. I got into the habit of carrying a gun and not sitting in lighted windows. My reputation was a disadvantage for a few years. But Cassius was less than thirty when he died, and had a full life to look forward to. And he was my brother. He had always taken my part and supported me in my mistakes. I was a young man too, you know, and full of delusions."

"What did my mother say when you'd done it?" Cass asked.

Lucius cleared his throat. "Oh, she was horrified. Horrified and pleased, I expect. Don Ygnacio told me I was a true Villanueva. He was incapable of higher praise. I thought my conscience might bother me, or my dreams be haunted, but nothing happened. I never had any regrets. All I remember now is the expression of complete surprise on Bob's face as he was blown to kingdom come. He wasn't pretty, and it makes me laugh . . ."

They crossed the restaurant and the lobby of the hotel and went out into the warm, dry, breezy darkness, imperfectly dispelled by widely separated gas street lamps. Stopping, Lucius sniffed the air. "Well, well," he said. "The end of a century. God save us all. The next hundred ought to be an improvement, don't you think?"

"Yes, sir."

"I'll say good night to you, Cass. May I add that I think it would be inadvisable to tell Doña Maria what I have confided in you?"

"I understand," Cass said. "May I ask one last question?"

"Why not?"

"Why didn't you marry my mother—afterwards? People thought you might. I wish you had."

"Jesus, Mary and Joseph!" Lucius laughed harshly. "I might have known you'd think of that one. Don't expect a sensible answer from me. I don't know. Here, shake my hand, friend, and forgive me for robbing you of your innocence. It's as fragile and vulnerable as a maidenhead and worth nothing if you keep it too long."

Cass waited while his uncle went from light into darkness, up the dusty street, and disappeared. He swore he would be a Brennan, an exact copy of Lucius Brennan, at any cost.

two

WHEN Cass came home, he could not get the gate open; somebody had fastened it firmly on the inside. He attempted to climb the fence, skinned a hand, and got caught on a nail and tore his pants. His hat fell off and the dependent string wound around one leg. In a rage, he beat on the gate and shouted to be admitted.

Juana, one of his mother's maids, appeared in dishabille and let him in. She looked shocked at his appearance, which did not improve his temper. While crossing the garden, he stumbled and Juana attempted to hold his arm and guide him. He shook off her hand and denounced her in Spanish.

His mother, wearing a wrapper and nightgown, was in the broad front room lighting candles. She was opposed to the use of gas and kept the old house very much as her father had thirty years before. There were still only a few glazed windows behind the heavy shutters, the wide plank floors (a rarity in the district in their day, when hard-packed dirt was considered adequate) were worn and grooved by the tread of many feet, the furniture had the stiff thick angularity of Spanish Colonial, heating in the winter was a matter of scattering braziers in the various rooms around the central patio, and the kitchen was primitive and tiled in vitreous blue squares brought from the forgotten workshops of the Mission San Gabriel. But Doña Maria was a good housekeeper. Her home was spotless.

She stood looking at Cass gravely and yet with sympathy, and he had to stop before going to his room. He never could quite make the adjustment necessary for accepting this woman as his mother. Thirty-six years had touched her so lightly. She seemed a girl, a contemporary of his—not a matron. Slim, small, delicate, with a lovely unlined full-lipped round-chinned face and abundant dark hair and wide-set dark eyes, she was prettier than anybody he knew. Her fine physical presence had an accompanying grace, an intelligence, a subdued humor, a will that was velvety but relentless. She was born to dominate. Even the new men in the Queen, the landowners and merchants and speculators, the overpowering gringos, accorded her respect.

"Did you have a good time today with your uncle?" she asked. Her English was accented, soft and musical.

"Yes," Cass said. "He introduced me to everyone after I marched. He made a great speech."

"So I have heard. But some were not pleased with it."

"He had to be interesting or they wouldn't have listened to him—it was too hot. Then we had supper at the Angeles House."

"Are you drunk?" she said.

"Of course not!"

"No? What did he give you?"

"Wine and beer," Cass said, and blushed.

"How can you tell if you are drunk? You have never been drunk before, have you?"

"No."

"Well, perhaps the drink did you good," she said. "You are nearly a man—within a few years of it, anyhow. Come to your room."

"I don't need any help, Mother."

"I can walk with you, can't I?"

They went out in the patio and crossed to his bedroom. Candles were burning in a wall bracket. He paused irresolutely, opening his collar. Doña Maria made no move to leave.

"Wash your hand," she said. "It is bleeding."

He gazed down at the abraded flesh and oozing blood, and simultaneously his stomach turned and his head spun inside crazily. Taking uncertain steps, he sat heavily on the bed.

"I think I'm going to be sick," he said. His intention had been to add that she should go, but he didn't actually want that. The words were unspoken and she stayed on, raising him from the bed and taking him to a basin, making him bend, cupping his jaws between her palms, abjuring him to spew until the sour mixture in his stomach was discharged. Then she cleaned up, washed and dried his face and hands, and brought a glass of milk for him to drink.

"I'm sorry," he said. "I can't tell you how sorry I am, Mother."

"Hush. You must go to bed."

She began to undress him and he protested, and she appeared surprised. He apologized and explained: at his age, in his room, it was not right—Juana or one of the others might surprise them . . . Her laughter cut him short. The sound of Doña Maria's merriment was brief and concentrated, as though she had too many serious concerns to be able to spare much time for amusement.

"I have bathed and cared for you and seen you naked most of your life," she said. "Have we changed so because you have grown larger and I older? You came from me. There is nothing about you I don't know. What is the sense to changing now? Because you are at an awkward age that will soon pass? What does it matter if Juana surprises us? You are not my lover."

He became very red and fell silent. Stripping him, she helped him put on a nightshirt. As she hung up the discarded garments he slipped gratefully into bed. She returned to his side and smoothed his hair and the covers.

"Does this happen to everybody who drinks?" he asked.

"No. There are some fools who never get sick. They kill themselves with liquor."

"Are you saying that of Uncle Lucius?"

Her eyebrows lifted ironically. "How could I? He hasn't yet killed himself."

"I wish I could bring you together. He doesn't feel toward you as you do toward him."

"I feel nothing toward him," she replied. "This is the only difficulty. I see him as a stranger, with certain defects." She stooped swiftly and kissed his forehead. *"Mi querido . . ."*

That she permitted herself the Spanish and the sentiment moved him. The great dark eyes on him were luminous with devotion. A knot gathered in his throat and kept him from speaking. He turned his face away, loving her tenderly and to distraction, as a baffled and partly encouraged lover might have. She must have divined the emotion he was trying to suppress and left, blowing out the candles and shutting the door behind her.

He lay in the darkness harried by a sense of failure. He did not like drinking and its aftereffects. He was no man yet. His mother meant everything to him, despite Uncle Lucius. And he was a damned crybaby.

The night's events had their inevitable sequel, for Doña Maria was a woman quick to seize an opportunity. With Cass in a humble mood, she proposed they take a trip to the San Cristobal. He could not think of a good reason for refusing, nor see the use of again telling her that he was insensible to the attractions of the rancho—that the inspiration and

36

happiness she received from each visit to her heritage were never transmitted to him. It was better to get the thing over with.

Early in the morning they went by railroad to San Fernando, leaving the little wooden station house near the Plaza, sitting on the red plush seat of an elegant parlor car bound for San Francisco. This was the one part of the ride Cass enjoyed, poised at an opened window breathing the locomotive's smoke and dodging its cinders as he exulted in the speed of movement and the clatter of the wheels and the whistle sounding frequent warnings. In moments the town was left behind, and then there were simply open bare brown country and stark tawny mountains, varied by an occasional broken-down farm house, until the platform and small station at the mission settlement had been reached.

Off in the distance lay the white arcaded ruins of San Fernando Rey, once next in prosperity to the equally ruined San Gabriel Arcángel. As his mother had informed Cass enough times, twenty thousand cattle had grazed in the huge valley, five thousand horses, three thousand sheep; under the Franciscans labored hundreds of Indian neophytes, and the mission ranchos stretched from Cahuenga to Triumfo, from Encino to the towering Sierra. In her girlhood Doña Maria's religious instructor had been a Father Igualdo, formerly of San Fernando, and she said he never tired of talking of his famous "long" building, two hundred and forty-three feet in length, with nineteen arches shading a tiled portico, thirteen years in the building. Father Igualdo had received important visitors in the largest *sala* in California, entertained them overnight, served them seven course dinners while his musicians played, and pridefully shown a soap factory and an aqueduct half a league long leading to a masonry dam in the hills. He had tanners, carpenters, weavers, masons, plasterers, saddlers, brickmakers, storekeepers, farmers, herdsmen, fishermen and pages, and orange gardens, vineyards, blossoms scenting the air, bells sounding the vespers, holy Mass to celebrate, good wine in the refectory, and savages called "gentiles" to bring out of the wilds for conversion and the supplanting of those under his care who died too rapidly of white men's diseases like measles and smallpox and syphilis and were buried in consecrated ground. It was a golden age of peace, religious zeal and prosperity, as remote now as the days of King Arthur and his knights of the round table, and Cass could not have cared less for either. The fabled monarch and Sir Lancelot and Guinevere had not vanished more completely than Padre Igualdo and his brethren in the robes, leaving behind monstrous adobe buildings converted into stables and grog shops.

Waiting in a buggy at San Fernando was Jim Dorcas, the raw-boned, sunburned Missourian who ran San Cristobal on a shares basis for

Doña Maria. He removed his hat to greet her, and ceremoniously shook hands with the young master. Doña Maria was given a hand up to the front seat and arranged her skirts, and Dorcas sat beside her. Already ignoring the conversation dealing with weather, crops and animals, Cass slumped glumly on the rear seat and closed his eyes to the dusty road and parched landscape. He refused to be drawn into the talk, and his mother sighed resignedly.

The bumpy wheel tracks, which led north at first, presently turned westward, threading a narrow pass in the smooth hills and entering a subsidiary valley. It was a long journey. Three hours passed before they entered the outer limits of the San Cristobal. A *vaquero* moving cattle to the watering trough beneath a windmill saluted them, and Doña Maria's expression brightened at the sight of the crossed arrows brand of the rancho. However, beef on the hoof had ceased to be the principal output of her land; competition was too fierce, prices too low, rainfall generally too scanty for proper pasturage. Wells had been dug, as many as she could afford, but San Cristobal was apparently deficient in underground deposits of water. Some of the countryside was hilly and eroded. At lower elevations orange groves, olives, and feed and vegetables could be cultivated; the higher levels were used for dry farming wheat and oats. Lately Dorcas had experimented with vines and walnut trees, not always successfully. An additional disappointment was the fact that well drillers on several occasions had struck oil instead of water, especially at greater heights where it was badly needed. Doña Maria contemptuously dismissed the black and sticky stuff, fit only for coating roofs and laying the dust on roads, and would not hear of the hopes Dorcas cherished for its future.

The better land nearer the coast, warmed by the sea air, was gone, sold in bitter times by Don Ygnacio and his son-in-law at twenty dollars an acre to satisfy creditors and pacify the tax collector; neither Cass's grandfather nor father were men to endure a lower standard of living when they had leagues of property to dispose of. In any event, the original fault lay with an early Villanueva, a cavalier who had chanced his luck in Santo Domingo and Mexico prior to accepting the first grant offered him by a Spanish governor eager to keep select parcels for his favorites. At that time, considering its extent and the wet winters which no longer seemed to come, the San Cristobal had served well and supported several generations of Villanuevas in a style that permitted them to live in the Queen or Santa Barbara and frequently go back to the fleshpots of Mexico City.

For over a decade Doña Maria had been fighting hard to keep intact what remained. She felt herself lucky to find Jim Dorcas, now a man in his fifties, to help her. He shared her allegiance to the soil, her delight in green and growing things, her faith in the eventual benefits of large holdings. If he did not have her almost mystical attachment to the ground her forefathers had held, he had at least a part of her stubbornness and eye for the smallest profit. Like her, he seemed undaunted by lack of wells, distance from reasonable transportation, and a population growing too slowly to create real demand for their products. He was a widower who had moved west to start a new life, his children grown, and it was rumored that he hoped to marry his employer and partner.

To Cass the enthusiasm of his mother and Dorcas, their dogged attention to duty, was incomprehensible. He had no feel for agriculture or rural pursuits. The nearly treeless grassy hills, the scrubby live oaks in the draws, the rolling miles of chaparral were antipathetic to him. Exposure to the outdoors from infancy, herding, harvesting crops, caring for animals, meant merely that he longed for town the more. He hated manual labor. The freedom of the open was unpleasant. No bond adhered between him and the Mexicans and *mestizos* who tenanted the San Cristobal from one generation to the next and awoke a spirit of *noblesse oblige*—to her financial loss—in Doña Maria. Those miracles of ripening grapes and fattening steers and tasseling wheat were not miracles in his eyes. The pride of owning miles of land left him untouched. The Villanuevas preceding him were puzzling and unlovable figures out of a remote age, doting on their silver-mounted saddles, dressed in embroidered vests and silk shirts and tight velveteen trousers split up the sides and elaborate boots and spurs, going to their balls and dancing the *contra danza* and the *jota* with women rich in silks and satins and jewelry; or spending their time drinking and gambling and racing horses instead of learning to read and write. The world had turned upside down. These *hacendados* on the far side of the globe, pretending to a nobility that was spurious, had long since been elbowed aside. Cass could not even imagine what they had been like.

The home valley, made green and fresh by an unfailing artesian spring, had half a century ago contained the sprawling adobe house of Colonel Jesús Antonio Cordoba Villanueva, Cass's great-grandfather. He was the gay successor to a number of previous Villanuevas who, in spite of their expensive tastes, were diligent about keeping the San Cristobal whole. They were *hidalgos,* proud, dedicated to their families, big-nosed, solemn and conscious of their worth if the darkening portraits Doña Maria had kept could be trusted as likenesses. Their wealth had been counted in hides and tallow and they had sent their younger sons to Mexico City or Madrid to be trained as soldiers, priests and officials, and married their daughters within the select circle of *californio* aristo-crats. Reputations for coveting land and laughing at religion did not bother them. Bequeathed to the colonel (who attained his rank fighting in the revolutionary armies against the Emperor Maximilian and suc-ceeded an elder brother killed by a falling horse) was a barony running through inland valleys nearly to the ocean. Jesús Antonio made the first serious inroads on the Villanueva wealth. With more retainers than many a European lordling, letting his *mayordomo* handle tiresome business details, building his great house and returning in splendor to the rancho, backing his fast horses and spreading his hospitality in all directions, he piled up debts and willingly signed notes whose com-pounded interest brought twenty and thirty per cent to gringo money-lenders. His fame waxed, his lavish habits were admired, and his credit grew shaky. Don Ygnacio, inheriting from the colonel, had some of the virtues of earlier Villanuevas, but time and luck were not on his side. In spite of a desire to preserve the San Cristobal, it declined in munificence and extent.

The colonel's lavish home had disappeared; only foundation stones remained to trace the U-shaped outlines that enclosed a patio with fountain, innumerable bedrooms, a dining hall which could accommo-date fifty persons, a wine cellar, a ballroom, a grand fireplace, and pre-sented wide cool verandas where he received his hordes of guests. Part of the outbuildings, much repaired, survived to shelter the present di-minished number of workers. In Jesús Antonio's time a small army had numbered among them *vaqueros,* artisans, riata makers, hide curers, tallow renderers, lumberers, *carreta* drivers, laborers, maids, cooks, and all the other humble folk as securely attached to him and his land as were the peasantry attached to a lord of the manor in the old country. The corrals were gone, the fighting cocks, the dogs and the flocks of sheep—Jim Dorcas enforced a Yankee order and economy to the extent that Doña Maria would permit. His plain frame house nearby was small and neat, devoid of gardens, with an incongruously steep roof for a valley where it had snowed twice in a century.

Doña Maria and Cass joined Dorcas at dinner, a midday meal cooked and served by a Mexican woman. Beef and beans were staples at San Cristobal now, and tortillas to soak up the gravy in the earthenware dishes; Jesús Antonio's silver plate and superb china went with Don Ygnacio when he moved to Los Angeles. No wine graced the table of the water-drinking Dorcas. The grapes the rancho produced were sold in wagon-load lots to the wineries in town.

When he had finished eating and, after obtaining Doña Maria's permission, lighted a *cigarillo,* Dorcas said, "Cass, aren't you going to come out here with me pretty soon?"

"I'm supposed to have more education," Cass told him.

"You can get plenty of educating on the San Cristobal," Dorcas said, "I guarantee you. The kind you'll need when you inherit it. Better start young. And I could use you, lad. I'm no chicken anymore."

Cass scowled down at his food.

"It's the same story," Doña Maria said. "He simply isn't interested. Each time we are here I hope he will find his vocation, but that never happens."

"Well, patience, patience," Dorcas said. "He was born to this. Or were you spoiled for ranching in the Sandwich Islands, lad?"

"No, I didn't like them," Cass said. "I wanted to come home."

"If you decided to live at San Cristobal," Doña Maria said, "I would stay with you. We might build another house."

Keeping quiet was Cass's best defense. He waited, avoiding his mother's eyes. She shrugged and said, "I'll have a look around, Jim. You needn't go with me. Cass?"

"Marching in the parade made my legs and feet hurt," Cass said. "I'm too sore for riding. I'll wait for you, Mother."

Doña Maria emerged from her room wearing the rakish costume Don Ygnacio had encouraged her to put on from childhood as long as she was within the privacy of his own domain. She had the sombrero, the short jacket, the tight trousers and boots of a *vaquero.* Clothed in them she looked incredibly young, lithe and inviting. Her hands were gloved, she carried a quirt, the silver rowels on her spurs jingled. Outside a white mare was waiting, and the same old, wrinkled, dour body-guard who had protected her when she was not yet of marriageable age. He carried his hat in his hand, and a Winchester rifle in a leather scabbard was slung to his saddle pommel.

Doña Maria required no assistance in mounting. She was an excellent horsewoman. Glancing at Cass, she said, "You won't change your mind?"

He shook his head. She rode off attended. In the distance he saw Dorcas pretending to be busy overseeing the digging of an irrigation ditch but eyeing Doña Maria. An inkling of how the Missourian must relish this invaded Cass's consciousness before he could reject it, and his face flushed. His mother's breasts bobbed under a thin silken blouse, her hips were firm, her legs slim and straight. He wondered whether she realized how well the strange clothing suited her and emphasized her fine body. If she wore the outfit deliberately and not in homage to the past, then she was something else than the person he loved and revered.

Cass spent five long disconsolate days on the rancho. His time was wasted wandering around the home valley, catching and releasing frogs in the little lake the springs fed, taming a piglet and trying to teach him simple tricks, and talking to an ancient pensioner who sat every afternoon on the front step of his hut to take the sun. The man had been Don Ygnacio's *mayordomo del campo,* in charge of all the *vaqueros,* and his exaggerated respect for the young master was flattering. Although Cass had little patience with his stories of the great days and ladies riding behind their *caballeros* in brocaded gowns to attend the *gran bailes* of Don Ygnacio and the horse racing and huge wagers and the music playing till dawn in the colonel's house until one night guttering candles set it afire, he was interested in reminiscences concerning his father and Uncle Lucius. Both were much men, by this witness, and a handsome pair, always in the company of each other. In that time Lucius evidently came often to the rancho. They enjoyed hunting and drinking, those brothers, and laughed and shot at targets and danced and held the bank in high-stakes monte games and smoked tobacco and did other manly things. The gentry rallied round them, their popularity and generosity was immense, they feared no man, and Don Ygnacio—God rest his soul—delighted in their company.

And the ancient uttered a curious remark that intrigued Cass: "Don Luis never brought a woman here. He came alone. It was as if they were a trinity, no disrespect meant"—he crossed himself—"Don Cassio, Doña Maria and Don Luis. Oh, they enjoyed life. They were young. Once Don Cassio said within my hearing to Doña Maria and Don Luis, 'Pity the lady of our dreams; she has married a family, not a man, and scarcely knows yet which Brennan to choose,' and the three of them laughed very hard. Then there was the killing and it ended. The land stank of dead beasts too. We wept."

At last Doña Maria surrendered and arrangements were made to return to Los Angeles. On the eve of departure, as his mother and Dorcas pored over the crude account books of the rancho, Cass discovered an element that piqued his attention. It was the columns of figures on the pages Doña Maria frowningly turned, listening to Dorcas's explanations. The slowness of comprehension the older people displayed, their inability to employ even elementary mathematical reasoning, astounded Cass. He had to intervene. They listened to him so wonder-struck he almost laughed at them.

For the first time he became aware of the deficiencies in his mother's education and judgment. She had the social graces, she was literate in two languages, her head was stocked with various experiences and she possessed a good memory, and she had read a few devotional books and knew her catechism. That was the extent of her formal training. There was an irony in his being controlled by a mother who knew far less than he, with only sixteen years to his credit. Cass began to regard more favorably the prospect of college; it could pay him realizable benefits.

"He must go to Santa Clara," Doña Maria said.

"Mother, there're schools in Los Angeles," Cass said.

"They are not like Santa Clara," she said.

"I say only the best for a lad with his brains," Dorcas added.

"Oh, lord!" Cass said. "If I'm so bright, I can make an ordinary school do." Later, alone with Dorcas, he said, "Please don't carry on about my helping with the books, sir. My mother will think I'm a genius and put me in Santa Clara if it's the last thing she ever does. I'd rather stay home and go to St. Vincent's. I didn't tell you anything an ordinary bookkeeper couldn't."

"You're right, lad," Dorcas answered, and grinned. "I'm not as big a fool as I look. But you're Doña Maria's son, and the San Cristobal is going to be yours. I have to admire you, don't I?"

Cass held his tongue. But his conception of Dorcas changed. He began to mistrust him. It was possible that the haphazard accounting had a sinister purpose. Perhaps he was stealing from Doña Maria and covering up defalcations in the books, or at least not turning over a fair share of any profits. In any event, Dorcas wasn't as naïve as he pretended.

Doña Maria was set on Santa Clara. When he resisted, she was willing to consider St. Mary's in San Francisco. His arguments for St. Vincent's ran into a blank wall upon his mention of Lucius's suggestion that he enter a law office and study for the bar; he thought he could manage both an education and the start of a career at home. She shook her head, lips compressed, and was silent for a while.

"I don't want to leave you," Cass pleaded.

"Or him?"

Spreading his hands helplessly, Cass hesitated, and asked: "What is the matter with him? Why do you hate him?"

He expected no reply, but to his astonishment she retorted, "I don't hate Lucius. I am afraid of his influence on you—that and nothing else. You ask what is the matter with him. Are you still so young you can't see for yourself?"

"I can't see for myself, Mother. What is the matter with him?"

"He drinks too much, he gambles at everything and has lost all his money, he associates with loose women, he is not a good Catholic. He's filled with grand schemes that never come to pass. People don't trust him." She paused, adding reluctantly: "I'd rather die than have you another one like him."

Emboldened, he said, "Was my father the same?"

"Does Lucius say that?"

"Well, yes."

A bitter half smile wreathed her lips. "So you get drunk together and are very manly. That impresses you, eh? Did he tell you how your father died?"

Cass nodded.

"Ah," she said, "how kind of him to disillusion a boy, to ripen him too soon, to poison his mind—"

"He didn't do that, Mother."

"Are you going to model yourself on Lucius?"

"No," Cass said. "He doesn't want me to be like him."

"Did you learn from him how he shot down the man who killed your father?"

"Yes. I was glad to find it out. I admire him for—"

"You are mistaken. There is no glory in vengeance. Lucius is a murderer too, and they talked of hanging him."

"It was a fair fight."

"In his eyes it was," she said. "Some people, when they bother to remember, are not so sure. Lucius had a shotgun and he surprised a man who may or may not have had a pistol in his pocket. It was an execution, in defiance of the laws of God and of the town . . . Cass, I have had enough of this discussion. I cannot make up your mind for you. There is only one question I can ask: are you willing to break my heart?"

"No, Mother," Cass said. "You know you can always win by asking that one question. But I—"

"No more, please."

At the first opportunity Cass went to talk to his uncle. Lucius's office was on the upper floor of a Main Street building, near the corner of Second. The sign on the door, in peeling gold letters, read:

BRENNAN & JENNISON

LAND AGENTS

CONSTRUCTION ENGINEERING

REAL ESTATE DEVELOPMENT

Inside, the single long room had a couple of desks, numerous scarred chairs, and maps on the walls of the county, the city and outlying townships. It smelled of cigar smoke. Copies of *A Glimpse of Paradise*, promotional literature and a magic lantern outfit were much in evidence.

Lucius was engaged in a confidential talk with a puffy, red-faced man when Cass arrived. Signing for Cass to wait, he continued the conversation. Half an hour passed. Finally the man took his leave, and Cass, who had moved a discreet distance away and looked out a window, walked over and sat beside his uncle's desk. Hat on the back of his head, coat off, sleeve cuffs inched up and protected from soiling by scarlet arm garters, Lucius was the embodiment of a busy land agent; he laid aside a pencil with which he had been making notes, took cognizance of Cass's despondent expression, and clucked sympathetically.

"Where have you been?" he asked. "You're a sad looking citizen."

"At San Cristobal," Cass said. "Then I've been arguing with Mother ever since we got home. What am I going to do, Uncle Lucius?"

"It's come to that?"

"Yes, sir. I can go either to St. Mary's in San Francisco or to Santa Clara."

"Did you mention my finding you a clerkship in a law office?"

"Yes. She just ignored me."

"What about the University of Southern California? It's not much to look at but I hear those Bovard brothers, the ministers, are doing a fine job."

"They're Methodists," Cass said. "Do you think my mother would let me go to a Protestant school?"

"How stupid of me. Well, St. Vincent's isn't run by the wrong kind of Christians."

"She says it's no good."

"Meaning I'm no good," Lucius said. "You're done for." He sighed. "Oh, choose St. Mary's—you'll have San Francisco to enjoy yourself in if the fathers ever let you out of their sight."

"All right," Cass said, and got up. "I'm sick of talking. I'll go as soon as she wants."

Gazing at him sadly, Lucius was about to say something when Kirby Jennison entered the room. He shook hands with Cass and inquired for his health and the state of his present position.

"He's badly off," Lucius interjected, "and almost resigned to his fate. How did it go, Kirby?"

"Sold, by God. At the price we stipulated. It went as smooth as rhubarb through the hired girl."

Lucius arose and seized Kirby by the arms and they did a ridiculous little war dance around the desk. In spite of his low spirits, Cass had to laugh at them. Then Lucius took a pint of whiskey from his desk drawer and they dignifiedly lifted the bottle to each other and took deep swigs.

"The boom is near upon us," Lucius said reverently. "Twenty-two thousand dollars for a hundred-and-seventy-five-foot city lot! Lord of Hosts, sustain us for a little while longer! We'll despoil the Philistines yet!"

"How?" Kirby demanded. "Where can we raise the money to buy property? Who would finance you these days, aside from me?"

"Somebody will hark to my rhapsodies," Lucius said. "I don't need a fortune; just enough for options will suffice, and coverage in a few choice locations. To hell with you." But he was laughing as he spoke, and swung Kirby around in the dance again.

The lot which had sold for the prodigious price, Cass gathered, was on Spring Street at Fourth (Spring Street had been Primavera once, and Doña Maria disapproved of the change in name), and Brennan & Jennison had turned a handsome profit. However, the implications were more important than the money—their judgment was vindicated, the sale established a record, and now they had proof of soaring real estate values. Golconda was only around the next bend if they stayed lucky and got out before feet were wetted.

"If they'll vote the water bonds," Lucius said, "if the Santa Fe comes in, if they'd pave the streets, if we can swing the cable railway deal—"

"Slow down," Kirby protested. "You're making me dizzy."

Brennan & Jennison were involved in the promotion of a cable-drawn streetcar system to supersede the horsecars, powered by electricity from steam-driven dynamos. The lines would climb west into the encroaching hills, opening up whole new residential districts. It was easy for Cass to see that his uncle was the brains and motive force in the partnership. He had the air of a prophet in talking of the cable railway.

"Then nothing can stop us," Lucius said. "And that means sewers, water pipes, curbs, sidewalks, paving, houses everywhere. Gas for heating and cooking, yes, but electricity, Goddamn it, for lighting purposes. It's coming and we have to get in on the ground floor. Why would a man stay in this ass end of creation if it wasn't for what he can do in the way of improvements and lining his purse? We've got to grow or atrophy."

"Wait a minute," Kirby said. "For every boom there's a bust, especially in this town. If enough people listen to you, they'll have the biggest collapse in history. Take it easy."

"Oh, ye of little faith!" Lucius told him. "Haven't I given you my word we'll have built our ark before the deluge falls?"

"Remember your past?" Kirby said. "You forgot to float an ark in '75. Things were going pretty good then, and you helped take the brakes off. How about the bank you started, the loans you granted without getting enough collateral, your confidence in booming values? You were

46

a big man until the bottom dropped out. Afterward nobody would touch you. The depositors in Liberty Consolidated got twenty cents on the dollar in the liquidation. Losing your own shirt didn't satisfy you—you had to lose everybody else's."

"The crash began in New York, not here," Lucius said. "It was nationwide and won't happen again. The fools wouldn't have brought themselves down if they hadn't persisted in the run on the bank. Anyhow, I'm through with banking."

"You sure are in these parts," Kirby said. "You're thought of as a *bandido,* not a banker. Stay away from counting houses or you'll go to jail next time. Except for luck and political pull, you might be in San Quentin now."

Lucius smiled at Cass. "Pay no heed to him. He's a character assassin, and a liar to boot. Cass, what do you want for a going-away present? What's your heart's desire?"

"Going away?" Kirby asked. Though well aware of Cass's situation, he assumed a polite surprise. "You aren't here to stay with your sainted uncle, boy? Has the great lady won again?"

"Yes, sir," Cass said resentfully. "I'm going up to St. Mary's."

"Why, the parting is painful to contemplate," Kirby said. "I must say, however, I think the lady's in the right. Considering how often the sins of the fathers are visited upon the children—"

Speaking softly, Lucius said, "We aren't in need of your reflections, friend."

"Oh?" Kirby said. "Sorry, Colonel. Your pardon. Do you object to my suggesting the best and most necessary present for your nephew?"

"No. What would it be?"

"The oldest of revelations. I don't guess he's experienced it yet, and he must be hungering."

"Bless me," Lucius said, and seemed amused. "I hadn't even considered it. You amaze me."

"Part of your duty, I'd say," Kirby said. "And it should happen under your supervision. He ain't likely to receive a gift of that sort at home."

"True. But I have some qualms, and we haven't heard from him yet. Cass, what would you like?"

"I can't think of anything, sir."

"Do you know what we were talking about?"

"No, sir."

"It's just as well," Lucius said. He held out his hand. "I'll surprise you one way or another. You'll hear from me before you go. Goodbye for now."

Cass shook hands with both men, a little annoyed by their mischievous smiles, and left glumly. On the walk home a weary resignation comforted him. At least the struggle was over.

Next day he attended early Mass at St. Vibania's Cathedral with his mother, and then sat silently through the breakfast that followed. She talked easily of commonplaces, ignoring his low mood. Presently he tired of her cheerfulness.

"I'm not going to break your heart, Mother," he said. "But let me go to St. Mary's."

She showed no signs of elation or satisfaction. "As you wish. I know Father Bernard there. He will guide you."

"All right."

"We'll go as soon as possible," she said. "The arrangements will not take long. I don't think you'd better go alone this time, and I will not leave you until you're settled and content."

Two days later he was a trifle surprised to have her affably tell him that she had received a note from Lucius. His uncle asked what her decision was on Cass's education and whether Cass could have supper with him that night. Her reply, unfinished, awaited delivery by Juana. Did he care to accept the invitation?

"Whatever you say," he replied indifferently.

"Are you angry with him?"

"No."

"Disillusioned? He hasn't been very helpful to you, has he?"

"No, Mother."

"I have the feeling," she said, "that the older you grow the less impressed you will be by him." She smiled. "I think you had better say farewell. He is your uncle, after all. But in my letter I'm going to request him not to get you drunk again."

In the evening Cass took a horsecar southbound on Main Street, got off at Sixth, and walked to his uncle's house. The horse and buggy Kirby Jennison owned was tied to the hitching post outside. Fidelia opened the door. She had the air of being in possession of an agreeable secret, and Cass took it unkindly. He told her if she called him *niño* he would trip her up as she served the supper.

"That I would call you a baby!" she said. "Tonight you are a man!"

"You are an old fool," he said, "and not humorous."

Lucius and Kirby awaited Cass in the fusty parlor, smoking cigars and drinking whiskey. Each appeared in a high good humor. Oddly, the moment Kirby had greeted Cass, he tossed off his drink and excused himself and left. Pouring liquor in a glass and adding soda water, Lucius casually handed it to Cass.

"I'm running a bit of a risk in offering you strong waters," he said, "but then running risks is my specialty."

"I'll stay sober, don't worry," Cass said. "Once was enough. I felt awful."

Fidelia summoned them to the meal, and Lucius continued the subject in the dining room. "My reason for exposing you to temptation isn't to lead you to your downfall," he said, and offered Cass wine. "All my knowledge of men and living has taught me that restraint is the result of exposure to folly—and the earlier the exposure the better. The worst sin is to resist any sin and have to practice an unhealthy self-restraint. It leads to narrow-mindedness, hypocrisy, delusions, and gives the transgression a false importance. Are you bothered by the demands of the flesh, Cass?"

Reddening, Cass said, "No . . . not very often."

"It's worse than needing a drink, I suspect. You've had a girl by now, haven't you?"

"Uh—no, sir."

"Not even in the Islands? I have heard they're full of generous brown beauties."

"They were pretty strict at the school."

"Don't be ill at ease," Lucius said. "The appetite is universal, I assure you. And it has to be satisfied. You've looked at the brown girls, haven't you, and wanted them?"

"Well . . . yes."

"And taken measures with your fellow pupils or alone?"

Cass nodded unwillingly.

"I trust you didn't acquire a taste for boys," Lucius said. "The Greeks and Romans have written of their advantages, but I'm damned if I could ever see what delighted them. Grown men misusing the young or themselves are somehow ridiculous. You agree?"

"I never liked any of that kind of stuff," Cass said.

"But you've abused yourself?"

"Not much . . . Doesn't it make you blind or crazy?"

"That's what we're told," Lucius said. "I'm not sure that the information is correct because in my early youth I was indefatigable in obtaining proofs of my virility, and yet my sight is good and I am only a little insane. Still, there's nothing like a woman to give pleasure. Cass, would you care to have a girl tonight?"

"Me?" Cass said. A choking sensation gripped his throat. "What kind of a girl?"

"Why, a handsome one purchased for the occasion."

"Sir—I wouldn't know what to do with her!"

"The girl will know what to do," Lucius said gently.

He stopped the questioning, pressed more wine on Cass, and spoke of women in general. His attitude toward them had the qualities of a benevolent tolerance. They were a mystery, but not a very intriguing mystery—not, in short, a worthy subject for intensive study if a man was absorbed in making his way in the world.

When they had finished eating, he took Cass back in the parlor and gave him a small glass of brandy. Obeying instructions to toss it off for a better effect, Cass gulped the fiery liquid. A hot trail burned far down in his throat and his eyes misted and a stunning vapor filled his nostrils. He noticed, when he could see again, that Lucius's head was cocked to the side in a listening attitude. Fidelia went to answer the door, and Kirby Jennison brought a small, very young girl into the room.

"This is Mariquita," he said. "Call her Molly for short."

She was perhaps fifteen years old, and wearing a plain dark dress and a shawl over her shoulders and clumsy white slippers. She had an olive skin and auburn hair loosely plaited down her back, an enchanting face with almond-shaped eyes and flattish cheekbones and a softly curved chin, and looked voluptuous in spite of her youth as her mixed race often did. In better clothing she would have been striking. Her manner was solemn and respectful, but she was not embarrassed.

"Are you satisfied?" Kirby asked.

"Splendid," Lucius said, and studied Molly from head to foot. "Just as advertised."

"Well, let's go," Kirby said. "He'll do better alone."

"Yes, of course," Lucius said. "Goodbye, Cass. Molly will entertain you while we're gone."

"You can count on that, boy," Kirby said, and grinned wolfishly. "Don't waste a minute of your time."

"Goodbye," Cass said, in a faint voice.

His uncle and Kirby left the parlor. The front door slammed. Cass stood gazing at Molly, his face red, his heart starting to pound. Appearing in the doorway and giggling, Fidelia instructed the girl to go upstairs and into a bedroom on the left side of the hall. Smiling cheerily at Cass, Molly turned and went out.

"Have you had a bath?" Fidelia said to her.

"*Sí, sí!*"

Cass remained where he was. "*Pronto!*" Fidelia said, and motioned to him. He put his hands in his pockets because they felt ready to tremble, glared at her, and followed Molly up the staircase. She entered the

50

bedroom, waited for him to come, and shut the door. The bed was turned down and a single lamp burned.

"Have you fear?" she said. "I am all right."

"I am not afraid."

"Good. I will make you very happy."

Stepping out of the ugly slippers, she removed blue garters and peeled off cotton network stockings. The dress was pulled over her head. There was nothing underneath. She reached up to straighten her hair with both hands and the movement lifted her full red-tipped breasts. Cass stared at her, forgetting to undress. Pulses sang in his ears.

"I will help you," she said, and knelt at his feet to untie his shoes. Then she rose and began unbuttoning his clothes. As they fell away she reached out and grasped him and laughed at his startled reaction. She pushed him on the bed and threw herself upon him, starting to breathe hard, and forced him flat beneath her and kissed him on the mouth until he was breathless. Her hands never stopped moving over his body. Rising on her knees, she poised above him and guided and sank on him and wetted him and accepted him with difficulty. Almost immediately he gave a fierce cry and seized her and was undone. After a moment of moving on him, her cry echoed his. They lay together in a close embrace panting until she freed herself.

On a marble-topped stand was a basin and pitcher, soap and towels. Molly washed them both. Cass touched her bosom and buttocks lovingly. She kissed him, not alone on the mouth, and he returned the kisses. He said he loved her, in Spanish, again and again. Her hand directed his to her secret places. Lying under him, her legs wrapped around him, she raked finger nails along his back and moaned and spoke of his splendid size. There was no quick conclusion now. He felt he had conquered everything. And the end was not yet; she fondled and kissed him and made him respond once more, and she said he was a bull and she loved him dearly. Tired shadows came on her cheekbones and she wept. He kissed the tears away.

"When will I see you again?" he asked.

"At any time," she said. "But the colonel must give me another ten dollars—"

Supposedly ready for departure, Cass walked painfully along Main Street to pay his uncle a visit, consumed by panic and disillusionment. Thus far he had managed to keep Doña Maria in ignorance of his revolting urethral discharges and fearsome swelling, but he was too ill to hold out much longer. He had heard enough of schoolboy rumors to have a good idea of what ailed him, and making the trip to San Francisco seemed impossible.

Lucius was involved with three strangers when Cass arrived at the office, and he had to sit squirming in a corner until the discussion of the terms of sale of an orange grove had been concluded. As he limped toward Lucius, the latter started to frown.

"I think it was Molly," Cass said. "I can hardly walk, and—"

"Jesus, Mary and Joseph!" Lucius said. Even his aplomb was shattered. "Come behind the desk. Sit down. Undo your pants."

"Do you have to look?"

"Yes, Goddamn it!"

Cass revealed his afflicted parts. His uncle paled and cursed. He got up, went to the doorway and stuck his head out in the hall, and shouted for the youth downstairs who ran errands for tenants of the building. When the boy came running, Lucius said, "Mr. Jennison is over in Pete Eggar's saloon talking to somebody. Get him here as fast as you can. Tell him this is a matter that can't wait." He returned to Cass. "Does your mother know?"

"Not yet. But it's getting worse, and—"

Lucius waved a hand to stop Cass, shook his head, and stared out the window. Afraid to say more, Cass folded his hands in his sore lap and waited. Suddenly tears filled his eyes and he lowered his head. Coming on them in haste, Kirby said, "Hello, young fellow," to Cass, and "What's the matter?" to Lucius.

"That little piece you handpicked," Lucius said, "the one fresh as a daisy who'd never been on the turf and hadn't even sold it yet, gave Cass a dose. He has balls as big as grapefruit!"

"Oh, my God . . ." Kirby said.

"I ought to shoot you," Lucius said.

"Give me your gun," Kirby said. "I'll do it myself . . . Her father swore on his word of honor—"

"I'm going to run him out of town," Lucius said. "And maybe you with him. You and your infant whores!"

Cass hadn't before seen him in so towering a rage—he was beet-colored and swollen and his eyes seemed to spit blue sparks. Colorless and grim, Kirby waited for Lucius to regain control.

"Let's go see Doc Kreder," he said, when he dared.

Lucius put on his hat. "Come on," he said. He reached out to touch Cass in sympathy and evidently thought better of it; his hand was withdrawn. "Stop crying, for Christ's sake!"

They went out of the building, hired a hack standing on the corner, and drove to a dilapidated adobe house on Los Angeles Street between two warehouses. En route, hooking arms with Cass, Kirby said, "This is something that happens to practically every red-blooded man. It don't really hurt you. A bad cold can be worse. I remember once—"

"Shut your Goddamned mouth," Lucius said.

The doctor's anteroom contained a pair of hangdog patients waiting, and one was at that moment exiting from a surgery adjoining. Lucius called peremptorily to Dr. Kreder, who stuck his head through the doorway. He was a portly, bewhiskered, middle-aged man in a frock coat, and availed himself of a pince-nez attached to a buttonhole by a black ribbon.

"Well, well," he said. "Mr. Brennan, I believe." He glanced at Cass and instantly understood. "And who have we here?"

"My nephew Cass Brennan," said Lucius. "He has a little disability we'd like you to examine."

"You remember me, Doc," Kirby said. "I'm Kirby Jennison."

"I never remember my patients, Mr. Jennison, for obvious reasons," Dr. Kreder told him. "But I do recall you . . . Come in, young sir."

He had Cass remove his lower clothing and climb on a table, and his examination was swift and deft. A treatment followed, and as he worked he talked: "Incurred from an amateur, I presume, young sir. How many gents have I warned through the years against them? 'Go to a regular inspected house,' I say, 'and pay your fee and achieve spermatic relief with safety. Don't try to save money by rolling in the brush with niggers and Indians.' But they rarely listen to me. The first bit of tail they fall upon seduces them and they are back here limping and in pain. I must have treated half of our population at one time or another."

He presented Cass with mercury pills and salves, instructed him on how to do for himself, prescribed a strict regime of diet, abstinence and rest, and ordered him to return inside a week. While Cass dressed, his uncle bit off the end of a cigar, lit it, and regarded the doctor gloomily.

"He has to go north tomorrow to school," he said.

"That would be inadvisable," Dr. Kreder said.

"His mother doesn't know. Can he conceal it from her?"

"I don't see how."

"Very well," Lucius said resignedly. "Here's some money. Call on me when you need more."

He led them out of the adobe. The hack, upon his orders, had waited. Lucius stopped, looked at the cigar in his fingers, and threw it away. He took a deep breath and straightened his shoulders under his coat.

"I can't go home alone and tell her," Cass said. "I just can't!"

"No, I expect you can't," Lucius said.

He got in the hack, ordered the driver to take them to the Plaza, and wrapped himself in his own thoughts and said no more. Kirby patted Cass's hand and stared at him in mingled entreaty and apology, apparently fearful of rousing Lucius's anger again if he talked. At Second Street he dropped off, mumbling a few indistinct words. The dreadful journey ended at Doña Maria's wooden gate.

"How are we going to tell her?" Cass quavered.

"I'll do the honors," Lucius said. "Don't whine when you speak. We're in the chamber pot up to our necks now, and we're going to have to grin and bear it."

Immediately they stumbled on Cass's mother in an old gown and with gloves on her hands, tending the thorny rosebushes and neat beds of flowers and shrubs delineated in bricks. She rose from her knees, forehead crinkling in surprise at the presence of Lucius.

"Good afternoon, Doña Maria," he said. "I regret coming unannounced, but I have to talk to you on an urgent matter."

She was looking in alarm at Cass, for his eyes were red and his lower lip trembled. "I'm at your service," she said.

"Can we find some privacy?" Lucius said.

"Let us sit in the summer house," she said, and took them along the brick path that intersected a thick carpet of blue flowering periwinkle and into the lath structure covered by vines. She had grown pale, and sat down stiffly on a bench. Then she waited resolutely for Lucius to go on.

"Cass can't travel to San Francisco at present," he said.

"Why?"

"Do you know what gonorrhea is?"

"No."

"It's a disease men get when they sleep with an unclean woman. Cass has it. I provided the woman."

Doña Maria grew rigid, and two bright spots glowed incongruously in her cheeks. Her hands, divested of the gloves, strained together in her lap and then became limp.

"He's been to a doctor," Lucius continued, "and the treatment has started. The cure is certain and rapid. In the meantime he has to have rest, quiet and good care."

"Why did you do this?" she said, her voice shaking. "To be revenged on me? To spoil what little was left to me?"

He grunted wearily. "No, nothing like that . . . I just don't know any better, I guess. And my luck is uncertain."

"Well, you have won him at last. Take him away with you."

"That's a foolish way to talk, Doña Maria. It's not his fault. You'll be punishing the wrong one."

"I won't have him in my house with that filthy disease!" she cried.

"Don't be a damned fool," he said. "You never had an overabundance of common sense, but at least you could always accept the inevitable. He's sick and sore and ashamed—and he's yours. You can't abandon him now."

"When you've done this to him, you don't want him—do you?"

"Listen to me—"

"Go away!" she shouted. "Never let me lay eyes on you again! I'll kill you!"

He raised his voice: "I'll make you a bargain, you shrew. Swallow this and forgive him, and I will swear to leave him alone—forever, if necessary—until you freely grant me the right to see him again."

"I despise you. You're filth!"

"And you're a bitch," he said. "Enough of a conscienceless, conniving bitch to accept my bargain. I can read it in your face. It's your opportunity to lash him to you for life and break his spirit. Well, you're welcome to him." He turned to Cass. "Goodbye, boy. God help you—and try to forgive me for an unpardonable mistake."

He strode out of the summer house. Doña Maria's eyelids had dropped and she seemed to be in a trance. Cass could not bear to look after his uncle. Moving to his mother, he dropped on his knees and buried his head in her lap and wept. In a moment her arms enfolded him, and her cold brow pressed against the back of his neck. She wept with him.

three

FOUR years later, a graduate of St. Mary's College, Cass went home again to Los Angeles. He was older, of course, perhaps wiser, and heartily sick of Latin, Greek, biology, physics, ecclesiastical history and liturgical music. The time had dragged, and he was often bored. As a product of Father Bernard, a relentlessly intellectual priest, he had theoretically prepared for the world. Actually, he felt less sure of himself than he had at sixteen. The attacks of melancholy from his adolescence still bothered him. And his faith had been undermined by rigorous schooling, for Father Bernard, who could relate all knowledge to his religion, had no idea of the doubts he put in the minds of his more logical pupils. Cass did not much like San Francisco, despite his mother's renting a house there and spending many months with him. Contact had been severed with Lucius, and Cass despaired of ever reviving their old relationship. He tried to banish his uncle from his thoughts.

What he came back to surprised Cass. Doña Maria had given him to understand changes had taken place, but their extent was greater than she seemed to realize. Everywhere were new buildings, homes, shops, roads. The last of the irrigation ditches, the *zanjas,* were covered over; electric arc lamps on tall masts glared down at night in the business district, and stores, saloons, hotels and some houses were illuminated by this fresh wonder; commodious two-horse streetcars had succeeded smaller one-horse models, and cable cars climbed gratingly into the western hills; sewers, piped water and gas were now commonplaces; the city had spread east on both sides of the river (which had lately flooded and swept away all the bridges) to embrace an East Los Angeles; the overflow of population was spreading to the southern flatlands; telephones were in use; and throughout the county people planted orchards and drilled for water and mapped townsites with fanciful names.

The streets were thronged. Midday siestas had gone out of style. Lured by bargain prices as the Santa Fe and Southern Pacific railroads struggled against each other, crowds of outsiders arrived daily on excursion trains; once during a twenty-four hour period fares were quoted at a dollar a head from Kansas City, and freight was carried for a dollar a ton. Tourists intending to stay a week or two lingered on to gamble in real estate futures. Boomers out of the Middle West joined them, eastern confidence men, respectable capitalists, promoters and salesmen. The magic words were "syndicate" and "subdivision." Newspapers sprouted full-page advertisements for new Edens, bands marched to proclaim the birth of more towns, charabancs filled in front of hotels to take the public to the latest development, gullible investors lined up a day ahead to buy unseen lots and sometimes sold their places in line for a hundred dollars to later arrivals. Lotteries were organized to dispose of land and sold out within minutes. Thrifty and needy visitors could live for days on the free dinners and suppers lavishly supplied by subdividers.

The very air seemed to radiate optimism and inflation. Brokers could be found in every block, and, less formally, hotel lobbies, barber shops and street corners served for transactions large and small. Bellhops, hack drivers, loafers and tradesmen dealt in the Queen's basic commodity or knew where to send the inquirer. That optimistic air was full of rumors which caused stampedes to favored localities. Auction succeeded auction. To give reality to a torrent of words spoken and in print, entrepreneurs raised hotels in pastures, built dummy narrow-gauge lines to forsaken hills, and carved out broad avenues to accommodate nonexistent traffic. Their poorer competitors simply employed maps and silver-tongued persuasion to dispose of deserts and mountaintops.

It was nearly impossible to find a room in a hotel or boarding house, and the populace swelled to an estimated fifty thousand. A million acres invited subdivision. Already the satellite towns of New Vernon, Lordsburg, McCoy's Addition to Broad Acres, Arcadia, Raymond, Glendale, Ivanhoe, San Dimas, Port Ballona, Southside, Ontario, Olivewood, Gladstone, Glendora, Azusa, St. James, Burbank, Oleander, Alta Vista, Bonita Tract, Walleria, Ocean Spray and Brennanville were in existence.

Doña Maria disapproved of a Los Angeles splitting at the seams, but the boom had touched her. A year before Cass graduated she sold her home at the Plaza for a tidy sum. Now she regretted not having waited for a bigger return. Although she would never countenance them, promoters in quest of more land had made offers for a part of the San Cristobal.

Cass and his mother lived at first in a select boarding establishment on North Main Street. She had hopes that they could go out to the rancho, but he refused to consider the move. Their relations were much altered; increased age and education had given him a dominance he could feel, and she was more submissive. He wanted to follow Lucius's suggestion of entering a law office as clerk and studying for the bar, and she presented no real opposition to the plan.

One of her friends from the past was Aaron Shapiro, a successful merchant whose new dry goods emporium was daringly situated far uptown on Fort Street at Third. She sent him a note explaining her son's circumstances, and Cass was invited to call at Shapiro's office in the store. It had been his daughter who portrayed the Spirit of Los Angeles in the Centennial Day parade, an incident Cass had not forgotten. A grave, elderly, bearded man, Shapiro listened sympathetically to Cass, seemed to approve of him, and promised to help.

Meanwhile, he had to wait. He was restless and lonely. The friends of his childhood were gone, and he was uninterested in Doña Maria's circle. There was nothing for him to do but walk the streets. Buying law books, he spent his days studying, and ate his meals in the company of widows and superannuated men. His only amusement consisted of accompanying his mother to Mason's Opera House for the plays and lectures.

His uncle was often in his thoughts. To have avoided knowledge of him would have been difficult. Brennanville, backed by heavy newspaper advertising, was reputed to be the new gem of the San Fernando Valley. Lucius courted publicity and generally outdid his competitors in the printed appeals. Cass read such things as:

Colonel Lucius Brennan, the great pioneer figure, calls your attention to Brennanville, realization of his dreams for Southern California. This is a MODEL CITY! View lots on green hills. Lovely acres in a perfect valley. Spacious *ranchitos* for the outdoor man. Best water supply. Sunny days, cool nights. Fertile soil, perfect drainage. Pure air. No fog. Frequent railway service to Los Angeles. The magnificent Xanadu Hotel now under construction. Come to HEAVEN ON EARTH while there is yet time! HE WHO HESITATES IS LOST!

WATCH FOR ANNOUNCEMENT OF OUR GIGANTIC AUCTION, COMING SOON! THIS WILL BE YOUR ONLY OPPORTUNITY TO BUY INTO THE IDEAL COMMUNITY!

Another broadside revealed that Lucius was availing himself of the talents of Virgil Hoch, who unabashedly signed his crimes against prosody:

> When blessed Comfort to the earth first ascended,
> To swell with joy the longing hearts of sensible men,
> In the fairest of scenes to which Comfort ever wended,
> His glad voice rang out again and again.
>
> As he reveled mid the glories of pure air and roses,
> Sure at last that he would never more roam,
> He said, "Here in Brennanville perfect peace reposes,
> So let me stay to build up my permanent home!"

As he strolled one day, Cass heard a band playing in a slowly driven dray decked with banners testifying to the advantages of Brennanville. Twice he observed Lucius at a distance, once hurrying along the sidewalk, another time engaged in an animated conversation with a group outside a restaurant. His uncle had not altered in appearance. He continued to wear the same old-fashioned clothing and to clip his beard short. Cass wondered if he had fallen out of the habit of carrying a pistol in his pocket. The tragedy with Molly had dimmed through the years, any resentment he had felt was forgotten, and he longed to go up and speak to him. But pride and the compact Lucius had made with Doña Maria kept him from acting.

Finally a message came from Aaron Shapiro. He had learned of an opening in the law firm of Blour and Regan. Cass was to apply at once; their offices were in the Wheland Building on Arcadia Street. Inside of an hour, Cass was at the suite. Only the senior partner was present, a thin, absentminded man who interviewed him in the reception room. Evidently Albert Blour had but a dim recollection of Shapiro, though he had handled legal matters for him. That he needed a clerk appeared to come as a complete surprise.

"But Mr. Shapiro said—" Cass began.

"You're a college graduate?"

"Yes, sir."

"Can you operate a typewriting machine?"

"No, sir."

"Have you read any law?" Blour said. "Or a form book?"

"Yes, sir."

"Do you know how to keep accounts, pay bills, make collections, write up a daily diary, and serve pleadings, notices of motions and briefs?"

"Not yet. But—"

"You are very inexperienced."

"Yes, sir," Cass said. "I could learn, though."

"You won't do," Blour said. "On the other hand, I suppose we've got to have somebody." He searched his vest, found a fifty dollar gold piece, and gave it to Cass. "Here is your first month's wages. After this you'll pay yourself when you divide the proceeds between Mr. Regan and me at the end of each month. See that pile of written sheets—the brief?"

"Yes, sir."

"Copy it. I want four copies. Use carbon sheets."

"Copy it on the typewriter?" Cass said.

"Precisely." Blour went in his office. In a moment he returned. Cass stood staring down at the old Remington. "I will give you further instructions as needed. What did you say your name was?"

"Cass Brennan."

"In your spare moments, Cass, you must study hard. It is knowledge of precedent that makes a lawyer, not brains or experience." Blour disappeared again.

In an hour Cass mastered the machine. It had only capital letters and was reasonably simple in operation. He was making good progress on the brief when a stout, red-faced man in a frock coat, gray trousers and Congress boots entered the reception room. He smelled of whiskey and had a genial air.

"Well," he said. "We have a new clerk, eh? Who are you?"

Cass explained, and shook the hand of Brian Regan. His name aroused Regan's interest. "Would you be any relation to Lucius Brennan?" he asked.

"I'm his nephew."

"He's a good friend of mine. A drinking companion. Why haven't I heard of you from him?"

"I haven't seen him in a long time," Cass said. "I've been away to college . . ."

"I'll have to tell him you're with us," Regan said. "Maybe we can get his business. He's going to need legal representation real bad at the rate he's going."

Stints at the typewriter were merely a part of Cass's manifold duties at Blour and Regan. Taking turns, the partners indoctrinated him quickly. His days were full, and Doña Maria grew indignant at the hours he kept. And he was too tired of nights to give her more than a hazy conception of his activities. She was incapable of grasping what he did in visiting courts when demurrers were argued, and how he prepared contracts, complaints, answers, opinions on titles, briefs, statements on motions for a new trial, bills of exceptions and notices of appeal. That he collected notes, hounded debtors and disputed the addition of the tabs Brian Regan signed with distressing regularity in saloons struck her as degrading. She could not understand how he took to the job; in her view, assisting Dorcas at the rancho would have been much better. Often he had supper with her and went back to the office to complete documents and to study. Although she complained at his absences, he overheard her praising his industry to a crony in the boarding house.

The partners were quite unlike, and their division of the practice reflected that. Regan handled criminal cases and suits concerned with battery, libel, divorce and revoked promises of marriage; Blour concentrated on civil actions, contracts and title searches. Despite his vague manner, he was prompt, exact and painstaking. Cass found Regan a problem. He was dilatory, drank heavily, stayed up late carousing, and constantly employed his clerk to get stipulations extending the time for pleading. The firm was profitable, but both men were so careless in financial matters that they always had need of ready cash. As a convivial bachelor Regan was a man for outright profligacy, and Blour had a wife and daughters with expensive tastes he made no effort to curb. However, Blour manifested more interest in Cass's progress, and he was grateful for the help. Because of the sympathy between them, he leaned toward Blour's end of the operation and discovered a liking for that area of the law.

But it was Regan who was instrumental in Cass's again meeting his uncle. To his confusion and delight, Lucius walked suddenly into the reception room one afternoon, wafting a scent of cologne and rubbing his bearded chin a trifle uneasily. He paused and stared at his nephew. Cass's fingers tangled in the typewriter keys and stopped helplessly.

"Are you sore at me?" Lucius asked.

Cass shook his head. "How could I be sore at you?"

"No aftereffects from that night?"

"They wore off," Cass said.

"What was her name—Fanny?"

"Molly."

"I meant to run her father out of town and forgot in the excitement," Lucius said, and grinned. "I didn't even get my ten dollars back. It was a hell of an introduction to manhood, wasn't it?"

"Yes, sir."

"Have you tried your luck since?"

"No," Cass said.

"I don't blame you . . . Are you happy here? Get along well with Regan? He's a good fellow."

"Oh, yes. Mr. Blour too."

"You like the idea of being a lawyer?"

"It's the best I can do, I think . . . I'm not like you."

"Thank God for that," Lucius said.

"I didn't mean it that way."

"You should have. Cass, I've missed you—as I did once before. I meant, lots of times, to write you, and somehow never got around to it. Or remember your birthday or send you a Christmas present or something. Well, you understand. I get mixed up in things and become forgetful—"

"I've missed you too."

"This coming together today is only a technical violation of the promise I made Doña Maria. I just happened to wander in and stumble on you, eh? Besides, it's a wonder we haven't met on the streets. How is she?"

"Fine," Cass said.

"God knows, I can't blame her for being angry with me for providing you with a dose . . . You've never been to Brennanville, have you?"

"No, sir."

"We're holding our auction out there Saturday," Lucius said. "I'd love to have you in on the excitement. This is the supreme test, you know. We've piled up the faggots and it's either going to be a hell of a blaze or we'll freeze to death. Couldn't you bring your mother? I'd stay away from you."

"I might talk her into it," Cass said. "I'll try. I'd give anything to come myself."

"Good. The excursion train leaves at ten o'clock. I'll send tickets to you. Let me know if I can help you somehow or other."

"Yes, sir."

"Shake hands with me," Lucius said. "I feel better, having laid eyes on you. Is Regan in?"

"He's in court."

"Tell him to come by my office. I might have a little work for him on title searches and contracts, now my nephew is on his staff."

"That would be Mr. Blour, Uncle Lucius."

"Very well. Give him my message. Goodbye, Cass."

"Goodbye, sir. Thank you."

By devious means, including a mention of the necessity for his learning some of the intricacies of land subdivision, Cass led into a proposal to his mother that they attend the auction at Brennanville. He said Mr.

Blour, who happened to do work for Brennan & Jennison, could procure them tickets; but he did not tell her of Lucius's visit. She confounded him by promptly accepting. "I have five hundred dollars I can spare," she added. "Perhaps we ought to buy a lot."

"What?"

"Not for sentimental reasons, Cass. But the town does have your name and has been founded by your relative. Values are going up. Everybody is excited about Brennanville."

"I never thought I'd hear you talking like this."

"I am trying to forget that disgusting incident," she said. "Lately I have given Lucius considerable thought. They say he's made an awful pile of money and hasn't married. Do you realize you are logically his heir?"

"But you always said he would die a pauper, Mother."

She shifted impatiently in her chair in the boarding house parlor. "I was mistaken. And I am not an obstinate fool, Cass. And I would do anything to ensure your success and happiness. You have seen him since you've been home, haven't you?"

Clearing his throat, he said, "Well, he came by the office to see Mr. Blour yesterday. We only talked for a minute. He says he will keep his promise about me."

"Did he still seem fond of you?"

"I guess so."

"We can't afford to lose him now," she said, as Cass gazed at her incredulously. "It's different—"

Next day, en route to the courthouse, Cass encountered Aaron Shapiro on the street. He was accompanied by his daughter, Rachel Marcus, wearing widow's weeds; a bride of a few months, her husband had died of pneumonia. She was darkly beautiful and remained the willowy goddess of the parade. Cass was in a mood to prolong the conversation, and answered all of Shapiro's questions with regard to his progress in the law office.

"Permit me to give you a word of advice," Shapiro said. "Mr. Blour has a good reputation, but Mr. Regan is entangled in debts and high living. He may be driven to making mistakes. The firm cannot last, in my opinion. I would take care, if I were you, to avoid the least suspicion when you are acting for it. After you have passed your bar examination you would do well to find another connection."

"My uncle seems to like Mr. Regan, sir."

"I regret to say that Colonel Brennan is not the best of guides in business conduct."

"What do you mean?" Cass said.

Rachel laughed, and said, "What my father means, Mr. Brennan—I'm sure he's too polite to come right out with it—is that your uncle's a crook. He can't be trusted. He'd do anything to get more dollars."

"My dear!" Shapiro said.

"Isn't it true?" Rachel demanded. "Haven't I heard you saying that for years? Am I lying?"

"I admit I have disapproved of some of his actions in the past," Shapiro said, "and his Brennanville syndicate dismays me, but he is no worse than most of the subdividers. We should remember he has done a good deal to develop Los Angeles."

"Yes," Rachel said, "if you choose to approve of his methods—closed banks, street railways that go broke, the sale of tracts in the hills where there's not enough water pressure, buying votes, and getting city contracts his partner Mr. Jennison cheats on."

"I think you've said too much, my dear," Shapiro told her.

"I'm very interested, sir," Cass said. "I hardly know my uncle, and I'd like to talk this over with you and Mrs. Marcus. May I come to your house some night, at your convenience?"

"Please do," Rachel said quickly. Her eyes conveyed a frank invitation. "My father is always busy, but I never am. And there are lots of things to discuss besides your tiresome uncle, Mr. Brennan."

"Come any time, Cass," Shapiro said. "I will do my best to protect you from my talkative and flirtatious daughter."

Cass watched them go. He thought Rachel enchanting, and her bias against Lucius only added to her piquancy. That he might be guilty of disloyalty didn't concern him. His uncle could take care of himself, and he certainly did not require the support of an obscure law clerk. Anyhow, he would probably find amusement in a pretty girl's indictment and admit to every accusation.

That evening he mentioned the incident to his mother. "You didn't defend him?" she asked. "Don't you care when he is maligned?"

"Why should I? It's the truth, I suppose. I want to hear more from Mrs. Marcus."

"Why?"

"Because she's beautiful and encouraged me," Cass said. "Isn't that reason enough?"

"Mrs. Marcus is a Jew."

"What difference does it make? Her father is rich."

"It didn't make a difference once," Doña Maria said; "it does now. You could hurt your career by falling in love with a Jewess. Los Angeles is full of Protestants from little inland towns where everybody is the same, and the feeling toward Jews has changed. Take Aaron's advice—he's a wise man—but leave the widow alone."

"I prefer to do as I please," Cass said.

Doña Maria smiled tolerantly. "You're a smart young man; smarter and more prudent than Cassius and Lucius ever were, or my father. These days a young man has to be. You'll always do what is sensible."

Distinctly annoyed, Cass suspected she was correct in her estimation of him. At sixteen he could model himself upon his uncle and vow to become another Lucius; at twenty-one, knowing them both better, the idea had a hint of the ridiculous.

On Friday afternoon Moses Smiley brought the tickets for Lucius's auction to the Blour and Regan office. As rosy, round and benign as before, he greeted Cass warmly. The Smileys now had been blessed with nine pledges of their love. He was auctioneering for Lucius and others, and in addition had accepted the pastorate of the Church of Universal Godhead. It was temporarily situated in the former hall of a fraternal organization on Pearl Street and rejoiced in a growing congregation.

"No doubt you wonder," he said, "at my abandoning Methodism. The reasons are twofold: I am much attracted to evangelism, and it pays better. While I was casting around for increased income, your uncle pointed out to me that Los Angeles is a city particularly well suited to the creation of novel forms of religious observance. We have strangers of every persuasion, many of whom are lonely, feel dispossessed, and are here looking for a change and the opportunity of starting all over again. I find them grateful, generous and in the market for real estate."

Cass congratulated him on his successful ventures. He could not decide whether Moses had the innocence of a wayward child or was a consummate scoundrel. No doubt he was the latter. But Cass liked him notwithstanding. And plainly the preacher belonged with the new Queen and Uncle Lucius.

"You might have a bidder in my mother tomorrow," Cass said. "She seems to have caught the fever."

"No, no," Moses replied. "I'm sure I speak for the colonel in telling her to abstain. Confidentially, we will have numerous agents scattered through the crowd making false bids, and the prices ought to go sky-high. Doña Maria might waste her money."

"Reverend Smiley, tell me: do you consider Brennanville a bad investment?"

Smiling blandly, Moses said, "I am no expert, Cass. But you know your uncle. He isn't always ethically perfect. Like his other friends and admirers, I turn a blind eye when his enthusiasm carries him away, and pray for his redemption . . . My boy, this has been a precious meeting. God bless and keep you."

Conveying Moses's warning to Doña Maria, Cass said, "Apparently Mrs. Marcus was speaking the truth. Uncle Lucius is dishonest. Everybody can't be mistaken."

"I am not surprised," she said. "But you may be his heir, and the guilt is his. Let him take care of what happens in the next world."

He laughed heartily at her. She flushed, and then joined him in the laughter. It amazed him to realize that months passed between episodes of genuine amusement they could share. And he saw, with a measure of apprehension, how she had altered in keeping with the newer, tawdrier ideals of the Queen.

Saturday morning a fife-and-drum corps in flashing blue and gold uniforms paraded along the thoroughfares carrying banners to announce the auction at Brennanville. The newspapers bore pages of advertisements to the same effect, and signs decorated windows and walls. Like gaudy pied pipers, the musicians led a growing stream of people to River Station, where a long excursion train hung with bunting awaited them. Lucius arrived in an open carriage, attired in black broadcloth and a ruffled shirt and boots and a tall hat, and his corps tootled and banged ecstatically. At his side was Kirby Jennison, fatter, wearing a thick moustache, the picture of ease and affluence. Together they shook outstretched hands and exuded a cordial benevolence.

Sitting at a coach window, Doña Maria stared and wetted her lips with her tongue. "If my father could have witnessed this," she remarked, "he would not have believed his eyes."

The trip to Brennanville resembled the first stage of going to the San Cristobal, except these days the countryside was no longer bare; houses had sprung up, groves and standing crops, and several small settlements. Roads marked the edges of ploughed fields, and men dug and sowed and pumped water from wells. South of San Fernando the train moved off on a spur track and approached the flanks of rising ground. Spring had been kind and clothed the land in green; the air was fresh and clear; and a gentle breeze blew. "Paradise," the signs proclaimed. Brennanville came close that morning.

Issuing from a baggage car, the fife-and-drum corps struck up "Yankee Doodle" and made for a great wooden building with crenelated towers, scrollwork traceries to relieve a yet unpainted surface, and wide verandas surmounting vast areas of steps. This was Xanadu, Brennanville's hotel. Adjacent to it stood a half completed three-story brick structure. Each edifice flew the national emblem. All around were graded streets; some had curbed sidewalks and lonely arc-light towers marching along them. Tapes attached to stakes marked lots, every one bearing a number on a neat sign.

The gay crowd straggled to the hotel, where carpenters hammered and glaziers fitted window panes and tea and coffee and pastries awaited the hungry on improvised tables of planks laid over sawhorses. A collection of chairs rented from funeral parlors and auditoriums was ranked about. In a discreetly placarded anteroom were kegs of beer and bottles of whiskey, presided over by a man in a white jacket and apron; the drinks were on the house.

Producing additional instruments, the fife-and-drum corps played suitable music in the vast lobby. Kirby Jennison led a party on a tour of the Xanadu, and Lucius took another outside to inspect the brick building (nobody was working on it), a park consisting only of weeds and dry earth at present, and various business and residential lots. Farther away were one- and five-acre "estates" and "ranchitos"; several buggies stood by with drivers to take the interested to them.

Doña Maria elected to go with those following Lucius, but she kept to the rear, leaning on Cass's arm. Though his uncle gave no sign of having seen them, Cass assumed he had. Lucius painted vivid scenes of the Brennanville to come in his best oratorical style—picturesque homes ranging from cottage to mansion, happy children playing in the flowering park, churches rising on ground set aside for them by the syndicate, the brick building and companions soon to appear filled by doctors, lawyers, dentists and commercial firms, a spacious railroad station to accommodate passengers enjoying the frequent service to Los Angeles, tourists reveling in the luxuries of the Xanadu (which would have mineral baths, a chef imported from Europe, and be conducted like an old world spa) and contributing to the prosperity of the community, and the carefree householder raising his own oranges and vegetables in the rich soil and perfuming the pure atmosphere with blossoms; over all would hover the blessings of peace and plenty, assured by the gentle unction of a climate unmatched by any other locality in the world.

"Consider the very names of the streets," said Lucius, and directed attention to the temporary signs at the corners. "Harmony Way, Avalon Avenue, Blessed Isles Street, Contentment Lane, Placid, Sleepy Hollow, Samarkand, and so forth. Friends, we have done everything in our power to bring you the promised land, the fabled abode of milk and honey, right here in Brennanville."

The forenoon was devoted to familiarizing the guests with the town. While the first batch was being indoctrinated, the train returned to Los Angeles and brought a second contingent, again stimulated by the fife-

and-drum corps, in charge of Moses Smiley. They too were taken on tours by the untiring Brennan & Jennison.

The bar in the Xanadu became more popular, and an eagerness swept the assemblage. Cass heard Kirby telling listeners that a good deal of the purely business property, sold in advance to eager speculators, would go on the market today providing the demand warranted; these early buyers, he said, were willing to sell off if they could make a decent profit. A special sale might be held at the close of the regular auction. Several men told him they were interested in nothing but commercial lots.

Bringing chairs to the veranda, Cass seated his mother and supplied her with tea. Her eyes were brilliant. "I had no idea it was this lovely," she said. "Don't you think Lucius's detractors are either mistaken or envious? Brennanville is bound to succeed." She glanced at him in sudden feminine appeal that was amazingly youthful. "Are you sure we shouldn't buy something?"

"I'm positive," Cass retorted gruffly. He felt he was head of the family now, and appreciated her dependence on him. But he wasn't as convinced as he sounded; the emotions Lucius and Kirby played upon were highly infectious.

Behind the hotel, underneath live oak trees, cooks were preparing a barbecue. Carpenters abandoned the Xanadu to set up plank tables in the grove and bring chairs; while the guests ate, they assembled a railed platform nearby and covered it with bunting. As the musicians performed, wine and beer were served to wash down the tender, spicy beef and thick slices of bread and mounds of beans flavored by a hot sauce. Then waiters brought dozens of pies and gallon pots of steaming coffee. The diners were considerately allowed a period for dozing or walking about to digest the food.

Then the musicians blew a prolonged fanfare. A man walked among the throng in the fashion of a town crier, ringing a bell and proclaiming the start of the auction. Lucius and Moses were already on the platform, and Kirby was climbing the stairs at the side. Fastened to rear scantlings was an enormous oilcloth map depicting every lot, acre, "ranchito," street and feature of Brennanville; a young man with a wand was ready to indicate exact locations when Moses gave the numbers. The barbecue crew brought chairs and the crowd gathered underneath the stand. Lucius stepped forward. Having seated his mother, Cass stood beside her and waited expectantly. He was reminded of the gathering on Centennial Day at the literary exercises—the undercurrent of excitement, the unease of the listeners, the threat of rising wind instead of heat, the same explosive combination of hope and disillusionment in himself. But now

Lucius, unless he had taken leave of his senses, was not going to inflict the truth on them.

His uncle removed his imposing hat and held it to his breast as he would have at the passing of Old Glory. "My friends," he said, "I intend to be mercifully brief. Today represents the culmination of my dreams. I have worked and slaved and sacrificed for this hour. Brennanville sums up what I have ever held dear: justice, peace, security, integrity, the commonweal, the good of my fellow man, the scriptural injunction to do unto others as you would have them do unto you. I want only that Brennanville will constitute my monument and such recollection as I deserve when I have passed on. Glory to the young Queen not far away, and may we be the brightest jewel in her diadem!"

There was heavy applause. Lucius bowed repeatedly, his white teeth flashing in his dark beard, and Cass stared at Doña Maria; her eyes had clouded, and she was gazing up at Lucius with slightly parted lips. After silence had fallen, he introduced the Reverend Moses P. Smiley, of the Church of Universal Godhead, who would conduct the auction. In his reversed collar and suit of decent black, Moses gave the proceedings a heartening gloss of sanctity. Said he: "Dear friends in Christ, if you think it odd for a minister to have taken refuge among the money changers in the temple, believe me I feel I am doing the work of the Lord here. Colonel Brennan, a Christian gentleman if I have ever known one, would have no other than a man of God to officiate at his crowning achievement, and I have come at his beckoning to complete the great task. As the Proverbs say, 'By the blessing of the upright the city is exalted, but it is overthrown by the mouth of the wicked.'" His voice grew louder. "Dear friends, the opening item on the block today is Lot 21, Tract A, Section One. Please direct your attention to the gentleman at the map. Mr. Kirby Jennison, chief planner and engineer of our city, will be happy to answer any questions you may have. Friends, what am I offered for a magnificent residential lot in the best section of Brennanville, fifty by one hundred, level and fruitful, supplied with every amenity, awaiting the nurturing hand of man? Do I hear a bid? Are the offerings to be forthcoming from you?"

They were. The bidding was at once spirited and unflagging, and the turnover rapid. A pink cherub who never became hoarse but was sweating a bit toward the close, Moses kept his audience under perfect control. He spurred them on, he exhorted them, he quoted the Scriptures, he blessed them, he banged down his gavel uncountable times. Clerks with receipt books circulated through the crowd, confirming sales and taking deposits.

Doña Maria's five hundred dollars would have bought little, and Cass

69

noticed her counting distractedly on her fingers, lost in awe. *"Madre de Dios!"* she said. "Lucius is receiving five thousand dollars an acre! Or is it ten thousand?"

Lucius went back to Los Angeles on the first train, which also bore Cass and his mother. Kirby arranged that, coming to them with bared head and introducing himself to Doña Maria. "I know you, Mr. Jennison," she said. "We have met previously. I am glad to see you again."

"Thank you, ma'am. I hope you have enjoyed the outing."

"It has been remarkable."

"The colonel's compliments," Kirby said. "He has taken the liberty of reserving a seat for you and Cass on the last car. I have a buggy waiting to drive you to the train."

Beside the end coach was Lucius being agreeable to a group of well-wishers, and Doña Maria smiled and waved to him—and Cass had to stifle an involuntary burst of dismayed laughter. Lucius promptly walked to the buggy, took off his silk topper, and handed her down. He appeared tired and drained, and not quite as erect as usual. "You are looking well, Doña Maria," he said.

"I can say the same of you," she replied.

"I was delighted by your and Cass's presence at our little auction today."

"Little, indeed! It was magnificent. I give you my best congratulations."

"Thank you."

"The bargain we made in my summer house is ended," she said, "if you choose. I am sorry for the harsh words I spoke then."

"And I am sorry for mine."

"Let us forget them—and the past. I commend Cass to you."

"You are more than generous," he said. "I'm very grateful, Doña Maria."

He was off the train before they at River Station, and had procured a hack. "Allow me to escort you," he said, and she took his arm. Cass walked behind them in a daze, not knowing whether to be overjoyed or disgusted by his mother's transparent duplicity. Lucius aided her in getting seated, gave the driver instructions and money, and turned to shake Cass's hand.

"Perhaps your uncle has a taste for your company," Doña Maria suggested. "Why don't you accompany him?"

"I would enjoy having him with me," Lucius said, "but I hate to deprive you of his protection. I'm sure he would prefer—"

70

"He'd prefer to stay with you. I'm only an old woman, going back to her boarding house to have a quiet supper."

"Not old, Doña Maria. Never old in my eyes."

She smiled. "I'm afraid your sight is failing, sir. Anyhow, take him with you. He is yours, Lucius."

They went to Pete Eggar's, and Lucius requested a private room. Pete himself brought a bottle of whiskey and chilled soda water. "Say I'm not here to the curious," Lucius told him, "and don't let anybody in except Kirby or Mr. Norcross." He drank a shot glass of liquor, chased it with the bubbly water, and stretched and groaned and rubbed his face and eyes with opened palms. He pulled off his boots and hoisted stockinged feet to a chair. "I'm done in," he said. "And I'm going to get drunk. And I'm rich!" Cass declined a drink, or a schooner of beer. "Splendid," he said. "If you don't really have a taste for it, you're better off without it."

After he had a few glasses of whiskey, his tenseness dissipated. He rang a bell for a waiter and sent him to a restaurant across the street for a supper of fried chicken, mashed potatoes and gravy, and a special dish of fried bananas they knew how to prepare for him. "I was in Central America on the way to California," he remarked, "looking over the opportunities. The natives seemed to live on these. I acquired a taste for 'em." He drank more, lit a cigarillo, and unbuttoned his vest and grunted comfortably as he talked in lazy accents to Cass. The heavy meal, following such excitements, made Cass sleepy. But he resolutely fought drooping eyelids and answered his uncle crisply. Something in his mother's abject surrender worried and angered him; he was unable to define his curious feeling of resistance, other than to tell himself he was his own man, too old now for being batted like a shuttlecock between two demanding relatives, and no toy to be picked up and discarded at will.

Lucius had a way of divining his thoughts, as proved from the past. He said suddenly, "Were you impressed by what went on at Brennanville today?"

Pouring coffee for them, Cass said, "My mother certainly was."

"You weren't?"

"Some things worried me."

"That it was rigged, you mean? Hell, that was nothing. Let me be specific. The property supposedly sold to smart speculators and then resold belonged to us—it's a good dodge for doubling prices. The reason I'm fond of Brian Regan is because he was once mixed up in a real estate development in Illinois and talked me into offering fifty foot lots; he told me the suckers like to be bunched in together, and I made half again as much money by listening to him. The Xanadu and the brick building will never be finished by us. The grass that may grow in the park won't come from our planting. Our syndicate is a facade. It consists of Kirby and me; we disposed of the others long ago by letting them have property in return for their financing. We got to use their names for window dressing, which was all we wanted. This was done on a shoestring, Cass; we risked hardly a red cent of our own. I bought the land for ten dollars an acre, on credit, and spent more in advertising than anything else. One ace is still up my sleeve, and I might get a chance to play it tonight. If I do, I will be guilty of a fraud I don't think I can be prosecuted for."

"I guess the ethics involved don't bother you," Cass said.

"No, the ethics do not," Lucius said. "This is a free country with boundless opportunity, dedicated to the principle of the devil take the hindmost—or dogs eating each other, if you prefer. I believe in unlimited enterprise, which has made us great and strong. But I couldn't believe that and still remain more than technically honest. I'm a Pharisee, Cass. Would you like to hear my secret? Do you remember your Latin?"

"I think so."

"Faber est quisque fortunae suae. Give me the equivalent in English."

"Well, loosely—fortune helps those who help themselves."

"That's close enough."

"I was talking to Mr. Shapiro the other day," Cass said. "He has a daughter, a widow; Mrs. Marcus."

"Yes, I've met her. She's a handsome girl."

"She says you're a crook. Mr. Shapiro half agreed."

Drinking, Lucius paused to wipe his mouth, and laughed. "I can't wholly deny it. Aaron is a very upright man. He might stand convicted of a little prejudice, though; he had funds in my bank in '76 and lost thereby."

"To tell you the truth," Cass said, "I didn't pay much attention to what she was saying. I just looked and admired. She could tell me the world was flat or the moon blue cheese and I wouldn't contradict her. But my mother says I can't pursue the subject because she's a Jew. Is that so?"

"In a way, Cass. The Queen small was cosmopolitan, and big she's a village. The new outsiders are in love with full pockets and hurting from raw Protestantism and the crucifixion of Jesus. You'd better forget her unless sleeping with her is enough."

"I didn't think you'd talk like that."

Lucius laughed again. "I know when to pull in my horns. The years make you sensible. You'll learn."

"Learn to be a coward and have no principles, sir?"

Hardening, Lucius said, "That's right. But you don't have to heed your elders. Doña Maria and I are only concerned for your future."

"Money makes strange bedfellows, doesn't it? I mean—"

"I'm aware of what you mean; you needn't elaborate."

"I don't think you are," Cass said. "All Mother dreams of now is my inheriting from you. That's more important to her than the San Cristobal."

"She's right," Lucius said, biting off his words. "Doña Maria is no fool." He poured whiskey, drank it down, and stared at Cass with a queer, instantaneous anger. Sweat glistened on the clean cheekbones above his beard. "Bedfellows, did you say? Your mother and I *were* bedfellows once. Do you have a feeling in your bones or are you only careless in your choice of language, you little bastard?"

Cass regarded him openmouthed. He took a deep breath, feeling a stinging in his eyes and a salt taste in his mouth. Feet thumping on the floor, Lucius straightened and turned away. The back of his neck was a fiery red. A cry of anguish and expostulation rose in Cass's throat, but his tightening throat muscles strangled it. The door burst open and a jubilant Kirby came in. "God Almighty!" he said. "That was *some* picnic today! I've paid everybody off, and—"

"Sit down," Lucius said. "Have a drink. There's plenty—my pure nephew doesn't touch the stuff."

"I could use a drop," Kirby said, and pulled over a chair and reached for the bottle. "And if there was ever an excuse for lifting a glass in salute to the bold colonel, Cass, this is the moment."

Lucius had recovered his composure, had his feet elevated once more, and was looking coolly at Cass and Kirby. "Assuming," he said, "that enough of our customers follow up their deposits with hard cash and we can unload the credit we've extended."

"They will," Kirby replied. "And suppose we can't dump the paper? We're still up to our asses in daisies." He raised his drink. "To you, sir, and to Mr. Hervey F. Norcross. I have a hunch Mr. Norcross will rush in where angels fear to tread."

"I'm beginning to wonder," Lucius said. "That eastern money didn't pick him for his innocence. He wasn't around today."

"A couple of his scouts were," Kirby said. "I saw them."

"If he was really panting," Lucius said, "he would have been present. I think Norcross is a man who trusts nobody but himself."

"All right," Kirby said. "We've lost Norcross. Let him go. You've got enough. You can't have everything."

Reversing the process, Lucius swallowed soda water and then a shot of whiskey. He said, "I want everything. I've had to wait and wait. I want the whole Goddamned hog before this boom falls apart. There's a Latin tag I remember which sums it up, and my nephew is learned, Kirby, as well as virtuous—he'll translate for you." He waited, summoning his memory. *"Crescit amor nummi quantum . . . ipsa pecunia crescit."* He gazed inquiringly at Cass.

"Uh, love of money grows as fast as the money itself increases," Cass said.

"Wonderful," Lucius said. "The benefits of education are there displayed. They teach you, among other things, how to understand real estate boomers."

A knock sounded on the door. There was a dead silence for ten seconds. Slowly, symbolically, as though washing them, Lucius rubbed his hands together. "That would be Pete announcing Mr. Norcross," he said. "Do the honors, Cass."

Opening the door, Cass found it was Pete, and a couple of impeccably dressed, hard-hatted men standing behind him. The older and fatter of the two, who wore gold-rimmed spectacles and had an imposing expanse of gray whiskers along his jaws, said, "I'm H. F. Norcross. Is Colonel Brennan with you?"

"Yes, sir," Cass replied. "Please come in."

Norcross shook hands with Lucius (he got up in his stocking feet to receive the visitors) and Kirby, and introduced his companion, a Mr. Dessing. Lucius presented Cass to them.

After looking askance at the nearly empty bottle of whiskey on the table, Norcross said, "I'm here to talk turkey, Colonel. I assume you are in a like mood."

"At your service, sir," Lucius assured him, "but I'm not sure it isn't too late. We have done so well today that my syndicate is highly encouraged. Kirby and I polled 'em when we got back from Brennanville and I don't know if they'll be willing to accept any kind of offer."

"Shall we sit down and delve into the subject?" Norcross said. "I might be able to sweeten the deal."

"I cannot understand why the offer needs increasing," Mr. Dessing said, "when in effect the colonel has already accepted."

"Provisionally, my dear fellow," Lucius said. "Provisionally."

"Provisionally," Kirby echoed. "I remember that."

"Sir, may I be excused?" Cass said to his uncle.

"You may," Lucius said. "Make your apologies to the gentlemen."

The last glimpse Cass had of them, they were sitting down around the table. Lucius seemed to have instantly thrown off the load of the liquor upon him, and Kirby was prayerfully mopping his face with a discarded napkin.

Cass slept badly that night. His mother was in bed when he returned to the boarding house, but he could not in any case have undertaken to talk to her. What Lucius had blurted out in his tipsy rage had demolished him. He found it impossible to comprehend, and intolerable; but in the depths of his being was a kind of foreknowledge which had lain undisturbed for years, awaiting this stroke of lightning—it was as if he had known and yet not known, and not wanted to know, and still anticipated the disclosure in his subconscious. The blasting light having illuminated his mind and soul, he could not willingly accept losing the comfort of darkness. To question Doña Maria was degrading, futile and impossible. It was sickening even to contemplate. He refused to think of her in that connection.

The succeeding forenoon brought Lucius unannounced to Blour and Regan's. He looked in fine fettle, if a little marked by fatigue, and perfectly at ease in Cass's presence. He wanted immediate entrance to Mr. Blour's sanctum, and they were closeted together for over two hours. When he reappeared, he started for the door without speaking to Cass.

"I've got to talk to you, Uncle Lucius."

Stopping, Lucius said, "Why?"

"Because of last night—"

"You needn't whisper. We are not conspirators. And I have nothing further to tell you. Don't, for God's sake, start talking to *her*—"

"I'm not going to!" Cass said. "But you've got to finish it—you've got to say right out—"

"I don't have to do anything," Lucius interrupted. "I was drunk last night and spoke in haste, and you are foolish to believe in that old nonsense of *in vino veritas*. Let it go, hear me? Forget it."

He left the office, and Cass slumped in his chair, his hands and feet chilling, his head paining him. Blour walked from his room carrying scribbled sheets of foolscap; twin pencils were tucked behind either ear. "This is incredible," he remarked. "Are you aware of it? Your uncle said you were with him last night."

"I left early," Cass said.

"They have sold all of Brennanville to an eastern syndicate and I am to draw the agreement. Fantastic! Fantastic luck. Where's Mr. Regan? Your uncle wants his advice on different matters."

"I don't know. He didn't come in this morning."

Groaning, Blour said, "What is on the daily calendar for him? Has he any cases?"

"Yes, sir. I appeared in court and made the excuse of illness. Judge Beandetti granted a continuance, but he was pretty sarcastic."

"Thank you . . . Well, if Mr. Regan does not show up by three

o'clock, you had better go to his hotel and discover what ails him."
Blour started to retire, snapped his fingers, and returned to Cass. "Another thing—the colonel is concerned about the state of your learning. He wants you admitted to the bar as fast as possible. Are you progressing in your studies?"

"I have been working hard, sir," Cass said.

"Are you ready for the examination?"

"I'm not sure, Mr. Blour."

"Come in my room."

Upright in front of Blour's desk, Cass was subjected to a worrisome, nerve-rasping inquiry. It resembled being on the witness stand, and Blour did not spare him. Many of his questions received no answer. Repeatedly shaking his head and sighing, Blour became glummer and glummer. "You're not ready," he said finally. "What have you done with your time, young man?"

"You have used it, sir! I have to sleep—"

"You can sleep when you are in better circumstances . . . Now, I intend to supervise your studies. We will meet each night and on Sundays until you are fully instructed. I beseech you to apply yourself."

"Well, I certainly appreciate your kindness, Mr. Blour," Cass started to say, "but I can't see why—"

"Don't waste your gratitude on me. Your uncle is paying handsomely for my coaching."

Though distracted in manner, Mr. Blour had a faculty for grim concentration when the occasion demanded. He kept after Cass—to Mr. Regan's huge amusement—for many weeks. Another clerk was hired to take over a portion of Cass's work while he struggled with books and endured the cross-examinations of his mentor. Mr. Blour began to brighten. Once he had subdued a desire to rebel, his pupil became reasonably apt. Neither further visits nor messages emanated from Lucius. That was a blessing to Cass, for he could not have borne the sight of him, and feared he might precipitate a second quarrel. His feelings toward his uncle had undergone a cataclysmic change. He was disillusioned and depressed. Their old relationship had died and could never be brought back to life. He thought now that he hated and feared him, yet he was not in a position to disdain his bounty—or to explain an open break to his mother. When she expressed gratitude for Lucius's interest and aid, the most he dared to do was silence her with a curt authority which caused her to show puzzlement and hurt.

Sooner than either he or Blour had anticipated, the ordeal was ended. Blour said simply, "I believe you are ready, and I have earned my pay. This is the last time I shall do any force-feeding in the legal line, whatever the emoluments. I don't think you will ever become a shining light in our profession, Cass, but I expect you to occupy an honorable niche. You'd better go to San Francisco with the next batch of candidates."

Doña Maria arranged to accompany Cass. They went north on the train, and the examination of the current eleven candidates was conducted by members of the State Supreme Court. Justice Ephraim Gideon interrogated Cass. His appearance was overawing, but his questions were perfunctory and easy to answer; he was no merciless Mr. Blour, earning a sizeable fee for stuffing a refractory goose. In essence, Cass had merely to explain the steps in foreclosing an unpaid note secured by a mortgage on real property. He sailed through in high style, and Mr. Justice Gideon complimented him on his ready replies. Next morning Cass returned to the court and heard his name read from the list of those admitted to practice.

Tears dappling her cheeks, his mother embraced him. "I am so proud of you," she said. "Now you can follow in the footsteps of your father."

He flinched. "He wasn't much of a lawyer according to Uncle Lucius."

"Lucius's word is not the gospel."

"You're sure of that?" he said.

"What do you mean?"

"Is he a liar as well as a crook?"

"Do you think that of him," she said, "when he tries to help you?"

"How can I avoid it? I know what I've seen and heard myself—and what I've heard from you, from him, from Mr. Shapiro—"

"I know. But he is a blood relation, and perhaps he loves you. You have to make up your own mind."

"I've made it up," he said.

"Then you won't care to hear my secret."

He started to sweat. "Secret, Mother?"

"I had a letter from him before we left Los Angeles," she said. "The firm of Blour and Regan is breaking up. Mr. Blour is moving to Sacramento, and Lucius wants you to form a partnership with Mr. Regan. He is willing to pay your share. His only proviso is that the partnership must be called Brennan and Regan!"

"No, I won't do it. Mr. Regan is drunken and undependable, and he has a bad reputation. If I can't be a lawyer on my own terms, then I'll try something else."

"Very well, Cass."

"Haven't you changed your tune? Uncle Lucius won't make me his heir when I go against his wishes."

"That's possible," she said. "But you will have the San Cristobal, won't you? And the tune is the same, only now you are saying what I have always said of Lucius—and you have come to this of your own free will. Don't you understand how hard I have tried, and how long I have waited, to bring you to this frame of mind? At last we are free of him, and I have not influenced you."

"Do you mean it?"

"With all my heart. Do you think I care for his dirty money if you don't?"

He caught her to him and kissed her forehead. It was like holding a girl in his arms; she was so slim, so small, so youthfully innocent in guise. The unmentionable thing had never happened. To renounce his uncle and implicitly believe that was enough. The stain would go away. As a secret, their secret, it would wither and perish. A bitter taste in his mouth turned sweet.

She pushed him back and peered at him. "You look too young for a lawyer. People won't trust in you. Shouldn't you grow some whiskers?"

"Oh, Mother!" he said. "For God's sake. I'll be old before you know it."

"So will I," she said. "Old and dead." And she wept again.

four

CASS was indeed old before Doña Maria knew it. During the next three years he appeared either for plaintiff or defendant in one hundred and twenty-six suits, and in addition drew innumerable contracts, wrote opinions on titles, and negotiated deals for clients. He had no partner, no clerk, no stenographer. All of the documents involved were drawn by him on the battered Remington. His office was two small rooms in the Temple Block called the "lawyer's block" because of its heavy occupancy by attorneys, crammed with books and papers and a few oddments of furniture. Many a night the lights burned in them until dawn. A mania possessed him: to succeed on his own, to owe nothing to any man, to achieve an uprightness that defied criticism and wiped out the past, and to escape from bondage. He stood willing to endure every hardship in return for a mystical freedom he could scarcely define.

There was a price to be paid for such benefits. He was usually red-eyed, nervous, harried, overtired and pretending to a knowledge and assurance he did not have. He had no social life and little relaxation. As he worried a good deal, his health suffered. Headaches threatened to shatter his skull, and he experienced stomach upsets. Hours of typing and correcting proof and digging in books seemed to dim his sight, and he started wearing glasses. Often he appeared in court snuffling and feverish, aching in his joints from persistent cold germs; but he rarely allowed ailments or fatigue to interrupt his work.

At first the going was hard. He would not take borderline cases, criminal actions, or represent people of whom he was doubtful. Sustaining his ideals and code of conduct meant small fees and handling the dull subsidiary litter of courts and commerce. The condition of the San Cristobal was unsatisfactory, and his uncle proffered no more assistance after an unhappy interview. But Aaron Shapiro remained his friend and adherent. He gradually turned over his own legal affairs to Cass, and brought him solid, continuing accounts, frequently against the grain of the clients he dragooned. Helping further was the growth of the Queen; the population was approaching the hundred thousand mark, and the smoke of industry could be seen on the horizon—iron foundries, flour and feed and planing mills, kilns and brickyards, pipe works, manufacturers turning out carriages and wagons, cigars, brooms, crackers, soap, ice, stoneware, mattresses, furniture, jewelry and shirts, and there were railroad repair shops, cold storage plants, tanneries, hat factories, pork packers, and distilleries and wineries furnishing brandy and the lighter potables, as well as breweries making beer. Each of these firms needed representation of one kind or another, and Cass's charges were suitably low.

Accepting his mother's advice, he grew a moustache and bushy sidewhiskers; to his despair, however, his facial hair was light in color and texture and looked weedy rather than imposing. He took pains to speak slowly and in measured tones, to affect quiet suits and plain vests, to employ pinch-on nose glasses, to stoop a little and move with a deliberation beyond his years. Doña Maria was charmed by his impersonation of age and stability. She was active in trying to drum up trade for him among her acquaintances, and these forays were frequently disconcerting to her. Outsiders had inundated Los Angeles, and the society and town she had known were rapidly changing. Of the ranchos, only the San Cristobal and three or four others remained intact and under original family control. Blood strains of the Spanish and Mexican landholders had been thinned or nearly obliterated by the dominant gringos, and the very names of the *hidalgos* were forgotten. She detested the recent arrivals, who were without roots or tradition, and generally spoke in the flat accents of the middle part of the United States; she thought them pushing, greedy and ill-mannered, and hated the city they were raising on the foundations of the pueblo and shoving toward the sea and the mountains. Mexicans had been elbowed aside into districts that approached ghettos, and the Latin heritage of the Queen was regarded with contempt. Wood, brick and stone were supplanting picturesque adobe walls and a stuffy order replacing a genial disarray. The peace and quiet, the sleepy ease, had vanished. If possible, she would have gone to the San Cristobal and not returned.

But Cass needed her. As soon as he was settled in the Temple Block, she rented a small house farther west on Temple Street, within easy distance of the courthouse, and resurrected Juana and a second maid from pensioned obscurity. Some household possessions dating to the day of Colonel Villanueva reappeared, and Doña Maria saw to it that her son had comfortable surroundings, nourishing meals, and no interruptions. She made few demands on him and had immense respect for his work. Their only amusements were tranquil conversations at meals (she never failed to breakfast with him), occasional visits to the Tivoli Opera House or other theaters exhibiting refined entertainment, and infrequent gatherings with old friends to bemoan the passing of a better time. Cass's reaction to the few girls of good background she presented for his approval was disappointing, but she believed the right wife would come along, and that a man was better advised to marry at the height of his maturity. She would, she said, save her energies for resisting a poor choice. Waiting in the wings was the San Cristobal, for which he was destined. In her dreams, Cass supposed, she envisioned him taking a bride there and staying; after, of course, he had risen to glory and riches in Los Angeles. At intervals she went to the rancho to confer with Jim Dorcas and try to wring more profits from its operation. He rarely accompanied her, and as rarely entertained clients and friends at the Temple Street house, for the folk he dealt with and liked were not impressed by the past his mother reflected and could not abandon.

Almost as soon as Cass had come back from San Francisco, the firm of Blour and Regan dissolved. His only duty to them was to discharge his stewardship and close out the tangled accounts. Brian Regan treated the dissolution lightly and began to welcome Cass in the role of his junior partner; his face turned red with displeased surprise when he was told the offer was declined. A faint smile on his lips, Mr. Blour listened in silence.

"Am I to understand," Regan said, "that you have a better offer than mine and your uncle's?"

"No, sir," Cass said. "I intend to attempt the practice of law on my own."

"Is that a fact?" Regan said sarcastically. "What a boon you will be to the Los Angeles bar. Well, you had better explain this to Lucius. I don't intend to."

"I'll explain," Cass said.

"Do it gently," Regan said, "and maybe he won't let you go hungry, boy. I bid you both good-day with a feeling of relief."

He flung himself out of the room, an odor of whiskey trailing in his wake. Sighing, settling his hat firmly on his head, Mr. Blour said,

"Goodbye, Cass. The best of luck. I think you have chosen the wise course. If you have too many difficulties, write me in Sacramento; I have no doubt I will be able to find you something."

Cass telephoned his uncle. These days Brennan & Jennison had removed to larger quarters on Spring Street and had a man clerk and a girl "typewriter" to handle inquiries and take care of the correspondence. There was a delay until Lucius came on the line. "Hello, Cass," he said. "I'd hoped for a telegram announcing your success. It did go all right up there?"

"Yes, sir. I'm sorry I neglected to notify you. I thought you knew from Mr. Blour how much I appreciated his tutoring and your other favors to me."

"It doesn't matter. Regan and Blour have parted, eh?"

"Yes, we just finished with that," Cass said. "Mr. Regan mentioned the partnership, and I'd like to discuss that with you in person. When can I see you, sir?"

"Come over tonight to my house. Will you have supper?"

"Thank you, but I'll come later."

"As you please," Lucius said. "Make it about eight."

A strange young Mexican girl answered Cass's ring that night. She was pretty and too flamboyantly dressed for a maid, and had a flaunting look to her. Another woman, also a stranger to Cass, peeked at him from the kitchen as he came along the hall. Lucius was in his bedroom, and Cass ascended the stairs and knocked on his door.

"Come in," Lucius called. He was seated in a chair at his writing table, coat off and vest and cravat unfastened, with a black cat in his lap and inkstains on his fingers. In the air was the familiar scent of cologne. He did not rise or offer his hand, but his smile was cordial. "Sit down, won't you?"

Cass took a chair. He glanced at the enormous bed to see if the Colt's pistol still lay under one of the pillows; apparently it was no longer in use.

Lucius laughed. "I know what you're looking for. I've put the guns away, Cass. This has become a civilized community." He put down the cat and uncrossed his legs. "Sometimes I'm inclined to regret the changes, like all aging citizens. Look what they've done lately—closed the gambling halls, paved Main, Spring and Fort streets at last, opened Los Angeles Street from Arcadia to Alameda, and wiped out Nigger Alley. And the lovely boom is starting to fall apart. One of these days I suppose they'll padlock the whorehouses. They might force me to move to greener fields if they don't watch out."

"I can't imagine the Queen without you," Cass said.

"Maybe I can think of a way to ginger her up. Have you ever had occasion to consider the oil business?"

"No, sir."

"It seems promising," Lucius said. "There must be a hell of a lot of oil underfoot around here, probably more oil than water. The process of finding, drilling, refining and selling it are all Greek to me, but I have never been deterred in the past by my ignorance. And the ups and downs in the trade don't bother me. Selling kerosene for lamps and greasing axles and laying dust on roads won't be the whole story in the future. Surely railway locomotives and steamships ought to be able to use the stuff. Kirby is working on the design of a compressed-air burner for firing furnaces at my suggestion. One encouraging thing is that he's opposed to the scheme. I haven't had an idea so far that he wasn't against in the beginning."

"Speaking of partners, sir—"

"You turned down Regan, eh? Why?"

"Oh, he told you?"

"No. But you have the expression of a man about to swallow a purge."

"Mr. Regan is unreliable," Cass said, and flushed. "Everybody says so."

"What you're trying to say is that he's a drunk. He isn't, not quite, although he will be presently. Meanwhile, he would serve your purpose in getting started—he has the reputation, the clientele, and a weakness to exploit. You could use him and discard him."

"I don't like that, Uncle Lucius."

Pushing the cat gently aside with a foot, Lucius arose and contemplated Cass for a moment. His expression stayed genial, his voice softer than usual. "Well," he said, "we have at any rate uncovered an honest difference of opinion. Whether you should remain as pure as the lilies of the field—or even where you got such notions—it is a debatable point, but I am not the man to argue it. I accept your curious highminded decision." In a gesture of dismissal, he walked toward the door. Cass got up and followed him. He added, smiling, "Tell your mother you continue as my heir, providing anything is left."

"Good night, sir. I regret having offended—"

"Don't descend to hypocrisy, Cass. By the way, did you notice my new maid?"

"Yes, sir."

"Delightful, don't you think?"

"I didn't pay much attention to her," Cass said.

"She's worth a second glance," Lucius said. "Especially when her skirts are up. She wears no drawers and spreads her limbs almost without invitation. Of course, nothing in the house has been dusted since I began sleeping with her, but even so she is an improvement on Fidelia."

"Where is she?"

"Downstairs in the room the new maid would have if she didn't occupy mine. Fidelia is suffering from the ills of old age. I have hired another woman to cook and provide for her."

"Couldn't she go to the county hospital?"

"Would you advise that, Cass?"

"Yes," Cass said. "I never liked Fidelia. She didn't know her place. I should think you'd jump at the chance to get rid of her."

"Ah, yes," Lucius said, and sighed. "With such virtue as yours always goes an inflexible set of rules. And a hard heart. But I am an erratic villain and lack resolution. Fidelia is a cross I have elected to bear. Good night, my boy."

"Good night, sir."

The Queen's real estate boom suddenly disintegrated. People left the city by the thousands, values collapsed, trade stagnated, the fanfaronade of the syndicates turned to whimpering, and the tracts and townships —including Brennanville—perished or subsided into small, somnolent wide spots in the road, their grotesque hotels and office buildings converted to storage, torn apart for the materials in them, or ruined by neglect and fire. For a time it seemed as if the ghost of Yang-na was back, and the confidence that men had lavished on the place was all in vain. But the boom, the like of which had never before been seen in America, was a spectacular emanation of economic growth and human energy that would not accept denial; the wave traveled far, and in receding left a substantial residue of families, houses, commercial structures, civic improvements and hard money. Stability gradually returned, spurred by fiestas, grandiose pronouncements in the newspapers, and the customary visitors in search of a warmer climate. Beyond the confines of the fluctuating town was the immovable asset of land tamed with water and fertilizers to year-round agricultural production. And nothing stayed dormant in the region. The outsiders flocked in again, new projects were afoot, oil gushed out of the ground, oranges ripened, the sun poured down.

Oddly, the collapse was helpful to Cass. It provoked a deluge of foreclosures, suits and complicated arrangements for the transfer of property; successive sales of lots, often improperly documented, encouraged endless title examinations; and there was no lack of litigation among bloodthirsty promoters fighting each other, their stockholders, and the tax collector.

One day he discovered Mr. Hervey F. Norcross and Mr. Theodore

Dessing in his office when he got back from court. They appeared dignified but uneasy, and Norcross resorted to a good deal of hemming and hawing before he disclosed his purpose. He had made certain inquiries, he said, and come to the conclusion that Cass's relationship with his uncle was not so close as to prevent his representing somebody in disagreement with Colonel Brennan.

"I'm afraid I don't understand you, sir," Cass replied.

"The fact is, Mr. Brennan," Mr. Dessing said, "we are contemplating an action against him and Mr. Jennison. They sold us an enterprise which was sadly misrepresented, and we feel we are entitled to relief."

"I should think you would prefer a lawyer with greater experience than mine," Cass said.

Mr. Norcross cleared his throat loudly. "We have retained Mr. Gorsch, and he welcomes your assistance. You will find us generous in the matter of fees."

"The fact is," Mr. Dessing said, "we assume you were with Colonel Brennan during the period of our negotiations and must have valuable information or the sources from which to get it. We feel your alignment on our side would have a moral effect."

"In other words," Cass said, "I am being asked to betray my uncle's confidence and testify against him."

"I assure you, Mr. Brennan," Norcross said stiffly, "that we have not contemplated going that far."

"You will," Cass told him. "I'm sorry, gentlemen, I know nothing of the Brennanville affair, and if I did I would not accept your offer for reasons which must be plain to you."

"You seem to me unnecessarily noble, young man," Dessing said. "What is the merit in protecting scoundrels?"

"The merit of not allying oneself with other scoundrels," Cass said. "Anyhow, allow me the luxury of declining bribery. There is the door. Get out."

Soon he had a call on the instrument newly installed at his desk. It was Moses Smiley on the wire, soliciting an appointment. "I'll be glad to see you," Cass said, "but if you are acting for my uncle I'd better tell you frankly that it won't do a bit of good."

"Please let me talk to you," Moses said. "Put it down to Christian forebearance on your part. I am a poor and worthy man, a good father—"

Cass laughed. "How many children do you have now?"

"Ten. Can you refuse a father of ten?"

They set an hour, and Moses turned up punctually. He caught Cass's hand in the pair of his and stared at him. "You have changed," he

85

said. "Grown older, stronger—and tireder. The whiskers are impressive. But somehow I would have liked to see you remain a boy, Cass."

"You're the same, Reverend."

"Yes, I go on as before, only oppressed by family problems and those of my evangelical mission."

"How is the Church of Universal Godhead?"

"I had to abandon that venture," Moses said, with not the slightest embarrassment. "It became relatively unprofitable, and the failure of the real estate market gave me pressing monetary worries. I am currently pastor of the Congregation of Jesus Christ and His Saints. We are building a sanctuary on South Flower Street. Mr. Jennison is constructing the building for us."

"Then you are still in real estate. Don't you share in the construction fees?"

"To some extent, praise be. Those little people I have to feed are always hungry. But, Cass, I didn't come here to speak of them or myself; I have business to transact with you."

Moses had brought papers relating to the formation of a stock company called the Sunset Sea Oil Products, which was to have Lucius as president and Kirby as vice president and general manager. The poetic name derived from Lucius's book, *A Glimpse of Paradise,* where he had referred to Southern California as "the land of the Sunset Sea." It was the wish of Brennan & Jennison that Cass take the necessary steps for setting up the company.

"I suppose this is in gratitude for my refusal to represent Mr. Norcross," Cass said. "Uncle Lucius heard about that, didn't he?"

"Well, yes," Moses admitted. "However, it's more than just gratitude. I'm sure he misses you, and regrets whatever impediments have spoiled your former close association. I expect this might be expressed as a peace offering. You'll note that counsel for the firm has been left blank—he hopes you will take the position. You are to name a fair salary."

"No, thank you."

"Will you represent him in the Norcross suit?"

Cass shook his head.

"What can I do to bring you together again?" Moses said. "I ask the question in my capacity of minister of the gospel, with no ulterior motives. There is a close tie between you that should not be broken beyond repair. Your uncle is lonely and growing no younger. He is eager to forgive and forget. Can you harden your heart against him, Cass?"

"I can and have."

"What is the real difficulty? Are you able to tell me?"

"No," Cass said. "It's a private thing, and this discussion is ended.

But I'll put Sunset Sea together, at no charge. Give Uncle Lucius my regards."

Cass was interested in the progress of Mr. Norcross's campaign against Lucius, but he took care never to ask questions or to express an opinion. It gave him pleasure to note that clients and friends fell out of the habit of connecting him with his uncle, and the similarity of their surnames ceased to excite interest. Eventually Norcross and Dessing and their hapless eastern syndicate got precisely nowhere. Lucius was reputed to have laughed at them, and the lawyers he hired were adept at evasions and delays. The suit failed to come to trial, and Norcross threw in the sponge and disappeared, a sadder and wiser man, leaving Dessing to liquidate the disaster at Brennanville.

The tentacles stretching between Cass and Lucius were not entirely severed. Lucius's Sunset Sea and nose for booms presaged another rally, and all at once the town was dotted with oil wells and Cass found himself engaged in organizing other companies. In the course of his work, and indeed in merely going to and from home, he could observe the effects of the new craze. Northeast through the hills ran a field which crossed Temple Street; drillers labored night and day, running an excess of their product into a huge and stinking sump hole, and bright flames of burning gas jetted from pipes standing upright. Derricks shot up in nearly every block in every neighborhood. Wells bubbled in front and back yards, and houses, fences, sidewalks and streets were smeared with the black gold. Outsiders and natives alike competed for stock, leases and promising locations. Cass was told that Brennan & Jennison had become a firm dealing primarily in oil properties and shares. Knowledgeable men said overproduction and a shortage of markets was sure to kill off the budding industry in a year or two, but meanwhile the stampede was on.

Indirectly, the petroleum speculation served to resolve a crisis at the San Cristobal. While Cass began to enjoy a modest prosperity, Doña Maria still contended with ebbing returns and rising taxes. They seldom discussed the situation as a matter of policy, and Cass accompanied his mother on her inspection trips not oftener than twice a year; his relations with Jim Dorcas were frigidly polite. Doña Maria postponed bringing up the subject as long as possible, but finally she was compelled to ask Cass's advice. He listened to her tale of woe and inspected a set of figures supplied by Dorcas. These were illuminating enough—the rancho was failing badly. Then she surprised him. "Is Sunset Sea Oil Products the company Lucius has?" she said.

"Yes. You remember I told you I did the legal work for him when it was formed."

"What have you heard from him lately?"

"Nothing," Cass replied. "Our telephone conversations ended when I finished the job and returned the check he sent me."

"I thought you might have had something to do with the geologist and not informed me . . ."

"What geologist?"

"He came out to the San Cristobal with Mr. Jennison," she said, "and they wanted permission to look for evidences of oil. Mr. Dorcas was quite excited and thought it would be all right for them to explore. He intended to write me about it and forgot. Now they are asking for a lease. Mr. Jennison's letter says they would like to drill a test well."

"Mr. Dorcas took a good deal on himself, didn't he?"

"He was worried, Cass, and felt it might help us. You know we have found oil when we were hunting water. What do you think?"

"Tell me first how you feel," he said.

"I hate those ugly derricks and the smell and spoiling the country-side."

"But you need the money."

"*We* need the money," she said. "The rancho is going to be yours. Would we make a lot?"

"That depends. They're overproducing already, and people say the market will slump. And the San Cristobal has to have oil."

"I don't want to do it. But what else can I do?"

"Sell off acreage," he said.

"No! I won't sell a foot. It must go to you the way my father left it to me. You can do as you please after I am dead."

This was the second time she had spoken of death to him—she was youthful in spirit as well as in body, and therefore he thought her immortal—and he glanced at her sharply. A whispering of loss and change rippled in cold flesh on his shoulders. He'd had a protracted, boring youth and aged artificially to escape a spiritual prison, and she was his young mother, almost a contemporary to be fought with and endured forever; but the years were overtaking her, and the signs of a long pursuit were to be seen in the gray strands in her hair and the checking of crow's-feet under her eyes. She moved with less abandon these days, and her voice had lost resonance and her opinions were not so final as they once had been; and he had heard no more of her riding around the San Cristobal in *vaquero's* clothing. She had given up bothering him to attend Mass with her, as though her own salvation at this hour was sufficient concern. Surely Jim Dorcas didn't watch her now in the fashion that had angered him . . .

"What are you thinking?" she asked.

He was startled, and masked the abrupt amazement and sorrow he felt. "I was considering the dilemma. If you are not going to sell or allow the oil prospectors to come in, there is something else you must do."

"Yes?"

"Stop attempting to run the place in the style of Don Ygnacio and Colonel Villanueva. Pare expenses. Quit unprofitable operations. Get rid of the pensioners. Send Mr. Dorcas on his way and find a good foreman who will work for wages. The age of the *ranchero* is over."

"Send Mr. Dorcas—?" Her lips parted in dismayed surprise. "I can't do that, Cass."

"I think he has stolen from you."

"Oh, that is not true! And the old people and the others—they belong to San Cristobal. They are from Don Ygnacio, their fathers worked for him. Where would they go if—"

"It is their problem," he said. "You will have to manage your land in the modern fashion or else lose it. Sentiment and talking of the Villanuevas won't do a bit of good. You cannot run a charitable home for agricultural workers under a dishonest incompetent like Mr. Dorcas and expect to survive."

Raising her hands to her forehead, she cupped the palms over her eyes and gently rubbed. He stirred impatiently. "Suppose this was done?" she said. "I can't do it. Would you?"

"Of course. Give me power of attorney to act for you—"

"No, the San Cristobal is yours. I ask only that you keep the boundaries as they are until I am gone." She lowered her hands and gazed steadily at him. "I will forget the other obligations, but not that one."

"You have my promise the San Cristobal will stay intact as long as I live. But I won't stay there, or become a rancher, or—"

"Then we are agreed," she said.

The title of the rancho passed to Cass and was duly recorded. A mood of resignation enveloped his mother; she had at last capitulated to the future. Casting about for an efficient deputy, Cass found a recent graduate of the Chaffey College of Agriculture at Ontario, a young man named William Sego, who produced an odd sound in his ears by repeatedly ending sentences with a "sir." Together one morning they took the road through Cahuenga Pass and northward along the San Fernando Valley, riding in a buggy behind a pair of horses. Bill Sego was thin, gangling, big-eared and enthusiastic, willing to listen, content with

89

his salary and the opportunity to put his training to the test, and Cass thought him an excellent choice. As they drove, he explained the background of the rancho and the purpose of their expedition.

Bill sawed on the reins. "Oh, yes, sir," he said. "I see. We're going out for the head cutting, the house cleaning. Well, that has to be done, naturally. As long as you do it—"

Smiling, Cass said, "I think I have the temperament for a headsman. Don't ever tempt me, Bill."

"No, sir," Bill said. "I won't."

The new route was far quicker than the older one via the railroad to the mission town. They were within the precincts of the San Cristobal by forenoon, and shortly after arrived in the home valley. It continued to sleep peacefully as it had in Cass's boyhood, and the same little army of retainers were on hand. In worse condition, the outbuildings survived, the chickens strutted and clucked in the dust, and the springs faithfully maintained the level of the small lake. The steep-roofed frame house was in grievous need of paint. Looking around, Bill took off his hat and massaged his straw-colored hair. "This could do with some changing, sir," he said.

"I want you to start all over again," Cass told him.

A Mexican came to take the horses, not recognizing Cass. Unwarned, Jim Dorcas was out somewhere, and a man was sent to fetch him. Bill and Cass sat on the porch discussing the work ahead, and then Bill went on a tour of inspection with the Mexican. Strolling among the huts, Cass recalled the ancient who had been Don Ygnacio's *mayordomo del campo* and remembered Lucius and his father and had told him the queer story of the beautiful girl marrying a family rather than a man and not knowing which Brennan to choose. Cass stopped short, the familiar bitter taste in his mouth. His father? Who was his father?

As he returned to the house, Jim Dorcas rode in and dismounted. They shook hands and entered the parlor to talk. "Well, stranger," Dorcas said, "you're an unusual sight out here. What brings you alone? Where's Doña Maria?"

"She preferred not to come, Mr. Dorcas. I'm the new owner of the San Cristobal. My mother deeded it to me."

"Ah?" Dorcas sat up straighter and studied Cass warily. He was balding and white-haired, and his seamed face was sunken from missing teeth. "Congratulations. I've been hearing fine things of you in the Queen, Cass."

"Thank you."

"The time's come, eh? I'll bet Doña Maria felt a kind of a wrench, though, stepping down. The Cristobal's always been her whole life. Are you finally coming home?"

"No, Mr. Dorcas. But I have a man who will act for me; Mr. Sego is from Chaffey College. We're going to have to make many changes."

"Such as?"

"Most of the people you've had are too inefficient and must go. Probably I'll plant different crops after Mr. Sego has analyzed the situation."

"What about me, Cass?"

"I'm afraid you're through. I regret the abrupt decision, which had to be arrived at quickly, and my thought was that a personal meeting between us would be less humiliating than a mere letter of dismissal."

"Doña Maria agrees with that?"

"I own the San Cristobal. Her opinion is no longer decisive."

"Don't you think you owe me a little?" Dorcas asked. "I've spent a good part of my life on your land. Going somewhere else now is apt to be hard for me. I never took in much money here. Isn't it a sort of a question of good faith, Cass?"

"Not to my mind, Mr. Dorcas. My concern is solely with the legal aspects of this. Your original agreement with my mother terminated years ago and was not renewed. Apparently you elected to stay on in an undefined capacity."

"I had Doña Maria's word. It was good enough for me."

"May I remind you again," Cass said, "that ownership of the ranch has changed?"

"'Ranch,'" Dorcas said. "Not 'rancho.' That's the new word, huh? That explains it. Aren't you forgetting the oil, Cass? Shouldn't I have a share of any discovery—a small share? I always had hopes for oil."

"You should have had a binding written agreement instead of hopes. I recognize no such obligation."

Dorcas motioned in the direction of the outbuildings. "Who's going to tell them they have to move? Not me, Cass. Your mother, maybe?"

"I'll take care of that," Cass said, and got up. "Mr. Dorcas, you have a month to wind up your concerns and vacate. I would appreciate your sending me the account books and a closing financial statement when you leave. If you feel you have a further equity which has been disregarded, I suggest you consult an attorney. But in the event you elect to do that, I am compelled to warn you I will take a very hard look at your accounting and do whatever is appropriate."

"That time I said I had to admire you . . ." Dorcas spoke a trifle thickly, like a drunken man; it could have been only the gaps in his dentures, and not liquor or shock. "You couldn't forgive me, could you?"

"Did you say that?" Cass said. "I can't remember."

He walked outside, looking for Bill Sego. He did remember, and he hadn't forgiven. Beside the lake he saw a dirty, dark-skinned child trying to catch the descendants of the frogs he had caught in what seemed another century. The interview with Dorcas and even revisiting the San Cristobal was surprisingly troubling and upsetting to him, and he felt a little creasing of sharp, evanescent pain in his chest.

When he got home, he proposed to report in full to Doña Maria. She shook her head emphatically. "I don't want to hear of it. Just tell me that it's done."

"It's done."

"There was no trouble?"

"Why should there be trouble?" Cass demanded irritably. "This was a simple matter of business, and inevitable. And in case you are worrying for your reputation, the blame rests on me alone—you are still the gentle mother of them all. Aren't you going out to say goodbye to them?"

Her eyes widened; she would never lose that incredible guise of springtime innocence. "Then it did hurt you, Cass?"

"Not at all!"

"No, I won't say goodbye to them," she said. "I am a coward. I may not go again to the San Cristobal. As long as it is there, that is enough for me."

"Sego has advanced an interesting idea," he said. "Range cattle are too scrawny and don't furnish good beef, which is why the choice cuts come to us from Chicago. It's his suggestion that we put in feed lots. He thinks we can easily raise the corn and other materials for fattening the animals. The principal objection I can see is the expense involved in getting more wells for irrigation and putting up fences."

"Fences!"

"Stop being the daughter of a *hacendado*. That's history now. Would you oppose my mortgaging the ranch to raise money for improvements? I don't foresee any danger in it."

"The *rancho* is yours," she said.

Her emphasis of the word, reminding him of Dorcas, increased his irritation. "We'll attempt to talk sensibly later," he said, "when you are not so concerned by the fate of Mr. Dorcas." He could not repress an extension of the thrust, and in a flash of disturbing insight perceived that he had always been jealous of her. "Your solicitude amazes me, Mother. Obviously he worries you more than anything else. Tell me, why didn't you ever marry him?"

"I might have," she said, "but for you—and lived where I belonged."

Hurrying up Broadway—which had been Fort Street, and was yet for Doña Maria—toward the courthouse, Cass was treated to a startling sight. Two men in a sedate black glass-enclosed electric brougham with rubber-tire wheels were purring through a tangle of carriages and carts, headed in the opposite direction to him; he caught only a glimpse of them. Seeing a horseless vehicle did not particularly attract his attention for there were a few in the Queen these days—including the smelly, noisy, disgusting affairs that resembled buggies without shafts for the horses and ran on kerosene or gasoline—but its passengers did. One was unmistakably Albert Blour. And the other—with high cheekbones and a strong jaw and a derby hat cocked high on his head—who was he? It could be none other than his uncle, beard shorn, dressed in the modern style, hand on the steering tiller of his electric car, still in the vanguard! "God save us all," said Cass, and laughed and went on his way.

Later in the week, his clerk announced a Mr. Blour had come to pay his respects. Cass arose from a desk piled with open books and sheets of neatly written foolscap and moved to the doorway of his office to usher in the visitor. Mr. Blour's absent manner had apparently persisted; he looked closely at Cass, seemed not to recollect him or the reason for their coming together, and fumbled for words. "Can't you remember why you're here, sir?" Cass asked amusedly.

"Forgive me," Blour said. "I simply didn't know you, and I was taken aback. What is your age, young—old man?"

"I'll be thirty-six soon."

Blour shook his head. "Time flies. In your presence I feel like one of the founders of the republic." He accepted a chair, regarded the paneled room with approval, and spoke briefly of himself. He had flourished in Sacramento, transferred to San Francisco, and presently divided his labors between that city and the capital; he had the privilege of representing a railroad or two and some other influential organizations, enjoyed a certain amount of behind-the-scenes political power in the legislature and elsewhere, headed the firm of Blour, Esdrick, Faber and Canzetti, and was in the southern part of the state on a business trip. "But mine is an uninspiring story," he concluded, "and yours is more interesting, I am sure. How is Doña Maria?"

"Very well. Incidentally, I saw you the other day in my uncle's electric car. I didn't realize he was so advanced and barely recognized him."

"I gather there is no contact between you."

"Almost none," Cass replied.

"That strikes me as unfortunate."

"I don't think we have much in common, Mr. Blour."

"Possibly not. But Lucius is rather an original, you know. He retains

93

an astonishing amount of youth and vigor. His farseeing inventiveness and business acumen are quite impressive." Blour's eyes twinkled. "Besides which, he is a generous contributor to the Republican Party Fund. Did you know Sunset Sea Oil products is erecting a five-story building on South Flower Street? It will be reconstructed from an unfinished church put up by some obscure religious group."

"I'm not surprised, sir, and I believe I know of the obscure religious group. The whole thing sounds very like my uncle. I fear I don't find him as amusing as you do."

"Well, good enough. Let us talk of you, Cass. I see I was wrong in my estimate of your legal abilities."

"No, I'm not a better lawyer than you anticipated. It's merely that I am willing to drudge twelve hours a day and never take a vacation."

"Still, I observe many signs of prosperity around here."

"They are late developments," Cass said. "This office and my clerk and stenographer date from six months ago; until then I occupied a hole in the wall and did every bit of work myself."

"Wouldn't you do well to take on a partner?"

"I haven't found a man who suits my taste."

"Mentioning partners reminds me of Brian Regan," Blour said. "He has fallen on evil days, eh?"

"Yes, drink finished him. He was disbarred for improper conduct, and has since spent his time begging and being in and out of jails and hospitals. Once he appeared here in a dreadful condition, drunken and unshaven and his clothes in rags, and had the gall to blame me for his woes. When I refused to give him money, he cursed and threatened me. I had a policeman remove him, but didn't prefer charges."

"That was good of you . . . I believe Lucius is paying his way now."

"My uncle has always had a penchant for strange benevolences," Cass said. "Possibly his conscience bothers him."

"I would suspect not. Cass, you aren't married?"

"No. I am giving the subject thought, however."

"Are you happy in your present circumstances?" Blour asked.

Removing his glasses, Cass rubbed the indentations on his nose. "That's a hard question to answer. So far I've done what I set out to do, but it's been a long servitude. Sometimes I wish I had more leisure and less ambition—and a chance to enjoy myself." He hesitated. "I hate to see my youth going."

"Who doesn't?"

"There seems to be a kind of upsetting influence around," Cass said, "and I'm not immune to it." He felt he could indulge in a trifle of self-revelation with this man he trusted. "All the new inventions, the growth,

94

the promises and prophecies made when 1900 rolled in—they work on my dissatisfactions, if I can call them that. And the Spanish-American War—" He smiled. "My mother was furious. The war was further proof to her of how the gringos had always plotted the robbery and destruction of the Spanish. But I half wanted to join the volunteers and be off. Or to escape. Who knows? Naturally, it was a state of temporary insanity. Nobody ever escapes. The shock that brought me back to the humdrum came in the realization that I was really already too old for soldiering or adventure."

"The California volunteers didn't accomplish much, if that's any consolation to you. Mostly they stayed encamped at the Presidio in San Francisco and died of fevers."

"Yes. But in your dreams you're a hero and don't get the fever."

"My dear Cass, permit me to get to the object of my visit. Have your political views remained unchanged?"

"Yes, I'm still a Republican. Don't ask me why, except that my father was a martyr to the cause and I couldn't bear Mr. Bryan's radicalism in the last election. Frankly, I have found that only local concerns interest me."

"You should take a wider view," Blour said. "Politics is a duty in this country, and can offer a rewarding career. Lawyers do particularly well at the hustings. Now, we need fresh blood in our organization. Do you have any of Lucius's talent for speechifying?"

"I haven't put myself to the test."

"I'm sure you'd qualify. What do you say to coming to Sacramento for me, performing a tour of duty among the legislators to learn the ropes, and then aspiring to office? I promise, in due course, to put my friends behind you, and I can provide a membership in my firm."

"You surprise me, Mr. Blour."

"It's high time you moved to the center of things. San Francisco is the place for a man of your abilities. What have you here? Oh, electric street railways and hollow real estate booms and a scattering of disconnected communities all over the county, but no real city and no real influence on the affairs of the state. This will never be more than the provincial focus of a farming area. You ought to have the advantages of wider horizons."

"Your offer is most flattering, but I—"

"Pardon me. Give it thought. How can you refuse offhand?"

"Because I'm part and parcel of the Queen, I suppose," Cass said. "My father was here before me, and my mother comes of people who settled here nearly a century ago."

"Nearly a century!" Blour said. "In New England that would be a joke. Nobody's part of Los Angeles, Cass—everyone has come from somewhere else and is an outsider among outsiders." He got up and took his hat. "Please consider my recommendation. When you're of a mind, come north and talk to me."

"Did my uncle suggest this?"

"Well, only collaterally. We had other business to transact, of greater importance to him. But I may say he has not lost interest in you and thinks of your future."

"I'll give your proposal consideration," Cass said. "Thank you, sir."

After Blour had gone, he sat at his desk and did give the proposal consideration. For five minutes. The idea of his leaving the Queen was preposterous. He could not tolerate the thought of being anywhere else. At the root of this quick, irrevocable decision was, inalienably, his uncle. How could he strive against him if he was far away? Then the reason for the striving was gone, the possible victory rendered impotent. As he reflected and recoiled from his conclusion, the familiar devil, the nightmare in broad day that produced sweat and sickness and a pain in his heart, returned; he struggled to rid himself of the evil.

Although his considering was through, he mentioned the matter to Doña Maria. She looked incredulous, and said in tranquil dismissal of such an absurdity: "Politicians are thieves who rob the innocent, especially gringo politicians, and you pride yourself on being a man of principle. How could you ever agree to do Lucius's bidding? Besides, you have the San Cristobal."

His uncle continued impinging on his life. One day an elderly Mexican came to Cass; his name was Arnulfo Ruiz, and he had a will he wanted recorded and administered. Since his command of English was hazardous, he preferred to talk in his own language, and Cass, whose Spanish was rusty from long disuse, had difficulty understanding him. Ruiz had been a close associate of Madam España, formerly keeper of a celebrated and expensive house of prostitution on North Main Street. She had just died in the midst of luxurious retirement, and her passing had not gone unnoticed in the newspapers. Everybody from the half-world in the old days of the Queen knew her. The girls she sold were South American and French importations, champagne flowed in her red-and-gold plush parlors hung with huge oil paintings devoted to indecent subjects, and the distinguishing features outside her establishment were a pair of locally famous couchant stone lions salvaged from an early railroad station that burned down. In her prime Madam España was noted for taking her girls on rides Sunday afternoon in open carriages, all resplendent in lawn and lace and shaded by frilly parasols, for the inspection of the interested and the scandalizing of the better

96

element. She herself was remembered as a beautiful woman, and had sold her favors to wealthy clients for large sums. The sealed envelope Ruiz handed Cass contained, he said, the Madam's posthumous instructions.

"Why do you bring this to me?" Cass asked.

"She requested it."

"I can't understand that. I have never known nor acted for her."

"I think you will understand when you open the letter," Ruiz said. "See? It is addressed to you."

Cass slit the flap of the envelope. On a sheet of elegant initialed notepaper were scrawled a few lines bequeathing the worldly effects of the woman known as Madam España to Lucius Brennan, Arnulfo Ruiz and the Church, and naming Cass Brennan executor of the will. At the bottom Madam had signed her true name, Susie Figueres. Aware of a smiting from the past, Cass put down the paper and gazed at Ruiz.

"Is it as she told me?" Ruiz said. "Have I twenty-five thousand dollars?"

"I am not acquainted with the value of Madam's assets, but you are willed that sum in this instrument—if it is valid."

"It is valid, and I have twenty-five thousand dollars."

"What did her wealth consist of?" Cass said.

"She had the house near Westlake Park. We lived there. The rest is in the bank, money and government bonds. Will you do this for her and Colonel Brennan?"

"You know he is mentioned?"

"Oh, yes," Ruiz said. "He was a good friend and she owed him much."

Hesitating, Cass perceived the connection was oddly moving and fantastic and somehow just, and too close for comfort. "I will do this," he said. "Give me your address that I may notify you."

Upon the completion of legal requirements, he telephoned his uncle. "What a pleasure to hear from you," Lucius said. "I trust you are flourishing, Cass."

"Yes, sir. I understand from Mr. Blour that I needn't ask you that question."

"No, indeed. I am holding up magnificently for an old man. How is Doña Maria?"

"Very well, thank you," Cass said. "Uncle Lucius, this is not a social call—"

"I didn't flatter myself that it was. Were you interested in what Blour had to say?"

"No, sir. I don't care for politics, and I intend to stay in Los Angeles.

I am calling to inform you that I have been appointed executor of the estate of Susie Figueres and you are named in her will."

There was a silence on the wire, and then Lucius began to laugh. His amusement was so hearty it ended in a coughing fit. Holding the receiver away from his ear, Cass waited resignedly.

"I beg your pardon, Cass," Lucius said. "But that was funny. I'll be damned! How our chickens come home to roost! She insisted on your appointment, eh? The old whore had a sense of *noblesse oblige*, by God! Did she leave anything?"

"Your share of the estate may amount to a hundred thousand dollars. The remainder goes to the Church and Arnulfo Ruiz."

Lucius whistled. "She was smart as well as adept at pleasing men. And a miser, of course. Arnulfo was her pimp for years, and ran her temple of Venus."

"I will inform you when the requisite steps have been taken, Uncle Lucius."

"All right. No doubt this astonishes you, Cass. As I recall, I never got around to telling you about it—or didn't care to. The truth is, Susie had some bad moments after Cassius was shot and I disposed of Chawed-Nose Bob. My supporters were all for riding her out of town on a rail in a coat of tar and feathers, but I cooled off and came to the conclusion that persecuting a little drab wouldn't help Cassius's memory or please his shade. So I befriended Susie. Hatred's akin to love, you know, or anyhow curiosity is. Before long—"

"If you will excuse me, sir, I am due in court—"

"This won't take a moment more, Cass. As I said, before long I was sampling what had engaged my brother. I must admit he was a good judge of talented performers. Susie had a way of allowing easy entry and then squeezing the member exquisitely—using a set of muscles in her vagina that most girls don't have or can't learn to employ. A man would lie with her and roar like the Bull of Bashan. No wonder she commanded high fees and could leave a fortune."

"I see," Cass said. "Well, you have profited by my father's indiscretions and your own, Uncle Lucius. Congratulations."

"Thank you, my boy," Lucius replied. "The path of the transgressor is not always too stony, it seems. Convey my best respects to your mother. If she has a change of heart regarding oil exploration on the San Cristobal, tell her not to forget me. I'm still interested."

"I am now the owner of the ranch."

"Ah? Well, it's high time. Perhaps you are not as old-fashioned as Doña Maria. Can we get together on a deal?"

"We cannot. I am just as old-fashioned."

Lucius laughed. "I do believe you are, Cass. You've always been too damned sedate. But consider: you remain my heir. Doing me a substantial favor of this kind couldn't hurt you."

"Let me tell you something, sir," Cass said, and perspiration started out on his brow. "I don't want to be your heir. I disapprove thoroughly of you and all your works. You are not my father, Goddamn it, and I am sick of your nasty insinuations. I reject you—reject you—do you understand?"

"Don't shout at your uncle," Lucius said mildly. "I understand. You're showing the Brennan temper, Cass, and it doesn't become a pillar of society like you. Your disregard of my advice saddens me. Why didn't you resist questioning Doña Maria?"

"Goodbye, sir!"

"Shame on you. It was the wrong thing to do."

"It was the right thing!" Cass retorted. "She as much as told me you are a liar as well as a thief."

"Certainly. And she is a lady and correct. Isn't that the answer you expected and wanted?"

"Goodbye, sir!"

"Goodbye, son," Lucius said, and chuckled.

Summoned to Aaron Shapiro's store, Cass found Rachel Marcus with him in his office and was pleasantly distracted. She looked fleshier than when he had last seen her, and was now all curving, satiny olive skin and gleaming white teeth and black hair and black brows beneath which flashed black eyes, at the apex of a handsome maturity. The lure she had for him was fully restored as he held the white-gloved hand she offered, and he detected a coquettish invitation in her manner. Disgusted by the tedium of his labored, uneventful days, he made an instant resolve to pursue her whatever the consequences and even at the risk of alienating her father. Smiling, Rachel said, "I always thought you such a boy, Mr. Brennan. You aren't any more. What blooming sideburns! You resemble that general from the Civil War."

Cass felt himself reddening, and yet he was pleased. "I have that aspect to impress clients like Mr. Shapiro, Mrs. Marcus. My heart continues to pound as it did when I was a boy if I meet a beautiful woman, so I must not have changed entirely."

"Indeed?" she said. "I accept your flattery, sir, and take note that you may forget old acquaintances but not how to pay lavish compliments."

"How could I forget you?" he said. "You are very much mistaken

99

on both counts. If I am a slave to my profession, believe me I would rather be your slave."

"Listen to him, Father!" Rachel said. "There's no end to either his praises or his whiskers."

"Express definite displeasure with my facial adornments," Cass said, "and off they come."

"No, no," she told him. "You make me feel a queen about to order heads to roll, but I would not change you in any respect."

"Now I am flattered," he said.

"Rachel, my dear," said Shapiro benevolently, "if you have a defect, it is that of constant flirtation. I don't think your wiles suit your condition or the occasion."

"I stand corrected, gentlemen," Rachel said, and lowered her eyes demurely.

Without preliminaries, Shapiro explained the purpose of the meeting. He and a group of associates were going to form a new bank, to be called the Los Angeles National Savings Bank, and they intended that Cass would handle the incorporation proceedings and thereafter act for them as counsel. "The era has arrived, I feel," he said, "when banking must play a stronger role in our community. We are undercapitalized here for the expansion we contemplate, and too dependent upon eastern financial interests, which persist in exerting a misguided and ignorant control. The Los Angeles National will be a bank for Los Angeles, not a mere clearing house for outside money. Furthermore, we will emphasize a savings department, not as a novelty but as a coming necessity—and on such funds deposited with us we intend to pay a stated rate of interest at regular periods. Banks are now too prone to a concentration on commercial accounts and the making of loans; there is no reason why the accumulations of the laborer and small merchant cannot be consolidated and put to use in advantageous situations. I have every expectation that the Los Angeles National will supply a vital need."

Cass agreed with him, of course, and said he was honored by the trust placed in him. Unobserved by her father, Rachel mimicked the way his white beard waggled as he talked. She made a face at Cass; then she winked at him. He had difficulty keeping his composure, but he had to, for Mr. Shapiro had developed a degree of pomposity with advancing years and might not have relished any levity on his part.

"That is not all," Shapiro said. "Cass, I want you to buy stock in the bank—I have reserved a block of shares for you—and sit on the board of directors. I have other plans for you as well, but allow me merely to say at present that I cannot imagine a better investment for a young man in your position."

100

"Your word is my law, sir," Cass said. "But there is the question of ready money with me. How great an investment will be necessary?"

"Seventy-five thousand dollars. You have my guarantee that within five years your stock will have doubled in value."

Cass frowned. "I haven't anywhere near that kind of sum at my disposal, Mr. Shapiro."

"I urge you to do everything in your power to raise it. You can borrow on your land, can't you?"

"Unfortunately, it is already mortgaged to pay for various improvements."

"Well, under ordinary conditions my friends and I could assist you," Shapiro said, "but now we are too heavily committed in the bank. The most I can do is hold the shares for you until we are nearly ready —perhaps five or six months. Cast around, see what you can do."

"Yes, sir," Cass said. "I'll try not to fail you."

An assistant came in to request a decision from Mr. Shapiro, and he excused himself and departed, saying his daughter had a problem to take up with Cass. She sat quietly for a moment or two. He pondered his next words, unable to formulate them; he was nervous and eager, and wanted to take her with him at once, anywhere, and talk to her and listen to her laughter and gibing and forget his cares.

"What I have to ask," she said, "is scarcely worth the trouble of a stockholder and member of the board of directors of the Los Angeles National Savings Bank."

"None of that has happened yet."

"It will, Mr. Brennan."

"I wish you'd call me Cass. Shall I tell you a foolish thing? I'm far more interested in your concerns than in my own."

"Good heavens! You are a master of rhetoric."

"Only with you," he said. "What can I do for you? I'm prepared to kill dragons or fly through the air without a balloon."

"It is nothing that daring," she said. "I am going to be married again, and I have some property my first husband left to me. My father is a very cautious man, and he thinks I should be protected in the event I find difficulties in my second marriage."

"Married?" He realized his expression betrayed his shocked disappointment, and strained to make it blank and looked away. To add to his bitterness, he saw that her flirting had been unfeeling and in the nature of a small revenge for his previous slights. "Oh, yes. That is easily arranged, Mrs. Marcus. I am glad you are ending your widowhood. Who is the lucky man?"

"Samuel Eindhoven. Do you know him? He is a commission merchant."

"I don't believe I do."

"He has plagued me for the last three years, and he says he loves me to distraction and would lay down his life for me. But they all have said that. Do you suppose he is telling the truth?"

"I'm sure he is," Cass said.

She clapped her hands together imperiously. "Can't you look at me, Mr. Brennan?"

He turned toward her, and she sighed and shook her head. "If you will send me a letter," he said, "itemizing your property and—"

"Why did you avoid me? I tried to entice you once."

"I was busy . . ."

"Why?" she asked. "Because I'm a Jew?"

"Certainly not. I—"

"You needn't be ashamed. Don't you know the Jews are even more particular than the gentiles? They are chosen people and aristocrats, and they don't like intermarriage any better than your people. Probably my father would not have encouraged your attentions to me; he isn't that fond of his first Catholic protégé. You were wiser to forget me."

"It's not because you're a Jew," he said. "It's because I'm a fool and listened to fools." He got up awkwardly. "I'd better go. We'll talk on the telephone about your property. I hope you are very happy, Mrs. Marcus. Goodbye."

He went out and down Broadway, wrapped in a haze of melancholy and discouragement. A sharp pain coursed between his shoulder blades and his breath caught. He swore he would marry, and soon, at his own pleasure, and repel anyone's opinion to the contrary.

five

THE Los Angeles National Savings Bank was established, and commodious ground floor space rented in a building on Spring Street between Fourth and Fifth. Aaron Shapiro pressed for the seventy-five thousand dollars which was Cass's contribution. Grimly clapping his hat on his head, Cass made for the one quarter where he might hope to borrow seventy-five thousand dollars without collateral—a square, ugly, reinforced concrete building (a startling novelty in the town) which housed the Sunset Sea Oil Products Company. He went unheralded, and discovered that Lucius was home ill. A clerk suggested that he see Mr. Jennison instead, and Cass followed him unwillingly.

Kirby inhabited a large, barren room, where he sat behind a desk devoid of papers gnawing on the end of a pencil. His moustache was white, his hair nearly gone, and he had taken on an alarming amount of weight. "Bless your heart," he said cordially. "I haven't seen you since the night we took those Chicagoans into camp. Say, Lucius and I sure appreciated your standing by us when they wanted to use you in the suit. What brings you here, my boy?"

On impulse, Cass explained his errand. "I swore I wouldn't come begging," he concluded, "but Uncle Lucius is my last chance."

"Why shouldn't he give you a hand?" Kirby said. "He can surely afford it—even old whores leave their savings to him. Go out to his house right now and talk to him."

"I hate to, Mr. Jennison, and doubly so when he's under the weather. If I could only think of somebody else—"

"Me, maybe?" Kirby sighed. "I suppose I could come through, but I don't think Lucius would like that. My hunch is he'll jump at the chance

103

to tie in with you again, and I can't afford to do anything that might offend him at present. Just between us, I want out of Sunset Sea if I can escape with a whole skin."

"That's astonishing news," Cass said.

"Not too astonishing when you know the facts. Cass, I'm going to need a lawyer. Are you available?"

"Truthfully, sir, I already have more than I can do."

"Don't want to get mixed up in it, eh? Well, he just might leave you something some day. I don't blame you."

"That's not my reason, sir. Believe me."

"Oh?" Kirby said sourly. "I'll take your word for it, Cass. This is a hell of a business, this oil business. You never know where you are. It's one gamble after another, and you can lose your shirt overnight. I'm getting old and tired and sensible, and Lucius thinks I've lost my nerve. Maybe I have, Cass."

"Have you discussed this with him?"

"Well, I've made two or three half-assed attempts, but he only laughs and says he can't get along without me, which is a lie. I can't help but figure he just hates to part with any of our winnings."

"I hope you're mistaken," Cass said. "Have a serious talk and put your cards on the table. You won't need a lawyer."

"The hell I won't," Kirby said. "I don't trust the son of a bitch now— not that I ever did much. And I better get paid off while we're still in a liquid condition. You know what he's doing? He's bought two refineries out in Puente, he plans to build a pipeline from them to Los Angeles, and down on Alameda Street he's adding more damned storage tanks. All the time he keeps buying and selling leases and drilling new wells, half of them dusters. He went to New York last year looking for help and hired a bunch of Pennsylvania highbinders away from the Rockefellers. Ever since he got the idea of storing crude in tanks when the price was down to ten cents a barrel and then forcing an artificial shortage and cashing in, he thinks he knows everything. The trust and old John D. are gunning for him. As sure as God made little apples, they'll catch up with Lucius and wipe him out."

"Yes, I imagine that could happen."

"*Will* happen. And I don't care to be his partner when it does. Look here, Cass—you represent me and use your influence with him, and I'll do you a favor in return. If Lucius refuses to pony up the bank stock money, I will. Is that fair?"

"Yes, sir," Cass said, and his spirits soared. "Fair as fair can be. What do you want of my uncle?"

"I'll show you," Kirby said, and shouted to the clerk outside his office.

"Now, listen, my boy—if I have to raise seventy-five thousand dollars, I'll expect a nice easy five per cent and the pledging of your bank stock. You understand that, huh?"

Cass understood. The clerk brought a balance sheet for the company and Kirby gave an exhaustive outline of what he considered his fair share. They spent a long time going over the various aspects, and Kirby reminisced at boring length.

"It's never been an equal partnership," he said. "I'm willing to admit that. But I want half for the risks I took. In the beginning I was the only man who would gamble with Lucius. If I went into court with him and told what I know, he might end up sitting on a very sharp tack. Strictly between us, though, my rock bottom figure is a third—in cash, not paper and promises. He can have my Sunset Sea stock at the going price. Try to keep him from getting lawyers of his own. He'll listen to you, Cass. I'm depending on you."

When the estate of Susie Figueres was settled, Lucius's portion included her house. Since then Cass had heard of an extensive reconstruction, the sale of the home on Sixth Street, and a move by his uncle into grandeur. He took a streetcar to the Westlake Park area, which was perhaps the most elegant of the newer suburbs. The Figueres place was familiar to him through his handling of the will, but he failed to recognize it upon arrival; supplanting a rococo edifice of towers and minarets and stained glass windows and filigreed porches was a simple white structure, almost devoid of ornament, of shining stucco shaded by lacy pepper trees, the approach set off with a low stucco wall and a wrought iron gate. The flattened roof was of red tiles, the extensive garden a profusion of flowers and shrubs, the coach house prefaced by a paved courtyard. The house had a certain confusion of design, yet the total effect was agreeable. Porches had disappeared, the windows were in the form of Moorish arches and had iron grilles in front of them, and at the rear was an elaborate plaster pergola and a fountain playing in a tiled circle.

The gate was locked, and Cass had to ring a bell. A Chinese houseman appeared, listened expressionlessly to Cass's name, and shuffled inside. Several moments passed. As he started to fear for his reception, Cass saw his uncle hasten out and come to unfasten the gate. They gripped hands. In a dressing gown, trousers and slippers, Lucius showed his age and declining health at close range; he was thinner, bent, slower in movement, clean-shaven, with concave cheeks and luxuriant hair turned white. But his blue eyes were bright as ever, and possibly a trifle filmed by moisture. Cass was aware of a touch of sorrow at what the years had wrought, and of the revival of an affection he had not expected.

"By God," Lucius said, "I was wondering when you might turn up to see Brennan's Folly." He gestured toward the house. "This, I mean. Come in, Cass. You must forgive the unintentional discourtesy of Hannibal—that's my chink. He understands virtually no English."

"To be honest," Cass said, "I wouldn't have blamed you for turning me away."

"You have forgotten me. Don't you remember how I never held grudges? Besides, what we disagreed on is ancient history."

The foyer they entered was tiled and resonant. Beyond lay a huge room with a ceiling two stories up, a great fireplace, and a balcony running around the second floor. Heavy, carved, dark furniture in a medieval style and brilliant hand-woven rugs decorated the vast space. The pictures on the walls were dark with age, their surfaces cracked, and depicted saints and mythological horsemen and several classical ladies in a dishabille that did not conceal buxom charms. Thick velvet draperies kept out the sun, and gas mantles glowed in spreading fixtures of forged iron. It was June and the morning clouds had gone inland, but a fire burned in the grate.

"Sit down," Lucius said. He took a chair near the fireplace, pulled a rug over his knees, and lit a cigarillo. "Tell me about yourself. How is Doña Maria?"

"The same," Cass replied. "A little older."

"As we all are." Lucius frowned. "Especially you, Cass. What have you done with your youth?"

"Buried it in an office, I guess. Uncle Lucius, I hope you aren't seriously unwell."

"Oh, no. Just the Goddamned ailments of age. My kidneys ache and I wake up of nights and pull my pot from the cabinet and pee liquid fire. My doctor advises against strong drink, which is my one consolation. Will you have a drop of the creature?"

"No, thank you."

"I shall." Lucius clapped his hands sharply and a diminutive Chinese woman materialized from nowhere. "This is Lucrezia Borgia, Cass. I haven't the least idea of what her real name is—something unpronounceable. She's Hannibal's wife or sister or cousin or concubine or whatever. I've never got it straight, and it doesn't matter. They're good servants, answer to the name I happen to call them, and keep quiet." He raised his voice, which had lost its deep timbre and sharp articulation. "Whiskey, Lucrezia! Soda water! Chop-chop!"

106

"Are you sure you should go against the advice of your doctor, sir?" Cass asked.

Lucius chuckled. "Wait until you meet my doctor. She ought to be along shortly."

"*She?*"

"I knew you'd be astonished. Yes, she. The Queen has 'em these days, you know. At least one. Mine is named Alice Chambers. I assume you have never been examined by a female physician?"

"No."

"And I can tell from your expression that you don't intend to be," Lucius said. "Well, every man to his own taste. It's a damned queer feeling when you have your clothes off and she has her hands on you. I'm inclined to wish that I was younger and could surprise my doctor by having a splendid erection while under her ministrations. Unfortunately that time is over, and I have to content myself with whiskey. I wouldn't be surprised if I were Allie's only male patient. No doubt she doesn't take them if they are likely to prove dangerous."

"I can't say I approve of the innovation, sir."

Glancing at him curiously, Lucius smiled. "No, I suppose not. But I am very modern in spite of my advanced years. I ride in motorcars and go to watch the Kinetoscope at Talley's Electric Theater on Main Street and yearn to have an airship. I wish to God I didn't have to die and could stay around for more miracles. Those in the Bible don't compare to the modern kind."

Cass matched his smile. "You haven't changed, have you, Uncle Lucius?"

"No, nor you. Nobody changes, really."

Lucrezia returned with a silver tray, set it beside Lucius, and whisked off. He poured liquor in a glass, added soda water, and looked inquiringly at Cass. "You won't reconsider?" he said. "This eases a long passage."

"Thank you, but I haven't indulged since you instructed me."

"I cured you of a lot of vices, didn't I? You aren't married, I know. Do you indulge in any whoring?"

Cass shook his head. "I haven't time. However, I wish I was married. Don't you think I've waited long enough?"

"I'm not a reliable oracle on that subject," Lucius said. "Matrimony never appealed to me."

They chatted easily of the past while Lucius finished his drink and the little cigar. His memory was surprisingly good, and obviously his interest lay in what he called "the good old days." "It's strange," he remarked. "I'm better at resurrecting the events of thirty years ago than I am at recalling what happened last week. Does your mother ever ramble on like this?"

"Quite often," Cass said.

"And you get tired of it?"

Cass shrugged. "Occasionally, sir."

"I'll stop while I still have your attention," Lucius said, and grinned. But the return of Lucrezia bringing strong green tea in eggshell-thin green cups and delicate sugar-powdered cookies reminded him of the Chinese quarter in Nigger Alley, and the opium dens, joss houses and laundries. He smelled again the strange scents that had delighted him nearly half a century before, and heard the firecrackers popping. "In '71—damn it, the low numbers of this century depress me—yes, in '71 they fought a tong war and had the bad luck to shoot some white men while resisting arrest. That started a riot, and before it ended more than twenty of the Chinamen had been strung up or shot full of holes. I remember hearing the alarm, getting my six-shooter, and running down Main Street to the Plaza. On one of the few times in my life, I enrolled on the side of law and order and helped the sheriff put the lid on. The black mark the Queen got all over the country for the massacre rather surprised us. We thought everybody knew she was a wide open frontier town."

Abruptly, while Cass prepared to introduce the subject of the loan he required, and possibly Kirby's defection, Lucius arose and insisted on taking him for a tour of Brennan's Folly. There were ten bedrooms, sewing rooms, anterooms, dressing rooms, a billiard room, a library with hand-wrought beams, a dining room fit for state dinners, a solarium supplied from a greenhouse on the grounds, and a huge, empty, dim last-minute addition to the west wing suitable for conversion to a ballroom. The second story of the coach house included servants' quarters, and below, instead of horses, were stabled an electric brougham and a six cylinder Franklin touring car. Hobie, Lucius's Negro chauffeur, clad in a smart double-breasted gray uniform and billed cap, was presented and started up the gasoline carriage for demonstration purposes.

"It can go forty miles an hour," Lucius said, "and make the damndest noise you ever heard. Hobie has killed more dogs and chickens, and scared more teams, than any nigger in the county. Once a farmer chased us firing birdshot after we'd run over his prize pig, and Hobie broke several world's records getting out of there."

Hobie smiled and looked proud.

The house struck Cass as folly indeed, and an absurd extravagance for an old bachelor. He did not like the unornamented design or the queer furnishings. Susie Figueres's spindly love seats and gold hangings

108

and crimson plush in the previous incarnation were better, in his estimation, but he exercised a prudent restraint in commenting. Only the fountain and odd pergola, so much superior to his mother's little summerhouse at the Plaza, aroused his enthusiasm. Listening to him, Lucius leaned back on a bench and squinted at the chaste bulk of his castle.

"You don't sound too exercised," he remarked amiably. "Most of my visitors have been pretty cool, I have to confess. Well, it's foolishment. But late in life building is a great satisfaction, as you may find out. Seeing something rise from the ground, solid and permanent, gives you a grip on living. My intention was to sell Susie's palace, but suddenly the mania that troubled pharaohs and caesars took command of me."

Hannibal interrupted them, conveying a message in scrambled English which was unintelligible to Cass. "My physician has arrived," Lucius said. "Come help me greet her."

They entered by the solarium, where sun was streaming in on the plants and flowers, and Lucius halted and ordered Hannibal to bring the doctor there. "This is a damned cold house," he remarked, "and I spend much of my time sitting before a fire wrapped in a blanket. I forget how pleasant the sun room is."

Through the doorway came a small, sandy-haired, clean-featured, freckle-nosed woman, dressed in a sober gray suit trimmed in black braid, a saucy black straw hat perched on her piled-up hair, which had a distinct shade of red to it. Her skin was pale and softly luminous, her mouth thin-lipped and wide, and when she smiled her teeth were revealed as white, square and obviously strong. In one hand she carried a tubular black bag. Cass was taken aback at the shortness of her skirts; far from dragging on the ground in the current fashion, they were elevated high enough to reveal slender ankles encased in laced kid shoes, and apparently had no weights in the hem to keep them down.

Dr. Chambers greeted Lucius in a businesslike fashion and popped a thermometer in his mouth and began counting his pulse almost before he could introduce Cass, to whom she nodded. She peeled back his eyelids for an inspection, and examined his legs. Sitting beside him, she said, "The edema is better but you still show evidence of uremic poisoning. Is that whiskey I smell on your breath?"

"Just one, dear doctor, to celebrate a reunion with my beloved nephew."

"You must stop entirely. Let me feel your back in the affected area."

He loosed his trousers and lifted his robe, and she tested him for soreness. Pretending ecstasy at the pressure of her hands, he reported lessening pain. Quite unmoved by his gentle ribaldry, she proceeded to question him on bowel movements, digestion, discomfort in the lumbar region, and frequency of urination. "Are you experiencing burning sensations?" she asked. "What is the color of your urine? Does it have an odor?"

"Doctor, I seem to pee molten lava. The stuff is the color of an inferior port wine. It smells like the piss of a sick horse."

"You'd better furnish me with another specimen, Colonel."

Conversant as he thought he was with the changing times, and opposed to conventional prudery, Cass nevertheless stiffened at their colloquy. His uncle was being deliberately provocative, of course, and Dr. Chambers was ignoring him; but a woman had no right to put herself in such a vulnerable position by choosing to follow a man's profession against all established reason and custom. He turned away from them in disgust, pretending to study a plant.

Evidently the doctor was as adept at divining his thoughts as Lucius had once been, for, glancing at him, she said, "I put up with the colonel's crude gallantries because he is the only man I have met in Los Angeles who is not a fool. Someday he may be able to bring a blush to my cheek, and then the game will be over."

Lucius laughed. "You underestimate me. I am intent upon your seduction, improbable as it might seem. I am willing to pay any sum for a single night, doctor, after you have restored my health. A single night will satiate me, I suppose."

"Perhaps I underestimate you," Dr. Chambers said, "but I think you overestimate yourself. Plead for a quarter of an hour, a half hour at the most; you won't need longer."

"Touché, Allie. My God, you could be right, but let us put me to the test. What harm can befall us? You'll wear your magic ring, won't you?"

"Yes. If I didn't have it, though, I doubt that you would do me any harm."

"I may surprise you yet," Lucius said. "Tell my nephew of the ring . . . Cass, this is the greatest discovery since fire and the wheel. It will make adultery as feasible as cheating at cards."

The doctor looked steadily at Cass, who was bothered by embarrassment and a premonitory chill of alarm. "When I grew to know your uncle, Mr. Brennan," she said, "and was appreciative enough of his kindnesses in recommending other patients to me to tolerate his indecent language, our little game began. In the course of it I made the error of telling him I had fitted a ring to the mouth of my uterus, the kind of ring which has been used for centuries by women in India and the Orient to prevent pregnancy. He has never forgotten my confidence, and it is confidential no longer."

"The good doctor has introduced the custom here among some of

110

her trade," Lucius added. "Cass, we now have lovely women who can diddle with no thought of that disconcerting leap from bed to squirt water into their innards."

"Indeed?" Cass said, with difficulty. "How interesting . . ."

"Don't you feel you've done your utmost for today, Colonel?" the doctor said. "Mr. Brennan has turned the color of the red, red rose."

"Yes, Allie. You are imperturbable, I see. All right. Thank you for looking in on me."

"I'll return in three days. Meanwhile, rest, no liquor, plain foods, few condiments. Do not resume business until you are better."

"Please show the doctor out, Cass," Lucius said. "Then I won't have to bellow for Hannibal."

"I know the way, thank you," Dr. Chambers said.

Furious at his telltale face, Cass followed her. He opened the front door and allowed her to pass, and brought up the rear. He could not take his eyes off her. She was the size of his mother, finely made, but not beautiful as Doña Maria had been, or even pretty in the ordinary sense; and she had the same air of undeviating resolution.

Leaning on a pillar of the gate was a safety bicycle built to accommodate a rider in skirts; she strapped her bag to a parcel rack over the rear wheel, hitched up her dress in an indifferent display of ankle and black silk stocking and sat in the saddle. "Open the gate, if you please," she said. "And stop staring at me. I am not a circus freak."

"Please forgive me. It's curiosity on my part, not boorishness. I haven't met a lady doctor before."

"I am not a lady doctor. I'm a woman doctor, and the distinction is important."

"I beg your pardon," he said. "No matter what I say or do, I seem to offend you. But that isn't my intention. I'm not as prissy as I look."

"Very nearly, though, aren't you?"

"I suppose so. I'm open to correction, however."

"Oh, I don't mean to be rude," she said. "But in my profession I've been exposed to so many slights that I just can't endure any more. All I ask of men who can't stand women doctors is simply that they leave them alone. It's the lecturing and condescension that sets me frothing at the mouth."

"I have no prejudice, Doctor. My difficulty must be lack of sophistication."

"Good. Next time you are sick, come to me. I can use more patients."

"I'd like to look you up as a well man."

"Really?"

111

"Naturally with your permission, Doctor. I am unattached, and I notice you aren't wearing a ring."

"Your Rabelaisian uncle explained. It is in the mouth of my—"

"I do not maintain the same views as my uncle," Cass broke in sharply, "nor play blushing games with young women. You would have to consider me as a serious suitor for your hand and conduct yourself accordingly."

She exhibited astonishment. "For my hand . . . ? After one glance, you are considering marrying me?"

"Exactly. I have already waited too long to marry, and so have you. Instead of wasting time on silly preliminaries, we should be frank with each other and get right down to the object in view."

"Dear me," she said. "You're not only a prude, you're crazy!"

"It's a harmless form of insanity. May I call on you?"

"Well . . . once, I suppose. My callers never come a second time, Mr. Brennan. But you must learn to restrain this impulsiveness of yours."

"Expect me soon," he said.

She pedaled off, exposing more leg than he approved of, and he closed the gate and returned thoughtfully to the solarium. The process of finding a wife was under way. He had a feeling of satisfaction. Lucius was being served a fresh drink by Lucrezia. "What do you think of my medical adviser?" he asked. "Isn't she a caution?"

"She's queer but interesting," Cass said. "Has she a good practice?"

"No. People want women for nurses, not doctors. It isn't a line of work the distaff side shines in. I think her failure infuriates Allie. She blames our town."

"Is she capable?"

"As most of them, I expect," Lucius said. "I have no confidence in their pronouncements."

"So I observe."

Lucius grinned. "This dry country has always raised a fierce thirst in me."

"Dr. Chambers ought to consider following a more normal course of womanhood," Cass said.

"Marriage and motherhood, you mean? What right-thinking man would give that opportunity to an atheist, a suffragette, a fighter for equal rights, an enemy of the double standard?"

"I might."

"You astonish me," Lucius said. "Allie must run against your grain entirely."

"She might be susceptible to conversion."

"You're mistaken. And aside from saving a lost soul, where is the lure? She isn't even pretty."

"She's intelligent."

"Beware of that kind, Cass. Didn't I warn you about women?"

"Yes," Cass said, "and also arranged for me to get a foul disease."

"Oh, God," Lucius said. "The past does rise up to haunt me. I wish I could manage to make you forget that mistake."

"You can, sir. Lend me seventy-five thousand dollars, secured by stock in the Los Angeles National Savings Bank." Cass went on to relate Mr. Shapiro's offer, and his predicament with the San Cristobal. "I'll pay any rate of interest you require."

Lucius studied him a moment. "Is this the life you're set on—banking, cultivating the prosperous and running their errands? Should you commit yourself? Won't it be dull?"

"What else do you suggest?"

"For no particular reason, I'm reminded of Brian Regan. He died a few months ago, you know."

"To the relief of one and all including Regan, I imagine," Cass said.

"Not to mine," Lucius said. "I miss him. He had a colorful career and a bit of fun, despite the bottle."

"You must be joking, sir."

"I see that I am—to you. Well, never mind. Go your own way. You shall have the money, but there's a consideration. Open the San Cristobal to me exclusively. In proof of my confidence, the seventy-five thousand is your bonus. And I'll give you a sixteenth of the proceeds."

"My mother will object."

"Let her. She doesn't own the land, and you're in a bind."

Cass looked at him calmly. "So I am, Uncle Lucius. So are you if you want those rights. Because I insist on a fifth interest."

"Ah, me . . ." Lucius said. "Exacting a pound of flesh from your fond uncle, are you? Still, you show the right instincts. All right. Twenty per cent it is."

"I had a talk with your partner before I came out. He accuses you of recklessness. Is the trust after you?"

"With horse, foot and guns." Lucius grinned. "And my partner has never stopped accusing me of recklessness while he steadily enriched himself. Those leases you grant me must be transferable."

"Why?"

"Because I have the oldest shell game in the world in operation. I can't possibly buck the trust for long, so I'm going to swallow my pride and sell out for Standard Oil stock. My pride is a figment of the imagination, incidentally. The more I have, the more I'm a potential thorn in

113

their side, the better they'll pay. They don't waste money in fighting if they can settle equitably. Sure, there is some risk in assuming they will not change their usual tactics, but the profits are worth the courting of a little danger, see?"

"I see," Cass said. "Kirby doesn't, though. He wants out, and has engaged me to negotiate for him. Are you willing to settle?"

"I've been expecting that. Yes, I'll let him go. But he'd be better off waiting and cashing in with me."

"What are your terms? He asks for a fifty-fifty division."

"I'll appoint you my representative in this too," Lucius said. "He isn't entitled to a split, but I don't object. You decide, Cass. The difference will come out of your inheritance."

Cass wetted his lips. "I am empowered to accept a rock-bottom one-third in return for cash. Can you pay in hard money?"

"I can borrow it."

"On behalf of my client," Cass said, "I accept your settlement on a one-third basis."

Suddenly they began to laugh. "Did you catch the money fever from me?" Lucius said.

"Yes," Cass said. "Long ago."

That evening Cass went to pay Dr. Chambers a visit, having secured her address from his uncle. Lucius was sardonically interested in the outcome and made Cass promise to keep him informed of every development.

Alice Chambers occupied a small frame building on Wall Street. The front held a consulting room, the rear, living quarters. She came out of the back at Cass's ring, hastily pulling on a white coat. The air smelled of cooking. He looked around the shabby office.

"Oh," she said. "It's you—"

"Didn't you expect me?"

"Not so soon."

"You know," Cass said, "you've done a curious thing to me. I can't understand why it could happen, and all at once. But the moment I met you, I felt happier. I don't feel happy very often. Better yet, I had a new sensation of strength and power. Would you say that was love at first sight?"

"I think you're being foolish," she said, "and you're too old for acting like a boy."

"Well, bear with my foolishness for a while. You told me your callers came only once. Let me try for a record."

There was another woman with the doctor, who shared the rear sec-

114

tion of the building—a dull, quiet, shabbily dressed girl named Sadie Lewis, with dun-colored hair and downcast eyes. She worked for the municipality as a filing clerk and had been Dr. Chambers's first patient in Los Angeles. Somewhat ungraciously, the doctor took Cass to her living room and introduced Sadie. The meeting was awkward, for Sadie had nothing to say and stole unhappy glances at the intruder. A meal was ready on the stove, and she wore an apron.

"I'm sorry to be so late, Miss Chambers," Cass said, "but I was busy. May I take you to supper?"

"I am a doctor, Mr. Brennan. Do you resent addressing me by my title?"

"Certainly not, Doctor."

"What is this preoccupation with 'supper' in Los Angeles?" the doctor asked. "I feel I am back in Wisconsin. Doesn't anybody dine here? Do you still eat your big meal in the middle of the day?"

"No," Cass replied. "Two hours for a siesta has been out of fashion for years. It's just custom that makes us call it supper. May I take you to dinner, Doctor? Miss Lewis, will you excuse us?"

Sadie mumbled and flashed a mute appeal to Dr. Chambers. She paused irresolutely.

"The food will keep," Cass continued. "Indulge me this once. It's better to get it over with."

"His uncle is my patient, Sadie," the doctor said. "He might throw some trade my way. I won't be late."

Bound for the best restaurant he could think of, Cass said, "Do you owe Miss Lewis an immense obligation?"

"No. Why?"

"You seemed reluctant to leave her. You acted as I do when I have to tell my mother I can't be with her."

"You have that sort of mother?" she said. "Is she the reason you haven't married?"

"Perhaps. I don't really know. She doesn't look like you, but somehow she's remarkably like you. Hasn't my uncle ever mentioned her?"

She shook her head. "Only you. He laughed and said you were a graven image."

"I intend to change that," Cass said.

At dinner the doctor had part of a bottle of wine, which he did not share, and appeared to relax. She offered no serious objection to his calling her Allie, as Lucius did, or to talking of herself; in fact, in the latter she was explicit, the loneliness and segregation she had endured because of her views and training lending volubility. The daughter of a Wisconsin farmer, she had attended Oberlin College and then, over the strenuous objections of her family, enrolled at Rush Medical College in Chicago. Her mother had died early, and she had a stepmother and two half-brothers. She detested her home and the Middle West, and hated her stepmother and half-brothers. From sheer spite, her father had withdrawn financial support to thwart her ambitions and she had suffered privation in getting her medical education.

"But it may not be solely your doctoring," Cass said. "My uncle says you're an atheist and suffragette."

"I gather you are opposed to my opinions, so how can you have fallen in love at first sight?"

"I take into account your imperfections. They endear you to me."

"I have a secret to confide," she said. "This is our one dinner together. After tonight you won't see me again. I don't like you."

"Try not to jump to conclusions. Give me time. I'll grow on you. After all, it must have been fate that brought you to Los Angeles."

"Not fate, Lucius."

"My Uncle Lucius?"

"Yes. I happened to read that old, lying book of his, *A Glimpse of Paradise*." She snorted in disgust. "I believed all that stuff about a city where winter was unknown, where fertile land planted to grapes, citrus fruit, olives and nuts gave the farmer a yearly income of four hundred dollars an acre, where the sick came in droves to be cured. I wanted to live in a place without malaria, lung infections, scarlet fever and diphtheria. I thought I'd be happy and successful where there were just thirteen deaths per thousand of inhabitants and graveyards were superfluous. Oh, he is a dreadful liar! Mechanics, bricklayers, masons, cabinetmakers and blacksmiths getting six dollars for an eight-hour day! Laborers receiving four dollars! Beef ten cents a pound, a barrel of flour six dollars, a hundred pounds of potatoes a dollar, weekly board in a hotel or restaurant seven dollars! I thought I was going to a heaven on earth."

"That book was written a long while ago to help a boom. He must have been amused when he learned he'd lured you out here."

"I've never told him," she said. "I won't give him the satisfaction."

"How did you happen to meet him?"

"He read my advertisement in a newspaper and called me."

"We are the victims of fate," Cass said, "and had better not struggle."

They went for a walk afterward, and sat for half an hour in a beer garden and listened to the music. Allie was contemptuous of the Queen. "There is nothing here," she said. "No interest in the finer things, no art, no poetry, no culture, no awareness of the twentieth century. The climate

116

is too soft for real effort. This is just a great big village, fit only for sleeping and rearing children. It is full of dust and simple peasants."

"Why don't you leave?"

"I can't afford the train fare."

"I'll give it to you," he said.

"Oh, shut up!"

He smiled. "Now you're talking like a woman. That's better than when you talk like a physician."

They took a hack to her building, on better terms with each other. The moment they entered the office, the door at the rear opened a crack, a single eye of Sadie's regarded them, and the door closed. "She waits up for you as my mother does for me," Cass commented. "How old are you, Allie?"

"Twenty-six."

"You're too old to be watched over by a foster-mother again."

"And you're too old to be under the thumb of a real mother," she retorted.

"I was thinking that too."

"Good night, Cass. Don't bother me any more unless you are ill and need treatment."

But he telephoned her next day and was quietly insistent. She rebuffed him again and again. Even-tempered and patient, he sent flowers and candy and any knickknack that caught his fancy, and received curt, grudging notes of acknowledgment. The circumstance that she returned nothing encouraged him, for he relied on her poverty.

Presently she agreed to accompany him to dinner and a performance of *The Admirable Chrichton* by William Gillette and his touring company. Fortified by lessons from an upstairs "dance studio" on Main Street, he invited her to a Bar Association ball. She accepted immediately, to his surprise, and proved to be an accomplished dancer. She was unexpectedly attractive in her shimmering blue gown—which she confided that Sadie had helped her make, and shed tears upon—and they swung down the floor in the closest rapport yet in the measures of the polka and the waltz. Both of them were fond of "After the Ball Is Over" and "In the Good Old Summertime," and he discovered she could finger elementary tunes on a banjo and bought her one.

There remained the matter of the confrontation with his mother. She had taken notice of his absences evenings and weekends, of his purchase of a bicycle and the rides he went on to Pasadena or the orange groves of Hollywood, of neglect of his work and the occasional apologies he had to give on the telephone at home to impatient clients. Her pride kept her from questioning him, but she looked her disapproval. He knew she must assume he was in the toils of a woman whose identity he preferred to keep secret, and he was not at all sure she hadn't discovered who the woman was and had already mustered arguments against her. Yet the armed truce continued between them until he felt ready to reveal his decision.

His preliminary step was an approach to Allie. Their relationship could be said at that stage to have progressed to easy familiarity. She was accustomed to him. They were not affectionate, and neither had breached a cool reserve. In Cass's arms on the dance floor, Allie's color heightened and she obviously enjoyed such moments, but he suspected music and movement were the excitants and not his close proximity. When he spoke of an inevitable marriage she shrugged and dismissed the subject. He had fallen into the habit of kissing her as they met and parted, on the cheek or brow, and she submitted; he attempted no more intimacy than that, calculating his chances and avoiding the mistake of disgusting her. In any event, he was not greatly stirred by her in the physical sense. It was marrying he had in mind, and the pleasures and rewards of a sober and decent union. Her unheated acceptance of him was satisfaction enough. At this juncture he was gratified and reassured when she trustingly took his hand or clung to his arm. Propinquity was doing its work for him. One day he would get children on her in the conjugal bed. Their frequent quarrels, usually over politics or women's rights or moral questions, had become half amiable. He had never seen her cry.

"I want you to meet my mother, my dear," he said.

"I haven't the least desire to meet her. I'm not interested in Spanish families or an alleged aristocracy, and I won't be condescended to. What possible sense is there in my knowing her?"

"She is going to be your mother-in-law," he said.

"She is going to be nothing of the kind," she replied. "Now stop annoying me, Cass."

They argued a bit aimlessly through a period of a couple of weeks. From experience, he was positive he could wear down Allie's resistance. He had grown to know her well. She had strong convictions, and she was capable of brief, fierce devotions to ideas, but she was easily discouraged and bored. Achievement, or the illusion of it—even, possibly, in the case of her medical degree, he hoped—often ended the drive that motivated her. Aware of what he regarded as a typical feminine trait of being unable to resist distraction (not manifested, however, in his mother), he chipped away.

"I won't discuss it any more," she said, at last. "You are tiresome!

. . . Yes, I will discuss it. On Sadie's account. If your mother has to be included in our friendship, so does Sadie. She has sat home and waited for months. Why can't she go with us occasionally?"

"She can," Cass said. "Sadie is our *quid pro quo.*"

He hired a buggy and took the women on a picnic in the Arroyo Seco. When he suggested an escort for Sadie, Allie appeared startled; that was impossible; Sadie hated men and made no friends among them. She was miserable during the outing, talked in whispers to Allie, barely answered the remarks Cass directed at her, and once wandered off to hide and weep and be rescued by her companions. Allie reproved her on the way home and she wept again.

Pleased by the task of undermining Sadie, Cass persevered. The three of them boarded a red electric car which ran to Santa Monica and spent a summer day at the beach. Emerging from bathing machines, Sadie huddling behind Allie, the women took off their shoes and stockings and followed Cass into the surf. Their costumes, once more fabricated by Sadie, were of black twill and had shortened skirts, long sleeves and high-necked linen collars. Sadie wore a hat and veil, but Allie insisted on going bareheaded. The wading they did was soon terminated by Sadie's shrieks and her retirement to the bathing machine, where she stayed for a long time. Cass sat on the sand with Allie, who glowered at her shapely ankles and feet.

"She's crying, I know," she said. "I ought to go to her."

"Why?"

"She needs me."

"She doesn't need you at all," he said. "Sadie is childishly jealous, and her hatred of me is preposterous. Does she expect to keep you forever?"

"She had a sister who died," Allie said, "and she never got over it. Her family is back in New Hampshire; she has nobody here. She is afraid of men. I've taken the place of the dead sister, I suppose."

"You can't fill the place indefinitely. You have your own life to consider. It's an unnatural relationship."

Strangely, Allie turned crimson. "It is not! I am giving her the care she has to have. We live together because it is cheaper and more practical. What I do is my own business, Cass. You don't own me!"

"I know all that. But you can't throw away your best years caring for one silly hypochondriac. Allie, look at me . . . you're going to do what I want, aren't you?"

"I don't know—"

"Yes, you are," he said. "I love you, Allie."

She got up quickly. "I'm going to Sadie."

"Will you visit my mother? I've done my part."

119

"All right," she said. "It won't do any good, but I'll go."

At breakfast the following morning, Cass unburdened himself to Doña Maria. She listened to the story of his borrowing the money for the bank stock from Lucius and nodded approvingly; she had wondered what he was going to do, decided not to interfere, and yet hoped he would appeal to his uncle if no other source was available. The faintest of frowns marred her forehead when he went on to explain Lucius's stipulation that the San Cristobal be opened for oil exploration, and how the first derricks were about to rise on the ranch. "He is clever," she commented. "Well, be his friend and relative. You won't suffer for it. He is an old man, and sick."

"They say he's worth six hundred thousand dollars," Cass said. "Perhaps more."

Her breath hissed in quick intake. "Is that possible?"

"Oh, yes. If he sells to the trust and acquires good stock, his fortune may increase a great deal."

"Then humor him!"

Cass thought they resembled two conspirators, leaning toward one another over the table, voices lowered so the maids could not hear. He said, "He might be gulling me, Mother. The money could go to somebody else. Suppose he lives too long and becomes feeble mentally and falls under the influence of—"

"Suggest to him that he makes his will with you."

"No, I can't do that."

"Someday," she said, "I will contrive to meet him and sound him out. I could pretend—"

"No, he has told me I'm his heir. We'll have to be satisfied with that. If the trust develops the San Cristobal and we actually have substantial deposits, we will prosper enough."

"You will prosper. I am not interested, except in the fact that the San Cristobal stays wholly yours."

"It is mine," Cass said. "They can take the oil from the ground, but they cannot take the ground. My promise to you has been kept. I am sorry for the desecration, but I could not help myself—"

"That does not matter," she said, "and I don't question your action. Probably I will never see the desecration."

An awkward pause fell between them. She knew he had another subject to broach. He despised the signs of nervousness in him: the dry throat, the way he temporized. Only his mother could daunt him now, and he had to snap the chains. Their long, peculiar devotion and union faced a sad end. To anticipate a welcoming of Allie by Doña Maria was

120

impossible. His sole alternative was to make her understand she could accept the new order or be banished. He proposed to do exactly that.

"I intend to marry," he said, an unexpectedly harsh note in his voice. "I would like to present Dr. Alice Chambers to you. Will you receive her next Sunday afternoon for tea?"

She had expected the blow; her expression did not change, although her lips tightened for an instant and she carefully put down the cup she had been holding. *"Doctor?"* she asked. "A woman?"

"Yes. I met her at Uncle Lucius's. She has treated him."

"Oh? Is she of Los Angeles? I don't know the Chambers name."

"She is from Wisconsin."

"What of her family?"

"A father and a stepmother," he said, "and some half-brothers, I believe. It's of no importance to me."

"There is money, Cass?"

"None. And she is neither homely nor pretty, but something in between. She contents me, you see."

"A woman doctor—" Doña Maria said, and paused and wrinkled her nose. "I have difficulty getting used to these times. Has she accepted you?"

"Not yet. I am confident she will."

"I won't try to interfere in your life. No, don't protest. I know you will not permit it. You never would—only when you were young and helpless. I didn't abuse my power then, did I?"

"That is beside the point now, Mother."

"Very well. It no longer matters. But I might have been consulted. I have had ambitions for you—"

"You had better abandon them," he said.

"Yes, I expect I had."

"Forgive my speaking so frankly. I don't want to hurt your feelings. But an argument between us will be a waste of breath. My mind is made up."

"Yes," she said. "Your mind was always made up, like mine. I was too long in understanding that. Have the doctor come on Sunday."

Feeling relief and a twinge of conscience, he reached across to take her hand. The act of apology was unwise, but he was willing to attempt it. She gently moved the hand out of reach, and smiled. "It isn't necessary, Cass. You have put me in my place."

On Sunday, in a new pearl gray suit and detachable white collar and wash leather gloves and a straw boater with a gay band, Cass set out in rented equipage to bring Allie to the house on Temple Street. She wore

121

the latest in fashions of shirtwaist and skirt, and he fancied they were a smart pair as they journeyed up the hill. He was a trifle on edge, but relieved to observe that Allie seemed entirely at ease. Her only remark en route was, "I hope she doesn't like me. That will simplify matters."

Waiting for them in the parlor, the gathering white of her hair contrasting with the youthful though worn symmetry of her face, was Doña Maria. She greeted Allie in a kindly fashion, taking her hand without rising, and had Juana bring in a silver tea service. The trio sat erectly in their chairs, balancing cups and saucers and discussing the weather, the latest local news, and some aspects of living in Los Angeles. Cass was dreadfully bored. Then it began. He had thought it might, and almost welcomed the diversion.

"May I call you Alice?" Doña Maria asked. "I am old-fashioned, and it doesn't seem quite proper to me to call a young lady 'Doctor.'"

"You may call me anything you wish, Mrs. Brennan," Allie replied indifferently.

"My name is Doña Maria, please. It is a title of honor from other, better days, if I might be permitted a little vanity. Has Cass told you of our family, Alice?"

"Yes, Doña Maria."

"Of Colonel Villanueva and my father, Don Ygnacio, and of my husband, who died for the government cause during the North-South War?"

"Yes, Doña Maria."

"I'm afraid Allie isn't much interested in California history, Mother," Cass said.

"I am not at all interested," Allie said.

"Really?" Doña Maria said. "We are a very old family, Alice."

"We are all supposed to be descended from Adam, Doña Maria," Allie said. "That is a still older family."

"No doubt. But I should think you would like the details of the family into which I am informed you are marrying."

"You have been misinformed, Doña Maria. I haven't any intention of marrying into your family."

"Eh?" Doña Maria said, and assumed a brighter look. "But my son has told me—"

"He keeps insisting I marry him, and I do not share his feelings. He takes too much for granted, Doña Maria. One of the reasons I came to you today is to assure you that I have no designs on him."

"This is part of her charm for me, Mother," Cass interjected, and forced a smile. "She is as forthright as you are."

122

"Well, that is most kind of you, Alice—taking me into your confidence. Don't you feel you could learn to reciprocate his affection?"

"No, Doña Maria."

"How strange. Perhaps it is a mother's natural emotion, but I think he is a fine man. His appearance is pleasing, he is highly regarded in his line of work, he is the owner of the Rancho de San Cristobal, and I can give you my vow that his private life is blameless."

"Oh, I am sure he is a compendium of male virtues, Doña Maria. But I regard him as dull. He is too old for his years, and stuffy. Even his looks are against him, in my opinion; those whiskers are ugly, and I don't like men who wear glasses. Only rarely do I enjoy myself with Cass. If he wasn't so persistent I would have forgotten him long ago. There is another reason for my refusing him: I have been trained to earn my own living, I prefer it that way, and I don't have to marry the first man who asks me as many women do."

"Ah, yes. I have never met a woman like you before, Alice. Are many the same these days?"

"Very many, Doña Maria. And more are coming. I have worked for, and hope we may soon achieve, complete equality with men."

"I am amazed," Doña Maria said. "It was not so when I was your age. Such a thing was unheard of. Women accepted their lot and took comfort in babies. Will this time you speak of, the equality, come soon, do you think? Do the gringo men—the Americans—accept your kind of woman?"

"They are beginning to, Doña Maria. What other choice do they have?"

"Will you have children, Alice? Is a woman's life complete without them?"

"I am not sure," Allie said. "Some men go through life without children, or at least children they acknowledge. Why should every woman have to bear to be complete? Preventing conception is easy. Men have lovers and change their minds, or sip the flowers and fly away. Women need be no different."

Cass stared at his mother. She was unshocked, and obviously fascinated. "Is this possible?" she said. "You are remarkable, Alice. As a doctor, you have been trained in these matters?"

"Yes, Doña Maria."

"A world of that sort would be delightful! Do men accept you as a physician? I do not mean my brother-in-law, Colonel Brennan, but others—like—like—"

"Like your son?"

"In a word, yes." Doña Maria smiled faintly.

"They do not welcome us except in special cases. That is their means of keeping us in subjection, Doña Maria—of keeping all women in subjection. I don't have much to do, and my pay is small, which is the reason I have allowed Cass to pay court to me; I need the extras he supplies. Someday, though, he and the rest of them will have to admit us as full human beings."

"I believe we have covered that subject," Cass said. "Can we change to another?"

"Observe, Doña Maria," Allie said. "See how the masters try to preserve their illusions?"

"I see," Doña Maria said.

The conversation continued in a more normal vein. Amused, relieved and dimly resentful, Cass perceived that his mother was enchanted by Allie. And he thought that Allie, having come with the deliberate intention of alienating Doña Maria, had also encountered turned tables and acquired a respect for the older woman. To watch them together was to be reminded forcibly of similar strains of temperament; even the same slimness and strength in fragility was a characteristic of both of them. He was brushed by a vagrant tip of insight; he loved his mother for her very formidabilities; he had to love Allie for identical reasons.

As they prepared to leave, Doña Maria said, "I have physical troubles I cannot discuss in front of my son. And I don't want a man examining me. Alice, will you come to me as a doctor?"

"I shall be happy to, Doña Maria."

"Goodbye, Alice. Kiss my cheek, please . . . Thank you. I wish you would marry my son."

"I would like to please you," Allie said, "but you make it too hard, Doña Maria. I have a better reason for refusing him than any I have given you. He loves Los Angeles. I cannot stand the place. How could I go on living here the rest of my life?"

"I understand," Doña Maria said. "I hate the Queen too."

At the conclusion of an exhausting conference in Lucius's office in the building on Flower Street, Cass ushered out the frock-coated gentlemen from New York and sank in a chair. He and his uncle looked at each other wearily. Lucius lit a cigarillo. "What do you think?" he said.

"You could have done worse."

"Will you join me in a drink?"

"No, thank you," Cass replied. He rubbed his aching head. The Sunset Sea Oil Products Company, nearing the end of its earthly existence, was a fearsome and wearing problem; still worse was the struggle he had

124

to make against an odd new attitude of accommodation and generosity in Lucius. "You could have done better, too."

"I've lost my spark, Cass. I'm an old man, and the almighty dollar isn't as mighty as it once was to me. Let them have a few advantages."

"It's your wealth, not mine."

"Yours, my boy. I'm a man of my word . . . Let's get out of here. Drive home with me; I don't want to go alone."

They climbed into the electric brougham and moved almost silently to the west. "Look at the goddamned town grow," Lucius said. "Before long we'll have solid tracts from here to Vermont Avenue. I should have been wilder in my early predictions."

"If the city doesn't stop expanding and annexing new territory, we're going to be swamped by increased taxes."

"No, no. More citizens will pay the freight. They and more street railways—give 'em transportation and they'll spread out."

"Not unless the height limit on buildings is restricted to a hundred and fifty feet," Cass said. "With the crazy prices on downtown property, the next thing will be skyscrapers."

"After the earthquake in San Francisco?" Lucius demanded. "You're being unrealistic. We're perched on the same earth fault, and everybody knows we could be next. Height limit law or no height limit law, you're bound to see a flat, wide Queen."

The moment he was home, Lucius had Hannibal bring him a whiskey and soda. There was an urgent message, and he had to retire to a telephone, glass in hand. Cass waited in the solarium, petting a spotted cat who was determined to be friendly.

"Here's a good omen," said Lucius, upon returning. "That was Mathis, my driller—he rode in from the San Cristobal to the nearest phone. The second well has come in. It's nothing to mount a celebration on, but Mathis estimates it is flowing at close to two hundred gallons an hour."

The talk shifted to other matters. Suddenly Lucius said, "How are you getting on with Allie?"

"Why do you ask? Has she talked of us?"

"Yes, she was out here inspecting my damned waterworks the other day. She says she hasn't seen you lately."

"Not for three weeks," Cass admitted. "You've kept me busy, and lately she has been putting me off."

"Well, what happened?"

"Nothing unusual. I'm perplexed."

"Confide in your Uncle Lucius. Have you gotten between her legs and taken the bloom from the rose?" Cass shook his head. "Do you remain in love with her?"

125

"Yes."

"And you're despondent."

"Not at all," Cass said. "I'll have my way. She's been presented to my mother, you know."

He related the story of the meeting with Doña Maria, and Lucius laughed until he was forced to wipe his eyes. "That's the funniest thing I've heard in months," he said. "By God, the old lady has seen a vast new light in the universe!"

"I wish I knew what to do next," Cass said. "I've cleared the path, but—"

"You're a fool," Lucius said, "and yet entitled to your candied apple. Will you have the advice of a man who cut his teeth on Casanova's *Memoirs?*"

"Gladly."

"You can lose your luck playing a waiting game. Make your move, risk the assault. She must be as tired of the suspense as you are. If she refuses you, there is little hope; if you have her, you can then decide whether she is worth the bother of matrimony."

"You don't understand," Cass said, with dignity. "I have resolved to make her my wife."

"I understand this much: you are a pompous idiot, maybe a coward, and possibly your blood runs too cold. What do you think she is, a marble statue? Will she be swayed by closely reasoned argument and fall into arms that won't try to hold her? How can she take you seriously? She's waiting for evidence of a stiff member. You'll pay court forever!"

Cass flushed. "Very well, sir. Tell me how I can take her by storm."

"Take her out to the ranch," Lucius said. "Show her how rich you are —women are only interested in material things—they haven't the mind for abstract conceptions. I'll have Hobie drive you in the gasoline car. Arrange a picnic for two and decoy her into a secluded sylvan glade. I have found that many of the weaker sex will succumb in natural surroundings rather than behind locked doors in cloistered rooms; sunlight and a leafy bower suits 'em better than a mattress and pillows. Convince her of your passion and need, not your Goddamned rectitude and respect for her. At the crux of the proceedings, place it in her hand. Normally, once it is in their grasp, they will find a haven for it."

" 'It'?" Cass said. "What are you talking about?"

"Your penis!" Lucius said disgustedly. "Large, rosy and quivering. If you have less, go back to closely reasoned argument or feeding her potato salad."

126

More in propitiation of his uncle than anything else, Cass invited Allie on a picnic at the San Cristobal. She agreed to go without much urging on his part. The date was set for the following Sunday. "I'm curious about those thousands of acres," she said. "I've heard innumerable descriptions of them from Doña Maria."

"You're taking care of her?"

"Yes. Hasn't she informed you?"

"No," he said. "I haven't pried—she'll talk of it when she feels like it. Do you regard her condition as serious?"

"Surely you wouldn't value a medical opinion from me!"

"You are her doctor."

"Oh, she has various aches and pains and small swellings," Allie said, "which are probably rheumatic in origin. They will increase with age, and I am giving her treatments for them. I believe her other ailments are unimportant. She might live to a hundred. Don't worry."

"Thank you, Doctor," he said.

On Sunday Hobie, in goggles and a leather cap, arrived at the Temple Street house in the Franklin touring car. Doña Maria came out on the front porch to watch Cass's departure, smiling nervously. Although he had been in several automobiles, Cass had never taken a long trip in one, and he sat on the rear cushions and braced himself with a degree of trepidation. However, the sensations of movement were pleasant, Hobie seemed skillful at guiding the towering monster, and they were at Allie's building within moments. Hobie pressed the rubber bulb of the horn in salute, removed a robe that covered the picnic basket in the seat beside him, and dismounted to escort his new passenger.

Allie emerged wearing a voluminous linen duster (sewn, of course, by her companion), a hat and veil, and heavy gloves. From the front window, swathed in a curtain, peered Sadie. Handed up by Hobie, Allie settled next to Cass and was enrobed. Hobie adjusted controls, cranked the engine, and took the wheel. Allie waved to Sadie. She looked a bit frightened, and Cass took her elbow reassuringly.

In no time they were climbing through Cahuenga Pass, overhauling the horse-drawn traffic, tooting at passing motorists, and chasing the dust clouds of the cars which had gone before them. As they descended into the San Fernando Valley, Allie removed her hat and veil. It was her first real journey in a motorcar and she was enraptured. She exulted in the speed at which they traveled and urged Hobie to greater efforts. The dust and noise were of no consequence to her. Cass watched her in amazement; he had not before seen her so animated, sparkling-eyed and pretty. Her hair, disordered by the wind, tumbled down, and she let it hang, held loosely with a ribbon. Even when a front tire struck a stone and deflated rapidly, causing them to swerve and nearly leave the road, she did not show concern, and watched and asked questions of Hobie as he jacked up the axle, pried the tire off the rim, patched the inner tube, replaced the tire, and pumped it up.

"Oh, how I would like to have one of these!" she said to Cass.

"You shall have one," he told her. "Or two. Or three."

She reached out and caught his hand, touched by his yearning generosity; but then she relinquished it, almost flung it away, as if she had betrayed herself. His swelling heart went flat in the fashion of the tire, with a rush, leaving crumpled and forlorn the knowledge that he could sway her by the exertion of will and tenacity and by no other means.

Despite the accident they swept into the home valley in less than half the time consumed in his previous trips. While the Franklin bumped through vistas of decaying cornstalks and among cattle feeding at bins, Cass's eyes were searching the higher levels. The sight of a pair of ugly wooden towers, of rusty pipe and machinery, of storage tanks and gouged earth stained black, of a boiler and piston casing puffing steam and a walking beam rocking back and forth, gave him a queer feeling. A metamorphosis of the San Cristobal was in the making. On the *hacendados* and their endless leagues had been inflicted a final indignity; they were being rushed into the discard of history by a dirty, wasteful technology that would have stunned and sickened them. The disgraceful litter of man's ingenuity did not dismay Cass, however. In his nostrils was the sour smell of the land's entrails siphoning upward, but it was the smell of profit and victory.

Warned in advance by letter, Bill Sego awaited the motorists on the stoop of Jim Dorcas's old house. With him was his thin, gawky bride, for he had recently married. He looked drawn and worried, and his face was beet red from the sun. The autumn heat had a stifling quality, and the air was still. Hobie was sent to a tenant's outbuilding for rest and food and to procure a five gallon can of gasoline, and the others went inside a dusty living room to drink iced tea. Ethel Sego took Allie back to freshen up, and Cass and Bill returned to the porch. A bellowing motortruck, chain-driven, on hard rubber tires, rolled by, carrying a bewildering load of equipment that resembled a junk pile. Displaced soil formed a thin curtain and slowly subsided.

"They're spudding in another hole tomorrow," Bill said. He managed a pained smile. "That's how they talk. They're a rough bunch. They get drunk at night and chase our women. We have to lock up."

"I'll have a talk with the foreman before I go," Cass said. "What's his name?"

"Mr. Mathis. They're talking of putting a derrick right down by the pond, sir. I don't know how that will affect the water."

"Never mind the water."

"I'm having trouble keeping my help, Mr. Brennan."

"Do the best you can. This will come to an end very quickly, or else be so important nothing will matter."

"It isn't the right way to run a ranch, sir," Bill said.

"On the contrary," Cass said, "it's the finest of all possible ways—if they discover enough oil. Have you had any luck with the irrigated pastures?"

"They're going to put a pipeline through my best one if they get three more producing wells."

"Good. We'll pray for them. Bill, I want to take Dr. Chambers on a picnic, as I wrote you. I'd like a buggy and a docile horse."

"Yes, sir. Is she—is the young lady a real doctor?"

"Yes, with a diploma to prove it. Where can I find a beautiful and private spot, with shade and a brook?"

"Well, this isn't a good season for picnics," Bill said, "and the streams are mostly dry. I guess the oak glen is your best bet. It's where they say the outlaws and Sonorans and raiding Indians from the Mojave used to hang out in the old days. Do you remember it?"

"No. Draw me a map."

"I could easily send a man with you—"

"Three's a crowd," Cass said. He felt heat in his cheeks as he spoke, and disliked the impression he conveyed. And yet, at that instant, he started to take his uncle's suggestions seriously.

"Yes, *sir*." Bill pulled a pencil and paper from his shirt pocket. "I get you."

The women joined them while Cass was studying Bill's drawing. Bill went off to procure the buggy, and Ethel tried haltingly to make conversation, awed by Cass, eyeing him furtively in a manner that reminded him of Sadie. He cut her short in his impatience and took Allie on a tour of the oil workings. Most of the crew was absent, but Ted Mathis, a burly middle-aged man with a pipe in his mouth and the crisp accents of a Down-Easter, presented himself and furnished explanations. He grinned at Cass's complaint about annoyance of the ranch women. "It's only the Mexicans they're running after," he said. "But I'll see what I can do, Mr. Brennan."

"Thank you," Cass said. "If I hear of further incidents, I shall aid your efforts by sending a deputy sheriff. Is that clear, Mr. Mathis? I own the San Cristobal, you know."

"It's clear," Mathis said. "I know you own the ranch, Mr. Brennan."

Presently Bill drove the buggy up to fetch them. Allie's face was flushed and Cass was sweating, and they were grateful for the interruption. After Bill had been dropped off at the house, they waved to Ethel and drove into an arroyo.

"Poor Ethel," Allie said. "She is very unhappy here."

"Why?"

"It's a dreadful place, can't you see? What is the affection Doña Maria has for the ranch? I thought it would be attractive, as Wisconsin or Illinois farms are. Is there nothing in California but this brown and dried-up country and barren hills and mountains closing in everywhere?"

"When the rains come," Cass said, "you will find a miracle taking shape—"

"Once a year, for a little while in the winter! I am sick of these small miracles!"

"But look." Cass's hand swept around them. "Sixteen thousand acres. Oil. Cattle. Grapes. Corn and wheat and rye and oats and citrus fruits and olive groves. I'm a rich man."

"Then why is Ethel worried for her husband's future?" Allie asked. "He desperately wants to talk to you, and you scare both of them. He thinks he is failing. Isn't the ranch losing money?"

Cass laughed. "As long as he remains scared of me, he's perfectly safe. He is honest and I trust him. No, the San Cristobal is doing sufficiently well under the circumstances, and with enough oil reserves it will give me a great fortune. But I don't intend for him to know everything. He won't share in my bonanza. His reward will be to sit someday behind a desk, wearing a white collar and faithfully minding my interests."

"Doesn't he deserve more?"

"I don't think so. This is mine. I put him where he is. He has been paid for what he contributed. Let him worry. It'll keep him on his toes."

"But according to you," she said, "you have an abundance. Haven't you enough? Can't you share it? Is it necessary to worry the Segos to extract the last drop of blood from your turnip?"

"You don't understand these things," he said. "You're a woman. I'll never have enough. One day, though, I'll give it all to you and your children, and then you'll realize what I've done."

She looked at him and shook her head. "You were meant to be rich, all right. Let's go back. I don't like it here, and I don't want to have a picnic."

"We'll soon be there, and it's a lovely spot."

He slowed the horse and scrutinized Bill's map. A warmth not of the sun was invading him. This was his land, his riches, his picnic place—and

130

so immense were they that maps were needed to find them. For the first time in his life the San Cristobal was truly his. He swore it would belong to him and his issue forever, buttressed by enormous wealth, in a way that defied death and gave a recurring life which could alone spring from earth exploited and held. The dimmest memory of the oak glen rose in his mind, a paradise awaiting him; and overlaying the vision was another of Doña Maria on her white mare, clothed as a *vaquero,* firm breasts moving under a silk blouse, lithe and long-legged, silver rowels on her boots and a quirt in her hand—and she merged into Allie, just as shamefully inviting, lighted by the glow of dreams. Glancing at Allie, he felt quickening blood and desire instead of the usual calm resolution. She observed his changed expression.

"You look as though you might have sunstroke," she said.

"May I loosen my collar and take off my coat and vest?"

"You'd better."

The little *cañada* was as attractive as ever, to his profound relief. Under gnarled live oak trees the shade was deep, grass kept alive beside the trickling stream, and an afternoon breeze conveyed a hint of salt moisture from the ocean beyond the mountains. Cass watered the horse, hobbled him, spread blankets for them to sit on, and emptied the picnic basket. There was a bottle of wine kept cool in a damp gunnysack for Allie to drink, and thin sandwiches and pickles and cheese and slices of tongue and salad and a frosted white cake. Their appetites were good in spite of the heat they had endured. Then they dozed, his head in her lap. Dry leaves rustled and the branches of the trees sighed, but otherwise the silence was absolute.

In changing positions, Allie came into Cass's arms. He lifted her to him and kissed her on the mouth. Her lips pressed firmly on his, unsoftened, and she did not resist. He kissed her repeatedly, his loins starting to ache. Neither of them spoke. The high-necked dress she wore made it impossible for him to do more than caress a rising layer of whalebone over her breasts. When his hand fumbled under her skirts—without movement or protest on her part—his fingers were lost in manifold layers of cloth. Sweat dripped down his face, and he rubbed it distractedly with a shirt sleeve. She remained calm and inert, her eyes closed.

"My God," he said despairingly, "what am I going to do?"

She opened her eyes. "I have on underwear, a corset, knickers, a corset cover, two petticoats, a dress that buttons up the back—"

"Sadie dressed you for this!"

"I can't undress here, Cass."

"Please!"

"No."

"I'm going to marry you!"

"No," she said. "It just won't work. Somebody might come by. I'd be a mess going home, and the Segos would know—"

"To hell with them."

"No."

"Please!" He was tearing at himself, and he grabbed her hand and brought it to him.

"What an ugly red thing," she said, unsurprised. "It is enormous. Did your uncle tell you to do this?"

He regarded her groggily, bathed in perspiration.

"It sounds like him," she said. "What fools and beasts you all are!" The cold, dry hand was not withdrawn. "Well . . . this might help. Is that better? Tell me if I hurt you . . . No, don't hold me . . ."

When he had finished groaning and quivering and reaching blindly for her, she arose and knelt at the stream. He rearranged his clothing and sat elbows on knees, his face in his hands. She came back and stood before him. "Are you ashamed?" she asked.

"Yes."

"You must have done that to yourself innumerable times. Were you ashamed then?"

"Yes."

"You shouldn't be. It is a natural thing."

He uncovered his face and gazed up at her fearfully. "I love you. Can't you take pity on me?"

"Pity?" she said. "I never feel pity. And I don't love you. But I think I understand you, Cass. Your uncle told me of the Mexican girl when you were a boy, and what happened afterward. He believes you are afraid and not capable of loving a woman, and blames himself for the accident. Are you afraid?"

"No."

"Has there been anybody since the Mexican girl?"

"No," he said, and got up and dusted his trousers. "That's enough, Allie. I have failed today, through listening to Uncle Lucius and his nasty suggestions, but I haven't really failed—failed in myself. I'll go back to waiting. I can wait longer than you."

"You are awful!" she cried, and her voice cracked and she started to sob.

Within his breast something shattered and flung tiny glinting brittle particles, shattered as glass would, and set up a thousand fiery points of pain that coalesced in an overwhelming agony that drained his soul out of his body and left him open-mouthed and keening in surprise. The unendurable lasted for a tenth of a second. It was the concentrated torture and slow death of a lifetime. As it stopped, the relief was, by contrast, equally unbearable. Shock and aversion and a horror which loosened his bowels and bladder halted breathing. He sank into a bottomless dark sea.

Before sunset they were again in Allie's office. The curtains rustled at the window as they entered, and Sadie fled. Very tired and still pale, with a great hollow feeling in his chest and a churning in his abdomen, Cass began an apology for his conduct and the fainting fit.

"Don't bother about that," Allie interrupted, and picked up a stethoscope. "I want to examine you. Open your shirt."

"I am perfectly well," he said. "Put that away. I don't need an examination."

"From me, you mean?"

"I mean nothing of the kind. Don't be so sensitive. I have recovered completely. It was only a combination of the heat and my—excitement—and eating a heavy meal."

"You might be mistaken," she said. "Your symptoms were peculiar when I revived you. It could have been a serious attack."

"Nonsense! I don't intend to dramatize a case of heatstroke." He smiled. "Your aid and sympathy are appreciated, doctor, but I'm not in need of your services. Thanks just the same."

"Promise me you'll have somebody else look at you."

"I can't promise you anything, my dear," he said, "except that I'm going to stay out of the noonday sun after this."

"All right," she said, and put the stethoscope on her desk. She paused. "Cass, I can't see you any more. Now we must part."

"Why? What happened today will not happen again. You have my word."

"That doesn't matter. I would have gone to bed with you long ago, if you had wanted. It's of no importance to me. But I—"

"We are being overheard, Allie!"

"I don't care. I will not marry you. I don't love you, and I am happier alone. We would never get along. I want to pursue my career, even if I starve." She was speaking faster: "You are a Catholic. I hate all religions. I don't want children—"

"You can be persuaded of many things," he said. "Allow me time. I will not give up, Allie."

Tears coming in her eyes, she said, "What is there about me that attracts you? I'm not good-looking, I don't care for you, I only take your presents and—"

"I don't know. But I do know I can't live without you."

"You are insane!" She gasped, and had to stop for a moment; he watched her steadily and humbly. "Will you lend me a thousand dollars, Cass?"

"Yes."

"Don't you want to know what the money is for?"

"No."

"It's so I can go away from here and forget you. I detest this town and I detest you!"

"I understand," he said. "But you might feel grateful some day, or need more help, and come back to me. I'll wait and hope."

"Oh, my God! . . . What must I do?"

"Have pity on me."

She walked to the rear door, half turned, and could not look at him. Tears streaked her white cheeks. "I'll marry you. It's no use, but I'll marry you . . . Leave me alone now."

His empty chest filled to bursting, with pain and delight and a fine soaring burst of conquering pride. He was too full to answer her and headed for the outside. The rear door closed behind him. Instantly came the sound of Sadie addressing Allie; she half spoke and half screamed, in the wailing crescendo of an enraged cat. Cass stopped, barely able to hear Allie attempting to quiet her friend. It did no good. Sadie called Allie fantastic names—bitch, whore, horse droppings in the street, a liar, a traitor, a dirty, nasty, panting slut who would allow any man to have her. Then Sadie shrieked in pure fury and Allie gave a cry of startled hurt. Racing back, Cass wrenched open the door.

A paring knife in her hand, Sadie crouched before Allie, who had her right palm pressed on her left forearm; blood bubbled up beneath her fingers, and her mouth was contorted and open in a grimace of utter astonishment. Sadie wheeled to confront Cass and yelled unintelligibly. "Drop it," he said. He was consumed by a cold rage. "Drop it or I'll knock your head off."

She retreated, stabbing at him clumsily and shouting her hatred of him. As he followed, Allie cried, "Cass—no, no!" He deflected the stabbing hand with one arm and struck Sadie savagely on the side of the head with his other fist. She fell to the floor. He kicked the knife from her grasp, picked her up by the slack of her clothing, shook her until her crimson head rolled wildly on her shoulders, and, deaf to Allie's expostulations, carried her to the kitchen doorway, threw her into the yard, and fastened the catch. Returning hurriedly, he saw Allie going into the office. She took gauze from a jar and pressed it to her wounded arm.

"Let me look," he said.

134

"Did you injure her?"

"I don't know. I don't give a damn. Let me look."

"It's only a gash," Allie said. "When the hemorrhaging stops I'll see if it needs suturing. Take care of Sadie, please."

The blood-soaked gauze raised a queasiness in him, and he went out and opened the kitchen door. Sadie had disappeared. Rejoining Allie, he said, "She's gone, so I couldn't have harmed her much. What happened? Why did she go off her head?"

"The bleeding has stopped," Allie said. "Wash your hands . . . Now, I don't have to be sewn. Press the incision together with your fingers. Hold it while I plaster it. I don't want a scar."

"You can't stay here tonight. Come home with me, and my mother will take you in. We'll explain to her and Hobie that you had an accident with broken glass—anything."

"That might be better."

"You're a brave woman," Cass said. He was sweating, and an undulation of pain ran from his neck through his left shoulder and down into his arm. "Allie, why did she do that? She must be mad as a hatter."

"I provoked her deliberately."

"How?"

"The whole affair is my fault."

"Why?"

"There's a reason."

"What reason?"

"You would not like the reason." Allie regarded him sharply. "Are you feeling well? Do you have the pain again?"

"No," he said. "I'm fine. I've got a little touch of indigestion, but this has been a long day. I'm glad it's finished." He took her right hand and patted it. "Everything is settled, my dear."

"Everything," Allie said. Her eyes held a pity she had disclaimed feeling.

six

CASS and Allie were married by a judge in his chambers (at the insistence of Allie, who would not have a religious ceremony, and with the approval of Doña Maria, who seemed to find everything about her daughter-in-law agreeable) and left on a honeymoon trip to San Francisco. From there they went inland and saw the Falls of Yosemite and motored down the San Joaquin Valley in the Franklin, sent to them with Hobie by Lucius. They were away three weeks. In that period they reached an agreement of sorts, or perhaps it was an armed truce. Mrs. Brennan stopped being Dr. Chambers. Two months later she discovered she was pregnant, and laughed at the spectacle of Cass's extravagant gratitude. Devoted and indomitable, he felt briefly that there were no more worlds for him to conquer.

In Los Angeles his work had piled up to unmanageable proportions. He was forced to consider taking in a partner or partners. In addition, he had to establish a new household; although Allie was willing, Doña Maria refused to live with them, and he and his bride stayed first in a hotel. Another complication was Lucius, aroused by the marriage and determined to forward the career of Cass.

His largesse began with a considerable reception he gave for the newlyweds at "Brennan's Folly." Refurbished from top to bottom, staffed with more servants, the ballroom completed and equipped with an orchestra, the house was thrown open and everybody of consequence in the Queen invited for the appointed evening. Allie didn't wish to appear, and Cass was both pleased and annoyed. But Doña Maria, whom Lucius had chosen to be his hostess, would not hear of demurrers and took firm charge. Since her influence on Allie was powerful, there was no further resistance.

Attired in full dress, a ruffled shirt and flowing Byronic black tie, Doña Maria at his side, Lucius greeted the flower of the city and presented Cass and his wife. A conglomeration of the vanishing old and the overpowering new, the social mixture was less than ideal. The remnants of the earlier settlers, mainly burdened by age and poverty, huddled together and contemplated a horde of outsiders in loathing and envy. Except for the professions and certain business circles, nobody really knew anybody else; an established, recognized society was as yet nonexistent. The Jews Lucius invited, including Aaron Shapiro and his wife, were universally shunned by the new people, whose prejudices had been formed in the midlands of the United States. Notwithstanding, the party went forward. Hospitality was lavish, champagne corks popped, and dancing grew energetic. The pace was hot until the small hours, and the last of the celebrants left after breakfasting at dawn.

Lucius and Cass enjoyed themselves because their objectives lay in the same quarter. Suddenly Cass realized he was an important man, and Lucius took delight in a dazzling manifestation of his riches. What they meant to accomplish was well done. No one could mistake the Brennans for an ordinary family after that. They had made a splash in their own pond and been accepted on the level they desired. Of his mother's attitude, Cass could not be sure. If she found pleasure in her son's glory, she must also have suffered a revulsion at seeing the extent to which her world had dissipated. But she was undoubtedly cheered when, in the course of the night, Lucius mounted a chair, obtained silence, and gave an announcement in his florid manner.

"My friends," he said, "I ask your leave to say a few words, in the humble expectation that you will accord them the charity you would the mouthings of any ancient basking in the glow of his loved ones. This occasion is very important to me. You must know the pride and joy I feel in the union of my nephew with his beautiful Alice, and the expectation I have of our family—which is not unknown in these parts—continuing to furnish the Queen with sturdy citizens. Surrounded by my friends and good companions, I would like to say hail and farewell. *Ave atque vale,* in the words of the Romans. You are in my house for the last time." He paused to let that sink in. "The reason is simple; henceforth it will not be my house. It is my wedding present to Cass and Allie. They can do it far more justice than I. Will you join me in a toast to the new owners?"

Applause sounded, and glasses were lifted. Astonished, Cass looked vainly for his mother; she was hidden in the throng, probably exhaling

137

a long sigh of relief. Allie whispered in his ear: "I don't want his damned house!"

"We'll discuss it later," he said, and gripped her arm and propelled her to his uncle, where she added her thanks to his. The essence of benign magnanimity, Lucius walked her aside for a private talk.

Later, dancing with Allie, Cass asked: "What was the conversation with Maecenas?"

"He wanted to know if I was happy. I said no, and that I didn't care to accept his damned house."

"Did you need to be so frank?"

"Yes, I needed to. He said please to take that damned ring out of my uterus and give him a grandson and I didn't have to keep the house. Is he your father, Cass?"

"Of course not. I think he's a little drunk tonight."

"He's very drunk. I suppose he can't be your father. He wouldn't have sired a stuffy bore like you."

"Thank you, my dear. Won't you accept the house? I wish you would."

"You're going to get his money. Isn't that enough?"

"Are you drunk too?"

"I wish I dared to get tipsy," she said. "I haven't quite got the nerve."

"We'll discuss this when you're in a better mood," Cass said.

He surrendered her to another man and went to make the rounds, talking to as many people as possible. It was the only means by which he could get to know those he proposed to cultivate and use and impress himself upon. Unlike Allie, who was shy and lacked reserves of banalities, he did not think the affair dull. He had no desire to engage in arguments or display a facile brilliance, and he enjoyed the company of leisurely folk from his own strata without much of importance to say. To be well dressed and prosperous and in the proper surroundings, dealing with safe subjects and assured of a decent reception, was enough for a man to require of fortune.

Cass and Allie never did debate the issue of "Brennan's Folly." Soon their removal to it was an accepted fact. Allie's pregnancy changed everything. She went dutifully off to confer on details with Lucius, who was enraptured by the news she brought, insisted on having Doña Maria join the proceedings, and told them he intended to retire. Shortly after, Cass had him to lunch at the Athletic Club, where he had recently become a member. Lucius stopped in the middle of eating and looked around the crowded dining room incredulously. "My God, how time passes!" he said. "A few years ago we would have been meeting in a saloon. I've always been in favor of improvements, but they're coming too fast. I'm starting to resent them."

"Do you know what amuses me most these days?" said Cass. "It's how you and my mother have got together. You're pretty thick, aren't you?"

Lucius grinned. "Well, I've acquired a certain respectability in her eyes, if that's what you mean. We wouldn't qualify as bosom chums, though. Our relations are formal and correct. She has forgiven but not forgotten. For your sake, she's willing to stomach me." He went on to say that he wanted Cass to draw him a new will, naming Cass and his children as heirs; then he was going on a long trip to Ireland, England and Europe.

"That surprises me," Cass said. "I can't visualize you leaving the Queen."

"Wouldn't you go if you had the chance?"

"No. This just suits me. Where could you find a better place?"

"You're a hopeless provincial, Cass. I want to visit County Mayo and look at our origins and find out whether the old is superior to the new."

"The new is superior, I'm sure."

"It won't be new forever," Lucius said.

"I think it will," Cass said. "Los Angeles can't age. Some impossible turnover happens every decade."

They talked of the family, and Cass was aware that their relationship had almost returned to the easy warmth of his boyhood. "It's funny how we've pulled ourselves together," Lucius remarked. "Crazy as it might sound, Doña Maria is close to Allie. That's all to the good. Having a grandchild from a woman she approves of is a great joy to her. The Villanuevas and their paltry glory are an illusion, but she thinks she's part of a dynasty. I have to laugh at her pretensions, and still I don't mind sharing in them." He chuckled at the idea.

"Well, we've made it go—each in his own style."

"Your style is not so much different than mine. We've both taken what we wanted."

"Perhaps," Cass said.

"And used whatever came to hand. Oh, don't pretend to an exalted virtue with me. Consider poor Allie, for instance. Is she happy with you, Cass?"

"I don't know."

"You know," Lucius said. "She isn't. The Brennans don't have any luck with their women. But does it matter to you? Are you happy with her?"

"I'm too busy to consider the question," Cass said. "Besides, I don't know what happiness is."

"You'll learn," Lucius said. "Happiness is what you can't buy or steal."

Having engaged in correspondence with Albert Blour and having seen him in San Francisco during the honeymoon, Cass had occasion to explain his predicament to him. The result was that a young lawyer named Burton Lely paid him a call. Cass liked his looks and the apprenticeship he had served under Blour, and offered him a partnership and a one-fifth interest, which Lely accepted. Simultaneously, Cass had been negotiating with an older, established member of the bar, Harold Baltim, once a deputy district attorney, and well connected in political circles. Baltim agreed to a partnership with a two-fifths share. The firm of Brennan, Baltim and Lely engaged spacious offices in a modern building on South Spring Street.

Lucius meanwhile was intriguing in another area. One day Aaron Shapiro telephoned Cass and arranged to meet him at the Los Angeles National Savings Bank. They retired to a private room to confer. Somewhat enfeebled physically, Mr. Shapiro was nevertheless sharp as ever mentally; he had left the retail trade, but he was still active in banking and other endeavors. The proposal he presented to Cass was flattering and lucrative: his brother David Shapiro, the bank president, wanted to resign and devote himself to interests in San Francisco, all of the board members were convinced that Cass was his logical successor, and now an expression from him was in order before the offer was formally tendered. "I must confess," Shapiro added, "that this is less spontaneous than would first appear. I've done a good deal of politicking in the last few weeks. But you are aware of the confidence I repose in you. You've been my most successful protégé, Cass." He smiled. "How many times have I wished you were not a gentile!"

"I'm proud and honored, sir," Cass replied. "However, you are asking me to make a difficult decision. You know my position. I have just organized a new law firm—"

"It can continue to handle the bank's affairs, and we expect you to act personally for us in legal matters."

"That's very generous of you. But I can't help wondering if I am the right man. My knowledge of banking is considerably less than encyclopedic. My age must be against me—"

"No, not your age," Shapiro said. "I'm afraid, like most of us, you regard yourself as eternally young. You're over forty, aren't you?"

"Yes, sir."

140

"That will do. You're ripe enough."

"Begging your pardon in advance," Cass said, "are you able to give me any of the details concerning my selection?"

"Well, I suppose good lawyers are suspicious by nature . . . The fact is, your uncle has campaigned for you. His influence is considerable. In recent months he has become one of our largest depositors."

"Ah, I see. I wish he had taken the trouble to consult me first. Being master of my own fate is one of my little peculiarities."

Shapiro sighed. "I assumed you had reconciled your differing points of view long since."

"We have. But I cherish my independence. And I seem to remember you weren't a devoted admirer of my uncle."

"Wasn't I? I can't seem to remember. Conditions have changed, haven't they?"

Returning to his office without committing himself, Cass called Lucius. "I hear you are putting fingers in my pie again," he said.

"Aaron talked to you, eh? Do you object to my interfering?"

"Would I dare? Is it 'Aaron' now with you?"

"We're fast friends," Lucius said, "and both rich. What do you say, Cass?"

"I haven't reached a decision."

"You're not much of a lawyer, really, except in the administrative field, and you have the presence and tastes of a banker. The job makes the man. Rise to the occasion."

"I'll consider it overnight," Cass said.

"You will come around," Lucius told him. "Don't forget Liberty Consolidated in '75. Living that down for the Brennans won't hurt. You have Doña Maria's dynasty to take into account, remember."

Cass carried the problem home with him. His mother urged him to accept. Allie declined to venture an opinion. "Why should I care?" she asked. "I'll only be at home with your baby."

"That will satisfy you, Allie. Wait and see."

"No it won't."

"But you must be interested in my future," he protested. "You're going to share it with me."

"We haven't any future," she said. "At least I haven't."

He pondered, steadily discarding self-delusions; the truth was that his independence and ethical aspirations had been cast upon a junk heap of other youthful toys, and the end of this was absolutely predictable. He would take a position influence and favoritism had procured him, and recognize the cynical primacy of his uncle—and that was that. But Allie's attitude concerned him. She wasn't happy. Nor was he, and only took

comfort in her surrender and the prospect of children. The partial satisfactions extended to him barely helped to ease the bewilderments of
trying to understand and soothe her. The marriage had suited him, and
he regularly paid his devotions to her. She submitted without protest, but
her response was negligible. That did not quench his ardor, fortunately.
To have the fevers and transports of another Molly, he thought, would
have sickened and rendered him impotent. A cool and precise union
devoted to his pleasure and relief was almost what he desired. It was
simply that he could have done with more tribute to his power of loving.
Passion lay beyond his expectations; if Allie would just show affection and
a measure of gratitude, he'd be content. Something irritatingly necessary
was missing.

He adored her thin body and bony hips and small breasts. Her physical imperfections passed unnoticed by him. She had a girlish, undeveloped quality which was queerly exciting, as though he was a boy again
and had found a girl of his own age to enjoy. The swelling of her previously flat belly from his seed infused him with pride. At moments, pene-
trating her, he had intimations of a mystical, complete consummation
that always slipped out of reach. The complement of ultimate bliss, he
supposed, had to come out of her means of reciprocation. Once he
questioned her while lying in her arms.

"Oh, finish it," she said, "and get up. You're too heavy and I'm tired.
You sound as if this was the first time."

"It's always the first time for me."

"Then you're an idiot."

"No, tell me," he said. "You don't seem to feel me. Is it impossible
for a good woman like you?"

She began to laugh, and buried her face against his chest. When she
could speak, she said, "Dear God, I'm nearly sorry for you! I could feel
if I cared to. I won't permit it."

"Why?"

"I don't know. Because it's you—or me—or us together. We don't
belong . . ."

"How can you resist? I would think—"

"Do I have to be honest? I think this is terrible. When you come
blundering at me, I do mathematical problems in my head or imagine I
am performing a total splenectomy. It makes this no more important
than a bowel movement or filling my empty stomach."

"Why, Allie? How can you talk that way?"

"Because I don't love you. I don't want to love you. I can't love you."

"Have pity on me," he said, in his former manner. "Nobody else will
do for me. You can't refuse me now."

142

But there it remained. She would not say another word, and the subject was dropped. He accepted her coldness as one of the many compromises life had forced on him. The ideal was unattainable and best forgotten. He would have laughed at somebody accusing him of harboring a grand and misplaced passion.

Still, he had wispy visions of happiness and fulfillment. Daylight, practicality and expenditures of energy put these irritations to rest. He never shook off the feeling of urgency, of having to run faster and work harder. He called it ambition. It was bound up now—but buried deep in his being and resolutely ignored—with fear of the great pain he had endured while on the picnic at the San Cristobal. The pain had not recurred. He was convinced it had not happened and could not come again, and as impossible as that Uncle Lucius could be his father.

Cass Brennan became president of the Los Angeles National Savings Bank, and he and Mrs. Brennan took possession of Lucius's house. Lucius departed by railway for New York, there to board ship for the Atlantic crossing. A stream of letters detailing his experiences flowed back; he seemed to have acquired an elderly man's compulsion for self-revelation (in elegant language and script) and a deploring of the standards of comfort he encountered away from home. Despite insufficiencies in sanitation and the exactions of dishonest merchants and hotel-keepers, he stayed on for months, alternately fascinated and repelled by the hegira. Presents regularly arrived for every member of the family—shawls, capes, furs, dress goods, jewelry, Swiss watches, wine and canned delicacies.

With little time to give domestic affairs, Cass was amazed at the transformation his uncle's house underwent. Some of the alterations he thought unnecessary, but he did not protest, knowing Allie had come there unwillingly. Hannibal and Lucrezia Borgia were gone, their places taken by a German man and wife, with an Irish girl for an upstairs maid. Hobie remained, as Allie's favorite, and Cass bought a second auto, an imposing black Locomobile, and sold the electric brougham. After Hobie had driven him to the bank each day, he was assigned to Mrs. Brennan, who had a passion for motoring. Twice a week she visited her mother-in-law in Boyle Heights and they went on an outing; at Doña Maria's insistence, Cass had pensioned Juana and her assistant, and his mother moved to a boarding house on the high ground across the river, tenanted by old people of origins similar to hers, where Spanish was spoken more often than English.

Cass wondered what Lucius would make of his house when he came back. The dark ponderous furniture had disappeared and the oil paintings were off the walls, superseded by fumed oak and chintz and bright curtains and papers and China bric-a-brac and pale pastel scenes of knights and ladies and lorn maidens standing atop battlements listening to troubadors. Sunlight struck through every window, flowers in profusion filled vases, and electric fixtures cast a sharper radiance than the wrought iron chandeliers with gas globes Lucius's architect had believed proper for domestic illumination. A self-playing piano, the delight of Allie, occupied a corner of the living room, tinnily rapping out "Sweet Adeline" and "In the Shade of the Old Apple Tree." She was not a meticulous housekeeper, and the litter of her temporary interests—books, paints to apply on teacups and saucers, a rug-weaving loom, watercolors, cylindrical rolls of celebrated operas for an Edison phonograph, a dress form on which ill-fitting garments were adjusted and then thrown away —lay about unregarded. Disliked by Cass and his wife, the three cats Lucius had specified they must keep for him roamed in furtive observation of the new tenants, digging claws into upholstery and mewing sadly.

Changes multiplied; the burgeoning firm of Brennan, Baltim and Lely continued, and Cass grudgingly parted with half of his interest, divided between the two active partners. At the bank he soon found his administrative feet and took charge. Since much of his work was representational and social contacts were important, he proceeded to spread himself, learning to play golf at the Los Angeles Country Club, and enrolling in the Cotillion Association, the Golden Pioneers, and various civic and fraternal organizations. He fulfilled numerous speaking engagements. His days lengthened and grew more crowded. People began to say he had inherited the silver tongue of his uncle; he became a spokesman not only for the bank, but for the class to which he belonged. The Chamber of Commerce depended on his vigorous participation. He sat in the councils of the Republican Party, was an officer in the Clearing House Association, and presently assumed the chairmanship of the powerful labor relations committee of the League of Commerce and Industry. As an acknowledged community leader, he tried most of all to appear a sound man who inspired confidence. In his talks he espoused the Golden Rule and conservative business practices, and his philosophy embraced strong stands against revolutionary labor unions, socialistic trends of government, and agitators in general. His one embarrassment was a lack of religious affiliation, something his closest admirers quietly deplored. Mrs. Brennan, however, flatly refused to join him in any kind of formal worship. Having no vestige of faith left himself, he could not very well smother her with convincing arguments to the contrary. In the avoidance of unfavorable comment, he took to attending Episcopal services at least once a month; the Catholics were a minority in the

144

Queen now, and he saw no good reason for reentering a sect which was regarded with suspicion by many of his friends.

Nothing but the best of doctors would do for Allie, and the fashionable practitioner at the moment was Eldred Loren. A thin, smiling, youngish man, formerly established in New York and a graduate of Harvard Medical School, he was a bachelor and the darling of dowagers and their daughters. His bedside manner did not work on Allie. At their first meeting, Cass stood outside a closed bedroom door while Dr. Loren concluded his examination, and then heard them wrangling in terms that were incomprehensible to him. Loren emerged from the room dabbing at his brow with a handkerchief. "I didn't realize your wife was a physician too," he said. "She gives me the impression I'm unneeded."

"That's her way," Cass replied. "Humor her, please. How is she?"

"I can't find anything wrong—except with her temper. I hope you appreciate the fact that if I deliver the child, I will have to follow procedures specified by her, and I find we are in professional disagreement."

"Oh, when the time comes—"

"I beg to disagree, Mr. Brennan. She has pronounced opinions and none of the usual fears or feelings of dependency. Her grasp of the act of parturition is exact and complete, even if, in my view, her suggestions are too radical. I believe you should put one or the other of us in charge of the case."

Cass went in to Allie. She lay staring malevolently at the mound of her abdomen rising under the bedcovers. He attempted to remonstrate with her.

"Dr. Loren is a quack," she said coldly. "He hates women doctors. I know more than he does, and I will have nothing to do with him."

"Allie, darling—"

"This is my baby, and my case. I can use a midwife, if necessary, and direct her. I'm not going to a hospital and I won't have any of Loren's chloroform."

"Allie, dear—"

"I'll prescribe for myself," she said. "Tell Loren he can be a consultant and I will give his advice a hearing, and that is all. If it's beneath his dignity, let him go."

Returning with her message to Dr. Loren, Cass evoked his laughter. "This is the queerest one yet," the doctor said, "in a city full of eccentrics. All right, Mr. Brennan. I shall serve as a consultant, but you must understand the responsibility is not mine."

In ensuing weeks, notwithstanding their bad start, Dr. Loren and Allie became good friends. Her pregnancy progressed without incident or complaint. Loren dropped by more frequently than necessary, and Cass sometimes listened to them talking of Loren's other patients. Evidently he was seeking Allie's advice. "I must say," he remarked to Cass, "that Mrs. Brennan is well grounded in medicine and has a flair for doctoring. I find her conversation most interesting. Marriage's gain is medicine's loss, I think."

"I wish you wouldn't encourage her, Eldred," Cass said. "Frankly, her profession has been a sore point with us. You wouldn't want me to have to assert my authority again, would you?"

The doctor glanced at him queerly. "Asserting authority with her wouldn't do any good. I've discovered that."

When Cass mentioned Loren's esteem to Allie, she shrugged. "Oh, he's an inveterate flatterer," she said. "It's his principal stock in trade. And I'll bet he's a seducer, too. They tell stories of him around town. Probably he hopes to give me another child when this one's been delivered."

"Allie!"

"Doctors are human. Or nearly so. But don't worry, I'm too sick of your attentions to encourage others."

Once Dr. Loren questioned Cass on the state of his health, and the latter was evasive. This forced the doctor into direct queries regarding hollow sensations in his chest, radiating pains in his arms and shoulders, and shortness of breath while exercising. He mentioned a pallor Cass had when very fatigued, suggested an examination, and asked if he had ever experienced a seizure that brought agony and unconsciousness. "You've been talking to my wife," Cass said. "Confess it."

"Well, yes. Her observation of you has given her certain opinions. Why don't we have a look at you, Cass?"

"There's no reason for it. I'm bothered by a little indigestion if I overwork. I had heatstroke on a picnic with Allie a long time ago, and it frightened her. Believe me, I am perfectly well. I don't have 'seizures,' as you call them."

"I'm sure you don't," Loren said. "But an examination won't do you any harm."

"Someday I'll pay you a call," Cass told him. He hated the subject, and wanted to escape. His breath did catch in moments of stress or exertion, pains did slither in his upper extremities on occasion, and a void did come under his ribs. But the great pain had gone. It would not return. He had forgotten and refused to be reminded.

Lucius came home, grumbling and tired, and much fatter from high living. Paradoxically, the first long vacation in his life had further aged him. His white bristly brows jutted out untended, and beneath his eyes were dark pouches. He did not see or hear as well as before and walked stiffly, balanced on swollen ankles. Europe, confusing and strange, had aroused his ire. "All they think of is war," he said. "Pretty soon they'll have one. You see nothing but uniforms—the men are dressed up like peacocks in braid and blue and gold and scarlet, with swords and decorations. And the lower classes are shifting about and talking revolution and making trouble. There's no respect these days for good sense and moderation. They listen to the fools and agitators, and either they're rich as Croesus or dirt poor. The Balkans, the Balkans, that's all they talk of. I sailed to Dalmatia from Venice. You should see the lazy, worthless bastards rolling in their own filth. They're worse than the drunken hollering Irish we stem from. Thank God we've got the Atlantic Ocean between us. We ought to cut off the old world entirely and never get mixed up with it again."

He wished to see Allie immediately, and Cass took him to the house. The new decor barely elicited a second glance from him. "It looks fine," he remarked, as Cass awaited his reaction. "Brighter and merrier. The damned place was like a tomb when I had it. Where are my cats?"

When he had greeted and petted them, he climbed heavily upstairs to Allie's bedroom. She was sitting in a chair reading, clad in a silk wrapper that failed to conceal her unhandy proportions. Kissing her cheek, he sat down and grinned at her. "You're a sight," he said. "The same as any peasant girl in Italy—every one of 'em has a big belly. My respect for Italian men has increased enormously. They are always ready. The minute a woman has been delivered, or a girl is out of her swaddling clothes, somebody mounts her."

"Cass is always ready," Allie said.

"That ought to please you."

"It doesn't."

"Tell Allie about your trip, Uncle Lucius," Cass said.

"She doesn't want to hear of it," Lucius said. "Do you, Allie?"

"No," she said.

"Why doesn't it please you? Isn't he any good?"

"I don't know. I'm not interested."

"I'll be damned. Well, if he can't interest you it means he's no good. I wish I could have had a try, Allie."

"So do I."

"Can't we raise the conversation to a higher plane?" Cass asked.

"I'm afraid not," Lucius said, "with me here." He pointed a finger at Allie. "When are you going to drop it?"

"In a week," she said. "Not more than ten days."

"Then will you start treating me again? I need you. I'm pissing old port wine."

"Providing my husband doesn't object." She looked inquiringly at Cass. "May I have two patients—me, and the man pissing port wine?"

Cass nodded. "Excuse me. I have some telephone calls to make. I'll leave you to your charming reunion."

They laughed together at his retreat. Lucius was closeted with Allie for a long time. He descended the stairs looking less grumpy. "I missed her," he said. "You know, she's something different, and she improves with time like a good vintage. I'm surprised she married you."

"You're going to become a critic of mine too, I presume?" Cass said.

"No, but I'm also different. Allie and I occupy a common ground."

"Well, you and I have various matters in common. Do you care to catch up on our business?"

"Lead on, MacDuff," answered Lucius.

Everything that had happened in his absence was covered. He approved of Cass's plan to revive Sunset Sea as a private holding corporation for the assets of the ranch, which had become increasingly important with the discovery of a second producing field; the separate sections were labeled Cristobal I and Cristobal II, and a pipeline built by the trust was pumping the crude to a new refinery by the sea south of Santa Monica, thence to be put in the holds of freighters and tank ships for wider distribution in several forms. The agricultural end of the San Cristobal had grown less feasible and profitable, and Cass proposed to shift Bill Sego to Los Angeles and put him in charge of the corporation, with an underling to oversee the ranch. This structural arrangement had tax and inheritance advantages.

"We'll divide the stock among you, my mother, Allie and me," Cass said, "and ensure control for the two of us. In the event we are both incapacitated or die, a trust instrument will permit my law firm and the bank to administer the estate. Since I am trying to build up the trust department of the bank, I am particularly eager for it to have a share."

"We're going to have a hell of a lot of money," Lucius said. "It's rather surprising. Don't give me too much control. I'm getting close to my dotage."

But he was exaggerating, and easily grasped Cass's concerns at the bank. He manifested his flair for anticipating the future by musing on what would happen next. The town was broadening, spreading, sprawling out. It would never be a city in the accepted sense of the term. In a great basin readily accessible anywhere, untroubled by hampering winters, settlements flourished at random and arose on impulse, tied together

148

only by adequate transportation. Except for oil, there was no real industry here, and therefore no requirement for concentration. Look at San Gabriel, Puente, Hollywood, the beach communities, the villages dotting the San Fernando Valley. Interconnection of these multiple hamlets would one day constitute the actual growth of Los Angeles. Coming from the packed, almost distilled confines of European cities, and the metropolises of the eastern United States, made the contrast acute to Lucius. The Queen was unique. Nothing on her lines had ever existed before. She represented freedom, space, disjointedness, a kind of urban anarchy. He had no fear she would stop expanding and adding to her population; maybe the automobile, with an increasing promise of reliability and lower price, was the solution to pulling together an entire galaxy of as yet unrelated suburbs.

"Bear with my rambling," he said. "I'm still talking about the bank. What you'll need are branches. A single office won't do. You ought to put your mind to the problem."

They discussed the working man. Lucius agreed with Cass that he was getting too big for his boots, attracted by crazy ideas of equality and socialization which were foreign to American conceptions of thrift, individual enterprise and pride in craftsmanship, and plainly in need of restraint. The Queen would suffer if she turned into a union labor town like San Francisco. Ever since the big railroad strike of 1893, which was put down with troops sent by the United States District Court, this had been an open shop town. It was necessary to keep it that way. "Let 'em show respect for their betters," Lucius said. "What we've accumulated we got by hard work and superior ability, and we don't intend to surrender it. They listen to immigrant troublemakers with immigrant ideas and then start spouting treason. No nation in history managed to hang together unless it regarded private property as sacred. You've got to knock sense into their heads. But the union jackals are not the worst— the damned radical politicians, promising bread and circuses, are the main danger."

To Cass's relief, his uncle had no intention of remaining with him. He was ready to establish residence in a comfortable hotel at Fifth and Spring streets, without servants, motorcars and possessions that wouldn't fit in a trunk or suitcase. "I've had my fill of plenty," he said, "and I'm through with worrying. You carry the load. I'm going to live in one room the rest of my life, smoke and drink whiskey, walk down Broadway and watch the pretty women, and think what I've saved by wanting nothing more."

Cass sent him off with Hobie and reflected long on the subject of branch banks. The idea had enormous merit. He had toyed with the innovation himself, but Lucius had put it in proper perspective. In the night he awakened to Allie's restlessness and promptly resumed the same train of thought.

"The baby's stirring," she said. "Oh, I'm weary of this! Why do the higher vertebrates have to take so long? If I were a cat I would have had at least two litters by now."

"We must send Uncle Lucius his cats," he said. He scarcely heard her. The bank was going to have kittens.

"Go to sleep," she said. "You really have nothing to do with this, aside from the grunting and sweating and a little semen."

"I don't think we should discuss our marriage in those terms, my dear," he said, and turned over.

Dr. Loren guessed that the child would be a boy, they nearly always were in first births, in his experience. Besides, weight, size, movements and so forth indicated a male. Allie said it would be a girl. It was a girl. She was delivered at home, without anesthesia and without difficulty, advising her colleague between each spasm. Having paced a groove in the carpet of the upstairs hall, Cass found his wife pale but calm and assured, about to have a glass of champagne with Loren. He held his tiny, red, wrinkled daughter, consented to take a few swallows of wine with Doña Maria and Lucius, who were hurriedly brought to the house at midmorning by Hobie, kissed Allie, and went off to work. To begin with he was tired and less elated than he had expected. The cigars he distributed at the bank, and the congratulations which poured in on him, restored his morale. But he wished he could have had a boy.

There were immediate problems. One was the matter of a name; no consideration had been given to it beforehand. Cass considered calling the baby Maria Elena, after his mother. Lucius objected to that as being old-fashioned. Doña Maria favored Concepcion or the name of her own mother, Pilar, in tribute to the Villanueva line. When Lucius hooted at her, the old folk engaged in a rambling dispute. "You always hated and envied Don Ygnacio," Doña Maria said. "He was an aristocrat and you were a gringo, an outsider. Confess it. Now you would take out your spite on an infant. You disgust me."

"Aristocracy, my foot," Lucius retorted. "Don Ygnacio was a descendant of hungry *paisanos* out of Spain in a hurry who were strangers just ahead of me and used Indian women to fill out their ranks. This child is of good white stock, thank God."

"You lie! And you have had every kind of woman, white, black and in between. How can you afford to talk?"

"Would you make a Mexican of her? You're insane. Call her by an

150

Irish name—call her Mary, for God's sake. That ought to satisfy a Catholic grandmother."

"When we had the land and the wealth," Doña Maria said, "before we were robbed by the gringos, who pursued me? The Brennan brothers! The child is part Spanish, not Mexican. She has the blood of the *conquistadores.*"

"My brother pursued you," Lucius said. "His taste was not above criticism, nor his judgment either. You pursued me."

"You were a drunken boor. You smelled of whiskey and perfume. I laughed at you!"

And so on. Bored and annoyed, Cass glared at them and started to dread his own old age. They had become duller-witted and petulant, and ridiculous in the bargain. A mere wisp of flesh in her black dress, his mother still retained a kind of cool beauty, however antique, that was irritating to him. Her dignity, courage and authority were undeniable. And Uncle Lucius had his panache despite the weight of the years; he was tall and imposing yet, splendidly dressed, and bright-eyed with deviousness and humor. But each seemed to Cass to have shrunk spiritually, as if they had embarked on return journeys to their childhoods, and without having surrendered an iota of the power and influence they intended to keep wreaking on him.

He put a stop to the wrangling and could not resist the opportunity to scold them. Their answer was to regard him in astonishment and disdain, and he felt shame and anger. In desperation, he said the naming would be left to the child's mother. They shrugged and abandoned him to his ignorance and perversity. When he confessed his woes to Allie, she was scarcely helpful or sympathetic. "Try to get them in agreement," she said, "and accept their choice. They're not used to listening to opinions from you."

"Don't be ironic, my dear. This is a serious question. I want a traditional, American name for our baby—even something elegant."

Allie smiled at him wickedly. "What about John Alden and Priscilla? That goes right back to the beginning. Call her Priscilla."

"Priscilla . . . I like that. It has a ring."

"My God, it was intended as a joke!"

"It's no joke to me," Cass said doggedly. "Priscilla sounds dignified and thoroughly ladylike. Priscilla Alice Brennan—how does that strike you as the name for a gentlewoman?"

"Go away, please," Allie said. "I'm tired of you."

He informed his mother and uncle that Allie had decided upon Priscilla Alice, and they promptly increased his irritability by applauding Allie's good sense. Another problem was the christening. His wife would have no truck with such outmoded customs. Doña Maria plumped for the true faith. Tongue in cheek, Lucius suggested Reverend Moses Smiley and his latest affiliation, the Church of Higher Astralphysics and Universal Good. "He comes to my hotel to shoot bolts of good into me and cadge advice on investments," he explained. "His disciples all get together and do their astralphysics and send out healing rays. Moses conducts them like an orchestra. He might give Priscilla Alice exactly the start in life she needs."

"You are a heathen," Doña Maria said, "and your jokes are not funny. A priest—and nobody else—has to baptize the child. She comes from the Villanuevas."

Lucius laughed at her and Cass temporized, but on this issue she could not be subverted. She had endured the loss of grace by her son; to have her granddaughter robbed of the hope of heaven at the outset was unendurable. Catholics held the key to redemption and eternal life: it was that simple.

The christening was delayed a month. Custom and his social position forced Cass to act, and he resolved to take Prissie to the Episcopalians. Doña Maria received the news with a baleful expression. "So you will send an innocent baby to Purgatory," she said. "You are a fool and a coward. If you do this, I will never forgive you and I will not set foot in your house again."

Arguing with her was useless. She stamped out and did not return. Attempting to telephone her, Cass heard a series of clicks in his ear. Allie was sent to Boyle Heights in a peacemaking role and reported Doña Maria welcomed her visits and wanted to see the baby, but that her relationship with Cass had come to an end unless her will was done. His anger rising, Cass mustered friends and defiantly bore Prissie to an Episcopal cleric; Allie stayed at home feigning illness. It was Cass's last time in a place of worship. He had had his fill of religion and its disputes. The break with Doña Maria, after a week or two of regrets, was rather a relief; Allie could keep up the connection, and he was frankly tired of the difficult old lady. Her purpose in his life had been served. He was too busy to concern himself further.

"You just can't and won't understand her," Allie interrupted, in the midst of Cass's explanation of his feelings on the subject. "I've begun to think you *are* Lucius's son. Neither of you has the slightest tincture of mercy in your makeup. You don't need anybody else, except to use as may be necessary. Your money and how well you get on in the world are the only essentials. What happens on the outside is important to you, and that's all. Doña Maria is reaching the end of her life. She has arteriosclerosis and can't think as clearly as you. And are you *always* right? Why shouldn't she cling to her religion? What else does she have? Has it made her any worse than you or Lucius? Don't you have a speck of pity for her?"

"No more than you have for me," he said, and felt with an abrupt disquiet that he had not defeated her, but only temporarily smothered a will as implacable as his mother's; he loved her, and yet she was as alien to him as Doña Maria.

"If I had any," she said, "it is gone now."

Happily, Prissie constituted no problem. She was a model child, unemotional, content and healthy. She rarely cried, was slow to talk or even give vent to a baby's babble, and seemed able to amuse herself. Her look was not that from the Villanueva side of her ancestry, to Cass's unspoken relief; she had the sorrel hair, thin-lipped wide mouth, pale skin and clean features of Allie, and, he supposed, a substantial part of her mother's temperament. He intended to be a fond and devoted father, but leisure was hard to come by, and an infant's hours did not coincide with his own. Mornings the Negro nurse Allie had engaged brought Prissie to him at the breakfast table to hold in his lap for a few moments and nights he bent over her trundle bed to give her a kiss she was too sleepy to be aware of. On Sunday mornings he had half an hour or more to devote to wheeling her in a pram around the garden. His manner with children, he thought, was not very good. Prying their attention from incomprehensible concerns was difficult, and Prissie obviously shrank from his awkward displays of affection. He renounced the attempt to win her at so early an age and resolved to wait until she had grown enough to appreciate his interest and attention. It annoyed him a little that Lucius, with the time and an apparent aptitude, had better luck in impressing himself upon Prissie. So did his wife, who seemed not especially engaged by the child. And he heard at second hand that Doña Maria had enjoyed a great success.

The fact was that Cass looked beyond a mere daughter. He wanted another baby, in the hope of acquiring a son. Pleading with Allie, he had difficulty putting the symbolistic importance of a male heir into words. More eloquence would not have helped him, for she was uninterested in adding to the family. She dodged increased responsibility and told him children bored her. The adventure and novelty of one pregnancy was sufficient. He argued that their wealth and position, not to mention the background of the Villanuevas, required a sizeable brood. What was the use of acquiring what they had, within the framework of a town like Los Angeles, unless there was a continuity and the sense of a spreading tribe? She looked at him quizzically, restraining amusement. His ambitious goals were preposterous to her; he doubted if she could understand them, and certainly they had no validity in her scheme of things.

Sometimes Cass tried uneasily to plumb the depths in Allie. He was always unsuccessful. Eventually he presumed no depths existed—just ennui, inconstancy, and a fevered longing for the impossible. Perhaps those were the principal attributes of a woman, and his experience with her no unusual one. He decided to accept his plight in a spirit of resignation. But still he loved her, and would in the end have done anything she demanded.

Meanwhile, there was his work. It absorbed him to the point of exhaustion. Nothing was easy. The establishment of his first branch bank, in Pasadena, occurred during the panic of 1907, when eastern financial interests called in their deposits and loans and abandoned the west. Harassed by a shortage of money, Cass had many anxious moments. Only by pretending the utmost vigor and confidence could he keep his equilibrium. At the same time, he became the city's main opponent of labor unions. His legal experience was used to frustrate organizing and quell strikes. The Clearing House Association required his attention, he was active in the enforced liquidation of weaker banks, and he joined a battle with the railroads regarding unfair freight rates that favored San Francisco. Poor economic conditions the following year did not keep him from opening a second branch in the port town of San Pedro, now annexed to the Queen; he had to subdue the resistance of his board of directors in order to go on with the program of expansion, ruefully aware that he was exhibiting a taste for risk as keen as that of Lucius's before him. With the arrival of summer, he found himself embroiled in the campaign to ensure the election of William Howard Taft, the choice of the Republican convention in Chicago.

Death attended birth, and the past began to vanish. One day Kirby Jennison appeared in Cass's office; he had become appallingly fat, he wheezed painfully, and the round bare dome of his head was sheened by perspiration. "I thought you were living in the east," Cass said. "When did you get back?"

"Last year, but I've been laid up for a while. It was too damned cold in Rochester—I went to Florida twice. Everybody I'd known was dead. I'm living here with a step-daughter."

"Have you seen Uncle Lucius?"

"No," Kirby said. "I have a bone to pick with him. How is the son of a bitch?"

Cass smiled. "Fine, thank you, Kirby."

"He ought to have passed long ago, considering the life he's led. Listen, I've got to talk to you, Cass. I think I'm entitled to more than

154

I got out of that partnership. Oh, no reflection on you—you're my friend. But you know that compressed-air jet I put together for him. He holds the patent on it. And he's manufacturing it."

"Yes, through a subsidiary company he doesn't own. You agreed to surrender rights in the patent, you remember."

"I didn't realize what I was doing," Kirby said. "And Sunset Sea—that's in operation again."

"Only in essence as a dummy corporation to hold assets for the San Cristobal."

"I was part of Sunset Sea, and I didn't get my rightful share. I want you to tackle Lucius for me, Cass."

"I'm a banker these days," Cass said, "not a lawyer."

"All this means is talking. He'll listen to you. Surely you can spare a couple of hours for a man who helped to raise you from a pup, Cass. I only want a fair shake."

Cass sat looking at Kirby. He was at once amused and disgusted. The greed that persisted beyond every other emotion sounded a warning in him, and yet aroused an anger. To dispatch this old man was to kill the old man coming in himself.

"Better say something," Kirby said, "or I'll begin to figure you're not my friend. Or were you ever my friend? Was I a sucker to trust you that first time? You can satisfy my curiosity one way or the other."

"You were well paid," Cass replied, "and you haven't a legal leg to stand on. In the settlement I was not your friend but your lawyer. I did the best I—"

"You're a liar. You cheated me. The only thing I thought you had was honesty—that you weren't like your Goddamned father—"

"My uncle, if you please."

"Don't pull a poker face on me," Kirby said. "That cuts a little, don't it? Did you think I never heard those stories of what happened after Cassius got killed? You are a smaller copy of Lucius, more mealy-mouthed and straiter-laced—that's all. He made his kind of Christian out of you, didn't he? It took quite a few years, but he succeeded. Money talks, huh? You must be his bastard. You are a bastard!"

"Anything else, Mr. Jennison?"

"Yeah. Tell me why I was such a blind fool. You had everything to lose by playing fair with me."

"Let me give you fair warning: what you say to me in here I am willing to forgive and forget because it has been spoken in the heat of reckless anger, but if it is repeated outside these walls I shall sue you for libel."

Kirby heaved up from the chair. He was panting. "You'll hear more

155

from me, damn you. I'm going to get a lawyer. Robbing me won't end up a paying proposition!"

"Good day, sir," Cass said. Pain tightened viselike in his neck and spread with rippling fire through shoulder, elbow and burning fingers. He closed his eyes and waited until it and Kirby had gone.

Less than a month later Kirby was dead. Not informed by Cass of his belated threats, Lucius attended the funeral. The ceremonies provoked his macabre risabilities. "One of the few compensations connected with nearly attaining the Biblical three score and ten," he remarked at a subsequent luncheon in the Athletic Club, "is having the lightning strike your contemporaries and miss you—and then enjoying the spectacle of their burials. You should have seen Kirby's, Cass. There weren't above twenty of the bereaved, including his family. The poor devil had a casket the size of an outhouse laid flat; he must have grown to the size of an elephant in his last days. He had some pseudo-grandchildren, but they couldn't have been any comfort to him. Both of his step-daughters married Americans, and still their offspring are all a shade too dark. I think I was his only sincere mourner. Somehow I've always missed old Kirby, in spite of his being cowardly and a pinchpenny. I must say he did display the cunning and ferocity of a cornered rat when I had led him far enough into a cul-de-sac and turned him round. I damned near laughed aloud, though, when the minister praised his contributions to the Queen and the oil industry. He took and never returned, and worried all the time. None of his savings went for luxuries or whores, and I bought the drinks. I wonder what he had in mind? Whatever it was, it didn't pan out."

"Perhaps to be the richest fat man in the world."

"Or to escape me and my plans. He has."

"May he rest in peace," Cass said. "I'm glad he's gone."

Lucius glanced at him in slight surprise. "You'll be saying the same of me presently. A quiet conscience is one that has no reminders."

Not long after, Aaron Shapiro followed Kirby to the shades. A stroke of apoplexy felled him as he prepared to take his wife with him on a farewell visit to his native Poland, for going to Europe had become a popular movement in Los Angeles; people were aware of gathering tides of unrest in the world and experienced the desire to see the great monuments and cities before they crumbled under the onslaught of a new cycle of disasters. But Mr. Shapiro went off in a hearse instead of in a North German Lloyd ship. Cass did not regret the end of his benefactor too keenly. Of late, having grown increasingly senile and eccentric, he had been something of a nuisance. He showered unsolicited advice on Cass, he disapproved of the branch banking ventures, and he was worried by Cass's uncompromising stand against union labor. Forced to show respect and gratitude, Cass suffered from a fretted temper. He was now firmly entrenched and didn't require direction from old fogies who had lost touch.

Unlike Kirby's obsequies, the last respects paid to Mr. Shapiro were considerable. The commercial lords of the town turned out en masse. Among them, in the largest synagogue of the Queen, sat Lucius and Cass, surrounded by venerable gentlemen in long black coats and skullcaps. Everybody wore a hat. The service was long and emotional. By prudent exercise of honesty, fair dealing and sensible generosity, Aaron had contrived to make himself respected, honored, even loved, and genuinely regretted. Tears were shed for him, which embarrassed Cass and amused Lucius. From the gallery reserved for women descended Rachel Eindhoven, and Cass stopped to express his sorrow. She was heavy and a bit shapeless, no longer fit material for an eastern potentate's harem, and surrounded by children. He wondered what he had ever seen in her. She presented her bulky husband Sam, who, despite the best efforts of his father-in-law, had not managed to amount to much. But Rachel retained a glint in her eye, and the ghost of her former flirtatiousness. "I hardly recognize you any more, Mr. Brennan," she said. "What happened to those fine silky whiskers you used to wear?"

"I had to shave them off, Mrs. Eindhoven. My wife objected."

"Well, being clean-faced makes you look younger. Did she object to you looking so old?"

"No," Cass said. "She felt they were unsanitary."

"Such a queer reason!" Rachel said. "I would have curled and perfumed them for you."

He thought she might have, too, and was curiously struck by her remark. It summoned a strange longing for Allie in him, and an impatience with her as well. If only she could have had the softness and compliance of a Rachel! Then he might have discovered complete happiness and needed nothing else—not money, position, the anodyne of overwork, the gathering haste . . .

Returning Lucius to his hotel, Cass went upstairs with him. Moses Smiley awaited them in the corridor. "The clerk at the desk told me he expected you to return momentarily," he explained to Lucius. "Am I intruding in your hour of sorrow?"

"No, come in, Reverend," Lucius said. "Shoot me full of astralphysics rays. Make me resemble St. Sebastian and his arrows. I'm in need of them and a stiff drink."

As he grasped both of Cass's hands in ecstatic pleasure, Moses blessed another of their precious meetings. He was almost unchanged in the

157

midst of flux and dissolution, rounder perhaps than of yore, but rosy and bright-eyed. "One immediate question," Cass said smilingly. "How many children have you?"

"Thirteen, my dear friend. Alas, there will be no more."

"Really? Why?"

"Mrs. Smiley has undergone transubstantiation. She is of this earth and yet not of it. Hadn't you heard?"

"I forgot to tell him," Lucius said, as he poured whiskey in a glass. "She went to the well once too often, Cass."

"I am very sorry to hear of her death," Cass said.

"The thirteenth was an unlucky number for me," Moses said. "But Mrs. Smiley had a rebirth and is now part of the all-pervading astrality and universal good. She is near and directing powerful rays at her loved ones. We rejoice in and for her."

"I take it you have found the secret of immortality and discarded evangelism," Cass said.

Moses nodded solemnly. "Yes, sir. To be blunt, the role of an evangelical preacher in Los Angeles is unprofitable. The chapel-going public expects new sensations. My astralphysics discoveries in theology have proved to be just what they needed, and my present congregation is the most active I have ever encountered."

"The collection plate sails through the air," Lucius said, "sustained by an effort of will. I've been there and seen it."

"Your uncle delights in gibing at me," Moses said. "However, the rays have benefited him."

They talked for a while of old times, and Moses inquired for Cass's mother, his wife and child. The cluttered room smelled of cologne and the ammoniac fumes of cats, and by shutting his eyes Cass could have transported himself back to the house on Sixth Street. He consulted his watch while Moses spoke movingly of Kirby's transubstantiation and promised to beam the combined emanations of his flock toward the graves of him and Aaron Shapiro; he doubted, though, if astralphysics could prove helpful to those of the Jewish persuasion.

"Speaking of beneficent rays," Lucius said, "you'd better expose yourself to some, Cass. You look tired. Get down off that white charger of civic virtue and take a rest. The people and the bank and the Republicans and the laboring man can do without you for a few months. Don't risk transubstantiating along with Kirby and Aaron."

"I've never felt better, Uncle Lucius."

"Well, you impress me as being peaked and pale. Allie is worried about you. Consult her."

158

"I must get on with my business," Cass said, and arose. "Forgive me, gentlemen."

"Please," Moses said, and took Cass's hands again. "Whenever you are weary and failing, come to us. I can promise you reinvigoration. We are in a mansion on Bunker Hill, and our electric cross can be seen throughout the city. We're a practical group, dedicated to universal good. There is nothing sectarian about us. You can go on practicing your own faith and yet enjoy the help of astralphysics. Meanwhile, I will have Mrs. Smiley aim her rays at you."

"Thank you, Moses," Cass said. "I shall count on her intervention."

"Stand quite still at intervals," Lucius said. "Don't put Mrs. Smiley to the bother of shooting at a moving target."

That night, Moses's transubstantiated wife or not, Allie brought Cass to their room for a private conversation before dinner. She had incurred an abrupt change of mind and was willing to give him another child; in return, he must agree to take her to Europe. "What occasioned this?" Cass asked. His heart pounded and strained in exulting expectation.

"I don't know," she said. "I want a change of air, and you should have a rest. Lucius tells his traveling stories and they inspire me. Soon we'll be too old for having adventures. Have I your promise?"

"I can't go now. So many things are unfinished . . ."

"When can you go?"

"Well, in a year," he said. "Not sooner. I wish I could—"

"I want to go first, and come back and have the baby."

"My dear, it's impossible. Give me a chance. You know how entrapped I am."

"If I have a son," she said, "will you promise to go as soon as we can leave him? Within six months after his birth, at the latest?"

"Yes, even if you have a daughter, Allie."

"I'll have a boy. Swear it."

"On my word of honor," he said. "Darling, you have made me very happy. I wish I could express my—my—"

He couldn't; the words choked him. Affection became importunate desire. With the fumbling eagerness of an adolescent, he wheedled her into removing her corset and drawers. An intense excitement lay in the making of a new baby, and he was quickly spent. Resting beside Allie, he felt her gently holding his scarcely lessened member and the pouch beneath it. "If a man hangs like that," she said, "why isn't he given the temperament to go with such things? You could have made twenty women happy and fathered a dozen sons."

"I don't make you happy."

"That's different. The fault is mine."

159

"Let me try again," he said. "Your hand gives me the temperament."

She submitted and helped him without a word. The second entry of her resulted in a tremendous increase in sensation. But he was savagely disappointed even at the height of a lingering discharge. Allie remained unmoved, her eyes wide open and fixed upon a distant object. He said, "What are you thinking of? The what-d'ye-call-it—the splenectomy?"

"This last month I've been making hats. I'm not very good at them. I thought of making a hat."

"Can't you think of *me,* for God's sake?"

She shook her head and smiled. At the meal which followed downstairs, he slumped in his chair and his hands trembled from the effects of nervous exhaustion and he had no appetite. He caught a glimpse of his bloodless face in the mirror over the sideboard and looked quickly away. A vast, dispiriting hollow formed in his chest. It was the indigestion tormenting him once more.

Yet the fear that attended these manifestations did not deter him. In succeeding weeks his demands on Allie were constant. He spurred himself, trying desperately to elicit a response from her, and she offered him neither resistance nor communion. She told him she was pregnant, and still he refused to desist; the haste was on him again, more insistent than ever.

Then the great pain returned, while he sat peacefully on a Sunday out by the plaster summerhouse with Prissie playing in the grass at his feet. He was reading a difficult brief his law partners had sent him and penciling notes. Suddenly he started up, a scream rising in his throat, a thousand jagged edges of glass lacerating his heart, and the ghastly suffocating agony pitched him headlong on the lawn and into depths of the black sea.

Awakening, the fumes of smelling salts tickling his nostrils, he saw he was in bed. Sweat had soaked his shirt, and he was depressed and without the strength to move. He gazed at Allie, who was bent over him; in the background stood the German manservant and Hobie, apparently employed to carry him inside. A tear dripped from Allie's chin and struck his lips. "You don't deserve this," she said. "Not this—"

Because he was a week in recovering, and his wife would accept no less, Cass went to Dr. Eldred Loren and had a thorough examination. "Well, Dr. Brennan is correct in her diagnosis, as usual," Loren said, and smiled. "She told me what she thought a long time ago."

"What is the matter?" Cass asked.

"Well, it isn't indigestion. Some vascular changes have taken place in you, my friend."

160

"What does that mean?"

"Specifically," Loren said, "you've got angina pectoris. It's uncommon at your age. Did you ever have syphilis?"

"No, gonorrhea at an early age. I don't think I had—"

"Are you sure? Syphilis is a factor."

"I can't be positive," Cass said. "Anyhow, the sickness was cured. How does angina pectoris affect my ordinary life?"

"You must rest more, and avoid stress, anxiety and over exertion. I advise a simple diet and keeping your bowels open. I'm going to give you some sodium nitrite to take three times daily, and perles of amyl nitrite to carry with you—in the event of another attack, break one open and inhale the fumes. Normally that will give quick relief."

"In short, you are saying I've got to become a semi-invalid and give up most of my work."

"Not precisely. But you must slow down and lead a much easier existence. Dr. Brennan will tell you how to proceed."

"That's impossible. I have far too many interests and obligations—"

"You could die of one of these seizures, you know," Loren said.

"Then I'll have to die. Eldred, I don't want a word of your diagnosis to go to anybody else."

"Very well. But you had better not be a damned fool."

Cass would not discuss his condition with Allie or appeal for her advice and sympathy. She offered none. Despite his brave words in Loren's presence, he began unobtrusively to slow his pace—to delegate authority at the bank, refuse the taking on of fresh commitments, reduce the speed with which he walked or climbed stairs, avoid worry and dissension, and curtail the parties given in his home. He ate carefully and seldom played golf. By unspoken agreement, Allie aided him however she could. It was she who always made sure the perles of amyl nitrite were in a pocket of any garment he happened to be wearing.

Certain events compelled him to depart from the strict regime. His membership in the Municipal League and the matter of an unsatisfactory mayor supposedly allied with elements in the red-light district drove him to the forefront of a fight that led to the official's resignation. Lucius was revolted by this triumph of public morality. "Ever since poor little Molly," he said, "you've hated whores. Women, maybe, for all I know. You've had your chance for a belated revenge, eh? It makes me sick to think a relative of mine—a Brennan, God save the mark—is opposed to fornication. You'll end up by eradicating every bit of the Queen that was. Next it'll be prohibition. You don't drink and you don't copulate, do you? Why not have the city council put up stocks, brand adulterers with a scarlet letter, and duck the tosspots in a pond?"

Listening wearily to Lucius, Cass was half disposed to tell him of his ailing heart and how, perhaps, it was a legacy of the night with Molly. But the revelation would give him no comfort, and only distress the old man. The battle was his alone.

The reverberations of the municipal scandals had barely subsided when Allie bore a seven-pound six-ounce boy, once again with speed and ease. The infant appeared to resemble Cass, as far as new babies resembled anything human, and he was overjoyed. He took care, however, to restrain his emotions; now he had, more than ever, a reason for living. In pursuance of calm, he merely informed his mother by letter of the birth, extending no invitation, and did not receive a reply. Their alienation was complete, and he was indifferent to the idea of reviving any association. He toyed with the idea of naming the boy Cass, which would have been fitting, and finally decided against a name he had never liked. Nor was the name of Lucius acceptable, for many reasons he was opposed to elaborating upon. His choice at length was Albert Chambers Brennan, out of gratitude to Allie, and possibly in memory of that early model of his, Albert Blour, with whom he was still friendly.

Albert had no christening. The question went unanswered, left conveniently in abeyance until forgotten. He was remitted to the care of Lagonda Brown, the Negro nurse whose father had named her after a foreign bicycle which had excited his admiration, and Prissie promptly became Cissie and Albert was addressed as Brother except on state occasions. Cass coddled and adored him, but he was careful to show Cissie extra attention, even if she did not represent the shining promise of his son.

He spent an increasing amount of time with the children, not alone for the peace and comfort they brought him, but in a search for another kind of love. His bewildering and incomplete intimacy with Allie had come to a full stop. She would no longer occupy his bed, and slept in a separate room after Brother's birth. Her excuse was the condition of his heart. He suspected she was punishing him, and an irrational fury paled his face. It was his first real anger directed at her. "What is your actual reason?" he demanded. "Is it because you've guessed I can't take you to Europe quite as soon as I promised?"

"No. I don't think you should travel until your health is improved."

"My health is fine! Tell me are you finally so disgusted with me that—"

"Of course not," she said. "Why should my letting you do something that doesn't matter to me make any difference? I have told you the truth. Look out for that rage—it isn't good for you."

"Then why do you put me in a rage?"

"It's better than having you die in my arms."

"You're lying," he said bitterly. "Nothing I've done, nothing I can ever do, will win your love. You've finally come to hate me."

"My God, I don't! I don't! I pity you . . . I've come to that now."

"Oh, go to hell!" But in a moment his patience had reasserted itself, and he was apologizing. "I'll take you abroad. My word is good. Please, Allie. Give me another six months. Then we'll stay as long as you want—"

"We've got to stop talking," she said. "Leave me alone. Go sit down and rest."

His neck hurt, his shoulder and arm, and his fingers burned and stiffened. He waited grimly through weeks which stretched into months —and the great pain was put off. Dr. Loren said he was improving. He considered his situation and made a cold decision: to be a vegetable, to lie down and surrender to the faulty thing beating in his breast, was utterly unacceptable. Carefully, almost craftily, he concentrated on forgetting; as of old, the evil did not exist when it was ignored. The best of forgetfulness was achieved in work. He would exert himself until he had another warning or met his fate.

Labor agitators were hard at it in the Queen, unsettling the working man and raising specters of terrorism and anarchy. Cass took up the challenge. His League of Commerce and Industry committee, well financed, imported Pinkerton men and plug-uglies experienced in strike-breaking. He had the backing of Lucius, who feared a revolution. "Look at what they've done in Europe," he said. "In the east—the mines, the steel mills, factories—every Goddamned place there's an opportunity for mulcting the people like us. I tell you they're on the march, and it's now or never. They'll pick us cleaner than carrion crows can if we don't put 'em out of business."

"When we're finished," Cass said, "Los Angeles will still be open shop. You can depend on that."

Within a couple of weeks of Brother's first birthday, in the late spring, the conflict came to a head. During the night, asleep in bed, Cass was awakened by a reverberating blast. He felt the house shudder and groan, and heard the clatter of breaking glass and china. Putting on a robe and slippers, he ran into the hall. A smell of burnt black powder was in the air. His first concern was for the children, who were crying but unharmed, tended by a mud-colored Lagonda. He turned to discover Allie behind him, and grasped her convulsively. "I wasn't touched," she said calmly. "Let's go downstairs. There might be a fire."

Cass had thought from the beginning it was a bomb. He was not mistaken. The front windows lay in shreds on the carpet, the door was shattered and hanging on its hinges, plaster had fallen everywhere. A section of the garden wall was blasted out, and the gate a jumble of twisted metal. The servants joined them below, coming from the coach house, and only Hobie was a casualty; he had a gash from running in his bare feet. While Allie patched his wound, Cass ascertained that the telephone was in commission and called the police. Neighbors were gathering, and Allie admitted some of them. One man, aroused by the sound of a speeding automobile, had witnessed the tossing of an object from it and then seen the explosion. Countenances were white, hands shaky; it was like the outbreak of a war. No fire had ensued, and an obliging, knowledgeable fellow turned off the gas at the main.

The telephone started ringing. A hollowness spreading in his chest, Cass sat down and talked to his friends, associates and the newspapers. A colleague of his on the labor relations committee, a newspaper editor, had been bombed at his house and his dog killed. Another bomb placed in the railroad shops had failed to go off. A warehouse on Los Angeles Street containing nonunion goods had been wrecked by an explosion and was burning, and its watchman was badly injured. Expressions of confidence and sympathy deluged Cass, and eternal vengeance was sworn. He began to sweat, and had to wipe his face repeatedly.

The police arrived, and reporters and photographers; three Pinkerton detectives sent by the League posted guard. Lucius appeared in a taxi, unshaven and tieless, his Colt's pistol in the waistband of his trousers. He tried to give Cass a smaller revolver. "The dirty bastards will stop at nothing," he said. "Put the women and children in one room, and I'll sit outside the door. We may have to sell our lives dearly."

"You're an old fool," Cass said irritably. "Don't you realize that?"

Lucius subsided and grinned. "Perhaps I am, Cass. But this is more fun than what I've been doing for the last fifteen respectable years."

Allie kept suggesting that Cass retire, but he had to confer with the law officers and many others, and issue a statement to the press. One of his partners, Burton Lely, came by to make sure he and his family were unharmed. The mayor sent a personal messenger, who had to be given a reply. Additional police augmented the Pinkerton guards, and Cass ordered the cook to distribute coffee and sandwiches. Tearful and trembling, she quit on the spot, and her husband departed with her. Allie went in the kitchen to fire up a wood range that still remained, and Lucius accompanied her to help with the food and drink, his gun transferred to a hip pocket. To Cass's eyes he looked years younger, suddenly sprightly and gay, scenting the breeze for more trouble like a warhorse brought out of a dull pasture.

There were reports that the streets were full of armed men. Every policeman and fireman was on duty. The governor was in touch by telephone, ready to impose martial law and call out the National Guard. But a silence fell, and nothing happened. Information poured in to Cass. As he had presumed, this was no insurrection. A few madmen had vented their wrath and fled. They had wrecked their cause by scattered and senseless acts of violence, and he would be victorious in the morning. It was his best moment yet. He relaxed and stopped sweating.

Finally the house was cleared. And then Doña Maria made an entrance, hobbling on a stick, clad in impeccable black, her white hair newly arranged and held in place by a jewelled Spanish comb. She took Allie in her arms, permitted Cass to kiss her cheek, and gazed with distaste at Lucius. She was unemotional and unafraid. Her presence gave Cass new assurance, and the reunion caused him to blink back grateful tears. "I had to come," she said, "in spite of my oath. We are a family, and the children must be protected. Only they are important. If they mean to massacre us—"

Cass smiled. "The gringos, you mean, Mother?"

She spat out the words, a decorous facade of forty years' duration crumbling: *"Sí, los gringos!"*

Nearly pleased by what the bombing had wrought, Cass supervised the upstairs maid in preparing rooms for his mother and uncle. The Irish girl had been hiding under a bed for a long time unnoticed in the confusion, and was full of apologies. In a strange mood, Cass joked with her and put an arm around her shoulders, and she stared at him in pitiful astonishment; he was tired of being an angry, responsible and dignified man, but she would never understand.

Few windows remained whole. Outside in the soft night the shadowy forms of the guards could be seen, one pulling on the glowing stub of a cigar. Nocturnal birds chattered under the eaves. Cass thought how lovely it was, what a kind land, what a good city, what a better life he could lead; somehow, abruptly, the race he was running was over, and he could stop to enjoy the littler things he had missed. To rest, to sleep, to put aside care . . . he had done more than enough, in too short a time . . .

He waited in Lucius's room until he came, and watched while his uncle prepared for bed, undressing, putting his false teeth in a glass of water, laying one gun on a nightstand and a second under his pillow, and pulling a nightshirt down over his protruding belly and spindly shanks. Suddenly they shook hands. This was a coming together, a joining of spirits, and all the years and all the difficulties were erased in an instant. Lucius opened his mouth to speak, thought better of it, and turned his head quickly away and waved a negligent farewell. As he closed the door, Cass had a last sight of him—a fine old man he loved, settling to his rest, grunting and content—and hid tears he could not help shedding.

Cass wiped his eyes and went in to kiss his children, already asleep, the noise and their fright forgotten. His heart swelled at the sight of them. They were innocent and untroubled, oblivious to the perils and sorrows which stretched ahead. God help them, they had to grow up. But he would spare them many of the difficulties and disillusionments and compromises that had plagued him. They would learn from him; he had important lessons to teach, of humility and patience and sober content and sympathy and how to avoid the perils of greed and lust. Theirs would be a better life than his. Only Cissie and Brother were important, as his mother had said. That importance was his excuse for having struggled hard and long, and without the glory he had hoped for. Casually, incomprehensibly, he was aware at last of being happy and fulfilled.

Returning to his own room, he observed that he was still in nightwear and a robe. He laughed aloud. There was a knock on the door, and he went to open it. Allie came in, tired and bedraggled. His arms enfolded her and he held her tightly for a moment. "Doña Maria has gone to sleep," she said. "She hates the Americans, but she is not afraid of them."

"It's all right," Cass said, in explanation of everything.

"Now you must go away from here for a while."

"Yes, I know that. Forever, if you want."

"What?"

He touched her hair, reaching out hesitantly. "I'll explain later—but this is done with. I'm finished, as of tonight. Whatever I do in the future, it won't be this, or like this. Give me two months to show them I'm not afraid, then we're off. We'll have to take the children; I can't leave them."

"That's better," Allie said.

"If you will just love me a little, I'll change. It won't be the same again."

She smiled. "I'll love you a little. It's high time, isn't it?"

"Will you come in here and sleep with me? Only lie beside me? Every moment since I have known you that I've been away from you, I have been lonely."

"Don't make me pity you."

"No, this is different. Don't you see?"

166

"Yes," she said. "I'll be back in ten minutes, when I have washed myself, and I won't leave again."

Cass took off his robe and sat on the edge of the bed and stretched luxuriously. He expected to sleep well, to awaken in a new set of circumstances, to already have consummated the beginning of another life.

The great pain clasped him, and he fell on the floor. In blind agony, his breath gone and the screaming that would out reduced to a gobbling sound, he squirmed toward the chair on which the robe was folded; in a pocket were the perles of amyl nitrite. It was a thousand miles away, as far beyond reach as true happiness, and his strength was used up. He was received by the dark sea with the endless depths.

PART TWO

Queen of the Heavens

one

In his youth, Brother did not regard himself with high favor; that came later. His nickname seemed condescending and derogatory, and Albert sissified. Before he arrived at a school-boy Al, he was successively Little Albert, Master Albert, Albert the Terror, and had a number of other names even less complimentary. When he grew old enough to command respect, he styled himself A. Chambers Brennan and never was Albert again. Friends called him Cham, and a literate companion in college dubbed him "The Great Cham of Tartary." He rather fancied that.

As a child he failed to arouse wide enthusiasm. His mother, with whom he was on nothing more than polite terms, did not show him any special favor. Lagonda Brown, his nurse and companion, had trouble getting him to behave. Hobie, the first chauffeur, who stayed on until the war began, was given to spells of not speaking to Albert. The servants barely tolerated him. He fought with his playmates and screamed at the mere sight of a dentist or Dr. Loren. Looking back, Albert had to concede that in those days, what with crying rages, insanitary habits and abounding energy, he must have been a little hard to take.

Cissie, the sister three years his senior, was the center of his life. They were inseparable until schooling parted them. She was the one person he wholly surrendered to; different in temperament, she was unreflective, decisive, without personal doubts or the capacity for complaining. Although her devotion to him was unquestionable, she was his severest critic and beat him up regularly, and he feared as well as loved her. It was she who stopped his baby squalling, sucking his thumb, and wetting his pants and bed. A silent, secret, consecrated rebel, the injustices of their elders meant less to her than to him, and she had a

171

practicality and common sense which overrode his clumsy methods of trying to get his own way. Unlike him, she rarely pondered on her looks, her boredom and the tyrannies of mere living; she was the soul of motion and command and impenetrable reserve, and nearly always secured his obedience.

Miss Holmes, Albert's homeroom teacher at the James T. Blaine Elementary School, motivated his casting up of some accounts at the age of twelve. Youngish, crisp, intelligent and good looking, she was adept at imparting the rudiments of intellectual curiosity to her charges. Alone among the faculty, she thought Albert had promise, and treated him with a patient sympathy. In return, he regarded her with a shameful, undefined yearning, and tried to please her. Thus, when she suggested in the beginning of the term that each member of the class prepare an autobiography to be read aloud to promote better understanding and appreciation of one another, he took the assignment seriously. Miss Holmes was advanced for her era, knew something of group therapy, and had been enlightened by the revolutionary psychological theories of Sigmund Freud; unknown to Albert, she intended to write a doctoral thesis on just such grubby bundles of contradictions as he.

He determined to furnish a well-rounded portrait of Albert C. Brennan. It seemed to him very important. He brooded on his position and attainments, not to mention his physical appearance. No question of it, he had many advantages; his family was rich and well known, he was big and heavy for his age, and very strong, and good at soccer, football, basketball, handball, baseball and boxing and wrestling. Nobody at James T. Blaine, including through the eighth grade, could really lick him. Except for Cissie, who didn't seem like a girl, he hated girls. He owned a superb lightweight English bicycle, of a kind practically unknown in Los Angeles, and rode it everywhere—downtown on Broadway where palm trees in concrete boxes decorated the curbs and watering troughs for horses were disappearing, out west through the barley fields to the suburb of Hollywood, along the double row of mansions tenanted by millionaires on the high ground of West Adams Boulevard, across the river by bridge and into the gathering slum that was now Boyle Heights, southward over flat wastes broken by Chinese truck gardens, and occasionally to the sea at Ocean Park or Venice, the latter a quaint monstrosity of canals and gondolas in imitation of the Adriatic city, but unhappily pocked by oil derricks. His enthusiasms were not confined to sports; he liked, surprisingly, to read nearly anything except textbooks, help the chauffeur work on the Brennan motorcars, row the boats and fish for carp in Westlake Park, catch halibut and tomcod off the wharf at Santa Monica, cheer for the Vernon team (his idols) in baseball games at Washington Park, and swim in bathhouse pools.

For obvious reasons, Albert did not propose to mention his close association with Cissie, which he considered necessary but perhaps an indication of a fundamental weakness. There were other interesting aspects to take the place of that. For instance, he lived in a larger house than any of his schoolmates. The Brennans had the San Cristobal, a famous ranch to which he had been many times. It was full of cattle, fields of hay, orange groves, olive trees, a forest of wooden towers, and had a sour oily odor and resounded to the chugging and clatter of steam engines and walking beams. Three automobiles graced the coach house, a Pierce-Arrow, a Franklin, and a Ford the servants used; presiding over them was a chauffeur named Hank Isbrow, who had driven in road races. The cellar was filled with whiskey and wines laid in before the imposition of prohibition. When the Brennans entertained, which wasn't often, everybody in the town of consequence came to drink the champagne and dance to the orchestra.

Brennan males were celebrated for their selfless heroism. Albert's father had died in 1910, a victim of Bolsheviks and their bombs, and his father before him had been killed by rebels during the Civil War. His mother had died in the influenza epidemic of 1918. As an orphan, and a rich one to boot, Albert thought he was deserving of pity and attention. Especially since he had to put up with Grandpa Lucius, actually Albert's great-uncle, an immensely old, white-haired, bushy-browed, energetic man, a relic out of the past whom he regarded in a general mood of fear and wonderment. Grandpa was lordly, infirm, uncertain in temper, and smelled of booze and cologne. He was alternately pleasant and generous, dictatorial and angry. His conflicting instructions were hard to follow, and Albert detested exhortations to instantly grow to a maturity beyond his years and at once understand complicated business matters he was unable to make heads or tails of.

In a room upstairs—which she rarely left, and then in a wheelchair, for she was crippled by rheumatism—dwelt Grandma, who was not Grandpa's wife but the mother of Albert's father. A quiet and gentle old woman, tiny and frail, she spoke little and often appeared not quite sure of where she was or what she did. She doted on her grandson, and to his discomfort he had frequently to sit with her, holding one of her withered hands and trying to make conversation. Grandma was a Villanueva, a distinction that was of no importance to Albert, and had a forbidding looking middle-aged female nurse with whom his relations were strained. He had nothing against Grandma, but she was an awful nuisance.

Other than Cissie, Albert's closest friends were Harry and Tom Sego, the sons of Mr. William Sego, who ran the Sunset Sea Corporation, and Hal Baltim, Junior, son of his late father's law partner. He was the acknowledged leader of this group, and catered to, which he regarded as his rightful due. Nevertheless, if he had been restricted to one companion, again not counting his sister, he would have chosen Lagonda Brown, who understood and admired him. She alone besides Cissie, from the days when, not much more than a child herself, she had bathed him and changed his diapers, had his love and confidence; now, loyalty undiminished, she kept his clothing mended and covered up for his lapses in manners and intelligence and insisted he drink plenty of milk and nursed him through runny-nosed periods. Lagonda swore Albert was handsome and smart, destined to be a replica of Grandpa, and certain to ornament Los Angeles business and society. Cissie did not share his confidence in the judgment of Lagonda, and that was one of the few points on which they differed.

With other adults Albert continued to encounter disappointments. They often accused him of being insubordinate and a smart aleck. Picking his nose, failing to bathe and keeping white mice and lizards in his bedroom inspired a resentment he resented. Aware of his importance through the lectures of Grandpa, he tended to answer criticism with criticism. Mrs. Godby, the housekeeper, considered him one of the crosses she had to bear. The cook, Mrs. Gonzales, abhorred his thieveries in the kitchen—he was always hungry. He was not a favorite of the housemaids because he never wiped his feet in wet weather and left dirty hand-and-finger imprints on doors, walls and cupboards; also, he knocked down things in the course of running through rooms. In the coach house he was more acceptable, but Hank Isbrow tired of his begging to be allowed to surreptitiously drive the Ford and condemned his overbearing confidence when he was permitted to help with small repairs. Mr. Sego was patient and polite with him, no doubt on orders from Grandpa, although sometimes he wore a look of suffering. Albert annoyed Mr. Baltim and delighted in it, spurred on by Hal Baltim, who perceived that Albert had an immunity he had not. On the other hand, Albert got along well with Mr. Burton Lely, junior partner of his late father, who was an easy, smiling man and didn't seem to take things too seriously.

All in all, Albert thought he was right and they were wrong. He didn't much like grown people and wondered if he could get even with them when he grew up. His great-uncle kept telling him of the huge responsibilities he was going to have to assume and how he must prepare himself, and quickly, but Albert paid little heed. The bent of his aspirations would have astounded and enraged the old man. While the great war was on, and especially when it promised to last forever, he had intended to become a soldier and hero, outshadowing his father and grandfather, probably in the French Foreign Legion or the British Royal Navy because he liked the uniforms. Now that it was over and the opportunity lost, going to the movies had supplied him with a different goal. Despite the lure of *The Perils of Pauline,* he enjoyed even more the jungle serials featuring Art Acord (it made no difference that Cissie told him they were made right out by Lincoln Park in Colonel Selig's zoo, and were no closer to Africa than Albert was), and had virtually made up his mind to roam the dark continent as a professional adventurer in whipcord breeches and riding boots and topee, a revolver slung around his waist and a rifle in his hand, forever hearing the mystic strains of "Hindustan" in his ears—as played on the piano by the deft man who was down in the front of the theater beside the screen. Failing that, he was willing to join the Secret Service and track down the unknown villains whose bombing of the house had caused the death of his father, thus confounding such carpers as Mr. Baltim, Mrs. Godby and Mrs. Gonzales, or join the Vernon team, preferably playing third base, and dazzle everybody at the James T. Blaine Elementary School, no doubt making them sorry they hadn't cultivated him while they still had the chance.

Putting all this down on paper was harder than he had assumed. He gnawed off the end of a pencil getting together a few consecutive sentences. They sounded awfully silly when he read them aloud. He sought Cissie, took her into the privacy of his room where the mice wiggled their pink noses and the lizards crawled, and requested advice. A slim, angular, sandy-haired girl, freckles banded across her nose, she listened to him disgustedly. "You're stuck on Miss Holmes," she said, "and you'll make a fool of yourself. I know her. She was always getting her classes to do stunts before I graduated."

"I'm not stuck on her. You're crazy."

"Then what are you blushing for? Do you think maybe she'll take you on her lap if you're a good boy?"

"Get out," Albert said. "This is the last time I ever talk to you."

"Listen to me, stupid. Just put down your name and where you live and how old you are and how you like baseball. And say you're nuts about school and learning a lot and wouldn't be in any other homeroom —so you'll get a good grade, see?"

"You think that's best, huh?"

"I don't think, I *know* it," Cissie told him. "Try showing off for Miss

Holmes and you'll feel like you're back again peeing down your leg in front of everybody."

That clinched it. Albert stared at her in horror.

So the autobiography actually amounted to nothing. But it had the effect of focusing Albert's mind on the family, and in the course of further talks with Cissie he learned a good deal. Her three years' seniority, a capacious memory, and a sharp eye for detail were most instructive.

The bombing was a landmark among the Brennans; everything dated from before or after that, like the birth of Christ in world history. Albert had no recollections of the event, but Cissie could recall hearing the explosion, being comforted, how her brother wet his bed, the arrival of Grandpa Lucius and Grandma, how she was roused to be told of her father's death, and seeing the extent of the damage in the house. She remembered their mother kissing the cheek of their father before the undertakers took him away; she might have done the same, but the act filled her with repulsion and she fled. Their mother was very brave and quiet, and hardly cried at all. She prepared some sleeping medicine for herself and went to bed. Grandpa and Grandma sat up in the living room talking. If Albert wanted to find out any more about them, he'd have to talk to Lagonda, who, when the children were settled, went downstairs to try to bring a little order in the place.

Albert spoke to her. Lagonda said: "I wasn't there long, and mostly they talked in Spanish and I didn't understand a word. The colonel, he had a gun in his pocket and was drinking from a bottle of whiskey, and the old lady, she cried a little and seemed to be scolding him some. I heard her say this is what they got for sinning, and he say it was so long ago he couldn't remember if it ever happened. She say it happened all right, and she would never forgive him."

"What happened, Lagonda?" asked Albert.

"I don't know. What you think happened?"

"Oh, what's the difference. They're so old, they probably went crazy and just talked."

"Maybe," Lagonda said. "The colonel say, who said love was immortal? He had forgot everything. It was funny to think they were young once and now were going to bury the result of being young. And Doña Maria, she say they'd lived too long. Then she cried again, and the colonel put his arm around her."

"Okay, okay," Albert said.

"You know something, Albert? I think the colonel is real close to you. Don't just uncle him, see? You think of him as real close."

176

"Why do you say that?"

"Never you mind why I say that," Lagonda said. "I got my reasons. You think of him as real close."

Albert was bored by her Delphic pronouncements and preferred the more lucid explanations of Cissie, who was not a sentimentalist. She had decided, from what she'd heard, that their father was already sick, and the bombing merely served to finish him off. Grandpa and Grandma were delighted at having the chance to come back to the house, and availed themselves of the excuse that they were needed to stay on. Their mother probably accepted them because she couldn't do anything else. The details of their father's funeral, which Grandpa had handled, were still fresh in Cissie's mind. There was a graveside ceremony instead of services in a church, and a funny little preacher named Smiley, a friend of Grandpa's, made a long speech on sending out astralrays and doing universal good. Grandma was scandalized by this, and got sick and went to bed right afterwards for a long time. Their mother certainly wasn't crushed by grief. She had dry eyes at the funeral, and Cissie could not think of a later occasion when she cried or mentioned their father. He was just gone, and that was the end of it.

Probing his memory, Albert couldn't remember her talking of him either. In all honesty, he did not miss her much, and she had made no great impression on him. He recalled her reading, listening to phonograph music, and doing watercolors she promptly destroyed—and somehow avoiding him and his sister. Still, she had done her bit for them, taking them to the movies, to concerts, on automobile drives, and interesting herself in their schooling. Grandpa had decided they ought to go to eastern boarding schools, which pushed Cissie to the brink of mutiny and started Albert howling and begging and to reviving the custom of wetting his pants; whereupon their mother stood him off, and the children were allowed to continue attending the local grade school and come home of nights. Undoubtedly she had loved them, but they hadn't constituted her whole existence by any means.

Cissie said Grandpa had already retired before their father died, and when that happened he had to resume an active life and take charge of the family businesses. Everybody knew of the change in short order, for he smoked cigars and drank liquor and shouted on the telephone and generally kept the place in an uproar. Mrs. Godby was hired by him as housekeeper, and their mother had nothing further to do with domestic arrangements. Because he refused to go downtown to an office, Grandpa was always home, and a constant stream of visitors entered and left from morning till night. At intervals he gave parties, citing the necessity of keeping alive the Brennan name and fame, and paraded Cissie and

Albert—until the latter developed into something of a social menace and had to be kept under cover until his brashness subsided.

Albert had a long history of being under Grandpa's thumb. He envied Cissie, whom the old man usually ignored. Unlike her, he was called on to listen to those hortatory lectures. The changeable moods of Grandpa baffled Albert; he never knew precisely where he stood. Touring the San Cristobal together, his great-uncle taught him to ride and handle guns and gave him half a glass of beer to drink every night, and their relationship was fine. It also flourished the day Albert got a bloody nose in a street-corner altercation, and Grandpa at once conveyed him to a Main Street gymnasium and had a rubbery-faced man teach him the elements of boxing and wrestling. If his mentor was in sufficiently good health, Albert could count on going to ball games, duck hunting, fishing and even a trip to Santa Catalina Island in a yacht. But contrasted to these halcyon times were the meetings in Grandpa's room, where he vainly attempted to establish a marriage of minds with Albert and discover an intelligence in him that didn't exist. Growing balky, Albert glumly endured torrents of instruction and considerable abuse.

Each birthday after Albert's eighth, Grandpa would call him in for a tête-à-tête. He kept hoping the boy had attained a maturity in excess of his years. "You must understand, Albert," he said, "that I am a leftover from a remote era. My days are numbered. It is up to you to carry on for our tribe, in spite of your youth. God knows how much longer I will last, at least in a state of sanity. Any moment you may have to assume your burdens. Put your mind to it, Goddamn it! Napoleon was a child general, Wolfe conquered Quebec and died at a tender age, Alexander the Great was a stripling. If we were ordinary people, you wouldn't be called upon to make this effort—it wouldn't be necessary. But it is necessary. We have the wealth and the opportunities. You have to fit the occasion. Given a touch of luck, you will be the best man the Brennans have yet produced . . . Don't sit staring at me open-mouthed, you horse's ass. Straighten up and anyway pretend you know what I'm talking about!"

He tried to indoctrinate Albert with his pronounced views. His *bête noires* were President Wilson and his Fourteen Points, women who smoked cigarettes, and William Gibbs McAdoo's handling of the railroads during the war. Crossing the Atlantic to aid the Allies was in his estimation an act of criminal folly. He grew empurpled while speaking of red anarchy, Communist propaganda, labor union dictators, prohibition, dishonest officeholders, Democrats, income taxes and the spread of pension systems. His voice soared as he inveighed against the World Court, praised the Ku Klux Klan, and excoriated William J. Bryan. At

178

the end of all of these sessions, he said mournfully that he hoped he passed on before the whiskey in the cellar was gone. Sometimes he became confused in his utterances, repeated himself, and once dozed off in the midst of a complicated explanation of how he had dealt with the Brennan capital. Assuming this was a normal disadvantage to living Albert bore up as best he could, listening groggily.

Mr. Sego and Mr. Lely assured him that he must take such lapses into account and not be fooled: Grandpa was still strong, acute, and remarkably capable. "His opinions are uncompromising," Mr. Sego said, "but they are well founded. He is a violent man, yes—only remember he dates from a violent time. His confidence in you is great [an outright lie, Albert believed], and he has a strong affection for you [which was doubtful]. Listen to him and learn. And don't think he isn't making money for you."

Of course, Mr. Sego was a prejudiced witness. Even Albert could tell that. Grandpa had taken a fancy to him and delegated a lot of authority. Harry, Mr. Sego's eldest son, told Albert of Colonel Brennan giving his father stock in the Sunset Sea Corporation, which hadn't happened when Albert's father was alive.

Grandpa's temper was very uncertain. Once he said, "My God, you've got no more expression on your face than a stinking Indian! Does anything I say to you get through? What have you in your skull for brains—soup? Can't you answer me?"

Suddenly maddened, Albert cried, "I don't care what you say! I'm not listening! If I could understand, I wouldn't!"

"That's better," Grandpa said, and grinned, showing the shining white teeth made by his most recent dentist. "Anyhow, you have some guts, and maybe you won't always be stupid. I'd rather see you brave than cowardly smart; the timid, no matter how bright, never can take a plunge and do really well . . . You're beginning to resemble me, boy. But for that I'd have you taken out and drowned."

Mr. Baltim simply ignored Albert's whinings, but Mr. Lely was sympathetic and less platitudinous than Mr. Sego. "I know it's difficult for you to swallow the colonel," he said, "particularly at your time of life. And it isn't your fault, it's his. But you've got to take into account his advanced age and impatient nature. When your father died he was in retirement and going downhill. Coming back into action has been a strain on him. He worries about your future and your sister's and feels you are the only one he can depend on. For your own protection, you ought to do everything possible to help him. Take into account, please, that every day he is living far beyond his strength and performing feats he couldn't have managed ten years ago—all in your behalf. Thanks to

179

him, you're going to be dirty rich. You have heard the old saw concerning the error of looking gift horses in the mouth, haven't you?"

Albert speculated on the relationship between Cissie and Grandpa. She would not discuss him. It was hard for Albert to believe that she resented her brother being the favorite. He thought her coldness toward the old man might have come from the time when he was five and their mother wanted to marry Dr. Eldred Loren. They had no inkling of a crisis until brought to an upstairs sitting room, where Dr. Loren, Grandpa and their mother awaited them. The war in Europe had yet to start, and life had been serene and quiet.

Their mother launched into an elaborate explanation which was fairly clear to Cissie, but confounded Albert. She was lonely and tired of living in seclusion, and concerned by the children's lack of a father. Dr. Loren had done her the honor of asking her to be his wife, and she felt she would like being married to a doctor; she was a doctor herself, as they knew. However, she wasn't going to do anything to hurt or worry them, and she had to have their assent to her marrying. Would they like to have Dr. Loren as their new father? Were they agreeable to moving to another house? One of these days Dr. Loren might want to return to New York; was that all right with them?

Albert looked wildly and indecisively at Cissie, who was pokerfaced. Never having known his own father, the conception of acquiring another was neither repellant nor realizable. He liked the doctor well enough, without really knowing him. Loren was merely a threatening presence when he was ill and confined to bed, and otherwise forgotten. That their mother desired to live with him, and take them along, was something he'd need years to come to a decision on.

"Before either of you answers," Dr. Loren said, "I can assure you I'll provide a good home and all the love you're willing to accept from me. I'll try to make up for the loss of your real father without doing any disrespect to his memory. If you'd like, I will give you my name."

Cissie started to reply to him, and Grandpa cut her off. "No, this won't do," he said. "We're not taking Loren into the family or sharing what we have, and I won't surrender the children. And they belong in the Queen by right of heritage—they aren't going to New York. I know what you're after, Allie. You couldn't forgive Cass for taking your profession away from you, and now you see a chance of picking up where you left off with a partner more to your taste. But it's too late. You made your choice years ago. If you had half a marriage with Cass, what will you have with Loren? Nothing better, I'd bet. Forget it."

"Colonel," Dr. Loren said, "why not allow the children to answer before you make up your mind?"

180

"The hell with their infantile opinions," Grandpa retorted. "You are not going to be cut in on the riches Cass and I have piled up for them. You are not going to take them away from here or from me. Defy me and you'll be sorry. I have control, and you'll spend ten years in court fighting for them and one red cent of their inheritance. They're Brennans, and they'll stay Brennans."

"I'm not interested in their money," Dr. Loren said. "Can't you think of anything else?"

"Not when there's a possibility I might have to part with some of it," Grandpa said.

"Cissie, Brother—" Loren said. "I'm afraid your great-uncle is being very unfair. He is more concerned for himself than he is for you or your mother. Now, your grandmother approves of the marriage. She isn't strong enough to come here and tell you that today, but you can take my word for it and ask her later."

"Doña Maria has no idea of where she is or what she's doing," Grandpa said. "The kids know that."

"Cissie?" their mother said. "What do you think?"

"I guess you ought to marry him," Cissie said. "He's all right. I don't mind having a father, and I'd like to go to New York."

"You're a damned little fool," Grandpa roared. "Brother, do you want to leave home and go clear across the country and have to find a whole bunch of new friends? Do you want to stop being a Brennan and lose me? What of the hunting and fishing trips we're going on, and the motorcar rides, and the times at the ranch? Your father was a good man and gave you the chance for a fine future, here where you ought to be. Will you like having another name and living back east in snow and cold?"

"I wish you'd say something to the boy, Allie," Loren said. "In my position it's hard to speak—"

"Perhaps it is too late," their mother said.

All of them gazed solemnly at Albert. At first he felt courageous and important, and then started to tremble. A wave of distorted images and conflicting emotions plunged through his mind. Grandpa meant nothing, but neither did Dr. Loren. And he could not leave the town, the house, the ranch, everything he knew and loved. Blubbering, he implored their mother to let him alone. He said he hated Dr. Loren and didn't want a second father. He threatened to get sick if they took him away. As a last resort, he wet his pants. He threw himself on the floor in the puddle.

Their mother closed her eyes. "Take him out, please, Cissie," she said.

"What is the verdict, Allie?" Grandpa asked. "The little bastard made it plain, didn't he?"

181

"It's too late," their mother said, as Cissie wrestled Albert to his feet.

"Well, I expected no more," Loren said quietly, "with such an important thing as a fortune involved. Money talks louder than I can."

"You must understand," their mother said. "I can't jeopardize the future of Cissie and Brother, and I can't desert them. Blame Lucius, not me."

"I do," Loren said. "And I understand. May I still be your physician?"

"You may be anything your heart desires," Grandpa said, "except a member of my family."

Outside, the door shut on the adults, Cissie slapped Brother with such vigor that she sent him sprawling. On his hands and knees, he tearfully begged her pardon for a fault he did not know he had committed. "You're just dirty and foolish," she said, "and afraid of Grandpa. He's no better than you are. Get up—I want to knock you down again."

Albert rose and received another felling blow. As he lay weeping, his sister said, "Grandpa can make everybody do what he wants. Everybody but me."

Nothing further was said to them about the marriage. They did not discuss it with each other, and Grandma, lost to the world, never mentioned the subject. Dr. Loren's visits were less frequent, but his manner toward the children remained unchanged. Their mother appeared the same to Albert, and made no allusion to the scene in the upstairs sitting room, although he rather expected a chiding for dampening his pants. For his part, he was afraid to attempt an explanation or apology, and within days had forgotten the incident.

Cissie's help wasn't necessary to him in recalling the death of their mother. He had passed his ninth birthday by then, and the memory was vivid and sometimes troubling. It was mingled with fragments of times which were stirring and pleasurable—the Red Cross Parade of forty thousand marchers, the Liberty Loan drives, the fear of nearby Mexico helping the enemy, the shipyard his great uncle invested in where Albert saw the building of steel ships, Cissie and the women in the house (not their mother) rolling bandages and knitting wool mufflers, the vegetable plot hastily installed in the rear garden and tended by Hank Isbrow, and the Thrift stamps he bought in school. Troop trains left, bands played, women wept. Looking forward to joining the fray in a few years was an agreeable means of daydreaming. As a patriotic small boy, Albert was alert for signs of German sabotage and possible I.W.W. conspirators, who were reputed to be firing the barns and haystacks of farmers. There were military camps in Arcadia at the old racetrack and at San Pedro, and men drilled in the Armory in Exposition Park. Even the Armistice was not too disappointing. With Cissie, he fled from the house, despite orders to the contrary, when the siren on the roof of the Los Angeles *Times* gave the signal, and joined the wild mobs on the streets. The clamor of the yelling and tolling bells and auto horns and music and parades continued for hours; streetcars stopped, business houses closed, and bunting and flags broke out all over. Many were injured, but Albert and his sister managed to avoid getting hurt. Coming home at last, they found Grandpa drunk, the servants gone, and only Grandma's forbidding nurse at her post. Their mother, not bothering to reprove them, made them undress and bathe and prepared supper before they fell into bed.

Albert paid little attention to the influenza epidemic. Germs or microbes, or whatever it was, were outside his scope, and he enjoyed disguising himself by wearing a gauze mask. For a while the schools were closed, and he ran amok with Cissie, who had a girl's bicycle and was willing to accompany him anywhere. She was accepted as an equal by the other boys, and could play games skillfully and had plenty of physical endurance. If a fight developed, she could be counted on to take care of herself. Discipline was erratic in the Brennan household, with Grandpa enforcing the rules by fits and starts and refusing to give the servants any authority, and Albert and Cissie abused the latitude given them. They rarely gave thought to their mother's views; she was much in her room, books strewn on the counterpane of her bed, and seemed to have become nearly as nonexistent as Grandma.

One day in winter, with the scourge of influenza lessening, she fell ill. Dr. Loren, having seen the housekeeper through a mild bout, said there was no cause for worry; nevertheless, he watched her carefully, for the infection appeared to spare the very young and very old and strike hardest at those in middle life. Warned to keep a safe distance from her, Cissie and Albert were taken to her to pay their respects. Their mother looked tired and pale, and spoke to them in a hoarse voice. A nurse was attending her. While he shook a clinical thermometer, Dr. Loren frowned. After she had hoped they were behaving themselves and regretted she could not give them a kiss, he said: "I don't like that attitude you have of a Dickens heroine, Allie. You know patients full of resignation worry doctors. Brace up."

She smiled and said, "I feel exactly like a Victorian maiden. If the pneumococci or streptococci don't get me, I'll probably just pine away from ennui. It's been too long and too dull, dear doctor."

"Stop that!" he said. "You aren't badly off."

Grandpa entered the room in his stiff-legged fashion. "How are you, Allie?" he asked. "You've got to get up and take care of me. My waterworks have gone to seed again."

"Count on me," she said. "I can't afford to neglect my last patient."

"There's something else," Grandpa said, and paused until he had cleared his throat. "We haven't seen enough of each other lately. I've been too damned busy. But you know how I feel about you. You're different. Maybe I have a little sense of guilt. Don't give me any trouble."

"Is that an apology?" she said.

"You could call it that," Grandpa said.

"I accept it as such," she said. "Lucius, you have finally shocked me. You win."

"No, you win," Grandpa said. "I want you at my funeral. Please remember."

Albert and Cissie did not see their mother again until she was in her coffin. During the night she took a turn for the worse, and next morning Dr. Loren telephoned for an ambulance and had her removed to a hospital. Through the following two days Grandpa was up and about at all hours, drinking whiskey and smoking, and the children were warned by Grandma's nurse not to mention to the old lady that their mother was ill. Suddenly they were called from school, met by Grandpa and Hank in the Pierce-Arrow, and driven rapidly across town. At the hospital they had to stay in a waiting room while Grandpa visited their mother. He came back to them sallow and bleary-eyed, and his hands shook while he lit a cigar. Dr. Loren followed him.

"You tell them, Goddamn it," Grandpa said.

Kneeling before them, Dr. Loren took their hands. "I'm terribly sorry," he said. "Your mother is dead. You must be brave and accept the fact. She had pneumonia, and there was nothing I could do."

Cissie began to cry, to Albert's astonishment. He joined her in tears. If she wept—which was almost never—then it was all right for him to express a confused and unbelieving grief.

"Now I am up shit creek!" Grandpa said, and left them. Hank took them home, and the servants showed great consideration, even to Albert. Where Grandpa went was not disclosed. He failed to return until late the next afternoon, haggard and angry.

"She's gone," he said, having had them sent to his room. He sat in bed with a cat in his lap and a glass in his hand. "We did the best we could. This is the last time we are going to discuss it. For Christ's sake don't go around wringing your hands and bawling like calves. It happens to us all. She was a good woman and deserved better, and she missed something in life. But that's not our fault. We've got to stick together and keep what we have. You're the new generation of Brennans, and you'll have everything. Live up to that fact. Now, get out of here."

184

He proved himself a man of sentiment, however, writing to their mother's family in Wisconsin—nobody replied to him—and observing a wish she had expressed to Dr. Loren in her last hours that her body be cremated. Her ashes were interred in a grave adjoining that of her husband in Rosedale Cemetery. No service was held, and only Grandpa and Dr. Loren observed the cremation.

Grandpa was caught up by the novel process and added a codicil to his will instructing his executors to give him the same treatment after death. Still in a mood of penance and conciliation, he went to Grandma to inform her of her daughter-in-law's end, had second thoughts, and resorted to the merciful lie that she had gone home to see her ailing parents. During periods of lucidity, Grandma continued to inquire from the children and others for their mother, but she was never told the truth. Gradually she seemed to forget, as did Albert, whose conception of what had happened was hazy and not stimulated by great interest or sorrow. He was somewhat astonished to find that Cissie went on mourning, and would break into tears at the mention of their mother's name; he hadn't realized she was so touched, nor as feminine as she revealed, and she fell a little in his estimation.

Next Memorial Day, whiskey on his breath and chomping a cigar, Grandpa ordered them to accompany him to two cemeteries, Rosedale and an old Roman Catholic one on Buena Vista Street, where their grandfather Cassius, great-grandfather Don Ygnacio Villanueva, and divers other ancestors were buried. They put flowers beneath the headstones and watched as Grandpa stood and looked glumly at the grave of Cassius Brennan, muttering to himself. When he'd had enough, Grandpa said, to nobody in particular: "Never again. Why should I have been spared? It's sufficient to ruin your faith, if you had any. If there is another world, God knows I don't want to meet them and have to justify myself or try to lie my way out of it. To hell with the past—it's unhealthy!" And they did not observe a second Memorial Day, although Albert knew Cissie sometimes went to Rosedale alone carrying flowers she had picked in the garden.

His sister fascinated Albert. He regarded her with great respect. Her influence on him was undiminished. He tried to understand her, naturally taking into account that she was a girl and getting to a certain age. Happily, he had not yet seen her sewing, playing a piano, learning to dance, or flouncing around in elaborate dresses in the revolting display her contemporaries made. She still could fight like a cat, all spinning speed and teeth and claws and pure ferocity, and bat a ball and run

185

bases. Hank appreciated her helping him work on the autos, an honor Albert had yet to win. Having her was as good as having a brother.

Cissie's ambitions outdid his own. When she had been a mere babe, in 1910, Grandpa, forever charmed by new inventions, took her to the famous air meet at Dominguez Field. She had seen a Frenchman named Paulhan establish a record by flying forty-five miles in a Bleriot monoplane, and Art Hoxie, a Pasadena boy, crash and lose his life right in front of the crowd. The day had made a lasting impression on her. To sail through the air, to fly, to leave the earth and taste an unearthly freedom lay in the core of her dreams; no matter that she was the wrong sex, that Grandpa had lost interest in what he called airships and thought they had no future except in war and indignantly rejected her plea that he arrange for her to ride in one, that a woman piloting a flying machine was patently ridiculous. The frail contraptions of coated cloth and wooden spars and myriad wires and clattering engines had lighted a fire in her heart. She read everything she could on the subject. With cleverer hands than Albert's, she built kites, little hot air balloons that actually rose, and models of airplanes fighting on the western front. Rubber band-powered designs made in her workshop in the coach house soared from one end of the garden to the other. Once Mrs. Gonzales, peering out of a kitchen window, was struck by a tiny replica of a Fokker triplane and had hysterics for half a day, with no meals until the following morning as a result.

Cissie impressed and worried Albert. He had a secret fear of heights, and just thinking of flying made his stomach billow. The idea of being a Charles Nungesser or Captain Eddie Rickenbacker in devil-may-care boots, leather jacket and helmet was intriguing, but to risk your neck in peacetime was silly; he reluctantly discarded any thought of participating in his sister's plans, if she were foolish enough to go ahead with them someday. That didn't stop him from admiring her for having visions which paled his own, and caused the careers of federal agents and jungle adventurers to seem humdrum.

Albert's lone confidant was Lagonda. He could tell her anything. She was a large, raw-boned, blue-black young woman with honest brown eyes, kinky hair and liver-colored lips.

"Well," Albert said, "I could be a turd, but I won't be. I'm strong and I don't get sick, and probably I'll turn out to be a good ballplayer. Still, I wish I looked a little better."

"I never seen no better looking boy than you," Lagonda said. "Don't you pay any attention to what I say?"

"Oh, sure. I got a pretty good build, I guess. I'm getting bigger all the time. But I'm short on brains."

"Who say so?"

"Grandpa."

Lagonda shook her head in exasperation. "The colonel don't hold with nobody. You're smart. Mark my words, you'll turn out to be smart as any of them, maybe smarter. Don't worry your head. Pretty soon you'll be as tall as him. He calls me a foolish nigger and laughs at me, but I know better than he does about you."

"You never know where you are with him," Albert said. "Do you think we look alike?"

"I do, I do."

"I hate to hear you say that."

"Why?" Lagonda said. "Old like that, he's a fine looking man. He ain't sweet, but he looks like what he is."

"Well, let me get on the Vernon team and hit a couple of home runs and they'll all change their tune. But I wish I could be more like Cissie, even if she is a girl."

"Don't say that. She's a queer one, like her mother. Nobody knows what goes on in her head. I love her, but she ain't like you."

"That flying, though," Albert said. "What do you think about that?"

"I don't know. I don't think of it. It makes me dizzy."

Albert was on the brink of telling her it made him dizzy, too. He decided against going overboard. Some confessions were not good for the soul. Lagonda urged him to wash and put on a clean shirt, and he complied from force of habit. She dried the back of his neck and behind his ears, saying, "Cissie forget that stuff. There comes a time when girls forget everything except one thing."

"Not Cissie," Albert said. "She's the farthest from a turd I ever saw."

"Don't use that word all the time."

"Why not? Everybody does. Lagonda, I'll tell you something—I might grow into a turd, but I'll be so rich they won't dare laugh at me. Isn't that right?"

"Yes," Lagonda said. "Old colonel, he fix that. But you won't be no turd, mark my words. Someday they'll be laughing on the other side of their faces."

Dr. Loren came with increased frequency to the house, treating both Grandma and Grandpa. The latter's ailment was hemorrhoids, which gave him fits and soured what little milk of kindness remained in him. Presently he had to go to the hospital for an operation. He returned after a few days in a high temper, and his painful arising and sitting were comical to watch; but Albert was careful not to exhibit his amusement. Grandpa cursed his "fiery ass" and compared it to Job's boils, to the scandal of the housekeeper and cook. "Nothing on this planet compares to the horrors of advancing age," he said. "Who in his right mind, contemplating the old crocks around him, would care to live past forty? The Spanish Inquisition could not have devised a torture to match my fundament! Every defecation is an auto-da-fé!"

Yet his handicaps increased rather than diminished his energy. Complaining of sleeplessness, he roved through the house nights, smoking, drinking and concocting fresh schemes. However balmy the temperature, he was cold, and took to wearing knitted vests and a vast shawl around his shoulders. His cheeks sank and exposed two huge cheekbones, which loomed over the uncertain, nervously constant movement of his jaws as his false teeth threatened to pop from between his lips. When creaking legs restricted his movements, he established a headquarters in the solarium, with a pale and unhappy young female stenographer to take his loud dictation and a telephone beside the half-reclining chair he ordered built along the lines of the chairs he had found comfortable on shipboard. Amid glittering sunlight, waving plant fronds, and the mingled smells of fertilizer, cologne and cigar smoke, he received Mr. Sego and Mr. Lely more often and kept them longer in business discussions.

While Grandpa flourished, Grandma gradually slipped away. Her grim nurse stopped wheeling her in the garden, and the food trays brought upstairs were untouched. Mrs. Gonzales, who was the nurse's only friend in the establishment, relayed word to Mrs. Godby that Grandma had had another severe stroke and was in a sad state. And Dr. Loren informed Grandpa that he feared he had discouraging news. "Jesus, Mary and Joseph!" Grandpa said. "What else have you ever brought me?"

Attended by Albert and Cissie, he grunted up the steps for a ceremonial visit. Albert, lately introduced to the history of ancient Egypt, thought Grandma, swathed in bedclothing, resembled a mummy except for the exposed, wasted countenance and dark purblind eyes which moved blankly from face to face. She was, unexpectedly, talking a great deal in a whispery voice, but she had reverted to Spanish. The two words Albert could distinguish were "San Cristobal" repeated again and again. "What is she saying, Grandpa?" asked Cissie.

"Nothing sensible," Grandpa replied. "Something about the ranch and wanting to see it. I think she's afraid we've lost the land."

He sat down beside the bed and addressed her in her own language. She kept on speaking, apparently not to him. He shook his head in irritable despair. "What are you saying, Grandpa?" asked Albert.

"I was telling her I loved her once," Grandpa said, "or thought I did, and that now my heart is filled with regret and sorrow. By God, it is.

But the poor old soul can't understand a word." He glanced up at the impassive Dr. Loren, standing in the doorway. "The only satisfactory deathbed scenes you come on are in plays or books. You don't get them in real life."

"True," the doctor agreed. "Dying is a slow process, like birth—a going to sleep. One is not here one minute, fully awake, and gone the next."

Grandpa got up. "Well," he said, "she's had a long journey and she's worn out. She needs a rest, so let her go to sleep. It wasn't the best possible journey—and I had a hand in determining that—but I suppose none of them come up to expectations . . . You kids: say goodbye to her."

Neither Cissie nor Albert were of a mind for weeping. "We're always saying goodbye to somebody around here," Albert said rebelliously, and was treated to a malevolent glare from Grandpa. He sat at the side of Grandma and held her cold, chalky fingers. In the background was her forbidding companion, dissolved in tears. Grandma had relapsed into silence, but she seemed to recognize Albert and started talking in Spanish again. She looked to be trying very hard to tell him something. She said "San Cristobal" several times. Then she grew quiet and closed her eyes. They did not open when Cissie took Albert's place. Rising and falling, Grandma's breast showed how difficult it was for her lungs to get the breath of life into her. Dr. Loren suggested that the visitation had gone on long enough.

"Come with me, kids," Grandpa said. "She doesn't know us anymore. She's already over on the other side."

They were all back in a few hours. Grandma was harshly breathing her last. Grandpa went to the telephone and called a priest. He was a young man in a queer round hat, and appeared a bit rattled. Albert watched in fascination as the priest anointed Grandma's forehead with oil and gave absolution. Kneeling at the foot of the bed, Grandpa listened to the prayers for the dying, crossed himself, and joined in saying "Hail Mary, full of grace . . ." The priest had to help him to his feet, and Grandpa wore a strange, hurt expression for a few moments.

Scarcely believing what he had seen, Albert later devoted some thought to Grandma and the way she kept saying the name of the San Cristobal. She must have meant the ranch because St. Christopher wasn't her patron saint. But why? What did she have to do with it, except that he had heard she lived there as a girl? She had not been to the ranch in years. It was mystifying.

Grandpa turned from reverence to the business of giving Grandma a proper send-off. "This is a means of making up for omissions and the committing of flagrant evils by the living," he said to Albert, who had to wait some years before the intrinsic sense of his uncle's remarks were clear. "All the ancient peoples followed the custom, so why the hell shouldn't I bow to an atavistic impulse? They laid 'em in pyramids and long boats and in marble sarcophagi beside the Appian Way and burned 'em in great funeral pyres, surrounded by their gold and jewels and slaughtered animals and servants. I wish I could dress Doña Maria in rich vestments, fill her pockets with oil leases, and kill her Goddamned nurse to put at her feet for the crossing of the Styx." Later he said, with a certain satisfaction: "Now we will witness the last uprising of the earlier outsiders. Every poor Spanish-Mexican bastard in the county is going to show up."

It was a splendid funeral. Grandma had a solemn High Requiem Mass at St. Vibania's Cathedral, and was interred next to her husband in a towering rose-colored vault in Buena Vista Cemetery. The newspapers carried extended accounts of Doña Maria, those aristocratic first citizens, the Villanuevas, the San Cristobal, the martyred Cassius Brennan, the heroic son who followed in his footsteps, and that living pioneer legend, Colonel Lucius Brennan. The mass of floral tributes was overpowering, the messages of condolence endless. In somber black, and sporting a ruffled shirt and a silk hat, Cissie and Albert accompanying him, Grandpa was a distinguished figure at the services. Universal respect bemused him. "My God," he said, "I'm all alone! Everybody else has died off. There's no one left to remember my sins. I've become respectable."

When they were home, and the luxurious wake to which Grandpa had invited more than two hundred people was ended, Cissie said to Albert, "This is an unlucky house. Nothing good ever happens here. I don't want to stay in it any longer." He was surprised and hurt. It seemed to him perfect, other than for the volcanic presence of Grandpa, and Grandma in her room or in her grave was surely of no importance. There was plenty to eat, servants to pick up after you, Hank and the automobile, Lagonda . . .

He attempted to tell Cissie that, and she said, "Oh, shut up, you turd!" and went to Grandpa with a request that she be sent away to boarding school. Albert trailed after her.

"Why?" Grandpa demanded.

"I hate this place," Cissie said.

"And hate me too, I presume," he said. "Well, be patient. You have only one more to bury, and then you can turn the Goddamned house into a dance hall if you prefer."

"I don't hate you," Cissie said. "That has nothing to do with it, Grandpa. I'm serious."

190

"So am I," he said. "You don't much like me, do you?"

"Not much," Cissie replied, looking straight at him. Albert experienced a thrill of horror.

"Thank you for being honest," Grandpa said, and grinned coolly. "I could scarcely have hoped to have won your affection, even if I had wanted to—and I'm not sure I did—and anyway I'm too old to understand a girl two generations removed from me. But we have to get along, you see, because we belong to the same tribe—and because we have a hell of a lot of money. Let it go at that."

"Am I going away to school?" Cissie asked.

"I don't know," Grandpa said. He looked at Albert. "What do you say? Or are you about to also beg for freedom?"

"Oh, no," Albert said. "I don't want to go anywhere, and I don't think Cissie ought to either."

"Then it's settled," Grandpa said. "We've just heard from the future head of the family. You'll stay with us, Cissie, and make the best of it."

"Do you know how I'll make the best of it?" Cissie said. "I'll flunk every course in school."

"That suits me," Grandpa said. "Ignorant women are more acceptable than smart ones. Your mother was brainy and educated, and had an unhappy life. Since you resemble her too much for my taste, you'll probably benefit by being unlettered."

"I'll run off," Cissie said, and Albert shuddered.

"We'll get you back," Grandpa said. "But I admit I don't like the prospect of a public scandal. Albert, what do you think?"

"I think she's turning into a turd," Albert said bitterly.

"Really?" Grandpa said. "All women are peculiar, you know. Not a bit like us . . . Give me a week to consider, Cissie. I'll try to work out a compromise."

But it was Albert who did the compromising. Appalled at the prospect of losing Cissie, he invaded her room that night, begged her not to carry through the threats she had made, painted his own position in woeful colors, drew a portrait of Grandpa as a senile, nutty but kindly old man, unloved and unappreciated, and finally began to sob. "If you go," he said, "I'll have to go with you. I couldn't stay here with only Lagonda. They might put us in jail, Cissie!"

"Why don't you pee your pants?" said his sister in disgust.

His pleading knew no depths. "I think I might," he said. He prostrated himself for calling her a turd, and dwelt on the sad assumption that poor Grandpa would soon be joining their father and mother and Grandma under ground.

"He'll live forever," Cissie said. "I gave up counting on getting rid of *him* long ago."

"Cissie!"

"Don't you want me to tell you the truth?"

"Well, yes . . ."

She got up and started him toward the door. "All right. Quit crying, you big baby. I won't run away."

"You promise?" he said. "Cross your heart and hope to die?"

"Yes!"

"And you won't flunk out in high school?"

"No."

"That makes me feel better. Gee, thank you, Cissie. I—"

"I'm doing this for you," she said. "Because you're just a bowl of jelly. But you've got to do something for me."

"Sure, Cissie."

"When you're head of the family, the way Grandpa says—if you ever are—will you give me anything I want?"

"Anything," Albert said.

"Is your word good?"

"Not with anybody else, but it is with you. You know that."

She stared at him for a second or two, her expression gradually softening. Gently, with her fingers, she wiped the tears from his cheeks. Then she kissed the tip of his nose. "I'm sorry I beat you up all those times when you were little," she said. "You're okay, Al."

His heart was full of love for her. And some of that affection was transferred to Grandpa, perhaps on account of the lovable character he had given him; he was a bit taken with this new conception of the old bastard. On his part, Grandpa seemed to try to live up to the softer role, restraining his criticisms of Albert after the row with Cissie and rather cultivating him. Their relations steadily improved. Albert's advice was asked in regard to his sister, and he divulged that he had persuaded her to cool off, which evoked flattering expressions of esteem from Grandpa.

"You're invaluable," he said, among other things. "Give me more of your counsel, Prince Albert. What shall we do next with the young Victoria? She's a dirty-necked tomboy and has a big head. Without a mother, she has no one to model herself on in this house—Mrs. Godby is a foolish old bitch with airs and pretensions beyond her station. Public school is doing nothing for Cissie, from what I can see. And pretty soon she'll have to become a gentlewoman. Have you a suggestion?"

Albert felt set up by the responsibility conferred upon him, but he was nonplussed. There was a Westlake School for Girls, Grandpa went

192

on, the creation of a pair of respected ladies from the faculty of the University of Southern California. Maybe they could file the rough edges off Cissie. The moment Albert heard she might enroll as a day scholar, he was for the move. Grandpa sent him to Cissie to propose it, advising caution and diplomacy. Albert thought he conducted the affair with skill. His circumlocutions were immense. Rome wasn't built in a day, and he proceeded slowly, prepared at any moment to cry or to depict Grandpa as a broken-hearted and dying old devil. Pulling out the tremolo stops was unnecessary; Cissie accepted the idea without argument, evidently on the basis of any alteration being for the better, and changed schools. Eager to report to Grandpa, Albert watched for improvement in her. It was hard to discover. Cissie was possibly a little neater and sometimes she brushed her hair, but grease still lay under her fingernails and she never brought home friends of her own age or evinced interest in the usual concerns of normal young ladies. Nevertheless, Albert told Grandpa a different Cissie was developing, happier, not so absentminded, and less likely to spit in your eye—he had suddenly discovered the smooth efficacy of telling people what they wanted to hear and the pleasures of not giving a damn about the truth.

One day in the solarium, a shawl draped on his shoulders and steel-rimmed spectacles perched on his nose, Grandpa drew his tufted eyebrows together and said: "Albert, what do you think of me?"

Albert was startled. "What do you mean, what do I think of you, Grandpa?"

"Precisely that. You needn't be polite. What are your feelings toward me?"

"Well, I don't know . . . I don't think about it. You're my grandfather and everything—my great-uncle, I mean."

"I'm sure I'm your grandfather, your real grandfather."

"You are?" Albert said. That was exceedingly difficult to comprehend, and he wondered if the old boy was having another of his flighty spells; he was nutty at times.

"We won't go into the Goddamned thing," Grandpa said, "but I am. Will you take my word for it?"

"Yes."

"You actually believe me?"

Albert nodded, secretly stirred and curious, and yet not terribly interested.

"Does this change anything between us?" Grandpa asked.

"I don't know . . . should it?"

"Consider it this way: I'm a poor old son of a bitch with one foot in the grave, and you are my only connection with the future. Cissie doesn't care for me. She won't remember me or take into account anything I've done, and days come now when I think I want to be remembered—even remembered with some degree of fondness. As my brain softens, I seem to be trying to clasp hands with you, Albert. Do you like me?"

"Sure I do."

"We've grown closer of late, haven't we?"

"Yes, we have," Albert said.

"I resembled you once," Grandpa said. "My life was ahead of me and endless, and I thought of women and money and power and being different from the damned fools around me. Maybe you are a throwback. If you are, a little of this might make sense. If you can come to love and remember me and continue what I brought to your father and you, I could have a taste of immortality and lie quieter where I'm going. Do you feel that's possible?"

"I guess so."

"Do you understand me at all?"

Albert stared at him. A dawning, puzzling, amorphous comprehension flooded him. Without doubt, without the need for explanation, he perceived this old man was part of him and unique and precious and the essence of his blood and bones and memory. It was like a shaft of brilliant light piercing him. His eyes filled with tears. He longed to say something which was unsayable, to reach out and touch his grandfather. Grandpa's eyes were wet, too.

"Take my hand," he said.

They gripped hands. "I don't like you," Albert said. "I love you, Grandpa. I didn't know it before, that's all."

"Yes," Grandpa said. "I thought it might happen. With you here, I didn't waste everything, did I? Albert, there's just one path through this. Be your own man. Your father never was. Be me again. Live as long and as hard as you can. Piss on all of them."

Their hands parted, and the moment passed. It was never repeated. When Albert considered it afterward, he could not completely appreciate what had happened to him. But he had crossed the line. Grandpa's elliptical message had got through. He was not exactly Lucius Brennan again, but he was a Brennan, and to the manner born.

two

As a sophomore at L.A. High—not the old redbrick one on North Hill Street, but the dignified new edifice out on Olympic Boulevard—Albert blossomed and acquired confidence. The days of dampening his pants and weeping were put far behind. He played football and baseball, didn't exactly star in track, belonged to the Debating Society and the Student League, and was elected vice president of his class. Stylish in bell-bottom trousers, he considered himself something of a man of the world and was justly popular. He had discovered girls without falling in love, and sang bass in a quartette that entertained at dances. With a cut-down Ford roadster capable of forty-five miles an hour and a generous allowance to spend, he thought life full and rich. His academic standing, unfortunately, was not very impressive.

Time was a problem with him. He simply didn't have enough of it. An athletic program required many hours, he had social obligations, Grandpa required his attention, as did Cissie, and he could not neglect Hal Baltim, Junior, his best friend. Nor was Lagonda ever slighted, although she had, to his secret hurt, become Mrs. Ferris Washington and went home to her bridegroom every night after doing the washing and cleaning to which she had been consigned when Albert and Cissie grew up.

Responsibility did not suit Albert, yet he had it forced upon him. Somebody had to take care of various everyday details, and he seemed to be the only candidate. A Graduate of the Westlake School for Girls and now enrolled in a business college (she had refused to go to a university), Cissie offered scant aid; she was annoyed by domestic crises and disappeared at the slightest hint of them. Grandpa was Albert's main problem; he had participated avidly in the mushrooming boom of 1923, but in the next year a prolonged sinking spell apparently robbed him of most of his powers, and he spent months confined to his room. His conversation became disordered, he could not concentrate, and even signing his name was difficult. Notwithstanding, he refused to surrender control, and Albert had to act as intermediary with Mr. Baltim and Mr. Lely, not to mention with Mrs. Godby, Mrs. Gonzales and the maid assigned to help Lagonda; it was Albert who decided on menus, called plumbers and electricians, settled the frequent disputes between Hank Isbrow and the housekeeper, ordered the house painted, brought urgent bills to his drowsing grandfather, and gave consideration to the future of Cissie.

Then, amazingly, Grandpa emerged from hibernation in 1925 and proceeded to enjoy an Indian summer. He was approaching his eighty-sixth birthday: walking was hard for him, he was quite deaf, and distressingly lank, but his head grew clear again, he could see fairly well, and his appetite for whiskey and cigars returned. The cellar had become depleted, and his first decision was to establish relations with a bootlegger Dr. Loren disapprovingly recommended in lieu of providing unlimited supplies of prescription liquor. Established once more in the solarium, bellowing into the telephone on the assumption that everyone he talked to was just as hard of hearing, he entered zestfully on a program of harrying the Messrs Sego, Baltim and Lely.

Though pleased by Grandpa's return to an indecent sort of activity, and grateful for relief from household and business burdens, Albert found there were disadvantages to a phoenix rising. The old man leaned on him and was too demanding. He needed company, and Albert was his mainstay. To refuse him was unthinkable. Cissie stood willing to have breakfast and dinner with him, and no more; the remainder of her leisure she spent by herself. Stoically, Albert resigned himself to the task of amusing Grandpa.

Among his duties was that of driving Grandpa around in the Ford roadster, for he had taken a liking to both the car and inspections of the city, and declined the services of Hank. Every day Albert could spare, until Grandpa's curiosity was exhausted, the pair of them covered a confounding sweep of loosely joined suburbs from the mountains to the sea. Driving was fun, and cutting classes, missing out on baseball practice, and allowing a budding romance or two to languish was not overly onerous, but Albert's interest in Los Angeles quickly subsided. That the great bowl of land had been occupied and reduced to an unappetizing conglomeration of houses, buildings, factories, stores, streets, and traffic appeared to him self-evident and not surprising, and the wonderment of his passenger struck him as a little crazy. Tremendous growth had occurred during his own few years. For example, the high school he attended was, when Cissie first went to it, far out of town, and after the streetcars the students then used put Western Avenue behind, only open fields and isolated dwellings met the eye; now neat residential blocks and an array of cross streets intervened, and the rabbits and gophers had vanished. What was so remarkable about that? Why shouldn't people move in and settle down?

Grandpa told him, upon his venturing an opinion. "You're a newcomer, Albert," he said, "and I've been here overlong. My God, who would have thought it? I made a speech once, I think it was on the hundredth anniversary of the town, and advised 'em to keep booming. Suppose I could have told them we'd have a million inhabitants by 1925! They would have committed me to an insane asylum. I was a promoter who cashed in on the optimism of '87 and got out hurriedly. Later on ruin came. Everybody lost hope and decided the Queen was through. But 1887 didn't hold a patch to 1923. Can't you see how improbable this place is? Everything's new each twenty-five years—citizens, spread, values, the things we live with. When I came here they used adobe for building, open ditches carried the water, bandits roamed the highroads, a steamboat was a novelty and railroads a dream. Now we've got radio, autos, telephones, electric lights, women in one-piece bathing suits, and the Goddamned government at war with people distilling whiskey. And there's more money to be made than ever!"

"Haven't you got enough?" Albert asked.

"That's a silly remark," Grandpa said. "Nobody ever has enough. You can make me look like a piker if you have any brains. This is Golconda—it's going to be the biggest city in the country in another century. All you have to do is ride the tiger."

He marveled at the harbor where ships could bunker crude oil for ten cents a barrel, at the forest of derricks on Signal Hill outside Long Beach, at proliferating Santa Monica, at the plushy suburb of Beverly Hills, at the sweep of Wilshire Boulevard, at the southward plains still undeveloped, at the gathering decrepitude of East Los Angeles in which lived the poorer immigrants and minorities cheek by jowl with flourishing industry, at the expansion in the San Gabriel and San Fernando Valleys, and at the mansions wintered in by eastern capitalists on the rim of the Arroyo Seco on the edge of Pasadena.

"West Adams Boulevard is finished," he mused. "The potentates from the Middle West who got rich selling groceries, harness and oranges are dying off, like the *hacendados* before them. And Orange Grove Avenue can't last—a trust-busting government and taxes will take care of it.

Where will the next bunch of outsiders go? West, I guess, toward the ocean breezes. Baltim says the business area won't grow past Figueroa Street, and then move south; but he's always wrong. Albert, your father had luck putting branch banks in the sticks, perhaps with a shove from me. The sticks didn't stay that way long. This isn't going to be a city on the design of any other. The Queen won't have a heart or cohesion, or the same people from generation to generation, and it'll copy the snake and grow a new skin every ten years. The center will lay wherever you persuade 'em to go, and force continually outward when men have to buy cheaper land. She's a huge, fat queen, a whore, ready to lie down and spread her legs anywhere for new lovers. She no longer needs a bed and a house and pimps to bring in the trade. Growing up late, she can afford to break all the rules. She's how cities will look in the twenty-first century, I think—a thousand villages and encampments, constructed to last out a mortgage in a mild climate—held together by telephone wires and rubber-tired wheels and entertainment sent through the air. San Francisco is pretty. Los Angeles is a phenomenon."

To Albert's relief the expeditions ended suddenly, and Grandpa went back to his financial pursuits and lying in his room, earphones clamped to his ears, listening to the radio that had such an enduring fascination for him. But the indoctrinating of Albert did not stop. The sentiment their relationship had developed was Grandpa's hold, and he never relaxed it. Slow-acting and imponderable, the training and views he imparted were nevertheless powerful. Despite unconscious resistance and a lack of interest, Albert's character was subtly formed. He developed independence, a ruthless quality, a seasoned hedonism, a conception of his own importance, and an appreciation of wealth. Quite early he realized he didn't have Grandpa's brains, his energy and prescience; this unabashed bit of self-knowledge tended to promote a stubborn cunning in him that he hoped would substitute for intellect. He slowly built up nerve and a hidden assurance.

The day arrived when Grandpa, with characteristic speed, decided on Albert's career for him. He solicited an opinion from Albert, but it was obvious that he had already come to a decision. Having abandoned dreams of playing for the Vernon team or prowling jungles, the victim had little to offer in rebuttal. "I haven't thought about it, Grandpa," he said. "Do I have to at sixteen? I wouldn't mind being a movie star, though. They make good money and have fun."

"You horse's ass!" said Grandpa. "Well, that just shows I have to act for you. We'll make you a lawyer, I expect. Your father's firm is waiting to receive you. What d'you say?"

"I guess it's all right," Albert replied. "But I can't give you ironclad guarantees. I'd have to get through law school, you know, and they say that's tough."

Grandpa thought that was only a detail; if he resolved that Albert was going to be a lawyer, then by God he'd be a lawyer. To say the firm awaited the scion of the family was something of an overstatement, however. Called over to hear a statement of his intentions, Mr. Baltim and Mr. Lely looked shocked. Lely, who was fond of Grandpa and inclined to a philosophic acceptance of his fancies, put up courteous token objections; but Baltim, a tall, thin, precise man, with the bare brow and righteous indignation of the public prosecutor he had been, hotly opposed taking another Brennan into the fold. He glared at Albert as if he conceived him to be the author of the outrage.

"Why?" Grandpa said. "You're still Brennan, Baltim and Lely and need another of us. We own a fifth. The name lends you prestige, and there is a sentimental value, too."

"I beg to differ, Colonel," Baltim said. "To imply a mere beginner, a youth, as titular head of the firm will expose us to ridicule. You are allowing pride to blind your judgment. It is nepotism of the rankest kind."

"What is nepotism?" Albert asked.

"There!" Baltim said. "Need we say more?"

"I won't enlighten you, Al," Lely said, and smiled. "Anyhow, you are going to discover the meaning without fail."

"I'll explain, Albert," Grandpa said, and a grim cast settled on his features. "Nepotism happens to constitute one of the many advantages of being a descendant of the successful and is another variation of the phrase 'money talks.'"

"Your explanation may not be clear to Albert," Baltim said, "but it is to me. Or was it intended for me?"

"Oh, I can be clearer with you," Grandpa told him. "Either take the boy in when he's ready or the firm will cease to exist. I'll purchase Burton here for his partner, and transfer my business to him. And then I'll devote myself to reducing your income. I can take the bank away from you, of course, and no doubt I can influence some of your other clients. If I have to blacken your name a little, I don't mind that either."

"You're an old man, sir," Baltim said, "and I forgive you such childishness. Let me remind you that the days of your freebooting are over."

"You think so?" Grandpa said. "I don't. I'll crucify you, you son of a bitch."

"Wait, wait," Lely said. "Please, gentlemen. After all, Albert is with us."

Crimson and furious, Baltim said, "I'm sure the colonel has raised the lad in his own image and that he's prepared for anything. Burton, what do you say to this? Are you going to desert me?"

"Not willingly," Lely said. "Why don't we count our blessings, Harold, and prepare to welcome Albert in the firm?"

"*If* I make it through law school," Albert said. "I warned Grandpa on that."

Baltim cooled slightly. "I hadn't considered that aspect," he admitted. "Albert may not be qualified for our profession—or conceivably for any other . . . Thanks for reminding us, my boy."

"You're welcome," Albert said.

"Shut up, Albert," Grandpa said.

"Colonel," Lely said smoothly, "it would hardly do for our young man, fresh from a bar examination he may not pass, to start as senior partner with us—we don't want them laughing, do we? Can't we become Brennan, Baltim, Lely *and* Brennan until Albert is prepared to take his rightful place in the firm?"

"Better yet," Baltim said, "why can't we go on without change and announce Albert's entrance in an associate's capacity?" He flinched. "Then in the years to come, after appropriate seasoning, he can succeed to the position his father occupied."

"I like Lely's suggestion," Grandpa said. "You can't have too many Brennans. We'll draw up a private agreement to the effect that Albert becomes head of the firm five years after he enters practice, providing he so desires, and that the second Brennan will be reserved for a son of his in due course."

"Oh, God . . ." Baltim said.

"Now there's an equitable solution," Lely said. "As a financial associate of the colonel's in various enterprises, together with Harold"—he paused significantly—"I don't feel we can afford to disagree. We have hired a couple of young lawyers and promised them limited partnerships in time, but their names need not appear in our title. The Brennan name does have magic."

"Does it?" Baltim said. "Well, we'll see. But I would not care to be requested to hand over to Albert the extra two-fifths interest we now share, would you, Burton?"

"That's yours," Grandpa said. "Don't worry, I'm not grasping. This is a question of the fitness of things."

"Yes, yes," Baltim said. "The fitness of things . . . Ha!"

"Albert," Grandpa said, "I think that's all we need you for. Your future is assured. Shake hands with your partners and run along."

Albert received a heartening grip from Lely and a limp one from Baltim. As he left, Grandpa was saying he would "sweeten the pot." He didn't want the boy launched on the lifework he had selected over any dead bodies.

In bringing order and direction to the family, Grandpa presently got down to an examination of Cissie's position. Albert was a consultant. "What is she up to?" Grandpa said. "What does she want? When I try to talk to her, she evades my questions. I've got to do something for her."

"Why, Grandpa? She's getting along fine in college."

"College, indeed! Is a business course suitable for a laborer's daughter the best we can manage for her?"

Albert thought uneasily of recent conversations with Cissie. She still meant to be a flyer, even at the cost of leaving home. It took every blandishment he could conjure up to prevent her from acting immediately. "Well," he said, "she's got to have some interest."

"It ought to be marriage, damn it," Grandpa said. "At nineteen, and an heiress, she should have young men following her everywhere. Why isn't she a debutante, being presented, taking a place in society? I've offered to encase my aged bones in a boiled shirt and give parties for her, and she will have none of it. Hasn't she any of the ordinary reactions of women?"

"Well, she's different. She—"

"You're close to her. Tell me what she says. She must have plans."

"Uh . . . she doesn't say," Albert said.

"She never brings anybody here, man or woman. Does she have men friends?"

"None I know of."

"She's in her room every night, except for going to a movie with you. What the hell is she doing?"

"Reading, I guess." Albert sighed, dreading closer interrogation. "You know how they are—they paint their nails and fix their hair—"

Grandpa shook a gnarled, admonitory forefinger. "Not her. You're stalling me, Albert. She's a copy of Allie, who didn't give a damn for feminine occupations. Does she really look terrible or is it that chopped-off hair and the shapeless dresses and a waistline a foot below her navel? Is her appearance so much against her she can't interest boys?"

Considering—for virtually the first time—Cissie's looks, Albert believed she was presentable. She was tall, wide-shouldered, narrow-hipped and long-legged, with bright blue eyes and a cleanboned freckled face and a closely cut mop of unruly brown hair usually combed only by her fingers. In male clothing she might have been taken for a graceful, delicate boy. Compared to the little Charleston-dancing pigeons who rolled their stockings below their knees and lathered on the lipstick, who wouldn't prefer his sister? "She's as good looking as most of them," he said.

"Then why hasn't she got suitors?"

"I guess she's got to find a guy who slays her."

"*Slays* her!" Grandpa said bitterly. "You can't even speak English. Listen, I'm going to have to marry her off. Who can we find worthy of the honor? I want somebody rich, handsome, potent and respectful. Have you any friends that would qualify?"

"Well, Hal Baltim or the oldest Sego kid—but they don't like her—"

"No, no! Not those puking infants from third-rate families. Her children have got to have a father with a recognizable name. You must help me hunt for him. We can't just put an advertisement in the newspapers, Goddamn it."

"Sure, I'll look around, Grandpa."

"Wait a minute. Is it possible she's found a man and is sleeping with him? Companionate marriage, maybe, as advocated by that damned judge from Denver—Ben Lindsay? In my day there were moral standards, but now—"

"Cissie? Oh, gosh no!"

"You're too dim-witted to trust. Does she smoke cigarettes?"

"Oh, no."

"Do you?"

"Oh, no," Albert said.

"Don't sit simpering and blushing like a schoolgirl who has had her titties handled," Grandpa said. "You look so guilty I'm inclined to believe you. But the truth is I've allowed you and Cissie to run wild. Your father belonged to things and led an ordered, respectable life, and for your sake I should have gone on in the same vein. I expect I'd better get you and Cissie in that hunt club in Pasadena, and the Cotillion Association and the Golden Pioneers. If only I was steadier on my pins, we could start lunching once a week at the Athletic Club. How about your playing a little golf and meeting some of the gentry?"

"I have to stick to baseball and football, Grandpa."

"Yes, damn it. You were born too late and I was born too early. Well, we shall make do with what we have . . ." Grandpa studied Albert closely, and his voice sank to a confidential level. "Favor me with your confidence, my dear boy. I'm a broad-minded man. Does Cissie happen to have a close friend who is a member of the fair sex?"

"I don't think so. Why?"

"Your mother had, before she married—Cass got a strange letter from the woman which I have kept. I always considered myself well versed in the peculiarities of human kind, but I must confess I was a trifle innocent of knowledge in a certain realm until your father had me read the letter and told me of his problems. Then I chanced to remember having been in a temple of joy where a couple of devotees of Sappho stripped to the buff and made love for the delectation of a paying audience. The effect was peculiar and disgusted me. Only later did it occur to me that the practice might be widespread. Which brings us to Cissie, Albert."

"Yeah?"

"You understand what I'm talking about, don't you?"

"What's Sappho?" Albert asked.

"The hell with it," Grandpa said. "I haven't sufficient time remaining to me for the instruction of babes and sucklings." He suddenly glared at Albert. "My memory betrays me these days. Have we ever had a talk on the subject of women?"

"No."

"My God! Methuselah probably went through this." Grandpa groaned. "Here I am knee-deep in a second generation, and once again called on to impart wisdom. What can a man say who hasn't had a satisfactory erection since Teddy Roosevelt's administration? And Goddamn him too for attempting to undermine the fortunate few! Uh . . . do you play with yourself?"

"Oh, no."

"You're a liar."

"Yes, I am," Albert said.

"Stop it," Grandpa said. "Aside from the customary objections, it's a fearful waste. There's a better way. Are you aware of that?"

"Well, I suppose you mean—"

"Precisely. Are you acquainted with any whores?"

"No," Albert said. Technically he was not, if the criteria involved acceptance of a fee. And he couldn't see the advantage to informing Grandpa of Hilda, a fifteen-year-old at high school who wore no teddies and had the habit of flipping her brief skirts to show her hairy crotch and give the boys a thrill. Hilda was constantly available and untiring. She furnished condoms, which she fitted personally. She exacted no payment. Whenever the spirit moved him, Albert took a bottle of expensive Canadian bourbon from the cellar, bribed Hank in order to use the Pierce-Arrow, picked up Hal and Harry Sego and perhaps one or two others, met Hilda on a street corner, and drove to an abandoned gravel pit on South Vermont Avenue. There Hilda accommodated her lovers without even removing her slippers. Nobody would call her a beautiful girl, but she was certainly better than nothing. Having her was not an unmixed blessing, for she was damp inwardly and outwardly, often became very agitated and broke wind while wriggling on the rear seat of the car, and refused to take off her clothing. Albert conceived of love in tenderer, more ethereal aspects, and intended eventually to rise to better companions. Someday, given the opportunity, he could see himself seducing a golden-haired college undergraduate at a summer resort in a luxurious hotel, or satisfying some hotbox of a married woman in her own bedroom behind drawn shades. Surely a bed would make a difference, and less sheer excitement might lend charm. What's more, these ideal encounters would transpire in the nude. Meanwhile he had driving urges to placate, and the comparing of notes with Hal and Harry enlivened conversations. Also, drinking whiskey and smoking cigarettes between sessions of pumping at Hilda were pleasant. She made for a confraternity at the school, as well; since she was a freshman, calculations were that she would have screwed every boy in the student body not hopelessly backward, ill, in training or smitten with religion by the time she graduated.

"You're sure?"

"Yes."

"Good," Grandpa said. He seemed weary and baffled. "Stay away from prostitutes or you're apt to get something you won't relish. Keep your pants buttoned, hear me? If I can live a few years, I'll select the right wife for you, and you can bring to her all the reserves she'll need to keep her busy and content. Grit your teeth and bear it. I don't know what else I can tell you for now. Exercise a lot and take cold showers."

"All right," Albert said. He was relieved to observe that Grandpa had evidently forgotten Cissie.

"You don't suffer, do you?"

"No."

"Splendid," Grandpa said. "Quit flogging yourself, understand? If you have any questions, feel free to bring them to me." He yawned. "We'll talk again soon. Has this been helpful?"

"Oh, yes," Albert said.

"Very well," Grandpa said. "I'm going to bed. Tell Mrs. Gonzales to send my supper up on a tray. Talking to you has made my God-damned back ache."

But next morning he remembered Cissie. Digging into a cantaloupe at the breakfast table, he said to her: "Albert and I have been discussing you. We think you ought to find some beaux and buy a new wardrobe and titivate yourself."

"Do you?" she said. Her forehead wrinkled as she glanced at Albert, and he stuck out his lower lip defensively and looked helpless.

"Well, don't you?" Grandpa demanded.

"No," Cissie said.

"Do you realize," Grandpa said, "that being a stenographer is one cut above being a chambermaid? You're rich and bear an honorable name, for Christ's sake. Where's your sense of duty?"

"I won't always be a stenographer," Cissie said.

"I suppose you believe in that nonsense of having a career," Grandpa said. "When are you going to discover you are a woman?"

"I've already discovered I'm a person," Cissie said, "which is something you won't concede me. I even have certain rights. What I do is my own business."

"Not till you're of legal age," Grandpa said.

"I'll wait," Cissie said.

"Let's not have a fight," Albert said. "We don't have to get excited—"

"Cissie," Grandpa said, "you are a pain in the ass. You have been since you were born, and I'm sick and tired of your insolence. Either recognize my authority or—"

"I don't recognize it," Cissie interrupted. "I never did. I won't do anything you say, and you might as well get used to the idea."

Grandpa glared at Albert. "What have I done to deserve this?" he said. "My life has been devoted to you. I am only trying to do my duty—to help, not to hinder. Oh, 'how sharper than a serpent's tooth'!"

"I haven't done anything," Albert said.

"Your duty as you see it, Grandpa," Cissie said, "is to have your own way. You're a slave driver. You're selfish and autocratic. But that won't work with me. Concentrate on Al—he's always been your darling, and he's licked. Leave me alone, please!"

"Go on in that fashion, Miss," Grandpa said, "and I'll make sure you are not left a penny. By God, you'll need a career in order to eat—or else beg from your brother!"

"Money, money!" Cissie said. "It's your only claim to fame. Can't you think of anything else? Do you go on living so you won't have to part with it? I don't give a damn for your precious money!"

"You watch your Goddamned language in my presence!" Grandpa cried. "There are no emancipated modern women in *my* house!"

"No, just slaves," Cissie retorted.

"All right!" Grandpa said. "You're going to be eliminated from the will as fast as I can get Burton Lely over here to change the terms. Put that in your pipe and smoke it!"

"I'll have a cigarette instead," Cissie said, and suited action to words, lighting, for the first time in the Brennan ménage, one of the cylindrical bits of paper Grandpa abhorred.

It came from her purse, in clumsy haste, and the match nearly went out. His reaction was swift and violent; he kicked back his chair, rose, staggered, and had to put a steadying hand on the table; partially recovered, he seized the half of melon on his plate, hurled it against the wall, and went weaving from the room.

"He had it coming," Cissie said, and coughed on swallowed smoke. "Did you have to go nuts? You're just making it harder for me."

"Oh, you'll manage. Keep sucking around him."

"He's all we've got left. Maybe he is a little crazy, but he means well. Don't you care for him a bit?"

Cissie shook her head. She was pale and her eyes were glinting, and the smoke from the cigarette curled upward past her face. Albert said, "I might run away and join the navy. I'm getting pretty fed up with trying to keep peace in this family."

Instead of going to school, he stayed under cover until he judged Grandpa might have subsided enough to be approachable. The old man was in the solarium, a cat occupying his lap, a cigar clenched in his uncertain teeth. Hesitantly, Albert said, "Can I talk to you for a minute?"

"Of course. Sit down."

"I'm sorry about Cissie, Grandpa. I know she didn't mean what she said, and every girl smokes cigarettes now. If you could forgive her this one time—"

"She's a kind of a firebrand, isn't she?"

"Well, she's got a big mouth. But she isn't as bad as she sounds."

"She is guilty of grave disrespect to the aged," Grandpa said, and grinned. "My feelings were almost hurt."

"Please don't cut her out of the will," Albert said.

"Did you believe that stuff? I'm positive she didn't. I cannot do a damned thing except prevent her from sharing in my portion—you and she are entitled to the income from a trust set up by your father years ago, and what your mother and Doña Maria had went into it too. At age thirty-three for Cissie, and thirty for you, control of the principal will be divided between you."

"Oh. Then there's nothing to worry about."

"You're very unworldly, Albert. Why haven't you ever thought to question me on how and when your inheritance would come to you?"

"I don't know."

"Maybe we have arrived at the moment to enlighten you," Grandpa said, "and you can convey the information to your hard-hearted sister. Discretion on when to start paying you from the trust has been left to me, but the moment I die, providing you are of age, the executors—Baltim and Lely, and the Los Angeles National Savings Bank—are authorized to hand over the income on a monthly basis. Do you have any idea of the amount of the trust?"

"No."

"Six million, perhaps a little more."

"That's quite a bit," Albert said. He wasn't very exercised; he had always had everything he wanted, and presumed such would be the case forever.

"By stipulation, half of the earnings of the trust are ploughed back into reinvestments, but you and Cissie will have a voice in the selection of them. Plenty of cash is available for emergencies and the payment of taxes."

"It sounds neat, Grandpa."

"What I've mentioned doesn't take into account my private capital, which I withdrew from the family assets when Cass died. My speculations have been generally successful." Grandpa petted the cat and beamed. "Damned successful. In fact, I have made a veritable pisspot of money."

"I'm glad."

"You should feel a modicum of joy because I intend, only to put a spoke in Cissie's wheel, to leave my gleanings to you."

"Thank you, Grandpa."

"When do you want it?"

"Oh, any time. Whenever you decide—"

"On my death, I guess," Grandpa said, "whether it occurs tonight or several years hence. The former is more probable, but I think public gaiety might benefit by the spectacle of a high school boy, none too intelligent, in possession of a king's ransom. I've been too Goddamned sedate for too long, I suspect. Am I not entitled to a last posthumous fling?"

"Sure."

"Unfortunately I won't have the opportunity of learning if you are an idiot. I fear you are, Albert, and that the brains and resolution in the third generation of Brennans have been transferred to the female side."

"Probably you're right," Albert said. "I've always looked up to Cissie. But I'm doing the best I can. You still like me, don't you?"

"That's the funny thing—I love you. You're my joy, if not my pride. These last years would have stretched out interminably without you, Albert."

Grandpa blinked his eyes, leaned forward, tipped the indignant cat from his knees, and gripped Albert's shoulder; his white fingers had a surprising strength. Heart swelling, Albert looked at the fantastic old man in open adoration. "I must be an idiot, Grandpa," he said. "Otherwise I wouldn't tell you what I'm going to."

The cigar allowed to grow cold, Grandpa listened to a betrayal of Cissie's ambitions. He had his usual bland, alert gambler's expression, and the imperviousness to surprise he unfailingly manifested, which made it difficult for Albert to calculate how the secrets he had impetuously and emotionally decided to reveal were being received. But the risk seemed worth running. His grandfather was—oddly enough, when the quarrel with Cissie was taken into account—in the best of all possible moods. In concluding, Albert coppered his bet. "Don't get mad," he added. "Or if you do, get mad at me. I'm the stool pigeon."

"I'm not mad. I appreciate your confiding in me."

"I can't tell you how set she is on flying."

"Aviatrixes—isn't that what they call 'em?"

"Yes. There are some already. They get their names in the papers—"

"She'll break her neck."

"I admit that's what I'm afraid of, Grandpa. But she's so stubborn and determined—"

"Let's help her break her neck," Grandpa said. "She's got a stiff one, the little bitch, and it'll serve her right. You'd better go to school."

Happy at the outcome of the gamble, Albert encountered Mrs. Gonzales as he left the house. She was in a mutinous frame of mind. "Throwing food," she said. "Yelling at the top of their voices. Running out of the room and not touching nothing on their plates. Have they gone crazy?"

"What they do is nothing to you," Albert said.

"Eh?" Mrs. Gonzales said. "Who you think you talk to? That spot on the wall where he threw it—huh? He want another breakfast, you think? The old fool! Let him come ask for it! You think I stand for anything?"

"I'm late for school," Albert said. "Excuse me. I'm awful sorry, Mrs. Gonzales."

He was held in no better esteem by Mrs. Godby. She and the cook reproached him for every outrage committed by Grandpa and Cissie; his role of go-between had become that of perpetual apologist. Despite the chancy victory in the solarium, he wondered about fleeing to join the navy. And his resentment slowly warmed as he recalled Mrs. Gonzales calling Grandpa an old fool.

Grandpa was not a man to wait upon the order of his actions. "These are my declining years," he was fond of saying, "and among other things I decline to act rationally." That night, after an awkward and silent dinner, he requested a private interview with Cissie. She said talking further wouldn't help. He replied, in his high-handed manner, that it damned well might. Bristling visibly, she followed him upstairs. Albert skulked along the second-floor hall, a prey to conflicting emotions; he feared they would clash again and ruin his amazing peace, and yet he recoiled at the prospect of Cissie being freed to break her neck. The meeting lasted over an hour. As Cissie reappeared, Albert popped from an alcove to intercept her. "Well?" he said.

"I think he's lost his mind. I can fly and do whatever I want. He'll pay for it. According to him, we ought to be friends. I gave him a kiss on the cheek when I went out . . . Al, is he nicer than we ever thought?"

"Sure he is. I told you that."

"I suppose I have you to thank," Cissie said grudgingly. "How did you ever find the nerve and brains to tell him?"

"I'm braver and smarter than I look."

"Yes, but you took a terrible chance. I might have had to kill you for squealing."

"As long as it's you killing me," Albert said, "I won't mind."

Cissie's eyes grew damp as she stood on tiptoe to kiss his forehead (which caused him to realize how tall he was getting, as nothing else had), and vanished. He tapped on Grandpa's door and heard an invitation to enter. Grandpa had changed to a nightshirt, put his teeth in a glass of water on a bedside stand, and was reflectively scratching his behind; his free hand held a pint of whiskey, the cork of which was drawn. "I understand it went all right," Albert said.

"Yes," Grandpa said. "It always does when you give people what they want. Albert, what do you see in her?"

"I don't know."

"Come on."

"Well," Albert said, "she's different. She looks clean and she is clean, and she means business. She's got an idea of something—I'm not just sure what—but I trust her. I can't really express it . . . When I was little, she took care of me. I didn't have anybody else. I need somebody still."

"You've expressed yourself," Grandpa said. "You were born to be a follower, and you'd best accustom yourself to marching in the ranks. She's going to wear the pants here."

"Let her," Albert said.

In a few days, out of business college and transferred to the first flying school Grandpa found in the pages of the telephone book by means of searching with the aid of a magnifying glass, Cissie literally was wearing pants, a pair of faded jodhpurs she had used in riding at the ranch. Her new school was located on South Western Avenue, a level, dusty area containing three shabby hangars and a rutted field where the airplanes took off and landed. Albert went out with Grandpa and Cissie the morning she matriculated, and was distressed by the machine that carried her on a maiden ride, an insubstantial little biplane seemingly held together by a maze of interconnecting wires, oil spotted and scarred from long, hard use. The shock of seeing Cissie in helmet and goggles, denizen of a different world and somehow abruptly beyond his reach, remained with him for a long while.

Cissie's instructor was, to Albert's surprise, a woman named Sarah Godowsky. She wore shapeless, dirty coveralls and was middle-aged and weatherbeaten. In her plain face was something of a motherly aspect, which reassured Albert. Hank Isbrow, an airplane buff now luxuriating in the role of expert adviser to Grandpa, said Sarah held one of the lowest numbered piloting licenses in the country, was the first woman graduate of the Glenn Curtiss school, had tested experimental ships for the government during the war, and had logged hundreds of hours in the air. "Miss Cissie will be safe with old Sarah," he went on. "I've seen her doing her tricks at several air shows. She flies like a bird."

"You have, eh?" Grandpa said. "No doubt Cissie was along on those occasions?"

"I won't lie to you, sir," Hank replied. "She was. It was on account of her that we went. I didn't see nothing wrong in it."

"Oh, you bastard!" Grandpa said.

"Yes, sir," Hank said. He grinned almost imperceptibly, catching the twinkle in the old man's eye.

"Did you know of those expeditions?" Grandpa asked. "Were you on any of them, Albert?"

"No," Albert said. "They're news to me." They were, and he felt hurt at hearing of his exclusion from that part of Cissie's life. He could only suppose she had kept him in the dark in order to spare him the moral problem of whether to inform on her to Grandpa, although surely she knew she could trust him. Still, he had peached on her just the other day . . .

She was settling in the front cockpit of the biplane. As Sarah Godowsky was about to climb to the rear seat, Grandpa strode out to talk to her. "What did you say?" Albert said, when he came back.

"I told her to give Cissie a rough ride and all the trimmings," Grandpa said. "If her stomach comes up in her throat, maybe she'll abandon this foolishment."

"Grandpa, are you having another nutty spell?" Albert exclaimed, heedless of the consequences. "That—that birdcage might fall apart!"

"You think so?" Grandpa said grimly. "Well, *that* would change her mind for her, wouldn't it?"

"Oh, don't you worry, sir," Hank said. "She's in a good little ship, even if it don't look pretty—an Air-Traveler—they must have built a hundred of them back in Bridgeport. Everybody learns in 'em. They're much better than the ships left over from the war with those big heavy unhandy Liberty engines. That's an Anzoni powering her, made right out in Burbank. Five cylinders, air-cooled radial, pulls seventy horsepower."

"I feel kind of sick," Albert said.

A mechanic rotated the propeller and then spun it sharply. Standing with clenched fists, Albert watched the Air-Traveler with the Anzoni in the nose waddle and bump to the end of the field and turn about. The noise of the engine rose from a staccato popping to a roar; next moment Sarah and Cissie were trundling clumsily toward a distant barbed-wire fence and a line of telephone poles and beanfields where squatting Japanese toiled. The tail of the biplane left the ground. While Albert's eyes blinked, Cissie was in the air and flying off under a serene sky. His damp and knotted fingers relaxed. There hadn't been much to it after all.

He and Grandpa inspected various airplanes under repair in the hangars or tethered outside them, Hank serving as cicerone, and talked to an odd collection of leather-jacketed young men, apparently without means or employment. Their principal occupation seemed to be squatting on the ground and holding long conversations incomprehensible to the uninitiated, illustrated by expressive hand gestures that simulated the motions of flying. The Godowsky Aerial Instruction and Charter Company consisted of several battered airplanes, a littered and unswept office in the corner of one hangar strewn with dog-eared books and papers, a collection of tools and drums of gasoline, Mr. Godowsky (an unclean fat man who was an aircraft rigger), two mechanics, and a stray cat which won Grandpa's interest, and smelled richly of hot oil and the dope applied to canvas surfaces. Wiping his hands on a piece of waste, Mr. Godowsky shook hands with each of the visitors and welcomed them to the brotherhood of aviation. His wife, he said, was a real hummer. She was sure to make their young lady a hummer too.

"This is a dump," Albert said, once Godowsky had returned to his twisting on wires. "He must be starving to death out here. Couldn't Cissie go to a better school?"

"I like it," Grandpa said. "The desperate always give satisfaction."

Nearly an hour passed before Cissie returned, and Albert's worries had become acute. The swooping, floating landing, even worse than the ascent, made him hold his breath and brace against a supporting wall.

Grandpa scrutinized Cissie. She was pale, but it was the pallor of triumph and delight. "What was it like?" he asked.

"Like I thought it would be," she said, "hoped it would be. It's not less, it's more . . . Like the day you took me to Dominguez Field when I was a child. I fell in love with airplanes then. Remember?"

"Vaguely," Grandpa said. "What a talent I have for handing apples to Eves!" He wrote Mr. Godowsky a check as an advance on Cissie's tuition, ordered Hank to bring her out every day and stay with her, and paused a moment to reflect. "I believe I might have a ride," he said. "There must be more to this than just a feeling of insecurity. Hank, have you ever been up?"

"No, sir," Hank said. "But I sure would enjoy going."

"You are about to," Grandpa said. "Albert?"

"Not me!" Albert told him.

Cissie was installed in the hangar office to read a textbook, and it took the combined efforts of Godowsky and Hank to hoist Grandpa into the fore cockpit. Mechanics rolled out another airplane, and Godowsky followed Sarah aloft with Hank as passenger. Albert went in the office and sat down and looked solemnly at his sister. "I think you're both crazy," he said. "Grandpa shouldn't be flying in his condition."

"I'm happy," Cissie replied, "and so is he. And you're a coward."

"I'm a live one."

"You'd make a perfect old woman."

"Somebody has to hold the family together," Albert retorted.

Grandpa resumed a footing on earth looking rejuvenated, and Hank was pleased and grateful. "It's remarkable, by God," Grandpa said. "Unquestionably you could find a passage in the scriptures prohibiting man from taking to the air—those Hebrew prophets were against everything —and certainly Icarus broke his ass, but I found the experience unique. If I weren't too old to travel, I'd take an airplane and sally forth. And what a means of seeing the Queen! We covered the city in the space of a few minutes, at the rate of eighty miles an hour, Sarah says. Think of that. It's a big town, by God, and never did I think I'd be able to look down on it from the vantage point of an eagle. To come, as I have, from riding in a cart with solid wooden wheels and ungreased axles, behind a team of oxen, to flying through the air at high speed is a hell of a tribute to man's ingenuity and my endurance. One has little sensation of height except in rising and descending. The feeling of freedom and having risen above ordinary concerns is very marked. No wonder birds are so Goddamned cheerful and sing their songs!"

Everybody went home in good spirits. Hank requested permission to spend his time at the field learning to work on airplanes in order to be

212

of assistance to Cissie. "She'll have a ship of her own pretty soon," he said, "and I can take care of it."

"I presume that is the next step," Grandpa agreed. "All right, Hank, your offer is accepted. If Godowsky wants payment for your training, I'll foot the bill."

"How can I ever thank you, Grandpa?" Cissie said. "I never realized you were this way."

"I am a dear, kind old man," Grandpa said. "Try to keep that thought in mind."

"Oh, phooey," Albert said.

Though he worried for Cissie, Albert was solaced by how his rash indiscretion had promoted the unity of the Brennans. Grandpa, given a fresh interest, closely followed Cissie's progress. Their long talks in the evening dealt only with flying, and Albert was freed to return to his own concerns, for Cissie actually superseded him as favorite. His nose a trifle out of joint, he confided the news of her new educative venture to Hal Baltim; he thought it almost shameful to have a nutty sister, and hesitated before unburdening himself. Surprisingly, Hal was impressed. So were the Sego boys when they were told. Grandpa handled the disclosures to the Messrs Sego, Baltim and Lely. Sego was shocked. Lely received the information with raised eyebrows but without comment. Baltim shook his head and mentioned the incidence of senile dementia and a new generation utterly lacking in discipline and stability.

Hal took to dropping by the house uninvited to see Cissie. Ignoring Albert except for the most perfunctory civilities, he invited Cissie to dinners, dances and parties, and was refused. Albert heard he had been seen at the Godowsky field and became outraged. Finally Hal suggested that Albert get another girl, act as his John Alden with Cissie, and the foursome go to the movies. "Have you gone off your trolley?" Albert demanded. "What's so wonderful about Cissie? You never used to like her."

"I was a blind fool," Hal said; he had a taste for the language he read on motion picture subtitles. "She's a real good scout now, a perfect mate. The red-hot mammas are tame compared to her. She sets my pulses racing."

"And you're upsetting my stomach," Albert said. "That flying has made a sucker of you."

Putting a hand on his chest, Hal said, "Call me a plaything of fate if you want, but I see Cissie as a kindred soul. I plunge into the limpid pools of her eyes and everything goes black. You know something? She arouses my passions."

"Leave her alone," Albert said. "See? She's not your type."

"Leave her alone!" Hal said. "Ask the sun to stop rising! You're a cigar store Indian, a clod. I ought to hang one on you for insulting me. How can we be friends—a poet and a peasant?"

"We just stopped being friends," Albert said. "I may be a clod, but there is going to be no double-dating with my sister."

He could not endure the thought of Cissie falling for Hal. And he wondered at his motives. The truth was he didn't want her committed to any of his friends; she was much too good for the people he knew. If she succumbed to romance, he would be out in the cold. A sickening shame possessed him when he conceived of her marrying and lying in bed with somebody. Harboring those emotions was crazy, he knew, and a highroad to the nuthouse, yet he simply could not entertain the idea of losing Cissie. She was his alter ego, his crutch, his guarantee of a spiritual safety. Life without her to care for and commune with looked intolerable. Someday the ideal man might appear, the prince and hero, and then he was willing to step down. In the meantime he intended to hang onto her. His need was greater than that of the others. It was a secret need, though. He divulged his thoughts to nobody. Even Lagonda remained ignorant of them. Brothers were not supposed to feel that way about their sisters, and he suspected he was nursing a profound and disgusting weakness.

Lagonda was bewildered by Cissie. "I don't know," she said. "Don't ask me no more what I think. I can't figure her out. That flying—what it get her? Where she going, to the moon? Who marries girls that ride around in airplanes?"

"She doesn't have to marry, Lagonda. I mean, not right away."

"Is she getting younger? What else do girls do but get married?"

"Oh, you say that because you're married," Albert said irascibly. "The minute somebody's done something, he thinks everybody should do the same thing. You could have got along all right here with me. We didn't need Ferris Washington."

"We sure didn't," Lagonda said. "Only it's too late now." Ferris, ordinarily a bricklayer's helper and part-time waiter and peddler and houseboy, had given up working once he was assured of Lagonda's future with the Brennans, and she had experienced some disillusionment.

Hal appeared to achieve no success in his advances, and one night in Cissie's room Albert ventured on a discussion of the matter. Cissie laughed. "*Him,*" she said. "He's only a kid. I was being nice to him. I won't ever love anything but what I'm doing."

"You like me, don't you?" Albert asked.

"That's different. You're my feebleminded child."

"Gee, thanks!"

214

"You know how I mean it," Cissie said. She was busily engaged in rubbing and trampling on a knee-length leather coat she had bought, endeavoring to make the garment give the appearance of long use so as not to excite humorous comment at the field. Pausing in her destructive efforts, she gazed at Albert narrowly. "If I wasn't your sister I think I'd be your mother—or your wife. We couldn't do without each other . . . Is that good enough for you?"

"Yes."

"Tell Hal to go chase himself. I don't care to have to say it to him. I'm tired of his hanging around."

Unspeakably relieved, Albert telephoned Hal. "I told you that you were off your nut," he said, in conclusion. "She's in the market for a grown man. Next time pick on somebody your own size."

"You dirty bastard," Hal said. "I'll bet you helped to disillusion her. Okay. Turn your knife in me. Finish the job. Why doom me to an early death or the drunken oblivion of the gutter? Go to hell."

A bit later, however, they resumed the friendship, took Hilda to the gravel pit, and Hal recovered his spirits and aplomb.

When she had received sixteen hours of careful instruction from Sarah, Cissie had the controls turned over to her and was sent up alone. She came home prancing and announced she had soloed. "You may think you have been lonely," she said, "but try taking up an airplane with no one in the other seat. Oh, boy!"

"I wish you'd thought to telephone us or put it off a day," Grandpa said. "Albert and I would have liked to watch."

"I didn't dare," Cissie said. "I might have lost my nerve. It happened all at once. We were practicing landings, and suddenly Sarah got out and told me to go ahead. Just like that. The next minute, not thinking, I was pushing the throttle and heading for the trees."

"Were you scared?" Albert asked.

"For two seconds," Cissie said. "After that I was terribly busy. I wasn't up more than ten minutes. Then I made a nice three-point landing and Sarah gave me a kiss."

"As long as it wasn't Godowsky . . ." Grandpa said. "Now what?"

"More training," Cissie replied. "A ship of my own. Once I really know my stuff, I want to go to that aeronautical school in Glendale for navigation and instruments. Sarah is not equipped to teach me the advanced things."

"Good enough," Grandpa said. "But where does this lead to? I can't see you becoming another Sarah, out in the beanfields teaching fledglings. Where are the other jobs for women in flying? Or are you planning some stupendous flight across an ocean in the style of Alcock and Brown? Maughan's already done this continent, you know."

"We're at the beginning, Grandpa," Cissie said. "This is lovely and *new,* and there is no end to the possibilities. It's not where you go, it's how long you take and how much you can lift off the ground. They've circled the globe and been to Australia and Capetown and Tokyo and Alaska, but not easily or fast enough. The men are better than the airplanes. And no woman has competed with them. Can't I prove I'm better than they are?"

"No," Grandpa said. "You're up against too many of 'em. Still, it might be fun trying—"

"What's going on here?" Albert exclaimed. "Are we out of our minds? Cissie has to stay here. This is her home. She can't make those crazy, dangerous flights! She was just supposed to learn to fly to keep her happy—my gosh, she's been up in the air once, and you're talking of—"

"Shut up," Cissie said. "Grandpa, I've got to learn my trade. The airplanes are improving. Perhaps I can help improve them. In a few years they ought to be able to go anywhere at high speed, safely and comfortably. That's what I must do—have the best of airplanes built and establish the records and prove myself. It will be like Columbus finding a new world, or Balboa looking at a new sea."

"Or like the ordinary rich man," Grandpa said, "buying a ranch, getting horses, and improving the breed. Except that the rich man doesn't tempt fate by riding his improvements. Well, you'll have the money and I won't live to stop you in your madness—if I were willing to, and I suppose I wouldn't be. How will you achieve this? By becoming an engineer?"

"No, that's too slow," Cissie said. "Flyers have to be young, and anyhow I hate mathematics. I'll find the builders and fly what they give me."

"And end up famous," Grandpa said, "alive or dead?"

"The risk is the best part," Cissie said. "It keeps your blood circulating. I'd rather be dead than half-dead."

"Oh, for pete's sake!" Albert said.

"Cissie, you seem to be harboring legitimate ambitions," Grandpa said. "And, of course, the customary mental confusion which goes with an urge to excel. If you have no desire to add to your riches or live in happy obscurity, I presume an aerial crusade is as sensible a solution as any. Let me wish you luck. When you've found the airplane you need, tell me."

But he was being disingenuous with Cissie, which Albert discovered in their next private conversation. "She's still an adolescent entertaining dreams of conquest," Grandpa said, "and, for her purposes, a member

216

of the wrong sex. You should have been the sister, Albert, and she the brother."

"I'm beginning to think so," Albert said.

"I can't hang on much longer, so the responsibility for her will rest on you." Grandpa grimaced. "You're the homemaker and guardian of our domestic gods. She won't gain access to a sizeable amount of money for ten years; while she waits, no doubt impatiently, you must calm her and douse any schemes that might endanger your inheritance or result in her death. Are you aware of the decision resting with you?"

"Yes."

"Time may bring her circumspection," Grandpa said. "On the other hand, don't over-do the quenching process. Her mother had a spoiled life because your father was too authoritarian. Give her an illusion of freedom, but retain control of the finances—that's all that counts." He sighed. "We can hope she'll begin to show normal inclinations and turn to the delights of copulation and childbearing."

"She doesn't have to do that," Albert said. "I can handle her."

It was a halcyon period. The morale of the household improved immensely. Grandpa was quieter and less troublesome, and Albert's duties were not so arduous; as Cissie went on flying the Godowsky equipment without incident and Hank became her devoted adherent and a good aircraft mechanic, he settled into a fairly comfortable routine. He could afford to spend more time on athletics, on Hilda and other girls, and even a few hours in studying, and yet not feel the family structure was suffering from his neglect.

Mrs. Godby herself took note of better conditions. A stuffy woman with an archaic mode of speaking and an imposing bosom on which was pinned an over-large gold watch, she said to Albert: "There has been too much dissension among us. I am glad to observe it has declined. The colonel is now bearable without being in one of his sinking spells."

"It's none of your affair," Albert said.

"I am forced to make it my affair, Mr. Albert," Mrs. Godby said, "when altercations assault my ears and eccentricities impede my housekeeping. Although only an employee, I take an interest in the well-being of my employers."

"Okay, okay," Albert muttered.

"My satisfaction would be complete," Mrs. Godby continued, "if Miss Cissie would stop playing tomboy in those flying machines and assume her rightful place in society. May I cherish the expectation that you will make every effort to bring the young lady to her senses? Allow me to add the foregoing is stated with the utmost in goodwill."

217

"I'll try," Albert said. "I've tried everything else, haven't I?"

"In passing," Mrs. Godby said, "or *en passant*, as the French say, permit me to remark that your intimate friendship with Mrs. Ferris Washington is not in the best of taste, Mr. Albert. At the risk of inviting your censure, I would like to aver that your conduct is undignified and unworthy of your position. Worse, it gives Mrs. Washington illusions not suitable for a humble colored person and weakens the discipline I must enforce."

"Listen to me," Albert said. "You can offer all the advice you want to, but leave Lagonda alone. Is that clear?"

"My, my," Mrs. Godby said. "We seem to have another budding colonel in our midst. Yes, sir, you have made yourself clear."

Yet such passages were only minor irritations. On the whole, events moved forward nicely. Albert graduated from high school—by the skin of his teeth—and received a red Kissel roadster to mark the occasion. The second night afterward, fortified by bottled lightning pinched from the cellar, he wrecked the car against a tree in a skid on wet paving. His brow and nose were cut, and Hal Baltim, occupying the front seat beside him, banged his skull on the windshield. Mr. Baltim was enraged and complained to Grandpa; he felt his son was being led astray. Dr. Loren, who sewed and bandaged Albert, said, "This will heal. The injuries you receive from your grandfather will not."

Shaken and humble, Albert paid no heed to the encouraging words of Cissie and Lagonda. He went to Grandpa as to an executioner. The ensuing scene was astounding. Grandpa was sympathetic, amused and half admiring; he agreed to have the Kissel repaired, uttered not a sentence of reproach, and scarcely bothered to dwell on the dangers of reckless driving. His glee at the indignation of Mr. Baltim and Hal's alleged double vision and prostrating headaches was ill concealed. He asked Albert if girls had been with them.

"No, Grandpa. We were coming home."

"You'd already dropped off the girls?"

"Well, yes."

"You'd been drinking?"

"Oh, no," Albert said.

"Tell me the truth."

"Well, we'd had a drink or two."

"My liquor, I suppose?"

"Uh . . . yes."

"That's intelligent," Grandpa said. "You can go blind on some of the stuff around these days. Albert, are you diddling many women? I'd hate to think driving and booze are your only interests."

218

"I'm getting my share, Grandpa."

"Oh, God! Sometimes I dream of a stiff member. For years I had difficulty buttoning my pants while just thinking of the next exercise in store for me. Don't waste a single opportunity. A long dry spell comes to every man. Aside from gathering wealth, no other diversion compares to venery."

"I certainly like it," Albert said. "They do, too."

"Yes, heaven bless them," Grandpa said fondly. "Nothing interests them more. Albert, you have become a real Brennan! I salute you."

Albert began to think his luck had changed, and could be pushed. Hal was going to the University of California at Los Angeles as his father had; but Albert wanted to attend the University of Southern California, which had a better football team. Furthermore, he had conceived the plan of first taking a liberal arts degree with easier courses that would enable him to concentrate on sports and a varied social program, and then study for the law. This would put off the appalling prospect of Brennan, Baltim, Lely and Brennan for at least six years. He dared to ask Grandpa's approval of the swindle. "The point I'm concerned with," he said, with a false unction, "is getting a full education. I've got plenty of time, don't you think? And I'll be in the firm the rest of my life."

"I see no objection," Grandpa said, "and I'm glad to hear you are starting to take an interest in intellectual pursuits. Perhaps you are not the dullard I have assumed you are; you might be the kind of individual who develops slowly. In any event, I am entitled to a little misguided optimism. By all means grow into a well-rounded man, if that's possible."

"Thank you, Grandpa," Albert said, and squeezed himself to be sure he wasn't dreaming. "I'll make you proud of me yet."

He was positive the fates were smiling on him—and he was in error.

Cissie went off to Glendale for navigational, instrument and radio instruction, still attended by Hank, who was enrolled in a mechanic's class at Grandpa's expense, and Albert entered U.S.C. The elder of the Sego boys, Harry, was there, preparing for a career in accountancy and business administration, and a friendship that had cooled to some extent was renewed. Albert found Harry in many respects a better companion than Hal; he was a tall, pale-haired, licentious youth with a proper spirit of subservience to the Brennans and a deep contempt for everything else, including his father, authority of any sort, and steady work. His intelligence was high, his methods were devious, he had hardly to crack a book to get by, and he stood ready to administer scholastic aid to Albert. They were soon inseparable and joined the same fraternity. The intimacy Albert had with Hal declined. As a matter of fact, Hal was beginning to take himself pretty seriously. He talked of the state of the nation, of man's obligation to his fellow man, advocated the spread of trade unions, questioned the sanctity of capitalism, and aired other views which would have sent Grandpa into a soaring rage. Some of these eccentricities had contrived to alienate Mr. Baltim (a feat Albert could not overlook as being on the credit side), and Hal was considering a break with his family and going it on his own.

"He's a chump," Harry Sego said, when he and Albert discussed Hal's case. "His ethics have gone to his head. Dishonesty is the best policy, and moral and political reform are for people anxious to work and suffer. God knows I hate his father as much as I do my own—both are fogies who belong in the age of the covered wagon—but they have to be used. Why bite the hand that's feeding you?"

"I never trusted Hal," Albert said, "since he got a crush on Cissie. The guy is undependable. Besides, he runs down America. What's wrong with a country where everybody is getting rich in the stock market?"

"I agree with you," Harry said. "Certainly he ought to insult his father, but not enough to have to take a job. That's stupid."

"Maybe that crack he got on the head in my car changed him," Albert said. "If I thought I was responsible for him going off his rocker I'd be very happy."

The metamorphosis of Albert was thorough. By degrees he turned into A. Chambers Brennan; smoked a pipe; cut his hair shorter; carried but did not read a magazine edited by Henry L. Mencken, and did read *College Humor*. He wore suede shoes and jackets of a material unmatched with his pants, had entrée to a speakeasy, and affected a world-weary smile. Explaining the alteration in his name to Grandpa was somewhat rough. "What's the matter with the one you have?" Grandpa asked.

"I never liked it."

"Why? It's plain, pronounceable, easily remembered."

"I think it's commonplace," Albert said. "Anyhow, Chambers is a family name—"

"Chambers," Grandpa said, "is a word reserved for lawyers' offices in England, butlers and maids—derived, I expect, from a chamber pot —and you're also full of shit. And a man with an initial prefacing his name is likely to be a bucket-shop operator, an unsuccessful politician, or the president of a backwoods college."

"I'm called Cham at school."

"Sham, did you say?"

"You needn't act nasty, Grandpa."

The old man looked at him and groaned. "Oh, what the hell. Call yourself anything you want."

220

"I've got a right to be an individual."

"Or a pretentious fool. As you wish—you're Chambers henceforth. If occasionally I am remiss and address you as Chamber Pot, put it down to my failing wits and your marked resemblance to a useful vessel. And get out of here."

"Thank you very much, Grandpa," Chambers said, and departed.

Popular, rich, carefree, hulking, brave, gallant and none too acute, with a peculiar but lovable sister and an immortal grandfather, Cham went out for freshman football. His intention was to emblazon the name of A. Chambers Brennan alongside those of Red Grange and the Four Horsemen of Notre Dame. In the first serious scrimmaging of the season, while he was playing fullback on the third string, he was downed, damaged and carried off the field on a stretcher. The infirmary passed him to Dr. Loren, who called in a bone man. At the beginning of the ordeal, despite pain in his knee, he was rather caught up by the glamour of injury and crutches and the flattering attention he evoked; but X-rays and treatment did not bring recovery, and he had to leave school, come home, and take to his bed. Grandpa was annoyed and concerned, and Cissie spent every evening in Cham's room. The knee grew worse.

"My big fear," Cham said to Grandpa, "is that my career in sports may be over."

"Jesus, Mary and Joseph!" Grandpa said. He gazed at Dr. Loren, present for an examination and discussion. "Why couldn't they have banged him on the head instead of the knee? He would not have noticed."

"He's already on crutches there," Loren said. "Colonel, I'm afraid an operation is indicated."

"Operation?" Cham said. "Oh, no you don't!"

"Oh, yes we do!" Grandpa roared. "You can't spend the rest of your Goddamn life in bed!"

A specialist came from San Francisco to prod at Cham, and he concurred with Dr. Loren. Over the patient's protests, he was put in the hospital, anesthetized, and carved upon. He awakened to a long misery, and presently learned he could not go home; the leg had failed to mend properly. Grandpa poured abuse on Loren and his colleague, and additional orthopedists were summoned. They talked of ostempyesis, osteochondritis and leaking synovial fluids. More surgery was necessary.

After a bout of self-pity, Cham settled down and accepted misfortune. He acquired his mother's habit of strewing the counterpane with books, having quickly tired of listening to a radio, and read omnivorously. The pages of print he consumed, the breaking of an aversion to sitting still, the feeding of an expanded curiosity, enlarged his vision and quickened his responses. But his great consolation was Cissie; she never left him if he had need of her, she patiently listened to his complaints and despair and returned soothing answers, and he later learned she was in the operating room in sterile cap, mask and gown during both the surgical episodes. "I might end up with one leg," he told her. "Then what is going to become of me?"

"I'll be around," she said, "to push your wheelchair or whittle you a pegleg. I won't leave."

"Not even to fly?"

"No."

"Well, don't forget," he said. He hastily closed his eyes, squeezing teardrops from them. Her lips settled on the tip of his nose. It was endurable as long as she abided by him.

The second operation produced rapid improvements. Cham was allowed to return home, and a distraught Lagonda nursed him day and night. In the middle of his convalescence, Grandpa suffered a sinking spell, apparently the victim of tension and worry. Able to hobble about on crutches, Cham went every day to his grandfather and sat beside his bed. The old man lay still most of the time, his face a beaked, waxy, white-tufted immobile mask, wrapped in a strange somnolence. He recognized people and was capable of speech; it just seemed that he had decided the effort of being fully alive was too much for him and had retired to a half-sleep, a cocoon of silence and dreams where he could recruit his worn-out body. Weeks passed before he roused. Replying to Cham's worried questions, Dr. Loren shrugged and said, "He's nearly eighty-nine years old. There isn't much left, and perhaps he won't bother to awaken again. Let's leave him undisturbed and see."

One day, though, Grandpa resumed living. He sat up and stretched and yawned and called for a whiskey and soda, and ordered Cham—who was off the crutches now—to walk up and down in front of him so he could study the extent of the disability. "You move better than I do," he said. "Don't complain."

"They say I'll always have a stiff knee. That means no more football or baseball."

"Devote yourself to whiskey and women, then. I told you not to complain."

"Believe me, I'm not kicking," Cham said. "Why would I, with you feeling better? That's all I ask, Grandpa."

"Would you miss me, Chamber Pot?"

"I couldn't get along without you."

"I'll be damned," Grandpa said. "Is it possible I'm going to linger on until I'm a saintly figure, loved by everybody? I'll have to mend my ways if there's any chance of beatitude."

He wasn't really the same as he had been. The chilliness that had made his bones ache for years was succeeded by a consuming inner heat, and he mentioned crickets rasping in his ears to Loren. "Arteriosclerosis," the doctor replied. "We all have it, in varying degrees, shortly after youth ends. Time is irreversible. You must accept what you have left."

"I've got Goddamned little," Grandpa said, "which doesn't include a trace of sympathy from you. Can't you forgive my preventing your marriage to Allie? How would you like A. Chambers for a son these days? You might have had him, you know. Or Cissie flying airplanes. Haven't you any gratitude?"

Loren smiled. "Absolutely none. To tell you the truth, I've always partially blamed you for Allie's early death."

"That's unscientific," Grandpa said. "However, you never were much of a doctor. Why didn't you go back to New York and stop being the specter at my feasts?"

"I wish I knew," Loren said. "A miasma floats in this raw and hopeless town—few can muster the energy to leave. Perhaps it is the climate. The inhabitant is robbed of initiative."

"You could have married," Grandpa said. "Don't try to make me believe you've been mourning Cass's doctor all this time. Or would a wife have hampered your manful attempts to deflower every young nurse you've met?"

"No, Colonel," Loren said. "The climate is at fault—the insipid weather and the sheer weight of Los Angeles."

"Don't disparage the Queen," Grandpa said. "She doesn't age like the rest of us. Chop off her tail and she grows a new one. She's forever young and having illegitimate babies. I think the only enduring love I've ever had is her; my taste in whores always ran to the big, blowsy, careless kind. God knows I wish I could stay to see her become respectable. The apotheosis is yet to arrive. She'll be a marvel."

"Forgive me, Colonel," Loren said, "but your glasses are too rosy in color. In my opinion the great village has outgrown its purpose and function, and decay must set in—or an ice age will come to freeze our dinosaur. Even if she lives up to your expectation she won't be a marvel, only a monstrosity."

"Behold the carpers!" Grandpa chortled. "They never would listen to me, and the great village always made fools of them. And I'm much richer than they are."

"I hope your money is a comfort to you now," Loren said.

223

Grandpa squinted at him thoughtfully. "Not exactly. It was mine to use and not to keep. But where I've been and what I've done and how I've watched the cloud-capped towers rise—that's a comfort. It was a muddy puddle, it's grown to a lake, it will be an ocean. My manhood and visions went into it, in a half-assed, dishonest fashion which should have been better and was the best I could manage. Don't you like to belong to something?"

"I belong to myself," Loren said.

"Chambers," Grandpa said. "Consider the man. His instincts are refined. He has integrity and is relatively poor. He knows the Hanging Gardens of Babylon and the Colossus of Rhodes and the Tower of Babel are gone, that crumbling ruins mark the passage of the Pharaohs and the Caesars, that finally dust covers everything. He couldn't take a risk. He does not want ephemeral dreams to come true just because they're ephemeral. He can't understand how sheer, stinking *bigness* is enough —it doesn't have to last—and makes men ten feet tall in finding what they've done. He won't allow the validity of leaving behind you a temporary memorial of buildings and money and land and corporate entities and gushing charities and the ghost of a fetid Indian town blown to gargantuan proportions, tamed, cleaned, watered, lighted, fit for accommodating a million people in the sort of comfort they haven't previously known. The hell with him. He has no feeling for the subjugation of hostile planets. How would you like him for a father at this late date?"

"He once urinated at the mere thought," Loren said.

"I would again," Cham said, "with the same problem."

"Ah," Grandpa said, and regarded Cham warmly. "The Brennans, they have a certain peculiar quality. Piss on all of them, as it were. Decently Latinized, that could go on the family escutcheon. I feel reassured."

"So do I," Loren said, and got his hat and black bag. "Your recovery seems complete, Colonel. You've had more farewells than Tosti, haven't you? Good afternoon, gentlemen."

Yet Grandpa declined. When he walked his legs would buckle under him in a disconcerting fashion, and he rarely went out of the house. He abandoned the solarium, had a telephone put in his bedroom, and sparely ventured the trial of getting up and down the stairs. Each night Cissie and Cham ate with him on the second floor in a card room which had been converted to dining. Cissie was back at her studies in Glendale, and Grandpa urged Cham to return to the university, but the start of a new semester failed to intrigue him; having lost touch, he had lost interest, and he hated the thought of parading his handicap around the campus. Even the frequent visits of Harry, bringing the latest gossip and a collegiate air, did not inspire him. His solace for the accident was that servitude in Brennan, Baltim, Lely and Brennan had been deferred for years.

While he hung in the wind, his education proceeded. Grandpa, evidently sensing the presence of the dark angel, was at some pains to explain the state of his investments—which Cham alone would inherit —and his thoughts on the future. He had gone on riding the cresting boom that exploded in 1923. The variety and extent of his speculations were bewildering. He had money in the oil fields of Signal Hill and Huntington Beach, in shipyards, in a sash and door mill, in Wilshire Boulevard and Beverly Hills real estate, in a steel rolling mill in Torrance, in a new hotel on Flower Street, in a huge cemetery in the San Fernando Valley, in a loan company, in a combined cannery and fishing fleet at San Pedro, in a motion picture studio called the Xanadu Amusement Producing Corporation, in a gambling house that operated with the tacit consent of the police, in a San Francisco bank (headed by an old man named Albert Blour, a friend of Cham's father) which might merge with the Los Angeles National Savings Bank and by virtue of many branches dominate California financing, and in the stock market. "Confidentially," he said, "I filched some of the assets of Sunset Sea to back my play, maybe illegally—I wanted to find out if I had retained my touch when I should have been doddering. The touch was still there, and it doesn't matter now. I've got over ten million to put in your hands."

"I wish you'd mentioned the movie company," Cham said. "I'm interested in pictures. When can I see how it's done and meet the actresses?"

"Don't try my patience," Grandpa said. "You can go out whenever you like and see the Goddamned empty studio we built in Long Beach. That's my one investment which hasn't paid a handsome return. I kept hearing how the Queen was the film capital of the world and that two hundred million dollars was going into films every year, and I thought I'd better get on the bandwagon. But I was too old a dog for *those* tricks. It's a lunatic lottery run by Jews, a gold field wide open to claim jumpers—they're all thieves, liars, blue-sky stock peddlers, jewelry salesmen, glove merchants and highbinders. They take gambles no sane man would consider and thrive on bankruptcies. Even an experienced crook of my caliber was an innocent child to them. Never put a penny with them as long as you live or I'll come back to haunt you. Hear me?"

"I hear you," Cham said. But being a constant lover of the silver screen who had progressed from jungle serials and *The Perils of Pauline* to *The Covered Wagon* and *A Woman of Paris,* he felt a keen disap-

225

pointment at having missed the disasters of the Xanadu Amusement Producing Corporation.

While prospering extravagantly, Grandpa had pondered on what lay ahead. Dim though his eyes were and his race nearly run, he was always impatient with the present. A long life and many vicissitudes had taught him to be suspicious and prudent. He mentioned the geese which had guarded the town of Romulus and Remus and quacked a bit himself. He had kept cool with President Coolidge and admired the administration, but he suspected Coolidge had made a mistake in recommending investment in the severely inflated stock market. To his way of thinking, the wringer was again about to be brought out—the modern version of the guillotine. Having read of, or remembering, the panics of '37, '57, '73 and '93, he was prescient and pessimistic. And the troubles of 1913, induced by Woodrow Wilson and his Goddamned low tariffs, were just behind him. The Democratic party and its bias against sensible protection for the farmer and manufacturer did not present the only harbinger of possible approaching evil. Widespread extravagance and high prices raised storm signals too; they were the causes of the deflation of 1920.

"During the last four years," he said, "the people of the United States have incurred private and public debts that stagger the imagination. The stock market has gone crazy. A day of reckoning is near, by God. Wage earners are going to be hard hit and banks will fail. Unions have enslaved the country. Politicians are corrupt. Spend, spend, spend is the order of the day. We're the helpless prey of Communists and agitators and an autocracy of officeholders. Who knows when we'll fall before another invasion of carpetbaggers and have to live under the rule of criminals and niggers?"

The question, not exactly rhetorical, seemed to demand an answer. "I don't know," Cham said. "Pretty soon, Grandpa?"

"Goddamned soon, maybe," Grandpa said, and scowled. He paused to search his mind, as if uncertain of the facts. "Your father got killed trying to stop the bastards, and his father before him. You have to stand fast, Cham. It's a question of dollars and cents."

"I will," Cham said. He meant it. The old man was an infallible oracle.

"Now . . ." Grandpa said. He rubbed his head. "How the hell can I think with a whole chorus of insects in my ears? Listen, a tinpot government sworn to ensure the comfort and confidence of every lazy profligate in the union is the problem. We need a businessman to run the administration and cut the costs in half. That man Hoover they're talking of might fit the occasion, if the Republicans can hang onto power. Don't neglect working for him, and contribute to his campaign."

"I'll work for him," Cham said. "You contribute."

Grandpa looked at him and smiled. "I might, Cham. I'm sure a big wind is coming up, a cold and cutting wind. It'll separate the sheep from the goats, the wise men from the suckers. Plenty of grinning fools are going to hurt bad for a while. But don't get scared. Values always return, like the birds in the spring and the way of a man with a maid. The Queen may stumble, but she'll march on. Still, I have a hunch the hour has come to take in sail. What do you advise?"

"Well, with a wind," Cham said, "grab your hat." He tried valiantly for intelligence, not caring much for the future, yet striving to please his grandfather. "Sell out?"

Beaming, Grandpa said, "Precisely, Chamber Pot. The more water wrung out, the harder cash will feel to the holder thereof. A man might buy in again when the gale drops, for a fraction of what he had invested. Shall I remove us from peril?"

"Sure," Cham said.

"If I am mistaken," Grandpa said, "curse my name at your leisure. All right, we'll liquidate. Everything goes but the fundamentals—the oil, which can wait in the ground; the cemetery, where the trade is always steady rain or shine; the real estate, an essential nobody can pick up and depart with; and the bank stock as a pledge for the generation after you. Hold tight to the gold I'll provide. The government can't afford to let that lose its mystic virtue. Gold is the elixir of life. I have served Mammon indefatigably, and I will serve him to the end, praise God." He waited a moment, collecting his thoughts. "The petroleum reserves at the San Cristobal are going, and the chances of hitting any more pools are slight. In a decade the jig will be up. But don't sell the ranch, Cham. It is a good luck charm. It has been our backbone." He passed a hand over his eyes and appeared to remember something far, far off. "And it was the great love of Doña Maria. She'll sleep better knowing it's yours and I have kept what small faith I had to offer her."

"I'll hang onto it," Cham said.

"Promise me," Grandpa said. "I have to sleep too."

"I promise," Cham said.

Through sheer expenditure of will, and possibly by force of habit, Grandpa moved down once more to the solarium and began shouting on the telephone. Mr. Sego arrived, Mr. Lely, and in due course Mr. Baltim. Lely was enigmatic, and Sego and Baltim, as advisers and keepers for an aged eccentric, protested vigorously. The nation had reached an apex of strength and stability; the cornucopia was bottomless; and the colonel in his wavering dotage was sinning against his heirs.

"Jesus walks on the earth again," Grandpa said ironically, "but we'll hold with the apostles and deny Him. Let the cock crow thrice. I've heard optimists before."

All the ventures which did not suit his convenience were cashed in at handsome profits, sold to eager investors. He ignored the arguments of Baltim and Sego in behalf of changing his will: A. Chambers Brennan, whatever his age, was going to have a spectacular inheritance.

That special night, Cham got up and prepared to leave his grandfather. The old man sat propped by pillows in bed, the light of the lamps shining on his unkempt white hair and casting shadows under the high span of his cheekbones. He looked haggard and weary, as though the simple movements of lying supine and pulling up the covers were beyond him. "Can I help you down?" Cham asked.

"I'll stay up for a while," Grandpa said. "I hate waiting."

"Waiting for what?"

"Oh, waiting. My life has passed like a dream, Cham. But if it was a dream, will I awaken? I don't want to, I'm too tired for that."

"Don't talk foolishly, Grandpa."

"One thing is nice: I'm not afraid. I never really was afraid in all my years. I kept anticipating and hurried. That was comforting. To look back, to settle down, is a hell of a waste."

"You'd better go to sleep. Do you want a drink of whiskey?"

"No. It's lost its taste. And I've got to stay here, my back against something, in a position of defense. No use giving up when I've held out this long, is there?"

"No. Shall I turn out the lights?"

Grandpa shook his head. "They'll go off by themselves. I'd rather see the light as long as I can. The darkness could last forever."

"Grandpa, you're giving me the creeps. Get some rest. I'll drop by first thing in the morning."

"The other world—suppose there was one? Wouldn't that be a hell of a note? I'm not interested, Cham. I enjoyed this one. It was just to my satisfaction. I was unworthy, but I outlived all of them. Now I've had enough."

"I'm going to bed. Do you want anything?"

"A kiss. Maybe it's unmanly, but imprint it on my forehead. Thank you. *Ave, Caesar, morturi te salutant.* Do you know what that means?"

"No."

"Your father would have. Good night, Caesar."

"You're acting funny, Grandpa. Shall I call Dr. Loren?"

228

"No. I can do this by myself. It is nothing unusual, and I have deferred it unnecessarily. Good night."

"I might come in later. Good night, Grandpa."

The last Cham saw of Grandpa, he was still upright, his head turned toward the nearest lamp, greedily taking in the illumination.

three

THIS was not one of A. Chambers Brennan's good days. He was awakened early in the morning, roused by the monotonous click of pruning shears; it was Jesús Algonrones, the Mexican gardener, faithfully at work reducing the shrubbery. Cham turned over, covering his head in the sheet, and essayed sleep again. He could not even doze. The noise of the shears was succeeded by the rasp of a rake and the squeaking of a wheelbarrow. Rising, going to the window, Cham leaned out and blearily discerned the outlines of Algonrones. "Jesús!" he cried. "For Christ's sake go somewhere else! I'm trying to sleep!" But the gardener, who neither spoke nor understood English, removed his straw hat, bowed, and addressed a cheerful greeting to Cham. "Oh, go to hell," Cham said, and went back to bed.

The possibility of further slumber was remote. He lay and brooded, his stomach sour at the prospect of having to contemplate his troubles so soon in the day. Birds sang and sunlight streamed through the window. Lighting a cigarette, he held up a bare foot and meditatively flexed the toes. They afforded him small comfort. Without knocking, the maid opened the door and entered. Unlike the other help, who lived over the coach house, she was quartered upstairs nearby. She was nineteen years old, black-haired and black-eyed, and in her nightgown, which was a long, nearly transparent piece of material with untied blue ribbons at the neck and waist, purchased for her by Cham; it did not very much conceal her firm, pointed breasts and rounded belly and flanks and a dark triangle she seemed to flaunt. Her name was Concepción Algonrones, she had left the state of Guadalajara at the age of ten, and she was Jesús's daughter.

"I'm busy," Cham said. "Go do some cleaning."

"Too early," Conny said. Approaching the bed, she peeled off the nightgown and crawled in beside her employer.

"What brought you here?" asked Cham.

"I hear you hollering at my father," she said. "I tell him to go away."

"Well, I'm busy," Cham said.

But Conny, who had attracted Cham's attention months before when Jesús Algonrones was driving around the Westlake district in a battered flivver truck, accompanied by his entire family of seven, in an effort to find work of any kind, was not a sensitive girl and possessed a single-minded devotion to what she was best fitted for. If her brow was a little low, her hips heavy and her conversation limited in scope, she nevertheless had an amoral curiosity and busy hands and lips. Inevitably Cham succumbed to what were more demands than advances. Helpful and kind, Conny reduced him to a mindless delirium which could be heard elsewhere in the house.

"Every morning . . ." Cham said presently. "Like the gardening. I'll be dead in a little while."

"You die happy," Conny said, and went smilingly in the bathroom, returned to put on the nightgown, and started for the door.

"You might as well stay," Cham said. "I've forgotten my own name."

"No, I get newspaper," Conny said. "You want breakfast?"

"Oh, stay awhile."

"I got to clean. Breakfast?"

"All right," Cham said. He added aloud, to himself, when the door had closed on her: "Now, where was I?"

He hadn't the least idea. It was a poor way to start a busy and eventful day. That state continued until Conny returned, in a neat uniform, and gave him the newspaper and a lingering, pulling kiss that lifted his lips quite away from his teeth. A cursory inspection of the front page elevated his blood pressure. From Washington, Franklin D. Roosevelt and his bright young band of revolutionaries were engaged in ripping the country apart and setting it on the road to collectivism. One sensation followed on the heels of another; a man scarcely had the respite to draw a long breath. Every hour witnessed a new proposal that would have horrified the founding fathers of the Republic. An age of sober self-reliance and sturdy independence was going down the drain with a rush. "Thank God Grandpa didn't live to see this," Cham said, for the thousandth time. Hiding in a room, lying in bed—but with Conny—looked to be the only method of recoiling from such horrors.

There was a knock on the door, and Ferris Washington, clad in the black jacket he wore daytimes, brought Cham's breakfast on a tray.

Actually, he was Ferris Washington, Junior (the elder Washington lived on Central Avenue and stood on the tail-end step of a garbage truck six days a week), a slim, good-looking, affable Negro. Though his name was something of an affront, Cham nurtured a deeper grudge against him, for Ferris had proceeded to make Lagonda pregnant and terribly complicate the affairs of the whole household—this after Cham had, upon the death of Grandpa, fired Mrs. Godby, Mrs. Gonzales and the spare maid, and appointed Ferris butler and Lagonda housekeeper-in-ordinary. Since he would not consider parting with the ashamed and apologetic Mrs. Washington for a moment, she had kept at her duties until the last gravid moment, been rushed to an obstetrical clinic (Cham's own hospital would not accept Negroes, nor did Dr. Loren deign to treat Lagonda, and Cham had fallen into an enormous rage) in Cham's new Duesenberg, and Ferris was allowed to see his son and wife only when his employer was damned good and ready. Unfortunately, being bound up with Lagonda meant that Cham, who brought the coffee-colored infant back to his house and hired a nurse and emphatically vetoed the name of Ferris Washington II or III—nobody seemed sure which number was correct—and ordered the kid christened Albert Cassius, had to manifest at least some politeness to the grandparents. Thereby he found himself going to the growing black belt of small bungalows and haphazard stores and auto repair shops and pool halls and evangelists' tents situated beyond Washington Boulevard in order for the garbage collector and his wife and countless brothers and sisters and cousins to admire a grandson with a fairy godfather; happily, all of Lagonda's relatives were immured in Mississippi and too illiterate even to write a letter. Cham drank beer and ate spareribs with his new circle of acquaintances; he didn't care how he was treated, but he insisted that Lagonda be extended the respect due a lady who had produced the dauphin. He intended to take full charge of Little Albert, and Lagonda was in entire agreement. Both of them looked upon Albert's father as an intruder and an unnecessary evil, and he was humbly conscious of his position. Lagonda soon discarded the nurse, but she did require another maid to assist her, and that was where Conny came in. She began occupying Cham's bed very shortly, and all would have gone well, because Conny was a willing worker, except that Lagonda felt she was not good enough for the master and held various moral scruples. That tended to mitigate her own apologies for having allowed Ferris to win and impregnate her, and led to certain wrangles between Cham and her on ethics and methods. However, their affection was not impaired; it was only that they reached, by virtue of time and individual outlooks, a basis of complete equality.

232

"I hope you are well this morning, sir," Ferris said.

Not condescending to answer, Cham arranged himself in bed and waited until Ferris had suitably braced the pillows. Across his lap slid the tray; whatever Ferris's other deficiencies, and they were many, he had the deft touch of an experienced waiter. No cook had replaced Mrs. Gonzales, and Lagonda, despite her official position, functioned in the kitchen. She prepared a superb light, crusty French toast, and the usual breakfast confronted Cham—the toast, bacon, plenty of syrup, orange juice and coffee. Under Lagonda's regime he was gaining weight, but she claimed he was looking better than ever, and it was easier to buy looser clothing than to protest.

"I didn't see nothing in the paper today that was too bad, sir," Ferris said.

"That's because you can't read," Cham said.

"Yes, sir," Ferris said. "Will there be anything else?"

"Send Lagonda here in a few minutes," Cham said.

He ate every bite, mopping up the syrup, poured a second cup of coffee from the pot, and lit a cigarette. Food was nearly as great a distraction as Conny, and thus far he had put off the reckoning he had to face. Picking up the newspaper, he considered the latest outrages of the New Dealers again. But that was nearly worse than grappling with his own predicament. The agonies of a nation given over to apple selling, lines of relief applicants, indigents building all manner of public works or leaning on their shovels, innumerable alphabetical agencies infringing on the rights of the well-to-do, inane songs coming from radio sets requesting a spare dime or inciting people to fall in love on the basis of dropping commodity prices, and smart Jewish lawyers burrowing under Capitol Hill and stabbing at the Constitution reduced him to a dull despair. Lamenting the good old days was foolish, he knew, yet he could not resist a familiar comfort. The fabric of Cham's life had disintegrated after Grandpa's death and the onset of the ill wind he predicted. Nothing looked the same any more, or certain and safe, and the world was in a flux. The fun was gone. He longed to return to his adolescence and a time of sugar-daddies and flappers and speaks and bathtub gin and prosperity and optimism and fashionable disillusion and a kind of golden youth that would never be repeated. And to return to Grandpa, naturally. The old man had been a rock which could withstand the most devastating flood . . .

Cham sipped the tepid coffee. The future Grandpa paid court to repelled him. It bulged with responsibilities, decisions, worries, crises, unpleasant emergencies. There was the immediate problem of Cissie, now come to a head; the complaints and expostulations of Sego, Baltim and the bank trustees; the irritations of running a household and avoiding human entanglements he regularly fell into; and the sandpapery obligation of having millions of expectant, wholly liquid dollars to wet-nurse. He hated having to do anything, especially if the action involved study, appraisal, judgment and perilous deciding. The weight of the universe had descended on his unwilling shoulders. With his stiff leg, sluggish thought processes, sketchy education, immaturity and sporadic energy, he felt himself incompetent and unworthy. He knew everybody expected him to fail, to make a mess of things. He could rarely arrive unaided at a sensible conclusion, and his councillors had contempt for him. Even Burton Lely, ordinarily patient and sympathetic, hinted that Cham was a pitiful successor to a pair of remarkable, driving, intelligent Brennans and rather gloomily quoted the phrase "from shirtsleeves to shirtsleeves in three generations." If the corps of advisers had not thought Cissie a still poorer prospect, Cham was sure they would have attempted to put her in charge. Only the training Grandpa had imparted, plus stifled resentment and stubborn courage and cunning, sustained him, but he was already resigned to failure: what remained was simply a matter of degree.

Conny came back in the room carrying a mop. She put it aside and took the tray off the bed. "You want to do something?" she said.

"No, for God's sake," Cham replied. "Beat it."

"Remember Sunday. You promise."

"Sunday? Not this coming Sunday?"

"Yes," Conny said. "You promise. My father, he has told his friends—"

"I can't. I thought it was the Sunday after—"

"No, no. You promise!"

Cham hesitated. She might cry; she might throw the tray. Discipline was hard to impose on bedfellows. His intimate association with the maid also embraced a companionship with Jesús Algonrones, who was proud of his daughter and her success in the house. A courtly and quietly dignified man, he wanted nothing from Cham but the opportunity to exhibit him in his own home as an honored guest. That involved Cham's going at intervals to Belvedere on the east side, where the Algonrones, presently ten strong, not counting a variety of relations, occupied a small frame bungalow with a potted geranium on the front porch. His appearance always signaled the beginning of a party enlivened by music, dancing, chili and beans, tequila, beer and muscatel wine. Normally Cham went first for a ceremonial walk, Conny hanging on his arm and dressed in her finest, a gesture which raised the prestige of the family

234

in the neighborhood. Then everybody drank and sang and danced and got *boracho,* one of the few Spanish words Cham recognized. He enjoyed himself at these gatherings, and even forgave the tipsy *paisanos* who came up admiringly to say they had known Conny since her childhood and she was always pretty—pretty enough to be a whore—and he was a lucky man. In truth, he had better times at the Algonrones' and the Washingtons' than at the California Club or the Athletic Club or the stately dinners to which he was no longer invited. People in his predestined orbit bored and annoyed him, and he was too rich and secure to have to do what did not interest him. There was no need for him to conform; he wouldn't ever be looking for a job or a loan, or a girl with money to marry. Yet he could not evade his obligation to Cissie, and his social eccentricities were contributing to her isolation. She had no ordinary life. Unless she could meet the proper kind of men, and pick one of them for a husband, what sort of an existence was she going to have once her youth had vanished? With her odd unworldliness she couldn't do for herself, and it was up to him to manage for her. She wasn't getting any younger, her neck was in peril, she seemed to lack normal feminine characteristics, and her cronies consisted of Hank Isbrow, an unsuccessful aeronautical engineer named Dugald Stuart, a number of impoverished pilots, Luigi Anzoni the aircraft engine manufacturer (with a wife and five children), and newspaper reporters and photographers interested in aviation. Who among them was worthy of marrying a golden princess? Cham frequently wondered whether he might have to achieve reformation and conformity to provide a model and inspire his sister. It was a hell of a sacrifice to have to make.

"You promise!" Conny said again.

"All right," Cham agreed sadly. "Maybe I did. I'll be over Sunday."

Conny blew him a kiss, nearly dropped the tray, clutched the mop, and departed. Through the open doorway walked Lagonda, and wheeled to gaze somberly after the maid. "I know," Cham said. "You don't like her."

"I like her okay," Lagonda said. "She works hard. But she not fit company for you. This is not polite and nice. I'm surprised Miss Cissie don't give you a talking to."

"She doesn't notice. Have you heard from her?"

"No. I phoned Glendale and she hasn't come in."

Cham leaned forward, reaching for a cigarette. "Do they think anything's wrong?"

Lagonda shook her head. "She radioed San Francisco tower and ain't overdue yet."

"I'm sick of waiting around and holding my breath!"

"So am I. She'll be going across the water next. You know what I heard her saying to Mr. Stuart? India! Australia! That's too far. You have to cross oceans—I looked at a map."

"Well," Cham said, "I have to get down to cases with her . . . don't I?"

"You sure do."

"I'll just say no. Just like that. No. Cut off the money. Grandpa said to. It's for her own good. What else can I do?"

"Nothing," Lagonda said.

"She'll be sore."

"Sweet talk her."

"What if she walks out?"

"She won't do that."

"No?" Cham said. "Would you like to bet?"

"No."

"Lagonda, this is a mess."

"She going to kill herself! What good will that do her?"

"We've been through this before."

"Maybe we better keep going through it," Lagonda said. "You want her blood on your hands?"

"I'll get tough," Cham said. "That's all. There it is, take it or leave it. Cold turkey. Like Grandpa used to. Right, Lagonda?"

"Yes. You better get up and dressed. Reverend Smiley is coming first."

"Oh, Lord. I wish he'd stay away."

While Cham was shaving, Lagonda poked her head in the bathroom to report that Cissie had landed and would be home later. He breathed a sigh of relief, put on his clothes, and went downstairs to receive Moses Smiley in the library. As ever, Smiley was punctual to the second. A small, fat, white-haired man, he had been one of Grandpa's close associates in real estate ventures in the remote past, Cham understood. After that, embroiled in other concerns and hampered by ill health, Grandpa had seen little of Smiley. But he had entered into partnership with him in the development of the vast San Fernando Garden of Immortality, the largest park of repose, as the advertisements read, west of Chicago. Cham wished Grandpa had not chosen to retain his interest in the cemetery. Reverend Smiley bothered him. In spite of his advanced years, he was unquenchable, and he had six vigorous, inventive sons to support the improvements to the Garden assiduously planned and brought to Cham's attention. As sole holder of a half interest, with power of veto, Cham was constantly having to cast his vote on new

236

projects or present each quandary to Mr. Sego or Mr. Baltim. Because the Garden was profitable in a dizzying fashion, they rarely opposed Smiley's recommendations, but their amused condescension and contempt for the burying trade was irksome.

The current meeting was no different from any other. Admiring and affectionate, never less than worshipful, Smiley took the hand Cham offered him and pressed it to his bosom with both of his. He was accompanied by one of his boys, Norman by name (Cham had failed to get them straight; they were all little and rosy, clad in dark suits, indefatigable, tremendously cheery, soft-spoken and devoted to the pursuit of the dollar), who had a briefcase full of papers. "I know this is going to be a precious meeting," Reverend Smiley said, "and infinitely productive. You look to be in fine fettle, my dear friend."

"I'm all right," Cham said. He did not add that Smiley's inquiries and comments regarding his health induced nervousness in him, and that he had a marked distaste for the mere mention of their damned graveyard. Despite the steady, lucrative custom Grandpa had anticipated, Cham had been out there only once, forced to go by the pleas of his clerical co-owner. No doubt the great expanses of green lawn and groves of trees and placid lakes containing picturesque waterfowl and uniform, small, pure white marble markers studding gently sloping hillsides were charming, but his taste didn't lie in the direction of the hereafter; in his time he'd had enough of death and dissolution, what with Grandpa, Grandma, and his father and mother, and he didn't want to be reminded of the common fate, particularly in relation to Cissie—she seemed to him especially vulnerable, and he could not bear to think of it.

He shook hands with Norman, and they sat down to a discussion. The Smileys spouted figures and presented myriad sheets, drawings and plans. Half listening, Cham perceived that nothing but death and interment in his own handiwork would ever stop the flow of Moses's ideas. He already had the replica of a Saxon church that graced a rise in England's Kersey, a mausoleum, a columbarium, a building for reducing citizens to ashes which resembled a Greek temple, and an undertaking establishment pedimented and colonnaded like the Parthenon. His principal architectural specialist was a designer of sets for motion pictures, and the fellow shared the catholic taste of Moses; every new structure differed from the others in style, period and materials, and Reverend Smiley intended eventually for his park of repose to be a show place where tourists, visitors, the bereaved and prospective clients might repair to delight their eyes and uplift their spirits. "Departure," he frequently said, "need not have the customary sad and depressing aspects. It can be soothing and inspirational. Where is the sting at the end of earthly life is surroundings beckon imperatively and promise eternal peace? What is this passing but a sleep before immortality? My dear friends, the leaving of life for death can be made a thing to look forward to by application of good sales methods." Cham hated to hear him following that line; when he paid attention, Moses was nearly persuasive enough to still his beating heart.

Now Moses wanted to put an insurance company on the grounds—in an office disguised as an Egyptian temple, on the lines of those found at Karnak. The subject had been debated before, and he was bent on demolishing Cham's past objections. A proud boast of the Garden of Immortality was that everything in connection with what the management called "the sweet transition" could be taken care of right on the grounds; a single telephone call would do the trick; there were no gatherings in the distasteful neighborhoods funeral parlors generally inhabited, no processions behind hearses in crowded streets, no slow wending into a grubby ordinary cemetery crowded by monuments to forgotten generations. But insurance—policies that not only provided for the living, but included provisions for superb burial of the insured in the West's loveliest park of repose—that was an item they could no longer afford to ignore. Where would you find a better atmosphere in which to sell it, or customers more conscious of its necessity? The formalities had been complied with beforehand: the State Insurance Commission was agreeable, a staff could be put together on short notice, and the underwriting money was readily available. However, Moses believed so profitable an adjunct should remain in the hands of the Smileys and Cham. All he desired was a solid contribution from Cham to put a foundation under that temple of Karnak.

"Lucius Brennan would have approved of this," he said, and looked accusingly at Cham. "I wish he were sleeping with us. It is one of the great disappointments of my life that we do not have him."

"I've told you," Cham said. "He was cremated. That was his wish."

"We have our magnificent columbarium now," Moses said, "a copy of Westminster Abbey in miniature. Why can't we move the colonel to an honored niche which will be forever his?"

Cham was tired of lying, and a trifle confused by the urgency of his problems. He hesitated, and said, "Well, it's a kind of a secret we've tried to keep, but I guess it doesn't matter—I'm getting fed up with the questioning. Before Grandpa died he talked alone to Cissie and asked a favor of her; I didn't know about it till afterwards. He liked the Queen and wanted to stay with her, all of her. So Cissie and I paid off some people at Rosedale and had his ashes taken from the urn and put in a shoebox. Then Cissie went up one morning in her plane and scattered him across the whole town. She waited till a day when a hard wind was blowing. He's everywhere, and you can't get him back."

"Why, bless me . . ." Moses said. "Thank you for your confidence, Chambers. It was a brave gesture, and befits him."

"Just think," Norman said, "part of him is probably with us at the Garden, Father!"

"We did what he wanted," Cham said, and sighed. "Listen, where were we?"

"The Garden of Immortality Insurance Company," Moses replied. "It is a mighty work, and surely the Lord's. And I am positive we will coin money. The depression does not keep them from dying. In fact, it has helped our business; many are glad to go from such scenes of misery. Protestant Christians may economize on clothing, food and automobiles, but they insist on having their loved ones sleep comfortably. Cham, what do you say?"

"Here are some figures—" Norman began, extending a sheet of paper.

"Never mind that," Cham said. He studied Moses wearily. "How much, Reverend?"

"Not more than six or seven hundred thousand," Moses said. "I will provide the rest. Once we are in business, the actuarial tables will work for us."

"If I agree to this," Cham said, "what are you going to be after next? You just won't rest. You've got to promise me—"

"I do, I do, my dear friend," Moses interrupted. He counted off on his fingers: "My other requests are modest, and can come slowly, out of the profits—that I guarantee. One: a tidy Roman amphitheater as found in Asia Minor, where we can celebrate Easter and hold other sacred services. It need not be of marble. Let me emphasize that we must bring our customers to us and impress them with our advantages, and we are doing this in competition with theaters, movies and sporting events. Some form of display and entertainment is absolutely essential."

"Okay," Cham said. "But out of the profits."

"Two," Moses went on, "a marriage chapel—for we should deal with the inceptions of life as well as its conclusions—on the order of a New England church, which can be cheaply built of wood and appropriately weathered in advance. I would suggest an illusion, at least, of a village common, with a plain spire and a few sheep grazing. Lambs gamboling are always reassuring to the uneasy."

"Out of the profits," Cham said.

"Yes, sir," Moses said. "Three: a museum of religious objects from throughout the world, not excluding relics of the Hindu and Islamic faiths, housed in perhaps a small approximation of the Louvre in Paris."

"They could build us another Winged Victory at a studio plaster shop," Norman said. "I don't think that would sound a wrong note, do you, Mr. Brennan?"

"Not if it was out of the profits," Cham said.

"Four," Moses said, "a new water tower for when we open the Slumberland, Infinite Grace and Blessed Quietude Tracts, built to resemble the Leaning Tower of Pisa." He spread his hands. "Other than those, only more roads, underground pipes for watering, drains, trees, *perhaps* the largest of Wurlitzers for our Westminster Abbey, and an advertising program which will influence people to bring their departed to us from over the whole continent."

"Well, I guess I'll go along with you," Cham said. "Out of the profits . . ."

"May heaven bless you," Moses said. "Ploughing back our takings is only good sense, and we are avoiding taxes, raising future values, and benefitting our fellow mortals. And certainly neither of us needs the income—even I, with my many mouths to feed." He paused delicately. "Don't you wish first to confer with Mr. Sego or Mr. Baltim? When I have started on this I wouldn't like to have your decision reversed—"

"It won't be," Cham cut in. He scowled, nerving himself for an astonishing cold plunge which had been confronting him for a long time; he suddenly was in no mood to bear further affronts or to live in befuddled misery and fear. "I'm deciding on things from now on. I don't need anybody else's say-so."

"I feel that is wise," Moses said. "That was well spoken, my boy. Dependency was never a Brennan characteristic." He rose. "This *has* been a precious meeting. I know we are going to realize a fortune insuring and disposing of the grieving souls who come to us for surcease."

He went out, at once grave, reverent and merry, accompanied by his grave, reverent and merry son. Cham followed them to the front door. Again Moses clasped his hand with the pair of his. "If I seem to have a monomania with respect to our Garden of Immortality, Chambers," he said, "I hope you will forgive me. Please remember it is the culmination of my life's work, my legacy to posterity—just as the development of the Queen was Lucius's. I trust your feeling for our little land of blessed repose will grow."

"Oh, sure," Cham said. "It will."

"The Garden is waiting to receive me when I go to my reward," Moses said, "and it is waiting to receive you and your sister—without charge, of course, and in whatever fashion you choose to slumber—in an urn, a crypt, under the wide and starry sky—"

"Yeah," Cham said. "Uh-huh. We'll talk about that later. Good-bye, Reverend. So long, Norman."

"We are at your service at the Garden, Mr. Brennan," Norman said, and pumped his hand cordially.

Crossing the living room, Cham encountered Lagonda putting a new bulb in a lamp. "What's the matter?" she said. "You look as if you'd seen a ghost."

"I have. Mine, I think."

"Don't talk that way."

"Who's next?"

"Mr. Dunstan from the bank. In ten minutes."

"Oh, God." Cham returned to the library, tilted back a chair, and sat with his feet on a table. The smouldering rebellion in him, rampant and satisfying, was also frightening.

Mr. Dunstan, of the Trust Department, was punctual too. A busy man, neat, indeterminately aged, wearing the high collar that marked his occupation, he had no leisure for raillery. The depression had left its scars on him; he was nervous, suspicious, and painfully exact. Often at odds with Sego and Baltim, his opinion of Cham—never stated outright, but plain enough—was low and declining. Although the Sunset Sea was his only concern, he could not repress an abiding horror at Lucius Brennan's madness in leaving a large fortune outright to a backward young man. Heaven knew the trust was hard to administer, what with the obsessive and obstructive caution shown by Sego and that law firm, but far worse to Mr. Dunstan was a nightmare vision of Cham running berserk with the crazy old man's millions.

Their conferring proceeded according to rote. Dunstan had papers for Cham to sign, certain prefabricated conclusions for him to approve, and complaints to air regarding his fellow trustees. And one important matter to bring to Cham's attention, which dealt with the proposed merger of the Los Angeles National Savings Bank and the Golden West Trust and Savings Bank of San Francisco to form a state-wide giant that would be controlled by a holding corporation known as the Trans-California Corporation. The legal and financial intricacies of the combination, long in the incubation stage, were bewildering; even Dunstan was bemused by them. He did not stun Cham with the details, and he was against the plan. In his view ancient Albert Blour, ready for retirement, was attempting to leave behind him an imposing empire, a monument to his ego, which carried with it many elements of risk.

"I won't crush you with facts and figures, Cham," he said indulgently. "They would only give you a headache. Just let me say that the timing is wrong. There's no assurance that Roosevelt can pull us out of this gigantic slump with his bare-faced socialistic measures, or that we will not endure worse horrors in the future. California is in a shaky condition, the east still dominates the money markets. Those powers will certainly resist our homegrown octopus. Another feature I dislike is our loss of autonomy—under the contemplated arrangement, executive power will shift from Los Angeles to San Francisco, which is something none of us can regard with equanimity; we've lived long enough under *that* shadow."

"Grandpa liked Mr. Blour," Cham said.

"Far be it from me to criticize your great-uncle, but I think he was often swayed by his emotions. We can't allow our hearts to guide us in the dollars-and-cents realm, can we?"

"I don't know. Mr. Blour helped my father and was his good friend, I've heard. I think my first name comes from him."

"That isn't too pertinent, eh?"

"Well, I don't like the name . . . What do Sego and Baltim say?"

"*Mr.* Sego," Dunstan said, emphasizing the honorific, "is not a trustee, although naturally his interests are involved. For that reason, I have not consulted him. Mr. Baltim professes himself to be still undecided, and I haven't yet come to grips with Mr. Lely. I imagine they would like to contradict me, but they can't go against common sense. Your prejudice in my favor will help to decide them. Stick with me, my boy. It's the safe course."

"I am not your boy," Cham said coldly. "I'm almost twenty-four years old."

"Oh?" Dunstan forced a smile. "Pardon me, Cham . . . Look here. Let's talk facts. Your opinion is solicited simply as a courtesy to you. Decision rests with the trustees. Of course, we want you and Cissie to be happy, but I'm sure you are as aware of your relative youth and lack of seasoned judgment as we are. If it were not for the unfortunate strains set up between me and Mr. Baltim and Mr. Lely, and Mr. Sego, who usually adheres to their views and attempts to influence you, we'd have no reason at all for these consultations."

"Yeah."

Dunstan began to look disconcerted, which had not happened before in their dealings. "I can inform you in confidence that the Shapiros are in no mood to surrender their authority to San Francisco. They are going to oppose the merger. I maintain you are better off aligned with them. The bank stock held by Sunset Sea may be the deciding factor finally. Winning the gratitude of the Shapiros is not to be sneered at, eh?"

"No," Cham said, and regarded Dunstan with a fishy eye. Swept on by an undercurrent of resolution, he had already made up his mind;

242

oddly, the dull, blind hardening of will gave him perception, blandness and a faculty for devious invention. "Say, who is the head Shapiro at the bank now?"

"Oh, the place is crawling with them. Old Aaron made very sure his progeny were well taken care of. I should think Irving is spokesman for the tribe. He isn't the oldest, but he is the brightest. Irving was Isadore, you know." Dunstan smiled. "He didn't like his first name either."

"Irving Shapiro . . . Uh-huh." To circumvent any suspicions he might arouse, Cham changed the subject and told Dunstan of the insurance agreement he had entered into with Reverend Smiley.

The man from the Trust Department thought well of the scheme. "But I am more venturesome than the esteemed Mr. Baltim," he said. "However, you made a mistake, my boy. Don't fall into the error of underwriting the company to the tune of better than half a million. Have that queer little preacher handle the economics and any risk. Besides, you're sure to have a negative answer from Mr. Baltim when he hears that part of the deal."

"He's not a trustee of the money my grandfather left me."

"You take his advice, don't you, Cham?"

"I just stopped."

"Oh?"

"I just stopped taking yours, too," Cham said.

"Oh . . ." Dunstan said. It appeared they had nothing further to transact, and he departed, frowning and preoccupied.

"Goodbye, Dunstan," Cham said at the front door. "Thank you." The trustee pressed his lips together involuntarily, and went away without replying.

Cham wandered through the house to the rear, and was intercepted by Lagonda. "Now what?" he asked.

"Have your lunch," she said. "What you want?"

"Maybe some pork chops and a candied yam—and a salad."

"I think you eating too much. Sometimes it riles the blood and makes thinking hard. I'll fix you a sandwich. Go play with Al till it's ready. I got him tied in the back yard."

"Who's coming after I eat?"

"Miss Bresca."

"Oh, God," Cham said. He walked outside and found Al fastened to a twenty-foot length of clothesline knotted to the bole of a sycamore. The small black child with the round head and inky curls and great round brown eyes which had scarcely any white showing pulled a little wagon behind him containing a wooden duck. He welcomed Cham gladly. Sitting down, Cham cradled Al in his lap and they hugged each

243

other. They had an extended conversation about birds and trees and worms in the lawn. Al called Cham "Daddy" and seemed to have little use for Ferris Washington, Junior, a circumstance that pleased the master of the house.

Presently Lagonda came to the kitchen door and called him to lunch, and he kissed Al and went in the dining room, occupying a chair at one end of the enormous table, lighted by the glow of an Italian chandelier introduced by Allie Brennan when she had changed Lucius's home. The chandelier had always irritated Grandpa, for reasons he did not disclose. Since Cham lunched alone, Conny substituted for Ferris, who employed himself on those occasions in cleaning silver or taking Lagonda's grocery list to the store.

Cham ordered a bottle of three-point-two beer, and as Conny served him, reached up under her dress and caressed a solid thigh. The contact was soothing to him. Her drawers were conveniently loose. His hand moved higher, and she reacted at once. So did he. "Do you want to do something?" she said.

"No," he said, and released her. "This is going to be a hard day."

"I'll come in tonight."

"Wait till morning. Do you want to kill the goose that lays the golden eggs?"

Conny laughed and said, "That never killed anybody."

As he dawdled over a cigarette and coffee, Lagonda entered the room. "I hear Miss Bresca coming," she said. "You better get along."

"There is no rest for the wicked."

"You wicked all right. Just like your grandpa."

"I wish I could be like him," Cham said. "Do you think I could, Lagonda?"

"Maybe," she said. "I hope so, even if that is wishing an awful lot on somebody."

Making his way thoughtfully to the library, Cham sighed in the realization that he was no Lucius Brennan. The old man had been a great oak, a thundercloud, a vital force. Cham felt glad that Grandpa could not see him now—assuming Grandpa couldn't, scattered everywhere as he was.

Miss Bresca strode in, an elderly, bespectacled, gaunt virgin, carrying documents tucked in manila envelopes. She worked out of the Sunset Sea office, operating in conjunction with Brennan, Baltim, Lely and Brennan, and her relationship with Cham was brisk and tightly disciplined. Her job consisted of keeping close watch on every cent allotted to the Brennans (Cissie rarely met Miss Bresca, and many painful scenes devolved on Cham), auditing their expenditures, conveying the admonitions of Sego and Baltim, and reporting back to headquarters the commission of any follies. Sometimes she took down in shorthand the few letters Cham had to send. Because she had a high devotion to her tasks, and was vigilant and incorruptible, he hated her. He strongly suspected she couldn't stand him. As an acknowledged spy and tale bearer, she neither gave nor accepted quarter.

Miss Bresca had the falsely hearty manner of a nurse, and invariably opened the proceedings by saying, "And how are we today?" But this wasn't going to be one of their regular days. Until then Cham had been overawed by her, and their relations, while acid, were correct. Today she seemed a fit subject for immolation. He grinned sourly and said, "We are fine. How are you, you old battleaxe?"

"Wh-what di-id you s-say?" Miss Bresca stuttered.

"You heard me."

Bright color surged through Miss Bresca's cheeks. "I don't have to take that, Mr. Brennan."

"Are you sure?"

"Have you been drinking?"

"No," Cham said. "But why don't you go tell Sego and Baltim I've been hitting it up anyway?"

"Why do you act this way?" Tears blurred Miss Bresca's eyes. "What have I done to you? I get thirty dollars a week for doing what I'm told."

Cham licked his lips and groaned. "I'm sorry, Miss Bresca. It's just that I hate everybody except my sister and two or three other people."

"I hate everybody. If I had as much money as you've got, I could speak out too."

"Well, then we know how we stand," Cham said. "Our minds run the same. I've got nothing against you—you can't help being an old bag and a nuisance. And I can't help being a slob. Want to shake hands on it?"

"Yes."

Cham released Miss Bresca's hand. "Now. Give me the checks to countersign and anything else you have. No lectures, understand? How much I spend from now on is nobody's damned business. Just keep the accounts, see? I want to hear no more from Sego or Baltim. If I have any letters I'll write them out and send them to you to type. Tell your bosses if they have complaints to send them to me in the mail. Get in and out of here as fast as you can—once a month. Am I making myself clear?"

"Yes, sir."

"Okay. While I'm signing, call the bank and see whether you can reach a guy named Irving Shapiro for me."

In a few moments Shapiro was reached. Miss Bresca, looking tremulous and shiny-eyed, handed Cham the instrument. "What a pleasure to talk to you, Mr. Brennan," Shapiro said. "My grandfather and your father were close friends. I've had many dealings with your late great-uncle. I can't tell you how many times I have considered giving you a ring—"

"But you always called Baltim instead, huh?" Cham said. "Or Sego."

"Well, since Mr. Baltim has sort of been regarded as guardian of you and your sister—"

"I've got money of my own. Haven't you heard?"

"Of course, Mr. Brennan. But I thought Mr. Baltim was advising you —and Mr. Sego—"

"Why don't I call you Irving, and you call me Chambers? I was Albert and got rid of it, and I hear you got rid of Isadore."

"That's true," Irving said, and laughed. "I'll be glad to call you Chambers."

"Irving, look. Dunstan was out here. He says you are against the merger."

"We are, Chambers. And we're counting on you to—"

"Don't count. I'm for it."

"Really? But Mr. Baltim has led me to believe—"

"Forget him," Cham said. "I have. What I think you'd better do, Irving, is go along with me."

"I'm afraid that's impossible."

"All right. I appreciate your being honest with me, Irving. Then I'm going to pull my holdings out of the bank and—"

"You can't change the trust," Irving said.

"I mean Grandpa's money. When I'm thirty I take over my part of the trust, and my sister will assign me her share. The trust will go out of the bank too. In the meantime, I'll get hold of Mr. Blour and sign something to the effect that he can have my stock the minute I get hold of it."

"You'd sell it?"

"Sure, Irving, if I have to."

"May I come out and talk to you, Chambers? Any time you say?"

"No. There's nothing to talk about. Grandpa wanted the big bank. He liked big things, Irving. Take this up with your family and see what you can do."

"I will," Irving said. "Chambers, you surprise me. And you've given me a serious problem."

"I'll be darned," Miss Bresca said, as Cham hung up.

"I've got another idea," he said. "I haven't heard from Harry Sego since he went east. Where is he?"

"Home." Miss Bresca sneered. "Working for his father."

"That doesn't sound like him."

"He couldn't get any other job. He's awful, Mr. Brennan. No girl in the office is safe if he's around."

"Not even you?"

"Well," Miss Bresca said slowly, "he put his hand on my behind one day when I was leaning over . . ."

"In some ways," Cham said, "you've got to admire him."

Miss Bresca shook her head. "The only good thing about him is that he has more contempt for his father than the rest of us in Sunset Sea have."

"What is Tom Sego doing?"

"Studying at U.S.C. He's trying to make up for his brother."

"Where's Hal Baltim?"

"I don't know. Mr. Baltim never mentions him."

"Gee, we really scattered," Cham said. "Maybe I'm not the only one who is a mess . . . When you go back to the office, ask Harry to come over here. Right away."

"I will," Miss Bresca said. "Mr. Brennan, I'll have to tell them how you're cutting up. If I don't—"

"I know. That's all right."

After she had done, panic seized Cham. He walked aimlessly about the lower floors. Grandpa had said he should be his own man; his father had never been, as Grandpa had. "Piss on all of them," Grandpa said.

He went in the kitchen, where Ferris was polishing crystal goblets and Lagonda was putting clean paper on shelves. Jerking a thumb, Cham sent Ferris into the butler's pantry. Then he told Lagonda what he had done. "Am I nuts?" he said. "Something got me by the throat and wouldn't let go."

Lagonda considered, thoughtfully rubbing the hands with startlingly light palms. "Don't worry," she said. "They been taking advantage of you. I've noticed. It's time you got up on your high horse."

"You think Grandpa would believe I'm right?"

"Yes."

"I'm not going to fool around with Cissie either," Cham said.

But shortly after, his heart quickly sank, for Cissie appeared with Dugald Stuart in tow. The fact she had him along boded ill, and Cham greeted them distractedly; he might have put off any conclusion, except that Cissie said they wanted to talk to him at once. Some memory of Grandpa yelling into the telephone and dominating his associates moved Cham to lead them to the solarium. It wasn't that he was afraid of the engineer, because Dugald was an unimpressive figure—Cissie, a tall girl, topped him by a couple of inches, and he was small-boned, quiet, neatly dressed, with a trim little moustache and light brown hair precisely parted in the center, causing him to resemble a young clerk or shop-keeper; what counted was that he and Cissie were stanch allies and conspirators since he had built an experimental airplane for her, and his being present meant another frightening proposal was about to be launched.

They sat down in the sunny glassed room, and Dugald looked ex-pectantly at Cissie. Slim and freckled, weathered a bit, hair untidily hacked off and rumpled, wearing her customary outfit of checkered shirt and loose slack trousers and unpolished jodhpur boots, she still seemed sixteen years old and an undeveloped boy. Her blue eyes were marvel-ously clear and had an absent expression, as though concentrated on a distant point beyond the horizon. There was dirt beneath her unpainted fingernails and an oil stain on one knee of her pants. A first sight of her, even after a short separation, always brought a tightening in Cham's throat. He felt she was the best and most attractive human being he had ever seen, and could not possibly explain to himself why he idolized her.

They talked at first about the flight from the north. Cham had diffi-culty realizing that just a few hours previously Cissie had been in Seattle, poised at the end of a runway. The swift transit down the coast, at heights of seven or eight thousand feet, was impossible for him to visual-ize. His detestation and fear of the B-1 (Brennan One, named by Du-gald for Cissie), a low-wing, single-engined, two-place, metal-clad monoplane, was intense. In it Cissie had flown innumerable test flights, and been to Arizona, where she encountered an oil leak and made an emergency landing at an Air Corps base, nonstop to Mexico City, where she nearly crashed taking off overloaded in the high altitude for the return trip, nonstop to Miami, nonstop to New York, and across the continent, with an unscheduled descent in the desert near Yuma when headwinds exhausted the fuel. Cissie was a minor celebrity in the news-papers and a favorite of the photographers, who found her clean boy-ishness appealing. Once reporters had tried to talk to Cham about her while he awaited the end of a flight in Glendale, and he mumbled in hopeless, worried confusion and had been rather an object of fun—the docile male member of the family standing by until the aggressive modern female ended her adventuring. However, Cissie was not a noto-riety seeker and avoided the press when she could. All of her journeys were unheralded, she refused to be timed for records, and both she and Dugald insisted the B-1 was purely experimental.

Neither Cissie nor Dugald sounded very bucked up by the airplane's performance. The round trip to Seattle was uninspiring to them. "I car-ried ballast that indicated another twelve hundred miles of range," Cissie said, "but that's nothing. She's stable and solid on the controls, she'll climb to eighteen thousand feet, she'll lift maybe ten thousand pounds, she'll cruise at a hundred and seventy miles an hour moderately loaded. The new three-blade constant-speed propeller helps. But we haven't got enough horsepower."

"Or enough engines," Dugald said.

"Three hundred and fifty, with another thirty for takeoff," Cissie said, "just won't do."

"What's the matter with three hundred and fifty horsepower?" Cham demanded. "My Duesenberg's only got two sixty-five."

Cissie glanced at Dugald. "It's ignorance, not ill will," she explained.

"No, it's ill will," said Cham, with a rush; he had to take care not to stumble over his words, and was aware that his face was growing heated. "I'm fed up, Cissie. The time has come to call a halt. You've had your fun and your own airplane built to order and made the trips and risked your life. I want you to come back to earth and start acting like a girl. Lagonda agrees."

"Lagonda!" Cissie said.

"You're dirty and you look like hell," Cham said, "and men don't pay any attention to you. You are a Brennan. You've got to live up to your responsibilities."

"Who are you to criticize?" Cissie said. "Since when have you been living up to your responsibilities or been a Brennan—whatever that is? You don't work, you sit around this house most of the time, you sleep with a Mexican maid, your best friend is a Negro nurse you had as a child who's still nursing you, and the trustees of the estate think you're an idiot."

Cham gazed at her incredulously. "I'll be a son of a bitch!" he said.

"You are one," Cissie told him.

"You'd better wait outside, Dugald," Cham said. "This is going to be a real family fight."

"No, stay here," Cissie said. "You're part of us now."

"How is he part of us?" Cham said. "Building that damned B-1 didn't make *him* a Brennan."

"Oh, stop sounding like Grandpa!" Cissie cried. "And stop trying to act like him! You're not the type!"

"I'm not, huh?" Cham said. "Just you wait and see!"

"I'd rather go," Dugald said, and turned white and got up.

"Stay!" Cissie commanded. Dugald reluctantly sat down, his head lowered.

Fumbling in his wallet, Cham brought out a small item clipped from the newspaper. "Look at this!" he said. He extended it to Cissie, who refused to as much as glance at it. "You didn't care to let me in on the news, did you? How do you think that made me feel?"

"What are you talking about?" Cissie asked.

"Sarah Godowsky, that's who!" Cham said. "She got killed the other day. Don't tell me you didn't hear of the accident."

"I heard," Cissie replied indifferently. "She had bad luck and used bad judgment. She blew a cylinder head on takeoff and tried to turn around and come back. She spun in. Why are you so excited?"

"If it could happen to her, damn it," Cham said, "with all her hours and experience, what do you think will happen to you? Do you expect I can stand just passing the time waiting for the bad news—or Lagonda either, for that matter—the two of us just waiting to hear that you have—"

"Oh, shut up," Cissie said. "You're an old woman, and Lagonda is nearly as foolish as you are. Poor Sarah was flying worn-out equipment and getting on in years for a pilot. She wanted to avoid washing out a plane she couldn't afford to replace. I'm not doing that kind of thing."

"Not much you're not," Cham said. "You're flying stuff this Dugald puts together that nobody's been up in before. You're lifting weights and going places Godowsky never did. And what are you trying to prove? That the Goddamned plane will fly? Well, you've proved that. You and Dugald say the B-1 is a frost. Where're the aviation records you've established?"

"Uh—we haven't tried for records, Cham," Dugald said. "Oh—excuse me. This hasn't been properly explained to you. You see, we have a much larger conception which has yet to be proved. The main reason for building the B-1 was to test the airfoil—"

"Listen," Cham said, "you stay out of this. All I ever get from you is a lot of crap about wings and slots and wing loading and air density and lift coefficients and cambers—and every time you get me mixed up to the hilt you look at me as if I was an ape and pull out your damned slide rule. I've heard the words you use so much I can remember them, but I don't know any more than I did at the start. All right, I'm ignorant. But I do know you can kill my sister playing expensive games that don't make practical sense, and I know I'm head of this family."

"You're not head of anything," Cissie said, "and if you keep on being rude to Dugald, I'll knock you flat."

"Go ahead," Cham said. "Take a sock at me. We're not kids any more. I'll give you a thick lip for your trouble."

"Please, please," Dugald said. "That's not the way to talk to each other—"

"A fine girl you turned out to be," Cham said bitterly. "I love your

250

sympathy for poor old Godowsky. She was the biggest thing in the world to you a few years ago, and now she's dead and you act as if somebody had run over a dog."

Suddenly Cissie turned from him. She buried her face in her hands, and her shoulders shook. Cham stared at her, a tingling in his eyes, and he scratched himself erratically. He wanted to hold her in his arms and didn't dare.

"She took it hard," Dugald said. "But you can't talk about it, Cham. Somebody is always having bad luck. That's part of what we're doing . . ."

"Well, I apologize," Cham said. "But that doesn't alter cases. She's got to quit."

Cissie straightened and lowered her hands. They looked at each other steadily. Using a sleeve, she dried her eyes.

"Grandpa warned me," Cham said, in a voice that would not remain steady. "He told me you'd need disciplining."

"I won't quit," she said.

"I'll stop the money," Cham said.

"Let us finish it," Cissie interrupted. "Cham, we've only begun. I want Dugald to build me the airplane he's been dreaming of for five years. We've proved the airfoil and most of his theories, and that's what we're interested in—not setting records somebody would wipe out in a month or two. If he can make his drawings and figures and blueprints come to life, we'll have a plane everybody will buy. It won't be a stunt, but a new means of getting from place to place. Dugald's the man who set me straight: it's Grandpa's improving the breed."

"I'm not interested," Cham said.

"The airlines would want the ship," Cissie said. "Look at them—they haven't the equipment they should have, and still they're flying from coast to coast and in countries all over the world. Their business is growing every year. Everybody sends his important letters airmail. Someday all the people will be flying when they have long distances to cover. You don't need roads or railroad rights-of-way or anything—just beacons and radio communication. Don't you want to get in on that?"

"No," Cham said.

"Cham," Dugald said, "I think I can build an airliner that will cruise at better than two hundred miles an hour on twin engines, carry twenty-five passengers, lift thirty thousand pounds including its own weight, fly above twenty thousand feet, carry gas for twenty-five hundred miles, and be completely reliable. I don't think—I'm sure of it. So is Cissie. Let me build one. Give us a chance."

"The answer is no," Cham said.

"All I'd do is test it," Cissie said. "Help Dugald. Then I'd be satisfied. I wouldn't go anywhere."

"I said I wasn't interested," Cham told them. "How much would it cost?"

"Three hundred thousand, I suppose," Cissie said.

"That's for the first model," Dugald added. "Development work comes high. We can reduce the prices on subsequent models—"

Cham's breath caught. "Three hundred thousand! Do you think I'm as stupid as I look?"

"You sound as though you are," Cissie said.

"Thank you very much," Cham said. "Okay, I'm stupid. But it's my money." He glared at Dugald. "How much would you put in, genius?"

"I have two hundred dollars," Dugald replied. He smiled and shrugged. "And I'd have to quit my temporary job in the drafting room at Pilcher Aircraft and lose that twenty-eight dollars a week."

"There," Cham said to Cissie. "Does that answer the question?"

"It's your funeral, Cham," Cissie said. "We'll have to get on without you. We can raise the money somehow."

"I'll bet!" Cham said. "Give me a few examples how."

"Sell the project to an aircraft company," Dugald said. "Let somebody in with a chance to buy us out if the plane is successful. Of course, we'd lose everything eventually—"

"Forget that," Cissie said. "We'll hang onto it, Dugald. I believe I can raise a cash loan on my part of the trust. And there are other means of making money. I've had plenty of offers to fly in dope and uncut diamonds and Chinese from Mexico—"

"Wait a minute!" Cham said.

"Don't yell, baby," Cissie said. "You can keep your skirts clean. I'm going to move from here, and I'll change my name if you want me to."

"My own sister . . ." Cham said. "You're making a nervous wreck of me!"

"Why don't you pee your pants?" Cissie asked.

"No, I think I'll cry," Cham said. He thought for a moment he was going to.

"Remember when I planned to run away that time?" Cissie said. "You talked me out of it. And you promised that if you were ever head of the family in the place of Grandpa you'd give me anything I wanted. You said your word was good, not with anybody else, but with me. Only your word isn't good."

"It's good," Cham said. He loosened his tie and collar and rubbed his warm forehead. "Three hundred thousand, did you say? Why so much? The B-1 only cost—"

"We'll explain it to you," Cissie said, and darted up and kissed the end of his nose. "But you've got to pay very close attention."

"You think I won't for three hundred thousand dollars?" Cham said. Naturally Dugald had a briefcase, and out of it he was pulling a wad of drawings and sheets of figures. Cham moaned. "Everybody who comes in here has a bunch of papers!"

When Cissie and Dugald had left Cham, Loganda came in to say Harry Sego was waiting in the library. He'd been there for an hour. Tired and dazed, Cham regarded her disconsolately. "What a day," he remarked.

"I heard your hollering," Lagonda said. "Did you settle things with Cissie?"

"Yes."

"How?"

"Well, we had it out."

"Is she going to stop flying?"

"You could say that."

"Maybe I could. What do *you* say?"

"Well, she's not going to fly over any oceans or anything. I put my foot down. Dugald's going to build her a new plane—"

"What?"

"This is for carrying passengers. The airlines might use it."

Lagonda sighed. "I feel sorry for you."

"Everyone does," Cham said. "And that doesn't make it any easier, Goddamn it!"

He went in the library, and Harry got up from the desk to shake hands; he was thinner than ever, his blond hair needed cutting, and he had a wry, dispirited grin. "I've been reading your mail," he said. "It isn't very interesting. How did you get so fat, Cham?"

"High living. How did you get so thin?"

"Low living. I was in New York for a couple of years, starving in Greenwich Village. I picked the wrong kind of times for being independent."

"And now you're home with daddy," Cham said. "How's it going?"

"I have to eat. You've never been east, have you, Cham?"

"No. I'm satisfied here."

"With your money," Harry said, "you could sure enjoy yourself in Manhattan. The women, the food, the theaters, the booze! But it takes dollars in the pockets. Don't you ever dream of a bigger life?"

"I've got too much to do."

"Really? I understand from my father that you're a no-good bum."

"That was yesterday," Cham said. "Do you want a job with me?"

"Why not?"

"I'll give you two hundred a month."

"Consider me hired. What do I do?"

"I need advice and somebody to run errands. The guy also has to admire me, and I would like a little outspoken praise."

Harry grinned. "Laid on thick or thin?"

"Thick," Cham said, "as long as I'm paying for it. I haven't had many compliments so far . . ." He considered; oddly, a multiplication of problems energized him, and he discovered the bits and pieces of Grandpa's instructions were coming in handy. "I've got to have a lawyer too, and I won't want Lely or Baltim. Do you know of anybody?"

"How about the other Baltim? He's out of school and practicing in a little hole in the wall on Main Street. His old man and him are in opposite camps."

"That sounds interesting. Ask him to come here tomorrow."

"Right, boss. When do we show up?"

"About ten o'clock. I don't rise early."

"I can't wait to get back to the office," Harry said. "Miss Bresca came in with the first news and my father turned purple, but just think what'll happen when I tell him I'm quitting to go with you! He'll choke, I hope. What's got into you, Cham?"

"I don't know. You think it's a good idea, don't you?"

"Great idea. I'm curious, though—you sound like you had plans. Where do we go from here?"

"I'm going into the airplane business," Cham said, and was faintly astonished at his own words. "I've been sitting on my duff too long. My sister's a flyer, you know, and she's got a hungry aeronautical engineer on the string. We have to build a new kind of plane, better than anything seen yet. It'll cost a fortune."

"And then what?"

"Everyone will buy it. The airlines, see? We'll have a company. We need better engines and a factory and—" Cham trailed off, shaken by the implications of the enterprise. The details showered on him by Cissie and Dugald were just beginning to take form. His sister and the engineer talked glibly and dealt in perishable, rackety dreams that all led to an improbably golden afterglow which might never shine. In between were enough pitfalls to entrap a herd of elephants. He could see them, and Dugald and Cissie could not. Despite their special knowledge, they were babes in the wood. Still, what could he do? It was for Cissie, who was nutty. But it was Grandpa's money, and his heritage and training forced him to realize he had to rise and fight for every penny. Nothing could be

254

wasted. If they must fail in a foolish endeavor, they must fail as cheaply as possible.

"You're as crazy as they say, aren't you, Cham?"

"You just lost your job."

"You didn't hear me," Harry replied carefully. "What I said was that it's a great idea. Who else could think of such a thing? You've got a mind of your own, and there's no other one like it. All I can do is sit here and admire you."

"That's better," Cham said. "You're rehired."

Scarcely was Harry sent off, slightly flushed in anticipation of the thundering knock he was going to deliver at Sunset Sea, when Burton Lely made an entrance. He was smiling and apparently unshaken, but underneath his calm facade lay a degree of astonishment and anxiety. Cham took him for a walk in the garden, feeling the necessity of movement, and picked up Al, out for a pre-bed run after his dinner. Carrying the boy in his arms, he limped around the plaster summerhouse, the quietly disgusted Lely at his side. Until Al stopped chattering, they couldn't talk sensibly. When he had dozed off, Lely said, "I suppose you know why I'm here in such haste."

"Miss Bresca spread the alarm, huh?"

"Yes. What prompted your revolt, Cham?"

"I'm sick of being treated like a high school kid," Cham said. "Today I happened to spit out the bad taste."

"Probably we have patronized you. Have I been as bad as the others?"

"No."

"Well, I'll apologize for all of us," Lely said. "You must take into account that we've watched you coming up from infancy, always in the shadow of your prodigious great-uncle, and somehow we've made the mistake of not taking you seriously."

"Anyway, I looked stupid."

"Now that you mention it—yes."

"And acted stupid," Cham said. "A guy with bad habits."

"I'm not here to criticize you, Cham—only to offer amends—"

"Don't bother with my feelings. I wouldn't go to school or work, I sleep with the maid, I've got Lagonda and this black baby. Cissie's mentioned my failings."

"Has she? I thought her devotion to you was blind." Lely paused and rubbed his chin. "You aren't perfect, God knows. Are you going to change your ways?"

"Some of them."

"Good. Cham, Harold Baltim was going to rush here and lecture you.

I argued him into letting me come instead. Perhaps you'll tell me what you have in mind."

"In a minute," Cham said. "I want to settle one or two things first . . . Mr. Lely, why do you suppose Grandpa left me his money?"

"It was his idea of a joke, I presumed—and to spite your sister. And he was, to put it delicately, in a declining state. Am I wrong?"

Halting, Cham cuddled Al and frowned in concentration. "I think so. Grandpa didn't have any declining state. At times he had to rest, but that was so he could come back stronger. At the end he was all right. Just tired. I believe he gave me the money because he thought I was another Brennan. He told me to be my own man."

"I see."

"He was too big, and I was too small. To keep peace in the family, I played dumb. It made things easier. I've fooled a lot of people. I'm willing to go on playing dumb if it'll help. But I'm not as dumb as I seem."

"I'm starting to believe you," Lely said.

"I don't really agree with anybody," Cham said. "I don't believe anything I've heard. I don't need anyone and I don't care what they think. Underneath I've always felt that, but I never bothered to think about it until now. That's the most I can explain."

"That's sufficient."

"My idea is to be like Grandpa. Only I have to be different, see, because times have changed."

"Good heavens," Lely said. "Here we go again!"

Cham proceeded to explain his decision regarding the bank merger. In a stroke of cunning, he mentioned that Mr. Dunstan thought his fellow trustees were his enemies and not too bright. Color heightening a little, Lely agreed with Cham that Dunstan had the wrong approach; he was taken aback at Cham's handling of Irving Shapiro, and yet promised to bring Baltim around to his views. He listened intently to an explanation of Cissie's plans and how Cham meant to implement them. "Who is this Stuart?" he asked.

"Well, he studied aeronautics at M.I.T. He's worked for Glenn Martin and Boeing—they build airplanes."

"I'm aware of that."

"Cissie says he's a genius," Cham said.

"Her conviction is enough for you? Or are you so experienced in this you can determine for yourself?"

"No. I trust her."

"I thought you told me," Lely said, "that you didn't need anyone and believed nothing you heard."

256

"Cissie is different."

Lely sighed. "It's a queer method for getting into business, Cham. The expense seems inordinate, the risks enormous, and your experience nil. I know you love your sister, but—"

"You don't approve?"

"I think not. But I know even less about the aircraft industry than you."

"I have a hunch you can buy anything," Cham said. "Brains, love, faith, success and respect. Grandpa worked on that theory. You have to stay in one place, like Los Angeles, and fight it out. All you need is the capital and the nerve. I've got both."

"You have something else," Lely said. "That old man's conquering hedonism. I hadn't realized it before."

Cham didn't know what hedonism was. But he did not bother to ask.

Cissie had Dugald stay on, and that night dinner was a gay occasion, which the participants took as an omen for the future. The future—Grandpa's charmed future—got hold of Cham too, watching the high spirits of the others. He recalled Grandpa saying things always went well when you gave people what they wanted, and laughed and ordered Ferris to serve wine. The only bottles which could be found contained the sweet muscatel favored by the Algonrones, but it went down easily.

Talk centered on the B-2, and Cham found himself as impatient as Dugald and Cissie. The question of where to build the ship revived his memory of the Xanadu Amusement Producing Corporation, and he searched among papers in a desk drawer in the library. Grandpa hadn't been able to cash out that sad venture, or the eighty acres surrounding it. Evidently his real estate agents could find no one interested in buying three empty, windowless, barnlike structures two stories in height and a number of small shacks used for offices and dressing rooms. The ground about lacked a good well and was thus unsuitable for cultivation. Motion picture production had long since shifted to the west end of the city, or into the San Fernando Valley, and there was little manufacturing in Long Beach. Rather than compound his losses, Grandpa had kept the property and paid the low taxes. Occasionally, Sego had sent Cham a letter advising a sacrifice sale, which was ignored along with most of his other communications. "It sounds ideal for us," Dugald said. Cissie insisted they see the studio, at once.

There was some doubt that they could get inside, for Cham had no keys and the realty agents were unavailable; nevertheless, they piled in his car and set out, seen off by a disapproving Lagonda. A half moon shone and the night was clear, and long before they had crossed the southern flatlands and reached the graveled street, the square, ugly buildings could be seen silhouetted against the pale sky. Encircling the lot was a high wooden fence, sections of it broken and rotting, and in front stood an elaborate gate flanked by a kind of sentry box, both forced open by vandals. The corporation's sign overhead was faded and nearly indistinguishable. Driving inside, the three of them employed the flashlights they had brought for an inspection. Windows were shattered, doors hung open, filth in corners stank, tramps had employed anything they could wrench loose for their cooking fires. An onshore wind carried the acrid odors of an oil refinery at the harbor a few miles beyond. Vast, echoing, spooky black vistas inside the buildings made Cham uneasy, but Cissie and Dugald examined every foot of them and went out in the fields to pace off a runway. They returned to Cham, who remained in the Duesenberg phaeton playing the radio, and reported themselves very pleased.

"We can not only build it here," Dugald said, "we can fly it from here."

"We'll build a hundred of them," Cissie said.

Cham was listening to a rendition of "The Music Goes Down and Around," his favorite number. He nodded absently. His partners, as he had suspected, were Hansel and Gretel and would bear close watching. He would have to take charge unobtrusively. But that he did not mind.

"We'll have to get a sign right away," Cissie said. "'The Stuart Aircraft Company.' How does that sound, Dugald?"

"Well," Dugald said, "I—"

No longer wool-gathering, Cham said, "No, 'The Brennan-Stuart Aircraft Company.' How does that sound, Dugald?"

"Oh, fine," Dugald said. "I—"

"It's for Cissie, you know," Cham said. "Sentiment, huh? You don't mind?"

"I think Dugald ought to have his name—" Cissie began.

"Then it's settled," Cham said. "You're satisfied, aren't you, Dugald?"

"Oh, yes," Dugald said. "All I ask is to build the plane—"

"Okay," Cham said. "I'll have the company put together. I'm tired. Let's go home. Dugald, you drive."

He lay on the back seat and closed his eyes. Tired as he was, though, he couldn't doze off. What he had let himself in for had the irritating urgency of a dozen mosquitoes buzzing around his head—and in it. Despite indolence and distrust, he was compelled to rise and attempt to shine. Already he had decided to appropriate fifty-five per cent of the company; he could not entrust control to anybody else. Grandpa, he thought, would have grabbed at least sixty-five per cent.

Opening his eyes, he perceived another problem. Cissie's left hand was on the nape of Dugald's neck, vaguely caressing him, and they were talking softly; no doubt of the damned B-2. So that was the way it was going. Did Cham want his sister to marry the guy? No. Dugald was not high enough by a couple of inches, and too unworldly. And he had only two hundred dollars to his name. Well, Cham would handle that contingency when it arose. Suddenly he felt he could handle nearly anything, like Grandpa.

His bedroom seemed to him the best haven of his life, as it often had. Cham didn't even clean his teeth. When he had been to the toilet and peeled off his clothes and was hunting for pajamas, Lagonda walked in; she delved in the correct drawer and handed him the night garments. "You ought to give a little warning," he said. "Here I am bare naked and—"

"What's the difference?" she said. "There's nothing here I haven't seen."

"What do you want?"

"I don't know about you. Are you sure everything's all right?"

"Yes."

Lagonda tucked him in bed and turned off the top light. In an afterthought, she kissed his forehead. "You better be careful with the old man's money. He wouldn't like it being lost."

"He wouldn't like it just doing nothing either, would he?"

"I guess not."

"Listen, I can think a little," Cham said. "What you've got to do here is have the climate on your side. Everything else changes, but it stays the same. I learned that from Grandpa. The other day I was reading a piece in the newspaper. Do you realize something new's happening in Los Angeles again?"

"No."

"Well, it is. The oranges and real estate and tourists are old stuff. And this depression isn't going to last forever, in spite of Roosevelt. We've got close to half of the airmail traffic in the United States flying in and out of here, more planes and licensed pilots than any other state, thirty aeronautical schools, four aircraft engine factories, plenty of fields, seven scheduled flying lines, nothing but sunshine, and everybody but you and me wants to get his feet off the ground. Detroit has the automobiles and Pittsburgh the steel and Chicago the hogs and New York the trade. If I was to go into business, why not make airplanes? This is the place for them."

"If you was crazy," Lagonda said, "that's exactly what you should do.

Good night." She went to the doorway, and turned and stared at Cham. "It sounds as if the colonel was back."

"I wish he could hear us," Cham said. "He liked new ideas. Good night."

He said to himself luxuriously, "What a day!" and reached out and put out the lamp. Conny entered, barefooted and wearing a long robe. She removed it, disclosing that underneath was only her. "You want to do something?" she asked.

"Not me," Cham said. "I've got too much on my mind."

But she climbed in with him anyway, and favored him with those peculiar, sucking endearments. Soon he was entangled in a hot, wet embrace. Yet at the very instant he bellowed in the brief, miraculous, epileptic ecstasy, he had not divorced his subconscious from consideration of the queer voyage on which he was embarked. That had never happened previously; a nostalgia for a lost innocence and comfort and security stirred him. A driving practicality unknown until now caused him to abandon the generous spread-eagled refuge she made for him and say, "All right, don't lay there. Get in the bathroom. I don't want any cream-colored little bastards in Belvedere to worry about."

He was a changed man. Even Conny, hams bobbing as she obediently trotted from the bed, could see that. In a moment her surprised sobs mingled with the sound of running water. Taking partial note of her grief, he supposed he might have to get rid of her in the course of time.

four

PATIENCE Cham had in abundance, at least until lately, and the quality returned to him once he was free. Living with Grandpa and preserving the family had taught him the virtues of holding on. He needed all his training in his dealings with Dugald Stuart, who was a perfectionist and had no sense of time. "Someday I'm going to kill the little bastard," Cham said presently to Cissie. "I can't trust a word he says. He keeps bringing up new things. He's lied to me."

"He hasn't lied to you," Cissie replied. "You're just too dense to appreciate what he's doing, and he couldn't tell you the whole story in that one evening. Unless we have the wind tunnel tests we'll be going off half-cocked."

"Time is money!"

"Quit thinking of money. Think of the final result."

That was difficult for Cham to conceive: the B-2 assembled and flying, with Cissie at the controls, or not flying, and Cissie in mortal danger. He gave up attempting to envision the end; it was enough to concentrate on the step-by-step process and confront the daily problems. Besides patience he had tenacity, and, his sister's exhortations to the contrary, he never stopped thinking of money. It was well he did not. In the end, direct expense on the single prototype amounted to nearly half a million dollars and he had another three million invested in airline stocks.

Slowly, unwillingly, tentatively, Cham was led into constructing a radical form of transportation. Not led really, for he was compelled to make most of the decisions. Dugald was the pied piper who preceded him, aided in his siren's music by Cissie. Like a gambler seeking to overcome a losing streak, he kept doubling his bets and waiting for

261

fortune to smile on him. The wait was long and painful. Originally Dugald had guessed the B-2 would require six months to put together; it required more than a year.

First came the wind-tunnel affair. The help of a group of scientists in Berkeley was enlisted, and Cham found he had to finance a series of tests of a scale model of the airplane. Cissie repeatedly flew Dugald in the B-1 to Berkeley, and they seemed always to return with disclosures of fresh complications. "We're not trying to find out the secrets of nature," Cham said. "We're trying to build this one damned plane. I don't intend to pay for advancing general knowledge." His protestations were to no avail. The great fan blowing little flecks of wool attached to the model in the chamber continued until everybody was satisfied and each fact had been checked, verified and calculated.

Then there was the matter of the engineers Dugald needed to assist him, men he had known and trusted in the past. They were scattered around the country, and required inducements and guarantees to come to Long Beach. Bringing them together consumed costly weeks. Meanwhile the abandoned movie studio underwent a transformation—the fence was repaired, the buildings cleaned and painted, a runway scraped, graded and equipped with drainage. At Cham's insistence, Hank Isbrow was installed as foreman; he had considerable knowledge of aircraft by now, in the practical sense, and was a firm partisan of Cissie's. But he had nothing to do. Everything waited on the dragging labors of the fellows with the sketching pads and slide rules.

Cham went only once to the Brennan-Stuart Aircraft Company. Hank took him on the tour of inspection because Dugald and Cissie were busy in some kind of meeting in a crowded little office, and Cham looked glumly at the clutter of tools and materials which were arriving, the machinery and hoists being installed, and the long straight stretch of gashed earth bisecting the acreage. "We'd be better off making pictures," he commented.

"No, sir," Hank said. "Don't you believe that, Mr. Brennan. This is going to be the greatest thing you ever did. When people used to ask me what Cissie's brother was in, I couldn't say nothing. Now I can tell them—"

"Now you can tell them he's a nut," Cham said. "If Grandpa hadn't liked you, you'd be looking for another job in the next five minutes."

Dugald appeared to invite Cham to his office; the neat young men in the white shirts and ties, pencils clipped to their pockets, waited politely for the outsider to join them. Refusing, Cham got in the Duesenberg, drove home, and went to bed with Conny.

The airframe, as the engineers referred to what Cham in his innocence had thought was the B-2, constituted a mere part of the total effect. Transport planes were too noisy, the comfort of the passenger was a prime consideration, and a study of soundproofing was in order. Experts from the California Institute of Technology were summoned. Retractable landing gear and the hydraulic systems to power it caused harrowing delays and many revisions of equipment. Blueprints rose in towering stacks. Even the chemical toilet in the cabin aroused controversy. Gathering fabric and carpet samples and watercolor paints, Cissie clumsily set about designing the interior decor, assisted by Lagonda; their combinations were not satisfactory, and a thin, impeccable, offensive man who specialized in such projects was called upon to finish the job. He spent three months fabricating a tall, deep chair that would afford a comfort never before known to air travelers. Belts easy to attach or release would hold the customer securely on takeoff and landing and during spells of rough weather. Everyone connected with B-S (a contraction of the company name that provoked inevitable comment) had to try the chair, including Cham. It was brought to him by Dugald, and, feeling a fool, he had Lagonda, Ferris, Al and Conny precede him. They all thought it was wonderful. He sat down and scowled, and said, "It's comfortable, I suppose. What do you want them to do, go to sleep or ask to live up in the air? Never mind how I feel. I can promise you *I* won't ever be sitting in any Goddamned B-2."

Weights in excess of six tons necessitated special tires, and an engineer was sent off on detached duty at a rubber company. Ventilation and lighting posed difficult questions. The cockpit, bristling with dual controls and radio equipment that had to have constant testing and a temperamental new automatic piloting device, was built in simulation and redesigned six times. Baffles were installed in the tanks to keep the fuel from slopping around. De-icers which worked erratically were put on a model wing and taken to an ice-making plant for testing. A change in the wing flaps sent Dugald and a few of his merry men back to Berkeley for further investigation. Bolts failed from overstress, transfer pumps grew balky, the fabric surfaces on the empennage wrinkled under high pressures, Hank had trouble riveting the aluminum sheets of the skin, the electrical systems developed shorts. Every item, and there were thousands, had to evolve on a lengthening schedule of trial and error.

Through compounded confusions moved a serene, happy and confident Dugald. He never lost his temper, raised his voice, or exhibited a trace of dismay. Four hours of sleep a night failed to diminish his energy. Not the smallest detail escaped his attention. Each bit and piece going into the B-2 had his personal touch. While Cham chafed and complained, he smiled and soothed. Of course, it wasn't his cash disappearing down the drain. At his side, constantly supporting and defending him, was Cissie. Some of his gentility must have passed to her, for she started treating her brother with an indulgent sympathy during their arguments instead of threatening to hit him. Her forebearance bothered Cham. He fell to brooding about her and the engineer, and took his suspicions to Lagonda.

"Bull-Shit Aircraft," he said morosely. "How did I ever get into this, Lagonda? A year from now they'll still be talking of how a part won't fit and they'd better go to another laboratory for a few months."

"They'll get it done. It don't come easy."

"What does Cissie see in the guy?"

"Maybe nothing," Lagonda said. "They just want to build an airplane together. Leave 'em alone."

"Nothing, my arse! One of these days we're going to have a worse worry than the B-2. The two of them will be coming to us to say they want to get married."

Lagonda pursed her lips. "I don't think Cissie's got that on her mind. She isn't a regular kind of woman."

"I think she is," Cham said. "I saw her patting his head once. What can we do if they fall in love?"

"Nothing."

"Would you let her marry *him?* He's undersized, broke, too slow and good-natured—"

"Don't try to be like your grandpa and butt in," Lagonda said. "We've had plenty of managing other folks' lives around here. You leave them be."

"How do you feel about him, Lagonda?"

"He's a good man. He works hard. His manners is nice. If Cissie was interested in him, I wouldn't have any objections. I think he has a fine brain, which is better than yours or mine."

"He's got to have a giant brain," Cham said. "I'm betting a big piece of Grandpa's money that he knows what he's doing, and I'm getting in deeper every hour. Why should I have confidence in him? Because you worked it out on your ouija board? It's been wrong other times. The thing is, if I back out now everybody will say I was a sucker and as stupid as they always thought. If I go on, I may be a bigger sucker. Which is worse?"

"I'll tell you what's worse than either," Lagonda said. "Turning him down and losing Cissie. You couldn't stand that. So what choice have you got?"

Cham sighed. "Anyway, that makes it easier for me, huh? Well,

264

Grandpa liked a gamble. I'll see if I can't give him a hell of a run for his money."

Cham's two lieutenants were Hal Baltim and Harry Sego. Superstitious devotion to the past kept him in the house, transacting business as Grandpa had, having people come to him and talking on the telephone. He needed underlings to negotiate for him. Hal had at first refused Cham's offer. A call to him in which Cham dwelt on their boyhood friendship quickly took a turn for the worse. "Don't get sentimental, Great Cham," Hal said. "And don't attempt to do me any favors on account of our growing up together. You're the wrong sex for playing Lady Bountiful."

"Mean as ever, huh?" Cham said. "Harry told me you were. I wouldn't have bothered to ring you except that I hate your old man as much as you do. I thought it might make him gnash his false teeth harder if he heard you were working for me."

"I admit that's a good reason, but it's not good enough. We're worlds apart, Cham. I'm a labor lawyer, and opposed to every damned thing you stand for. My life is going to be devoted to the poor and downtrodden. Whatever the cost, I intend to fight for social justice. I won't accept big accounts. The laborer, the prostitute, the poor Mexican and Negro—those are the clients I deal with. My days are spent in Municipal Court defending the forgotten man."

"Don't quote Roosevelt to me, for Christ's sake!"

"You see?" Hal said triumphantly. "We are divided by an ethic that will tolerate surrender by neither side. You represent the kind of reactionary I most abhor. To my mind, you are the epitome of capitalism's last excrescence."

"Listen," Cham said, "you still talk like a movie subtitle. Where do you get your language since the talkies came in?"

"You're a mastodon inhabiting a jungle we are rapidly clearing. Enjoy it while you can, Cham. The hour of retribution and economic equality is on the way."

"Goodbye, you crazy son of a bitch!"

But Cham could not leave it at that. Grandpa wouldn't have either; he remained dominant and had what he chose, even if he permitted his puppets a few liberties. And Cham kept the desire to surround himself with the vestiges of his happy youth, as a token for a comfortable future. He asked Harry if Hal was married. Harry said he was not, and that Hal was interested in the common man, not the common woman. "I think I've got an idea," Cham remarked.

He mentioned Hal to Cissie. She appeared to have difficulty recalling him. Her eyebrows rose when Cham asked her to telephone him and renew the offer. "You needn't get mushy or anything," he said, "but let him know you're in on the deal and would appreciate his helping out."

"Are you drinking now like Grandpa?" she demanded.

"No. I'm serious."

"This is ridiculous. I always thought he was a fool, and I certainly won't call him. Besides, why him of all lawyers?"

"I don't know," Cham said. "Put it down to a hunch. Probably he's not very bright, but he's honest or he wouldn't talk that way. I've known him for a long time. I can trust him."

"Well, tell him that yourself—the good part, I mean. He'll change his tune. Surely you don't want your sister flirting just in order to—"

"Cissie, look. I've done quite a lot for you and that mad scientist of yours. Maybe it won't turn out any better than it does in the moving pictures. The monster in Long Beach may kill all of us, but I'm willing to go ahead. Did you ever hear of returning favors?"

"You've got me," Cissie said, and smiled sadly.

The tenor of her conversation with Hal was not reported to Cham by either of them, but inside twenty-four hours he was in Cham's service for a modest annual fee. Unfortunately, he provided no flattery of the sort Harry gave in abundance. His high moral standards threw up frequent obstacles. For a while he was a bore, lecturing extemporaneously on the inequalities in a social and economic system he deplored. The Queen was to him an untidy, loathsome octopus, tentacles spread everywhere over innumerable dusty miles, battening on open-shop labor, police brutality, the cynical fleecing of tourists, and lying claims of the boosters. The depression had filled him with exaltation and a high resolve: the abuses and villainies of a hundred years of robber barons and a shameless exploitation of natural resources were going to be cured in the white-hot crucible of want, hunger and orderly revolution. Hal could catch the reflected radiance of Utopia just over the next hill. He dearly loved New Dealers, labor organizers, fallen women, petty thieves oppressed by magistrates, Mexicans, Negroes, Jews, and the Russian proletariat.

Much of this was unsettling to Cham, and even revolting; but he bore it stoically, since Hal—in spite of taking on, with maturity, part of the pinch-faced, bald-headed ascerbity of his father—reminded him of the green years and contributed to his assurance. And Hal was careful and dependable, followed orders, stood above suspicion, and, worried by inexperience, secretly took perplexing legal tangles to Burton Lely. "He is an interesting case," Lely wrote, betraying Hal to Cham by letter. "I

266

believe he might do well as a liberal politician if it were not for his squeaky voice and a constant expression of smelling something bad. As a lawyer he leaves a lot to be desired, but he is a good negotiator and draws a tight contract. You can rely on him. If I have the time, I will seduce him and effect his conversion to that profit system he cannot abide."

One of the qualifications for being a subordinate of Cham's was a willingness to forget hours in attending him. He had fallen into the habit of sleeping later in the mornings and staying up longer at night. Others had to suit their lives to him, and he disliked being alone. A pliable bohemian, Harry accommodated easily to the arrangement; he had nowhere else to go, and appreciated the supply of whiskey in the house. The presence of Cissie kept Hal from rebelling until the routine was fixed. Apparently her attraction for him had not been dulled by separation. He patiently awaited her return at night from Long Beach, talked to her whenever he could, and accepted the presence of Dugald as a necessary evil. The few words she vouchsafed him, and an occasional smile, seemed to sustain him through protracted evenings with Cham. His duties frequently took him to the factory, which meant more opportunities of being in her company.

Cham perceived his whole hold on Hal was through his sister, and that amused him. That was how Grandpa operated. But he felt discomfiture when Cissie suddenly began to take notice of her old swain. Then she went out with him to dinner and the movies, somehow looking, in ordinary gloves and high heels, as though she were arrayed for a costume ball, and Cham was enraged and robbed of an attendant. "You don't have to overdo it," he told Cissie. "I have the guy pretty well trained. Smile at him once in a while and listen to him shoot off his mouth, and that's enough."

"You're taking advantage of Hal and I feel sorry for him. What you do to Harry doesn't matter—he's greasy and crooked and doesn't care— but Hal is different."

"You make me laugh. I'm only doing what Grandpa would have done."

"Did you ever stop to think," Cissie said, "that you're just a shadow Grandpa's throwing behind him now he's gone? How did he ever have such an effect on you? Haven't you got a personality of your own?"

"He had enough personality for both of us," Cham replied. "And I owe him something I've got to pay off. It has nothing to do with Hal. Forget him."

"I like him."

"Are you kidding? You couldn't be serious. I'd lose my mind!"

Cissie grinned. "Anyhow, I want to hear how the proletariat are getting along."

Cham took counsel with Lagonda. She showed a reluctance in their conversation which worried him. "You're holding out on me," he said accusingly. "Is this how you treat your best friend? Are you going to stand by not saying a word while my sister maybe falls for a lousy revolutionist?"

"Well, I guess I got to tell you her secret," Lagonda said, after consideration. "She say for me not to say, but how can I fool you? You're my boy."

"Then go ahead and say."

"She thinks Mr. Stuart is taking her too much for granted, and if she goes out a little with Mr. Baltim, he might wake up."

"Oh God," Cham said. "It's worse than I thought. That means she's really interested in the little genius . . ." He reflected, discovering a new cause for hurt. "The thing I don't like is how she has secrets with you I'm not in on."

"We're both women," Lagonda said. "What you expect?"

"From women," Cham said, "I expect nothing. The less you have to do with them, the better off you are."

Lagonda mentioned Conny. They ended by wrangling, because Lagonda felt Cham was in no position to criticize his sister's taste in companions. He left her nursing a wounded ego, and entertaining certain intimations of fatality. Maturity had lessened the shamed, grasping quality that lurked in the love he had for Cissie, but he could not yet bear losing her. He gloomed at a sense of breaking ties, of loss and change; when she had gone to Dugald part of him would be torn off. She understood nothing of this, nor would have cared if she had. His loyalty was absolute, and hers a sometime thing. They were sliding away from each other. And the sweat and agony would be his alone.

But there were plenty of distractions to take his mind off Cissie. One was the problem of engines for the B-2. Dugald awarded the contract for them to Luigi Anzoni, largely through the representations of Cissie and Hank Isbrow. On Anzoni's drawing boards lay plans for twin nine-cylinder radial giants, air-cooled, geared and supercharged, having a dry weight of no more than twelve hundred pounds, and theoretically capable of developing a thousand horsepower apiece. Cham took the ebullient preliminaries with a grain of salt, and he was not mistaken. The tall, dark, dramatic native of Milan was a dreamer and visionary, and quite impractical. In a first version, his engine hacked and coughed and spit out shredded valves and stripped gearing, and broke off supercharger blades. Metallurgists and carburetion experts had to be brought to Burbank at Cham's expense. A new engine was built. It pulled in excess of the thousand horsepower on a dynamometer for five minutes and, as Anzoni proudly strutted and thanked his patron saint, suddenly blew pistons and cylinder heads and sent everybody running.

"Send the guinea bastard to me," Cham ordered. Both Cissie and Dugald looked crestfallen. Their instinct was to place the contract elsewhere, with a big manufacturer; but it was very late—they had spent too much time and money with Anzoni.

The interview was short and unpleasant. Proud and forsaken, Anzoni admitted he was out of capital. He had to have more engineers. Testing would take months. "I am a man of principle," he said. "There is only one Anzoni. The best will not do. I seek perfection, Mr. Brennan. I will find it."

"Not without money," Cham said. "I want to buy fifty-five per cent of your business and bring a man from Connecticut to take charge of the plant."

"Never!"

"Then beat it. The deal is off."

"The contract terms haven't been met," Hal said. "I'll mail you formal notice of termination."

"You are killing me," Anzoni said.

"I wish we could," Cham said.

"Start up the motor again," Harry said, "and stand close to it. That ought to take care of you."

"You are gangsters!" Anzoni cried. "Young thugs." He wept and pounded on his ribs with a fist. He cited his record as an aviator for Italy in the World War. He described his wife and children, and offered to bring his decorations for them to see.

"He's an enemy," Harry said.

"He hasn't got a dime," Cham said.

Wiping his eyes, Anzoni got down to cases. The discussion was rancorous and passionate. In return for sixty thousand dollars, he sold the controlling interest in his firm and accepted the alien from the east. He knew he was finished, looking at the hard youthful faces confronting him.

"You have torn my heart out," he said.

"If we had," Cham said, "I'd feed it to you."

"Cissie and Dugald—" Anzoni said in his bewilderment. "Where are they? They are good people. We understand each other. What has happened to me? Santa Maria!"

When he had gone, the conspirators were not jubilant. "You haven't bought anything," Harry said, "but it's too late to stop, I suppose."

"The engines may never run," Hal added.

"They'll run," Cham said, "if we have to gold plate the Goddamned things. It's the only way to get my investment back." He recalled that Grandpa liked diversified holdings. He was diversifying, all right.

Cham received a letter from Albert Blour. The old gentleman had retired, leaving a highly successful Trans-California Corporation to mark his passing out of the scene, and he wanted to thank the son of his former protégé for aid in subduing the Shapiros. He remembered Cass Brennan well and fondly, and also the celebrated Colonel Brennan. To know they had been succeeded by a man as able as they had been, in the best family tradition, made Blour happy. Had his health permitted, he would have paid a call on Cham in the south; as it was, he hoped Cham might find the opportunity to come to San Francisco and talk to him. He would be honored to see with his own eyes another Brennan adding to the luster of the name.

The letter raised Cham's laughter. Here was perhaps the first praise he had ever known. It started him thinking, for Blour mentioned that he was spoken of as something of a mystery man who transacted business from concealment in the manner of Lucius Brennan, and wielded a secret power. Blour thought that of some advantage to Cham, and possibly a useful character to assume, but he urged him to come out eventually, assume his rightful place as a leader in the community, exercise political influence, and travel to broaden his conceptions. Naturally he couldn't know Cham was a mere victim of Cissie and circumstances, and might soon be revealed as a sad example of how to misuse inherited wealth. But what was in store for him, win or lose? Cham didn't care to go on living this sort of life forever. He had been nowhere and done nothing. Even the concept of going to San Francisco to meet Mr. Blour was quite incredible. Being a community leader or concerning himself with politics was of no interest. He decided that when he had fulfilled his obligations, he would quit and go see the world, thoroughly and at length. Los Angeles was not everything to him anymore, as it had been to Grandpa and his father.

The change in Cham's attitude was a result of unending evolution in Los Angeles. The Queen of his childhood and youth had contrived to disappear. What had been superimposed on the remains of a great, easy-going village did not please him. He suspected that Grandpa, for all his delight in the new, might have been displeased too. Depression had slowed but not stopped an accelerating tempo. Open spaces were being filled in, hills studded by houses. Streets were crowded, traffic signals sounded bells and raised stop-and-go semaphores, small markets and corner drugstores vanished under the impact of cut-rate merchants and chains. The spacious homes raised at the turn of the century, with attached lots devoted to trees and flowers, had given way to innumerable narrow bungalows shaded by wide front porches, each having a set of concrete tracks leading to a garage in the rear. Multiple occupancy in a denser town resulted in the creation of medium-sized brick and stucco apartments and double lines of side-facing bungalow "courts" separated by a central walkway. Buildings steadily grew longer and higher and marched west on every main thoroughfare, blotting out a feeling of clear skies meeting the earth. In Cham's very neighborhood, evidences of rapid decay were plain. The well-to-do burghers of Grandpa's day had died off or moved away, and their dwellings were being razed to provide sites for clubs, hotels, hospitals and department stores, or converted to nursing homes, offices, abodes of palmists and nature healers, and the sprawling expanses of car dealers. The interests of the automobile, whose use and maintenance had become an article of civic faith, were paramount; nothing was allowed to impede easy movement for motorists. The body of water in Westlake Park, as well as the park itself, had been parted like the Israelite's Red Sea to allow a straight connection of Wilshire Boulevard with the downtown area. Silent nights and a midday lassitude induced by brilliant sunshine and the last memories of Yang-na were forgotten.

Irked by growing pains and formless expansion, the Queen seemed irritable and edgy, waiting for a new revelation. A time of selling orange groves and praising the climate and tending the sick was finished. Those simpler devices had sufficed for Lucius Brennan and his generation, but they could not support the tremendous fat lady magicians had conjured up.

Driving about in periods of restlessness, Harry or Hal accompanying him, or little Al, often alone, Cham chafed and was sour. The people were different again. Another inundation of outsiders had altered the composition of the city. During Grandpa's latter days, they had been prosperous middle westerners with funds to invest, and the wealthy from the seaboard states in search of gentle breezes; their contribution inclined toward solidity, conformity, religious observance and the pastoral airs that went with Iowa homesteads and the spare white-painted aspect of New England villages. Now the influx, spurred by hunger and cold, was from the industrial towns where the tall chimneys had stopped smoking, the ghettos of New York, the plains of Texas and Oklahoma, the backwaters of the deep south. These people were untidy and ill-mannered, talked in strong regional accents, and had poverty written on them. The babies brought in their battered cars were legion. Out of

271

the migration had risen a different town, mirroring the prime ingredients of the new wave—a cheaper, louder, gaudier, more disquieting Queen, settling into ethnic districts, making slums of the quondam residences of retired farmers, showing the profound disparity between the rich and the poor.

Cham drove and pondered. Jews gathered in the west end, Negroes in the south-central portion, Mexicans in East Los Angeles. Downtown were colonies of Japanese and Chinese. Other groups were too small or scattered to be significant. Enclaves of the rich had formed in Beverly Hills, Bel Air, Chapman Park and Pasadena. On the whole, the city was still white, Protestant, peaceful, unsophisticated, uncultured and conservative of view. Smallholders predominated. Only the existence of a separate, relatively small but important motion picture industry contradicted the Queen's mid-country bloodstream and image, bringing her attention, tourists and wealth. She was raw, she had grown like a tropical plant, she was unplanned, she was mostly ugly and treeless and bedizened by a bewildering array of building styles. Through sheer energy and proliferation, she aroused curiosity and critics; generally she was thought vulgar, mean, disorganized and even ridiculous, as in Grandpa's salad days. Except for a few consciously preserved buildings and an area adjoining the Plaza, none of her Spanish and Mexican colonial past survived. That she was a portent and manifestation of an urban future (in the meaning of the dreams of Lucius Brennan), motorized and mechanized and reduced to a shabby mediocrity blown to gigantic proportions, seemed to be forgotten. And her old weakness remained evident: the iron and coal deposits, the navigable rivers, the strategic geographical assets were still wanting. Manufacturing had come to her, and agriculture had increased, but more than a million in population appeared to await the introduction of some economic miracle— they could not go on indefinitely selling real estate and taking in each other's washing. The climate would not prevail forever.

Cham was unable to clearly define most of these things to himself. He could only feel them while trying to think in the fashion Grandpa would have. For the first time, he had a distrust of Los Angeles. Behind that, bred in the bone and inculcated by the old man, was a concern for his possessions. They were part and parcel of the Queen. If she failed, they would fail. The Brennans had fought hard to come up in the world and gain what they had. For him to lose the fruit of their efforts was the worst of betrayals. How could he, lame in leg and brain, protect himself?

Suddenly he had the great conviction he was doing precisely as he should. He stood at the inception of a marvel and ought to extend rather than retrench. He was sure Grandpa would have approved of him, and nothing surpassed the honor and satisfaction of that conclusion.

Faithfully, Conny kept asking Cham if he wanted to do something. His response was usually immediate. But their relationship was changing. Often he was incapable of participating wholeheartedly, being preoccupied by other matters, and she complained of his bulk and weight and inattention. It was true that he was considerably fatter and had been forced to buy new clothing. He tried calisthenics to pare down, which bored him, and hurt his game knee playing strenuously with Albert in the garden. Sweat rolled off him, but not adipose tissue. Dieting shortened his temper and fatigued him, and Conny bewailed his declining interest in her. Unless they were in bed and engaged in sexual intercourse, they could only argue for diversion. Cham realized he was tired of her, and that she was getting restless. "We're like an old married couple," he told her. "I'm sick of those big tits always stuck in my face, and what I've got is the same story to you. If we have to spend the time just talking, we'll end up killing each other."

Conny burst into tears and ran out of the room and out of the house, and was gone for two days. Before she returned, Cham had Jesús Algonrones brought to him, in company with a young man from Belvedere to serve as interpreter. Jesús remained on his feet, hat in hand, waiting on the orders of his patron; he was agreeably surprised when Cham had him and his escort sit down, and ordered Lagonda, who had been in conference on the situation and knew her advice was being followed, to give them muscatel wine. "You treat me as a father-in-law," Jesús ventured. "But I suppose this is impossible, eh?"

"Absolutely impossible," Cham said to the interpreter. "You know that, Jesús. You wouldn't want it yourself."

He was answered at length by Jesús. "Is it all right if I give you a synopsis of what he says, Mr. Brennan?" the interpreter asked. "He's kind of long-winded and flowery."

"Yes, for God's sake," Cham assented. "I don't want this to go on until night."

"Yes, sir, Mr. Brennan," the interpreter said. "Well, he agrees with you. It wouldn't be wise. He understands. Where he came from, the big landowners hardly ever married the peons. He's very grateful for what you've already done. But he's worried about what else you could have called him in for. He hopes the gardening and housework are okay and you are happy."

"I'm happy," Cham said. "The reason we're here is because I think Conny should get married. My idea is for her to have a good husband with a steady job and no bad habits. If Jesús has the right man in mind, and the man is willing—and if Conny is—I'll start them off in married life with a nice piece of change."

"How much?" the interpreter said.

"Try the idea on Jesús first," Cham said. "We can't do anything unless he's for it."

Jesús was charmed by the offer. His daughter having a dowry was the height of his ambitions. He blessed Cham for his kindness and generosity. "And he wants to know how much," the interpreter finished.

"You mean you do," Cham said. "Tell him to find a husband who will satisfy Conny and I'll hand over ten thousand dollars."

"Holy Mother and all the angels!" the interpreter said. "How about me, Mr. Brennan?"

"Talk to him, damn it," Cham said. "He's going to be the one with the say-so."

The colloquy between Jesús and the interpreter was extended, interrupted only when Cham's gardener got up, eyes wet, and gave him an *abrazo* and kissed him on either cheek. Cham was embarrassed. "What's going on?" he asked, as the conversation continued.

"Everything's fine," the interpreter said. "He likes me. I'm practically a cousin of Conny's, see? She likes me. We'll get married right away, you can send us your check—"

"Wait a minute," Cham interrupted. "How do I know what Jesús is saying? You could be inventing this?"

"If I get the old guy to give me a hug and kiss," the interpreter said, "the same as he did you, will you believe me?"

"I might," Cham said.

Upon being instructed, Jesús smiled at Cham, lifted his glass to him, nodded vigorously, and embraced the interpreter and saluted him. He then stood with his arm around the boy and wept. Reassured, Cham interrogated the interpreter. His name was Ralph Inocencio García, he was the proper age, he had regular employment in a packing house, and he looked healthy and cheerful. He said he would be true to Conny and love her madly. He had been born in Los Angeles and finished high school. It struck Cham that he wasn't a bad bet, assuming Jesús had not been misquoted.

"We haven't got out of the woods yet," he said. "Somebody has to break the news to Conny, and I told you she must be satisfied. If she's too upset to marry or unhappy with you, I won't force her into anything. There's not going to be any strong-arm stuff."

"I'll talk to her, Mr. Brennan."

"Where is she?"

"At home."

"Well," Cham said, "give her my regards and say I'm sorry. Maybe you can make up for what I've done . . ."

"I'll try."

"But she has to come to me herself and let me know the marriage is all right. Otherwise I won't pay off."

"Okay," Ralph said. "Leave it to me."

Cham experienced some difficulty getting rid of Jesús. He wanted to be certain there were no hard feelings. He needed assurances concerning his gardening job. He wished to invite his patron to a prenuptial party in Belvedere where everybody would get *boracho*. In the doorway he gave Cham a second *abrazo* and kissed him goodbye.

"Anyhow you done it, and that's a relief," Lagonda said, having followed events from a concealed vantage point. "That Mr. Algonrones" —she couldn't abide the gardener's given name—"sure is crazy about you, isn't he?"

"You shut up," Cham said. "He's damned near as affectionate as Conny." They both laughed.

Next morning he heard a vacuum cleaner running outside his bedroom door. He sat up in bed apprehensively. A little to his surprise and sorrow, Conny knocked before entering. She wore her maid's uniform, and her lower lip protruded. On her face was the expression of an unruly, disillusioned child secretly grateful the punishment hadn't taken a more severe form.

They looked at each other in silent embarrassment, scarcely conscious of the relief felt at the peaceful and tired conclusion of something past a mutual relevance. "I hope you're not going to cry," Cham said.

"Oh, no."

"Are you still sore at me?"

Conny shook her head.

Clearing his throat, Cham said, "I—uh—thought this was the best way . . ."

"All that money—" Conny said. "How could I stay sore at you? I'm not worth half that much."

"You're worth twice that much. It's only that we've been friendly too long and . . . and you know."

"Uh-huh."

"You're happy with Ralph?"

"Oh, sure. I know him since I am a little girl."

"He—he doesn't mind about me?" Cham asked.

"Not when he's going to be rich."

"Jesús and the family—it's all right with them?"

"They're proud of me." A hint of a smile came on Conny's lips, and she shrugged. "Who do you think you're dealing with, the Rockefellers?"

"Well . . . fine. Take care of yourself, Conny. Have a lot of babies."

"Couldn't I keep on being your maid? I like the job."

"No. Ralph might think—"

"He won't think. It's hard for him. Listen, we could do something once in a while if you wanted. It might be nice."

"Nice," Cham said, "but pretty lousy. You take me for a real bum, don't you?"

"Okay. Goodbye . . . You want to do something for the last time?"

"Uh—no. Thank you very much."

"I worked hard around the house, you know," Conny said. "Even Lagonda won't say I didn't. Listen, I don't care about ten thousand dollars. It was you I cared about. It's not my fault I don't know nothing and I'm a poor *muchacha.*"

"I know," Cham said. "That's what hurts."

Conny turned quickly from him and left the room. The vacuum cleaner resumed its whining. Cham sank in bed and groaned.

For a few days he was in a bad humor and sorry for himself. He didn't exactly miss Conny when she had gone, but the lack of a familiar presence. Considering his situation, he reached the conclusion that men differed fundamentally in their tastes. Grandpa, he remembered, had liked women but not a woman, and remained unmarried. Cham felt he was cast in the same mould. A wife offered no advantages he could discern, and simply promised the inevitable satiation he had come to with Conny. Hereafter he would sample the crop and make no commitments. Yet the continuum of the Brennans had to be taken into account. Those possessions could not be left to foreign hands or the God-damned government. That, Cham decided, was Cissie's obligation. He was content with little Al, and would have to marry off his sister and prevail upon her to give them heirs.

His vague plans were promptly taken from his hands, and twisted in a fashion that depressed and angered him. It was not that he hadn't anticipated such a crisis, but the sudden reality was very provoking.

Dugald Stuart requested a private talk. Assuming a new defect had arisen in the infernal B-2, Cham wearily received him. The circumstance of Cissie's not being a party to the meeting kindled his fears. They were immediately confirmed. "She has proposed to me," Dugald said. "I was surprised, Cham, and couldn't give her a ready answer. I told her I had to have your reaction first. Sometimes I've thought you don't approve of me."

"Proposed *what,* for Christ's sake?"

Dugald blinked. "Why, marriage of course."

"I just wanted to be sure," Cham said, and had sensations of the ground sliding beneath his feet. He tried to sound a note of sweet reasonableness. "It's not that I don't like you, Dugald. But I've had bigger ideas for my sister. She's a Brennan. You know what I mean?"

Smiling wryly, Dugald said, "I suppose I do . . . Not that you make much sense to me. I can't seem to feel the Brennan aura. What gives you the sacred quality, Cham? All the money?"

"All the money you're spending."

"You'll get it back tenfold."

"Even if I do," Cham said, "that still doesn't make you the answer to a maiden's prayer—or mine either. Look, be sensible. We're an old Los Angeles family, and we've done quite a lot around here. Cissie is a real heiress, a prize. She deserves a husband who is in her class. I don't mean to be offensive, but who ever heard of a nobody like you?"

"As long as you're being frank," Dugald said, "I presume I can take the same line. I think you're indulging in delusions, Cham. According to my understanding, the aristocratic Brennans have been here for less than a hundred years. They have consisted of real estate operators and lawyers who happened to inherit a Spanish land grant by marriage. The first Stuart landed at Jamestown when this continent was settled. Since then my branch has lived in New Hampshire for twice as long as your family has lived here. I'm not too old, I have a good education, and my habits and manners are better than yours. Why is Cissie beyond my reach?"

"You're shorter than she is, damn it!"

Dugald laughed. "She doesn't mind."

"I don't have to explain to you. I don't want you as a brother-in-law, and that's enough. I'm backing you, see? How would you like to have me pull the rug out from under you?"

"You're in too deep for that, Cham. By the way, I'm not too sure I care to have you for a brother-in-law. I think my family would approve of Cissie, but you're another matter."

Sitting in silence, Cham considered hitting Dugald. But it wasn't feasible. Cissie would be outraged, and besides, too much depended on the guy. He clasped his hands in his lap and stared at the floor.

"I like you," Dugald said finally, "and I regret having been so rude. I hope you'll forgive me. But you asked for this, Cham."

"I thought you were grateful to me."

"I am. Very grateful."

"Another thing," Cham said. "Why did she have to propose to you?

It should have been the other way around. Who are you to be snooting my sister, you bastard?"

"I'm not snooting her," Dugald replied. "It's just that I was too busy with the B-2 to think of anything else."

"I'll bet! You haven't been leading her on or anything, have you?"

"Don't be a complete fool, Cham!"

"Well, you heard me," Cham said. "I'm against her marrying you. Now what are you going to do?"

"Nothing. The next move is yours."

"Mine? Why mine?"

"Because," Dugald said, "I'm willing to abide by your veto, but I don't intend to be your stalking horse—or fight your battles for you. Go tell her why I can't accept her proposal."

"Not me!"

"Why? Are you afraid of her?"

"Don't strain your luck," Cham said. "I'll be taking a punch at you yet . . . No, I'm not afraid of her. Where is she? I'll straighten her out."

"In her room, I suppose," Dugald said.

"Wait here," Cham said. "I'll come back, and I might want to kill you."

He went upstairs and knocked on Cissie's door, and she invited him to come in. She was lying on the bed, fully clothed, her hair tousled and smudges of tiredness under her eyes. He sat down and looked at her and said, "I got the bad news."

"What's bad about it?" she said.

"I think you could do better."

"I haven't time."

"Why him?" Cham said. "Or why anybody right now?"

"Shall I be honest with you?" Cissie said. "I can't love anybody very much, or forget everything else for him. It's not in me. The most I can really love is what I'm doing. Oh, I love you. But that's different."

"Then why—"

"Because Dugald and I are together constantly. We have the same interests. He's the smartest man I ever met, and I admire and respect him. I would not want to part from him. If I don't marry him, how can I be sure we won't eventually break up?"

"That's a hell of a reason for marrying a man," Cham said.

"Women have married for worse reasons. It will be much handier for us, Cham. We ought not to have to go to different beds each night—we could keep on talking and having ideas and making notes."

"Gee, that sounds romantic."

Cissie laughed. "Anyway, I'm with him all the time. I might as well be his wife. Probably people have started talking about us, and you're going to resent that, aren't you?"

"He got uppity with me when I mentioned the Brennans and so forth."

"You're an idiot."

"I thought when I moved out Conny," Cham said, "that you would be pleased and maybe we could be closer again and—"

"I don't care what you do as long as it isn't bad for you. Conny wasn't a problem to me. You're confusing me with Lagonda. You have a right to do as you think best, and so have I."

"Well, I depend on you, and I was hoping you depended on me. We've always sort of stuck together. I believe we could be happy, the two of us—"

Sitting up, Cissie gazed at Cham queerly and said, "You sound funny, Brother. Not like a brother. Something has hung over us since we were children—something not too nice. Perhaps we'd better settle it. What are you trying to say?"

Cham felt his face reddening and felt an artery ticking in his neck. "I don't know. But we're not going to settle it."

"All right. Then stop talking that way. We either have to come out in the open with it or forget it."

"We'll forget it," Cham said. "I don't think about those things. That could make me sick."

"Yes. Me too. But it's possible."

"No, no . . ."

"The Brennans you take such pride in," Cissie said remorselessly, "were a queer bunch. You know that as well as I do. It would be possible."

"No. Shut up."

"Then this is the end of the dreams of being happy together—just us. Only speak up. I would never desert you, any more than you would desert me. If we have to go the end, let's go. I won't marry Dugald unless you consent to it."

"Okay," Cham said, and took a handkerchief and wiped his forehead. "Marry him."

"That's final?"

"Yes . . . I've got a favor to ask. Have a baby. The family shouldn't stop. Grandpa would be disappointed."

"I don't care. I don't like the idea, and I'm too busy. You have them. Get married yourself."

"I'm not the marrying kind—I'm the same as Grandpa. And I am the wrong one. You have the looks and intelligence and all the rest of it.

Dugald is bright, and we have to use him . . . You can do that for me. I'm giving up all I've got . . ."

Cissie was quiet, watching him. She rubbed her mouth with the back of her hand. "When I have the time, Cham. You'll have to wait."

"Not too long. Promise?"

"I promise."

They both rose. "I'll go back and tell the little bastard I'm happy," Cham said. His sister moved forward, kissed him on the nose, and put a hand between his shoulder blades and shoved him into the hall.

Dugald was pacing at the foot of the staircase, evidently more nervous than he had been willing to let on. Descending slowly to him, Cham stuck out his hand, and Dugald grasped it. "You could turn out the most expensive groom anybody ever bought," Cham said.

"She won the argument, eh?"

"There wasn't an argument. We discussed it. Both of us thought you'd do."

"That's pretty decent of you!" Dugald said.

"Don't get huffy," Cham said. "I'm trying to act pleasant. Why can't you act the same?"

"I feel as if I were a dummy in a department store window. She did the proposing. You had to decide whether I was possible. While I was waiting that Negro housekeeper of yours came by and questioned me. It seems she approves, which makes the vote unanimous!"

"Now that I come to think of it, you do look a little like a dummy."

"One vote hasn't been cast," Dugald said, and flushed. "Mine."

"Yours?" Cham said. "Are you joking? You have to have us, and we could do without you. Go on, beat it. I'm not in a very good temper tonight."

Livid and shaken, Dugald retreated to the hall, snatched up his hat and coat, and departed. No goodbyes were exchanged.

In the morning Cham awakened at eleven, scratched and grunted, and gave consideration to the previous night. Distasteful as it was, it constituted an established fact. Recalling the splendid obsequies Grandpa had arranged for Grandma, he wondered if he ought not to rise to the occasion in behalf of Cissie and Dugald's wedding. The strain would be awful. He hated the very thought of it. But maybe the honor and standing of the Brennans was at stake. That vaunted Stuart family could come to the affair and find out Cissie's brother was no ordinary slob. And what about an appropriate wedding present for the bride and groom? Grandpa had given his house to Cham's father and mother, but turning over the old place a second time was obviously impossible. A new home was a good idea, though, and in the tradition . . .

280

He rang for his breakfast, and Ferris brought the tray. Cham contemplated it unhappily. By degrees Lagonda had reduced his first meal of the day to a couple of boiled eggs, a cup of black coffee and a slice of unbuttered toast. With breakfast came a telephone to be plugged into the wall. Cham rang Hal Baltim's office. "How did you come out with Dugald last night?" Hal said. "What's the latest mistake he's made?"

"Listening to Cissie," Cham said. "She told him he has to marry her. He wanted my blessing."

"Oh." There was a considerable silence.

Cham's spirits climbed as he imagined Hal's misery. "You're not surprised, are you?"

"Not too surprised," Hal said flatly.

"You didn't have a chance, actually."

"With you against me? No, I suppose I was cooked."

"If it's a comfort to you," Cham said, "I would have taken you instead of him."

"You couldn't afford to."

"He is not that important."

"He represents half a million of your dollars," Hal said. "I've grown to know you, Cham. To retrieve them you'd sacrifice your sister, your honor, your immortal soul, anything. All you've got in the world is what you have in the bank and what you've invested unwisely."

"I forgive you those cruel remarks," Cham said. "Your tender feelings are hurt . . . Since I've lost Cissie, I guess I'm losing you too, eh?" This was the moment he had anticipated and savored, the resolution of his theories. Poor bewildered, bereft, disappointed, abandoned Hal was the test case. Either Cham's creatures could be bought, dominated and used, as Grandpa had thought, or power was an illusion that blew away in the first cold breath of contrary fortune.

The wire hummed faintly. Hal did not speak. Waiting, Cham ate a spoonful of egg and sipped coffee.

"No," Hal said. "They're going to be married, but we're already married. I'm accustomed to you now. You need me, and I need you. And I've got to stay to see you fall on your damned ugly face."

"Suppose I don't fall?"

"Then you win. What I'm pushing—honesty and decency—is no good. I'll come over to your side and agree that only money counts. You can act the Roman emperor and I'll be your slave."

"That's my boy," Cham said. "Grandpa always talked of the Romans because his father liked them . . . Come by this afternoon, will you? I've got a few things for you to do."

He hung up. Despite the tasteless eggs and the unadorned toast, life was still interesting.

Lagonda intruded hastily, and she had tears in her eyes. "You got a telegram," she said. "Mr. Stuart and Cissie are married. She flew him up to Yuma in the B-1 before daylight. Where's Yuma?"

"In Arizona," Cham said, and choked on a bit of the hard bread; Lagonda pounded his back. When he had his breath again, he said, "Would it be too much trouble to let me see the wire?"

"I left it downstairs . . . Our little girl is gone."

"Little girl! She's bigger than you are!"

"Don't holler," Lagonda said.

"Why are you crying? You told me you liked the genius."

"Everybody cries at weddings."

"They couldn't wait for us, could they?" Cham said sourly. "We don't count. She had to go rushing him off and do it in secret. Well, the hell with them."

"That's no way to talk."

The bright morning was dimmed. His life was a desert. "Everything's finished," he said. "I'll never be the same again."

The greatest crisis of all was brewing, and apparently only Cham anticipated it. He summoned Hal and Harry and put the question to them: everybody mixed up with Bull-Shit Aircraft had to assume the B-2 would live up to expectations. Very well. Consider it a fact. There still had to be an airline to welcome and presumably, after testing, accept the ship. What airline was waiting? Who was ready to put on the necessary stamp of approval? Considering the nature and purpose of the B-2, nothing less than a continental organization would do. Orders from individuals, or the amount the government might buy, were not enough. From Dugald, Cham had learned they would be compelled to sell the planes at a loss until sufficient production was obtained. B-S might have to build thirty before showing a profit. And foreign sales were unlikely to come until the B-2 had been espoused by an American airline.

Brennan-Stuart was entering the fray very late. Boeing had a satisfactory transport in service. Fokker was building a three engined prototype that promised much. Even if the B-2 was as good as Dugald promised, an enthusiastic reception had somehow to be guaranteed. Few within the industry knew what they were doing, and Dugald was no salesman or publicist. Where were they going to find a sponsor?

"My God, he's right," Hal said. "I haven't thought beyond flying the thing . . ."

"Maybe we can depend on the story of the better mousetrap," Harry suggested. "The world will beat a path to the door at Long Beach."

Cham dismissed the supposition impatiently. Leaving the debut of the B-2 to chance was foolish. Somebody had to canvass the airlines and awaken interest. Dugald and Cissie needn't be distracted with these details. The task was delegated to Harry. The last to leave that night—it was already morning, and beginning to grow light—was Hal. Yawning in the doorway, he said, "You're a mystery to me, Cham. I've got to stop underrating you. Everytime I'm convinced you don't know what you're doing and just lunging around for Cissie's sake, you start making good sense. You won't work and you're ignorant, but your instincts are automatically right."

"It's my money," Cham said. "I have the responsibility."

Harry was sent to New York on a plane. The journey frightened him, and he wrote home pitifully of rough weather and the uncertainties of air travel. His brushes with airline executives in the east proved uncouraging. They were accustomed to doing their development and purchasing through committees, on a competition basis, and preferred to rely on established manufacturers. None of them manifested interest or confidence in the maiden efforts of tiny Brennan-Stuart. Anzoni was an unknown quantity in the realm of high-output engines. Acceptance of the B-2 might consume years, and obsolescence was stunningly fast in aircraft. Too young and inexperienced, Harry did not inspire respect. He came back riding on a train.

Cautiously broaching the subject to Cissie and Dugald did Cham little good. His sister, almost to his relief, had moved from their house to share a tiny apartment in Long Beach with the bridegroom. They ate their meals out and came home only to sleep and return hastily to the plant. Oblivious to Cham's concern for the reception of the B-2, they could think of nothing but finishing and flying it. Cham took care not to complain. To have scolded them would have been like badgering children.

The problem obsessed him. When a solution began to shape up and Harry grew aware of what the boss was thinking, he was appalled. Cham's path out of this was dazzlingly simple: gain control of an airline. "You're nuts," he protested. "It's a fantastic risk—you'd be betting a fortune on this one damned airplane. The B-2, whatever Dugald claims, isn't the answer to everything. And do you want in a shaky business you know nothing about?"

"Shaky to you," Cham said. "You are afraid of flying, as I am. That's because it's new. It won't be new long. I could get out in a hurry—"

"Without your shirt. It's like buying a locomotive to get the whistle.

283

You're not putting the cart before the horse, you're putting the airline before the airplane."

Cham smiled wintrily. "You're starting to have a talent for phrase-making. Find me a cheap airline, just in case."

There was one airline available in the transcontinental field, investigated and denounced by Harry. Its name was Columbia Air Transport, a recent combination of Columbia, running between New York and Chicago, Parker Airways operating in the middle- and southwest, and Eagle Airlines, which linked Dallas and Fort Worth with Los Angeles. Organization was poor and uncertain, equipment inadequate, prospects dubious. The surgery involved in joining three independent outfits, with the eastern end alone in sound condition, had barely saved the patient, and was killing the financial doctors concerned. A fresh separation was indicated. Only an infusion of new, fearless investors could retrieve the situation, and perhaps then only temporarily.

"I think I might buy into Columbia," Cham said. "We could furnish them with B-2's on credit. We won't have any trouble picking up stock at bargain prices."

"We sure won't," Harry said.

"If you intend to make a fool of yourself," Hal said, infected by Harry's panic, "at least get into a line that isn't falling apart."

"I couldn't have control in a good one," Cham said.

"Columbia will fold before it means anything," Hal objected.

"Suppose the B-2 is as good as Cissie claims?" Cham said. "It ought to save an airline."

"You're ready for the asylum," Hal told him.

Hal confided his fears to Burton Lely. This brought an unprecedented visit to Cham by both Lely and the elder Baltim. They were grave and soothing in conduct, as though dealing with a lunatic. Cham received them at noon in pajamas and a robe—plainly a shocking sight to the lawyers. In his capacity of senior partner, Baltim led the attack. But he was astonishingly gentle, and Cham was surprised to hear him begin with thanks for Cham's rehabilitation of his son; it seemed Baltim was greatly in his debt for that, and thereby doubly devoted to the welfare of a young man he and Burton had once hoped to welcome into the firm; only a deep sense of obligation would have compelled him to come offer unpalatable advice; besides, he had happy memories of his friendships with Cham's father and great-uncle, and trembled at the spectacle of Cham imperiling the equity they had built up through the exercise of prudence, wisdom and concern for their descendants.

"I realize I have not always been entirely sympathetic to your mode of living and limited aspirations, Cham," Baltim said. "That has changed,

284

I assure you. Your influence on my wayward boy has caused me to see you in a different light. And I respect your love for Cissie and her husband, and your trust in them. Not many brothers are capable of your selfless generosity. But you must not be generous to a fault and ruin yourself. Please understand that Burton and I are motivated solely by an interest in your welfare."

"Okay," Cham said. "I believe you, Mr. Baltim. Get to the point."

A trifle disconcerted, Baltim said, "According to Hal, you are contemplating buying into Columbia Air Transport. If my informants are correct, it is a feeble and loose amalgamation of disparate companies which fell into trouble the moment it was born. I think public acceptance of air travel is far off and perhaps will never come. Profitable operation of an airline is something for experts in the next generation. I beg you not to indulge in outright folly."

Cham looked at Lely. "How about you?"

"I am in general agreement with Harold," Lely said. "I'm also franker, for which indiscretion I trust you will pardon me. You haven't the stock in trade for a boy wonder, Cham. You're an innocent begging to be plucked—a youth of vast inexperience living in an old house, blinded by an affection for your sister and no doubt encouraged by the buccaneering expeditions of Colonel Brennan—an impetuous boy, I fear, advised by a couple of other boys only slightly better qualified. Don't throw away your inheritance. You can be happy and useful without gratifying your sister's expensive whims and posing as a Southern California Haroun-al-Raschid."

"Who?" Cham asked.

"The caliph from the *Arabian Nights,* you will remember," Lely said, and smiled.

"Oh, yes," Cham said. "Sure. My mother read some of the book to me once. But I got the real version later. It was dirty."

"We needn't indulge in a literary discussion," Baltim said. "Let us hew to the subject. Cham, take care. Accept inevitable losses and confine them as much as possible. Don't actively enter into a hard world where you are sure to endure grave hurt and disillusionment."

"The money isn't sacred," Cham said. "Dugald Stuart tells me that."

"He would," Lely said. "He's using you."

"You're mistaken," Cham replied. "I'm using him. Or else I'm terribly mistaken."

"I hate to observe these evidences of pride and overconfidence," Baltim said. "Can't we hope you will find it possible to take a rest and allow us to guide your destiny?"

"Give me a chance to think it over," Cham said. He was flattered by their concern. Both looked worried and upset. Grandpa's money *was* sacred.

The lawyers were followed shortly by Bill Sego, thin and glum, his straw-colored hair reduced to a fine sprinkling of gray around the lower edges of his head. This time Cham was not surprised to learn that a father was indebted to him for snatching a defiant son back from the edge of perdition. His new character excited his wonderment and re-pressed laughter. It was a lovely misconception. To be thought well-meaning and stupid besides was the best gambit he could have invented.

Sego spoke of Sunset Sea. The corporation was in good condition, although it lacked the importance of the days when oil production was heavy. He advocated a return to intensive agriculture on the ranch. If not that, real estate development might be in order; the growth of the San Fernando Valley was encroaching on the San Cristobal's borders.

"No, leave it alone," Cham said. "My grandmother wanted us to keep the place—she believed it was our luck. So we'll hang onto it and pay the taxes. Change will come of itself. All we have to do is wait."

Sego objected. He had served the previous Brennans well, and he had the knowledge and training. Cham was neglecting him. Colonel Brennan had allowed him a free hand. After all, Cham was still a youth. He ought to be glad to delegate authority. "I'm counting on you not losing your temper," he said. "From what I hear, you badly need my advice. Oh, I remember you put me in my place a while ago, but—"

"Wait a minute," Cham said. "I don't lose my temper. Why should I? People do what I say."

Sego gulped and rubbed his hands nervously. "Cham, you don't hon-estly intend to get into the airline business, do you? That would be mad-ness. Think of the colonel and how he'd feel. You've done too much for your sister. You're wonderfully kind, and you've already heard how I appreciate what you've done for Harry, who is the big disappointment of my life—"

"You have a bigger one coming," Cham interrupted. "I'm going to do even more for Harry. I want to make him head of Sunset Sea. You're kind of old and out of date, Mr. Sego. Are you willing to step aside for him?"

"No!" Sego almost shouted. His hands started trembling. "No, I'm not willing! This is a dirty trick."

"Not for your own boy?" Cham asked.

"Cham . . ." Sego said. "I've done everything I could for all of you Brennans. Don't throw me on the scrap heap now."

"It's time you had a rest," Cham said. "Like the San Cristobal. I've been thinking a lot about you. My grandfather made you wealthy. You won't have any worries in retirement."

286

"Harry is a fool," Sego said. "He has used his association with you to conspire against me. You'll be sorry you ever listened to him. Give me a chance—"

"You're through," Cham said, "as of the first of next year. We don't have to argue, do we?"

Sego gazed at him in silence. Tears came into his eyes. He got up, started for the door, and turned around. "You are your father all over again," he said.

"No, Grandpa," Cham said.

Sego shook his head. "Your father, I tell you. He was cold, remorseless, insincere, egotistical—"

"Have it your own way," Cham said.

"Lucius Brennan was a gentleman," Sego said. "He had compassion and a sense of humor. After him came the little mean men." He wheeled and blundered out of the room.

Cham had no confidence in the warnings thrust on him, but united opposition increased his uncertainty. Harry and Hal continued their glum resistance. Even the disclosure that he was going to succeed his father in Sunset Sea failed to cheer Harry. "Why?" Cham said. "You can't really care what happens. You're a crook and a liar, no better than I am, and anyway our agreement was that you admired me. That goes for my ideas too."

"You're great," Harry said. "The fat financier, the giant mind. But I do care what happens. You've bought my loyalty. Everybody sells it, and nobody can avoid belonging to something or somebody. You worry me. I'm concerned for your stinking money. I want to see you safely out of this."

Hal talked in the same vein. "You are narrowminded and unlearned," he said, "and crude and politically impossible. You're full of prejudices and pure ignorance. You don't often make sense. And yet you do some things right. You love Cissie and Lagonda and little Albert, and you shouldn't. You are honest with yourself, and you know you're a chowderhead. You have a queer sense of humor, and you're different. All the damned Brennans have been exceptional. They fasten on people like leeches. I feel responsible for you."

Cham laughed at him.

He never told anyone how he arrived at the sticking point. It was simple. When he went to Cissie's apartment he noticed she had a kitten. The tiny creature inhabited a cardboard carton in the kitchen, and raised its head over the rim to regard Cham with huge, curious eyes. "He wandered into the factory last week," Cissie explained. "I thought

Grandpa might have wanted him taken care of. His name is Icarus."
Cham thought he perceived an omen.

The other clincher arose from one of the girls the obliging Harry supplied Cham with now that Conny was a married woman and just a dim memory. To avoid the probable displeasure of Lagonda, he went afternoons once a week to Harry's apartment on Alvarado Street, pulled the shades, and copulated with a new young woman each time. Harry employed only whores, the freshest of the lot, and tried them before turning them over to his employer. Those unable to pass his exacting standards were discarded in advance. Cham was known to them as a Mr. Brown, and the bargaining and payment were matters Harry handled. He thought highly of Harry's selections and grew to look forward to each Thursday. Los Angeles was an excellent town for that kind of amusement, since many handsome girls came to Hollywood attempting to get in the movies and were frequently down on their luck.

The day he resolved to try to assure the future of the B-2, Harry had provided him with another excellent doxy. Her name was Catherine, she was large and well-made, she was a waitress in a cocktail bar when she was not engaged in prostitution, and she had rare charms which intrigued Cham. For instance, her toenails were painted, her hair was bleached nearly white—"platinum," she called it—and she had stained the nipples of her breasts the same shade as her toenails and fingernails. As she undressed, Cham observed that she had gone to the extra trouble of bleaching her pubic hair platinum too. Catherine was agile and effective and exhausted him, and he stayed beyond his usual hour to enjoy her tricks. Yet she was not overly professional, and exhibited an affection that warmed the encounter. She urged him to come to her bar when he could, and gave him the location. She flattered him, commenting on his endurance and skill. She said he was heavily hung and a man among men. She laughed at his jokes and offered her steady services at a substantially reduced rate. And she wanted him to call her by her nickname of "Cat."

Cham snapped his fingers. "That's it," he said. "I'm being pushed. You've settled it."

"I've settled what?" asked Cat.

"Lately," Cham said, "I've seen a real pussy, and then yours. My grandfather liked both kinds, and I think he's trying to tell me something."

"You're crazy," Cat said. "But you're funny."

Frightened and complaining, Harry was sent east by airplane to buy Columbia stock. On the west coast, Hal would act for Cham. "One of you has got to be on the board of directors when there's an opening," Cham said. "Toss a coin. I want absolute say-so, see? Don't stop buying until you have what I need, and the right people are in my pocket. And don't talk."

The news got out, though, perhaps through the agency of Bill Sego, or Baltim and Lely, and Cham had one more visitor, Irving Shapiro, a thin man of indeterminate age with a narrow head, tight black curls, and sharp dark eyes. The weather was warm, and Cham took him out in the summerhouse. He held little Albert in his lap and waited for Irving's protests.

"He's not yours, is he?" Irving said.

"If he was mine," Cham said, "he wouldn't be that black. But he is mine, in a way. Did you come here to talk or only to be nasty?"

"You've got me wrong. I've always wanted to meet you. Your forcing of the Trans-California matter made me sore, but now I'm grateful. It was the best thing that could have happened to us. What I'm going to say next will surprise you."

"No it won't. Everybody's grateful to me and wants to help with his advice. You're about to say you've noticed my money leaving the bank and you know where it's going and you've got to tell me I'm foolish and should stop."

"On the contrary," Irving said, "we respect your judgment. I happen to think you are another edition of Colonel Brennan and the rest of the Shapiros don't dare disagree with me. I've done some investigating, and I have the impression your airplane is likely to be revolutionary; I believe you are much too smart to waste large sums of money merely in pleasing your sister. And I share your confidence in the future of transportation by air."

Cham's jaw dropped. When he could speak, he said, "And I thought I was all alone!"

"You are not. How would you like us to assume half of your investment in C.A.T.?"

"CAT! That is how the initials go. By God, it never occurred to me!"

"I beg your pardon?"

"You can have half. I like you, Irving. Let's call each other Isadore and Albert in private."

Irving smiled. "I don't mind if you'll promise to be as lucky as your great-uncle."

"I'm lucky," Cham said. "You can depend on that. I'm lucky because I have a nutty sister and a stiff leg that keeps me home thinking, and a brother-in-law who might be as smart as they say and because everybody but you thinks I'm dumb. Don't worry."

After Irving had gone, Cham stumped up and down the garden with Albert in his arms. He was very pleased. He felt the fairy kiss of fortune. And he did not deserve it. That was the crowning feature.

five

THE moment for which Cham waited impatiently and with dread arrived—the emergence from a chrysalis of wooden props and chain hoists and high metal stands and hydraulic jacks of the six-and-a-half-ton metal moth called the B-2. Men stopped clambering over her, and the hiss of blow torches and the rapping of rivet guns ended. Undercarriage down, resting on her fat main gear tires and tail wheel, the airplane was pushed out of a building where tall sliding doors had replaced the solid wall built by the Xanadu Amusement Producing Corporation. All Cham's hopes were now laid on the line, as well as his reputation and Grandpa's money. But these were nothing compared to the safety of Cissie.

It was a hot, clear September morning. Everybody connected with Brennan-Stuart Aircraft was present, from Dugald to the old man who swept the floors. Hal Baltim, a member of the board of directors of a properly conditioned Columbia Air Transport, appeared in his official capacity. The Shapiros had been informed of the event. Harry Sego—ignoring the possibility of failure—had invited newspaper reporters and photographers.

Sweating and ill-tempered, Cham paid his second visit to the aircraft factory, bringing Lagonda and little Albert in his car. He sat in a stifling bungalow, drinking soda pop and smoking cigarette after cigarette, scarcely bothering to reply to the consciously cheerful Hal and Harry. People wandering about outside stared in at him curiously. Once, Lagonda employed a towel to mop his wet face, and he said, "Leave me alone." He wouldn't hold the excited Albert in his lap. Harry tried to persuade him to pose for pictures and talk to the newspapermen.

Cham cursed him and turned his back on the press. Swaggering and confident, Luigi Anzoni entered the bungalow. "Get out of here," Cham told him. "Come back and bother me when it's over. Or else start running for your life."

He barely glanced at the monstrous B-2 as it rolled by, enroute to the field. It was his personal white elephant, a mainstay of his most fevered dreams. The plane was too large, too heavy, a mass of complications and worries, perhaps destined to be a blot on his conscience, fearsomely shaped and wrought for a purpose he did not approve of —even if, finally, he might profit by this forced encounter and realize hidden, unspoken conceptual things within himself. Sometimes he felt he understood the adumbrations of the B-2 instinctively, and better than anybody else; but that did not make him like or trust it, or enjoy the activity and decision it had thrust upon him. Only on one point did he feel secure: Grandpa would have underwritten the adventure; the bigger the project, the newer, the more grandiose, the better pleased he was, and whatever happened today his treasure would not have gone for any piddling enterprise.

Dugald and Cissie came in, Hank Isbrow bringing up the rear. Cissie wore shapeless, unpressed pants, a checked red-and-white shirt unbuttoned at the collar, and her old scarred jodhpur boots. Her hair was disordered and stringy. Yet Cham, staring at her, not rising from his chair, was aware that she had never looked more radiant—freckles fading on her flushed face, blue eyes gleaming, her slender body taut and braced for impossible feats. She bent and kissed him on the nose and thanked him and whispered for him to wish her luck. "Piss on all of them," he muttered. "It'll fly. Nothing will go wrong."

"No," she said. "But if it ever does I want to be cremated, just like Grandpa."

"Oh, God . . ." he said. "Did you have to tell me today?"

"I didn't want to forget," she said, and grinned.

Dugald gave Cham a pair of binoculars for observing the flight, saying the ship would stay close to the field at first and not attempt to climb very high. He was dry, serene and confidently gracious. Cham, who was none of these, said, "Use them yourself, you bastard. I don't intend to look."

"I can't," Dugald said. "I'm flying copilot. The man we had for the job is ill."

"Oh," Cham said, and was crushed. For some reason that made him hate Dugald. Perhaps it was because he wished he had the valor to insist on making the flight himself.

Shaking Cham's hand, Hank said, "You won't ever have a greater day than this, Mr. Brennan. It was you that made it possible. Wait'll you see what you've bought. Maybe the colonel didn't think too much of you once, but wouldn't he be proud today?"

"Leave him out of it," Cham said. "And beat it, will you?"

Dugald said a radio ground link with the airplane had been set up in a hut at the edge of the runway and that two-way communication would be constant. He and Cissie and Hank left to run up the engines, and Anzoni strutted along beside them to oversee the ground tests. Cham stayed where he was. He shut his eyes and dumbly waited, shaking his head at Lagonda's pleading for him to come outside. She took Albert and departed. Hal followed them. Only Harry remained, silent and on edge. Sweat rolled heavily off Cham.

His ears were assaulted by the whine of a starter, and an engine began its pulsating bellowing. The other joined in the din. This went on forever. Shifting in the chair, Cham pulled sticky cloth off his body, squirmed from his jacket, and loosened his tie and collar. "Why don't they do something, for God's sake?" he asked.

"I'm going to see what's happening," Harry said. "You're the greatest man since Jesus Christ, and that includes Franklin D. Roosevelt, but I can't stand the suspense. Am I excused?"

"Excused?" Cham said. He closed his eyes again. "You're fired, you son of a bitch."

The interminable roar was at last cut short by popping and a dread, aching silence. Harry returned. "I know," Cham said. "They can't get the Goddamned thing to run on the ground, let alone fly through the air."

"Wrong, my lord," Harry said. "They're putting in more gas. Cissie says the cylinder head temperatures and manifold pressures are fine, whatever they are, and now she's going to taxi up and down. Hadn't you better watch?"

"Not me," Cham said.

But when the engines resumed thundering, Hank dashed by, in a tearing hurry, the kitten Icarus in his hands, and said, "She had me get the cat from her car for luck. He has to take the ride, too. On account of Grandpa, she told me to say. And she's asking where you are." A force beyond Cham's ability to resist impelled him to his feet and through the doorway.

Everyone was lined up beside the runway or gathered round the hut with the tall aerial above and the radio equipment inside. The buttons on his shirt pridefully straining, Luigi Anzoni walked to and fro, head inclined toward the sound of his product. Hank climbed a ladder into the cabin, holding Icarus, and slammed the door shut. Cham glared at the great shiny apparition, its smooth snout high like a supercilious camel, its propellers whishing and cavitating. In the nose, a side window open, Cissie waved a red and white arm to him. Waddling and bumping, she ran the B-2 from one end of the field to the other, sometimes fast, sometimes slow, back and forth, back and forth. Her flat, disembodied voice could be heard in the radio hut on a loudspeaker as she reported to the assembled engineers there. Cham suffered a profound and wrenching disappointment. Obviously something tremendous was the matter. Still, Cissie had sense enough to remain on the ground. "The hell with it," he said, and resigned himself to being a fat fool and a disgrace to Grandpa and returned to the bungalow without looking back.

Running madly, Albert slung over one shoulder, Lagonda appeared. "She going!" she cried. "She going! Right now! Don't you dare sit there, Chambers!"

Cham lurched upward, the great muscle in the middle of his chest flailing, grabbed the binoculars, and raced for the field. On the far end of the runway stood the B-2, straining and quivering, engines rising to a maniacal pitch. Behind the blurred props sailed long streamers of dust like dancing veils. Brakes released, his monster trundled forward, gathering speed. Only a thousand feet down the runway it surged into the air. Cissie's voice, metallic and calm, reported instrument readings in the radio hut. The crowd cheered. The wheels stopped spinning and rose, tucking themselves in the engine nacelles. Photographers clicked their cameras.

A screaming note intruded, far more piercing than any of the other sounds. The airplane slowed, staggered, the near wing dipped and righted. It was one of the engines. Sweat filming his eyes, Cham glared into the cruel white light. The screaming ended; the B-2 was leveling off and the noise was reduced by half. Slowing lazily, halting, the propeller nearest to Cham presented straight-on, helpless blades to the wind. Holding three hundred feet of altitude, Cissie went steadily westward. Cham attempted to use the binoculars, could not achieve a focus, and threw them to the earth. From the spectators came a mass groan, and simultaneously he heard his sister's voice; her words were without excitement, casual and unhurried, but to him it seemed he was hearing the last of her, as though she were already behind the curtain of the next world. He thought he would melt and run, racked by a remorseful agony, bleeding inside and wild and confused and mortally frightened and absolutely incapable of accepting the fact of Cissie being injured or killed.

Beyond his ken, lost forever, Cissie and the B-2 and Hank and Dugald and Icarus and his hope and joy and reason for living turned into a droning sliver of the sun's reflected radiance.

Shepherded by Harry, a thin, prissy-looking engineer came to Cham's side. "She lost the port engine, Mr. Brennan," he explained. "There's nothing to worry about. She'll go out, make a couple of gentle turns, and come in low and slow for a landing. It's a fine tribute to Mrs. Stuart's skill and the stability and reserve power of the aircraft that on takeoff, at under five hundred feet, fifty per cent power failure couldn't stop them. You must be very pleased with how—"

"Fuck off," Cham said, in mortal rage. "Who asked for your opinion?" He gazed at Harry with bloodshot eyes as the engineer recoiled, and then went away. Cissie could be heard talking again. "The engine . . ." Cham added. "Even if she gets back, I'm going to kill Anzoni."

"They say it's not the fault of the engine," Harry said. "The propeller went out of pitch and started overspeeding. She had to shut down and feather it quick."

"What does that mean?" Cham said. "I'll kill him anyway. I'll kill everybody, Goddamn them to hell!"

"Hey—" Harry said. "Hey! You can't cry out here in front of everybody. The experts claim there's no danger. They think the plane is much better than it looked on paper. Don't act like a baby."

"I'll slug you!" Cham said, and Harry backed away. He bumped into Hal, who was hurrying up. Behind Hal was Lagonda, toting Albert. The child was laughing and clapping his hands, and he called to Cham and wanted to kiss him. By an effort of will, Cham bent forward and allowed himself to be kissed.

"You won't believe this, Cham," Hal said. "They're dizzy in the radio shack. Cissie says the thing was designed to fly on a single engine and she's going to fly it. She is gaining altitude and heading for Catalina Island. The good engine isn't overheating or on too advanced a power setting. Everything is fine."

"Out over the ocean?" Cham said. "Oh, Jesus Christ!"

He wheeled and hastened to the privacy of the bungalow. Hal and Harry returned to the radio hut, but Lagonda followed Cham. She closed the door and set Albert on his feet. He was highly excited and wanted to talk about flying and the airplane, and endeavored to climb in Cham's lap. Cham shoved him back. Opening the door, Lagonda put the boy out, threatening him with punishment if he strayed far. "This ain't a thing that ought to happen twice," she remarked.

"Leave me alone," Cham said. "I'm sick."

"We better go watch and wait."

"I'm going to stay here."

"Well, I'm not," Lagonda said. "She's as much mine as she is yours, and I'm not afraid to look."

Cham waited, his stomach roiling. Extending his wrist from a crumpled sleeve cuff, he fastened his eyes on the handsome aviator's watch Cissie and Dugald had given him, which glowed in the dark and measured elapsed time and had a sweep second hand that had grown paralyzingly slow. The heat was suffocating. Nobody dared to interrupt him. He wiped his wet cheeks and gave up the idea of puking.

Then he detected the distant murmur of the B-2. It approached in a steady fashion as he held his breath, roared, abruptly subsided, roared again briefly, came singing down, and the tires yelped on the runway. An uneasy, hesitant silence was broken by a mixed round of cheering, applause and laughter. Cham sat where he was, lacking the strength to rise.

Lagonda opened the door. "She coming," she said. "They had to take pictures. She asked for you right away."

"You look two shades lighter," he said. The joy in him was difficult to contain.

"You look terrible. Chambers, we were foolish. You know what they say? This wasn't nothing. Just a regular testing. Little things go wrong, but that doesn't mean nothing . . ."

"The hell it doesn't. To us, anyhow. Where's Al?"

"I don't know," she said. "I forgot him."

She left, suddenly tearful, and Cissie came in. Cham gazed at her tremulously. Cissie had Grandpa's ability to repel tension, and, like him, she never sweated. She smiled and said, "Wipe your face."

He mopped with a handkerchief. "How was it? I couldn't keep watching."

"All right. It's the best airplane in the world, Brother. You didn't waste his money."

"That propeller—"

"That's nothing. They'll have it repaired in an hour."

"You shouldn't have gone out over the ocean."

"Why not? Catalina's a pretty sight from the air, and she flies better on one engine than most of the others on two. I was safer than I am at home in bed."

"Which reminds me . . ." Cham said. "How's the genius?"

"Dugald is satisfied," Cissie said, and laughed. "Satisfied but not surprised, and not a bit scared. You should have seen him pushing buttons and hitting switches when we lost the prop—he's a better pilot than he thinks. And he *is* a genius, Cham. We can hold to his coattails and ride to glory."

"The son of a bitch has aged me ten years."

"You'll be more dignified if you look older. Get up and button your collar and fix your tie. The newspapermen want to take your picture and get a statement."

"From me? You're crazy!"

"You have to do it. Don't argue."

"Wh—what'll I say?"

"Tell them," Cissie said, "that in your opinion we have the best airplane of its type ever constructed. That it will revolutionize air transport. That you were well aware of the performance factors in advance and felt no surprise or worry."

Cham's lips moved as he silently repeated her words. They were still moving when he accompanied his sister outside and faced the representatives of the press. He hooked arms with Cissie and the pictures were taken. He was asked to comment.

"In my opinion, gentlemen," he said, "we have the best aircraft of its kind ever produced. The B-2 will revolutionize air transport. No doubt you will wonder if I was concerned for Mrs. Stuart. I was not— not at all. She is the only pilot I would have trusted with this airplane. As for the B-2 itself, I was well aware of the performance factors in advance and wasn't the least bit surprised or worried. We make aircraft here which are safe under any circumstances." Cissie showed her pride in him, and he glowed; he had risen to the occasion, as Grandpa would have. Furthermore, he was convinced he could rise to future occasions. The past was buried. He was A. Chambers Brennan, not Albert or Brother-the-pants-pee-er. A great barrier had been surmounted. The monster was his friend. And he practically owned it.

Neat, moustached, cool, not a hair out of place, the kitten perched on a forearm, Dugald joined them for a photograph. "Icarus didn't fly too near the sun this time," he said, and smiled. "Are you happy, Cham?"

"I am happy in our association, I can tell you that," Cham responded. "With the blessing of Columbia Air Transport, we are going to put the common man in the air."

The atmosphere was charming, and Cham couldn't believe his emotions of a few minutes ago. Hank Isbrow shook his hand and said, "Mr. Brennan, when that prop ran away I thought we were gone, and after Cissie headed for the island I prayed a little. I'm ashamed I didn't have more confidence. I should have known nothing the Brennans do goes

297

haywire. I bet you're proud of yourself. The old man must be looking down at you and thinking what a wonderful boy he raised."

"Looking up, you horse's ass," Cham said. "Even I'm not that sentimental about him. He never went where he wasn't welcome."

Before she departed, Cissie whispered in Cham's ear, saying, "As soon as the prop's corrected we're going up again. Want to come along?"

"Oh, no," Cham said. "I just like the idea, not the thing itself. I'm going home."

Modestly gay, he thanked several attentive young engineers, gathered up Lagonda and little Albert, and made for his car. A party of Shapiros drove through the gates, captained by Irving. "I understand we're late," Irving said. "Unfortunately, we were delayed by a meeting at the bank." He presented his relatives to Cham. "How did it go?"

"According to plan," Cham told him. "We had some difficulty with an overspeeding prop, but it was easily remedied by my sister. The B-2 will revolutionize air transport." Some of the Shapiros were looking critically at him as he held the black child in his arms; he ignored them. "Of course, I was well aware of the performance factors in advance and felt neither surprised nor worried."

"You have good performance factors yourself," Irving said. "Only you don't sound quite the same as before."

"I probably won't sound the same again. This is where I came over the top of the hill."

"Sound the same just once again—for me. Cham, is it all you hoped for?"

"More," Cham said. "The luck didn't play out. You've backed the right horse, Isadore."

"Your word is good, Albert," Irving said.

"You better button your coat," Lagonda said. "You'll catch cold the way you been sweating, Chambers."

"Okay," Cham said. He handed her little Albert and fastened his jacket. "Let me turn you over to one of my assistants, gentlemen, for a tour of the plant . . . Hey, Harry! . . . I'm sorry I can't go with you, but I have an engagement in town."

"Yes, Mr. Brennan," Harry said, and came hurriedly to them. He was introduced and given the job of escort.

"Be sure they meet Mr. and Mrs. Stuart and inspect the aircraft," Cham said.

"Yes, sir," Harry said.

He went off with the Shapiros, and Cham got in the Duesenberg with Lagonda, Albert between them. As they started up, Luigi Anzoni approached, smiling and waving. Cham stopped the car.

"It was the propeller, not my engine," Anzoni said. "What do you think now?"

"I think you're a guinea bastard," Cham said, "and lucky to be alive."

Flushing, Anzoni said, "Very well, Mr. Brennan! Sell me your interest in my business. I promise to pay you off inside of a year."

"In another year," Cham said, "I'll have you crowded out of the company and looking for a job. You're already out of date. They do things by committees these days, and it takes more money than you can ever raise to put an important deal together. Without the people I brought in, you'd be flat on your ass and the B-2 wouldn't be flying. Get the hell away or I'll run over you."

He drove through the gates in a hurry, and the tires slid on the graveled street. "That's the last time for that place," he remarked thankfully.

"Why you say that?" Lagonda demanded. "You coming into your own there."

"I'm going out of my own," Cham said. "For keeps. I'm tired, Lagonda. I've done all I'll ever have to do, or will do."

But his abdication was a slow affair. First there was the question of more operations at Brennan-Stuart. Cissie and Dugald came to Cham's house to deal with that. Dugald wanted to hire additional workers, retain his staff of engineers, and start full-scale production on a B-3 series—for he had in mind a whole raft of improvements while the B-2 was still scarcely off the ground. Cham listened in astonishment to Cissie disagreeing with him. "I don't think we can ask Cham to get in any deeper in speculation," she said. "He's done what he agreed to do. Let's wait until the CAT tests are finished and we have firm orders."

"Darling, you're being unbusinesslike," Dugald protested. "We know we've succeeded. CAT won't give us trouble. We've got to keep moving. Besides, I can't afford to break up the crew I've put together. I might not be able to get them back in a few months." He appealed to Cham. "Don't you feel I'm right?"

"That's a foolish question," Cissie said. "He's going to agree with me whatever you say."

"All right," Dugald said. "If it's a family affair, I'm beaten."

"We'll have Harry try to find us some business," Cissie said. "Then you can go ahead."

"With the one model we have to show at CAT's disposal?" Dugald asked. "You're talking nonsense. Why not say we're going to shut down and have done with it?"

"Consider it said," Cissie replied. "Don't play the small, spoiled boy, Dugald."

"Pardon me," Dugald said glumly. "I won't bother you or your brother, dear. You have your testing to do, Cham has his money to count, and I'll go sit with folded hands."

"Oh, quit arguing," Cham said. "You're supposed to be happy with each other."

"Are we?" Dugald said. "I'm not a bit happy at this moment, Cham."

"I am," Cissie said. She grinned. "I have that airplane to fly, and I don't want my brother worrying. The Brennans come first, really."

"So I see," Dugald said.

"Can I talk?" Cham said.

"No," Cissie said. "It's settled."

"By all means," Dugald said. "Go ahead in your blindness and agree with your sister."

"I don't agree with her," Cham told him. "You'd better start building B-3's as you planned. Put together ten or so of them and then we'll figure how we're doing."

"Wh-at?" Cissie cried. She was dumbfounded.

"The Goddamned thing flew on one engine," Cham said. "You went to Catalina. It'll be all right."

"You don't owe me anything more," Cissie said.

"This is not for you," Cham said. "This is for me."

"Cham . . ." Dugald said.

Cham looked at him. "Yes?"

"Oh, I keep misjudging you," Dugald said, and his unease was pained. "I wish I could stop it . . ."

"Underestimating, you little bastard," Cham said. "Everybody has that trouble with me. But don't let it bother you. It doesn't bother me."

When Cissie took the B-2 east she was accompanied by Harry and Hal, as well as Dugald; Cham's two henchmen had orders to stay until they were certain CAT approval of the airplane was assured. Somewhat to Cham's envy, Harry was beginning to lose his fear of air travel. Part of his new attitude was the veneration the B-2 inspired. Even in its infancy the ship became a legend. And Hal embraced the opportunity to fly with Cissie; his earlier calflike adoration of her had turned into warm, admiring, unselfish loyalty that was too good to be true and provoked Cham's suspicions. "What's the matter with you, Hal?" he asked. "Don't you ever get over high school crushes? Are you hoping you can outlast Dugald and move in on her?"

"Would you object to that, Prince Charming?"

300

"I sure would. I've got her married off and Dugald came through and it's finished. I don't need any more problems."

"Then let me try to explain," Hal said. "She's a fine lady. Nothing can touch her as far as I'm concerned. She'll always be my best girl, in a funny way. I'd cut off my right arm to help her, and expect nothing in return. I almost like it being like that . . . You can't understand, can you?"

"No," Cham said. "You sound drunk. But I'll take your word for it. Only keep your hands off her if you ever find an opening, see? I'll kill you if you don't."

Dugald soon returned to the west coast bringing encouraging news. CAT officials had been bowled over by the B-2's potentialities. They were assigning their chief pilot, Frank Beeson, to join Cissie in the testing. Hank Isbrow and two expert mechanics were dispatched to New York to make sure the ship remained in top mechanical condition. And a slick, articulate young man named Aaron Eindhoven had arrived there to monitor the Shapiro interests. Cham mentioned this on the telephone to Irving Shapiro.

"He's a grandson of the first Aaron, your father's mentor," Irving said. "This Aaron is trained as an economist and may be the pick of our crop. His mother is Rachel Eindhoven, and we're told your father was once rather sweet on her. We felt we ought to have a man checking on Columbia for us, as you have Harold Baltim, Junior. It even occurred to us that Aaron might assume an official position with the company later."

"Why not just use us for keeping up on things? Aren't we partners?"

"Certainly we are, Cham."

"Then why are you buying stock on your own?"

Irving laughed. "You're a suspicious man! For two reasons. One, to take some of the burden off you. Two, because taxes being what they are, we believe we have to get into risk financing and new products. Aren't you in the same position?"

"I suppose I am," Cham said. "I hadn't thought about it until you explained it. I was only preparing for the B-2."

"Come now," Irving said. "You're much too smart to be operating without an overall plan. I can see your hedging in the airline investment, just as you have in aircraft and engine production. You want a bite of the future, but not too big a bite, in case indigestion goes with it. We approve of your strategy, Cham. However, you are diversified and we have only Columbia and must protect our investment. One of these days, with the fate of the B-2 settled, you might be pulling out

301

of CAT. At such a time we'd have to know we had a strong voice in the management."

"Yeah, I see . . . That makes sense. I probably will dump CAT as soon as I can."

"I don't blame you. You have more than enough in the flying business already, Cham. Thanks for the tip."

Their conversation ended on a friendly note, but sensitive antennae in Cham had been alerted. Obviously the promise he sensed in CAT through undefined instinct was also apparent to the Shapiros through a process of study and carefully applied logic. The value of their judgment was worth taking into account. They were no longer passive participants, merely following his lead. Buying more stock than he shared with them meant they were ready for a full commitment, perhaps with the eventual idea of controlling the company. Probably their knack for smelling out money and the fruits of transition was more acute than his. They had the brains and the organization, but Dugald's revolutionary airplane was his, and he was entitled to all of the profits.

Like a slow dawning, the concept of advancing instead of retreating came to him. He considered what Grandpa might have desired him to do. The answer was easy: the old man would have wanted him to be the richest Brennan ever, the most feared, the greatest success. He would have sniffed at the risks involved, especially when the reward was imposing. And there was the question of the Queen also—Grandpa's darling. She ought to have, and needed, a shot in the arm. Maybe she ought now to leave the ground and soar like a Goddamned angel . . .

Retirement was forgotten. Cham lay in bed a good deal, wiggling his toes and staring at the ceiling. The best reason possible for jumping into CAT with both feet was because the Shapiros wanted it. According to Irving, under different circumstances Cham could have been half Jewish. That was almost insulting, and he had indignation as well as avarice to spur him on. With neither Hal nor Harry available, he tried out his ideas on Lagonda.

"I thought you was going to quit," she said.

"Well, I might turn a couple more tricks before I quit."

"A whole airplane line isn't like a toy, Chambers. Will it pay?"

"It better."

"Haven't you got enough money?"

"For me, yes," Cham said. "But Grandpa would have liked more."

"You not making sense," Lagonda said, "or saying what you deep-down think. Say it."

Cham rubbed his belly and scowled and belched. "They're crowding me. They really think I'm an easy mark. If they'd leave me alone I'd be all right. What if they cashed in on something I thought of first? It's mine, see? And Irving said my father was sweet on one of their women. I don't like that. Besides, they're Jews . . ."

"You got no better reasons?"

"No."

"You're crazy."

"Okay."

"Okay," Lagonda said resignedly. "You won't never need a better reason than that."

Talking long distance to Harry and Hal in New York, Cham asked for an opinion. Their advice was to avoid any conflict and stand pat. "Suppose the Shapiros do eventually control CAT," Hal said. "What do you care? You will have sold them as many aircraft as they can handle. Let them have the airline and its worries."

"Don't spread yourself too thin," Harry said. "I thought you were going to sell out anyhow once the future of the B-2 was assured. If something goes wrong—if the public just refuses to get up in the air—then it will be their funeral instead of yours."

"I was waiting to hear that," Cham said. "Thank you very much, fellows."

"Good lord!" Hal said. "He's finally listening to us."

"No, I'm not," Cham replied. "I only said I was waiting to hear what I expected. Look, buy me stock, every share you can find, and don't worry about the price. I'll match anybody's bid. I want to own CAT. Piss on all of them."

"When we come home," Hal said to Harry, "we'll learn the men in the white coats have come for him. I hope they put him away soon."

"Him?" Harry said. "The great man? The boss? Don't you know he can't do anything wrong?"

Fresh involvements did not expunge Cissie from Cham's mind. Not only her flying concerned him; he also began to worry about the state of her relationship with Dugald. Along with nearly everybody else, he had achieved a kind of mystical confidence in the plangent B-2, but still it was his beloved sister tearing through the heavens in the first untried version. Frank Beeson beside her, and a flight engineer in the cockpit to check results, she broke speed records for land airplanes, lowered the time from coast to coast, took off at high altitudes carrying ten tons of ballast using a single engine, set new marks for endurance and distance, easily exceeded two hundred miles per hour in consistent operation, and deliberately made a wheels-up belly landing to demonstrate inherent fuselage and wing strength which resulted in no more damage than bent propeller tips. When she should have come home, she embarked on a new project, which had the backing of CAT, called cruise control—a method of determining the most efficient and economical power settings for the B-2 at any height and under any given set of conditions. Her absence stretched into months, and Cham saw her only once during this period, while she was briefly in Los Angeles during a round-trip transcontinental flight. Frank Beeson, a genial, hawk-faced, narrow-moustached man, was always in her company, exciting Cham's suspicions and ire. Beeson seemed on intimate terms with Cissie, and his constant, nearly disrespectful bantering evoked her smiles and amusement as nothing else ever had. Both flyers struck Cham as over-tired, nervous and unhealthily intent on what they were doing. They treated him and Dugald as well-meaning strangers. Plainly the airplane had become theirs alone.

Cham's temper wasn't helped by Dugald's attitude. Apparently he saw nothing odd in his wife occupying a hotel room next door to Beeson overnight instead of coming home to Long Beach, and then leaving at daylight sans farewell for the hop back to New York. "Are you nuts?" Cham asked. "Here she is with this guy Beeson more than she is with you. She ought to be home. The Goddamned plane will do everything you claimed it would—we all know that. CAT is not going to turn it down; I practically own the airline. She snoots us and you keep smiling. What kind of a man are you?"

"A broad-minded one," Dugald said. "The sort who would marry Cissie. You pretend to toughness, Cham, and the fact is you are a howling romanticist."

"Am I?" Cham said. "Well, I never did understand you, but I thought I knew her. I'm no longer so sure as I was about that. She still has Hal Baltim following her around like a dog, and according to him he's been seeing her in New York. And now there's this Beeson bastard. I always believed she was a simpleminded girl with one ambition—"

"She is," Dugald interrupted. "You were right the first time. The men in her life—Beeson, Hal, even you and me—are a small part of it. I'm willing to face that, and you are not. She has the B-2 and flying and a few rosy visions, and the rest is largely waste to her. Cham, don't you think you ought to resign yourself to that, as I have?"

"By God," Cham said, "I bet you wouldn't mind growing a couple of horns someday, would you? If I knew Hal or Beeson had made the grade with her, I'd take them apart. What would you do, offer your congratulations?"

"Don't continue thinking that way," Dugald said. "You'll get sick. You're her brother, not I."

"Yeah, yeah," Cham said, and turned crimson and furious. "I'm not a gentleman, so maybe I can speak out. You're saying she's cold and clammy, aren't you? Did you know that before you married her?"

"Yes," Dugald said. "Since you're not a gentleman by your own confession, I can give you a straight answer. Yes, I did. The physical part of our marriage means little to us; we have a different kind of loyalty to each other. That does not prevent me from loving Cissie for what she is and can be. Nor from trusting her."

"Anyhow," Cham said, "with her in the bag you got to build your Goddamned airplane and prove you were a genius. That's worth putting up with a wife who might be accommodating other guys, huh?"

"I realize you're a barbarian," Dugald said, "but even my patience has limits. Insulting your sister would mean nothing to you, of course, but may I remind you that you are slandering my wife?"

"Oh, I *do* beg your pardon!" Cham said. "Now get out of here, you son of a bitch, or I'll flatten you!"

His intimacy with Dugald, always fragile, terminated with that episode. Thereafter they maintained a cool correctness which involved no social occasions and was devoted to business, mostly transacted on the telephone. Cham's anger ebbed, but he readily perceived Dugald had a contempt for him, and in return he could not forgive his brother-in-law for having failed to make Cissie happy. He refused to acknowledge that any fault could be laid at her door. Lagonda, who had the dispute described to her, chided him for his blunt, profane statements. "It don't matter so much what you say, it's how you say it," she commented. "Making such remarks about Cissie is awful and they sure ain't true, but you have to shoot off your mouth, don't you? Why you use that awful language? It makes people mad at you and they think you're a slob. Do you have to swear all the time?"

"That's how Grandpa talked," Cham said, in complete explanation of himself.

"I knew it," Lagonda said, and shook her head sadly. "I just knew it. That old man won't never leave us entirely."

The longed-for event, Cissie's homecoming, was a disappointment to Cham. She appeared at Christmastime, and her fatigued, dispirited, almost unamiable mood was in marked contrast to the holiday atmosphere. She came back on a wave of success. The results of the B-2 testing had been stunningly good. Columbia Air Transport's acceptance was both eager and laudatory. Twenty B-3's were ordered and ten others put on option. Even Dugald was flattened by the victory, and Cham, although essentially unsurprised, was charmed by the additional orders which poured in, many from foreign countries. Suddenly Brennan-Stuart became the largest manufacturer of aircraft in the world, and the plant at Long Beach mushroomed in size. In less than a year sales totaled six million dollars. Dugald doubled his engineering staff, hired fresh drafts of skilled and semiskilled workers every other month, founded a selling force, and began advertising his product. Soon he was branching out into other types of planes, including military models, and bidding on government contracts. True to his word, Cham never returned to the factory. Increasingly he left its direction to his brother-in-law, and only scanned the financial reports and listened to bits of news given him by Hank Isbrow and Harry and Hal.

He thought Cissie would resume her place at Dugald's side, but that was not the case. She looked thin and tired, and betrayed scarcely more interest in Brennan-Stuart than Cham. Her participation in the B-3 test program had been vetoed by Dugald, who felt she needed a rest; she told Cham her husband was going to borrow Frank Beeson from CAT to ferret out possible defects in the new ships.

"I agree you could use a vacation," Cham said, "but the little bastard needn't think he can shove the Brennans out in the cold at his pleasure. If you want to test the B-3, then by God you're going to test it."

"No, no," Cissie said. "Hiring Frank is as much my decision as Dugald's. I don't care for the job."

Cham eyed her sharply. "Why? This doesn't sound like you."

"I don't know . . . I suppose I'm tired. The excitement's over, Brother. The thing is proved. All the rest is just repetition and drudgery. I was first—and that's enough."

She spoke with sadness and a sense of loss that was very apparent to him, and he was concerned for her. She seemed at a loose end through the holidays and well into the New Year, and apparently did little beyond occasionally flying the B-1 and serving as a hostess at the business dinners Dugald gave in a new and larger apartment—gatherings to which Cham was not invited.

He discussed the situation with Lagonda. "Oh, she'll be all right," Lagonda said. "It was a lot of fun, but I guess it's over now she's won everything in sight. She will settle down. She got a good husband."

"You want to bet?" Cham asked. "Maybe he's a cut above Ferris Washington, Junior—I might concede you that. And it's all I'll concede."

Both he and Lagonda believed having a baby was the solution to Cissie's difficulties. However, she gave no hint of what she had in mind, and had evidently forgotten her promise to Cham. At length, he reminded her of their pact, and she exhibited confusion and grinned uneasily. "Why do you have to be so serious and have such a good memory?"

306

she asked. "I don't want to be tied down. Any minute now I may think of something fascinating to do."

"You gave your word."

"Then let me off the hook, please."

"No, I won't," Cham said. "You held me, and I'm holding you."

"That family dynasty idea is damned foolishment and you know it. The only reason you keep insisting is on account of Grandpa. Forget it or marry yourself."

He shook his head. "I've got to have something from you. It's all that's left between us. Your children will be different. I'm no bargain, and it'd be just my luck to marry some stupid whore. At least Dugald can fill your belly with brains."

"You put it beautifully, Brother."

"I don't claim to be a diplomat, but you owe me a good deal. I had to give you up. I stood that and kept my mouth shut. I'm entitled to see a few babies, even if their name won't be Brennan."

"Oh, you're impossible!" she said.

"Sure. I did the impossible, too—you pushed me into it. If nothing goes wrong we're going to be so Goddamned rich we'll make the other Brennans look like beggars in rags. There have to be heirs for that kind of money."

"Put it in bad investments and lose it."

"I couldn't if I tried," he said. "The pile has grown too big. It'll just keep adding to itself. You've got to provide the people to watch over it."

"Give it to charity or the government."

"Do you realize what you're saying? Do you want Grandpa to gather up his dust from all over town and come back like a cloud to haunt us?"

His urging notwithstanding, Cissie remained evasive and refused to commit herself. Months passed, and there was no sign of any addition to the family. Cham saw little of her; evidently she preferred to avoid reminders of her forsaken promise. He was lonely and in a bad temper, and almost yearned for the febrile excitement and companionship of the days of the B-1 and B-2. Accustomed now to having his desires satisfied, he wondered how he could bend Cissie to his will and ensure an orderly succession among the Brennans. The example of Grandpa presenting a house to his father and mother came to him again. If the gesture was grand enough, surely Cissie and Dugald would understand the importance and responsibility of their position and take steps to provide for the only kind of permanence humans could manage.

While he brooded on bloodlines and the eventual placing of a great fortune in the hands of a close relative or relatives yet to be furnished and set in motion on earth, he contrived, in the midst of a planned withdrawal, to entangle himself further as he attempted to amuse his difficult sister. The Anzoni Aircraft Engine Company was prospering in concert with Brennan-Stuart, and Cham's attitude toward Luigi became nearly benevolent; he encouraged him to experiment on a variety of relatively low-powered, in-line, inverted, air-cooled engines designed for light and medium-sized airplanes, and called upon Cissie to put them through their paces in the air. She showed interest, bought a small ship to serve as a testbed, and spent some time at the airport in Glendale flying the different models. In the meantime, pressed for working space and advised to expand nearer the sources of raw materials, Cham arranged with Anzoni to establish a branch of the company at Hartford, Connecticut. His main work force and principal engineers, as well as his imported manager, went east and Luigi was shunted into a comparatively harmless obscurity.

Abruptly, Cissie quit the project. Cham insisted on an explanation. "This is nothing," she said, sitting alone with him in the summerhouse, her hands twisting in her lap, attired these days in a smart silk summer dress and a hat. "In comparison with what I've done, I'm wasting time. You're making work for me as you are for poor old Luigi. We both ought to be put out to pasture . . . Cham, I'm bored to death."

"Why can't you do something for Dugald?"

"It's too big and complicated now. He doesn't need me anymore."

"Have a baby," he said.

"Oh, shut up!"

"I was talking to Jesús Algonrones about you the other day—"

She laughed. "Can he speak English yet?"

"No. He had another interpreter, a young boy. Conny's had a baby."

"Yours?"

"Don't try to be funny," Cham said. "I sent a check to help with the kid's education someday. You know, I started envying that lousy Mexican gardener. I told him how I wished you'd follow in Conny's footsteps. Jesús told me I ought to get Dugald *boracho*."

"What?"

"Drunk."

"You're pretty disgusting, you and your friends," Cissie said.

"No, Jesús was only trying to help. I wouldn't be surprised if he's more of a gentleman than I am . . . Cissie, are you scaring off the little bastard? Are you keeping him from taking care of you? Should you both have a few drinks and get down to business?"

"Go to hell."

"I'll tell you what Jesús asked me," Cham said. "He wanted to know if you're barren. If you are, he thinks you ought to go to the shrine of

308

Guadalupe in Mexico. Women come from all over and pray there and then conceive. Jesús swears it always works. Are you barren, Cissie?"

She glared at him, flushing, a shining of tears coming in her eyes.

"I've got to know," he said. "It's important to us."

"No, I'm not barren," she said. "I'll prove it to you."

He relaxed, feeling a spreading warmth of satisfaction. Like Grandpa, he could have precisely what he wanted.

Certain his sister would not fail him, Cham proceeded on plans for the splendid house. Among the scattered properties left by Grandpa were five acres of high ground north of Sunset Boulevard, within the limits of Beverly Hills. Accompanied by Lagonda, Cham examined and paced off the brushy slopes, which were elevated enough to afford a sweeping vista of the flatter portions of the city and the sea. The weather was cooler here, the surroundings plushier, than in his own decaying section. Unhappily, a good many Jews had settled in the town, including movie potentates and their henchmen. Still, it was not what Cham regarded as foreign territory, and he was consoled by the presence of reputable rich who chose the region in preference to less diluted compounds in Pasadena, the Los Feliz district, and a stately array of brick and half-timbered houses midway between Western Avenue and Highland Avenue. The larger part of Beverly Hills was, in strict truth, a well manicured, neat, profusely watered collection of little holdings, bungalows, plain two-storied houses suitable for bigger families, and small white-stuccoed and red-tiled apartment houses of discreet pretensions; it was only toward Sunset and beyond that mansions reared up, and they were infrequent. Size and expenditure were more likely to stand out here than in Pasadena or on Los Feliz Boulevard.

He did not act hastily. Driving around, usually with Lagonda, meditating, he inspected Long Beach, and the Palos Verdes area, where on highlands overlooking the sea considerable homes of a Mediterranean character were rising amid verdant shrubbery and curving roads bearing Spanish titles. Presently he came to the conclusion that Grandpa's land offered the finest prospect. Pasadena was aging ominously, as was the Los Feliz section, and the English-style residences lying past Western Avenue were too uniform and uninspired. In none of these districts was there a commanding view, or any greater spread than could be had by pairing two lots. Palos Verdes was remote, and Long Beach an unpalatable concentration of Iowans, beach-front hotels and amusement parlors for sailors of the Pacific Fleet on leave. Of course, Beverly Hills was a long distance from Dugald's aircraft plant, but an automobile would take him back and forth with reasonable speed. Recalling

Grandpa on the subject of obsolescence and change in the Queen, Cham concluded the five hilly acres had the best chance for longevity and appreciation of value.

He needed an architect. Harry, home from another expedition to New York, supplied him with one—his brother Tom, a graduate of the University of Southern California, and sorely in need of commissions. Tom had the family height, straw-colored hair and lack of weight, but none of Harry's venal pliability. Sullen and reserved, he fended off questions Cham asked, was completely unhelpful, and seemed eager to escape from the interview. His dismal manner titillated Cham. "What's the matter?" he said. "Do you think the idea's crazy? It's not for me."

"I know. But families don't live that way anymore. Did you ever hear of the depression, Cham?"

"Sure. Did you ever hear of the Rockefellers and Fords and Astors and what they're doing on the other side of the country?"

Tom stared at him. "You haven't got that much money, have you?"

"No, but I've got enough," Cham said. "Someday, with luck and enough growth out here and a cut in the Goddamned taxes, whoever follows me and my sister could look nearly as good as they do back there. So what's wrong with our setting up on a solid basis now?"

"Nothing, I guess."

"Only you don't want any part of me. Why? We used to be friends when we were kids. I get along all right with your brother."

"I just can't forgive you," Tom said, "for throwing my father out of Sunset Sea—if you care for the facts. Harry doesn't mind, naturally. He and my father never got along. And he took over Dad's job."

"You shouldn't grieve. Your old man isn't starving, is he?"

"He's doing something worse. Eating his heart out. All he ever cared for was living in the reflected glory of your father and the colonel. When you fired him, you spoiled the last part of his life. He's sick and miserable and disappointed; he has rheumatism so bad he can scarcely move anymore."

"To hell with him," Cham said deliberately. "He's old and out of date and incompetent, and he was always trying to tell me how to act. I don't care if he's stiff as a poker. Harry told me you were having trouble finding anything to do in these hard times, and I'm ready to give you a chance. Take it or leave it."

"I'll leave it," Tom said. "To hell with you, you fat rich bastard."

Cham laughed. "Listen, everybody is entitled to an opinion around me except Harry. He agreed to admire me when we first started together. You can say whatever you think if I hire you. When and as I'm convinced you know what you're doing, you'll have the same freedom of action I gave my brother-in-law. Where else can you get those terms?"

"Freedom of action? You're talking through your hat, Cham. And you're ignorant. You intend to build a monument to your thieving great-uncle and your pompous father and your sister and your own luck, and you'll insist on a stupid pile of Victorian granite or a great white house with a pillared portico right off the James River stuck incongruously on the side of a California mountain—"

"Maybe not. Tell me what's better."

"How could I make you understand? There's a new movement in architecture, but it'll never survive out in this dumping-ground of spoiled and misapplied ideas. In Los Angeles they build with boulders sunk in concrete and put up Moorish palaces topped by minarets and make restaurants in the shape of derby hats—"

"Yeah, yeah," Cham said. "But I might understand. Tell me the new thing."

"You wouldn't. It's light, clean, functional, unpretentious, rising out of the ground and yet belonging to it—glass and metal and aluminum and terrazzo flooring, roofs like wings, space and depth, the tidiness of a ship, the warmth of a mountain cabin."

"Like an airplane?"

"Well, yes," Tom said. "Like an airplane."

"That's all right. It could take longer to go out of style, eh? I don't want to get into a house that will have no value in twenty years; it should be ahead of its time . . . Think about this and give me some drawings. I'll pay you a thousand dollars for your ideas. If I decide to go ahead, you can have, within reason, anything you want. A chance to make your reputation. No restrictions on expense. And I never go back to what I start—it spoils my luck."

"I don't trust you."

"We'll sign something."

Unwillingly, Tom said, "I could try it, I suppose. I need the thousand bucks. But you won't own me."

"Sure I will," Cham said. "You're on the hook. People are bought by generosity."

Tom went to Beverly Hills to examine the property. His plans and renderings, even though he had nothing else to do, were slow in arriving. When at length he had them in hand, Cham was surprised but not shocked or repelled. It was a different sort of house, certainly, wandering in calculated disarray at varying levels, never rising to much height, inconspicuous and almost conveying the impression of being impromptu, white-walled, flat-roofed, crowning heights in the fashion of a set of defensive works; there were expanses of glass, skylights, cedars to be planted in marching columns, statuary in bowers, and a roughly paved courtyard; within, rooms opened on a garden, fountain and swimming pool, and life was meant to revolve around that green and watery portion of the outdoor world that had walkways protected from the sun by columned overhangs. Wherever one looked, one was compelled to see not walls or constricting obstacles but clarity and sweep, the distant ocean, descending and rising hills, a city outspread, an infinite detail provided by nature and man. Cham was stirred, and scowled and puckered his lips, trying to take in the conception entire. Misinterpreting his expression, Tom reached for the papers.

"You can keep your money," he said. "I knew you would have no sympathy for this."

"Wait a minute," Cham said. "We've got a ranch, the San Cristobal—"

"God, yes! It was my father's religion. I started hearing about it in my cradle. Before I was old enough to walk I was out there."

"You too?" Cham grinned. "I remember a picture—just a drawing —my grandmother once showed me of a house somebody had on the ranch, grandmother's father, I suppose. It was a lot like this, built around a patio or garden, with a fountain. The rooms had doors on the patio. Is that what you had in mind, the way they made them then?"

"No, this is Mediterranean—but modern. Inside you wouldn't use tile and wrought iron and those God-awful plaster fireplaces with hoods. It would be warm and gay, with pictures and wallpaper and fine woods and marble for elegance and copper and ceramic pieces for color. Or suit yourself. I'm not an expert on interior design. The main effect would be in having it clean and uncluttered and bright as fresh paint."

Cham strained in an effort at recollection. "I've seen something like it long ago. Who had this kind of house even before the Californians?"

"Along these lines, you mean?" Tom asked. "Oh, perhaps the Romans. The climate in southern Italy resembles ours. They had an atrium and lived around an inner garden. Judging from the photographs I've seen, you could find a remote ancestor of the house in the ruins at Pompeii; but nothing like it has ever been built in California."

"Except by my great-grandfather."

"If it helps your pride, take the credit."

"I will," Cham said. "Look, you have good notions. Not as good as Dugald Stuart has, but they'll do. I'll see whether he and my sister agree with me."

"They won't."

"Their taste is better than mine."

312

"I'm beginning to think," Tom said, "that your taste is quite discriminating. Maybe I was mistaken about you, Cham."

The smallest of indications, of portents, aided Cham in coming to a decision. He resolved to put up the house Tom Sego imagined because the San Cristobal had once seen its like, and because Grandpa's father loved the Romans and Grandpa himself was partial to them. A house that possessed such recognizable ancestors would surely invoke mysterious blessings. If Cissie and Dugald resisted him, he'd live in the place himself.

His sister brought the subject to issue by suddenly appearing on a rainy night, a suitcase in her car. She marched up to a bedroom and retired before Cham could get down to greet her. Having seen to her comfort, Lagonda sought Cham. Her face was pinched in worry. "It's gone wrong," she said. "Real wrong. I could tell that ten feet off."

"What?" he said.

"I mean with her marriage. You know what she say to me? She say, 'Lagonda, I'm going to live here again from now on. Put me in the biggest bedroom you have so I can spread out. And tell Cham to leave me alone until tomorrow.'"

"They've had a fight, huh? I suppose she's left him."

"She sure has."

"I've got to talk to her."

"No, don't," Lagonda said. "Wait until morning. She looks kind of sick and disgusted. You won't get nowhere with her tonight."

Cham was inclined to disregard her advice, but prudence held him back. He considered telephoning Dugald; pride and the expectation that his brother-in-law might show up to offer apologies and hold out an olive branch stayed his hand. His forebearance was rewarded. Dugald arrived in a couple of hours, as Cham, still in nightwear, prowled about the lower floor. By then, with a degree of reluctance, Lagonda had confided how, in helping Cissie undress, she had noticed she was pregnant. "Sweet Jesus!" Cham said. "Is it possible?" Doubt tweaked him. "Are you sure? Did she tell you she's knocked up?"

"I got eyes, haven't I? Her stomach is sticking out and her chest is getting bigger."

"I asked you—did she mention it herself?"

"No," Lagonda said, "and I was polite; but I know enough to recognize—"

"How many months gone?"

"Maybe two, three, I don't know."

"Oh, Lagonda! She could be bloated or getting fat or she might not have gone to the toilet for a while."

"Yes, sir. You content yourself, Mr. Chambers."

"Listen, I don't mean to sound nasty," Cham said. "But this is nothing to kid about. You know how important it is for her to have a baby. For the family's sake, I mean. It ought to be a boy. I hope to God you're right. Grandpa would have been pleased, wouldn't he?"

"That old man . . ." Lagonda said. "He left plenty of himself behind in this old house."

Clad in a misbuttoned, crumpled raincoat, a hat jammed down on his head, Dugald rang unnecessarily long. Cham hurried to the front door. They stared at each other, Dugald in open enmity, and Cham stepped backward so he could come in. "She's here?" Dugald said.

"Yeah."

"I presume the two of you have had a long and cosy chat, exulted again in being Brennans, and arranged to discard me?"

"No," Cham said, "we haven't talked. Lagonda put her right to bed."

"I suppose I'll have to believe you. May I speak to her?"

"I don't think so. Lagonda says she feels rotten."

"Does Lagonda decide everything for you?"

Cham lit a cigarette. "Damned near. Don't get shitty with me, Dugald. You're in here on sufferance. What did you fight about?"

Sighing, Dugald removed his hat and coat and lowered himself in a chair. He made no answer. Cham offered him a drink, and he shook his head. "Why'd you come if you're not going to say anything?" Cham asked.

"Isn't that what you've been waiting for, to get her back?"

"No. She belongs to you now. I gave up when you got married."

"Do you mean that?"

"Yes, damn it!"

"She's simply tired of me, I gather," Dugald said. "I never meant enough to her to matter anyhow; the B-2 was important, and that has been achieved. It's insulting!" He sat precisely and stiff-backed, his mouth a grim line under the neat moustache, a small and angry man. "We haven't been getting along well lately. I think she provoked me tonight in order to have an excuse to come running to you. I obliged her by not being able to hold my temper."

"Is she pregnant?"

"Yes. But that doesn't excuse her conduct toward me."

"The child is an excuse for anything," Cham said. "At least to me; and it ought to be to you. Still, I can't say I blame you for getting mad. You always were an extra spoke in our wheel. Probably I'm to blame for her attitude. I guess I'd better stop calling you 'the little bastard.' "

"No, no. Please go on. I don't expect anything else."

314

Cham grinned. "How did she set you off tonight? I've tried enough times with you and failed."

"You'll be happy to learn," Dugald said, "that she succeeded by using you—by an extra display of the Brennan arrogance. I have contempt for you. You're not an equal. But I have to take her seriously. And when she told me she was only having a baby because you wanted it, it was just too much—too cruel, rotten, disgusting, incestuous—"

"Okay. Don't holler."

"It would seem you are the father. She doesn't love me at all."

"She doesn't love anybody. Remember how you pointed that out to me?"

"I've changed my mind about that. She loves you."

"Shut up. You're feverish. The important matter is the child—"

"Why?" Dugald asked. "To preserve the royal line of lechers, drunks, petty despots and confidence men? Have you infected Cissie with your megalomania?"

"Quit picking on me, will you? I'm trying to help."

"Excuse me, your highness. I forgot I'd won your favor with the only organ you respect."

"I'm going to make you two presents," Cham said. "A wife, and a place to keep her. All you have to do is be pleasant and a hero and live up to the Brennan standard. Wait a minute." He got the drawings for the new house, spread them on a coffee table, and offered explanations.

Dugald looked and listened indignantly, and seemed somewhat confused. "No," he said. "I'm not your puppet. I don't want your house, Cham."

"Cissie goes with the deal."

"No."

"Come on," Cham said. "You want the baby, so you've got to have her. That's where I come in. You need me, and you can play being the hero later."

"You can't do any more with her than I can."

Cham sat down, lit another cigarette, and thought for a moment. His stomach turned over. But this was how Grandpa would have tied up the loose ends, and played God. "Well, let me try, Dugald. You take care of the family and making a good show, and maybe I can take care of you."

Staring at him, Dugald said, "You're a lunatic. Why bother with me or your strange sister? Get your own babies and continue the lucky Brennans. Live yourself in that stupid, pretentious house and crow on your dung heap."

"I'm the wrong one, as you know. I don't amount to a damn, in spite of the luck. It's got to come from the good side, Cissie and you."

"Cham, you're incredible. The most fantastic man I ever knew . . ."

"Shall I go up and talk to Cissie?"

"Yes, if you like."

"Don't go away," Cham said.

In the second-floor hallway, Lagonda confronted him. "Let Mr. Stuart do his own talking," she said. "You'll just make it worse."

"I got to do something nobody else can. This is terribly important."

"Please leave her be."

"I just can't," he said. "We have to think of the kid and how it's got to have parents and a family. Cissie and I didn't do very well without a father."

"This'll turn out a mess between you," she said. "Mark my words."

He knocked on the bedroom door. "I can't see anybody," his sister called.

"It's me," he said. "I've got to come in. Please excuse me." Entering, he saw she was sitting up in bed, in a nightgown, an open book in her lap. Her face was ruddy, as though an anger moved her, and her eyes were bright with lurking tears. He walked slowly over, pulled up a chair, and sat down.

"You're not welcome," she said.

"I know. But Dugald's downstairs."

"Tell him to go home and forget me."

"There's the baby—"

"That doesn't matter. It's for you."

"Oh. Thanks."

"I'm going to stay with you for the rest of my life."

"Good."

"I never should have left."

"No." He delayed, testing his nerve. She seemed so clean, immaculate and beautiful to him, and twice as precious in her sorrow and confusion and fruitfulness. The breasts under the thin fabric were swelling, the nipples hardening and growing dark. He thought he could taste her mouth, smell the scent of her skin and hair. Delaying made his head feel full to exploding. To think of Dugald being connected to her and spilling out new life nauseated him. A next, inevitable act was no less shattering than preparing to relinquish a leg or losing her to a husband or wondering if she would die in an airplane crash or thinking of Grandpa waiting for the lights to go out. But it was not the means, it was the end . . .

"All right," she said. "That's settled. I'm not at my best tonight, Cham.

Nothing has gone well for a long time . . . We'll talk it over tomorrow."

"What's your hurry?" he said. "Welcome home." He leaned forward and pulled her to him and kissed her on the lips. It was the first time ever for that. He could hardly speak afterward. "We don't have to fight the urge anymore, do we? I'm sick of holding out. The next kid you have will be mine." He kissed her again, pushed her head back, and put his right hand inside her gown and cupped and pressed one breast; with his left hand, he burrowed under the covers and the gown and tried to feel between her legs, but her thighs closed. As he fought for control, he was cognizant of a burning in his groin and mounting flesh and her lips melting on his and her knees beginning to uncover the wonderful hot secret place. Her coldness was a myth. The true warmth was reserved for him, and he experienced a great and bitter triumph.

She saved them, gasping and pulling free, and rolling farther away in the bed. There was a look of horror and shame on her face. Her skin was so pale the freckles stood out in inky blotches. "Oh, no . . ." she said. "No . . ."

"Why not?" He was trembling.

"That's the worst. The end. We can't . . ."

"Listen, we can't do anything else."

She shook her head and put a hand to her mouth, as if she might vomit.

"Then you ought to go with Dugald," he said. "Don't stay here or try to live somewhere else alone. I'd chase you into a corner and take it whether you agreed or not. I'd die to have it."

She sat watching him for a long while, and suddenly tears inundated her eyes. "And I would welcome it," she said finally. "It could only be welcome from you . . . Oh, my God! What is the matter with us?"

"We're not the first ones. It's happened before." He was no longer sure of his purpose, and had grown dizzy and sick.

"It's terrible. You know it . . . Please go. Give me a chance to get dressed and leave."

"You're certain that's what you want?"

"Yes! We can't be together anymore."

"Shall I have Dugald wait?"

She nodded, and he went out. He stood for a moment in the hall, hoping the color would go out of his face and his hands stop shaking. At the foot of the stairs waited Dugald, more anxious than he cared to admit. "You look like a man about to have a stroke," he said.

"We had a fight," Cham replied. "Bigger than the one you had with her. She'll be down pretty soon and go with you. Don't ask questions, just take her back."

"Yes, Cham."

"I'm going to call you a little bastard one last time. Pay attention to me, you little bastard. My influence on her won't ever bother you again. She's through with me. But don't let the victory go to your head. Don't doublecross me. If you do, I'll bugger you up good. You'll lose her and the kid and your airplane plant and die a Goddamn bum. We've got an agreement, see? Hear me?"

"I hear you," Dugald said, and smiled rather sadly. "I'm sorry for you. You've got a lot of sense and guts and devotion to a crazy principle." He stuck out his hand. Cham took it, pressed hard, and turned and ran up the steps and puffingly into his room and went immediately to bed, but not to sleep.

Later Lagonda came in, and stood and looked down at him. "She's gone," she said.

"With him?"

"Yes. What did you do to her?"

He told her in an elliptical fashion, knowing she must correctly suspect a good deal. Recounting it helped to ease the pain and clear away the foul mists and vapors, but a raw, ugly, impossible wound remained that would never heal. Lagonda listened with stiffening features, rubbing her chin, ignoring the shamed tears he shed. "You come of funny people," she said. "It ain't your or Cissie's fault. They were more good than bad, I guess; or it might be the other way around. But you can't help what they left you—money and blood and queer things in your bones."

"It was hard to do," he said. "Very hard. The hardest thing I ever did."

"Well, it's over and done with."

"She's through with me, Lagonda. She didn't know I was pretending. And Christ, I wasn't pretending when I got started! It made her sick. She's much better than I am. She couldn't have finished it, and I could —gladly. I'm going to be real lonesome from now on."

"Go to sleep, Chambers. I'll turn out the lights."

"You know something? I feel like peeing the bed. It's the only thing that could help to make up for what's happened."

"Go ahead," Lagonda said. She bent and kissed his forehead. "You're my boy, and you got one last dirty trick coming to you. Then you better change your whole nature."

The lamps went off. He thought again of Grandpa defending himself against the darkness. That old man had loved life more than his descendants did. The black didn't scare Cham any longer. The long dark could come to him any Goddamned time it wanted.

318

SIX

THE first visitor Cham had at the old Westlake house upon his return from Europe was Irving Shapiro. He appeared, in fact, almost before Lagonda had finished unpacking his luggage. With Irving was Aaron Eindhoven, looking enigmatic and also a trifle embarrassed. Despite the underlying tensions of the situation, Irving was polite and unhurried; he and Aaron gravely acknowledged introductions to Albert, slim and straight in his smart Dangerfield Military Academy uniform and holding back earlier tears of joy at Cham's reappearance, and talked without condescension to the little black boy. Then Ferris Washington, Junior, served tea and cakes prepared by Lagonda and took his son away.

Cham observed the exit of the Washingtons frowningly. "Maybe you're wondering why Al is in *that* school," he remarked. "Well, I'll tell you: I found out that if you're too dark a color in this town you have a hard time getting a good education."

"Considering the views you have expressed to me in the past," Irving said, "I wouldn't think that would bother you."

"It doesn't," Cham said. "Except in the case of Al. I certainly wasn't going to put him in a class with a bunch of dumb niggers. He's mine. But you should have seen the hair come up on their backs when I started inquiring at private schools. They gave every reason but the one that bothered them, including his tender age. I told them I wanted him started off right from the cradle, and the hell with the expense. I had to buy a Goddamned gymnasium for Dangerfield. Of course, I could have had him tutored privately, but I thought he'd do better around other kids."

319

"Are you sure of that?" Aaron asked. "He must be having his troubles as the one Negro in a select white academy."

"Probably," Cham said. "I notice his father is whining at what he has to go through. Al just grits his teeth and does it for me. I'll assure you of this: if it comes to a showdown, Al will be the only student left on that pisspot drillground when the shooting is over. All he has to do is mind his manners and keep his grades up. I'll kill him if he doesn't."

"I imagine you would, Cham," Irving said, and sighed. "And I have no doubt Dangerfield will end up in your possession, and Master Albert triumphant—and crushed, too, perhaps, by his foster-father. Under certain circumstances, your attitude and efforts would be admirable. In this case, I don't think they are. You don't care at all for the ethics of the matter, or for the distinctions made against Albert's race. The injustice is of no concern to you. The boy is your property and therefore must be accorded the respect you insist on. Am I right?"

"Yes," Cham said. "I'm dumb. I can't deal in generalities and noble slogans like the Goddamned Democratic administration, which I presume you admire. My business is protecting what I have and advancing my own interests. And I stick by my friends. They can be any color."

"Uncle Irving," Aaron said firmly. "Pardon me. The conversation is getting off the rails. Mr. Brennan's opinions are his own affair. We didn't come here to argue about them."

"I must say, Aaron," Irving replied with asperity, "that I am not surprised to find you defending Cham. After all, you are now his man. Or am I drawing the wrong conclusions from your recent meeting in New York?"

"He's my man," Cham said. "He can't afford not to be. On the other hand, I think I've got to have him, and the CAT stock he's going to get ought to prove it. The next thing, Irving, is to—"

"Just a moment," Irving interrupted. "I'd like to settle the issue between my nephew and myself in your presence, Cham." He looked hard at Aaron, who averted his head. "The family counted on you, you know. We felt our ties overrode such considerations as mere self-interest. But we were mistaken, eh? You went calmly over to the other side, the stronger side—when the price was right. I'm deeply disappointed in you, Aaron. We all are."

"Yeah," Cham said. "He went over to the Gentiles. Is that what pains you? You people are the narrowest-minded bunch in the world."

"Not as narrow-minded as you!" Irving retorted. "You are a combination of ignorant prejudices and absurdities, and absolutely ruthless in the bargain. No doubt what is beginning to happen to our people in Europe escaped you, or more probably you didn't care. Or did you approve? What would you have us do, scatter now and offer up our throats for the cutting?"

"Well, let Aaron scatter, anyhow," Cham said. "With his brains, he won't come to harm."

Aaron sat, head downcast. Leaning back, Cham lit a cigarette and shrugged. He felt half sorry for the two men. It was as if he had been untrue to Grandpa, or his father before him to the old man; the tribes should stick together. There was a moment of silence. Finally Irving said: "All right. What plot confronts me?"

"I had time to do a lot of thinking while I was traveling," Cham said. "I decided CAT should belong to me, or to us, I guess I should say. It mostly does anyway, but the management isn't completely under our thumbs. They're still running the line as if it was a great adventure and cost no object. A housecleaning is in order. I want Aaron for president and Hal Baltim for chairman of the board. Then they can put in their own people clear across the country."

Irving stiffened. "What?"

"I could force the deal myself," Cham added, "but I'd rather have Shapiro interests' help and a little peace and quiet."

"This is even worse than I anticipated!" Irving said. "No wonder Aaron defected. He is as mad as you are, Cham . . . No, I believe I can safely say you won't have us behind you. And I wonder if you can have everything your own way without us?"

"Why won't I have you?" Cham asked.

"Because we do not intend to put ourselves at your capricious mercy in CAT," Irving said. "Because we regard Ford Briggans as a perfectly suitable president of the line. He is a flyer, he pioneered the routes, he's honest, he understands every facet of the business, we owe him our loyalty—"

"We owe him nothing," Cham said. "If it hadn't been for the B-3, he would have come to his finish long ago. He's old and out of date and talks of wearing a leather coat and goggles and carrying the mail. From now on we only have to consider getting passengers around the country as fast as possible, on regular schedules, at the lowest possible rates, and not scare them. We have to try to get customers that would otherwise ride on trains or buses, or take their own cars; we're selling convenience and quickness, not high adventure. The romance is over. My brother-in-law finished that. Anything else on your mind?"

"I'm not convinced," Irving said. "And I have plenty else on my mind. I neither like nor trust Baltim. He is endurable as a board member, but not as chairman."

Cham grinned. "I tried to get him for president, and he refused. Then

321

I worked on Harry Sego; he turned me down, too. You know why? They're like me—they belong to the Queen. If it's in your blood, you keep heading west for the warmer climate. Neither of them cares for New York and the blizzards. Harry is glad to stay with Sunset Sea, and Hal thinks he can spend just part of his time in the east and let Aaron really run CAT."

"No," Irving said.

"Well, give me a reason," Cham said.

Hesitating at first, Irving said, "Youth, Cham. Youth. You're asking us to agree to putting a group of infants in charge. They haven't the experience or the judgment. Aaron is twenty-six years old. Baltim isn't much older."

"And I'm twenty-nine," Cham said. "That's the worst reason yet. The young used to run the world when people didn't live so damned long. What about the depression? You'd better turn things back to the men without the dry balls. My grandfather thought all a young man needed was the forcing and the chance. Hal's had that. Aaron's going to get it. When a war comes you'll be glad—"

"There's no war coming," Irving said. "Not for us. Roosevelt has promised—"

"Oh, for Christ's sake!" Cham said. "He promises anything. Remember how Wilson kept his promise in the last war? Listen, we need a war. Especially in Los Angeles. We're ready to deal in airplanes and armament and shipping—the kind of stuff they'll need in a new big war. This climate is ideal for trying out their stuff. We can sell to Europe as well. What else have we got to offer? More orange groves? Listen, without a war, a good big one, we're going to see the bottom fall out here. Pray for it, Irving."

"Good God!" Irving said, and silently stared at Cham.

"Aaron is one of yours," Cham said presently. "He'll always be yours, more or less. I'm not really crazy about him, if you want to know. But I have to take what I can get. He's being handed quite a chance on a silver platter, huh? Think it over. You don't find suckers like me every day in the week."

"Come on, Uncle Irving," said Aaron grimly. "You can't talk the bastard out of it, believe me." And he led his dazed relative off.

Irving returned in a week, after vainly attempting to force Cham to meet him in his offices at the Trans-California Corporation's Los Angeles building; but Cham refused to break his habit of having people come to him. Again Irving was accompanied by Aaron, who looked glum and in an ill humor. The reason for the latter's depression was quickly apparent. The Shapiros had decided against him and the Brennan interests.

Cham did not argue the point. "Okay," he said. "The decision is yours to make, even if it may involve Aaron's scalp. I'll try to swing CAT on my own. If I miss, I'm going to sell out—and not to you."

"That threat worked in the bank affair," Irving replied, "but it isn't going to stampede us a second time."

"You did all right stringing along with me then, didn't you? I was twenty-three or something in those days."

"I think you were more sensible then than now, Cham."

"Suit yourself," Cham said. "Either CAT is going to be mine or nobody's in particular."

"You won't do that."

"Yes, he will, Uncle Irving," Aaron said. "I've been talking to Hal Baltim, and all the arrangements are made." His uncle rubbed his chin and glowered at the carpet. "You just don't understand him. He conducts business as if it was a gang war. Perhaps Uncle Samuel, Uncle Barry and Uncle David know him better. I was together with them privately yesterday. They're not so sure you're right in this."

Regarding Aaron coldly, Irving groaned aloud. Then he gazed at Cham. "Are you as lucky as ever?" he asked.

"Luckier," Cham told him. "And more generous."

"And even less scrupulous," Irving said. "You divide and conquer, don't you? Give me until tomorrow."

Next morning Burton Lely came to see Cham, apologizing for lack of an appointment. "You know you don't need an appointment with me," Cham said, and, somewhat surprised at the visit, ushered the lawyer into the solarium. As usual at any hour before noon, he was in rumpled pajamas and a robe.

Lely glanced around the sunny room and smiled. He remained slim and good-humored, but these days he appeared rather out of date with his receding, graying hair, high collars, and the brown, fuzzy fedora hat, a shade too small, he always placed squarely on his head. However, he did inspire confidence, which was part of his stock in trade.

"What memories this room arouses of the immortal colonel," he remarked. "He was an extraordinary man, wasn't he? Distance seems to lend perspective on him, or at least enchantment. My memories of him are a mixed lot, I'm afraid, but I imagine all of yours are delightful."

"Yeah, fine. I miss him."

"Ye-es. You'll never be moving from this place, I suppose?"

"I don't think so," Cham said. "It satisfies me."

"It's been ages since we've seen each other," Lely said. "You're looking well, Cham, and not much older. Are you content with yourself?"

"Sure. Aren't you?"

Lely laughed. "Indeed I am. You are fantastic. Not quite as fantastic as the colonel, but perhaps you will be . . . That incredible house Tom Sego is building in Beverly Hills is not for you, I take it?"

"No, for Cissie and Dugald," Cham said. "And the baby—or babies."

"I see. History repeats itself."

"I hope so."

"Well, down to business," Lely said. "I have two matters to bring to your attention. One is the Amalgamated Aircraft Corporation offer for Brennan-Stuart and Anzoni, which Hal has brought me in on. As he has told you, they are easy to negotiate with. You have practically a free hand in naming your terms. I suspect cash plus stock in AAC is your best bet. Mr. Anzoni has expressed himself as ready to retire and is willing to join you in the sale." Lely's eyes twinkled. "He says, in view of this development, that he holds no grudge against you."

"How nice of him. Do you like the deal?"

"I love it. You stand to make literally millions, with no risk and no further management worries. With AAC's great consolidation of related firms in the aircraft industry, I don't see how they can fail. I think their anticipations of a huge increase in government defense orders may be a bit too optimistic, but there's nothing dangerous in that."

"No, they're underestimating, if anything," Cham said. "We'll have a war sooner or later."

"You mean Europe, naturally. I don't believe we will ever again—"

"I mean us. That's Roosevelt crap about our staying out, just like the last time. He's starting to get ready, and eventually he'll have to use the stuff. But as long as we can supply it, it's all to the good. I can't wait for things to start. In my position it means nothing but money."

"Oh?" Lely looked pained. "I suppose one has to take the position where one sees the largest benefit, without recourse to conscience . . . Your researches abroad have convinced you of the inevitability of conflict?"

Cham shook his head. "My researches abroad were in eating and whores. The food is wonderful, except in England. The bathrooms are no good. Everybody charges too much. Switzerland is more like America than anywhere else. I bought a Rolls-Royce. Do you want to hear about the whores?"

"Not particularly."

"The English girls are the best. The streets are full of them. They'll do anything for a couple of quid. You may have heard that the French are in a class by themselves, but, discounting the brothel shows, they are nothing exceptional. The Italian whores are careless about bathing. Greek whores have greasy skins—too much olive oil in the diet, maybe. In Berlin they're all fat. You find bad teeth everywhere. In Cairo they have clean young boys they recommend instead of the women. I can't say I agree with them. Buggering a boy is not very romantic."

Lely stared at Cham. Then he began to laugh. Cham joined in the laughter. "But I kept an eye open," he went on, "when I wasn't on the lookout for more tail or a good dinner. They're in uniform again over there, and shaking their fists at each other. The Germans are beating and robbing the Jews, and in Italy they give castor oil to anybody who doesn't worship Mussolini. It's like what Grandpa saw when he went before the last war. I think he would predict another one, so I'm counting on it."

"Weren't your emotions aroused, Cham? Weren't you inclined to take sides, as so many of us are now doing?"

"Why should I care? They're only a bunch of foreigners. My ideas never went much beyond Los Angeles, and we need the business."

Shaking his head, Lely said, "Well, you had a considerable trip. It hasn't impaired the mystery you affect."

"Mystery? What's mysterious about me?"

"Oh, many things . . . My second item has to do with the Shapiro clan. For some odd reason, they wish Baltim and me to make an arrangement with you regarding the changes at Columbia Air Transport. Irving Shapiro informs me that their objections have been withdrawn. Evidently pride in the elevation of young Eindhoven to the presidency, coupled with his electioneering among them, has overcome their better judgment. I am told by Irving that you have ruined his position and he is no longer spokesman for the family."

"Good."

"They have a proviso, though. In the event you decide to abandon CAT at a future time, you must agree in writing to sell them a controlling interest."

"At what price?"

"I took care of that, Cham, despite their resistance. If it ever happens, the shares will sell for a sum mutually agreed upon."

"Okay, Mr. Lely."

"You seem to get whatever you desire."

"With enough money," Cham said, "nothing is impossible. Grandpa knew that."

He walked the lawyer to the door. Pausing, Lely set his hat firmly on his brow and shook hands. "You are the reincarnation of the old man," he said, and his eyes widened in a surprise he could not contain. "The contemporary version. There's no doubt of it."

"Thank you. I appreciate the compliment—if it is one."

"It is a compliment, Cham. At least to the line you so ably represent. To pass on such vigor, cunning, ability and callousness for three generations is an imposing feat."

"And the fortune," Cham said, and grinned. "Don't forget that."

"Increased in each generation, and added to immeasurably by you. No, we must not forget the fortune . . . I'm compelled to confess that I once thought the ability of the Brennans had ended with your father. How mistaken I was! Would you like to know that your former severe critic, Harold Baltim, has become your greatest admirer? His gratitude for what you have done for his son and namesake is rather pathetic. How to express his sense of obligation to you is his greatest problem."

"I give people what they want, by the double handful. There's enough for everybody—that's the secret of my success. Me and Roosevelt. Which reminds me: it looks as if we won't be providing anybody for Brennan, Baltim, Lely and Brennan. The firm had better be reduced to Baltim and Lely, or however you want it. You don't have to buy me out."

Lely studied him carefully. "Cham, I know you can afford generosity, but it is nonetheless impressive . . . No, thank you. Both Harold and I have our debts to pay. We'll leave the firm name untouched. Perhaps the next generation of Brennans will furnish us with partners. We may need them."

Flying in from New York, Hal Baltim joined Harry Sego and they came to Cham for a midnight meeting. He met them in his bedroom, unshaven and attired in a pair of cerise silk pajamas bought in Bond Street. He had spent the day in bed, twiddling his bare toes, staring at the ceiling, and contemplating things in general. "I think I might be getting a cold or something," he said vaguely.

They went over matters painstakingly, especially those relating to Sunset Sea. The holding corporation, now an excellent tax shelter, was bulging at the seams from CAT and Trans-California profits and investments Harry had made in everything from fruit processing plants to a company engaged in the manufacture of aircraft radio equipment; sensing future demand, he had even bought into iron-ore mines in Utah and a chain of food markets blanketing the suburban areas of the Queen. But, like his father before him, he was dissatisfied with the performance of the San Cristobal. Other than for a certain amount of marginal oil production and some farming operations that were only mildly rewarding, the ranch lay fallow. A single highway driven through the eastern end, however, had given Harry an idea. He scowled when Cham rejected his plan of setting up an industrial park for small manufacturing.

Laughing, Cham said, "Let's keep it for a pet. We need the losses and taxes for deductions. Don't be so ambitious. What's happened to you? Once all I could get you enthusiastic about was liquor and cheap broads. Now you only think of making money and being important."

"You reclaimed me, you bastard," Harry retorted, "and then forgot to do anything for yourself."

"Say, that reminds me," Cham said. "Aaron called me a bastard the other day when I was talking to him and Irving and I didn't even notice. I must be getting used to it." He was pleased at the memory of Aaron's instinctive slip, a tribute to the grand, unlovely character he had fashioned for himself. "I think we can make that yid one of us with a little work."

CAT business disposed of, Hal and Harry urged acceptance of the Amalgamated Aircraft offer. It was just too wonderful to pass up. Neither of them agreed with Cham on the inevitability of war, or considered the possible involvement of the United States, but they were alerted to the coming flood of government defense expenditures and argued for the advantages of an all-embracing corporation powerful enough to get a lion's share of the proceeds. "I hope you didn't mind me calling in Burton Lely on AAC," Hal said. "Explaining to you was too complicated, and we needed him in a hurry. My being in New York made it too difficult for me to handle alone. And, truthfully, we required somebody with more experience than I have. I had another, selfish reason for asking Burton to help, too."

"What reason?" Cham asked.

"I'll tell you later."

"Tell me now."

"Well," Hal said, "as soon as this CAT change takes effect and Aaron has a firm hold, I'm going to practice more law."

"Huh?"

A tinge of color came in Hal's face. He resembled his old man, Cham thought, grim and prissy and exuding an undeviating, prosecutorlike rectitude. "I intend to go in with Burton and my father. I, uh, made up with him. Having Burton in on the AAC matter helped clarify things." He coughed falsely, and wiped his lips with a handkerchief. "My father, the poor old bastard, is pretty pleased with the idea. He's not as young as he was once . . . You'd better be pleased too, Cham. It's your firm as well as mine."

"Sure, I'm pleased. What will you handle? Prostitutes and thieves?"

Hal grew redder. "Very funny. You cured me of that. Eventually I might take my father's place. You can find somebody else for CAT."

"This is beautiful," Cham said.

"Speaking of liquor and cheap broads, which you mentioned a while ago, Cham," Harry said, "I've got a little surprise of my own. You're going to have to find another procurer and apartment."

"Why?"

"I'm getting married. It'll be in the papers tomorrow."

"Gee," Cham said. "The papers!"

"On the society page," Hal said, and laughed. "You're always the last to know, Cham."

"Who are you marrying?"

"Well, a Partan. Jean Partan. We met at a Yacht Club dance in San Pedro a while ago—"

"The iron works," Cham said. "I'll be damned. The first Partan was a lousy blacksmith and spent his life shoeing horses and tightening up spokes in wagon wheels. He came here after the Brennan brothers. My grandfather knew him. My father was in the Golden Pioneers with some of them. What's she look like? I remember meeting some of their kids when I was a kid, and they were homely."

"She's all right," Harry said awkwardly. "I'd just as soon you didn't meet her."

"I don't blame you. Have you screwed her yet? Is she pregnant?"

"They came here after the Brennans. Isn't that enough for you, you tiresome son of a bitch?"

"Why, this is also beautiful," Cham said, and gazed happily at two flushed countenances. "It's been a beautiful night, hasn't it? I wish I didn't always have to spoil everything by helping my pissy friends. They grow up to be so nice. Listen, I don't need a procurer any more. I'm sick of broads. I think I shot my wad in Europe."

"Then heaven be praised," Hal said. "We're all taken care of, so let's call the meeting to order. Cham, you wouldn't give Burton an answer on AAC; he told me you ducked it completely. How about confiding in me? The deal won't remain at a white heat forever."

"I can't right now. I—"

"Is the fate of the genius bothering you? Don't let it. He's part of the transaction. They're mad for him."

"I'll let you know."

"Haven't you discussed it with Dugald?"

"Not yet," Cham said.

"Oh," Hal said. "Well, let me remind you that you have the over-

328

riding interest. And it's for his own good. He'd enjoy being rich, you know."

"Have you talked to your sister about it?" Harry asked.

"No."

A certain malice entered Harry's expression. "This gets beautifuller and beautifuller, Hal," he said. "He doesn't want to hurt the genius's feelings. Never mind whether that makes sense or not. The genius won't speak to him, but he's going to take that mansion in his kindly fashion. The pissiest one of us is growing up to be just as nice as we are."

"Up yours, matey," Cham said, and knew a burning was coming in his cheeks. "That's what they say in Great Britain."

Harry went home at four in the morning, but Hal lingered on. He and Cham had a drink of whiskey and went out in the garden for a last cigarette. Standing beside the plaster summerhouse, in a flannel bathrobe but still barefooted, Cham scratched himself dispiritedly and said: "How is Cissie?"

"You haven't seen her or the child?"

Cham shook his head.

"I saw her once," Hal said. "I went out to take a silver mug for the baby. She never looked prettier, Cham. Having a daughter did something for her. Cissie's softer and rounder—she has a glow. She's not boyish any longer. Dugald was there, and he seemed happy as a clam."

"She didn't mention me, I guess?"

"Uh . . . I don't think so."

"Well, that fight with the genius—" Cham said. "It hasn't helped any."

"The peace offering of that wonderful house ought to take care of any difficulties."

"Maybe. They sent me a cable when the kid was born."

"They've moved to Beverly Hills, you know. I'm surprised Cissie hasn't got in touch with you, Cham. If you don't mind my saying so, you ought not to stand on your pride."

"No." Cham put out his cigarette and lit another. "Tom Sego says they're always out checking on the house. At least that's going all right. How did the kid strike you?"

"Very nice," Hal said. "Another baby, to be honest with you. They must be pretty much alike in infancy." He stepped on the cigarette he dropped in a movement suggesting exasperation. "Cham, don't make me feel sorry for you. You've got too much, you're too nasty, you're not the type . . ."

"Did Cissie have the same old effect on you?"

"Yes, damn it. Worse than ever."

"Go home," Cham said. "We've been buggered, matey." He laughed to cover the effect of the melancholy in his voice, and walked to the front gate with Hal. Then he said, "Time's passing too fast. We've lost what we had. We're still young, but our youth's gone. Harry's getting married and you're going to be Harold Baltim, Junior. We all changed, and it makes my ass ache!"

Hal put a hand on his shoulder, and, after a preliminary twitch, Cham allowed it to remain there. Somehow it felt pleasant. That grasp and the tiny current which flowed between them was a final contact with his lost boyhood and Cissie and innocence and wetting his pants and a happiness he had tried so hard not to relinquish. Hal was conjuring up words.

"You haven't changed," he said finally. "You're the worst prick in town, and consistent to the point of insanity. What your grandfather accomplished by going around snorting fire and farting brimstone you are accomplishing by silence and hiding and building a mystery. He was a terrible old man, and you'll be another walking in his footsteps —and he would have been proud of you."

"Do you think so?"

"So help me God. Do you know how many people are fascinated by you? Do you realize how many newspapers and magazines I've fended off, trying to protect your privacy? Are you that naïve, Cham? Can't you see how a young man with fifty million dollars, living in a disreputable house, his closest friend a Negro maid, raising a Negro boy, staying up all night, never appearing in public or visiting any of his interests, transacting all his business by telephone, refusing to go to anybody, succeeding in everything and owning half of California—can't you see how *that* whets their curiosity? You're a success! You're a great man. You're a lunatic. You should be welcomed anywhere. Cissie and Dugald should be immensely proud of you. You are vulgar and intelligent and mean and generous and a villain and pitiable. Nobody is quite as different as you are. How the hell can anybody know how to accept you? Sometimes I have the crazy urge to kneel at your feet—and so does Harry and Burton and my father—and God knows who else. Without trying, you've made us love you . . . Oh, the hell with it. But how did you ever do it?"

"I don't know," Cham said. "I'm fat and lazy and not too bright. I've got a game leg. I used to pee my pants, and I didn't want to grow up. I just tried to please Grandpa and my sister . . . You think I'm the same?"

"Yes. Whatever that is."

"All right. Bugger off, matey."

"Good night, sweet prince," Hal said, and Cham went back in the house with his spirits rising. The others aged and altered, but the manipulator remained as he was. As Grandpa had made him. It would work out fine if he just had patience: the money, the family and the big fat Queen.

In renewing his ties, perhaps for superstitious reasons, Cham took Albert and his mother and father in the new Rolls-Royce drophead coupe with body by Mulliner (it had just arrived on a ship at San Pedro) to a gathering of Ferris's relatives at a fraternal hall on South Hoover Street. He was the only white present, an object of awe and adulation. He thoroughly enjoyed himself. Uniformed and immaculate, Albert was a source of fatherly pride to him and inspired general admiration. Ferris Washington, Junior, of course faded into the background, as he should.

It was at this event, immensely set up by Cham's warmth and graciousness, that Lagonda confided to him that she had been with Cissie before and after the birth of her baby. "Why didn't you tell me before?" he asked.

"I thought you might not like it," Lagonda said, "with the bad blood between you and Mr. Stuart." She added, a bit defiantly, "I couldn't help myself, Chambers. She was as much my child as you was. Leaving her alone at a time like that didn't make no sense to me."

"You're nuts. I'm glad you went, and I'm not sore at Dugald as long as he keeps his word and does what Cissie wants. Did he object to your being around?"

Lagonda shrugged in a politic manner. "Could be. But he say nothing. I didn't fuss with him, and I helped them move when Garnet and Cissie got out of the hospital."

"Why did they move?"

"I don't know. Maybe I do. I think I heard them say they wanted to be nearer the house while it was going up. Anyhow Cissie did."

"Well," Cham said, and was relieved. "That's better . . ."

He was moved to question Lagonda, and the details were encouraging. The pregnancy had been easy for Cissie. She had no difficulty in bearing Garnet. The child was pretty, a little doll, and had blue eyes and red-gold hair and freckles on her nose like her mother. Cissie loved her; you could tell that. Lagonda agreed with Hal that Cissie was better looking, softer, more womanly, less flighty and strange. She thought the Stuarts were getting along very well with each other, except that Mr. Stuart was hardly ever home, he was so busy.

"Oh?" Cham said. "Well, he's a genius, don't forget. How did he strike you with the kid? He like her?"

"Oh, yes," Lagonda said. "He very pleased. He plays with her every night." But her expression was enigmatic, and Cham felt uneasy. Still, he couldn't expect absolute victory. The little bastard was bound to rattle around in his chains some.

"Why'd they name her Garnet?" he demanded. "That's a funny name for a kid in her position. Garnet what?"

"They didn't tell me," Lagonda said. "She hasn't got a middle name."

"She should have been named from the family," Cham said. "Like Alice Chambers or something. Or my grandmother's name. You think there are more coming, Lagonda?"

"I couldn't say," Lagonda told him.

On the whole, Cham was satisfied. A girl instead of a boy had been a blow to him, but he didn't propose that they stop with one kid. The main thing was to keep the genius in line and have Cissie reasonably content and happy. If she could produce heirs more or less without strain and Dugald kept his pecker up, the rest ought to be easy. Possibly someday he could move in on them (Cissie was bound to forget that other mess, given sufficient time, and he had buried the old horror in himself so deeply it could be disregarded now) and sew up the family again, the way Grandpa had moved in on his father and mother. He wanted desperately to see his sister and her child, but he feared rocking the boat. Patience was Cham's specialty. He could outwait them and work his will. Time was on his side.

The following week he accepted an invitation from Jesús Algonrones and crossed the river to the east side. Belvedere turned out to view his British car and pay tribute. Albert was with him, uniformed again, and the reception of the small black boy was cordial and unforced; the kind of greeting, Cham had found, he received nowhere else he took his protégé. Those various withdrawals on the part of white people he knew probably contributed to the hermitage he had built for himself. He never analyzed the reasons for his attachment to Albert. Enough that Albert was the son of Lagonda, and that she belonged to Cham. Therefore Albert was his. To have been accused of pushing for equality for Negroes would have astounded him. He cared nothing about the rights of colored folk as such; only the boy, Lagonda, and to a vastly lesser degree, Ferris, were important to him. On the other hand, he had no inhibitions about mingling in the lower reaches of society. If his own kind insisted on snooting Albert and Lagonda, then, by God, his close friends would be niggers and Mexicans. He could afford it.

Conny—Mrs. Ralph García, that is—was at the party. She and her husband owned a large corner grocery store and a *tortilleria,* both purchased with her dowry. Prosperity and beans, rice and maternity had plumped out Conny to matronly proportions. She had poise and assurance, and a little boy at her side and a male infant in her arms. The reunion went off without incident. Cham admired the young Garcías (Ralph had to stay in the store, it was a Saturday and their busiest day) and boasted of Albert and Cissie's daughter. Conny paid Albert several compliments. Reflecting on the alterations wrought by time, Cham wondered how it was possible that Conny had ever shared his bed. They looked at each other in an unembarrassed fashion, coolly polite and tepidly interested, the memories of old ardors well submerged. Cham recalled what Lagonda had told him of the midnight meeting between Grandpa and Grandma when his father died. It was not so puzzling any longer. Lovers forgot as easily as the grateful or the bereft. But this revelation did not have a dispiriting effect on him; the process of obliteration was helpful and necessary. You were hungry and ate, and naturally you didn't remember back a thousand meals.

There was the usual music and dancing, but Cham took care not to invite the heavy Mrs. García to a turn around the floor. He ate chili and drank tequila and muscatel wine, and delighted his host by getting *boracho*. He couldn't recollect when he had had a better evening. As they parted, he and Jesús embraced one another affectionately. Beside the gardener was an adolescent translator, one of innumerable nephews, who said Uncle Jesús promised to be at work early in the morning.

"Not too early, for Christ's sake," Cham said. "And tell him to stay away from my bedroom windows."

"He means Monday morning, sir," the translator said.

Jesús made a speech on the front porch, with considerable fire and feeling. A sweeping gesture knocked over the potted geranium, and Cham realized his pal was also *boracho*. He heard several mentions of the Villanueva name. The onlookers applauded him and shook his hand and gave him *abrazos*. "What's going on?" he asked.

"Uncle Jesús says you are one of us," the translator explained. "Your family in the old days was by name Villanueva. They came here in the beginning like the *conquistadores*. They were *hacendados*. Uncle Jesús is proud to know you."

Cham smiled blankly at his admirers. He was pleased that his connection with the Villanuevas had been discovered, but it came as a shock to him to be reminded that he had Mexican—Spanish, rather—blood flowing in his veins. Being a Golden Pioneer was fine; acknowledging brotherhood with a bunch of Mexicans was something else. He was American, and the heritage from remote ancestors was nothing, aside from a dubious gentility it seemed to confer.

While Jesús added a footnote to his address, the translator obliged with a running commentary in English: "Uncle Jesús says there are more

Villanuevas right here in Belvedere. They came lately from the *Distrito Federal*. They are poor people. He asks would you want to meet them?"

"No," Cham said, and seized Albert's hand and began a quick retreat. "Hell, no. Poor Villanuevas are none of my business."

A gay young man blew on a trumpet, as in a bullfight, when they rolled off. Everybody waved and Albert stood up in the car and smartly saluted the crowd. Cham had a last glimpse of Mrs. García, entangled in her babies and looking puzzled. He speculated on what was going through her mind. Perhaps nothing; she'd always been stupid, stupider than he was. For some reason, tears came in his eyes. It had been lovely.

The lateness of the hour made for deserted streets. Enchanted by the huge, agile car, which was nearly without sound at any speed, Cham drove fast and erratically. On the upper reaches of West Seventh Street, a motorcycle policeman showed a red light and stopped him. The cop was impressed by the Rolls-Royce, but Cham's condition and the colored child in regimentals popped his eyes. Albert again arose and saluted, and appeared disappointed when the cop ignored him.

"Salute him back, for God's sake," Cham said testily. "You're both in uniform, aren't you?"

"Listen, Mister," the cop said. "You'd better get out and let me see how steady you are. You've been driving too fast and too far over on the wrong side of the road."

"Bugger off, matey," Cham said. "I have to get home."

"Come on, Mister," the cop said. "Don't take a hard line with me or I'll run you in. I can smell your breath from here. And who is that monkey in the fancy clothes?"

"Ah," Cham said. "Hunting for trouble, huh? You'll get it. Tangle with me and the next thing you know you'll be walking a beat in Watts with a club in your hand. Know who I am?"

"No," the cop said. "Who are you?"

"I am A. Chambers Brennan," Cham told him. "Esquire, matey. My family settled this Goddamned town and put it together piece by piece. They were here when your family was still climbing around in trees. They left me half of it, and the other half I could buy any time I wanted. Ever hear of the Brennans?"

"Yes, sir," the cop said.

Cham started a weary sigh which ended in a belch. It wasn't worth the effort. Wiping his lips with the back of his hand, he reached in a pocket, fished out a twenty dollar bill, and shoved the money into the cop's nerveless fingers. "Here," he said. "Stick that up your ass and let's forget it. I'm in a hurry."

334

"I can't take a bribe, Mr. Brennan," the cop said.

"Of course you can't," Cham said. "That's for the policemen's fund. Good night. Salute the kid, will you?"

Slowly, unsteadily, the cop raised his hand to his cap brim. Albert returned the courtesy in the best style of Dangerfield Military Academy. He was very happy. "I like him," he said. "He was good to us. Did you see his gun? I hope we meet some more policemen."

Shifting gears, gunning the engine, Cham said, "If we do, I'll make them salute you. I could make them all salute you. This is my town, Al."

It was his town. On the long trip to foreign parts homesickness had often assailed him; he missed the Queen's ill assorted, tawdry charms —the lengthy undeviating streets with their third-rate shops, the hayseed populace, the swarming automobiles, the barren hills, the benign and overflowing sunshine. Traveling gave him an insight into what a city could be, but it also brought him a keener appreciation of what he had left. His love of the Queen was renewed. She was still young and whorish and full of surprises. The pace was slower, the vistas remained larger. Now two million people were here, enjoying, like Cham, a villagey life in the midst of a juvenile giantism. A war was going to make a great lady of her. To hell with damp, dark London and silvery Paris and the Roman grandeurs along the Tiber that had always awakened an echo in Grandpa; or the miseries and claptrap along that other river, the Nile, where curious kings had mated with their sisters. The Queen had no splendid buildings or palaces or magnificent boulevards or heroes buried in immense tombs or a river worth mentioning or a homogenous past or a history that inspired respect—she was raw and makeshift and temporary and the child of expediency, mammon, wheeled traffic and deficient taste—but she was better than all the rest. As Grandpa had said, she was the future, fleshed out, boldly ugly and dynamic, for the rest of the world to see. If they didn't like her, they still would have to accept her.

"I think I have to pee, Uncle Cham," Albert said.

"So do I," said Cham happily. "Hang on, matey."

At home, Lagonda was not as annoyed with Cham as he had expected. There was an air of haste and elation about her. Albert was snatched from his charge and placed in Ferris's care. Cham was marched upstairs to his bedroom and quickly disrobed. He went in the bathroom and thankfully made water and grinned at his image in the medicine cabinet mirror, where it faded and rippled as if he were seeing it underwater. Coming out, he said, "I'm crocked, Lagonda."

"I know," she said. The telephone was plugged in and she had it in hand ready for him, and he was made to sit on the edge of the bed and she placed it in his lap. "*She* called. You are to call her back any time you get in. Now, try to talk straight. Don't act like a fool, Chambers, please."

Abruptly his hands trembled and he sweated. Only one "she" mattered to either of them. He had waited so long. "What did she say?" he asked.

"Nothing much. Oh, nothing's wrong. She wants to talk to you. Shall I get the number?"

"Yeah, you'd better." Cham licked his numb lips. He heard Lagonda saying, "Here he is, Miss Cissie. I hope he can make sense."

The treasured light, direct, measured voice sounded very small in his ear: "I suppose you've been hitting it up again. Where, Brother?"

"Over at Jesús's. He had a party."

"Shame on you. Did you see that maid you were always fooling around with?"

"Yeah. She's a fat housewife now."

"You have the most terrible taste," Cissie said. "Cham, I had to speak to you. It came over me all at once. Obviously you were never going to call me. Why?"

"Well, I didn't know . . ." he mumbled.

"How was Europe?"

"Okay. How's the genius—and the kid?"

"Fine. Don't you want to see your niece? You're responsible for her."

"Lord, yes! When can I come?"

"Tomorrow," Cissie said. "Any time you wish . . . I've missed you . . . missed you. Why can't we let it rest?"

"Oh, to hell with that," he said. "I'll be by in the morning, first thing. Good night, Cissie. Hearing you is the best sound I've heard in a long time."

"Good night. Good night, Cham. I—I couldn't go to sleep until I'd talked to you . . ."

"Not bad to go to sleep on, huh?" Lagonda said. She smoothed Cham's pillow before he laid his head on it, and remembered to unbutton his pajama coat because he always tore off the buttons in rolling about in his sleep. "Just you wait till you set your eyes on that little angel."

"A look at Cissie is good enough," he said drowsily.

"Listen. You hear me? We don't need no more of that. You finished it once. Leave it alone."

"Yes, yes, yes! Don't keep talking about it. I'll have those Goddamned dreams again."

336

Next morning, after an early breakfast, he took the Rolls and drove to Beverly Hills. His tongue was thick, his stomach sour, and he had a nervous headache; all due, he told himself, to a hangover, not to the prospect of meeting Cissie.

The Stuarts lived on the second floor of a commodious two-story flat building near the center of town. A maid admitted Cham to a good-sized, sunny living room furnished in a nondescript fashion. Cissie came in from a hallway. She wore loose unpressed slacks and a blouse and sweater, but her hair was longer and neater than he remembered and she had on lipstick. They stood and stared at each other. She was heavier now, softened, less taut in carriage. Yet in the piercing blue of her eyes was a melancholy that dashed his spirits. She had lost her boyish quality; she had become a woman, and somehow, to his sorrow, was not quite as special to him as she once had been.

"Hello," she said. She stayed her distance, and waved to a chair.

"Hi," he said, and sat down. She remained standing, and thrust her hands into the pockets of her trousers. "Look," he said, "it doesn't have to be this awkward. We're not enemies or anything . . . I've got a hell of a hangover."

"Do you need a drink?"

"Yeah, a short one. Whiskey."

Cissie brought him a shot glass of bourbon and a chaser. He tossed off the whiskey and the water, and blinked his eyes and made a wry face. She smiled suddenly and sat down across from him. "You haven't changed," she said. "You're much too fat, Cham, and your clothes look funny. Why are they so skimpy?"

"They're British. I think they save on cloth that way."

She laughed. "You've got to make Lagonda stop feeding you for a while. Are you drinking a lot?"

"No," he said. "I got drunk last night with those Mexicans, that's all. You're different from the last time I saw you."

"Not underneath. I'm getting fatter too."

"Ah? Are you happy? Has the kid made a difference?"

"Yes," she said. "I'm very happy. Do you want to see her?"

"In a minute. I've got some things to talk to you about. First, the house. Do you like it?"

She nodded. "It's going to be lovely."

"The genius feels the same way? Does he get along with Tom Sego?"

"He's satisfied. Sometimes he argues with Tom, but they don't have serious fights."

"Did you move here because of the house?"

"Yes, we thought we might as well get established in this area."

"Then Dugald isn't making a real fuss?"

"No."

"Okay," Cham said. "As long as he knows which end is up. It ought to be quite a place, from what I hear. Uh, worthy of you."

"Haven't you ever seen the house?"

"Not since they were just building the forms for the foundations."

"Cham, you must see it. Dugald has some questions to ask you—I'm supposed to be the go-between—"

"The hell with it. It's not for me. He can do whatever he wants as long as he doesn't make Tom sore. I promised Tom a free hand—"

"All right," she said. "What else? What I think?"

"I suppose. Has anybody taken up the Amalgamated Aircraft deal with you and the genius?"

"Everybody. Hal, his father, Harry, Mr. Lely. I even had a telephone call from Anzoni the other day. He still hates you, I gathered, but he's willing to go along."

"Well?"

Folding her hands in her lap, Cissie gazed down at them. A bar of sunlight fell across her face, enlivening the golden dots of her freckles. "I don't know. Haven't we got enough money?"

"Maybe. How does Dugald stand on the question?"

"He only says it's up to you."

"If it was up to me," Cham said, "I wouldn't be fool enough to hesitate. But the decision is yours, I guess. I'm willing to leave it there. You know why. What do you say?"

She lifted her head and looked at him. "Why shouldn't you have the fruits of your risk? You were the soul of all we did. You had the faith in me."

He shook his head. "That doesn't matter. You belong to him now. The kid has changed everything. Say what you think."

"Well," she said, "it would clip his wings. He loves being important and his own man. Brennan-Stuart is his whole life. He works day and night, and the younger people think he's a god. In Washington he has lunch in the Senate restaurant and knows everybody worth knowing. The President has had him to the White House . . ."

"Why don't you get in on any of that?"

"Because I'm like you. Cham, he couldn't possibly have the same importance in a huge corporation. And you remember how strong-willed he is. He might not last long with a committee handling his ideas."

"He could learn discipline."

Sighing, she said, "Oh, sure. And become another edition of me, with

338

the excitement and fun all washed out. Sitting around waiting—for nothing. Shall we do that to him?"

"So you're very happy, huh?" Cham said. "I thought you sounded blue. What's the matter, Cissie. What can I do? What do you want?"

"Not this . . . not anything."

"Come on. You're not talking sense. We made it. You've got everything."

"That's the trouble, perhaps."

"Are you doing any flying?"

"Once in a while," she said. "I take the B-1 up and try to remember what it was like in the beginning. But I'm growing old and rusty, and trying to remember where I made a mistake and lost my momentum is useless."

"You're better off than you ever were. This is just in your head. You're safe now."

"Of course. Perfectly safe."

"I don't get it," he said. "Don't you love Dugald?"

"I like him. That's as much as there ever was. He used to need me, and doesn't anymore."

"Listen. We'll turn down AAC. The genius can keep on astonishing everybody. The house will make you happy. I guarantee it. Have a couple of babies. Pull up your socks."

"Thank you," she said. "You're the most generous man I ever met. You'll always give me what I want, won't you?"

"Yes."

"And I'll give you what you want. Shall I bring in Garnet?"

"Yeah," he said. He shifted in his chair as she departed, miserable and raging at his helplessness. He attempted to remember where he had made a mistake. She was right. They had everything, but it had gone wrong. Yet having everything couldn't constitute the trouble. That was denying Grandpa.

Cissie returned with the child, saying, "The nurse just finished bathing her. She isn't dressed for company."

"Hello, Garnet," Cham said.

"Hold her. She rarely cries, and she's never scared."

He took her, clumsily cradling her in his arms. She looked up at him in perfect, smiling confidence, and he was awed by the tiny fragile hand she raised to his cheek. Its touch was soft. Her features were regular, her chin rounded, her face heart-shaped, her eyes gentian, her hair a shade between copper and gold, and freckles ran across her nose and onto her cheekbones. She was Lagonda's little angel, all right. Her body, clad in only a didy and tanned by the sun, gave an impression of newness and perfection. Cham tried to remember if this was the first baby he had ever held. He felt indignation at Hal's inability to tell one infant from another. Garnet was beautiful; she was unique. He loved her beyond measure, most of all because she was cast in the mould of his sister. "Well," he said, "you can tell where this one came from."

"Don't you think she resembles Dugald more?"

"No, thank God."

"She's going to be small."

"It doesn't matter with a woman. You can be proud of her, Cissie. She is the prettiest kid I ever saw."

"I have no feeling of ownership," she said. "Garnet is the little stranger with a vengeance. I think of her as your baby when I stop to consider."

"I'd take her gladly."

"I wish I could give her to you. I would, but Dugald wouldn't agree."

"He's proud, huh?"

"Not proud, pleased. Pleased that we did a good job, that we had a female and therefore she can't possibly be another in the straight Brennan line, and satisfied with his part in it. She's a good model, like a B-4 will be some day . . . Do I sound as though my feelings are hurt? It's not true. They aren't. But I taught him to stick to business, and what he learns he doesn't forget."

"Why the funny name, Cissie?"

"Well, that was part of it. Dugald didn't care for a Brennan name, and I rejected his suggestions. He resents your influence, Cham. You know that."

"Yeah."

"We were quarreling, you see. Our fights are not the same as those of other people. We smile and never shout or threaten, and only try to cut with so sharp a knife that you scarcely know you're hurt until the blood shows. Nothing comes of the quarrels but scars. We have to be careful; if we were louder and less skillful, we might make up."

"Cissie, are you a little nuts?"

"I think so. Look at my family. Do you remember the ring you gave me on my fifteenth birthday? Grandpa let you pick it out yourself. It was set with a red stone. Sometimes I still wear it."

"My God, now I do. It was a garnet."

"Yes. It's my only jewelry except for watches and my engagement and wedding rings. I don't wear them."

"You weren't the kind of girl for jewelry."

"Except the garnet ring, from you. I wonder if Garnet will be that kind of girl? When she was born her hair was much redder than now, and after we could not agree on a name for her, I proposed we call her Garnet because her hair was almost the color of the stone in my ring. That was innocent enough, wasn't it? But Dugald understood the connection. One of our rules, though, is that if you have been outwitted and hurt, you don't make a fuss or acknowledge your wound. And you accept defeat and wait for your turn. Dugald said he liked my idea. He said it was in the Brennan tradition—the stone was not very valuable and its shade was vulgar. He said he had confidence his daughter would live down the name and the wrong part of her ancestry."

"Ah," Cham said softly. "What a nice life you've made for yourself, Cissie. The little bastard can't get his part straight in this, I think. He has the soul of an engineer. But he ought to watch it. Sooner or later my feelings might be hurt. If they ever are, I'll make hamburger of him."

"He's no more to blame than I am," Cissie said. "I also have the soul of an engineer, and what I've got I deserve. Perhaps we ought to have failed. Or not succeeded beyond reason. Then we could have clung together and had something to hang onto."

"Here, take Garnet," Cham said. "You've answered my questions and spoiled my day. I have to go."

The child had scarcely stirred in his arms, and she laughed and crowed as he handed her to her mother. Cissie swung her to and fro, renewing the delighted laughter, and kissed her.

"Well, she's happy," Cham said, and headed for the door. "That's the main thing."

"I didn't mean for it to be this way. What got us started?"

He paused, his hand on the knob. "The genius. He's responsible for our great success."

"No, it's something worse than that."

"Oh, let it go. Goodbye."

"I'll be cheerier next time," she said.

"There won't be any next time," he said.

On the landing outside, he stood entirely still for a moment and drew in a long, anguished breath. Tears lodged in his eyes. Nothing ever came out right. The cards were stacked against you. The more you gained, the more you lost. Only Grandpa was master of his destiny . . . He told himself his hangover was murdering him.

One morning in that hot autumn Cham awakened to the sound of thunder and heard rain pattering on the roof. A forked brightness pierced the drawn shades of the bedroom and another heavenly bang sounded. He was almost disposed to rise and watch the storm, but the effort was too great for his depressed state, and he turned over and closed his eyes. Lagonda entered without any preliminary courtesies. Nobody bothered to respect his privacy; it was the same as in the days of Conny. "Storming bad," said Lagonda. "This hardly ever happens. What does it mean?"

"It doesn't mean anything, for Christ's sake," he replied. "We won't be eating dust for a couple of weeks, that's all."

He knew she was a great believer in signs, especially ominous ones, and climatical manifestations were her specialty. It always annoyed and frighted him, because he could not rid himself of the conviction that she possessed some claim to second sight. She was black, she had instinctual perceptions, and she loved him. She worried for him. This thunderstorm was going to be bad medicine. Her concerned, apprehensive expression made him scowl. However, that could be explained by his recent visit to Cissie and subsequent dark mood. He and Lagonda had not discussed the meeting: he was unwilling to admit, or talk of, the unhappiness that afflicted his sister. To entertain doubts of the future was inadmissible. But his silence only increased Lagonda's unease. Probably she suspected they had quarreled, or the baby had proved a disappointment to him, or the little bastard was kicking up again, or . . . the rest was better left unthought. He might end up punching his best friend and nosy nurse right in the mouth.

To his astonishment, she pushed the plug at the end of the telephone line into the baseboard and gestured to the instrument on the nightstand. "You know I don't take calls at this time of day," he said. "Who's died?"

"*She* calling."

"Huh?" He hesitated, almost of a mind not to talk to Cissie. The situation needed more time, avoidance of any overt act, fresh patience—

"Hurry up. She sound as bright as a new penny. I never heard her sound so good."

"Then why do you look so damned hangdog?"

"It just don't seem right," Lagonda said. "The storm has come, too. Talk to her."

Picking up the phone, he said, "What's the matter?"

"Nothing's the matter, sourball! Did I wake you up?"

Her voice did indeed ring gaily in his ear. "No, the storm did. Why are you calling, Cissie?"

"To thank you. Talking to you did me a world of good, Brother. I'm going to follow your advice and pull up my socks."

"Well . . . now that's more like it."

342

"But you've got to come see my new house," she said. "If I can take pains to please, so can you. I have a lot to tell you, in private."

"All right. As soon as I can, I'll—"

"No. This morning. This very minute. I can't wait."

"Are you kidding?" he demanded. "In the middle of a Goddamned rain?"

"In the middle of a Goddamned rain. You don't have to bathe or shave. We'll be alone—they don't work when it's raining. Meet me in half an hour."

"I'm only half awake. I'll catch cold—"

"This is our one chance, you fool," she said. "Saturday afternoons and Sundays I go to the house with Dugald and Garnet. The rest of the time there are workmen around. I'm going away soon. My wish is your command, don't you remember?"

He put down the phone and arose grumblingly. Before he could go in the bathroom, Lagonda required an explanation. "She seems bright and has her tail up," he said. "I have to go out to the house and talk to her. She says she's going away."

"Going away? Where?"

"How the hell do I know? Wait till I find out, will you?"

"I don't like it," Lagonda said.

"So you don't like it. Leave me alone, huh?"

Cham was alone only long enough to relieve himself, and then Lagonda was with him, bringing linen. She disapproved of his merely rinsing out his mouth and washing his face and hands. "I haven't got time to take a bath and scrape off my whiskers," he told her fretfully. "She's in a big hurry for some reason."

"She wait."

"I haven't kept her waiting before, and I'm not going to start now."

"More's the pity," Lagonda said.

A bit self-conscious in his nakedness, as usual, he wondered how he could ever break her of constantly standing by. Her devotion superseded the proprieties and was somehow scandalous. He almost wished that jerk Ferris Washington, Junior, would assert himself and point out to his wife that the white baby she had raised was a man grown. They were not even equals, Goddamn it; she was the real authority in the union. Faithful to habit, she complained of the yellow stains he left on his underdrawers. "You should dry that thing better," she said. "If you was to use paper like women do—"

"I shake it," he interrupted, sullen in his rebellion. "That's all I'm ever going to do. Listen, don't stand there and stare at me right there. It isn't decent."

"Chambers, I've changed you a million times—"

"I know! But you don't anymore."

"Remember when you used to just hold still and wet yourself? Who had to take care of that?"

"All right! How often does that happen now?"

"All I ask is," she said, "for you to keep your pants clean. I do your laundry, don't I?"

"You just don't know your place," he said. "You just don't know it. That's what's the matter with you."

She brought him an older suit and shoes and a tie, and made him put on rubbers. Her fingers with the amazingly pink nails buttoned up the raincoat and put the battered hat on his head. She ordered him to drive slowly and not to stand out in the wet.

"I've nearly got the sense to come in out of the rain," he said. "Don't worry!"

He went out the back way muttering, and pushed the Rolls-Royce at too heady a pace westward on Third Street to spite his constant nurse. They resembled an old married couple, wrangling futilely. Apparently the spiritual union he had with Lagonda was the closest he would ever come to marriage; the thought gave him a pang of resentment and sorrow, and even surprise. But all that took his mind off meeting Cissie. He scarcely dared think of that, with the black sky above and the thunder reverberating through immense hollow caverns of air.

This was a city unaccustomed to water not pumped from the ground or brought from distant rivers, not regulated by flow through a pipe or hose, and strictly metered. When the rain fell, it came down with a sudden headlong rush, as if the clouds had been trapped and defeated and were eager for annihilation, and the gutters ran curb-high and huge ponds formed at intersections and people disappeared and the unhandy motorized movement became fantastically snarled. A bleary darkness settled on the buildings and houses, emphasizing their raw and ugly modernity. Without a blaze of light, the Queen was a dreadful, dripping old whore, clad in rags and abounding in sores and painted excrescences. Rain in Paris and London and New York lent a soft enchantment, dulled the grime, smoothed off the rough edges, seemed a natural element; here it was an intruder, a nuisance, a hindrance to a necessary velocity of movement, a traitor to the beaming sun and the generations of men who had guaranteed a violent paradise. Like the other inhabitants, Cham suffered the change impatiently and longed for more hot, unvarying, monotonous bright clemency.

Dirty spray spouted from under the fenders of the car. Cham dodged around corners and spurted water on stalled cars. He deluged a man in an old Ford with broken-windowed side curtains. The man shouted curses. Cham raised his right hand, the middle finger alone extended, and yelled, "Up you, matey!"

He turned north in Beverly Hills and climbed a hill. Grandpa's property had a high fieldstone wall surrounding it now, and impressive pillars flanking the driveway that led upward; the iron gates were swung open. Cham peered between the flicking windshield wipers. Excitement and dismay held him. He had never meant to see this place, except in Tom Sego's elevations; that was part of his good luck charm; or perhaps, some day, much older, he might go here to be accepted by the Stuarts, as Grandpa had come to the other house. Yet here he was, in the damp and threatening pearly light, defying fate. Heat was on in the car, and still he shivered.

In the paved area below the main level of the house, devoted to garages and servants' quarters and presently encumbered with machinery and the litter of building, stood the old roadster Cissie used. Cham parked beside it, got out unwillingly, pulled up his coat collar, and ascended steps to the broad brick terrace on the lip of the hill. He stood under an overhang and looked at the house. It seemed strange and barren and less than he had imagined. Through solid glass across the front he could examine a huge, empty living room, a great marble fireplace of rose-pink, pegged wooden flooring bleached to the sheen of birch bark. The smell of wet plaster was in his nostrils. There was no sign of his sister. He wandered around the side of the house, braving the wind and stinging droplets. A row of freshly planted young cedars gave protection.

Cissie appeared from a side entrance, having heard him squelching through the mud, and drew him inside. Her hatless head streamed water. The lower portions of her jodhpurs were soaked, and she was barefooted, with her pulpy shoes and socks carried in one hand; she tossed them in a corner laughingly. She had on a yellow oilskin slicker that dated from her days at Los Angeles High, complete with the signatures of fellow students. Her face was flushed, from exertion or emotion, and she could not seem to remain still. "You took too long," she said. "I've been all over the place."

"My God, that coat. I'd forgotten it."

"Oh, I hang onto things. I'm not sentimental, just saving."

"Have you got Hal's name there?"

"I forget. I suppose so. Come on. This is the kitchen we're in, by the way."

"You'll catch pneumonia without your shoes," Cham said.

"No, I won't. It's easier to plough around without them. Come on. I have a lot to ask you."

"You won't get any answers. I'm not interested."

"Don't you like the house?"

"Not now anyway. It looks like a Goddamned fort. It's like living out in the open."

"There's rain falling, Brother. The sun is hiding. You've got to visualize how it will be. It's your handiwork. We're all your handiwork."

"You said you had something to tell me," he said.

"Well, I have. I pulled up my socks, as you commanded. Only they got wet." She laughed.

"What's the matter with you?"

"Nothing! I'll tell you the rest of it in a minute."

Compelled by her nervous insistence, he followed her through the house, paying no heed to the explanations she offered and the questions she asked, beginning to feel a sickening excitement and fear, staring at her with lowered eyelids, heat burning his cheeks. He took off his coat, and she removed the slicker; there was only a shirt underneath, a red-and-white checkered affair of the kind she had worn when she flew the B-2.

Standing under another overhang, regarding the formless, mushy waste of the interior garden, Cham lit a cigarette and said, "Maybe it'll come out all right eventually. The best part is that it's like a house the Villanuevas had at the San Cristobal."

"You see?" she said. "We're an old family. We have a tradition. Which Villanueva was that? I never did get them straight."

"I don't know. Grandma's father or grandfather, I guess. It burned."

"What did they call it? We'll give this the same name."

"Who knows?" He cleared his throat. "Listen, do me a favor. Call this house Xanadu, for Grandpa."

"All right," she said. "But people will think the money has gone to our heads." She laughed again. "And I'll have another fight with Dugald."

"The hell with other people—and with him."

"We made up, you know. For the first time. It embarrassed both of us. Your influence, Brother. Dugald was touched by your supporting him in the Amalgamated Aircraft thing. That almost brought him to his knees."

"Then why did you say you were going away?"

"Oh, I'm going away with him. We had a long, serious talk, and he apologized and I apologized, and we each held the baby, and I cried —and we decided we had to make a fresh start. We'll take the honey-

346

moon we didn't have. We're going to Mexico and I'll go to the shrine Mr. Algonrones mentioned to you and pray and have a boy for you, Brother. What is its name?"

"Oh, Guadalupe. Let's get inside. This gives me the creeps."

They entered the cavernous living room, and Cham shivered. The rain had slackened, but the clouds continued to lodge in the hills; he was unable to make out the town below. It had gone wrong. His luck was leaving him, after many wonders. This was the House of Brennan, marooned on a mountaintop, built of gingerbread, an act of the imagination, a forlorn hope. When the sun reappeared, the house would vanish. "So?" he said.

"He's going to take off a whole month. That is very difficult for a man of his importance. You realize that, don't you, Brother?"

"Don't take that attitude. Maybe it can be fixed."

"Then we had a new fight," she said. "We are to fly the B-1 to Mexico City and come back slowly by train, seeing the country. He has found a buyer for the old ship in Central America. The man will come to Mexico and pick it up. I don't use the B-1 enough anymore to make it worth keeping. Dugald believes in getting the maximum use out of things. Old airplanes and old ideas are not important to him. His mind is on the next one, the B-4, which will have four engines. Only it won't be called a B-4. The number is CT-4. CT stands for commercial transport. Things have changed, Brother."

"What do we care?"

"I don't care if you don't."

"Okay, why the fight?"

"Oh, because I'm not sane. Because I have a child and a house and a brother and millions—and terrible worries. Because the B-1 was the first airplane we had and I was important then . . . Because Dugald and I hate each other."

"Don't go on the trip," he said.

"Why not? I have nowhere else to go. I have to get away, Brother. And I have to visit Guadalupe and make sure you have a boy."

Cham walked to a window and glanced outside. On the hill slopes the sumac and greasewood, the live oaks, and the eucalyptus trees planted by earlier hands, were flourishing in the miraculous damp. Vegetation inured to long droughts awaked in an instant to moisture. Such a deep green looked anachronous and insubstantial in the uncertain light. "I don't want one that bad," he said. "Listen, take it from me, this is the best place to live. I've been around now. There's nothing like Los Angeles. Forget your troubles."

"I hate it," she said. "I never felt I belonged, like you. But I couldn't

347

really escape. Everywhere looked better, even from ten thousand feet up. I blame Los Angeles for you and Dugald. I can't leave you, and you won't let me leave him."

"You can leave him. I'll help you. And I'll knock the little bastard off his perch as you go."

"No, that won't help. The game has to go on. I have a score to settle. Did you believe me when I said he was grateful for your refusing the Amalgamated offer? He knew I was responsible for your decision, and I couldn't help exulting. The cut was nice and deep. Don't you think he was clever in using the sale of the B-1 to get back at me? Oh, I could see the blood bubbling up, Brother, before I knew I'd been hit. It was a lovely idea. Now I've got to pay him off."

Cham turned to her. "My God, Cissie, what can I do for you?"

"You drove me back to him. Didn't you? That night in the bedroom —that was a trick, wasn't it? You were forcing me out. The Brennans—or whatever that crazy conception you have is—come first, don't they? I'm indebted to you and I have to make good. Garnet isn't enough, is she? . . . Tell me it was a trick."

He lowered his eyes.

"You put it in my head," she said. "It must have always been there, but you woke it up. Now it won't go back to sleep . . ."

He could not speak.

"I'm not happy," she said. "I never was. Was that the reason from the beginning, something I couldn't think of? *You put it in my head."*

Raising his eyes, he said in his agony, "Jesus, Cissie, can't I help you?"

"Yes, you can help me. Listen to my heart beating." She walked up to him, opening her shirt, pulling it apart. "It's beating for you. Do you think Dugald doesn't know that?"

Blinded and wild, he clasped her and began kissing her soft, warm breasts. She sagged and his arms tightened, but her weight overbore him, and he dropped to his knees and lowered her to the floor. Her eyes were tightly closed as he bent over her. Sweat dripped on her from his face. "You'll hang for a goat anyhow," she murmured. "Hang for a sheep instead . . ." He stopped her talking by kissing her on the mouth. She squirmed, loosening the jodhpurs, pushing them down, and the panties underneath. Pausing, he waited for the thunder and lightning that always came in the movies at such a moment. But there was only silence. The rain had ceased, and the wind stopped blowing.

Then he observed the vertical blue and red weal on her abdomen, and was shocked—so shocked he got up, staggering on his bad leg, the knee of which had been damaged in contact with the floor. She opened her eyes and stared at him. He ran a palm over his forehead, and it came away wet. The next instant she was scrambling to her feet, pulling up the jodhpurs, clutching the shirt to her. They were giddy and reeling. "Even that . . ." she said. "I can't have even that . . ."

"Your belly— What happened?"

"A cesarean. Garnet had to come out—"

"But Lagonda said it was easy. She said—"

"It was easy. It's nothing. That was part of my debt—"

"But you can't have another."

"Of course I can. I—"

"Oh, my God," he said. "You're the most precious thing in the world to me. I don't want you marked up or hurt or touched or ever anything but what you are, perfect and white and clean and—"

"And untouchable," she said, coming over to him. "Untouchable and burning up. What's the matter with you?" She felt for his groin. "Aren't you able anymore?"

Her grasping and holding him was like a touch of fire. He caught his breath, his brain racing backward in time. There had been nothing like this in their childhood, no peeping and questioning and touching, no ravaging desire and experimentation—it had all come later, in an avalanche, burying them. Now he knew why he hated to grow up then, why he wanted the sun to stand still; corruption had come with age, changing love to passion. A spasm shook him and the seed discharged. Out of him went something that could not be replaced. She started to laugh hysterically. "See?" she said. "It was wasted. Everything's been wasted."

"Beat it," he said, when his wind returned. "This is the last time. We'll never see each other again."

"No, never again."

"But I love you."

"I love you so much, so much . . ."

"I'm going back to Europe."

"And I'm going to Guadalupe," she said.

"Don't forget your shoes and socks."

She laughed at that, almost in falsetto, and fled. He closed his eyes so he could not see her. He heard the whisper of her bare feet, the rustle of the slicker. As he reasoned on whether he had the nerve to kill himself, another thought intruded: somehow he must clean his Goddamned drawers before going home to Lagonda.

The departure of the Stuarts to Mexico on a belated honeymoon became a public occasion. Reporters and photographers gathered at the Brennan-Stuart field, and radio announcers mentioned the event in their news broadcasts. Already looking antique, the B-1 was accorded the affection due a piece of machinery which had started an enormous industry in the Queen. A newspaper editorial argued that the ship ought to be sent to the Smithsonian Institution (which had not asked for it) rather than put into service in Central America. The pioneer Brennans received flattering notices; Cissie's early career as an aviatrix was dwelt on; and her husband was the recipient of outright adulation. The public relations department of Brennan-Stuart Aircraft had stimulated the press, and a clever, literate young man supplied Dugald with a short, gracious speech he made before he settled in the cockpit behind his wife. It was the end of an era, as a columnist put it.

That noon Cham switched off his bedside radio the moment he heard the subject mentioned. He was in a despairing mood and attempting to conceal it, and wondering how he could manage to tell Lagonda and Albert that he intended to travel again. His journey to the new house had been discussed only briefly, and he had been evasive. Lagonda had not pried or seemed suspicious, but an involuntary reaction on his part while explaining that he had fallen during a tour of the grounds in Beverly Hills and wetted his clothing revealed that something was wrong. "Just like when you was little," she had commented smilingly.

"Shut your Goddamned mouth!" he had shouted suddenly, and then was assailed by remorse and made clumsy, inadequate apologies. Thereupon she had stared searchingly at him, perceived he was lying and concealing evidence, and treated him with a cold, withdrawn suspicion.

She was late bringing his breakfast; not that he minded, for his increasing weight had limited the morning meal to unbuttered toast, two strips of bacon, and tea with saccharine. When she finally arrived with the tray, she said Ferris and Albert—who had not yet started the fall term at Dangerfield Military Academy—were listening to three different radios, and to as many stations, which carried accounts of Cissie's leave-taking. They had been doing that off and on since early morning, when they first heard an on-the-spot description of the takeoff. And there was a real nice piece about Cissie and Mr. Stuart in the morning paper, with pictures. She had it folded to the right page.

"I don't want to read it," Cham said.

"Your name is mentioned, Chambers."

"Never mind."

"They mentioned you on the radio, too."

He gulped his tea and belched and glared at her.

"I sure wish we could have gone out and watched," she said, "and took Albert. You didn't think it was right, did you?"

"I wasn't invited."

"Well, maybe if you played up to Mr. Stuart a little—"

"Keep talking," he said, "and I won't eat this crap."

Frowning and alarmed, she waited in silence until he finished, and was in the doorway, bearing the tray, when she turned to deliver a valedictory. "They're better off going away like that," she said. "That's the trouble, they've never been alone or had a chance to get acquainted. Cissie's thought of home too much . . . It'll be all right. You'll see."

"You think so?"

"No, I don't. You are not being honest with me. Do you think so?"

Abruptly, Cham was sorry for her. She didn't stand as straight as she once had, and a salting of gray was coming in her kinky hair; she was getting older. Her life was an absurdity of work, selflessness, worry and tiresome deference to everybody but him. Ferris was a horse's ass and poor Albert was the wrong color. He wondered if he could somehow take her to Europe with him. Yet how the hell could he, unless he had her bleached white? Bachelors didn't travel with homely Negro maids. And she wouldn't go anyway; the Queen claimed her, as it had the Brennans.

"Well, answer me," Lagonda said.

"It won't be all right," Cham said, and felt a chill in his veins.

Later on, he went out in the rear garden with Albert. They had mitts and a baseball, and Cham set about a continuing task of teaching the boy to field and throw a reasonably straight pitch. It disgusted him to soon be puffing and experiencing a sore arm. The days of his dreaming of playing with the Vernon team and surpassing the feats of Red Grange were a thousand years behind. Although Negroes were supposed to take naturally to athletics, music and sexual intercourse, he suspected that his protégé, whatever he might do with a trumpet or in bed, wasn't going to do much in sports; he was a thinker and talker, perhaps a charmer, but not well coordinated muscularly or instinctively quick. Albert, looking at imaginary men on first and third, watching for the signal Cham gave him from under his catcher's glove, winding up and then hurling erratically, kept right on talking. His mother had told him to keep his complaints to himself, out of respect for Cham's munificence, but he felt he ought to let his uncle in on the difficulties of attending the military academy. He didn't look forward to going back there, you could bet on that. And he wondered, if he had to go, whether he couldn't be driven to and from the school each day instead of being a boarder and just coming home weekends.

"Why?" Cham asked. "Listen, get it in the groove, will you? You haven't pitched a strike in five minutes."

"I don't have a roommate," Albert said. "Yes sir, I'll get 'em in. They

351

put me in a room alone. All the other guys have roommates. You know why I don't have anybody."

"Sure I do. But we agreed you were going to put up with that in order to get a good education."

"I'm all alone, Uncle Cham. They don't even talk to me unless they have to."

"So don't talk to them. Read. Learn more than they do. You talk too much anyhow."

"They call me 'Little Smoke' and 'Nigger-baby' right to my face."

"Okay," Cham said. "Pick the biggest guy you think you can lick, choose him, and beat the be-Jesus out of him."

"I don't think there's anybody I can lick. None of them are as little as I am."

"Kick somebody in the balls as a starter. That'll give you an edge."

"They would gang up on me. I don't like fighting."

"Learn to like it. Al, would you rather change to a school where you have to sit with a bunch of niggers?"

"No sir," Albert said.

"Very well," Cham said, and decided to get on the phone and give the headmaster of Dangerfield the rough edge of his tongue. "Come on, put some steam in your fast ball."

He worked up a sweat. Trying to field a bad hop tossed at him, Albert tumbled and fell on his head and had to be picked up, brushed off and comforted. Above one eyebrow was a small cut. Cham heard a feminine scream, and Ferris appeared at the service porch door and called sharply, "Al, you come in here and see your mother right away. Scuse me, Mr. Brennan." Cham's irritability, barely kept within bounds under the best of circumstances now, burst out in full vigor; he motioned roughly for Albert to obey his father and walked behind the plaster gazebo, unable to face Lagonda at the moment. It was not like her to raise a fuss over a small accident. The strain was beginning to tell on both of them, and he had to leave pretty soon. Groaning, he confronted the prospect of putting his affairs in order for a long absence.

There was the sound of the service porch door slamming hard, a discourtesy no doubt attributable to Ferris Washington, Junior, which raised Cham's heat, and immediately afterward it opened again. Cham detected what he took to be wailing and pricked up his ears. The skin on his neck and shoulders turned cold. He stood stiffly as Hank Isbrow, bald, burly, a bristly white moustache of the vintage of his rise to Mechanical Superintendent of Brennan-Stuart, came hurrying to him. The pallor in Hank's face matched the color of his vestiges of hair, and tears were rising in his eyes. He stopped three feet in front of Cham, incapable of speaking for a moment.

Wetting his lips, Cham said slowly, "Well? What brings you here? Did Bull-Shit Aircraft burn down?"

"You haven't heard, Mr. Brennan? No, you wouldn't . . . they sent it in to us first. But it's going to be all over in a little while . . . I thought I better come and tell you myself . . ."

"Cissie and the genius?"

"Yes," Hank said. "Oh, Jesus, Mr. Brennan! They went in—right into a hill and blew up. At Hermosillo."

"Where's Hermosillo?"

"On the west coast of Mexico, about five hundred miles from here."

"They're both dead?"

"Yes. It hit hard and exploded. It made a big fire, they said—"

"Why were they coming in there?" Cham said. "Trouble?"

"No. I didn't get all the facts, but no mention was made of trouble. They were traveling in easy hops and were going to stay with a friend of Mr. Stuart's who lives in Hermosillo. Something went wrong with the landing. I have to get more information . . ."

Cham studied his hands, which were quite steady, and proceeded to light a cigarette. He shed no tears and felt no real surprise, and the spreading numbness in him was comforting. *It had to end. This was how it ended.* What shame was there in feeling an outrageous, doomed, wearied, anesthetic relief? Turning from him, Hank blew his nose and wiped his eyes. "You got to hold yourself together, Mr. Brennan," he muttered.

"I'm all right," Cham said. "It had to happen." He refused to think of Cissie. "So the little bastard's gone, eh?"

Hank wheeled and stared at him. "Yes, he is. It just don't seem possible. He was cutting me down, trying to get rid of me—he only kept me on because of you—but he was a great man."

"Yeah."

"It wasn't the B-1. It's not my fault, Mr. Brennan. I went over the ship myself. It checked out perfectly. They were carrying a light load. With a pilot like Cissie—"

"Sure. Now, listen to me. Get a plane and send some people to that town. Find out exactly what happened. Bring the—the remains back."

"I'll go myself, Mr. Brennan."

"Make the public relations people protect me. I don't want to talk to anybody."

"Yes, sir."

"I mean right now for everything."

"Yes, sir."

They started walking toward the house. The cigarette burned Cham's fingers and he dropped it. A telephone was ringing. Ferris opened the door for them, tears running down his cheeks. "Mr. Brennan," he said, "I just want to say—"

"Don't say a Goddamned thing," Cham told him. "And don't answer the phone."

"All three is ringing," Ferris said. "I answered one. It's a newspaper, and—"

"Tell them to go fuck themselves," Cham said. "That goes for everybody. Where's Lagonda and Al?"

"She put him to bed and laid down herself."

"Okay, leave her alone unless she needs a doctor. If anybody comes to the door, throw him out."

"Yes sir."

Absently, Cham walked to the front door with Hank, as though he were ushering out an honored guest. "Mr. Brennan," Hank said, "the way I figure it is this: she didn't need as long as an ordinary person. Look what she did in a few short years—got Mr. Stuart to change airplanes from toys to necessities, proved they were as good as Mr. Stuart claimed by flying them, and made this town the biggest aircraft manufacturing center in the world. And she made us all happy too. Maybe she was too good to stay very long. The good Lord must have known that. He was glad to get her back. She's happy now, with Him . . . You have to think that way."

"Yeah." Cham looked reflectively at Hank. "Well, the little bastard wanted to get rid of the B-1. It probably reminded him of his unimportant past. He got rid of it."

Hank gawked and said, "You ought to think of the good things. Remember that field out on Western Avenue, and the first day? The little old Air-Travelers and Sarah Godowsky? Remember how pleased the colonel was when he went for his ride, and how he backed her up? She was going to India or around the world . . ."

Cham's eyes finally filled, and Hank dimmed and wavered in his vision. He blinked the weakness away and breathed deeply. "Get out, you son of a bitch," he said. "I want to hear from you tomorrow, not later. I've got to know *exactly* what happened. See?"

Hank nodded. "I'm on my way." He fled.

Walking carefully, stiffly, as if age had caught him, Cham went upstairs and into his room and locked the door. He sat on the edge of the bed and smoked another cigarette. A noise of digging came from the side garden; that would be Jesús Algonrones, starting late today to please his

354

employer. His advice could never be taken: Cissie wasn't going to Guadalupe. She was dead and in ashes on the side of a hill in Mexico. "I killed her," he said aloud, and the flat inflections of his voice scared him. "But that doesn't matter. I also killed myself." She was marked up from having Garnet, but she was worse marked up now.

Somewhere, in a closet or a drawer, or in a cabinet in the cellar, were Grandpa's pistols. It would be so easy to put the Goddamned barrel in his mouth and pull the trigger. What would the old man think if he could ever hear that his grandson had blown off the back of his head with one of his own guns? Cham got up irresolutely, worried by the intrusion of Grandpa. And then the name of Garnet recurred in his mind. Grandpa would have liked her, cherished her; she was the continuation of the line. Suddenly hurried, Cham plugged in the telephone and called Sunset Sea. Harry Sego wasn't in, and his secretary sounded evasive. "Look," Cham said, "I want him. This minute. Where the hell is he?" He was at the country club, playing golf with Mrs. Sego. This was Thursday, and he always took Thursday afternoon off for exercise— "No, don't you call him. Give me the number." The girl furnished the number in frightened tones.

At the country club they said Mr. Sego was out on the course, and could they take a number and have him call? They could not. "I'm Chambers Brennan," Cham said. "It's an emergency. Send somebody running. I expect to hear from him in five minutes. I'll wait."

He waited, shooting himself forgotten, his brain racing over what he had to do. Gasping and blown, Harry was speaking into the telephone within four minutes—he revived a nearly forgotten joke. "Great Cham of Tartary," he said, "you're a sadist. Don't you realize giving my wife a diamond necklace for a wedding present doesn't forgive this? I'm a bridegroom, damn it! And I didn't even get a honeymoon. I'm entitled to an afternoon off a week—"

"Cissie went on her honeymoon and she's dead."

"Huh?"

"She and the genius got killed in a crash in Mexico," Cham said. "I forget the name of the town."

"Oh, Christ!" Harry said. "Oh, Cham, I'm sorry . . ."

"Forget it. Listen to me. I want the kid. She's at their place in Beverly Hills. I think Lagonda told me she's in the care of a nurse and an aunt of Dugald's who came out from the east to look after Garnet—Lagonda asked for the job and got turned down, and her feelings were hurt. Get the kid for me and bring her here. Shove the aunt on her butt if she makes a fuss, and then get hold of Baltim and Lely and arrange the

355

legal part of it. Pay off wherever you have to—I don't care what it costs. Get that?"

"Yes."

"As far as you know, I've left town with Garnet. I'm not talking."

"Right, Cham, I—I—"

"That's all," Cham said harshly. "You better not miss on this job, sweetheart."

He remained locked in his bedroom the rest of the day, drinking from an emergency quart of bourbon hidden from Lagonda behind the tub in the bathroom. Once Ferris knocked on the door and attempted to speak to him, but he was told to bugger off.

As evening darkened the room, Lagonda called to him from outside and Cham let her in. She was grim and torn to pieces, and he was drunk. They looked at each other somberly. "I don't want to talk about it," he said.

"Neither do I," she replied. "There's a thousand phone calls and people at the door—I had to get a couple of my folks to help. You got anything to say to anybody?"

"No. Call Harry Sego and tell him to hire detectives to keep the bastards away."

"She's here. She's laughing and making noises like a chicken and playing with her toes. She's happy, Chambers. Wouldn't you like to see her?"

"Not now. There's something about her, Lagonda—she looks like Cissie. I can't right now . . ."

"Are you hungry?"

He considered, and experienced faint surprise. "Yeah, sort of. Bring me another bottle of whiskey. And don't argue, for Christ's sake."

"I won't," Lagonda said.

She abandoned his diet and served him spareribs in barbecue sauce and greens cooked with bacon and brought a wedge of pie with a slice of cheese on top, the sort of food she and her son and husband must be eating, stuff to crowd the belly and lull the mind, crisis victuals needed to sustain black poor folks in their trials. He was sleepless, despite gorging himself, and resumed drinking. But, with all his muzziness, he shifted his thoughts to how to provide for the light-haired, blue-eyed, perfect infant somewhere in the house: she was a Brennan, or would be, and she'd have to grow up so Goddamned rich nothing could touch her and make a splendid marriage and have kids of her own and continue a succession that was mysteriously important and must not lapse. There was no use thinking of Grandpa's guns. They were intended for enemies, not to put in your mouth. He had something to do for the

356

rest of his buggered-up life. To say his luck had played out was nonsense. He'd never had any; only a lot of advantages he had not managed to put together in a winning combination. If the fault was his, the hell with it. He had done the best he could. The baby was an absolute reason for still shuffling around.

Lagonda came in toward midnight to clean up and adjust the pillows behind his back. He stared at her groggily. "I'm not going to sleep," he said. "I've had enough sleep to last me for the rest of my life. When the time comes, instead of getting up I'm going to stay right here and pee the bed. Believe me."

"All right," she said. She leaned over and kissed his forehead. "Good night, Chambers."

Yet he slept after a fashion, and next day had a miserable hangover. Under Lagonda's urging, he accepted a New York telephone call from Hal Baltim and Aaron Eindhoven. Hal sobbed while he was speaking. "You ought to be glad it's finished," Cham said. "I am. I got rid of the little bastard and I have the kid. Cissie had no future, and I figure I have to pay for gaining some ground. Get busy dumping B-S and Anzoni on Amalgamated, but hold off closing until I find out what kind of wills Cissie and the genius left. If everything went to Garnet, I'll perform the trick of having myself appointed executor and have the whole package. We could come out of this having a commanding position in AAC, especially if we bought more stock on the open market. Maybe we can ease CAT into the combination. Let me talk to Aaron on that. You sound like you might be beating your breast for a while, and I need somebody who can think."

"You coldhearted bastard!" Hal said.

"Uh-huh," Cham said. "It's not the same as in those movies you used to see when you had pimples on your face. A guy can turn a dollar or two in these circumstances."

He conversed with Aaron, who was cool, correct and efficient, and arranged for him to inform Amalgamated Aircraft Corporation of his change of mind and propose a renewal of negotiations; Aaron was also to begin the first fishing for available AAC stock, and to explore and prepare a report on the feasibility of including the airline in what had taken on the proportions of a merger. Aaron was a bit stunned by the magnitude of Cham's conceptions. "You amaze me, Mr. Brennan," he said. "This is Napoleonic—and I don't expect it will work. Give me a month, at the least. Do you realize, on this basis, that we could almost talk to AAC as a coequal?"

"I will in a minute," Cham said. "It could work. All you need is a dead sister and brother-in-law and a Department of Justice that won't

357

step in and start hollering its ass off about violation of the antitrust laws. Don't forget to make some soundings in Washington. The genius had good connections there. Use his; he won't mind now."

"Yes, Mr. Brennan," Aaron said.

"You can start calling me Albert," Cham said, and nearly managed a wry smile. "And you better call your uncle Isadore, if that's necessary anymore, and see whether your tribe is willing to take another trip with me."

Now in charge of the Shapiro interests, with Irving relegated to the retail merchandising end, Aaron didn't understand the antique joke.

Gathering headway, Cham talked on the phone to Harry Sego, Harold Baltim, Senior, and Burton Lely. His path was clear enough. The aunt had offered a token resistance in Beverly Hills to the removal of Garnet, but she was a befuddled old lady and easily handled. Both of the wills of the deceased had been made through Brennan, Baltim, Lely and Brennan, the firm having done such outside work of Brennan-Stuart which was not handled by the aircraft company's own legal department. After the birth of their child, Cissie and Dugald had changed their wills with Lely; she had left half of her estate to Garnet, where formerly the whole had been bequeathed to Cham, and he was named sole executor in the event she died before the child was of age; curiously, Dugald specified Cham as executor of his holdings, which, other than for a few substantial gifts to members of his family, were to be Garnet's, even if his wife survived him. He did it, the document carefully specified, "in appreciation of the aid and financial support from A. Chambers Brennan during a crucial period in my life." The codicil went on to say that Cham was "to avail himself of and use his discretion" with the heritage of Garnet until she reached the age of twenty-five, with Cham committed to paying her schooling and ordinary expenses, not to exceed one thousand dollars a month, and required to furnish a detailed accounting of his stewardship to his niece and her lawyers. This moved Cham to speculation, while he counted his blessings. Had the little wonder with the accountant's appearance and neat moustache and iron will felt a rush of sentiment and gratitude? Had his dislike of his brother-in-law abated toward the end? Probably not. It must have been part of the weird contest with a wife who didn't love him, and the consignment of a child he had not much wanted—a child who was not, spiritually, his. Of course, he hadn't intended to die, but if he had to, depending on Cham was another quick stroke of the knife so keen the blood showed before the hurt was felt. Cissie was unfit to manage the money he would bestow on Garnet; giving her contemptuously to the enemy was preferable.

Hank Isbrow came in on another line as Cham was finishing off the second of two round-robin telephone conferences with Baltim, Lely and Sego. They were troubled by the scope of his plans with respect to AAC, into which he launched as soon as he knew his custody of Garnet and her parents' resources were secure. "I know, I know," Cham said. He was sitting in the solarium, hoping Grandpa's dust had accumulated from throughout the city and hovered in a protective cloud over him, and nodded when Lagonda tapped his shoulder and pointed to the instrument Ferris held ready. "But don't give me any crap. Do as I say. My luck is about gone, and I have to hurry. Listen, I got to get off here—another call is waiting."

He took the second phone. Somehow Hank had managed to reach him from Hermosillo. The connection was bad and each of them had to shout and then listen intently and ask for repetitions of words and phrases. "I just come in from the field," Hank said. "I'm in a hotel. Here's what happened. The weather was clear but a little gusty, nothing to bother her. Mr. Stuart used the radio and talked to the tower and got landing instructions. He didn't say anything about mechanical trouble and they tell me he sounded quiet and easy. The approach was normal, except a crosswind, coming in gusts, kept moving her around, and she couldn't touch down until she was halfway along the runway— it's unpaved. Remember the ship was loaded light. Well, she bounced the wheels but the tail was high, and she must have changed her mind. At the same time, the tower told her to get off and come around again, low and slow. She applied full power and went off. They got a lot of hills half a mile beyond the end of the field. It should have been all right. I've talked to ten people that saw it, and they all swear the engine didn't miss a beat. She wasn't carrying much weight. She was gaining altitude when she reached the hills. But she went in, Mr. Brennan —right into a hill—thirty feet from its top—went in with the throttle clear against the firewall—I found that part when I got up there . . ." He had to wait before he could resume. "I don't know, Mr. Brennan. I just don't know. Nobody else does either. I can't see how she stalled out. Maybe she pulled up too steep when the hill got in the way, but she had clear air between them. It might have been she didn't have enough flying speed to risk a bank right then. I just don't know. Maybe the wind flawed around and she got a downdraft. One of them said something on the radio a minute ahead of the crash, but it wasn't clear. They went in like a ton of bricks. They still had gas in the tanks. The B-1 blew up. Mr. Brennan, all that's left is melted aluminum and red steel and—and bones and ashes. Nothing . . . I sat down and bawled . . ."

Cham and Hank talked further, but there was little to add. Regulations caused difficulty and delay with respect to bringing back the remains; Hank thought he might have to wait a few days until the right papers were drawn and forwarded. Cham's rage ignited. "Tell those mother-loving sons of bitches who I am," he roared. "My grandmother was a Goddamned Mexican, a Villanueva. Tell them that, and to go bugger themselves. I want her home by morning, you hear me? I'll call Hal in New York and have him get in touch with Washington. The genius was important in Washington. Tell the Mexicans I'm going to have somebody big go to their Goddamned ambassador."

He hung up, trembling and red-eyed, and just as quickly regained his hollow calm. The rest didn't really matter; his dear love was bones and soot and melted puddles of aluminum thirty feet from the crest of a lousy Mexican hill now. But he telephoned Hal in New York and ordered him to appeal to that bastard Roosevelt if necessary. Or Eleanor, or anybody, for Christ's sake.

When the sunlight faded, he was exhausted and once more in his room drinking whiskey. He sat at the window gazing out at the lawn and shrubbery Jesús had faithfully watered, pondering dully on Cissie's end. It could have been an accident. She was a good and experienced flyer, and her luck was gone. Her reflexes would have made her fight for her life. The wind was the reason; the vast, impersonal, unseeable wind; the cold wind of death. It blew alike on the just and unjust, the worthy and the unworthy—and those with guilt in their souls. Or was the reason that little bastard? Was this the last, the keenest cut of all, with Cissie wielding the sharpest of knives? She drew real blood on him this time, more than he could spare . . . She had to go away, as far away as she could go. You could not go any farther than that. And she was sent by somebody, somebody who was the scum of the earth. *You put it in my head.* Those words would ring in his ears forever. And those other words on the radio—what were they?—the words nobody could understand. The genius begging for mercy, Cissie saying "touché" for the last time? He would never know. There was a hell of a lot he would never know.

Lagonda came in and turned on the lights and inquired about dinner. Swiveling in the chair, he blinked at her stupidly. "I'm not hungry tonight," he said. "Only thirsty. Don't argue with me."

"I'm not arguing, Chambers," she said mildly. "Quench your thirst. You should see her, though. She's awake. It might make you feel better."

"Not now," he said. "Not now. I've got plenty of time to see her."

"You didn't wet the bed last night," she said, and tremulously smiled. "You going to tonight?"

"No," he said, and smiled in return. "It's no fun any more. I'm up walking around a lot, and going to the john seems easier. I finally grew up, Lagonda."

"Yes," she said. "Everybody does . . . There's that old man downstairs, with his son. Mr. Smiley. He can't hardly see and I felt sorry for him. I had the detectives let them in."

He was prepared to bellow at her, but nothing came from his throat. She knew him better than he did himself, and they shared a sense of the fitting. The shade of Grandpa abounded in this old house. Grandpa was a man who adhered to the tradition of decently interring his dead. Cham got up and left the room.

Moses Smiley and a black-suited, rosy young fellow awaited him in the living room. No longer rosy himself, shrunken and dim of eye, Moses rose with some difficulty from his chair. His expression and that of his son's were very solemn. Cham endured a silent embrace and was surprised at the frailness of the old man's body. But the voice of Moses was as vibrant and rolling as ever. "My boy," he said, "I have come to you in your hour of need. If I do not bring consolation or surcease, I do at least hold to your lips a cup of love that is overflowing."

"Thank you," Cham said.

The son was introduced, and clasped Cham's hand. His name was Sisley. Cham was unable to determine where he ranked in the Smiley order of precedence, nor whether they had met previously; he assumed he was the youngest. Sisley said, in his father's style, "May our blessed Savior sustain you in this fearful trial, sir."

"May I say," Moses said, "in the words of the Proverbs, 'a little sleep, a little slumber, a little folding of the hands to sleep.' And from Job, 'there the wicked cease from troubling, and there the weary be at rest.'"

"'All flesh shall perish together, and man shall turn again into dust,'" Sisley added. "Job thirty-four."

"Yeah," Cham said.

"To have her go in the flower of her blooming," Moses said, "a young mother, leaving a helpless infant behind, rich, respected, much beloved, is indeed a great tragedy. I scarcely knew Miss Cissie, having only seen her on a few occasions in her childhood, but I have followed her progress and the renown she won for herself and marveled from afar. What an immeasurable loss! I can merely say to you that the Lord giveth and the Lord taketh away, and that His measures are inscrutable to the mortal eye. And then we come to Mr. Stuart, her husband, that incomparable—"

361

"Let's forget him," Cham interrupted.

"Of course, Chambers," said Moses briskly. "May I ask you, will we have your sister at the Garden of Immortality?"

"Nothing could be more appropriate, sir," said Sisley, in haste, "and it could not help but enhance our reputation."

"Okay," Cham said. "Your coming gave me an idea. I want the damnedest funeral that ever was for Cissie. Remember the one Grandpa gave for Grandma? Everybody in town turned out. This has got to be bigger."

"Now you are talking!" Moses exclaimed, and Sisley joined in his gratified smile. "Yes, sir, I do. I had the honor of attending those obsequies. They were grand and entirely fitting, yet I flatter myself that we can outdo them at the Garden. However, I do not recommend St. Vibania's, where the rites were held for the late Mrs. Brennan. That part of the city has deteriorated. What was Mrs. Stuart's faith?"

"I don't know," Cham said. "It doesn't matter."

"All to the good," Moses said. "The Garden is completely eclectic except for the Jewish faith, and we are considering a special section for the Israelites—there are a good many of the sect here now, and we are missing many opportunities for profit by this omission. On a better occasion, I must take up the matter with you, Chambers—"

"Don't get off the subject, Father," Sisley said.

"No, no," Moses said. "To horse. Chambers, this must be done in the highest of styles. Whom would you have officiate?"

"I hadn't thought," Cham said.

"Permit me to offer my services," Moses said, "out of my respect and admiration and love for the colonel, you and the family."

"Father, you can't even see," Sisley protested. "It will be too much for you."

"Don't worry," Moses told him. "I will memorize my text and go into training for the occasion. Fittingly, it will be my last appearance in the pulpit. What do you say, Chambers?"

"You'll do," Cham said. "Lay it on thick, huh? I'll get my people to send out the invitations. The rest is up to you."

"Depend on us, sir," Sisley said. "Nothing, absolutely nothing, will be lacking."

"Nothing, Chambers," Moses echoed. "Chambers, I commend your decision. By the way, I have followed a number of preaching styles in my clerical career. At this late date, with the weight of the years and broadened vision and my necessarily nonsectarian duties at the Garden, I am prepared to conduct services in almost any style. Which would you prefer?"

362

"You are the best in the evangelical vein, Father," Sisley said.

"Make it evangelical," Cham said. "Whatever the hell that is."

"Exactly," Moses said. "Evangelical it shall be, with all the stops pulled out . . . Could I inquire as to the condition of the remains? I understand it was a dreadful accident."

"You'll get just odds and ends," Cham said.

"Then I suggest our Westminster Abbey," Moses said. "There is a special, honored niche a step or two beyond the entry." He peered a trifle accusingly at Cham. "It was reserved for the colonel, you know. We will use a Grecian urn."

"Allow me to propose," Sisley said, "that, considering the extent of these ceremonies, we conduct them outside on our village common. It is appropriate in California, warmed by God's glorious sunshine. We will rig loudspeakers and an address system so nobody will miss a word."

"That is an inspiration, Sisley," Moses said. "Chambers?"

"All right," Cham said.

"May we also expect Mr. Stuart?" Moses asked. "He could be given a separate service or accorded a minor part in the farewell to Miss Cissie's eternal slumbers."

"Possibly," Cham said. "I'll check with his family and let you know. But I don't want the genius in an urn beside Cissie. Keep them separated."

"Yes, sir," Sisley said. "He will be moved farther along in our Westminster Abbey if he comes."

"Okay," Cham said. "Let's get going on this."

Moses pressed one of Cham's hands in both of his. "It has been a precious meeting," he said. "God bless you, my son. And reflect that the Garden awaits your gentle slumbers, as it does mine and those of anyone else who feels the call to everlasting peace."

"Me, too," Sisley said, with enthusiasm. "God bless you, Mr. Brennan. Your courage and restraint have been an inspiration to us. You will never regret putting your beloved sister in our care. Good night."

"Good night, Chambers," Moses said. "Rest well, in the satisfaction of having done your duty to Miss Cissie in the utmost. Incidentally, there will be no charge, and that includes Mr. Stuart, should he join us."

Cham went upstairs with dragging steps. Lagonda had disappeared, and the silence was oppressive. He heard the faint wail of a baby on the second floor and was startled, and downed a stiff drink. On impulse, he telephoned Tom Sego. "That was a hell of a thing to happen," Tom said. "I still can't quite swallow it. I'm awfully sorry, Cham. I liked her.

363

She knew what I was trying to do with the house. I think she was looking forward to living in it."

"Did you like the genius?"

"Well, he knew a lot about putting things together. He gave me some good ideas."

"Did Cissie say how she wanted the house done?"

"Oh, more or less."

"Do it that way. Finish it in the way she said, everything. Understand?"

"Yes, Cham."

"And then see if you can sell it for me."

"Really? . . . All right. I'll send you word when it's finished and you can see it. You've never been out, have you?"

"No," Cham said. "And I'm never coming. Goodbye."

He drank more and smoked, and welcomed a spreading warmth and confusion and despair and remorse. He began to contemplate his loss. Until that moment, he had not considered a life without his sister.

Then he remembered something Cissie had told him. If anything happened, she said, she wanted to be cremated. Well, that had been done. She had vanished, as Grandpa had vanished, ashes in a void. Putting his hands to his face, he started to cry.

Lagonda entered the room, and he dropped his hands and stared at her with bleary eyes. She had the child in her arms and she was smiling. He thought perhaps he had been saved.

PART THREE

Queen of Hearts

one

ONE thick smoggy midday Garnet Brennan went to a luncheon in a private room of a downtown hotel. It was the annual autumn meeting of an organization called Los Angeles Lovely, of which she was a prominent member. Many of the best people in the city belonged to LAL and contributed liberally to its treasury. It had been founded in 1954 by a group appalled at the spread of urban blight and the tastelessness of land developers and citizens alike, and had the highest of objectives, a certain cultural authority, the desire to plant trees and improve parks and design esplanades in the most unlikely of places, and often contrived to influence the Planning Commission and the City Council.

LAL was only one of many groups, civic and social, to which Garnet belonged, ranging from the Citizens' Committee for an Art Foundation to the Junior League; from Queen's Court Club (dedicated to recruiting and training better social workers) to the Golden Pioneers, whose winter ball was the envy of all the uncertified climbers; from the Single Gentlewomen—they did amateur plays nobody who was anybody could afford not to attend—to the Westside Painters Union, the oils and gouaches of whose members found their way to a spring fair on La Cienega Boulevard and were bought by obedient patrons. Garnet was a busy and fulfilled young woman. Her background and wealth were matters of record. She had achieved nearly all the desires expressed for her by Chambers Brennan. That she was still a spinster occasionally bothered him, since she was the lone remaining Brennan of a procreative age, but he was too selfish and suspicious of her suitors to complain much. Hampered by ill health, he had largely retired, and somebody had to watch the enormous Brennan store; his choice was Garnet, and

367

to his delight she proved to have both the aptitude and the application. Oddly, she did not have many aspirants for her hand. Perhaps the prospect of being united with a couple of hundred million dollars daunted them. Or perhaps Garnet simply lacked the time for dalliance. She had been raised, irrespective of sex, to inherit a definite position, to make up for various deficiencies of Chambers Brennan himself, to step into the shoes of his well-remembered father Cass Brennan—and she had more than met her obligations. At age twenty-six she had long since shown a precocity the tribe was celebrated for, although, of course, she could never hope to match the legendary reputation of Chambers Brennan, who had far surpassed his ancestors. But Chambers had every expectation that she would worthily supplant him and, in the bargain, gloss over any gaucheries he had committed on the way through life. Garnet was the public alter ego he wished he could have cultivated.

It wasn't that she was unfeminine or too devoted to business. She had plenty of women friends and registered well with men. Her manners were excellent and her attitude retiring. The blue eyes set wide apart in her head could turn cold and calculating, but rarely did. Wealth and responsibility was not a cross she bore. The pressures and demands of her daily existence failed to make her curt or unsympathetic. She had grace, a ready, wide-mouthed grin. Indeed, there was a dashing air about her which was intriguing. Physically she was small, two or three inches over five feet in height, and well-shaped and a little too thin. Her hair, worn full and puffed in the current mode, was an attractive shade of faded gold, assisted a bit by the hairdresser. She used no makeup except lipstick, and her clean-featured, good-humored, freckled face had a scrubbed, sandy look that was attractive. On her rounds she invariably wore a hat and gloves and Chanel suits in the daytime and smelled of Chanel essences; her dresses for informal gatherings were always basic black; for the formal occasions her gowns were from Balmain or Dior, some said a shade too far on the full-blown side—but then these critics resented the fact that she rarely wore them more than twice before they went to be auctioned off at a favorite charity. She walked quickly, on excellent muscular legs firmed by morning swims and exercises, high spike heels clattering in a cheerfully staccato fashion; her lack of height bothered her a little, though she never alluded to it. She spoke incisively but softly, in a pleasing alto voice, and the faint nasal overtones so many westerners gave their words had been carefully removed in good preparatory schools.

Above all, Garnet radiated confidence and a genial self-assurance. The conditioning of Chambers Brennan had convinced her she was of a special breed, and that sufficient money could solve anything. She was healthy and well adjusted. The ill health of her father had given her an extra strength. In the midst of outrageous plenty, her wants were surprisingly simple. She cared nothing for jewelry, and in an area devoted to the worship of the new and expensive motorcar she drove a four-year-old station wagon of common make that was normally in need of washing. She had been painstakingly trained for her exalted role—at Mayberry School, at Santa Maria School in Monterey, at Stanford University, and then at the Stanford School of Business Administration. She could read and understand a corporate report, discuss tax matters intelligently, play a piano adequately, quote modern poets, and she discreetly collected the works of Paul Klee with the idea of eventually bequeathing them to a local museum. She also could ride, fence, do acrobatic dives, handle a camera, and converse slowly in French and Italian. Older men and women liked her. What she intended to do in the future was of no consequence; the present was interesting enough.

On many a foray, civic and social, Garnet was accompanied by Junior Christopher, a tall, spare woman with white hair faintly violet from mysterious rinses and a ravaged, kindly, humorous countenance; she had been Garnet's mentor for nearly twenty years, along with her recently deceased mother, and was responsible for a lot of the patina her charge had acquired. Actually, Junior was Annice Christopher, Junior, her mother—upon becoming a young widow in San Francisco—having assumed the title of Annice Christopher, Senior, and prepared her daughter for a career as startling as her own. Senior, before changing to Christopher, had been a Comstock Lode, Washoe Valley Flaherty; her father, Patrick Shawn Flaherty, was once a United States Senator from Nevada and such a high roller that he managed to die broke in a mansion with solid silver doorknobs on Nob Hill in San Francisco. Having entered into a love match with a pale, haggard, interesting looking young actor named Paul Christopher, who neglected to inform her that he had tuberculosis, Senior was soon pregnant and bereaved—and determined to keep up a *noblesse oblige* it seemed certain she would have to relinquish. Nothing fazed Senior, nor Junior when her time came. Their standards remained high and they knew only the important people, in spite of Senior's having to be a pit boss in a gambling house at Reno while Junior was at Smith College, and Junior later going to Southern California and becoming a Theosophist and entering Yoga trances to sell real estate to the faithful. From that expedition emerged Junior's grand design of bringing culture and taste to Los Angeles. She became one of the first, and most successful, of the interior decorators who began to flourish in the latter 1930's. The colorful Christophers were promptly accepted by the Queen's uncertain and aspiring upper bourgeois. Their high background was appreciated; no circles were closed to them, and Junior practiced her arts among folk who could afford her high fees. Even a repetition of her mother's mistake, marrying a drunken movie actor who quickly departed her bed, failed to dim Junior's luster. In the course of her duties, she met Chambers Brennan; he needed somebody to reconstitute the old house near Westlake Park. The changes she made enchanted him. Raising Garnet in a proper manner worried him, and the suggestions of Junior and Senior, as well as their entrée to the better homes, were very helpful. A peculiar, close, trusting relationship developed between him and Junior. Besides, Lagonda approved of the Christophers. Chambers was permitted, and even indulged in, his eccentricities by elegant eccentrics who understood him. Presently Junior was put in sole charge of Garnet's development, and accompanied the Brennans upon a six-month cultural investigation of postwar Europe which Chambers supervised at long range from cafés and hotels and other places less public. At Junior's instigation, he underwent analysis and tried manfully to reform his habits for the sake of the niece he had adopted. His spells of depression grew more infrequent under the rallying of the two Christophers. When Senior died, he gave her a superb funeral; she was buried in the Garden of Immortality, in the Blessed Quietude Tract. When he decided to abandon Grandpa's Folly, Junior went with them to live in the penthouse apartment on Wilshire Boulevard and gave up the decorating business she had been plying with decreasing regularity. Some acquaintances half expected Chambers to marry what was perhaps his closest adviser; certainly he must have provided for her in his will.

Junior squelched these expectations. "Where would we go for a honeymoon?" she would ask. "To a sanitarium or the U.S. Mint? And what would we do? No, thanks. One lunge at matrimony was enough for me. I am content to be an old family retainer."

On the drive straight down traffic-congested Wilshire Boulevard from the Xanadu, whose sixteen stories of apartments were situated on a rise just west of the Los Angeles Country Club, Garnet had the company of Junior Christopher. Their slow progress through innumerable traffic signals gave them an opportunity for one of their confidential talks, which were always impromptu and usually frank.

Canted sidewise on the broad seat of the station wagon, long legs drawn under her, a filtered cigarette burning between her lips but not interfering with her speech (she never permitted herself this lapse of good manners except in the presence of intimates), Junior descanted on the previous evening she had spent with Chambers Brennan. "It was a television evening, of course," she said, "fitfully interrupted by conversation. His grace, when not answering back the tube, excoriating the commercials and shouting clichés along with the actors, held forth on you. As general *éminence grise* of the family, I think I should fill you in."

"Please do," Garnet said.

"Well, to begin with, Lagonda was with us, which means we were sitting as an executive committee."

Garnet smiled. "Oh, I see. That means a directive was issued and action is to be taken."

"Exactly. May I add a footnote? Your father seems to me crazier than he was a year ago. Don't I say that every year?"

"Yes, dear. Your footnote has been duly noted. Get on with it."

"The annals of the poor," Junior said, "are often simple and brief. The same thing can happen to the rich. Chambers has been brooding, apparently. He is more than ever concerned with his health and doubtful of how many years he has left. In his view, he is going to be forced to intervene in your affairs. I gather he plans to simplify your annals. Garnet Brennan was born, she attained maturity, she almost waited too long, she was married, she had a large family, and she died leaving a fortune."

"Oh. There we are. I wondered when Father would get tired of waiting. Did the committee pick my husband?"

"Yes. Your date last night. Our chairman has decided on him. Lagonda concurred. Garnet, how do you feel about Larry Smith?"

"You haven't mentioned how you voted."

"Amid gunfire, beautiful girls in peril, horses galloping, secret agents saving the nation and comedians telling jokes, it was moved and seconded—"

"Now, really," Garnet said, in quick impatience. "I can remember trusting you instinctively as I looked up from the cradle. Are you a coward?"

"I'm afraid I went along with the majority," Junior said. "Unstable or not, Chambers has a point, and you display a definite apathy. Something has to be done, I suppose."

"Shame on you. What was moved and seconded?"

"The customary procedure in these cases. Your father is suddenly going to be charming to Larry. He'll have a serious talk with him. Larry can go into Brennan, Baltim and so forth if he wants. The Smiths will be cultivated, all of them—"

"I don't care to become Mrs. Smith. It's too common a name."

"Garnet, don't sound frivolous. The committee would take a dim view of that."

"I'm quite serious."

"See here, I admire you not ever having the need to confide in anybody. That's a good quality in your position. But there ought to be limits to the impenetrability of your defenses. The committee is entitled to some explanation."

Garnet shrugged. "A Smith I'll never be. That's my explanation."

"Are you at all interested in Larry?"

"Yes. Enough, possibly."

Straightening, planting her feet on the floor, Junior said, "Then what's the difficulty, aside from the foolish thing of the name? Why isn't Larry a good choice? Suppose we consider a matter of the heart cold-bloodedly for a moment—just between us cats. The fountain of youth is not necessarily part of your inheritance, and you won't be the prettiest of pictures ten years hence, still doing good works and possibly developing many of the characteristics of an automated Hetty Green. Or are you secretly planning to run for office, go to Italy and design fabrics, or join the international set and establish branch homes in New York, Cuernavaca and Paris?"

"No, I wouldn't consider leaving here."

"Which brings us back to Larry. He's the pick of the litter, Garnet. You can't do much better. The family is good stuff. You'll feel at home with them, and they will not be overawed by you or Chambers, I hope. Larry is personable. His manners and instincts are good. I have no doubt he will be able to cope with your father. I like his heredity."

"You mean that in collaboration with me he ought to improve the breed?"

"It's a factor, dear. You mustn't make any unrectifiable mistakes." Junior ticked off points in Larry's favor on her fingers. "Hotchkiss, Yale, Yale Law School. The right clubs. He doesn't drink much and he likes the outdoors. No one could accuse him of being stupid. His ambitions, I take it, are not exceptionable. He isn't praise be, an eccentric, and none of his forebears seem to have had that handicap. Look, I'm going to have to recommend him."

"There's one trouble," Garnet said.

"Well, we are in an era of extreme frankness. Comparative strangers discuss the most intimate functions with an appalling abandon. Why not us? Larry has made attempts on your virtue and disillusioned you? He is too active sexually? He hasn't made any attempts? He is not active enough? You fear matrimony with him might be stately and dull? That he might be neuter or even a homosexual? That—"

372

"One question at a time, please."

"Forgive me. I suppose I have a touch of buck fever. What's wrong, pet?"

"Nothing too dreadful. Larry is kind, considerate and affectionate. He is not too pushing at close quarters. I have absolutely no reason to suspect, on the other hand, that his reactions aren't those of a heterosexual. He's interesting and vital. His family likes me and I like them. They are encouraging this. But brace yourself. My answer is going to sound Victorian."

"Let me anticipate it," Junior said. "He hasn't asked you to marry him. He's a bit spooky. You might frighten him by being too matter-of-fact yourself. Don't worry, the committee can handle that by certain devious maneuvers."

"No, no. I wouldn't hesitate for a moment if my mind was made up —I'd simply move in on him, or take to seduction, or rattle my money. Don't you realize I can have anything I want? Haven't you listened to Father?"

"Uh . . . yes."

"The fact is, my heart has not been touched. Doesn't that strike you as old-fashioned and rather appealing?"

"Bless you, it does. But—"

"I have worse to add," Garnet said. "It has never been touched, except by you and Senior and my father and Lagonda and Albert and the kittens. I don't think it's ever going to be. I've met a lot of young men by now, and none of them has moved me seriously. The spark is just not there. It may be environment and training, but I suspect it is inherited temperament. I might as well confess, hadn't I?"

"Dear God," Junior said, with horror. "No, don't. We can't have another Brennan eccentric. All your people were odd, and enough is enough. Even your father agrees on that. Senior would turn over in her grave if she—"

"Oh, come off it. I'm not an eccentric, and only half Brennan. The truth is I'm an ordinary gentlewoman, raised carefully by you and your mother, and not very emotional. I am well adjusted and possibly a trifle too hardheaded—I've had to be in the atmosphere of a luxurious asylum. My interests are diversified instead of being focused on one silly object. I'm happy and enjoying my peaceful life."

Junior stared at her. "I wish I hadn't encouraged you to unburden yourself. Experience should have taught me, Garnet; since Freud, one always discovers the most dismaying things. Now, in my downhill years, I shall have to contemplate a worthy spinster devoting her energies to—"

"You won't have to do anything of the kind," Garnet said. "I'm going to follow a normal course: I'll marry and produce children and live up to my endowment and conform. But as long as my heart is untouchable, I think I'd better pick my own man. I don't need one with money or social position—I have both. My father is too erratic for me to depend on his judgment, and your opinions are colored by his. I shall have to rely on myself. Larry won't do. Like me, he is part and parcel of this place, his family overpowers him, they would probably interfere with my freedom of action. What I want is an outsider, without strings, somebody I can almost treat as a protégé and command completely. I don't mean, of course, that he shouldn't be first class. But he ought to be at a level where he will feel gratitude, follow orders, and mind his manners. Someone on the order of Elizabeth Rex's Prince Philip, you know. I've given this a lot of thought, Junior."

"I see you have. Forgive me for allowing my jaw to drop in such an unseemly fashion . . ."

"And I'm aware of the necessity of haste. I don't care to start bearing children at a late and dangerous age. I believe to make the choice interesting, and to show what I can do, I'll pick a man—a suitable man, mind you—at random. Then we'll find out if decision and influence count. It ought to be fun."

"*That's* eccentric."

"No, it's only being businesslike under the circumstances."

"I can imagine how your father will receive some—"

"On the contrary, there's a hurdle my man can't afford to trip over. If he doesn't charm Father, he doesn't get the job. I'll put that to him in plain terms."

"'Job'!" Junior said, and her voice cracked. "You are balmy. You're the worst one of the bunch! I have unwittingly raised a wolf in my kennel."

"Don't blow those sobbing saxophone notes, please," Garnet said, and grinned. "I'm supposed to have a consort, not a husband, and you know it. My father is the authority for that statement, and you have always concurred. How else can I protect myself unless we procure Frank Sinatra or Pope Paul? The law of probabilities guarantees me a reasonable chance even in random selection. If I do happen to err, we can buy off the candidate and try again."

"You're a Brennan," Junior said. "The strain is imperishable! Your father will be stupefied. This isn't what Senior and I intended for you at all . . ."

They were at the hotel, and a doorman took the car. Toward the end of the busy lobby, through a wide, pillared entrance guarded by screens and tables at which sat secretaries checking membership and seating cards, was the Conquistadore Room with mural vistas on the walls of bearded, helmeted, sword-bearing men in body armor marching across a desolate terrain carrying the standards of the Holy Virgin and Castile, attended by robed friars and frowzy bare naked Indians with their private parts decently covered; on supporting columns were decorative designs of shields, lances, sheaves of arrows, aboriginal pottery, religious banners and the armorial bearings of Spanish grandees; the dadoes, except where scarred by serving carts, were of a Hispanic darkness, the carpet a sea of scarlet, the chandeliers a *churrigueresque* tangle of snaky arms swirling upward. In a smallish adjoining room was a bar decorated with bullfight posters, tenanted by the male minority of the Los Angeles Lovely faithful having martinis to nerve them for the encounter. The female faithful were content to have sherry, or nothing.

Garnet's and Junior's cards conveyed them to seats in the center, just under the broad dais that held the speakers' table and a lectern and microphone. They had the minute glasses of sherry served by a frugal management and greeted friends and acquaintances. Some shop talk of the enlightened civic sort was exchanged. As a veteran of these assemblages, Garnet was alert, informed and vivacious. Lighting a cigarette, Junior gazed around dispiritedly. "Other than for certain private rooms I did in the French Provincial era," she muttered, "this is the most ghastly banquet hall in Los Angeles. All those monks and savages and soldiers are out of scale. The lighting is obscene. Whoever gussied up those columns should be prosecuted. The—"

"You're being unfair to our romantic past," Garnet replied, "and acting professional. Some of my people crossed that desert."

"Thank heaven mine elected to stay home and be butchered at the Battle of the Boyne," Junior said.

The meeting was twenty-four minutes late in coming to order. It was opened by Mrs. Alexis Cadwalladar, a burly, middle-aged, untidy lady, celebrated for her triumphs in good causes, usually in the realm of public improvement; she and her husband were of pioneer stock (circa 1900) and richer than the Brennans, with land and livestock and General Motors shares and a brokerage house and a chain of supermarkets and fourteen statewide dealerships selling Buicks, and each of her feats was invariably a subject of loving wonderment in the newspapers, which were stimulated by a public relations firm Mr. Cadwalladar employed for that sole purpose—his wife was always being photographed receiving the congratulatory greetings of the City Council, the thanks of folk starved for chamber music, the plaudits of women's clubs who dubbed her Patroness of the Year, Patroness of the

Decade, Patroness of the Twentieth Century, and Madame Los Angeles. She harried those in the upper income brackets for breathtaking donations, headed the committees, danced the first dance at the charity balls with Alexis, and was on the telephone day and night. All she wanted in return was that her labors be acknowledged in print, and to appear in numerous gracious acceptance scenes on television and radio. Generally she was simply called Madam President, since she was president of nearly everything she entered, and liked speaking to admiring groups. Her oratorical efforts were substandard, and Junior was not part of her mob—there had been trouble once when she was doing one of Madam President's several houses. "That's what you can become someday, dear," she commented, "when old Caddy begins to fade in the stretch. But please don't let yourself run to blubber like her."

"It makes you think, doesn't it?" Garnet said.

In truth, it did give one furiously to think, as Junior was fond of saying in a phrase borrowed from the British. Garnet seldom wasted consideration on her future; there was plenty of assurance to be had, and a shining, indefinable height of accomplishment, automatic approbation, and a somehow guaranteed feeling of all's well that ends well . . . yet now she wasn't so sure, and frowned through Caddy's prefatory words, obscurely pained by a sudden, new, unwonted uncertainty and sensations of time having passed without meaning or satisfaction. How could this have happened? Nothing was really the matter. Perhaps it was the bother of inevitable marriage and motherhood. It had become an increasing hazard which she had avoided by inattention. But it was not a matter for outright worry or dissatisfaction, and she could settle the question quickly enough. She told herself she hadn't changed, and that she was quite content. Whatever she wanted was within her reach. But the mood would not pass. She was twenty-six years old, her temperament was cold, a mysterious talisman had eluded her grasp, and Junior's last remark still hurt. She had suffered a defeat she could not name, and defeats were her particular abhorrence. Something *was* wrong, damn it . . .

Madam President held forth in her usual style: more trees than ever were being planted, two underprivileged suburban communities had plunged willingly into debt to build pedestrian malls, billboards were being erased by sweet persuasion, signs used by discount stores and used-car dealers had been shrunk, architects encouraged to abandon plans for frightful glass cubicles devoid of ornament, numerous tract developers devoted to ripping apart the country with bulldozers and solidly paving it brought to heel, the Planning Commission stiffened by exhortation, the City Council badgered into passing ordinances which might preserve vestiges of a less constricted day, the Highway Commission beseeched to mask their spectacular cuts with ground cover, and citizens generally nudged into compliance and tidiness by a multitude of good-humored signs ordering them to put their beer cans, spent flash bulbs and mountains of paper into receptacles stationed everywhere by LAL. A single sinister note intruded: an evil Cuban thrip was suddenly attacking the heretofore disease-free *Ficus nitida* that LAL favored for metropolitan planting. Caddy was taking this up with scientists at the University of California at Riverside.

The treasurer's report was reassuring. By acclamation, the minutes of the last meeting and the program for the 1964–65 season were approved. Committee chairmen reported briefly under Caddy's watchful eye and were applauded. A woman in a preposterous fruity hat moved a gushing testimonial to Madam President, and it was seconded and the whole audience stood up to clap hands. Photographers appeared to flash their strobes, and Caddy was enveloped in a rain of darting lights, smiling and moved for the thousandth time. She made a gracious and confused little thank you for yet another honor and sat down, and waiters started serving the puree mongole, hearts of palm salad, squab à la niçoise with wild rice dressing, rolls and coffee, European ices, and assorted mints.

Garnet had been lost in thought. She scarcely followed the proceedings, although she was a member of the executive council. "You know something?" she said in Junior's ear. "I say to hell with LAL."

"You're getting the message," Junior returned. She started to look away, wheeled back on Garnet, and stared at her fixedly for a moment. In Junior's expression was a measure of apprehension and at least the stirrings of a presentiment.

Following the meal, Caddy introduced the customary featured speaker. Los Angeles Lovely dealt in what was known as "challenging" guests and paid good fees. It encouraged controversy and, to the distaste of some supporters, occasionally went far into left field. In their time, with appropriate thrills of disgust, the garden club members, clubwomen, social climbers, civically righteous and retired bankers had heard out disgruntled architects, worried biologists, manic city planners, anxious politicians, embittered men from the Atlantic Seaboard, traffic experts, hopeless demographers, a Scandinavian industrialist trying to dispose of a monorail system that had been rejected in South America, and any number of academic types brooding upon the more noxious effusions of a mechanistic civilization. Today's star turn was a Professor A. B. Wyitt, late of the liberal arts department of Laguna Seca Junior

College, and an alleged authority in socio-economic dynamics and urban redevelopment.

"This is going to be a tedious early afternoon," Junior whispered.

But Garnet thought Professor Wyitt looked interesting, if not promising. He assumed the lectern without notes, a tall, slim, good-looking, smiling man, boyish in appearance, whose age was hard to guess. He had light brown hair and light blue eyes, and wore the standard academic outfit of sports jacket, button-down shirt and skimpy dark slacks. Although he seemed a pleasant sort, not like many of the agitated types for which LAL provided a forum, he wasted no time on the usual preliminary jokes or raillery. His first words, delivered without a "Madam President" or other salutations, were arresting: "You people, presumably the influentials and opinion-makers in this disorderly collection of unlovely communities called Los Angeles, the victims of an unbridled growth, ought to be ashamed of yourselves. You've made a mess of it. You have raped and debased a pretty country and a promising city, and I doubt if there is any way for you to escape the consequences except by packing your air-conditioned automobiles with a few necessaries and fleeing at once, two steps ahead of an overwhelming deluge of men, women, children, pollution of air, soil, water and the mind, cars, trucks, police regulations, basic housing, third-rate schools, taxes, public indebtedness, scoundrelly super-patriots and universal vulgarity. The Queen of the Angels is indeed the first true megalopolis, stretching some two hundred miles along a superb, climatically serene coast from the Mexican border to a befuddled, fumbling anachronism known as Santa Barbara. If Los Angeles is the flesh and spirit of what is to come elsewhere, then men are well advised to push out into space. I call your attention to the irony of the fact that much of the thinking and tinkering necessary for interstellar voyages is being done in your own area. Is it possible the urge to depart has more appeal here than in cities less favored by sunshine, gasoline fumes and the quick buck artists?"

"Oh, boy," Garnet said, and was touched and amused. "Listen to him. He sounds authentically bugged."

A. B. Wyitt went on to deal with certain numbing facts. Los Angeles, situated in the most populous state in the Union, was second in size nationally and had nearly four million citizens. The people of the county (of the same name) in which it sprawled in an abandoned orgy of rapid accretion numbered almost seven million. No one spoke anymore of the city as such, for who could distinguish between a central section decaying and forsaken and the innumerable collections of tract houses attached to shopping districts in Alhambra, Artesia, Azusa, Bell, Cudahy, Covina, West Covina, Dairy Valley, Duarte, El Monte, Glendora, Ha-

378

waiian Gardens, Hermosa Beach, Hidden Hills, Huntington Park, Industry, Inglewood, Lakewood, La Mirada, Long Beach, Monrovia, Norwalk, a hundred mobile-homes estates, and fifty other puffy little enclaves, all merged one into the other and utterly undistinguishable? To the four points of the compass the bulldozers rumbled and gouged, removing orange groves and row crops and gashing the hills for building pads, and the paving contractors spread their acres of blacktop. Westward the tall buildings rose on bits of property far too valuable for anything but immense concrete rabbit warrens, poking up out of the smog. In Civic Center, amidst the blue-brown haze, the city fathers labored to produce great piles of stone and steel in a diversity of heavy, pudgy styles, crowned by a prevailing mediocrity. And parking lots served for the sweep of the eye—they were the important item, with white-painted lines for the cars to stand in.

"Only the police building is handsome," Wyitt said. "Is that intentional, the mark of a cellular society? Is planting trees the extent of your obligation to your successors? You haven't done much besides that, except talk."

New York alone exceeded the Queen as a financial giant. The third largest complex of the nation's manufacturing was here. Perhaps the future safety of the United States lay with Los Angeles, for the central coils of the defense industry—brain trust, allied universities, experiment, development and manufacture—were here entrenched. Miles of residences went up overnight, as nowhere else, and with them the highest rate of real estate foreclosure in the country. Employment, aerospace, agriculture, minerals, motion pictures, television, international trade, fishing, nondurable goods production, tourism, sports attendance, motorcar sales, homosexual activities: the Queen was queen of all. Her magnet was stronger than ever: the outsiders came in by the hundreds every day. Megalopolis would have fourteen million inhabitants by 1980, or considerably better than half the total population of California, and probably thirty million in the second decade of the twenty-first century. The sum total was staggering and incomprehensible. Possibly only a computer could see the picture as a whole. That would be appropriate in the hyper-city devoted to electronics and automation.

"However," Wyitt said, "give a moment of merciful consideration to your typical Angeleno, your householder and taxpayer. He's a suburbanite in this apotheosis of suburbia. He just came here, and so he is not responsible for the trap you've got him in. He is young—Los Angeles is a young town, new all over again and progressively younger in each fresh wave of immigration, and old solely in mistakes—and he has a wife and is breeding too many children. You'll have to supply schools for those kids, as nearly as you can at the rate of one a month, and add new colleges at tremendous expense from public funds to educate youth beyond its fundamental intelligence in order to equip it for the demands of a profoundly changing technology. Your man has been plunked down in a ramshackle social structure, without traditions or continuity; he lacks relatives and old friends and a definite niche in a pecking order to occupy, and his church, if any, can't satisfy him. The astronauts and the rockets have been out where God was always supposed to be and haven't seen Him. He must have abdicated, or anyhow abandoned Los Angeles. The Angeleno is afloat without rudder or sail on a heaving sea of emotional insecurity. He has no roots, no standards, no permanent goals; he's unattached and mobile—a third of the families move once every year. Materially he is well taken care of. He has a pasteboard, cut-out, assembly-line house built to last nearly through a twenty-year mortgage; a dieted, nervous wife, clad in pants somewhat resembling his own, interested in the P.T.A. and banning the bomb; his children are healthy, though jumpy from the violence they watch on television and the fierce competition in the schools. Doctors can assure him of a frightful old age of creeping decrepitude if he abstains from cigarettes and saturated fats. His assets include such items as an electric razor and toothbrush, a washer-dryer, a tape recorder, martinis, tranquilizers, and news magazines to simplify his opinions. Unemployment insurance, unlimited credit, pension funds and the promise of government medical care seem to take care of the future. He is living in the most modern city in the world, surrounded by all the dubious attributes of the new civilization. Carbon monoxide is the breath of life to him."

Wyitt thought the Queen did have a god of sorts, a Moloch, to whom incredible sacrifices had been offered. It was the motorcar. Everything bowed to its demands. The city was ripped apart, whole neighborhoods obliterated, natural beauties buried under tons of concrete, to afford swift, deadly, unending passage for the cars. To give them standing room required thousands of hot, bare, repellant surfaced acres. They clogged the streets, fouled the atmosphere, dimmed the sight, killed and maimed. Dedication to them was complete; every man was a priest. No right-thinking citizen would consider using a public transportation facility unless he was short of funds or deprived of his driver's license. In each heart the ultimate bliss was equated with three hundred horsepower, elephantine size, low lines unsuitable for human ingress and egress, bright paint and gleaming metalwork, and time payments. People were born in them, grew up in them, had intercourse and conceived in them, and of course died in them. But one day soon Moloch would command the last measure of devotion—stoppage, suffocation and ruin.

"He's a nut," Junior said softly. Garnet didn't hear her; she had her whole attention fixed on the speaker.

"You say you don't have extensive slums," A. B. Wyitt told them. "What nonsense! How many of you have really driven around your immense city, how many ever bother to leave your comfortable neighborhoods? You have slums everywhere. Only the climate has prevented them from becoming quite as dirty and distressing as those to the east. Your kind of disintegration is unique; you have *new* slums, areas which have fallen into disrepair within the space of a decade, through inadequate building codes, lack of planning and venal politicians. Look at Hollywood, Santa Monica, Venice, Hermosa Beach, Lincoln Heights, Boyle Heights, the great reaches south of Olympic Boulevard to the ocean, the dreary compounds in the San Gabriel Valley, the stark and treeless monotony of Orange County tracts which have aged a little, the stinking, explosive jungle that is Watts. You are consistently discriminating against and hedging the opportunities of that substantial part of your population composed of Negroes and Mexicans. So far you have been saved from their organized resentment by mere size and diffusion—nobody can mount a protest or a revolution in so vast and disorganized a place. The confusion and compartmentation and absence of cohesion fogs men's brains. But that won't necessarily last forever."

The professor's voice, which was gradually rising in volume, began to take on organlike notes. He had the quality of the evangelist in him, and his listeners, who were stiffening in a growing hostility and mild shock, nevertheless pricked up their ears at a change toward reasonableness and a call for enlightened action; they were accustomed to such appeals, some of them actually pitiful. Wyitt, harsh but never losing his good-humored air, obviously wanted to help them, however much they had provoked his contempt. He had suggestions. They could perhaps repair their errors and those of their unmentionable predecessors. The hodgepodge of disparate architectural atrocities could be stopped or refined. Urban redevelopment might yet save the atrophied, crumbling plexus of the Queen. A decent social order would cure the sickness of the Mexican and Negro minorities. Planning and severe new laws could blunt the rapacity and destructive instincts of the tract promoters. Ugliness was not an immutable law of nature. Asphalt could give way to the spaciousness of the Lord's own green and pleasant earth. Moloch and his foul breath was not irresistible. The lovely contours of the land did not have to vanish beneath the earthmovers and dump trucks. No Sermon from the Mount compelled the faithful to remove vegetation,

381

allow narrow streets, perch crackerboxes on hills, erect tall glass cubes festooned with aluminum, build miserable miles of identical tiny houses on equally tiny lots, block off every view with billboards and the astral glow of tubular glass signs, smother the central organism of a living city by splattering dismal replicas of it in miniature for a hundred miles. They were not bound by oath to prevent man from standing upright and having natural space for breathing and recruiting his soul. Nor had God enjoined against parks and healing profusion of nature. Sour water, littered sands and thick air weren't inevitable. The Queen was capable of reformation. She had risen repeatedly on her ephemeral ruins. It was still possible to make her the prototype of an incalculable new world.

"You are the influentials here," Wyitt said, "the people who should accomplish this. You could substitute grace and abundance and simplicity for disorder and an appalling, tasteless modernity. It's in your hands. But you have to take a stand against greed and ignorance and eyes that cannot see and minds that cannot understand the good of the multitude is the good of the individual. In terms of historical time, you have about five minutes. This is your last chance, and I advise you to apply yourselves right now to distinguishing between healthy growth and the unchecked spread of a civic carcinoma called megalopolis . . . Thank you for listening courteously to somebody who has nothing but contempt for most of the manifestations of your chosen abode."

The applause he received was scarcely shattering. Madam President did not bother to thank him, and declared the meeting at an end. Chairs scraped, voices made a babel, and LAL adherents headed for the exit.

"Shall we go up and kiss Caddy's ring and ask for her blessing," Junior asked, "or simply beat it?"

"Neither. Let's talk to the professor."

"Good heavens! Why?"

"I have an idea," Garnet said.

A. B. Wyitt was a hard man to lay by the heels. He was making his escape at good speed, in crabwise, scuttling motions, head lowered to avoid being recognized, when Garnet overtook him by dint of trotting and leaving behind the annoyed Junior. She had to grip his sleeve to bring him to a full stop, and he turned to her reluctantly and said, "No rebuttals, if you please, madam. You have your views and I have mine, and I don't blame you in the least for being a loyal citizen of this abortion. Let me go in peace."

"You sound excited," Garnet told him smilingly. "Why? I'm not here to defend Los Angeles—I just want to talk to you."

"Believe me, our talk would get around to rejoinders to some of my unpleasant remarks. I've been through these things before, madam."

"I'm not 'madam,' Professor. Mademoiselle, rather. It's an honest mistake, often made—but it seems to bother me. I'm Garnet Brennan."

His eyebrows lifted. "You pronounce your name with certain stateliness, Miss Brennan. Am I supposed to genuflect or something? I haven't the least idea who you are."

"That doesn't matter," Garnet said cheerfully. "You'll soon find out unless you bolt again." Junior came up, still in a bad mood, and eyed the professor coldly. "Professor Wyitt, may I present my friend, Miss Annice Christopher, Junior?"

"There's a name I seem to recognize," said Wyitt. "Perhaps I've read it somewhere. Are you connected with education, Miss Christopher, Junior?"

"Sex education, you might say," Junior replied. "For many years I was a member of the white slave syndicate in Buenos Aires. I am a celebrated madam, but not like Madam Cadwalladar."

"All the more credit to you, Madam. And is this young lady one of your girls?"

"Yes."

"No," Garnet said. "She's putting you on, professor. I—"

He snapped his fingers. "Now I remember. Unfortunately, I remember nearly everything. Miss Christopher was a famous interior decorator and arbiter of public taste and is presently an ornament of your dilapidated society."

"He's the same off the platform as on," Junior commented; but Garnet could see that she was pleased at Wyitt's recognition of her.

"Will you come in the cocktail lounge or coffee shop with us for a few minutes?" Garnet asked. "What I have to say might be of interest to you . . . A drink or coffee?"

Wyitt hesitated. "Coffee."

They went down in the coffee shop, which was below street level, and sat in a booth. The waitress brought coffee. Junior, who never had to concern herself about her weight, ordered a chocolate sundae to supplement LAL's spartan dessert. Wyitt gazed inquiringly at Garnet.

His mere inspection of her introduced a mild confusion in her mind. She was surprised. That he could exercise any kind of influence on her, especially on such short notice, was unaccountable. She did not think him impressive physically, his mental attainments were largely unknown to her, and certainly his manner was not ravishing. She put down the uncertainty to her present flightiness. The caprices and the mood were not entirely unwelcome to her. There were times, as with any other woman, when being unpredictable even to herself, and wholly feminine, was both satisfying and a safety valve.

To cover the brief lapse, she mentioned his speech. Somehow she managed to praise it without really intending to. Much of what he had said was true, she admitted. Many of his strictures were well-taken. No one could deny that he impressed with the vigor of his convictions. At that, Junior bristled; she said, between spoonfuls of ice cream and thick chocolate sauce, that the good professor was intemperate in his language and biased in the presentation of his material. It was always easier to criticize than to be constructive, and the last part of his rambling address had struck her as weak, inconclusive and hopelessly idealistic.

A. B. Wyitt shifted his attention to Junior, and Garnet felt a pang of disappointment. She was astounded. "You're right, naturally, Miss Christopher—" he began.

"Call me Junior," Junior interrupted. "If we're going to engage in an altercation, let's not slow it up by the use of ponderous honorifics."

"Agreed. I'm A.B. You are correct, Junior. My ending was windy and vague. But I have to deal in generalities like all politicians and teachers. Nobody will sit still for specific suggestions—that means work, worry and the necessity for immediate action. People want to hear sweeping charges and idealism from the lecture platform or the schoolmaster's desk, not compromise and simple, expedient programs. Of course my language is intemperate. I have to capture the attention of idiots. I resemble one of those itinerant preachers in the rural districts of the last century going around predicting the imminence of hellfire and brimstone. Any fat, satiated segment of a reasonably successful society enjoys being scared a little, and titillated to an endurable extent. It quiets their consciences and gives them a feeling of virtue at confronting alleged facts. And anyhow, they know, from their instincts and the lessons of history, that what they're enjoying on an alien planet is too good to be true and can't last long. They can only hope it won't be as bad as their paid lecturers and would-be reformers make out."

"Then you are about as sincere," Junior said, "as any other of the fakers."

"Oh, I have my moments, Junior. In various small instances I have stood on the side of the angels. Not your angels, I hasten to say. But I've never been put to the ultimate test. I have to collect my fees, and the entire affair gives me the idea that it's a prolonged joke. I suppose if confronted with martyrdom or substantial amounts of money, I would sign up with the embattled bourgeoisie."

"I like you. You're a nonhero, and very modern."

384

"I thought you didn't want to hear rebuttals, Professor," Garnet said, a shade irritably.

Wyitt smiled at Junior. "I'm a neo-existentialist. And I'm mobile. What's more, I enjoy myself in a disenchanted way."

"Bravo. How old are you? You must be older than you appear to have acquired common sense and disinterested dishonesty."

"I'm thirty-two. I think my lost innocence gives me a youthful look of innocence. I have a master's and a doctorate, neither from the best possible schools. I am a professional scholar, Junior—which means I have an excellent memory and a talent for picking off scholarships and grants from well-meaning foundations. If I had a taste for the physical sciences, I could probably have attained prominence by now in enlarging the destructive power of nuclear weapons or in strapping hapless astronauts into metal casings and sending them to the upper airless reaches."

"Yes, I remember your introduction to us, A.B. You're in social dynamics and scrapping old cities. Is it a good racket?"

"Not bad. I fell into that line of work by accident, though. My doctoral thesis was built around a jazzy title which I borrowed from somebody else—'The Shame of Our Cities.' Gathering the material gave me an aggravated case of ennui, and besides I was pressed for time. As a result, I didn't bother to write my paper in the standard academic jargon, and I went on so long and so easily that it was a book. I was bowled over by the enthusiasm it aroused—possibly because it was as easy to read and understand as Mother Goose. With a modicum of editing, it was published as a commercial item and sold well. This established me as an expert in a not-too-crowded field. But once was enough. I decided I would rather perish than publish. I don't enjoy being alone in my work, or having to push a pencil hour after hour."

"I thought—" Garnet started to say.

"I wish you wouldn't interrupt us, dear," Junior said. "He's fascinating. We can get to the bottom of this if he keeps on being responsive."

Wyitt didn't even bother to glance in Garnet's direction. "I'm at your disposal, Junior. Older women, I've found, are the only solution. But I must admit that ten years ago I would have hooted at the French conclusion to that effect, despite their having devoted centuries of enthusiasm and study to the subject."

"I'm twenty-six years old," Garnet said. She was ignored.

"I'm curious about the half-college old Caddy mentioned you'd been with," Junior said. "The one with the peculiar name. What induced a man with your resources to join some state institution set out, no doubt, next to a freeway, and probably dedicated to teaching life adjustment, defensive driving and dramatic arts?"

"Oh, that. Laguna Seca, you mean. It's in Orange County, and is named after a dry lake. It is a dry lake, intellectually and politically—very arid. However, I liked the young people. Some of them were active and nonconformist for a while, until the smog saturated them. I had a sense of destiny before a couple of accidents befell me. Also, I discovered most of my students could not spell or write English. Then a kind of sourness puckered me up."

"You haven't answered my question, A.B."

"I haven't, have I?" Wyitt said. "Well, I spent most of the first part of my life taking notes in classrooms, pontificating in seminars, and delving through stacks of books. Probably you aren't too familiar with the times, Junior; you may have lost touch. This is an era of woe and worry, real and imagined. Many men would like to turn their backs on it. Some embrace conservative politics and invoke the good old days and forget, and others enter the groves of Academe. I was one of the latter. If you don't quite understand, try to remember the Middle Ages."

"I resent that."

"I meant your recollections of what you've read. That was also a period of woe and worry. The brighter and more careful sort in those days went into monasteries and reduced the Latin tongue to ruins. It was better than staying outside and being picked off by the Black Death or by the men-at-arms of the local baron. Today there's the White Death, nuclear variety, forever impending, and the horrors of commuting. The analogy is fairly secure. Things change you know, but the more they change—and so forth. Men are still shrinking from the unutterable. So I managed to spend years hiding in a scholar's gown. You'd be surprised how easy it is to earn a modest living leaping from grant to grant. I can recommend the career to young fellows with good memories and eyesight, who don't aspire to riches . . . Where was I?"

"Nowhere," Junior said. "Get to Laguna Seca."

"Oh," Wyitt said. "I was out at the Huntington Museum in San Marino researching something—I'll remember what it was in a minute—wait a minute, it was for a monograph on Ambroise Paré, the father of modern surgery—I was doing the spadework for a colleague at U.C.L.A. who had to publish or else. Paré has always been a hobby of mine. You see, when you're in the scholastic dodge, you can pick up a good many odd jobs of the kind. I—"

"Come, come, A.B."

"I was getting to the point, I assure you. The fact is, I met a girl. I wanted to marry her. To do so, I had to stop being a mere student. I needed an honest, tangible job. Perfect bliss was worth a sacrifice, but I wasn't going to lose my head—I was willing to teach, and that was as

386

far as I intended to go. My doctoral thesis helped. Laguna Seca took me on, promising tenure, a challenge, an opportunity to mould humanity —God knows what else. I was almost pleased for a year."

"Did you marry the girl?" Garnet asked.

Wyitt gave her a brief, hard look. "Certainly. Why else would I end up in Orange County?"

Garnet's heart sank. She was disgusted and confused by herself. In spite of that, she blurted, "Then you're married?"

"Everybody is married," he said. "And *was* married. I'm a was. The former Mrs. A. B. Wyitt just secured a Mexican divorce in Juárez. I'm happy to say there are some doubts of its legality."

As she began automatically to smile, Garnet detected Junior watching her. She stifled a sigh that could only have been one of relief. She composed her expression. For a moment she thought she might come to hate her oldest and best friend.

"I'd like to hear more," Junior said.

"So would I," Garnet added.

"You've heard enough," Wyitt told them. "I can't imagine why I've talked as much as I have—it must be the phony air of sympathy Junior manages to exude, and because she seems old and wise. Does every interior decorator have that pose of breathless interest and solicitude?"

"If he or she or it doesn't," Junior said, "they don't stay in business long. It's a form of therapy for the client."

"You're the only person in months who has disapproved of me in a heartening way," Wyitt said.

"You amuse me," Junior said. "Practically nobody does anymore. That may be because I've met almost everybody . . . Let's see. You and Laguna Seca parted. Probably you're paying alimony. You have no visible means of support. How do you earn a living?"

"I bone up quickly on cities," Wyitt said, "if the lecture bureau tells me I might be invited to speak, and then insult them in lectures. I'm an expert, you'll recall. Occasionally I write a short article on social dynamics or overurbanization or redevelopment for obscure magazines and newspapers. For a while I considered setting up as a consultant for civic bodies, architects and tract promoters. This is an age of consultation—even the doctors and lawyers contrive mob scenes. My alimony payments are very low and I'm behind in them, and still I haven't been brought into court. I think Miss Calvert—that's her name again— simply wants to forget me. She has a good job and lives at home in San Francisco, and I believe she has lost some of her greediness. Then, too, she has a tremendous new feeling of obligation toward me. She claims to have saved my life. You know how binding a tie of that kind is."

"How did that happen?" Junior wanted to know.

"After we were divorced," Wyitt explained, "I was going to deliver a lecture in San Francisco, the proceeds to go to my ex-wife. Everybody pretends to admire the city, perhaps for the reason that it was once rather attractive—fifty years ago. My remarks were in my usual style, and I sent a tape in advance to Dorothy—Miss Calvert—I had dictated to a recording machine. She got on the phone at once and begged me either to modify my speech drastically or withdraw from the engagement. She told me San Francisco, unlike Los Angeles, which is too busy raping and burning to really listen to critics, has a virulent strain of chauvinism running through the inhabitants and falls into a rage at the slightest note of depreciation. According to her, I would be mobbed long before I had finished. She said she might lead the mob, from force of habit. I withdrew, more from cowardice than distaste for embarrassing her and her friends and family. Besides, I was impressed by her willingness to forego her share of the lecture fee. Do you feel Dorothy actually saved my life? The chance that she might have haunts me. I'd prefer to die."

"No," Garnet said. She refused to entertain any good opinions of Mrs. A. B. Wyitt, née Dorothy Calvert.

"No," Junior agreed. "They allow people to jump off their tiresome bridges in San Francisco, but they don't lynch them. I've lived there."

"I'm going," Wyitt said, and signaled the waitress. "You've been wonderful to me, and you're both terribly nosy. I have not been this truthful and indiscreet in years. It may do something for my awful maladjustments."

"Just a moment," Junior said. "You can't leave us dangling. Why did you give up the idea of becoming a consultant? That sounds profitable."

Wyitt watched Garnet pay the check. "I was hoping you'd take care of it, Miss Brennan . . . What did you say, Junior?"

"The consultant thing. Why not?"

"Oh, yes. You are entitled to one last answer. I had a better idea—I think I'll join the Peace Corps. Those emerging, murdering, chaotic African nations are calling to me. I'd like to go to Burundi, for instance. Do you happen to know the name of the capital?"

Junior shook her head, hiding a smile.

"Bujumbura," Wyitt said. "The ruler is Mwami Mwambutsa the Fourth. I have a hunch we would get along while I was building his roads or laying out a new royal latrine. And Rwanda is just next door. That's where the Watusi tribesmen come from. I'm tired of having disapproving black faces around me here. I'd rather be segregated myself.

If it gets too sticky, I intend to complain to the premier, Pierre Ngendandumwe . . . I may be a bit shaky on those pronunciations, and don't ask me to spell anything—but give me a week in Bujumbura and I'll be talking like a native and walking barefooted. I'm very adaptable."

"And pretty devious," Junior said.

"Goodbye, dear friends," Wyitt said.

"Don't you remember?" Garnet said. "When we met, I mentioned I might have something of interest to say to you."

"I'd forgotten. Try to be brief, Miss Brennan."

Garnet found she was strangely ill at ease. Junior stared at her, expectant and curious, and Wyitt seemed to give her no more than half his attention. "Well," she said, rather hurrying, and angered by her desire to please, "we have a ranch out in the San Fernando Valley—the San Cristobal—sixteen thousand acres, less the acreage which has been used for a freeway and other roads. It is a Spanish land grant belonging to my family, and was used in the early days for cattle raising and agriculture, although deficient in water. Then my great-grandfather struck oil and there were several producing fields for a long time. The oil is exhausted now, and the ranch has sort of gone to pot. None of us have been sufficiently interested in it, I suppose. But the land, while too hilly in places, is ripe for development. There is plenty of water from the Metropolitan Water District. It is the last large, untouched entity in the valley. My father has been stubborn about parting with it, but taxes and public pressure are forcing his hand."

"Why has your father been reluctant to sell it off?" Wyitt asked. "I should think a parcel like that—"

"Sentiment. The San Cristobal has belonged to us since the eighteenth century. Of course, it was once much larger."

"You don't feel the pull of sentiment, Miss Brennan?"

"I'm not sentimental. Neither are his business associates. We have all urged my father for the last ten years to open the area to development."

"You said you were twenty-six, I believe . . . At sixteen you were thinking of how the land could be used profitably?"

"I don't see why that enters into this, but I was. I have a practical turn of mind, Professor. Since the oil reserves played out, the San Cristobal hasn't earned its keep. The tax losses were useful up to a point, in our income bracket, but we are having trouble with the Internal Revenue Service. Their argument is that we're using the ranch as a device for the avoidance of taxes. Our attorneys think we'll lose before the tax commission, and eventually in court—with charges and penalties added."

"I see . . ." Wyitt said. "Where do I come into this?"

"Discounting your facetiousness about your knowledge and integrity, I thought you might try to make a good impression on my father and help him to come to a decision. How to utilize the ranch requires expert planning. With a sensible blueprint for action he could understand, he might really generate some enthusiasm. Perhaps you could take charge of the project. Wouldn't that interest you?"

"Why should it? If he's only going to sell it to the common run of developers—"

"No, no," Garnet said. "You don't understand. I think we should capitalize on the holding ourselves, and I want my father brought around to that view."

"Ah. What would you say the ranch represents in outlay or total value?"

"Better than fifty million dollars, I'd estimate."

"Hummmmm," Wyitt said, and his eyes widened. "I don't suppose you'd have any difficulty with the financing?"

"Not with my father interested and convinced. We would supply the underwriting ourselves. You see, this needs an aura of importance, dignity, necessity and civic virtue, both for my father and the appropriate authorities—we'll have to soften up the planning commissions, the Board of Supervisors, the City Council—I don't know who all. Perhaps we will need enabling ordinances and that sort of hanky-panky. It seems to me you might add an atmosphere of authority and respectability to the project."

Junior was beaming at Garnet, and nodding; in her approval was mixed a good deal of relief. She had plainly dreaded some kind of unhandy coup on Garnet's part, or worse in view of their recent conversation, and to learn this interview was nothing more than a business gesture was heartening. She had always sided with Hal Baltim, Harry and Tom Sego, and the others in advocating that the San Cristobal be converted to a paying proposition. Even Lagonda Washington had come over to their side, and in the beginning she had supported Chambers Brennan in his illogical refusal to allow a single foot's encroachment on the ranch borders.

"I must say you surprise me a bit, Miss Brennan," Wyitt said. "You struck me as plain and energetic, but hardly as a well-dressed tycoon. I—"

"You're not very complimentary, you know."

"I hadn't intended to be."

"Well," Garnet said, "I'm going to overlook your childish animus on the reasonable assumption that there is more here than meets the eye in a surface inspection. Do you want to see my father about this?"

"I don't know. Let me think a moment. Burjumbura is calling." Wyitt paused and studied Garnet suspiciously. "Brennan . . . I have an IBM-card index kind of mind, but it takes a little while to query the machine. Is it possible your father is *the* Chambers Brennan?"

Junior seemed to be enjoying Garnet's discomfiture. "Not really," she said. "He's her uncle, but he has adopted her."

"He must be a dreadful man," Wyitt said, "from what I've read and heard. Quite mad, isn't he?"

"Come on, Junior," Garnet said, and got up. "The discussion is over."

A. B. Wyitt sat calmly as she gathered her purse and gloves. Appearing reluctant to part from him, Junior eased slowly from the booth. "I'll tell you what, Miss Brennan," Wyitt said. "Put it down to mere curiosity. Let me meet him. Then I can decide. When shall I come?"

There was a pause. Garnet fumbled the gloves, and dropped one; Wyitt made no effort to retrieve it, and she had to stoop and get it herself. She straightened, a flush coming to her cheeks. "Tonight," she said slowly. "After dinner. It's the Xanadu, on Wilshire Boulevard. I'll prepare him for your particular brand of insolence. But I can't prepare you for him . . ."

As she had anticipated, he did not ask for a time or bother to say goodbye. He did, however, grin at Junior and blow her a kiss from the tips of his fingers. Garnet walked quickly, outdistancing Junior, and proceeded to compose herself. She rarely permitted anger to dominate her for long. Indeed, she was nearly immune to effrontery from her inferiors. And she had no superiors—Chambers Brennan had taken care of that. It was only that A. B. Wyitt had a knack for rubbing her the wrong way.

When Junior caught up, Garnet was at ease again and smiling. They strolled through the lobby, looking in a couple of shops. Junior suggested they go to Bullock's-Wilshire for some shopping. "All right," Garnet agreed. "I have a four o'clock appointment with the dentist in Beverly Hills. We can spare a few minutes."

"Speaking of dentists," Junior said, "and how they contrive to touch nerves, does the professor grate on you? And if so, why do you insist on feeding him to our domestic lion?"

"Oh, he's interesting."

"Ah? How?"

"He's a fraud. He knew who I was all the time. That's the oldest trick in the world, playing hard to get and trumpeting his independence. Men have tried that with me, off and on, for the last ten years. Aren't they immature, though?"

Junior shrugged. "Sometimes. But what are you getting to, love?"

"I'm curious to see how he'll react when I scalp him."

"Oh."

At the motor entrance, the doorman hastened to conduct them to the station wagon, which had not been put in the parking lot with the other cars but kept up front a few feet beyond the doors. Garnet tipped him and settled behind the wheel.

"Anyhow," Junior said, "this is no girlish fixation or iron whim, is it? Wyitt won't do, eh? I must admit to a feeling of relief. After that strange talk of yours about the law of probabilities and picking a consort at random, I was a trifle upset by your pursuit of the professor—especially when he took a shine to me and seemed briefly negotiable."

"He did not take a shine to you! That's part of his act."

"Certainly, dear. Well, he won't wash, as I mentioned. Now we must look further, perhaps in Larry's direction—"

"Not necessarily," Garnet said. "If he checks out in an investigation, I just might break, saddle and ride him. He has a slightly different approach. I find him refreshing, and it shouldn't be too easy, should it? These things have to be done methodically."

"Oh, dear!" Junior said.

Nine o'clock that evening came and went, and no A. B. Wyitt. Garnet started to simmer. Not that she looked forward to anything in particular, or cared greatly—but she would have burned at the insult of being stood up.

But, as she had thought, the professor wasn't that small-minded. At nearly ten o'clock he came up in the separate automatic elevator, located in an offset to the foyer, which served the penthouse in the Xanadu. By then, before he settled down to a night of television broken by reading scraps of books and magazines during the commercials, Garnet had talked to her father, apprising him of the guest. Chambers Brennan showed faint interest merely because visitors were rare and this one had a connection with the annoying question of what to do with the San Cristobal. Garnet often suspected that the neurotic seclusion he had imposed upon himself—except for a few close friends and business associates and a shifting corps of doctors—was an attempt to evade a responsibility that was becoming a bore, and that he secretly longed for some kind of escape, any kind. Unhappily, it was too late—habit, insecurity, ill health and comfort had enchained him and he never would find a means of escaping the prison. As long as he had her, Lagonda,

Junior and Albert, he would not change. Yet he couldn't afford, with his plans for the family, to keep Garnet indefinitely.

"Who's this?" he asked, when her quick explanation was finished. "A college professor? Why should I talk to him?"

"An ex-professor," she replied. "A lecturer now. He's an expert on urban planning. I felt—"

"The hell with him. We'll reach a decision about the ranch one day. We don't need any help."

"Nevertheless, Father—"

"Tom Sego has taken care of it, if we ever decide to move. I don't like your pushing me, and experts make my ass ache—"

"There's the language barrier again."

He grunted, and accepted her kiss on the cheek. "I'm sorry. Lately I've been backsliding at being a gentleman. I'll have to discuss that with Dr. Rommer . . . Why don't you bring home a man I could consider your marrying?"

"Junior told me of your discussion last night. I'm getting around to that."

"You're not angry at my interfering?"

"No, of course not," Garnet said.

"I don't much like Smith, but he's better than nothing. He—"

"Neither do I. Take a good look at this Wyitt and tell me what you think. Then I'll explain my theory."

"Huh?" Chambers said, and concentrated on her. "I thought you told me you just met him today and—"

"That doesn't matter. See if he passes muster."

"Well!" Chambers grew more cheerful; the unexpected and unconventional always excited his support and interest. "Now you've got me on the hook. I'll look forward to it. Where is he?"

"Coming," said Garnet, with an air of confidence she didn't entirely feel.

In due course the professor did arrive, and she answered the door herself. He was in the same clothing as at the LAL meeting, and a little bedraggled. Her slight involuntary frown did not escape him. "Sorry I couldn't go home to change, Miss Brennan," he said. "It's too far to Orange County. I came out here to U.C.L.A., picked up a colleague, and we dined at a pizza parlor. He filled me in on the Brennans."

"I don't mind your appearance if you don't," she said, "and I must know your colleague."

"You do. He's Dr. Fred Dirovac, of the history department."

"Oh, yes. We hired him and his bright young men to collect our papers and prepare the official family history when my father gave the city the

Brennan Memorial Library." Garnet paused, and added, "I hope Dr. Dirovac's report was favorable."

"Objective would be the word, I think."

She took him in the living room, and it pleased her to see him react to the extent and the sober grandeur with which Junior had invested the place; beyond the unbroken array of ceiling-to-floor glass walls was the terrace, the garden, the marble swimming pool and adjoining hot mineral bath, the steam room, and hints of the outspread city in the murk below. He sat down at her gesture, and she asked if she could get him anything. The scene reminded her of when she had welcomed promising (only they always failed to turn out to be promising) youths at her sorority house in the school years. Then a little pang of uneasiness and haste intruded; that had been so long ago!

"No, thank you," he said.

"Do you normally drink much, Professor?"

Wyitt shook his head. "I've never cared for the taste of the stuff, and the relief it affords is temporary."

"You smoke, I suppose?"

"I had a pipe at one time, to give me an academic look. But the residues that formed in the thing made me sick."

"I presume you have some favorite sports and hobbies?" Garnet said.

"Possibly, but I have no intention of confiding in you again. Would you mind telling me the object of this interrogation? Is it part of a briefing for the encounter with Chambers Brennan, or am I filling out a verbal employment questionnaire?"

"You mustn't be huffy, my friend. Or too much on the defensive."

He smiled sadly. "These evidences of great wealth are pretty overpowering. What other reaction could you expect from a poor scholar? Take me to your leader before I crack."

"I want you to myself for a moment," she said. "We had no opportunity to talk at the hotel. And stop that smart-alecky sarcasm! I might slap you."

"Oh . . . I beg your pardon. I thought you were far too self-contained to exhibit emotion. By the way, where is Junior? I like her."

"She spent the whole of yesterday evening with my father and is away for rest and rehabilitation tonight—dining with gilded friends in Bel Air. She was terribly curious, though, about your visit."

"Tell her I missed her."

"I shall . . . I take it Dr. Dirovac's estimate of us was not flattering."

"Well," A. B. Wyitt said, "he sounded factual. His impression of your father was that of an outright financial genius afflicted with traumatic neuroses and a family circle which defied description. He felt you were cold, contained and unfeminine. The Brennan Memorial Library struck him as useful with its collections of Californiana and Western Americana, but the building housing it in a Graeco-Roman style by your father's pet architect appalling. I must go there sometime."

"It has the finest collection of Frederic Remington paintings extant provided by my father."

"Dirovac forgot to mention that. Anyhow, cowboys and Indians, and even the appreciation of representational painters, are out of my line. The library was, I believe, erected on the site of your grandfather's house?"

"Great-uncle."

"That would be Colonel Lucius Brennan?"

"Yes."

Wyitt put fingers to his forehead and rubbed gently. "Let me consult my control center . . . The colonel was the notorious opponent of union labor and a highbinder in early-day real estate. His nephew was a labor-baiter, too. He lived to a ripe old age, didn't he?"

"That's right."

"And his brother was Cassius Brennan, who was murdered during the Civil War. He acquired the Rancho de San Cristobal through marriage with a Villanueva."

"Yes," Garnet said. "I have to confess I have not taken a great deal of interest in the family history, and no doubt Dr. Dirovac is better informed than I. As I remember, Great-grandfather Cassius was assassinated by Confederate sympathizers—he took the side of the North in the war."

"Forgive me. He was shot while in the bed of a woman of the town by another of her lovers. Dirovac told me you suppressed portions of the family history in the privately printed book issued upon the establishment of the library. And he said it was you who did the editing, not Chambers Brennan or good old Junior."

Garnet flushed. "The book was sponsored by the Golden Pioneers and had to conform to conventional views. I had no choice. My father took the eccentric position that the truth was more amusing than a discreet version, but the rest of us had to overrule him. Naturally, the burden of changing his mind and deleting Dr. Dirovac's more unpleasant researches fell on me."

"Incidentally, what got you started in this form of ancestor worship? Was it an offshoot of the library?"

"Yes, I suppose so. And pride in the accomplishments of several extraordinary men and women—for instance, my grandmother was probably the first woman doctor here—and the necessity of a record of

395

their contributions to Los Angeles. My great-grandmother on the Villanueva side, Maria was her name, married to Cassius Brennan, must have been an exceptional person. In spite of war and hard times, she preserved the ranch for her descendants. My grandfather Cass Brennan fought the anarchists and died as a result of their bombing his house. My real father, Dugald Stuart, revolutionized air transport with the design of his first commercial airplane, and my mother, Priscilla Brennan, was a superb flyer and helped him in his work. They were killed when I was still an infant, while flying together in Mexico . . . That will give you an idea."

"It gives me several ideas," Wyitt said. "One of them is that you don't suppose anything of the kind. And you are very well-versed in the family history, embarrassingly so, since your father—or uncle, I should say; this is magnificently confusing—insisted on turning over all records to Dr. Dirovac and giving him carte blanche. I suppose you had no conception in the beginning of what a trained researcher would uncover, or that Chambers Brennan's obsession with his ancestors and belief that they were the chosen people was more than a harmless mania that could be safely encouraged. Is it true the library sprang from the mere circumstance that Chambers Brennan had commissioned a statue of the Brothers Brennan from the Finnish sculptor Eino Nurri and the city wouldn't accept it and he had nowhere else to put it?"

"No!"

"Yes. Unquestionably. Dear Miss Brennan, take heart. Your people are no better and no worse, if more successful, than those in other families. It's just that the Brennans had the money and position to pursue the matter to the end and make the results public. I sympathize with your desire to keep the worst aspects unrevealed."

"Dr. Dirovac," Garnet said, "would be well-advised to keep his revelations to himself."

"And by the same token, so would I, eh? I told you he was an old friend—we cribbed from each other in examinations. This won't go any farther. Miss Brennan, was Dirovac correct in his belief that the famous Colonel Brennan was guilty of somewhat intimate relations with his brother Cassius's wife after Cassius's death and the second Cassius, that noted reactionary and money-grubber, was really the colonel's son instead of nephew? Is there actually evidence in the family correspondence that the woman doctor, your grandmother, was Sapphic in taste? You've got to forgive Dirovac. He lives an exemplary bachelor life and gets his vicarious kicks from dealing with the sins and errors of the dead. The taste for gossip-mongering comes automatically to professional historians."

"Come see my father, Professor. You won't last long, and I'm sorry to have put you to this trouble."

"I'm afraid not," Wyitt murmured, "but I am glad to have been of service to you. Isn't everybody, Miss Brennan?"

Chambers Brennan was in the game room, which Junior had fitted especially for his comfort and convenience; he spent the greater part of his waking hours there, and received guests or associates in it or in his bedroom. It had paneled walls of light wood, deep-pile maroon carpets, draperies in the same color, a broad desk, chairs in morocco leather, two maroon telephones, bookshelves to the ceiling on three walls, a pocket billiard table, a built-in stereophonic record player, and a horizontal bank of five television sets so that Chambers, if he was of a mind, could watch all the principal stations and broadcasting nets simultaneously. The fourth wall was composed of glass and afforded a view of the swimming pool and city; arranged along it were a variety of potted plants which gave the effect of a small solarium; there were no curtains and the transparent wall had a rose tint which was evident even at night.

Only one television tube was in operation, and Chambers was paying it small attention. He seemed to be deep in conversation with a white-haired Negro woman seated beside him, clad in a neat black dress and wearing a matched set of natural pearls just a little smaller than robins' eggs. Arising at the entrance of Garnet and Wyitt, Chambers cut off the television from a remote control and came to meet them. As he did, Lagonda got up and brightened the dim lights from a rheostatic switch on the wall.

Garnet assumed that Dr. Dirovac (whom she remembered contemptuously as a small, precise, nit-picking sort, both defiant of and impressed by the Brennan wealth and inclined to grovel) had fully prepared Wyitt for her father as well as regaling him with the more unsavory episodes in the family history. Yet she tried to regard Chambers as a total stranger would, as Wyitt would, fortified by Dirovac's impertinences and the general rumors which had long circulated about him. At fifty-five years of age, Chambers resembled the photographs and a portrait or two of his alleged grandfather in the latter's older days. He was thin now, which emphasized his height, and a trifle bent; loose flesh made creases and folds on his cheeks, and his eyes, red and tired from overuse, were full of a melancholy that served to dull the irascibility and malice that often animated them; his hair, kept very short by a barber who came to the penthouse once a week, stood almost erect and was thinning and nearly white, and he wore bifocal glasses with thick black rims and heavy bows. As usual, he was attired in a sports jacket, a white shirt open at the neck, and wrinkled slacks; slippers enveloped his sockless feet. Staring at him in this new fashion, Garnet experienced a sudden, painful, heart-wrenching illumination: he looked sad and ill and lost, and infinitely wearied. She thought him a nuisance and a monument, a familiar problem and something of a disgrace, her servant and impost and perhaps a joke—and he was none of these things, wholly, but the strangest and most desolate of men, as different from and superior to the common run of his kind as a man could be, the inmate of a prison he had invented himself, the victim of a discipline whose origins she could not even imagine. She loved him and owed him an unpayable debt, and he needed her.

She stepped forward abruptly and kissed him on the nose, a gesture of affection that always moved him to an inordinate degree, and he showed surprise. She said, "This is Professor Wyitt, Father. I've explained my purpose in bringing him here. I hope you'll find him interesting."

"Hello," Chambers said, and made no effort to shake hands. "Meet Mrs. Lagonda Washington, my best friend."

He watched as Wyitt smiled and took Lagonda's hand. How she was received by strangers often determined how long they lasted in his presence. Wyitt passed the test with ease. There was no self-consciousness or condescension in his acceptance of the old black woman. Lagonda asked if she could serve him coffee or a drink, received his declination and thanks, and started to excuse herself.

"No, you stay," Chambers ordered. "You ought to hear what we have to say. Sit down, everybody."

Taking a chair across from the desk, behind which Chambers ensconced himself as though to preside at a meeting, Wyitt sat and waited. On his face was a tinge of confusion. Her father conveyed a peculiar, unexpected air of dignity and weight that might easily enough be ascribed to his millions and the enigma of his seclusion, but she felt rather it was the worn, tired, unhappy mask he showed to the world, a mask that suggested he had experienced everything and understood the mortal predicament of everyone and could tell what he had learned when he chose.

"We have a regular routine to go through, Wyitt," he said. "Let's get rid of the spinach. Dismissing me is the first order of business. That's because I once made a lot of money and fooled a lot of people. I'm supposed to be nuts, but maybe fascinating and worth cultivating. How do I strike you? As a sound proposition or as a crackpot? You can say what you think. I don't mind."

Wyitt had no reply. A silence lengthened. Feeling pleased, Garnet sat on a couch beside Lagonda, who took her hand and absently caressed it. Garnet's earliest memories were of Lagonda. She had raised the new

398

white child with the same devotion and expertise as she had the previous generation. Her affection had been as freely and deeply given to the newcomer as to Chambers and his sister. The bonds of devotion between her and Garnet were just as strong as they were with Chambers. She was immortal and undeviating. Unfortunately, her husband, Ferris Washington, Junior, was not. Some months past, after a lifetime of lackadaisical and uncomplaining servitude to the Brennans, he had without warning or explanation defected. At present he was reported to be in the black belt off Western Avenue at an address known only to his son Albert, living with a woman half his age and drinking and carousing. This had caused Lagonda much pain, put Chambers in a rage for weeks, and given Albert Cassius Washington a divided allegiance that appeared to amuse him. Moderately strained relations still existed between Chambers and Albert because of his attitude, and Lagonda, torn by mingled loyalties, went frequently to her room to weep. Garnet herself sided openly with the errant Ferris, who had been slighted and put upon for years: to the contrary, Junior accepted the cause of the wronged Lagonda and spoke eloquently in her behalf. It was a mess, and the sensation of her father's hectic premature aging.

"I want you to take your time, Wyitt," Chambers said, "but we haven't got all night."

"I don't know what to say, sir. My mind was made up when I came in. Now I'm not so sure. I'd talked to Dr. Dirovac—"

"That pissy little bastard! You can do better than him. He couldn't find his ass with both hands and a flashlight."

"Chambers," Lagonda said, "you got to stop that kind of talk. I don't want to have to say it again. Your daughter is sitting right here listening. Hear me?"

"I hear you," Chambers said. "Excuse me . . . Listen, Wyitt. Reserve judgment. Tell me about yourself."

Speaking very quietly, Wyitt gave the same details to Chambers that he had to Garnet and Junior; but Garnet noted that this time he employed no irony and left out mention of the Peace Corps. Both Lagonda and Chambers frowned when he said he had been married and divorced, which obviously puzzled Wyitt.

"What happened?" Chambers demanded. "Why couldn't you stay married?"

"Oh, there were a lot of factors. We didn't have a community of interests. I made some social gestures my wife regarded as errors. Just put it down to a lack of harmony between us . . ."

"It's never that simple, Wyitt. You didn't have any children, eh? Why?"

399

"Well, we were only married about twenty months. We had to consider the question of finances—"

"You didn't try and fail, did you? It wasn't that, was it? And don't immediately tell me she wasn't fertile, either."

Wyitt colored, and Garnet was delighted. She saw his eyes dart to her, widening in abrupt understanding of the line of questioning and exactly why he had been presented to Chambers Brennan. For a split second he was dazed by astonishment, the next instant he looked as though he might break into laughter, and finally he was terribly annoyed—not with her father, but with her. A warmth of pleasure washed through Garnet. He had been paid off in full, whatever happened. Audacity had taught him a lesson. With a little luck, she might swiftly direct him to his proper station in life. "I'm reasonably sure we are both fertile," he said. "Not that I consider it your concern—"

"Uh-huh. How are you in bed? Any trouble getting it up? That bothers wives, you know."

"Chambers," Lagonda said.

"I got to get this over with, don't I?" Chambers said to her. "Do you want me beating around the bush?"

"Yes, I do," Lagonda said. "You beat around the bush after this."

Clearing his throat, Wyitt said, "I don't believe the former Mrs. Wyitt ever complained in that respect, sir. But she did complain about nearly everything else."

"Sometimes they suffer that in silence and then just leave."

"The former Mrs. Wyitt did not suffer anything in silence. I would have heard."

Chambers looked at him intently. "I tell you what I'm going to do, Wyitt. I'm going to take your word for it. I am assuming we are both gentlemen."

"Thank you, sir."

"Maybe I wouldn't qualify for a gentleman in the full sense of the term," Chambers said, "but my word is good."

"So is mine," Wyitt replied, "and I think you are a gentleman in the full sense of the term, Mr. Brennan."

"You can call me Chambers."

"I'm A.B. to my friends."

"What the hell does 'A.B.' stand for? It's unhandy."

"My given names are Albert Bennett—I had an uncle named Albert, and Bennett was my mother's maiden name. I don't like Albert, Bennett seems to be stuffy, and Ben is too folksy. So I'm A.B. I hope you don't mind, Chambers."

Her father gazed at the women, first at Lagonda, of course, and Gar-

400

net was revolted. She knew the significance of that surmising look and the raised, bushy, whitening eyebrows. It was an omen, the sort of random coincidence which had always governed Chambers's actions. And Lagonda, whose influence with him was immense, was sure to be impressed; she abided by such meaningless improbabilities and held them infallible as guides to conduct. If a natural phenomenon followed this—a storm, the resurrection of a missing object, a dream, a striking passage in the astrological pamphlets she consulted—Professor Wyitt would acquire a merit that nothing could erase. Garnet was aware of a sinking feeling; somehow she had set in motion a combination of events that might entrap her. In the presence of Chambers and Lagonda, reason took flight and absurd notions were commonplace.

"I can see you do mind . . ." Wyitt said. "Why?"

"How about that?" Chambers said. "Every once in a while you feel a tap on your shoulder, out of nowhere— Did you know about this, Garnet?"

"No, I didn't," she replied, "and now that I know, I couldn't care less."

"Ha!" her father said. "Lagonda, what do you think?"

Lagonda actually appeared rapt. "It makes you think all right, Chambers."

"Have I any chance of being let in on the secret?" Wyitt asked.

"Pardon me, A.B.," Chambers said. "You certainly have. My name is Albert. I never could stand it. In my young days I was A. Chambers Brennan for a while, and then just Chambers Brennan. And Chambers was my mother's maiden name, as Bennett was your mother's. Why, it all fits."

"It does?" Wyitt said. "Fits what, sir?"

"Well, there's the similarity," Chambers said. "Garnet picks up a young man—"

"I didn't 'pick him up,' " Garnet interjected.

"Sorry. You met a young man. He has the same given name I have, and the same problems with it. And his mother's maiden name—well, you see. The coincidence. It might not happen again with a million people. That means something."

"Probably not," Wyitt replied. "The odds against it happening are of interest if one likes programming computers for silly answers, but I doubt if any other significance can be attached. Still, I'm glad we have a common handicap, Chambers."

"We're going to have more than that, believe me," Chambers told him. "You're a little dense and not playing your luck, but you can be taught. Huh, Lagonda?"

"He don't see," Lagonda said. "That don't matter now. Leave him be."

"Yes, I wish you would . . ." Wyitt said, and stared at both of them.

Garnet shrugged in apology and explanation to him, and simultaneously her rancor stirred; he was poor and unknown and had come to them hat in hand seeking favor—or he should have, if he knew what was good for him—and she didn't intend him to regard her father and his principal adviser as a pair of comic items. They could be amusingly eccentric and impractical, but they were damned well entitled to everybody's respect. "Forgive me for intruding upon the world of ESP and haunted houses," she said, "but Professor Wyitt was brought here for a specific purpose. I'd like to get down to business, and I'm sure he would, too."

"I really don't mind staying in the world of ESP and haunted houses, Miss Brennan," Wyitt said, and smiled. "It has certain fascinations."

"You can dine out later on that," Garnet retorted, "like your garrulous friend, Dr. Dirovac. In the meantime, do what you came for."

Chambers laughed. "She has a temper, A.B. It runs in the Brennans, and you'll have to take it into account. As for me, I'm a joke. I enjoy the joke myself, maybe because it's not really on me but on everybody else. You know what I mean?"

"Yes."

"I think you do. But get the stuff for me, Lagonda, will you? We don't want Garnet freezing up on us. She's good at freezing." He paused for a moment. "You can say anything you care to, A.B. A little destructive criticism never bothered me."

Wyitt winked at him. "Miss Brennan needn't worry. I don't dine out on bad jokes."

"I believe you," Chambers said.

Lagonda opened a cabinet and produced a mass of papers which were in considerable disarray. The arguments concerning the fate of the Rancho de San Cristobal, and Chambers's intransigence regarding it, had been protracted. Long since Harry Sego, acting for the Sunset Sea Corporation, had hired a firm of developmental engineers to prepare a plan for the ranch. Experts in population trends and land values had contributed, and interested banks (including the Los Angeles National Savings Bank and the parent Trans-California Corporation) had submitted reports. Big realty firms were represented with thick folders. The Shapiro clan, again captained by Irving Shapiro, was willing to engage in the project. There were maps, geological surveys, drawings, photographs, aerial and otherwise, reports by city and county functionaries, lengthy typed suggestions from Harold Baltim, Junior and Senior, and Harry Sego and Albert Washington and ancient Burton Lely, who was

402

virtually retired, and even Aaron Eindhoven, president of Amalgamated Aircraft Corporation, and a complete architectural scheme supported by folders of elevations Tom Sego had been commissioned to do.

Sorting through the mess, spread out on the billiard table by Lagonda, Chambers betrayed his boredom and disquiet. His explanations to Wyitt were perfunctory. "This has been going on forever," he added. "It's too complicated. I can only understand simple things and give direct, quick answers. The ranch beats me."

"What you mean is, Father," Garnet said, "that you're a victim of superstition and inertia. May I offer a few pointers to the professor?"

"I'll make do with what Chambers has told me, thank you," Wyitt said. He read and shuffled among the documents, and the annoyed Garnet stood behind him with arms folded across her breast, Lagonda returned to the leather couch and sat down, and Chambers perched in a high chair with broad arms, one of several he had had especially constructed from models of those in the pool halls of bygone days, and took a cue from a convenient rack and sighted along it meditatively. Wyitt took his time in the examination, without comment, and Garnet shifted her feet impatiently.

"I tell you," Chambers said, "I get sick when we go through the stuff—a reflex. Like that Russian's dogs."

"Pavlov," Wyitt said.

"That's right. Do you know everything, A.B.?"

"Nearly everything. At least, I don't forget anything I've been exposed to."

"I think you're the kind of guy I need," Chambers said. "When I've needed a man I've always found him."

Finally, Wyitt was through with the inspection. His expression was noncommittal. "I'd like to take some of the things home with me," he said. "May I?"

"Sure. I'll give you five thousand dollars if you come up with a satisfactory answer for me."

"All right, sir."

"I'll tell you something else, A.B.," Chambers said. "I'm paralyzed on this. Whatever I've done, I was pushed into, and I went out of business twenty-five years ago. My daughter is the one who has to get some action. She's the Brennan now, and all I'm doing is delaying her— for a reason that maybe is not your affair, or maybe might become your affair. I'm just waiting to die and transfer the burden to her. Then she can act as she pleases; I don't want the responsibility. I'm over the hill."

"Oh, hush!" Garnet said. "I don't mind your ducking the issue, but don't resort to self-pity."

"You say what I would say," Lagonda said.

"May I see the ranch with you?" Wyitt asked.

"Not with me," Chambers replied. "Garnet will take you. I don't go anywhere."

"Why, Chambers?"

"Oh, for various reasons. I've been enough places. You know, I like a single place to sleep and work and live. So did my grandfather. I might have moved around more, but television came along and saved me. It goes everywhere, and the world looks better in that little square of glass. It's God-awful but powerful and Grandpa would have loved it —he took to things that are so big almost nobody can handle them. I never was ambitious. Television is enough for me."

"Ye-es," Wyitt said, and picked out the items he wanted to take, stopping at intervals to glance at Chambers. "I suppose I understand. There's too much outside. It grows like a tropical rain forest, beyond sense and expediency—like amoebae in a too friendly culture—past all understanding. You have to turn your back."

Chambers nodded. "That's good enough."

"I infer," Garnet said, "that the professor doesn't wish my guidance at the ranch. I'll arrange for somebody else to show him around."

"No, I'll take you as a substitute," Wyitt told her. "You're the heir-apparent."

"Can you play pool, A.B.?" Chambers asked.

"As a matter of fact, I can."

"How well?"

"Pretty well."

"I'm surprised, considering your history. How did it happen?"

"They always have billiard tables in the recreation rooms of the student unions," Wyitt said. "With my standard of living, I rarely had the money for night clubs or golf and tennis. Shooting pool was my sport. I even picked up a bit of spare cash at times."

"You won't here."

"I might, Chambers."

"Let's shoot a game or two. You don't have to run off, do you?"

"No, sir."

"Get a cue, Garnet," Chambers said. "Come on, Lagonda."

"I'm tired," Garnet said, "and I'm going to bed." She kissed Lagonda's cheek and her father's cheek, and after the barest of hesitations, extended her hand to Wyitt. He took it and deliberately looked solemn, to emphasize that he recognized the honor accorded him; she quickly freed her fingers. "Good night, Professor. Let me know if I can be of assistance to you."

404

"Thank you, Miss Brennan. Good night."

"I'm bored, too," Lagonda said, "but I'll stay a minute or two." She took a leather-butted cue which had her name on it.

"Rotation?" Chambers said. "That's the kind of game to get acquainted on."

"Whatever you say, sir."

"A.B., we play a dollar a point and five dollars to the winner. You say if that sounds too steep."

"That's agreeable to me."

Bemused and aware of a growing, unformulated, irritating worriment, Garnet left them. While thoroughly chalking her stick, Lagonda was saying, "We better lag for the break."

Garnet was scarcely settled in bed, emollient creams on her face and neck and elbows and evanescent oil on her cuticles, a book at hand and the radio turned to the news, when she was interrupted by a tap on her door. "Come in, Junior," she said.

Junior entered and crossed over to her, elegant in black lace net and diamonds and a lingering suggestion of perfume, a cigarette bobbing in her lips, and said, "Did he show up?"

"Yes."

"I presume he was decently humble and that our man on the roof nevertheless ate him?"

Garnet scowled. "No . . . he was nothing in particular. Rude to me, and friendly and easy with Father. They—they seemed to get along well enough."

"Bless me!" Junior said, and was unable to quell a flash of satisfaction. "The good professor simply doesn't like you. It's odd."

"Don't be a fool. He's working on a definite line of strategy."

"Absolutely. But he won't get anywhere, will he? He's overplayed his hand, hasn't he? You've had it, eh?"

"Yes."

"Be a little more explicit, dear. I can't go to sleep harassed by doubts or ambiguities. That momentary reversion to the Brennan line today, that mad impulse to pick a consort out of the blue is finished, isn't it? You've recaptured your customary sanity, haven't you?"

"Yes . . ." Garnet said.

"I'm happy with monosyllables, love, if they're the right ones. How long was the audience?"

"He's still in there, shooting pool with Father and Lagonda. I was bored and left."

"Really? That's quite fantastic. May we hope that A.B. has sufficient

405

charm to make Chambers part with that dreary San Fernando Valley acreage?"

"I don't know. I don't care."

"You're fretful," Junior said. "I'll run along, dear . . . unless you'd like to tell me what's the matter."

"I'll tell you what's the matter! A.B. stands for Albert Bennett. He doesn't care for his first name, damn him! You can imagine what Father and Lagonda are reading into that."

"Good heavens. We could have another regular in the pool hall. Garnet, I'm compelled to point out to you that you have brought this on yourself—"

"Oh, shut up."

"Of course. Bless your little untouched heart. I'm going—"

"I'm sorry," Garnet said. "Forgive me, Junior—I have a headache."

"I'll get you some aspirins—"

"No, no. How was the dinner?"

"I was with *nouveau riches*. They have inferior modern masters and peculiar furnishings, and the conversation was trifling. But it's better than looking at three TV sets at once."

Junior started out of the room. Waiting until the last instant, Garnet heard the word rise to her lips involuntarily. "Junior."

"Yes?"

"You're too smart to have prejudices without reasons. Tell me—aside from the fear that I have inherited the family madness, which I know I haven't—tell me, why do you prefer Larry Smith to Wyitt?"

Junior gave thought to the subject. "Well, largely because I don't know A.B. I'm dubious of people I don't know, especially when they're outsiders and not socially eligible . . . Because A.B. has been divorced, because he's penniless and obviously unbothered by it, because he hasn't been to the best schools, because he doesn't even have a bad tailor but buys off the rack. Because you must religiously avoid any eccentricities you might have acquired from a very rum lot and occupy the high position God and the Brennans intended for you. Because I love you in a preposterous maternal fashion and know you aren't the emotional type, and intend to spare you any difficulties or inconveniences. You were meant for the straight and narrow like that priggish Grandfather Cass of yours. Is that enough?"

"That's enough," Garnet said. "Good night."

"Good night, dear," Junior said.

Garnet dreamed. She was on an airplane, in a storm, and the flight was rough and upsetting. She wanted to get off, and getting off was

406

foolishly easy if only she could persuade the stewardess to open the cabin door, put down some steps, and allow her to reach the ground. But the stewardess was stupid and refused to help her. In the blind panic of entrapment and frustration, she had to suffer the tossing and imminent peril.

This was a familiar dream. She had been afflicted by it from earliest childhood, in a number of variations. At the inception of puberty, when she was amazed and disgusted and frightened by the beginning of menstruation, personality problems had severely shaken the discipline she was being taught. Worried, Junior had brought her to Dr. Erich Rommer, Chambers's psychiatrist. Dr. Rommer's chatty, probing questions were both unnerving and helpful. Oddly, since Garnet had determined while she was still a child (under the vacillating influence of her father) not to inquire into herself and to assume the purple of the Brennans early, the very bulwarks she put up against Dr. Rommer aided her in attaining equilibrium. He was a fountain of omniscience, given to Delphic utterances, and he attached considerable importance to her dreams, especially those which involved aircraft. He believed they stemmed from her early infancy, the result of the deaths of the Stuarts, and were reinforced by the many later allusions to them. Touched in the cradle, Garnet was dissipating in unconscious fantasy a horror and loss and even an angry guilt for intruding upon obsessed lovers who deserted her and found a new consummation in death. Garnet thought this was nonsense, and Dr. Rommer a fool; but the mere process of detesting and despising him, and giving misleading answers to his questions, helped condition her to the unhandy, weakening and often nerve-rasping ordeal of being a woman. In spite of Rommer's madly logical explanations, the dreams persisted.

Into the dream, always soundless, intruded a noise. It was repeated. Awakening, Garnet sat up in bed, perspiration cooling her upper lip. There was a knocking on her door, for which she was grateful; she looked at the illuminated dial of the radio clock and saw it was past four o'clock in the morning. Alarm succeeded relief: she wondered whether something had gone wrong in the household. She plunged from bed, struggled into a robe, and went to the door, forgetting to put on her slippers.

A. B. Wyitt awaited her, pale and drawn with fatigue, his tie gone and his shirt collar unbuttoned. "You told me to let you know if you could be of any assistance to me," he said. His speech was slurred.

"I meant during ordinary business hours," Garnet replied. "There's nothing the matter with my father?"

"Matter? The bastard has won three hundred and twenty-three

dollars from me! It would have been more, but I can beat Lagonda, and she dropped over a hundred dollars—"

"You're drunk."

"Not drunk, tipsy."

"I thought you testified that you didn't drink?"

"I don't, ordinarily. But I had to keep up with him."

"Why?"

"Why?" He gazed at her glassily. "How do I know? He wanted company. I was exhausted . . ."

"Well, what do you want?" Garnet asked.

"Will you lend me a couple of hundred dollars? I gave Cham a check to cover my losses. There isn't that much in my account, and I'd like to cover the difference in the morning. I'll pay you back within a week, on my word."

"Why not let the check bounce? My father doesn't need the money and he won't care. Or are you coming back here?"

"Assuredly I'm coming back, Miss Brennan," Wyitt said grimly. "For my money. I can beat him. I'm just out of practice—I need a few hours on the table to get into form. He's not that good at callshot. I—"

"Yet you call him a bastard."

"He likes it. One picks up the language from him."

"And Cham. Nobody has used his nickname for years."

"He asked me to, Miss Brennan, after Lagonda left. It seems she feels the diminutive is disrespectful."

"I think I have the cash somewhere . . ." Garnet said. She crossed to a bureau, searched in the top drawer, found the purse she had last used, and extracted a roll of currency. Returning to Wyitt, she counted out two hundred dollars and put the rest of the bills in the pocket of her robe.

"Do you always carry that kind of change with you?" he said.

"Usually. I'm accustomed to paying my own way."

"Shall I write out an I.O.U.?"

"That won't be necessary."

"This is a madhouse. Do you realize that? That's Nero in there, hitting combinations instead of tuning his violin. The conflagration in this attenuated, ugly Rome could come at any moment."

"I make it a rule," Garnet said, "not to argue with men who are stoned. You have the money, so shouldn't you run along? Are you capable of driving?"

"I'm not sure."

She sighed. "Come with me."

They walked down the long hallway, through the foyer, and to the rear. Flinching when Garnet turned on the main lights to supplement the night light, Wyitt stared around the tremendous kitchen. "Good Lord!" he said. "How many servants do you have, Miss Brennan?"

"Only three, now that Ferris Washington, Junior, departed. Lagonda tries to work, but my father won't let her."

The large chromium boiler suitable for a restaurant, which Chambers Brennan insisted be constantly in operation, yielded coffee for the two cups Garnet procured. Remaining on their feet, they sipped the rich, hot brew. "By the way," Garnet said, "where is my father? Looking at the all-night movies or still at the table?"

"No, he went to bed to read. Do you happen to know what he is reading?"

Garnet shook her head.

"Gibbon's *The Decline and Fall of the Roman Empire*—for the third time. He says his grandfather revered the Romans. Apparently he made an indelible impression on Cham. That would be the immortal Colonel Lucius, wouldn't it?"

"Yes."

"Only he was supposed to be Cham's great-uncle, unless the story of how he and Doña Maria—"

"Never mind," Garnet interrupted. "Your problem is Doña Maria's rancho. Have you read Gibbon?"

"I have, Miss Brennan."

"How much do you remember?"

"I've got a good memory."

"You remember enough, I'll bet, to help increase your chances of getting my father's patronage."

"Wouldn't that please you, Miss Brennan?" Wyitt asked. "Isn't that part of my act, to win Cham over in preparation for winning your hand? Unquestionably, you are as mad as everybody else in this penthouse, and don't you intend for me to be your husband if I can pass the tests?"

Garnet smiled. "That's right."

"Why, for God's sake? Have you lost an election wager?"

"No," Garnet said. "I had a rather amusing idea that already doesn't seem to work too well. An explanation of what I had in mind isn't necessary. I'm ready to abandon it."

"Good. Because I'm not going to be your husband, you know."

"Are you sure? You appear to have given the preliminaries a good try tonight."

"I am succeeding by indirection, Miss Brennan. I could have the prize because I don't want it. Fortune is a bitch, and gives a hard time to those who woo her—she's kind to the indifferent."

"And I'm a bitch, too, I suppose?"

"Why, yes," said Wyitt cheerfully, "now that I come to think of it. Only a bitch could nurture such casual, callous designs—or a howling eccentric."

"I am not an eccentric!"

"I fear I'd need more than a mere disclaimer, Miss Brennan."

She explained her situation and theory, in as few words as would suffice. He listened carefully, and then said, "You're nutty . . . absolutely nutty. I caught on when your father was questioning me, and I was furious with you. Suddenly it occurred to me that you had an antic sense of humor. Now I realize you're a stiff and straight from the family loony-bin."

"Get out," she said. "You're disturbing my rest."

"In a moment. I'm really bagged, Miss Brennan. Would you mind refilling my cup?" He stood holding the cup with both hands, sipping reflectively, steam wreathing his forehead. Her feet felt cold on the tiled floor. She should have left him, not in indignation or hurt pride, for she was conscious of neither, but simply because he was a lost cause and it was the middle of the night: instead, she remained, held by curiosity and perturbation and a nonsensical desire to watch him. "Still . . ." he began, "it's an interesting notion. Certainly I was relying on nothing better than the laws of probability when I took Miss Dorothy Calvert for my own. If the problem could be decently mocked-up and subjected to analysis, I presume one could come up with a reasonable fix on the results—"

A thin small voice was raised, no more than a slight wind playing on feeble reeds. Wyitt raised his brows. The call was repeated.

"That can't be machinery," Wyitt said. "You don't have bats flying around in this ménage, do you?"

"No, that's one of my children. Would you like to see them?"

"I'm ready for anything."

Garnet took him into a nearby room—not a room, actually, but once a commodious broom closet. Despite a ventilating motor whirring in the ceiling, the place had a feral, ammoniac smell. In a padded basket were six striped tabby kittens and their mother; all of them had yellow around their noses and a rich brown undercoat of fur beneath an outward darkness. The light going on made them stretch and blink and yawn and flex their paws. From a corner watched a large cat of the same lines, immobile and green-eyed.

"There is Odysseus, the father," Garnet said, pointing to the animal in the corner. "This is Penelope, his wife. These kittens are her third litter. Shall I introduce them by name?"

"If you please."

"Well, let me see. It's difficult to tell the sex of young cats—the veterinary had to come the other day and straighten me out. Reading from left to right, I think we have Circe, Achilles, Diomodes, Telemachus—uh, Helen and Icarus."

"Icarus? He doesn't belong in the Odyssey."

"You remember Homer, too?"

"Naturally," Wyitt said.

"I've heard my mother had a cat named Icarus, so one in every litter is called that."

"That would sound sensible among the Brennans, and even a knowledge of Greek epic poems. May I pick up Achilles? Will Mother—Penelope—object?"

"No, go ahead. Do you like cats?"

"I love them." He raised the ball of fluff to his cheek and held it there. Arising, Penelope regarded him somewhat anxiously; he reassured her, gazed into the blue eyes Achilles opened, kissed him when he gave the reedy cry, and restored him to his mother, who had immediately to clean her boy. "I've just realized something," Wyitt said. "These kids haven't got tails."

"No, they're Manxes. They're born without tails at all, like rabbits, or with only vestigial caudal appendages. They have high hindquarters and can jump to astounding heights, and they have broad heads and rather short ears . . . Probably I'm giving you information you already have in your control center."

He shook his head. "We don't have that on the tape yet. Go on."

"I'm amazed . . . Well, I suspect Manxes are descended from the smaller breeds of wildcat. They aren't very common. I've been raising them for years. Sometimes I show them. Except for Odysseus and Penelope and an occasionally perfect rumpy, I—"

"Rumpy?"

"There is a distinction, you see. A rumpy is a Manx with no tail whatever. They're the valuable ones, the show cats. Stubbies, those with tiny stubs at the end of their spines, are the common run of the breed. However, they are essential in the Manx world—you have to breed a rumpy with a stubby and hope for a maximum of rumpies, although the reverse is generally true. To mate rumpies with rumpies produces cats with weak bowels and other genetic difficulties. Don't ask me why."

"I won't, I assure you. What you've told me is sufficiently confusing. Would you mind indicating a rumpy?"

"Penelope is a rumpy," Garnet said. "You can verify that by picking her up and feeling her behind."

"Should I? It seems awfully forward—"

"If you're interested, don't try to be playful. This is no joke with me."

"I can see it isn't," Wyitt said, and stopped to stare at Garnet. Then he lifted Penelope, patted her and she purred, apologized to her, felt her rear, and restored her to the babies. "You're quite correct," he added. "Mother is as flat as I am."

"Now, take—uh, Helen. She's a stubby."

Wyitt took Helen, kissed her, and examined her lower end. She did not awaken, and presently Penelope had to clean her. "I understand," he said. "That poor girl has an embarrassing vertebra the size of a peanut . . . Don't they ever leave this room?"

"Of course. In the daytime they are given the freedom of the terrace and have a sandbox. As I was saying earlier, I keep only the parents, and an occasional rumpy, once the litters are sufficiently grown."

"What do you do with them?"

"Sell them and give them to friends."

"Sell them?"

"Yes, if I'm sure the buyers will provide a good home. Outstanding rumpies are worth a hundred dollars."

"Ah—" Wyitt said. "No doubt you put an advertisement in the paper, have the prospective buyers up to these hanging gardens of Babylon, and proceed to dicker—"

"You have moments," Garnet said, "when you are civilized and almost acceptable. But mostly you're aggressive and ironic and self-defensive, and that's tiresome. I think you are about to become tiresome again. Shall we say good night?"

"Good morning, you mean. Yes, Miss Brennan."

She accompanied him to the foyer and pressed the button for the elevator; the doors promptly opened, since it was standing where Junior had left it. Wyitt asked, "Who interested you in the *Odyssey?*"

"My father. It's his favorite story. Odysseus is his prime hero because all the gods were with him, except Athena at first, and she came around. My father says the gods were all with him, too, for a while. He weeps when he reads the scene where Odysseus's old dog Argus recognizes him when he comes back from Troy."

"Do you like any animal, Miss Brennan?"

"Yes. Didn't St. Francis say they are our brothers?"

"Are you a Catholic?"

"No. I tried to be when I was a little girl, but it didn't work. My family was once Catholic."

"What do you believe in? Robert Welch and the John Birch Society?"

"The elevator is waiting, Professor."

"I'm serious."

"I don't know. Has anybody got anything to believe in anymore? What do you believe?"

"Nothing," Wyitt said. "Oh, something, maybe. That we're all animals like Odysseus and Penelope and ought to try to rise above it. The sun won't stop giving off energy for billions of years and we still have time, no matter how discouraging it looks."

Garnet recognized that she had suddenly developed a nasty habit of speaking before thinking. Her next involuntary words were: "Are we going to the ranch today?"

He groaned. "Not today. I'm dead. But soon . . . I have to shoot pool with Cham tonight."

"I shouldn't endure you," Garnet said. "To tell you the truth, I don't know why I do. I believe it's because my father accepted you and trusts your word, and because you like him. I didn't anticipate that."

Uneasily, Wyitt said, "Neither did I. And I really like him. And I admire you, Miss Brennan, for making money from stubbies and rumpies."

"I also gave a hundred thousand dollars to the S.P.C.A. I'll need a few years to get even."

Wyitt abruptly knelt, lifted the hem of her nightgown, and kissed her right foot. She became rigid. The imprint of his lips gave her the most extraordinary feeling; a tingling, melting, glowing sensation ran upward from her ankles and calves and thighs and groin and abdomen and breasts and came heatedly to rest in the skin of her face.

Since he wobbled in rising, she had to offer assistance. She wondered if she ought to hit him. It didn't seem indicated. There was something ceremonial in his bearing. "Well, that's settled," he said, with an air of satisfaction. "It's the biggest tribute I'm capable of. Don't ask for more, Miss Brennan."

"Tell me, how did you find my room?"

"Cham told me where to go."

"How helpful of him . . ." Garnet said quietly. "Good night, Professor."

He attempted to smile at her as the elevator doors closed, but the facial movement ended in a yawn.

two

THREE weeks after the Los Angeles Lovely meeting, Garnet was forced to consider what had happened to her, and to fear for the future. The extent of the crisis was made clear to her, as well as the depth of her recent astounding vagaries, during a luncheon with Paula Sego, the in-between of Harry Sego's three daughters, who was four years younger than Garnet and the only one of them with whom she had formed a close attachment. By then she had witnessed a considerable change in the life of her father, was herself coming unstuck, had given A. B. Wyitt a Manx kitten named Circe (he wanted a family of his own and to be able to sell rumpies at a hundred dollars a head, and she agreed to furnish a male for breeding purposes when Circe was ready for maternity), had rejected an offer of marriage from Larry Smith, and had lost her virtue repeatedly. Blood would tell, apparently, and her Brennan heritage had at last manifested itself, whether or not she was capable of admitting the fact. And, unawares, she was approaching a massive betrayal.

She and Paula met at Perino's, a luxurious and quiet restaurant on Wilshire Boulevard, where they could sit in a large booth and have one of their long, long talks. These talks nearly always concerned Paula, a rebel and nonconformer and generally in difficulties, with a constant need of Garnet's amusedly objective advice. She relied on Garnet. The Segos, awesomely social and stultified and reinforced by the towering prestige of the numerous Partan ironworks family on the maternal side, seemed to bring out the worst in Paula; her peculiar behavior was emphasized because her sisters were models of good deportment and the eldest, a couple of years junior to Garnet, had married St. Louis brew-

414

ing wealth, settled gracefully into New York-and-Florida matronhood, and presented the gratified Harry Sego with a grandson. All this joy was dampened for him by Paula's loathsome eccentricities. Only Paula had been kicked out of two boarding schools. Only Paula had refused to attend the annual Las Jovenitas Debutante Ball and embark upon polite society. Only Paula was currently a dropout from the University of Southern California, hastened in the dereliction by perilously low grades. Only Paula had no perceptible place to go or any ambitions. Harry could not understand the young people she attached herself to; they were brash, uncouth, defiant, immoral, posturing and lazy. He hated their songs, language, clothing, customs and, above everything else, the contempt and ingratitude they manifested toward their generous elders. In his day, thank God, it had been different. At times he appealed to Garnet, an object of his admiration, for advice in handling his daughter, and beseeched her influence in calming the maverick.

Currently the errant Miss Sego was undergoing an avant garde phase, and was in marked contrast to her well-groomed dearest friend. Her lengthy and untidy hair, of a Sego shade of yellow, hung to the shoulders of her bulky, shapeless sweater, a wisp of rumpled skirt barely extended to the tops of childish round knees covered by black stockings, and her slippers were flat-heeled. An opaque substance caused her lips to shine eerily, deep artificial shadows hollowed her eyes, fake glued-on lashes nearly blinded them, and she had odd patches of Indian-like white paint applied to her cheekbones. She played a guitar reasonably well, had a vast repertoire of wailing folk songs, and boasted of smoking "tea" when she felt the urge. Her brushes with the opposite sex had begun at the age of fourteen, usually, Garnet gathered, on a plane of enlightened platonism that not infrequently degenerated into outright passion and invariably ended in ruin; ill luck ignored, she went on collecting friends and lovers and enemies, and each new acquisition was "like Endsville, man." Long since, moved by prudence and the wide disparity in their tastes, Garnet had abandoned double-dating with Paula, whose companions were apt to be bearded, unbathed, opinionated and riding scooters or motorcycles. They inhabited two different universes, and yet Paula's didoes secretly struck a chord in Garnet—she was sufficiently honest with herself to admire the warm heart Paula had, the generosity, the energy, the humorous stoicism, the willingness to accept consequences.

Each of them drank a martini on the rocks and ordered unfattening salads, and Paula said of her father: "He's bugging me again. I think I'm going to have to split for keeps, Garnet. I'm not all that bad, but he's out to escalate our beef."

"Yes, I've heard echoes. He phoned me the other day. It's a man again, I assume?"

"*The* man. Heavensville. I have never really been in love before—"

"Of course not," Garnet said. "What's this one do—write for the theater of the absurd, or is he going to Alabama to get killed?"

"Garnet, don't bomb me. I need sympathy and understanding. I'm just a wayward, overprivileged girl."

"All right. Does he have a beard or merely a goatee?"

"He's clean-shaven and working," Paula replied. "He has a wife and two children, and they're not making the scene together. He is a stockbroker."

Garnet stared at her. "I'll be darned! What *has* happened to you?"

"I've grown up. Life goes on. The full implications of what it means to be a woman—to be fulfilled—to—"

"Wait a minute. Where did you meet him?"

"At a sit-in at City Hall. We were helping CORE—"

"A stockbroker? What was he doing there?"

"They have their ideals too," Paula said. "He's Princeton '53 and tried to accommodate to the three-button image, but suddenly it came over him that his existence had to have meaning and purpose. He couldn't find either in religion, and turned to man himself."

"Good Lord . . ." Garnet said. "Has your father met him?"

"Once. He was pleased at first, and then he heard about the wife and kids—my man is no evader of issues. The next minute they were grappling with each other. You should have heard what Old Harry was blowing. And they started out discussing U.S. Steel and Zerox! I was so embarrassed for my father that I was still apologizing when we were back in bed. He sounded for a while like Harold Stassen scared by Harry Truman."

"Have you met the wife?"

"No. But you can imagine her, Garnet. I can. All systems with her are gone. They lived in San Marino, and she has the house and kids and his money and insurance. He's got a terrible little apartment on Sunset Boulevard with a sofa that makes up as a bed, like in a Statler Hotel. She keeps an autographed picture of Dick Nixon—that will give you the idea. No divorce is possible; she's a Catholic. His first name is Jerry, and he's trying to find himself. Garnet, I'm going to help him hunt until the real Jerry please stands up if it's the last thing I ever do." Paula recoiled. "Look, I haven't just confessed to main-lining or necrophilia. Don't take it so big."

"I'm sorry," Garnet mumbled, and composed her features. Her face felt as if the blood had drained out of it, and she was dizzy and had a ringing in her ears. The vertigo and shock passed quickly, but she knew she had been hit with a megaton force—the damning force of coincidence, similarity, mutual simplicity, human error, and womanly weakness. Every mistake of this sort was appallingly common, repeated to infinity. Nobody was immune to folly. She wasn't, any more than Paula. The full implications of her indiscipline and stark insanity descended upon her in black, suffocating folds. For a moment she detested her friend; Paula reminded her of certain facts she had refused to consider. "No offense. I fear I'm a little old-fashioned and—"

"Only finicky and delicate, Garnet. You are apt to shy away from the nastier truths. I don't know, maybe you can pull it off for a lifetime. I hope so. It must be nice to blow it as cool as you do, without even a roll-on deodorant."

Garnet dabbed her upper lip with a corner of her napkin. "Well, probably I am rather unworldly. When you contrast your uninhibited behavior with mine—"

"You might act as I have under the same circumstances."

"Really? What are those circumstances?"

"My problem can be summed up in one word," Paula said. "The usual, darling. I'm a girl. The word is sex."

"Oh?" The folds grew thicker around Garnet.

"How can I make it plain to you? You're the superior soul, the stainless steel blade good for thirty comfortable shaves. Garnet, there have been other times, as you remember. I'm an outgoing type. But Jerry is different. Like waking up after too many Seconals or finding you're Cinderella and the shoe fits or flying without an airplane. The center ring at the circus, getting off the launching pad. Oh, the real thing! What else can I say? It must be the same as getting a fix, which I've often considered—and then coming right home to Old Harry with my pupils as big as the Gabors' diamonds."

"I think you've said enough."

"One more little tidbit: Jerry is the kind of guy you could make out with in a phone booth. In fact, we almost made it the other night when I wedged myself in with him while he was calling a client. He has to work, you see, to keep Snow White and the two dwarfs in San Marino. We were in the booth, Garnet, and—"

"Please," Garnet said, "I'm an aging gentlewoman, far removed from your jagged world. I don't believe I should hear any more."

"Maybe not," Paula agreed. She pursed her shining lips and considered. "Gee, I don't know. Perhaps you have the best system. You'll never bomb out and break into perspiration when somebody merely suggests something, or have to leave home and go live in two rooms on

Sunset Boulevard and skip meals while the little woman is stuffing herself at the old homestead. But to cool it *that* much you have to be born with the temperament. I think you miss something, Garnet, I really do. On the other hand, you have peace and plenty. It may put you to sleep, but it doesn't wear you down. Are you going to marry Larry?"

Garnet shrugged, and then shook her head.

"Why not? You ought to make *some* kind of move."

"Uh, I prefer to keep on raising my cats. I might start a stamp collection."

"What will your father say? My God, we're always asking that question, aren't we? Why can't they draft people for euthanasia instead of the army?"

"He'll bear up," Garnet said.

"I'll give you this: you're the goddess of the squares. Old Harry reveres you. He says you are the one sane individual the Brennans have produced in four generations. He regards you as absolutely dependable."

"Hooray."

"Hooray," Paula said. "Those terrible refined Baltims speak well of you. Everytime aged Burton Lely totters over to our house for dinner he sings your praises. What a shame you don't have a married brother; you're good aunt material."

"Shall we have coffee?"

"Yes. Garnet, I love you. Why, I admire you. I say these things for your own good. For my money, you should go mistakewise to avoid being bloody perfect. Hopefully, there's little chance of your ending runner-up to the Virgin Mary. Why come in second as a Red Cross worker or president of the Junior League? Hang tough, don't just surrender."

"Coffee for two, please," Garnet said to the waiter she had signaled. "Large cups." Her delivery was so charged with emotion that the man glanced at her in surprise. Paula cocked her head to look at Garnet, who spoke rapidly to mask her confusion: "Let's change the subject, Paula. We're getting too serious. Do you want to drive me into a convent? What do you think of Martin Luther King?"

"He's the greatest," Paula said. "Next to Jerry. Wipe off your upper lip. Listen, are you having trouble adjusting? Or getting the flu?"

"I think I'm getting the flu," Garnet said thankfully. "I'm weak and trembly and feverish. I hope I don't give it to you." She thought if she didn't have the flu, she would welcome it. She had everything else, by George.

418

The disastrous chain of consequences began quite innocently the day following A. B. Wyitt's opening visit to the Xanadu penthouse. Chambers stirred roughly on schedule around four o'clock in the afternoon, and had cinnamon toast and tea with Lagonda. Garnet went to his bedroom, where, in pajamas, he was sitting reading the newspapers and cursing divers governmental manifestations. At that advanced hour she had already transacted a good deal of business, including a downtown trip to the Sunset Sea Corporation's building on South Spring Street (she did not subscribe to her father's practice of holding court at home), much local telephoning, the dictation of letters to a secretary who came each weekday morning, the writing of personal notes, the acceptance of several social invitations, an extended chat with one of the trustees of the Brennan Memorial Library over a luncheon, an agreement to be a patroness of a forthcoming art exhibition, and a call to New York to Aaron Eindhoven. The Sunset Sea conference had been devoted to routine affairs Chambers would no longer countenance, attended by both the Baltims—Harold, Senior, was semi-retired and trembling from Parkinson's Disease, but loyal to Garnet—Albert Washington and Harry Sego. Garnet always basked in a warm climate of approval and gallantry with them, and no one concealed his relief at not having any more to wait on her father and endure his varying moods. What was done these days was accomplished swiftly and efficiently; Garnet received an admiration without sycophancy; they were far beyond that stage. But they did marvel at her good sense and quiet control, and it was pleasing to be the only woman in the group, able to comprehend their male forthrightness, anticipate their wishes, and often outdo them in hardheaded reasoning. She relished her competence and success, though not unduly; what really comforted her was a conviction that the Brennan fortune, hedged and static through her childhood from a lack of interest and energy on the part of Chambers, was now unlikely to suffer under her stewardship.

Rising politely at Garnet's entrance, Chambers pulled up a chair for her and accepted a kiss on the cheek. Lagonda put a stray lock of the hair of her last child in place, squeezed her hand, and left the room. They sat down. "You got him drunk," she said. "He called on me at four in the morning, thanks to your directions. I had to sober him on coffee."

Chambers grinned. "I told him about my ulcer and how I had to drink my liquor in milk. He offered to stay with me, and I loaded his drinks as part of the experiment. He came off fairly well. He's good company—or maybe I'm just lonesome. Anyway, when we parted he told me he had to speak to you, and I didn't see any harm in that."

"Did you discuss the ranch?"

"No, he's got to think it over. Not that it'll do him any good."

"I was at Sunset Sea today for the weekly meeting," Garnet said. "Everyone was happy to hear I had a new man on the job and that we were going to arrive at a decision soon."

"Yeah? Well, don't rush it. I might drop dead and put you in the clear."

"Father, I'm determined to make that land productive. This is an absurd situation, and it's starting to cost us dearly. Worse, we're holding up logical development of the city. You've got to listen to reason."

"All right, all right," he said. "I'll come to grips with it pretty soon. Tell me about how you ran afoul of this new Albert. You promised to explain."

At Garnet's description of her theory of random selection of a consort, and Junior's perturbation, Chambers laughed. She could see he was amused but not convinced by her assumption of arrogance. And she realized that the coincidence of the first names and Lagonda's voodoo divinations must have had an effect on him. She was willing to allow that aspect to pass unremarked; anything which would lower his resistance to parting with the San Cristobal had a value.

"Listen," he said, "you may not be as flighty as you sound. If he hadn't already been married and failed at it, he could measure up. I like him, and none of the other bastards you've brought around were any better. You have got to marry and have some babies, Garnet. Or have the babies, at least; I don't much give a damn how."

"Are you recommending immorality to me?"

He gazed at her, a glaze of doubt and uncertainty behind his glasses. "I'd recommend nearly anything at this point. The years are passing, and you never seem to get interested like normal girls. When are you going to wake up? And suppose you simply don't have the urge?"

"Precisely what do you mean by that?" Garnet demanded.

"What the hell do you think I mean? You're an iceberg. You're only fuss and business. You're better friends with women than you are with men. That Smith character appears to suit you—he wouldn't cause any scattering in a nunnery if he'd been there a year. Right?"

She was astounded. "If I don't mistake your meaning, you've insulted me. I ought to break your spectacles and kick you in the belly."

"Oh, don't get sore. I was only kidding. I'm an old man—you wouldn't beat up on an old man, would you?"

Her face was flaming, and her temper with it. "I think that's the first unkind thing you ever said to me. But you have more than made up for omissions in the past! You're going to be sorry for this."

420

"Now look," he said. "I meant no harm. And I know I'm as much to blame as you are; I've always wanted you for myself. But there comes an end to everything, and I have to say what I think. Can you be surprised at my beginning to wonder about you? Your mother was funny and cold, my mother—"

"Please don't get into the matter of that letter your grandfather left in the files for Dirovac to uncover. Do you realize we're having our first big fight?"

"Oh, Garnet—Garnet—"

"Shut up," she said hotly. "You've spoken your piece. Now hear me. I was considering the abandonment of Wyitt until you were pleased to be honest with me. Your frank views have changed my mind. Wyitt will do—or anybody else in the right age bracket and capable of signing his name—provided he is able to learn what we must teach him and where his place is on the totem pole. The professor has some illusions of independence and he's a trifle insolent, but we can cure him of those naïvetés. He told me he is coming over here again tonight. Take care with him and bring him along, understand? I believe I'll use him. If I do, he will need some status and a regular occupation. Taking charge of the conversion of the San Cristobal ought to fill those requirements nicely. When I give up my freedom for duty and maternity, you are going to give up your superstitions and sixteen thousand acres. I phoned Aaron this morning regarding a check on Wyitt by AAC's security people, and he is sending me his Los Angeles man tomorrow. We won't do anything drastic until we're sure our boy is passable. Are we in agreement?"

"Absolutely," Chambers said. He was smiling furtively. "Now you're making the right noises. You finally sound like the rest of us."

"Excuse me."

"Where're you going? I want to talk more—I like you when you got your tail up."

"I'm going out," Garnet said. "Out. Out before I hit you."

Later a peace was negotiated between them by Junior and Lagonda, who learned of the quarrel from Chambers; he decided, upon reflection, that he had been badly treated and complained to everybody within earshot. "I realize you have grounds for anger," Junior said in the preliminaries with Garnet, "but you must remember your father has never been noted for his finesse. My efforts, and those of my sainted mother and Dr. Rommer, haven't tamed him, God knows. However, don't forget you are prodding him on that immense and dreary and symbolistic ranch, and in addition he is concerned for your future. He is an impatient man, and irrational, and aging in a spectacularly squalid fashion. Consider his handicaps and admit the validity of some of his statements.

Take it all into account and conduct yourself like the little lady you are."

"I imagine I can manage that," Garnet said. "But answer a question honestly. Have you ever had the suspicions of me that my father does?"

"What suspicions are those, dear?"

"You know damned well what they are! And so must Lagonda. He confides in you both—it's just that I had to wait, not being a member of the inner circle, to hear them."

"Well," Junior said, "I confess mention has been made of the subject. I laughed at Chambers and his grimy thoughts. Lagonda sat and glowered. However . . . you are a bit remote in manner. You informed me yourself that your heart had not been touched, and I think you were a trifle puzzled by the lapse. You are twenty-six and—"

"Have I ever conveyed the impression I might be more interested in another woman than in—"

"Garnet! We needn't investigate that aspect of you. Even if I had for one moment thought—"

"Answer me. Have I?"

Junior paled and averted her eyes from Garnet. "No. I pray you won't."

"Your prayers will win the day, bless you," Garnet said, and gritted her teeth. "I'm going to make a few changes around here. The honeymoon is over."

"I knew this was too good to be true . . ." Junior said quietly. "Attempting to civilize Brennans is wasted effort."

Nevertheless, Garnet went into her father's sanctum, offered half-hearted apologies, hugged him, kissed his nose, and smiled falsely. He was watching the broadcasting of news on three different television stations, which helped to keep the scene from getting out of hand and provoking more trouble. "This makes me very happy," he said, keeping his attention on two announcers and the film of a southern race riot. "I haven't been too well lately, Garnet, and I'd hate to go to my grave thinking you had the knife out for me. If I could live long enough to dandle a grandson on my knee—"

"Turn those contraptions off," Garnet offered, "and I'll put a Mantovani record on the stereo to accompany your solo. The one with thirty violins. Shall we weep together?"

"No, thanks," Chambers said. "Leave it lay where Jesus flung it. This is beautiful to me."

It was, too; that was evident. She studied him closely, nagged by vague suspicion. He seemed stronger and surer of himself, as though he had a concealed purpose. Perhaps his extended dormancy was coming to an end; he had often told her his revered grandfather was given to "spells"

422

of listless inaction, only to revive and strike out harder than ever, and Chambers was a man governed by genetic and historical precedent. Perhaps he intended to resume control of the family affairs, displacing her. Although they would miss her at Sunset Sea, she thought having her wings clipped might not matter particularly. She held no illusions about herself. A woman had to be twice as effective as a man to achieve the same results, and she wasn't dedicated to leaving her mark behind on balance sheets and in board meetings. An old maid with innumerable shares of voting stock and an unimpeachable position was still an old maid. But this perception of the limited extent of her ambition and resolve was disquieting to her. There was a lack of guts and energy, she saw; she was a female . . .

They all dined together amicably, Garnet, Lagonda, Junior and Chambers, served by the two Negro maids who were distant cousins of Lagonda; the cook was an uncle of Albert's on the distaff side. No mention was made of the ranch or of Professor Wyitt. Even the absence of Ferris Washington, Junior, never elevated to the rank of his wife and compelled to wait on her among his other duties as butler, was not dealt with by Chambers; normally he had a few animadversions on the subject at dinnertime. Shortly afterward Garnet and Junior departed for a concert, over the latter's protests; she was of the opinion that they might do better to hang about and watch Wyitt in action with the penthouse sage.

"I see no necessity for it," Garnet told her. "Let him sink or swim on his own."

"Suppose he swims?" Junior asked. "What if he settles the ranch thing? Would you be apt to go off the deep end again?"

"No comment," Garnet said.

"Mercy . . ." Junior said. "Why don't we drop by the Smiths on our way home? Larry would be pleased and flattered. And honored, so help me."

But they did not visit the Smiths in Hancock Park that night, and Garnet slept fitfully, rather expecting another visit from a tight Wyitt. She wasn't disturbed. In the morning Junior appeared with Lagonda in tow while Garnet was breakfasting off a tray in bed and announced the latest news was sensational. "A.B. got our monster back to earth," she said. "Re-entry was accomplished. Tell her, Lagonda."

"He's not really a good pool player," Lagonda said. "He thinks he's better than he is." She smiled. "He's not much better than I am, but I like him. The reason he lost less than a hundred dollars is because we quit early."

"Be patient, love," Junior said to Garnet. "She is getting nearer."

"He says to Chambers," Lagonda went on, "that they ought to see Century City even unfinished, with the tall buildings, on account of the San Cristobal—it would give them an idea of Mr. Thomas Sego's plans built up like. Chambers says no, he don't care, he sees all he wants of Century City from the terrace. Dr. Wyitt says—"

"He's not a doctor," Garnet said impatiently, "he's a professor—or was—a teacher in a junior college."

"He is a doctor," Lagonda said. "He told me so. Not the kind of doctor that cures you, no, but—"

"Apparently he effects his own type of cure," Junior interrupted. "Shall we get on to the trees and forget the forest?"

"Anyhow," Lagonda said, "they argued. Dr. Wyitt says he can't help Chambers if he's going to be a child. I thought that would mess it up, but it didn't. Chambers put on some socks and I wrapped him up warm and got him a necktie, and he went out. They didn't come back until a couple of hours ago. Chambers says Dr. Wyitt has a new Cadillac."

"Ah," Garnet said.

"Gives one furiously to think, eh?" Junior said.

"Yes," Garnet said.

That afternoon, having missed her regular morning swim from press of duties, she went in the pool to do her customary six fast laps, and was joined by her father. The sight he presented in bathing trunks was unprepossessing and always bothered him. His skin lay limply on him, his bad knee was enlarged and articulated poorly, and his legs were skinny and threaded by hardening blue veins. "You think it's fun to grow old?" he said. "I've got hanging dugs like one of those Goddamned women you see in African villages in the travel pictures. I can hardly walk, let alone swim, and I can't see two feet ahead of me without my glasses."

Swimming over to the shallow end to stand beside him, Garnet said, "But you can go out and stay all night."

He laughed. "Are the rumors circulating? Yeah, A.B. talked me into going with him. I finally saw Century City close up."

"Were you impressed?"

"Oh, it's not finished, of course, but I don't expect it'll finally be any prettier than A.B. prophesies. He's against Tom's plans for high-rise on the San Cristobal."

"I'm not," Garnet said, "and nobody else is. That's the only means of obtaining maximum utility and return from the land. I suspect Wyitt is inexperienced and visionary."

"Maybe not. Dreaming sometimes comes true, huh? This is a fantastic town, Garnet. Grandpa saw it all on the way. And it might be different and better if people went to the trouble—in the next ten years, and no later. It could be impressive."

"You've been sold a bill of goods. That is Wyitt's party line, criticism and optimism and pipe dreams. Cities are an organic development, coral reefs building where conditions are favorable, blowing wild. You have to take them piecemeal. Leave the dreaming to the people who don't have to count cost."

"Well, never mind now . . ." Chambers said. "Century City didn't use up much of our time, so I took A.B. on a tour of my own."

"Where?"

"Places I hadn't visited for too damned long—the east side, the cathedral on Main Street where they had funeral services for your great-grandmother, the poor lousy trickle of a river running in concrete and smothered by freeway crossings, and out south in the black country. Garnet, they're living like pigs there, in the midst of plenty. What the hell's the matter with this town? . . . I'd forgotten what it was to ride around and look at the Queen. She's too big to love anymore, but somehow you've got to respect her."

Garnet glanced sharply at him, pulling her bathing cap tighter. "I haven't heard you talking like that in years. The trip did you good."

"Well, it's everywhere—" he said, fumbling for his words. "Everywhere. Grandpa's lying in it, if he hasn't blown away. It's a whole chunk of our lives, the biggest chunk perhaps . . . out of nothing . . . out of a village I can almost remember seeing with my own eyes. A confusing thing . . ."

She was silent, waiting for him to speak again, caught up in an indefinable manner, hearing echoes too far off to be intelligible to her ears. The endless, impossibly complicated, gargantuan Queen directed her existence too.

"We had a gardener once," Chambers said. "You didn't know him. Jesús Algonrones. He's dead, but he has descendants. He was great for leaving reminders of him behind, which is one way to make your mark, I guess. They remembered me, and the poor bastards haven't changed much . . . Then we went to call on Ferris's folks."

"And got drunk."

"I did, probably. A.B. had to drive. He has a feel for this stuff, I can make him understand without talking. He showed me the Sunset Strip and the fairies and General Hospital and the poker parlors in Gardena and the all-night markets and we stopped in a joint on Western Avenue and watched clumsy dames take off their clothes—they were amateurs competing for a prize."

"I'm sure it was enchanting," Garnet said.

425

He looked at her, fingering an ear lobe, his shoulders hunched, his bloodshot eyes bright. "You don't get it . . . it's a living thing, immense, diverse, something you can't grasp. Six, ten—how many million people from here to the southern end of the country?—millions, bound up in it, making it, building it, tearing it to pieces, living and dying and going to hell and making money out of it, and maybe even loving it. And leaving it, one way or another, and coming in. They're stripping and swimming at the beaches and sitting in theaters and hollering in bed with women and hollering alone in hospital beds and sailing boats and working and stopped at traffic signals and taking dope and men are falling in love with men and they sit in their mansions and apartments and listen to hymns on Skid Row and get educated and figure out how to reach the moon or kill the Chinese and Russians all at once and hold up banks and—and everything. All here, you know, where once they thought a city couldn't be. All in less than a couple of hundred years. There must be some importance in that, some meaning, eh?"

"To you," Garnet said, and was repelled by what she thought was the amazingly pervasive propaganda of Wyitt. "Figure it out. You have the leisure. I've got to mind the store and stay sober—those were your orders when I was ten years old. I need exercise. Goodbye." She dived away from him, swimming under water, annoyed by her protégé's quick success. And she feared her father was getting dotty. She couldn't count on him as she had; he was growing old.

A. B. Wyitt called every evening, earlier than at first, and four nights in a row took Chambers out with him and stayed very late. He was unaware that a quiet, affable young man wearing a hat—a rare item in men's wardrobes in Southern California—had called on Garnet in accordance with instructions from Aaron Eindhoven. His card identified him as Edward Garrick, assistant chief of the Internal Security Division of Amalgamated Aircraft Corporation. Because AAC employed considerable numbers of people in positions of varying sensitivity with respect to the national defense effort, it maintained its own investigative units and an extensive records library, staffed by experienced personnel. Garrick, for instance, had formerly been an agent in the Federal Bureau of Investigation. Sunset Sea had on several occasions used the services of the Division when dealing in delicate matters, so Garnet knew she could count on full and painfully exact information, promptly supplied.

"My father is considering hiring a man," Garnet explained, "not originally from Los Angeles and heretofore unknown to us. His job would be confidential and involve great responsibility. That's why we would like to know everything possible about him, Mr. Garrick, and especially if the information he has given us is truthful."

"I'm sure we can help you, Miss Brennan," Edward Garrick said. "Mr. Eindhoven has instructed me to put all our resources at your disposal."

Slightly, inexplicably concerned at the possible outcome of the probe, Garnet gave him such details as she remembered of A. B. Wyitt, and they were many. Garrick took careful notes, retrieved his hat, and promised an early report.

"Oh, the sooner the better," Garnet told him nervously. "I—I have a feeling this—arrangement will come to a head shortly."

She was fully justified in making that statement, although her relations with Wyitt were perfunctory for the next few days. Then suddenly they became awfully sticky. Until the confrontation, she did no more than talk to him casually, for the most part in the presence of Chambers and Lagonda. Since neither her father nor Wyitt seemed to pine for her company and kept silent about their nocturnal expeditions, an increasing pique stopped her from questioning them or hanging about. It was impossible for her to believe, much less to admit to herself, that at intervals her eyes perhaps lingered on the professor in wonderment, stricken interest, and even mute solicitation. But there were times when his attitude suggested he was concerned, and outright annoyed, by her inspections. She could recall only two significant things he said to her during that interval. Once he wearily mentioned drinking with Chambers, saying, "Now Lagonda is putting vanilla extract and sugar and an egg in the bourbon and milk, and shaking it up on an electric mixer. It's like being entertained in a soda fountain, but you have a delayed reaction and your head falls off in the morning. Your father takes the mixture along with him in a thermos bottle when we go out. We're going to have a shambles here before long, Miss Brennan." Their second brush had more to do with Garnet than him, and concerned the sudden disappearance of Junior. He missed her, he said, longed for her advice and encouragement, and hoped she wasn't ill.

"She's in fine shape," Garnet replied. "Friends in San Francisco begged her to come to them, Professor."

"I wish you'd address me as Doctor," Wyitt said airily. "Lagonda does."

"I'll call you Wyitt," said Garnet, in abrupt, self-puzzling ferocity. "That's good enough for me, and it'll have to do for you."

He grinned at her and went off arm-in-arm with Chambers, who was beginning to display a paternal affection.

The truth was that Junior looked to be in poor shape, at least mentally. Her depression was caused by Garnet and her insistence that Junior go north and personally check on Dorothy Calvert. A long argument ensued between them, enlivened by some harsh words. "I am not a private eye," Junior said, "and I have never heard of the Calverts. They did not move in my circle. Why in the world would I want to meet the unfortunate woman, and what possible reason can you have for being curious about her?"

"I am acting for my poor foolish father," Garnet said. "Wyitt has to be checked out. That should be sufficient explanation."

"It isn't, love. Tell me more."

Garnet looked hard at her beloved mentor. "You're either with me or against me. It's a case of shape up or ship out, Mister."

"I'm against you unless you can give me a sensible reason for acting irrationally."

"Well . . . I've got to know . . . just got to know."

"Got to know what?" Junior demanded.

"Got to know something about her—" Garnet averted her eyes.

Carefully patting her violet hair with one hand, Junior used the other to put a lace-edged handkerchief to her nostrils. She did not conceal her horror. "This resembles the plague striking a happy household," she said, "and you brought the carrier home to us, Garnet. You're gone— over the dam. You're the bird watching the snake. Confess it."

"I'm afraid we've had it with each other."

"Garnet, you're getting as nutty as all the rest of them: You aren't really fond of him—you're simply out for revenge and to prove a point. Please stop before it's too late. Please let me help you!"

"This is my bedroom. Go somewhere else."

"Think of good old Larry Smith—"

"Do you want me to scream?" asked Garnet.

"No, no," Junior said, and protectively raised the handkerchief higher. "*I'll* scream. And ship out."

They ended the dialogue by weeping, and Junior promised to go to San Francisco. Garnet admitted she felt she was off her rocker. Dr. Rommer was mentioned. Muttering under her breath, Junior refused an offer of a ride to the airport, hastily packed a bag, aroused Lagonda's suspicions with her lame excuses, and departed in a taxi. Confused and frightened, Garnet sank into a brief apathy. Her father ended that somehow restful interlude at an afternoon meeting in the swimming pool; she was seeking him out these days, and contrived to take her exercise later and later. He said conversationally, "You're too thin, Garnet. Being that bony doesn't attract men."

"I'm willing to take the risk."

"I mean it. For instance, you don't attract A.B. He told me so."

428

Anger choked her. She could merely say, "Splendid!" and start off on her six laps. He halted her at the end of a round trip.

"Not that it matters," he went on, as if there had been no interruption in their talk. "I have a hunch A.B. is as weak between his legs as the Smith bastard."

"Father, I cannot tolerate your language."

He nodded amiably. "You're right. Excuse me . . . Do you know where I was the other night?"

"I have no idea."

"Down on East Sixth Street watching the winos. Then we went up in Griffith Park to the Planetarium, and out on Wilshire Boulevard where they're building the new art museum."

"How informative," she said. "Wyitt must be revising your whole scheme of things. What is his purpose? Purely educational?"

"Apparently," he said. "He turned down my offer of a job."

"Raise the price."

"I did."

"He's incorruptible," she said. "Forget him."

"Nobody is incorruptible. When you pay enough, anyone is available."

"Well, if he amuses you—"

"He does. It's funny—nobody else has. I suppose I ought to thank you."

"You're welcome. Buy him. Those little luxuries are nothing for you."

"I'll think over your advice," he said cheerfully. "But he might cost a hell of a lot . . . Last night we were at Los Angeles International. I saw the CAT jets coming in. There was a strange feeling in thinking how I've never been up in a plane. I kept remembering your mother, and thought how your father would sit bolt upright in his urn if he could see what he'd started."

"Don't tell me you are considering flying somewhere. Does the professor work miracles?"

"Sure. Why not? Once I have your future settled—"

"My future?" she asked. "Am I to understand you are going to take an active hand in arranging affairs for me?"

"Possibly," he said. "Maybe you can't manage for yourself. Then I could make a stab at doing something really big—something as big as Grandpa might have imagined, that I'd be remembered for—and get out. I could die somewhere else and come back here to rest with my sister. In the meantime I'd keep moving to ward off death. Junior and Lagonda would have to go with me, and you could have your own setup —that's how it should be. But what can I do to make them sit up and take notice? This is city for a hundred miles, with Disneyland and atomic powerplants and a million cars and air you can't breathe and no man afoot any more and raw guts enough for all the slaughterhouses in the world and those Goddamned airplanes roaring down like castrated bulls . . . I ought to leave a hero, Garnet. The other Brennans did. Any suggestions?"

She was too astonished to reply, and swam away on the six laps, having forgotten she had already negotiated two of them. At once glad and afraid, and wholly confused, she began to suspect the professor was a Caligari and the devil's advocate.

The fifth night A. B. Wyitt was invited to dinner, an unprecedented gesture of goodwill from Chambers, who rarely allowed the family group to be diluted by outsiders. Garnet dressed with care for the event, having been notified in advance by her father, and felt herself buoyed up with a curious sense of anticipation. A little to her surprise and modest approval, she found Wyitt clad in a dark suit, as a prospective applicant for her favors should be. He was, by George, coming around, and she might consider taking him. Lagonda wore her pearls and a new black garment she had sewn in her room and a look of repressed elation, and Garnet presumed she had heard something confidential and encouraging her father did not choose to spread further; instead of irking her, she found it was a relief to be spared fresh secrets.

But despite the auspicious start, the evening failed to remain in Garnet's memory as a few of her finest hours. Wyitt exhibited fatigue and an evident inner depression, and Chambers was harried by stomach gases and a fraying temper. While the first course of bay shrimp cocktails was being removed, Junior came home unheralded, obviously in an uncertain mood, and sat down with them in her rumpled silk suit and daytime jewelry. Chambers held forth in a carping vein: President Johnson had incurred his anger, he thoroughly approved of Barry Goldwater and regretted his hurried exit from Washington, the New York theater in his estimation was dominated by fags producing plays for other fags, he thought he detected a new advance of creeping socialism, the war in Vietnam was silly and Robert McNamara had his hair cut like a bartender's, the bathetic mysticism of the John F. Kennedy cult aroused his ire, and he resented attempts to go to the moon because California was losing out on contracts to make the hardware. Still worse than times out of joint, he had had an unfortunate session that afternoon with his newest doctor, a respected internist. "My heart flutters and misses beats," he said. "This abortionist brought a portable EKG machine with him. So what did he find out for a hundred dollars and a wasted hour? I've got gas! I'm not a cardiac case. I told him of an epitaph on a gravestone my grandfather remembered—all it said was, 'I told you I was sick.' This son of a bitch didn't even have the decency to laugh. One of these days I'll die like my father, of the same disease, and on my death certificate will be a single word, 'Gas'!"

Garnet sat in silence, accustomed to enduring these periods of mingled self-pity and truculence; they rarely lasted for long. Wyitt devoted himself flatteringly to Junior, saying he had missed her and asking questions about her trip. "My dear boy," Junior said glumly, "explain this devotion of yours to me. I am twice your age and getting very wrinkled, and my influence with the Brennans is declining steadily. What have I to offer you?"

"A mother's love and care," Wyitt responded. "Since Miss Calvert, I have been unable to love anybody until I met you. Now I long to sit in your lap and tell you everything. Or you can sit in my lap."

"I'll sit in your lap. Have you serious problems, A.B.?"

"Well, I haven't gas, but there are other difficulties. For instance, I'm growing awfully sick of Cham." Wyitt glanced apprehensively at Lagonda, whose dislike of nicknames for her lord was well known. "Chambers, I mean."

"Oh?" Chambers said. "What the hell have I done to you?"

"I think you're a hypochondriac," Wyitt said, "you've foully wasted years of your life sitting stupidly on your duff, your opinions derived from watching five television sets are utterly unacceptable to any reasonable man, and I'm sick of sharing your damned bourbon milkshakes."

Chambers grinned. "Is that all?"

"Yes, sir. And I presume that's all for me."

"Certainly not. I don't mind people disagreeing with me. You know that."

"Indeed he does," Garnet said. "Dr. Wyitt never misses a trick." She colored instantly; she had not meant to call him "Doctor." It was a slip of tongue and brain, but a significant one.

"We were interrupted, Junior," Wyitt said. "Tell me more of your sojourn in San Francisco. I'm eager to hear every smallest detail. By the way, you didn't happen to meet the former Mrs. Wyitt when you were up there, did you?"

"Yes."

"Eh?"

Garnet observed that Wyitt seemed as startled as she was, if not as outraged. She also saw that her father was interested.

"I made a point of looking her up," Junior said, "and I hasten to report to all those who might be interested." Even Lagonda was leaning forward, Garnet noted. "First allow me to deal with her family, which is tasteless, gummy upper middle class and dreadful. Mr. Calvert is a commission merchant and prides himself on belonging to the Bohemian Club, though God only knows how he got in. His wife is fat and dresses in a style suitable for a woman thirty pounds lighter. Her brain is vacuous and she works as a Gray Lady in a socially helpful, all-white, AMA-approved upper-bracket hospital. She has large, terrible jewelry and lives in a ghastly remodeled house on Telegraph Hill which has matting on the floor and Shoji screens and a fake Buddha put together and artificially aged by child labor in Hong Kong for American tourists just off a President liner; it stands in a minute garden, and the demented woman burns joss sticks as she serves cocktails. The quondam Mrs. Wyitt has two brothers. One of them is sorting vegetables and going on buying tours of the San Joaquin Valley for his father, and the other is an Air Force pilot—in Europe, I think. No doubt he effected his escape as quickly as practicable and will never return."

"Those are the Calverts, to life," Wyitt said. "Is there any heart here which doesn't bleed for me?"

"Mine," Garnet said.

"Say, that was a good idea, looking in on them," Chambers remarked. "Who put you up to it, Junior?"

"Don't ask foolish questions, Chambers," Lagonda said, and stared at Garnet.

"Uh, I thought I might be of service to you, sire," Junior said awkwardly. She went on: "Now we come to Mrs. Wyitt, or Dorothy Calvert. The damnedest things sprout from manure heaps. She is five feet, seven inches in height, leaned-down like a model, full-breasted and narrow-hipped, and impeccably dressed. She has bleached hair which looks real because of her fair complexion and blue eyes, and she's full of smiles and shining white teeth and enthusiasm. Miss Calvert is handsome, tanned and a good skier. Her beaux are legion. She is a receptionist in the main office of the Trans-California Corporation on Montgomery Street, and one of the vice presidents, between wives, is pursuing her. She has pity and contempt for her ex-husband. In reply to my deft questions, she said she cannot now understand how she ever happened to marry him."

"She was getting failing grades at the University of San Francisco," Wyitt explained. "I fell into the job of tutoring her. She's gay and vigorous, and not very bright. That's how one thing led to another . . ."

"Let's face it, A.B.," Junior said. "She looks good enough to eat."

"I know," Wyitt said. "I developed an appetite."

Putting down her fork, Garnet found that her appetite was entirely spoiled. And she hated Junior.

"Did she mention," Chambers asked, "how they came to break up?"

"Don't hesitate, darling," Wyitt said. "I want to hear too."

"No more questions, Chambers," Lagonda ordered.

Junior paused. "Well, her manners are commendable. She only said they were incompatible. She thinks A.B. is a harmless nut."

"That's not too bad a reading," Chambers commented. "But the 'harmless' worries me."

"A young lawyer panting after her," Junior added, "is preparing to file suit to collect the unpaid alimony A.B. agreed to in the settlement. He was generous to a fault, Miss Calvert admits, about money he didn't have. Sometimes she feels a bit guilty, but not guilty enough to waive payment . . . That's all."

"I suppose I'm going to jail," Wyitt said. "Having a number and a cell will be a relief. You'll wait for me, won't you, Junior? You care, don't you? Otherwise you would not have plunged into the Calverts."

"I do care, my boy," Junior replied solemnly. "And I'll wait. And I don't believe I'm the only one."

"You talk about President Johnson or the moon," Lagonda told Chambers. "We're tired of this."

As the dessert and coffee were served, Albert Cassius Washington showed up on another of his periodical visits. He was big, blue-black, handsome, well educated, brilliant, with closely cut curly hair and incisive features and more than a hint of his father's lackadaisical grace, and Garnet loved him dearly. For years he had been her careful, retiring cavalier, and the great joy of Lagonda's advancing years was the firm bond between her white and dark children; what's more, her permanent child, Chambers, had finally forgiven the boy for becoming an accomplished attorney instead of a great lover and athlete. Only the division stemming from Ferris Washington's abysmal treachery was yet in force.

Albert kissed his mother and Junior, acknowledged the latter's introduction to Wyitt, dropped a hand for an instant on Chambers's shoulder, and came around the table to pull up a chair beside Garnet. He kissed her cheek, and she held his hand. He nodded to the maid when she asked if he cared for coffee and the thousand island pudding Chambers was compelled to eat, and said, "I'm glad to meet you, Professor Wyitt. My understanding is that you're the man who is going to pull the rug out from under Chambers so we can dispose of the ranch."

"I'm not sure," Wyitt said. "Occasionally I've had the feeling I was brought into this to marry the heiress."

"Is that a fact?" Albert turned to look quizzically at Garnet. "You? True or false?"

"False," Garnet retorted. "I suppose I have to marry someone, but I'm not desperate yet. Can't you marry me, Al? You're the only man I've ever cared for. How many times must I ask you? Why do you draw the color line?"

"You know why, little one," Albert said, and smiled. "I can't take a prominent role in the struggle for civil rights and simultaneously get mixed up in miscegenation and selling out to the rich folks. They'd hoot me out of town from both sides. Do you want to wreck me?"

"I'll buy you Mississippi," Garnet said. "Then they wouldn't complain."

"I'll present your offer to CORE and SNCC," Albert said, "but I think they'll turn me down. This business is all involved with principles now. Would you consider being my back-street wife?"

"Yes," Garnet said. "Shall we start tonight?"

"That's not funny," Lagonda said sternly, "and you're both too old to act smart-alecky. Stop it."

"I'm mad about her, mother," Albert said. "I can't help it if I'm a darky."

"I love him, Lagonda," Garnet said. "I'm tired of fighting it. I can't go on."

"It's bigger than we are," Albert said. "Youth calling to youth."

"You're stinkers," Lagonda said. "Chambers, speak to them."

"Go ahead," Chambers said. "I like coffee-colored kids."

In the midst of laughing with Albert, Garnet glanced toward Wyitt. He was unsmiling and stiffening in his chair. He had been pinched; he was a hypocrite and a bigot where his feelings ran deep and instinctual. Most of his type were the same. They prated and postured and admitted to nobility, but they really couldn't accept an ultimate equality of races.

"We'll change the subject," Albert said. "Who has an interesting topic?"

"I would like to introduce a motion," Junior said, "commending the merits of a certain Lawrence Smith—"

"Wait a minute," Chambers said. "I'd appreciate a little news from Al. What is your worthless nigger father doing?"

Wyitt stiffened further and turned red. He looked angrily at Chambers. "That is intolerable," he said.

"No, it isn't, Professor," Albert replied. "But perhaps we owe you an explanation for that and what went before. We're all Brennans here, you see—it's the same as entering the priesthood. Am I to take it that you are a supporter of the aspirations of Negroes?"

"Yes," Wyitt said. "Heart and soul. Mind you, I realize I'm a whitey and the time for mere lip service is past—"

"You just put your finger on it," Albert said, "and simplified my explaining. Chambers isn't a whitey. He's one of us. He raised me as his son and put a permanent brace in my spine. His daughter is my sister. My mother is his mother. Her people are his friends. If he hadn't been jealous of my father, my father would still belong to him. Large sums of his money have gone to aid us in the fight you approve of. I'm a member of the firm of Brennan, Baltim, Lely and Brennan; either Brennan you care to choose, to all intents and purposes. Only my stubborn clinging to the Washington name keeps me from being completely a Brennan—Chambers has always wanted to adopt me. How do you think a Negro entered one of the oldest and most fashionable law offices in Los Angeles? Over several dead bodies? You're right. Chambers insisted . . . There's never been any difference in us, do you understand? A nigger can be uncomplimentary about another nigger."

Redder than ever, Wyitt said, "I stand corrected, Mr. Washington." Garnet thought she had not enjoyed such happiness since Junior, making a sweeping entrance to the Coconut Grove of the Ambassador Hotel, had put a heel through the hem of her ball gown and removed the entire rear panel from the waist down. "And I can recall recently meeting some of his cronies on Central Avenue. But he isn't consistent. In most matters he is a hopeless reactionary, an opportunist, a chameleon, a lunatic—"

"He can afford to be," Albert said. "He's got a black heart—or a white one—pick your own color. It's in the right place. He's sane, too. Saner than the rest of us. We're bits and pieces and trying to put on pleasing airs—and he is himself. That himself is wonderful. So wonderful he can stand off and look at himself, and laugh at the brickbats coming his way." He turned toward Chambers. "Now. You were asking about a worthless nigger, sir?"

Grinning, Chambers said, "Yes, I was. You know why I love you? Because you never objected to the names I picked for you. Listen, I want Ferris back."

"You won't get him," Albert said. "Neither you nor my mother, and I hope you're both sorry for how you drove him away. Not for the present, anyhow. He still has his brown girl and plenty of liquor and the food that best agrees with him, and he goes to the race track almost every day. He's a happy man after a lifetime of slights and neglect."

"And you're financing him."

"I am."

Chambers's grin had faded. "I don't care for myself too much, but he's making Lagonda skittish. Something's got to be done."

"Then swallow your pride and go talk to him. It's the only way. Promise him a little dignity and self-respect, you confounded wife-stealer and plantation owner!"

Chambers laughed, but the laughter was cut short when Lagonda got up, said, "I have to go. Excuse me," and left the room. He said, "She's going to cry again, Goddamn it!"

"I'll see what I can do with her," Albert said, and arose. "You've spoiled her past all reason, Chambers." He squeezed Garnet's hand fondly and dropped it. "We're equally at fault in this, however, I suppose—with my divided loyalties and you with your penchant for owning human souls . . . I'm sorry to have subjected you to a family scene, Professor Wyitt."

"I don't mind," Wyitt told him. "I feel that I belong, to a degree. But I'm not going to enter the priesthood."

"Of course you're not," Albert said, and smiled and went after his mother.

"Everybody come with me," Chambers commanded, and kicked back his chair.

They moved to the game room. At first Chambers was grumpy, fiddling with the FM tuner on a radio, switching on and off the television sets, walking uneasily out on the terrace and back; presently his temper improved, and he fell into a discussion with Wyitt, who looked at once gloomy and tentative. Garnet was in a soft glow of vindication. Assuredly the pretentious "doctor" had been cut down to size. She meant to fire a few more darts into him when the opportunity presented. Meanwhile she rebuffed Junior's conscience-stricken attempts at a rapprochement. "I was only joking at the table, love," Junior said in Garnet's ear. "Put my slight indiscretions down to wear and tear from that hegira you sent me on. It wasn't easy, believe me. I had to use mutual friends to arrange the introduction to the Calverts, and the preliminaries were appalling. The questioning was painful. I was obliged to confess that I knew A.B., and they promptly clammed up. It was like pulling teeth to charm them and draw them out. You should have seen me exercising my enormous savoir faire. No one else could have pulled it off. The one redeeming feature, the intriguing aspect, was Dorothy's being such a stunner—"

"I don't care to hear of her," Garnet said coldly.

"That's why you sent me, damn it!"

"Stop shouting in my ear, if you please."

"Look here," Junior said, "I'm engaged in apologizing, princess. Shall I prostrate myself?"

"No thank you."

436

"Am I to blame because Wyitt lost a raving, tall beauty? Would you prefer I lied to you? Have you lost your mind?"

"If I have," Garnet said, "you will be the last to know. Our intimacy is over."

Junior gave the impression she might dissolve in tired tears, and Garnet was stricken by a remorse she attempted to hide. The men were discussing Victorian novelists, a pet subject with Chambers, who read and reread Grandpa's favorite authors. As with virtually any area of knowledge, Wyitt seemed well informed on this; he even knew the less savory details of the private lives of the eminent men. Once the characters and plots had been disposed of, Wyitt related, to the delight of Chambers, how William Makepeace Thackeray had been bedeviled most of his adult years by a frightful case of gonorrhea and assiduously pursued French ballet dancers; how Charles Dickens hated his numerous real children, gave his fatherly allegiance to his books, took up with a young mistress named Ellen Ternan after he discarded his wife, and begot an illegitimate child; how the Brontës were all mad as hatters and given to unsanitary habits; how Dizzy married a woman much his senior and unquestionably nourished a mother fixation; how Willkie Collins was a bold seducer and actually found the woman in white on a London street one night and took her to bed with him for several years; how Captain Marryat indulged in strong drink and had delusions of grandeur; how Anthony Trollope cultivated the petty aristocrats of England and was snubbed by them and ended up a brokenhearted snob; and so on. Garnet could not make up her mind on whether Wyitt was discoursing nervously and distractedly or again feathering his nest with an old fool. Suddenly she felt fatigued and disgusted and announced she was going to her room.

"It's early," Chambers protested. "Are we boring you?"

"In a word, yes. I like my scandal fresher."

"Have you ever heard of any of the people we are discussing, Miss Brennan?" Wyitt asked.

"A few times," Garnet replied. "But I am more familiar with comic strips. Good night, whitey."

He flushed, which enraptured her. "We'll play pool," Chambers said. "Grab a cue, Garnet."

She kissed him, and said, "I couldn't bear it. Good night, Father."

"I'll run along with Garnet," Junior said.

"Please don't," Garnet said. "Stay and amuse Professor Wyitt and my father, please. You're so funny, dear."

She departed amid a silence, rather of the opinion that nobody liked her. It was close to the end, apparently. An end had to come. She thought that if Dorothy Calvert had not been five feet seven inches tall and glamorously lovely, she might have contrived to suppress the more sinister facets of her personality. But that did it. And she feared she was no brighter than Dorothy . . .

Garnet was asleep, after much reading to induce it, when she was roused by a tapping on her door. She turned the nightstand lamp on, slid from bed, and consulted the radio clock. Two-thirty in the morning was too early for another of Wyitt's visits; this would be the pestiferous Junior, unable to endure tossing among the covers and determined to have a peace conference. Staying the hand which was reaching for a robe, Garnet sank back to a sitting posture and mumbled, "Come in, you chump."

Wyitt entered, bleary-eyed, his shirt tieless and unbuttoned at the top, carrying his jacket, and regarded her reproachfully. "That's not a very warm welcome," he said.

She felt drugged and uninterested. "It wasn't meant to be."

"I'm bagged again, Miss Brennan. The dogged madman and I must have had ten bourbon milkshakes apiece."

"I couldn't care less. Get out of here."

He moved forward and sat groaningly beside her, discarding the jacket. Somehow his closer presence occasioned no surprise or unease; he was the harmless nut, and besides done in. Even her modesty didn't seem worth bothering about, although she was wearing the sort of nightgown she preferred, a short garment of sheer material that came only halfway down her thighs. She didn't reach for the robe. Why should she worry if the towering Miss Calvert had failed to madden him?

"I think I'm going to drop in my tracks," he said. "This might kill me."

"Then don't come back," she replied.

"I have to. I joined the club tonight."

"What?"

"Cham put me on his staff. I'm employed until further notice—I presume so I can pay my gambling losses. I dropped over two hundred dollars at the pool table and had to accept. Then your father got restless and turned on the late-late shows on two TV stations and is watching them. I couldn't stand it. How can anybody look at one old movie, let alone two at once? He's memorized them all by now. He speaks the lines before the actors can say them."

"He isn't interested in winning your money," she said.

"Of course he is. But I can beat him. Wait and see. He's so damned lucky!"

438

"No, this is good. It means he's serious about the San Cristobal at last. You must try to be bright and helpful, I'll coach you—"

"No, no," he said. "You don't understand at all. I have, God forgive me, persuaded him to come out of his cave. Do you remember anything of *A Tale of Two Cities?*"

"Not much."

"Well, it's in the beginning. They've freed Dr. Manette from a French prison and he's taken to England to his daughter Lucie. In the words of Jarvis Lorry, the banker, Manette is 'recalled to life.' Miss Brennan, those words are applicable in this incredible penthouse and I'm the new Jarvis Lorry. Cham has been recalled to life. I'm to blame. I plead guilty. But I knew not what I was doing."

"You *are* drunk," she said. "Stop being offensive."

"He used the words to me himself—'Dr. Brennan has been recalled to life'!"

"That might be good too."

"I've got to beat him," he said feverishly, "and I'm not improving. My stroke is jerky. I can't seem to handle the cue ball well enough to get position . . . Miss Calvert will want her money."

"Look, if you turned up here in an attempt to borrow from me to pay *her*—"

He snorted. "That would be the supreme irony, eh? You can't bear the thought of her, can you? Poor old Junior had to go to San Francisco on your account, didn't she—to case what I'd had? Shame on you! Are you jealous? Do you have an evil mind?"

"Professor, I warn you—"

"Don't worry. I'm not going to ask you to help out, and I'll repay the other loan in a few days."

Once more, to her horror, Garnet found herself talking without thinking, babbling like an automaton: "Did you—you enjoy it with her?" Her ears heard the words, yet she could not comprehend the fact that she was saying them.

"Yes. It was wonderful as long as we weren't talking. She has a magnificent body and lots of stamina and the brain of a bird and the orderly instincts of a cub scout den mother." Wyitt put an arm about Garnet, raised her face to his with his free hand, and kissed her on the mouth. She did not resist or try to pull her lips away. A tremendous, bewildering flush suffused every inch of her skin. He released her finally and gasped, reviving stale fumes of liquor. "It was precisely like that," he said. "I think you have an evil mind. What else were you imagining? Something on this order?"

With his hands on her, she managed to struggle feebly. The heat his

439

touching engendered in her was fantastic and debilitating. She retrieved her voice, but the phrase she employed was scarcely authoritative: "What are you doing?"

"Trying to find whether you are a rumpy or a stubby."

He was doing exactly that, and she had fallen backward on the bed. His caressing of a sensitive area made her give a tight little moan. She was perishing in a marvelous fire.

"You are a rumpy," he said. "We can show you. But you have to be mated with a stubby . . . That's a joke of sorts, Miss Brennan, and you're quite serious, aren't you? Let me have a kiss."

Weak and dissolving as she was, she tried to raise her head. He didn't mean that. His kisses rained on her everywhere, and in unimaginable places. She closed her eyes and gave up the ghost. Then he desisted. The lamp went off. Lifting her lids, she perceived his dim, standing figure, gyrating oddly. She could only repeat, "What are you doing?"

"Undressing. I'm going to bed—with you. Take off your nightgown."

Her nightgown was already wadded up in a circle under her armpits; she sat up swayingly and pulled it over her head. She could, under the circumstances, think of nothing else to do. A seam split and made a tiny ripping sound. The next moment her virgin bed had another occupant. He rose before her spectrally, on his knees, pushing her thighs apart, and she sank back in a watery, fluid manner, legs spreading. "Is this the first time?" he asked.

"Yes."

"You're more wasteful of your life than Cham. Well, surely you know the mechanics. Take it and guide it in. Try to help me."

Scarcely aware of what she was holding, she gladly obliged in her ravishment. The intrusion was a shock and a stifling, enjoyable surprise. He balanced over her, braced on his elbows, in an awkward position, and her accommodation of him was embarrassingly humble and eager. She waited for the pain and difficulty, resolved to choke any outcries. But he was careful and gentle and insidious and patient. "Am I hurting you?" he said.

"No."

"You're a skinny, active, athletic girl—that's taken care of most of the impediments. Now join me in this!"

Suddenly he was descending on her, clasping her, touching her at a molten core, and she buried her face against his shoulder and lost track of the sequence of events. She was in the airplane, as in the dream, but the stewardess was helpful. The steps went down. Safety was in sight. She achieved the most magnificent of escapes, and cried, mouth wide, against Wyitt's throat. The tension, the great quivering sensations, the

440

release were all unbearably keen, and nearly unendurable, and mercifully brief, and absolutely necessary. And afterward the slow, warm
waves of fatigued, quiescent relief that swept her, regular as the declining beating of her heart, were infinitely, softly satisfying.

He removed himself from her and put his head on the other pillow,
and said aggrievedly, "That's another thing about Miss Calvert. She
kept right on talking no matter what was happening to her. In her estimation the unadorned aesthetics of a fundamental act were not sufficient. She had to give it an air of phony grandeur, to be admired, to
elicit gratitude for the use of certain portions of her anatomy. It was
like a debate interrupted by unseemly yells of triumph, and too nerve-
wracking. You're different. You're as comfortable as an old shoe despite inexperience. You appreciate the opportunity. Thank you very
much."

Garnet felt too shattered and contented for a reply, and she was unable and unwilling to think. But she was dimly conscious of both satisfaction at the shortcomings of Miss Calvert and resentment of his
description of her own attributes. In a way, Miss Calvert's stand had
merit. It should have been more romantic. Weeping again, irrationally
happy, Garnet wiped her eyes and realized she did indeed feel gratitude. Nothing else—even the professor's crass sensuality—seemed to matter at the moment.

"I hope no one overheard us," he said. "Perhaps if they did they'll
attribute it to Odysseus and Penelope having a spat. Good night."

He was asleep and breathing heavily within seconds. Garnet's
quandary deepened. To tell him he'd have to go presented obvious
difficulties, and anyhow she didn't want to part from him. On the other
hand, having him with her when her breakfast tray was brought at
eight o'clock was not feasible. She shifted reluctantly, put on the light,
set the radio clock for five in the morning, turned off the light, and
snuggled against her companion. The very contact with his flesh was
immensely pleasurable. There was no use now considering the moral
and other aspects of . . .

A disc jockey talking and putting on a rock and roll number in an
all-night radio station awakened them before dawn. Wyitt rolled over,
said "Where am I?" and laid a hand on one of Garnet's breasts. He
added, "Don't tell me, I know," and kissed her, which made her extremely happy.

"You've got to go."

"Yes. But before I do—"

"Yes," she said.

His arms groped for her, and then retreated. "You realize who the victor is," he said. "Your father. He's moving his pieces on the chessboard again, and we are a couple of pawns. Do you understand how clever and unscrupulous he is beneath that veneer of crudity and obtuseness?"

"Oh, don't talk."

"We've been gulled, Miss Brennan. He intended that we land in bed together—the woman called cold and perhaps a lesbian, and the weakling intellectual who couldn't hold a beautiful wife. All we're doing is proving him wrong, exactly as he planned. This is no real coming together, but a—"

"You're worse than Miss Calvert," she said. "Talk, talk, talk. Can't you manage it again?"

"You are an authentic Brennan," he said. "No perceptible inner scruples. Whatever exists was put there for your taking . . ."

Three nights after, out of, as far as she could tell, sheer gratitude, she gave him a rumpy named Circe.

three

ONE morning Garnet took A. B. Wyitt to the ranch. He had been putting off the trip, as though reluctant to come to any conclusion about it, and he gave no hint of the suggestions he intended to make to Chambers. She refused to press him, and she was not suspicious; besides, they had plenty of other things to discuss. She assumed he lacked any new ideas, or was too inexperienced for a job of such magnitude: she would wait him out, intervening when necessary and becoming the power behind the throne. But she proposed also to sit on the throne.

They went in her station wagon, and the journey on the freeways required only twenty-five minutes. Wyitt, far from being in high spirits, commented on his transportation. He said, "This isn't a very good car."

"Not to someone who has a Cadillac," Garnet said. "I've heard of the luxury you enjoy. How do you manage it?"

"By lease. One hundred eighty-nine dollars every month, open end. Don't ask me what open end means. I haven't the slightest idea. And I think I'm behind on this month's payment. The car may slide from my grasp any moment."

"The wagon's paid for."

"I thought as much," he said. "But you are disapproving of my way of life, and your father, encrusted with prejudice, is fascinated with how I leap from cliff to cliff, reveling in the creature comforts and never taking a hard fall. Neither of you poor innocent millionaires has the smallest conception of the trust Americans have in their fellow Americans, or the credit they're willing to extend. I live on credit cards and shuffle bills as they come in, taking care of the most deserving of my creditors. The bank is glad to honor my overdrafts and scarcely bothers to listen to my pious promises of reform. My house is on an FHA loan, and those boys are amazingly patient. A building and loan company gave me an electric toaster for starting a small account. I don't need cash in my pocket—I have a Trans-California card, a Diner's Club, American Express, a layaway Christmas fund, Standard Oil and Union, a fly now and pay later—"

"Yes, yes."

"I can look forward to an old age pension, and the benefits of Social Security. Medicare is coming to repair my aging body. Until I landed the post with Cham, I was collecting my unemployment insurance. I haven't a care in this increasingly solicitous society."

"Oh, sure."

"When I get to seventy—"

"You won't live that long," Garnet said.

"Not if I continue associating with the Brennans," Wyitt said. "However, I propose to put a stop to our strange friendship very shortly, as soon as I have fulfilled my commitment to the ranch."

"That will just be the start of your work, if my father is interested."

"I don't think so."

"Why?"

"Wait for me to arrive at a conclusion, will you?"

"I feel you ought to marry me," she said.

"So does your father."

"Really?"

"Indubitably," he said. "Last night he took me on top of the mountain to show me the world, as Satan did with our Savior. I wasn't tempted either. I have my credit cards. I must say Cham was impressed, and possibly a little bewildered."

"In other words, you were still working on him."

He looked at her sadly. "You're uncommonly dense and insensitive, Miss Brennan. No matter how hard I try, I can't convince you that your assets aren't irresistible. Or that you can't have whatever you want. Yet it's true. I am not to be corrupted. My heart is pure. My strength is as the strength of ten—"

"Oh, shut up."

"Very well. Your crudities remind me of your father."

"I've just proposed to you," Garnet said, in as reasonable a fashion as she was capable of under the circumstances, "which somewhat surprises me. I suppose it's because we've had such . . . uh, fun together. But don't let it go to your pretty head. You'll never get a better offer.

444

And keep in mind this one isn't going to be held open indefinitely."

"Only until you lose hope," he said.

"So far you have good grades, Professor. That's why you're still in the running." She lifted a number of typed sheets bound in a plain folder from the seat beside her. It was the report on Wyitt, Albert Bennett, sent to her the previous day by special messenger from Edward Garrick. "Here. I've been reading this with great interest. On the whole you seem to have told the truth."

He opened the report, forehead wrinkling; she was unable to determine, from his expression, whether he was hurt, surprised or chagrined, or all three. "I see . . . Amalgamated Aircraft Corporation. Internal Security Division. You've left nothing to chance or a woman's homely intuition, have you?"

"I'm glad you didn't say a homely woman's intuition."

"You're fatter. That's an improvement, at least."

"I am attempting to meet your objections."

"Then begin using makeup."

"Read Garrick's evaluation of the research," she said. "You aren't the catch of the season exactly."

He put verbal footnotes to the crisp pages he turned, elegantly triple-spaced on heavy bond paper, inscribed with an electric typewriter. "I am an only child, but there was another one after me. She died at birth . . . They've misspelled Manatteoc, Minnesota, where my father had his medical practice . . . He was gone at thirty-seven, not thirty-eight —from pneumonia, not a heart attack—his heart failed because of the congestion in his lungs. Don't they bother to find the autopsy records? My mother is married to a man named Gesston, two *s*'s. She lives in Clearwater, Florida now; she moved from Miami two years ago. Shall I pencil in corrections and keep everything shipshape?"

"That won't be necessary."

"Holy smoke, they've even got the line from under my photograph in the high school annual! 'A.B. will succeed by indirection, he never follows a straight line.'"

"Apt, don't you think?"

"I disagree . . . They have some of my academic records fouled up . . . The financial statement is too generous; I'm much worse off than they indicate, and consider the situation I'll be in when Miss Calvert's legal admirer files his suit . . . Now this is pretty damned bad!"

"That would be the estimate of your character as deduced from interviews with associates and friends?"

"No. I'd say the estimate is pretty close to the mark. I am bright, somewhat irresponsible, given to short enthusiasms, and possibly not as serious as I should be. I do tend to evade difficult situations. Flight is my solution to them. But this security classification—'Not recommended for clearing above lower echelons.' I dodged military service by staying in the cloister, yes. Who didn't, if he had the brains? The Korean War was hardly a popular crusade—"

"Read on."

"Oh. Liberal tendencies. Inclined to espouse left-wing causes. Highly individualistic and betrays evidences of erratic behavior under stress of regimentation. Some display of rebellious traits. Short, unhappy marriage. What's the asterisk for? Oh, childless. Asked to resign from Laguna Seca Junior College faculty by Board of Regents for unbecoming conduct . . . Has Cham looked at this? Perhaps he ought to see it. He might want to make the entirely reasonable request that I stop sleeping with you before you conceive."

"Let well enough alone, please. He doesn't know we are—"

"They all know, you idiot. Even Lagonda—she has started scowling at me. Those mad cries in the night, the dark circles under your eyes, your constant expression of catlike satisfaction—"

"You're mistaken, I'm sure," Garnet said. "And don't worry over your character deficiencies. I'll take care of them. Marriage, money and social position will improve your security rating, in case you ever need a better clearance—and your manners too."

"Oh, God bless you, Miss Brennan," Wyitt said. "You are as generous as you are efficient, and as kindly as you are beautiful. I will say no more. It's such a relief to have everything laid on for one. No need to ever act on my own again, once I have you, eh? You're my schoolmistress rather than my mistress."

Garnet suspected that she practically had him. If the AAC Security Division précis summed him up pretty well—and she believed it did—then he wouldn't hold out long. Weaknesses overbalanced strengths in him, and he would succumb to steady, tactful pressure. When he was in her grip, she could hack something out of him as Eino Nurri brought bulging, powerful figures out of unpromising cubes of marble; it only took time and devotion. All she had to do was remain calm and stay top dog . . . For an instant, affection clouded her judgment. She stared at him and wanted to kiss him. He appeared youngish and troubled and tired, and she yearned to pet and pamper him. Even to defer to his wishes and accept his orders. There was a strange, wavering, womanly satisfaction in the thought of submission. But that was dangerous thinking. She couldn't afford sentimentality yet. First she had to bring him to heel and arrange the nuptials . . . But he was wonderful. His hands were gentle and delightfully exploratory. She loved the subtle intimacies

446

of the flesh that were growing between them. When he thrust into her the communion was inexplicable and all-embracing. He had a sense of humor and intelligence and a concealed slim taut kind of male power and singleness of purpose. With him she was happy! Her unscarred heart had indeed been touched by a shining, pristine love. Notes of victory and accomplishment sounded in her inner ears. He represented a splendid achievement; sufficient achieving for her, anyhow. She was, by George, as much a woman as Miss Dorothy Calvert or Paula Sego or anybody else—

"Look out for that truck!" Wyitt shouted.

She swerved into another lane, narrowly avoiding both a tanker's trailer and a car overtaking her. The man in the car cursed her, and the driver of the tanker shook his head in disgust. She blushed and said, "I was looking at you . . ."

"Well, stop it. I'd rather die in bed from too frequent sexual intercourse than out on a freeway." Wyitt unsnapped his seat belt, squirmed free of his coat, wiped his face with a handkerchief, and carefully refastened the seat belt and pulled it tight.

The day was clear and beginning to heat. From the mountains blew a rasping, sandy Santa Ana wind. At the elevation of the huge, roaring, multi-laned road, divided by fencing, the view was wide and stark. The San Fernando Valley presented a sea of residential roofs and jutting buildings and simmering black parking lots and streets knifing straight across the central zone; eastward stood knobbly hills with rocky outcroppings, and to the west their hairless, scarred counterparts, infested by houses poised on stilts against sheer drops and curving roads and homesites ripped from clayey earth and shale and whole rises truncated to ensure living room. There was a great curving dam to prevent floods, an artificial lake, faded skies overhead, uncounted thousands of cars, a pitiful scattering of starveling trees, a genial ugly air of haste and confusion, and evidences of an appalling energy. Everywhere the refrigerators ran, the traffic lights blinked red and yellow and green, the swimming pools glittered, the children yelled and played in their black-topped schoolyards, and the neat little lawns sucked up the drops flying out of the sprinklers. It was brown and ochre and partially green and purpley in the distance where a towering spine of rock and earth sealed off the deserts, and geranium ivy climbed and fought diligently to cover the wounds made by the earth-moving machinery and put out pinkish-crimson blossoms to astound visitors from cold regions. Civilization of a sort had come here, in a manic profusion that knew no end.

"My God . . ." Wyitt said. "In a short time there will be nothing but the dichondra, the sidewalks and curbs, the concrete, the supermarkets and the automobile dealers. And the apartment houses. And the signs. The hills will sink under the weight of the home owners and their appliances and wall-to-wall carpeting. These new people will never know how it looked once, dry and hard but bold and open, tough and serene. Won't they all go nuts without room to turn around where space was meant to be?"

Garnet was inclined to humor him. "Wait until you see the San Cristobal. It hasn't changed materially."

"But you're going to accomplish that."

"Certainly. What else can I do? You're supposed to sugarcoat the pill."

He shook his head and fell silent, and she turned off the freeway, circled to go through an underpass, and they arrived at the gates of the ranch, which had a large sign overhead identifying it and an imposing stretch of four-bar wooden fence painted white. Horses wandered in permanent pasture wetted by jetting irrigation devices set in portable pipes laid along the ground. A broad macadam road, with lights for nighttime on tall silvery standards, lay beyond the closed gates. Running on the wind was a muffled chugging sound.

"See the little box with the crossed arrows on the door?" Garnet asked. "That was the Villanueva brand mark. Open the door, insert this key, and turn. The gates will open. They're electric." Wyitt got out, did as requested, and the portals whined away from each other. She called to him, driving through: "Take out the key and come in. They'll close behind you." He joined her in the station wagon and they drove on.

The chugging grew louder, and then the walking beams, actuated by diesel engines, were visible on the hills and in the valleys, as well as the storage tanks and a pipeline plunging suddenly underground. Grading for cleared spaces where the drillers had worked, and the roads leading to them, were everywhere. "We still pump enough oil to make it worthwhile," Garnet remarked, "but I persuaded Father to remove the derricks and clean up a few years ago." She indicated a sign which read: Cristobal I. "That's where they first struck it rich, my grandfather and great-grandfather."

"Bless them all."

They rolled by bare fields, broken only by the hooves of animals. Then there were orange groves neatly tended, with white-painted concrete cylinders for flood irrigation, the propellers of the machines used for dissipating cold air turning idly atop their towers; abandoned walnut and olive groves, slowly perishing; and on upper levels the blond stubble of harvested wheat and oats. Here and there Mexican workmen could

448

be seen, and a tractor dragging a gang-disker behind it. The hot wind gathered strength, raking the parched earth, and gave off an acrid scent. "This is not charming," Wyitt said.

"You haven't been here long enough," she replied. "You're an outsider. They never understand the pull of dry country."

She turned into the home valley and Wyitt moved slightly in surprise, regarding the little lake fed by the artesian springs, more horses, and mules, burros, an array of period wagons, buggies, antique ox carts and stagecoaches in a long shed, and a great sheet-metal barn stocked with bales of hay; built onto it was a separate tackroom. A queer, small frame house, steeply roofed and freshly painted stood alone; nearby was a modern, rambling, white stucco ranch house and neat, semi-joined, motel style lodgings for the ranch help. It was a display of the utmost neatness and orderly labor, with washing hanging on a line and a baby or two in his carriage and a radio playing the music of a marimba band. And farther on, incredibly, rose the false fronts and weathered outlines of a vintage western town which had a saloon, a hotel, a bank, a Wells-Fargo office, hitching posts and watering troughs. In the extreme distance lay what seemed to be a Mexican village, merely a shell like the frontier settlement, crumbling and showing plaster rubble, built around a well in a plaza. Higher up were the timbered entrances to mines, the flume of a placer outfit, a length of unrelated adobe wall, a corral and loading chute, a suggestion of what could have been a Mexican church, and an ominous plank gallows. "Really . . ." Wyitt said.

Garnet laughed as she stopped at the ranch house. "Did my father neglect to tell you about our never-never land?"

"Yes."

"The television people come out here and film their horse operas. It was Harry Sego's idea to provide for them, and the operation turns a fair profit. TV pays better than crops these days. But you won't hear shooting or see any posses today; by this time of year they have made most of their shows for the winter season."

"And the little house?" Wyitt said. "The one from New Hampshire? It looks real and out of character."

"That belonged, I think, to a man who ran the ranch for my great-grandmother. I can't remember his name. My father wanted it preserved."

"I saw your great-grandmother's picture in the Brennan Memorial Library book. She was pretty—prettier than you."

"I'm afraid so."

"Scarcely more moral, though, according to legend."

"She was sedate in her old age," Garnet said. "There's hope for me."

449

Bud Madsen, a burly, fair-haired man, custodian of the San Cristobal, came from the ranch house to greet them. He conveyed them inside, where an air conditioner was running, and introduced his wife, who opened cans of soft drinks. A Mexican woman left off cleaning the parlor and went in another room, but the vacuum cleaner she operated kept whining and they had to raise their voices to be heard. Bud remarked that it was pretty quiet now, with nobody making pictures and the drought hurting. He had a herd of longhorn cattle the movie people doted on that he was trying to graze, and he thought before long he'd have to bring them down to the feed lot; without rain, they just couldn't find enough to put in their bellies. Mrs. Madsen said the dust was terrible for her housekeeping and apologized for the state of the furniture. "But it's better without the cowboys and Indians and crews and trucks and all," she added. "And the whooping and hollering. The paper cups and napkins and cigarette butts they scatter!"

Garnet explained their purpose in coming, and accorded Professor Wyitt's inspection a proper importance. "Oh," Madsen said. "I've been expecting this for the last five years, Miss Brennan." He grinned. "I figured it might give me a second chance to meet your father—I've seen him once in twenty years. He's sure not getting what he could out of the acreage."

"Professor Wyitt's going to make him see the light," Garnet told him.

"Well, I don't care for myself, you understand," Madsen said. "I've got two teen-agers, and they complain about the long ride on the school bus—they have to go clear to Las Flores—and not having the friends they should. The TV reception isn't too good on account of the hills, and my wife is lonesome and wants to live again in town before we get too old . . . But it does seem a shame in a way. This is the last piece of ground around here held by one family and more or less as it was a hundred years ago. It's too bad it has to go along with everything else." He grinned again. "But don't pay attention to me. My age is showing, and the San Cristobal grows on you."

"I agree with you," Wyitt said. "It is too bad."

"I don't, Bud," Garnet said. She smiled. "But then, it's our land."

She put her glass aside and got up, asking Madsen for the loan of his jeep; she didn't think the professor would care to tackle a horse. Wyitt shook his head hurriedly. Madsen took them back to get the jeep, and called their attention to four massive white oxen in the barn. "Clear from the south of Italy," he said. "They're for pulling carts in the movies, and luckily there was no need for breaking 'em in. I'm having my usual hard luck holding onto hands. Up the road they have a lot of small electronic plants, and nobody wants to get dirty or strain his back

450

or get his feet stepped on when he can make good money wiring circuits or looking through a magnifying glass at diodes and transistors. I really am behind the times."

Finishing petting the handsome, placid, foreign beasts, Wyitt motioned for Garnet to drive. He grabbed a handhold affixed to the dashboard and settled himself resignedly, his coat wadded behind the seat. Madsen waved them off. "Just a general tour, eh, Professor?" Garnet said.

"Yes, and let's not fall off a cliff . . . I presume you've been all over the ranch at one time or another?"

"Oh, yes, since I was a little girl—on horseback, which is the best means of seeing it. Senior, Junior's mother, was a good rider, and she used to bring me here every week. We'd put our lunches in the saddlebags and strike out into the blue."

"What does the San Cristobal mean to you?"

"What do *you* mean?"

"The valuation you put on it, spiritually, emotionally, financially—"

Garnet shifted the car into four-wheel drive in preparation for climbing and shrugged. "The financial will suffice. I want to cash in on it. I'm a practical woman."

"Cham ought to come here. I can't understand why he doesn't."

"Don't you know his superstition? He never returns to something he's started—or that started him. It would spoil his luck."

"He has broken the rule with me. I took him one night to the Brennan Memorial Library and he stood there lost in wild surmise like that guy lonely on a peak in Darien. The watchman wouldn't let us in—Cham had never seen the inside—and he acted Brennanish for a few minutes, but we saw in the forecourt that damned awful monumental outsize formless tribute Eino Nurri carved of the brothers. How did you ever get into that?"

"Well, Father reveres the family, as you know. On our European trip he saw Nurri's work and decided it was grand enough for his conception of Lucius and Cassius. He sent Nurri to Los Angeles with fifteen tons of marble and set him up in a studio. Senior and Junior approved, which helped. You remember the rest. The library was simply an offshoot of the twin figures, arms entwined lovingly, contemplating what they had wrought."

"You're more cynical than I am. You frighten me, Miss Brennan."

"Perhaps my attitude is Nurri's fault. After he finished with the brothers, he wanted to do me. I refused to pose in the nude, especially for a sculptor more abstract than Epstein—if I was going to be naked, I intended to look like Canova's figure of the sister of Napoleon."

451

"Pauline."

"Yes. I knew you'd know her name . . . We settled for a thin draping; it would not have got that far, but Senior and Junior thought I might be immortalized. One day I was alone in the studio with Nurri, I forget why—a moment of carelessness, I imagine. Anyhow, he was sixtyish and had white whiskers, but he started chasing me. I had to slap the poor old man."

"You're common clay, Miss Brennan. A clod, a philistine, a money-grabber. You have no finer instincts. I look down upon you."

"I told you—I'm entirely practical. I only dream of what I can put to use."

Wyitt suddenly cowered. "Watch out! You'll turn us over."

"Don't worry," Garnet said. "These jeeps are half mountain goat."

"That's another thing I don't like about you," Wyitt said. "You're braver than I am."

They saw places untouched by time and man, and the longhorn cattle looking thin and melancholy, and a couple of escapee horses that had particularly vexed Bud Madsen. The little car grunted and roared and scraped through the brittle ground cover, and dust cascaded on the riders. Gophers and squirrels popped in their holes, a sizable rattlesnake sunned himself on a rock ledge, a fox ran fast to obscurity, once Garnet halted so a procession of quail could bob across the pair of wheeltracks she followed. At last she stopped in a diminutive valley watered by a dying stream; there was shade under the wide spread of very old live oak trees, and a patch of browning grass. Wyitt knelt by the stream and bathed his face and hands and dried them on a handkerchief. "This is called the oak glen," Garnet said. "In the time of the Villanuevas raiding parties of Mojave Indians and the bandits from Sonora holed up here. I suppose it was pretty once, when the rains fell regularly, and according to family legend there was more precipitation then. Do you think if rocks and trees could talk they'd have some interesting things to tell us?"

Flicking his shoulders mutely, Wyitt sat beside her and clasped his wrists around his doubled knees. He was silent for a while, frowning, eyes narrowed. "Thinking?" she asked. "I was disappointed when you didn't bring a briefcase full of maps and take notes."

"I'm listening," he replied. "Listening to the silence. It's magical. Hearing the wind. Engorging peace and quiet and the luxury of being alone. How can a man and woman ever be alone in megalopolis? There're too many of us already. We are in a maelstrom of bodies and motors and noises and hurtling objects and smells not meant for human nostrils. We have found a sanctuary, Garnet."

452

"You called me by my given name. I'm making progress."

"I beg your pardon for the familiarity. Miss Brennan, I should have said . . . Miss Brennan, you don't share my holy exaltation. You have to rip this all apart, don't you?"

"Yes. I want to make more progress."

He looked at her in genuine sadness. "I feel sorry for you. No, envious. And sorry for myself. You belong here, now, this moment, and for a lifetime. This age is yours. The future is yours. It's not mine. I wonder if I belong anywhere. You can have your Queen."

Impressed, she knew not quite how, she leaned over and kissed his cheek. "I'm willing to share what I have. Belong to me. Why won't you marry me?"

"Belong to you . . ." he said. "That's the rub. That's where we differ."

"You'd better explain."

"Oh, I've heard the consort bit from Cham, and the theory of random selection from Junior. They laughed when they told me, but—"

"Aren't they the confiding sort!" Garnet said.

"I'm the wobbly sort. I invite merciful revelations. It's my sole talent."

"I'll shore you up. You need me, A.B. I'm no whining Miss Calvert. I'll put starch in you."

"The hell you will," he said. "You're a prize all right, but not for me. I've had one unhappy fling at matrimony and that's plenty. With Miss Calvert I was at least an equal, and her father was just moderately well heeled and an idiot, not a mad Croesus about to enjoy a renaissance through my supplications. With you I'd be a mere appurtenance, at stud until further notice, and God knows what Cham would do to me in the course of a few years."

"He's going away, isn't he?"

"Perhaps. No doubt as his immortal Grandpa went away, and then returned to direct the next generations." Wyitt released his knees, took Garnet's hand, and patted it in a consolatory fashion. "Look here, Miss Brennan—it's no go. We have had our hectic honeymoon, courtesy of Wilshire Boulevard's Nero, and there will never be any dull, repetitive marriage to spoil the memories. Forget it. If I weren't a weakling, I wouldn't be even this involved."

"A.B., I hate to sound like a daytime soap serial, but I have given you everything—"

"It wasn't enough. You're interesting without your clothing, but married couples are dressed most of the time. Infatuations wear off quickly. Consider it my fault and forgive me for backing out. Put it down to idealism, if you want, or a lack of ambition. Or remember the Security

Division's analysis: rebellious traits, evidences of erratic behavior, seeks solutions by flight. Are you determined to put me on the wing this moment?"

Garnet shook her head.

"Good girl," he said. "We have come to an understanding. The romance is over. Thanks a million for the tiring interludes in your bedroom. I advise you to concentrate on that Larry Smith Junior is forever selling, and you needn't inform him of me. Have you grasped the nettle, Miss Brennan?"

"Yes," Garnet said. "Shall we go on with the tour?"

Arising, helping her to her feet, Wyitt wore a dubious expression. "You resemble a dour family portrait . . ."

When they got back to the ranch house, Garnet refused Mrs. Madsen's offer of lunch and drove Wyitt along Ventura Boulevard. He insisted they keep going until they found a restaurant displaying the Diner's Club membership sign. "As long as we have reached an intelligent conclusion," he said, "I insist on paying. It's the gracious thing to do. Don't attempt to thank me."

The meal was leisurely and relaxing. Garnet enjoyed being with him, and she had fallen into the comforting habit of eating all she wanted. It seemed a new and inviting path to serenity. He began to talk of the ranch, and she stopped him. "No, let's conclude on us," she said. "We'll deal with the business end later. You know, this is our first real date—"

"And our last. You sound like a schoolgirl."

"Well, why not? I never was a schoolgirl, I suppose. Too many responsibilities."

"How touching. But it's difficult to feel pity for a rich steel butterfly."

"Mustn't be rude at the end, Professor."

"I beg your pardon," he said. "You make me nervous for some reason."

"I think I should have a reward for my good behavior. Other girls, before they give in, are courted and—"

"Miss Brennan, you are no longer a girl. You should have given in, as you put it, long ago."

"Still," she said, "all you've ever done is come in and sleep with me. No theater tickets, dances, parties, flowers, champagne—"

"I can't afford the niceties."

"Am I not entitled to one pleasant, ordinary memory? Why don't you take me out tonight? Then we can call it quits."

"I'd rather not."

"Please. Pretty please."

454

"Your father needs me."

"I'll talk to him."

"I'm doing this under protest," Wyitt said. "Make a note of that."

At the penthouse, Chambers wasn't hard to find. In pajamas and robe, unshaven and barefooted, he was restlessly pacing the living room, watched by Lagonda, who exhibited a coolness both to Wyitt and to Garnet. "I feel jumpy and trapped," Chambers said. "It's the bumming around with A.B., I guess. My Goddamned stomach is as sour as a persimmon."

"I'll get you a glass of milk," Lagonda said, and got up and left.

"She's sore at us," Wyitt said to Garnet.

Garnet ignored him. "You're up early, Father," she said.

"I told you," he replied. "I feel lousy. Did you see the San Cristobal?"

"Miles of it, in clouds of dust," Wyitt said. "I feel you ought to have a last look, Cham."

"All right," Chambers said. "I'll get dressed and go with you now. But I'm not going all over the place."

Surprised, Garnet said, "You've become a man of action. Why the hurry?"

"I have to make up my mind," Chambers said. "You won't rest until I do. Listen, I want Lagonda to go along, and Junior. We have to discuss it. Where is Junior? I haven't seen her this morning."

Lagonda came in with the milk. "She's at the Garden Club lunch at the Bel Air Hotel. Garnet is supposed to be there too."

"We'll pull her out on the way," Chambers said. "Get ready, Lagonda." He took the glass, sipped from it, and belched heartily. "Jesus, that relieved the pressure! Garnet, are you coming?"

"No, you'll have a full staff," she said. "Father, the professor has requested the honor of taking me out tonight. I've accepted his gracious offer. Can you spare him?"

"I don't mind," Chambers said, "if he brings you home early."

"She'll be home before you know it," Wyitt assured him. He made no effort to conceal his disappointment.

"Besides," Chambers added, grinning slyly, "she's not a girl anymore. Why should I be telling her when to get in?"

"Right," Garnet said.

"Wrong," Wyitt said. "She has the mind of a girl, a backward little girl . . ."

Shortly after, Chambers went off with his entourage, and Garnet retired to her room, put on a bathing suit and made for the pool, swam vigorously, showered, dressed in slacks and a sweater, insisted on an emergency appointment at her beauty parlor, and dashed out for a shampoo, rinse, set, manicure and a spell under a dryer. She was back at sunset and found Chambers and company had not returned. For an hour she devoted herself to business telephoning and neglected social obligations. The slips marked "Lawrence Smith—please return call" she swept into a wastebasket under her desk. Then she put on fresh underthings, including an uplift brassiere, tightened and straightened her sheer stockings, slipped on a clinging, low cut, soft red frock, and stepped into slippers with high spike heels. She carefully examined her image in a full-length mirror and thought she looked quite tall and soigné and sexy—and a bit nuts. Preparing for the undertaking had distracted her. Now her emotions rose; she would never be the same again, and things had come to a pretty pass. She was a wheedling, undignified, disgusting suppliant, not a victor but a vanquished. Even if she succeeded in trapping the professor, she would never regain her self-respect, inviolate soul or integrity . . .

Suddenly she sat down on a bench at her dressing table and wept. Tears were not the relief they should have been, for she was decked out in mascara and blue eyeshadow and a powder base and an overdose of perfume, and a lack of restraint would have made a mess of her. She had to hold tight, smiling and pretending and subduing a rightful sense of her own importance. The humiliation, the loss of an inner virtue and assurance, was awful; she couldn't conceive of what had happened to her, except for the shameful transports in bed, or how to recover her equilibrium. She was obliged to confess hers was an inferior mind. Fortunately it was single-tracked. That might save the day.

The voices of the dusty wanderers brought her up standing, and she walked out to meet them, draping a sable stole on her shoulders. They all appeared exhausted, and Junior had an air of nervous apprehension and her shoes were ruined. Although a peace between them had been concluded, she kissed Garnet's cheek tentatively; they had ceased being intimate, and Junior no longer dared to provide advice or express her fears. "You're lovelier than I've ever seen you, dear," she said. It plainly took a mustering of will to bring out the next words. "Do have a good time with A.B."

"Yeah, enjoy yourselves," Chambers said, and smiled significantly. "My back is killing me. I'm going to bed for a while."

"I'll rub it," Lagonda said.

"How do I look, Lagonda?" Garnet asked, and attempted without success to brazenly stare the enigmatic old black lady down.

"You look fine," Lagonda replied. "Kind of fancy, but fine. I guess you are fancy these days, Garnet."

"Explain that remark, please," Garnet said, reddening and raging.

456

"I got to rub your father's back," Lagonda said, and took Chambers's arm and pushed him ahead of her.

Over his shoulder, Chambers said, "Don't forget to turn up later, A.B. We've got to talk seriously tonight."

"Right you are, sir," Wyitt said. "We'll be home very early."

"Good night, dears," Junior said. "I'm going in to treat my bleeding feet and have dinner in bed." She ran a hand through her hair in a gesture of reckless despondency. "It was much nicer when his highness was an invalid."

Garnet followed Wyitt into the living room. He collapsed on the sofa and groaned. His clothing was rumpled and dirty, his trouser cuffs bulging with sand. A rim of black showed around his shirt collar. "Most of the time he walked," he said. *"Walked.* Walked and talked. We covered miles and listened to his maniacal boastings of the Villanuevas, Grandma, Cassius and Lucius. And how the second Cassius outsmarted everybody until he was fiendishly cut down by the forces of union labor and bolshevism. The return to his ancestral hardpan stimulated the old boy beyond reason. Why do I keep putting nooses around my neck?"

"Where are we going?" Garnet said.

"Why can't we just go to bed? You could rub *my* back."

"This is our last night. You agreed—"

"Very well," he interrupted. "I agreed. Let's go to dinner and a movie. I'm sure I can sleep through a couple of pictures."

She eased down beside him and took his hand. "Do you like how I look?"

"You're gorgeous. I hope that Smith fellow appreciates what I have done for you."

"I have an inspiration, A.B. Would you consider going to your house?"

"No."

"I'd love to see how you live, and I want to check on Circe. Couldn't we just put some steaks on the fire and have a salad? If any of your friends happened to be there, I'd enjoy meeting them—"

"Wait a minute," he said. "What are you leading to?"

"Nothing. I—"

"Out with it."

"Suppose I came to live with you in your house?" she said. "Legally, I mean. Fitted in. Observed all the amenities. That would constitute a public act of submission. Wouldn't it salve your pride, or spookiness, or whatever makes you want to run?"

He stared at her. "Why are you determined to marry me? I'm not worthy of you, I'm happy to say—you don't deserve me—"

"I don't know. Is it sex, the determination of the Brennans, taking the easy way out? You give the reason."

"You're the least of the Brennans, the end of the line. Do you realize that? You lack the imperial will."

"Well," she said, "I'm only a woman. I am the one serious mistake they ever made."

After unhappy consideration, Wyitt said, "Your suggestion isn't impossible. Perhaps you ought to visit Lakeland, where the deer and the antelope play. You might be surprised and cured . . . Let me call some people and then we'll take off."

While he was telephoning, Garnet slipped out and engaged in a last inspection of her enamelled beauty. Or standard appearance, anyhow. She didn't look like the same girl, and she was not—deflowered, rejected, overeager and slightly scared. But it was fun. Her past life, by contrast, struck her as dull.

In the Xanadu garage, Wyitt insisted on her taking the wheel of his convertible. He gave detailed instructions, climbed over the front seat, and lay on the rear cushion, rolling his coat under his head. "I've got to rest if I'm going to scintillate in our final evening," he said. "Don't talk, and don't play the radio. And drive carefully."

The trip on the Hollywood and Santa Ana Freeways was long and uncomfortable, and the traffic dense. At Civic Center she inched the huge, silent car through a tangle of intersecting, soaring, curving, spaghetti-tangled roads, eyeing the lighted hauteur of the Music Center and wondering whether, with Wyitt gone beyond recall, she could ever pick up where she had left off less than a month ago.

When she took the specified off-ramp in the wilds of Orange County, she had to wake Wyitt. He sat up and groaned. "Already?" he said. "I don't feel as if I'd slept five minutes . . . Straight ahead. Left at the next intersection with a signal. Lakeland revisited. Homage to Lakeland. Oh, God."

Everything looked the same: monotonous, all the buildings one or two stories in height, spangled by colored lights and defaced by signs, awash with motorcars; the camera shops, the jewelry stores, the frocks for teens, the barbers, the didy laundries, the cleaners, the auto dealers, the realtors, the doughnut shops, the pizza parlors, the medical centers, the bowling alleys, the chrome-and-plastic restaurants, the cheap furniture emporiums, the cocktail lounges, the beauty salons, the discount houses, the record sellers blaring monaural music into the hot, windy night. Wyitt became coldly loquacious. "Here we are," he said, "where you may find your spiritual home, Miss Brennan, in the avatar and exemplar of modern suburbia—where it began and from whence it will soon cover America, blotting out the curvature of the earth with its splendid, profuse, ugly, suffocating, four-wheeled, macadamized, over-crowded, healthful, energetic, misdirected and inane uniformity. The women wear tight pants, and cover the curlers in their hair with ornate mob-caps, and the men put on tight pants and white shirts to go to plants devoted to the care and feeding of computers and automated machinery that will soon put most of their contemporaries out of work and create a social system previously unknown to man and possibly inconceivable to him. Everybody is young; they all arrived here yesterday. They don't be-lieve in a divine being, but they know anything can be fixed by surgeons and psychiatrists and permissive prison wardens. They breed rapidly, diet, avoid dental caries, join in neighborhood associations, paint terrible pictures, pry into the lives of their offspring with eight-millimeter movie cameras, cheerfully accept identifying numbers from tax collectors in lieu of their names, exult in a sun stained yellow by emissions from in-dustry and internal combustion engines, and embrace a fashionable, status-seeking conservatism which is a direct denial of the principles and advances achieved by the generations ahead of them. Note the bumper stickers on the cars around us, Miss Brennan. Many of them carry signs saying 'Please, Uncle Sam, I'd rather do it myself' and 'Sup-port your local police.' Those are the Birchers and their sympathizers. They intend to impeach Chief Justice Earl Warren and keep the Negro in his place and hound the Communists into oblivion. Police, unlovely as they may be, are better than having a change or growth, and a police state is necessary to control a nation that has become an enormous, mill-ing crowd overnight. Orange County is one vast bedroom, devoted to copulation, raising children, shutting out the sane light of day, and whispering of counterrevolution. Here you will discover the latest ver-sion of the ineffable bourgeoisie, still battling untiringly for cheap re-spectability and a guaranteed safe conduct to the mortician—there are no undertakers here."

"You have the overtones of a man coming unstuck," Garnet said.

"No, that's farewell," Wyitt said. "I'm not long for this part of the world."

He was silent for several moments, sending her along a street of iden-tical houses, each lodged on a narrow lot. The front lawns were similar, the planting unobtrusive, the trees immature and sparse. Presently he said, "On your right is the junior high school; across the way the ele-mentary school. The senior high school is only two blocks off. During class hours the screams of the active, overburdened, overprivileged kids can be heard for miles. Not far away is Laguna Seca Junior College. Ev-eryone is entitled to an education which will keep him running in the

459

rat race and fit him for a calling that machines in another decade can do better and more cheaply . . . Look ahead: observe the home with ivy planted in the yard instead of grass and the struggling little cypress trees. Stop there. We've arrived."

Wyitt scrambled out of the car and held the door open for Garnet. She stopped and gazed at the house. It was low and painfully, shoddily plain, with a flat roof and a slab front door and square outlines and stucco walls and warping tongue-and-groove paneling across the street side underneath the windows. The porch light was on and a sound of recorded music wafted from inside. Her heart sank. "My neighbors," Wyitt remarked, "alerted in advance, are on the job. How do you like Model Number Two in the Lakeland Subdivision?"

"It's lovely . . ."

"I knew you'd be impressed. There are five models available for the purchaser, and prices range from eighteen thousand, three-fifty to twenty-six thousand five hundred. Model One is the basic offering; it has a single bathroom and no family room. Two has two bedrooms and two bathrooms, and an enclosed patio instead of a family room. Three has three bedrooms and two bathrooms, and an enclosed patio. Four has four bedrooms and two bathrooms, or three bedrooms and a family room, and five has four bedrooms and a family room with a toilet, or maybe it's five bedrooms and an enclosed patio and two extra toilets —I can't quite recall—at any rate, it's terribly grand. The exteriors vary from what is known as Hacienda Modern to Contemporary Traditional. You can almost tell them apart in broad daylight. For instance, Contemporary Traditional has a bricked doorway with a pointed arch, and the kitchen walls are papered. The fixtures are—"

"Thank you," Garnet said, "but I'd prefer to come back in the daytime and have you elaborate."

"Whatever you wish, Miss Brennan. Before we bought, the former Mrs. Wyitt and I went into the subject exhaustively. We looked and looked. That's why I am so well informed. Mrs. Wyitt was indefatigable."

"I'd rather not dwell on that either."

"Of course," he said. "Where was I? Oh, every buyer is furnished with a planting guide. Restrictions govern what you can put in the ground, and a Lakeland Residents Council enforces—excuse me—the ground rules. The purpose is uniformity. Nobody is empowered to take it upon himself to stand out by cultivating antisocial begonias or flowering peach trees."

"I see."

"The restrictions apply not only to obligatory grass and the height of bushes and the color of outside paint, but to other amenities—Ne-

460

groes, swimming pools, power tools that interfere with TV reception, garages converted to living quarters—"

"Hadn't we better go in?"

He nodded and smiled. "Would you care to hear how the *soidisant* Miss Calvert and I fell into profound disagreement?"

"No."

"I'll tell you anyway, Miss Brennan. It began with her referring to this as our playhouse and little dreamland. No sooner were we installed than she was planning ahead to a twenty-six five hundred number with four bedrooms and a family room and one or two extra toilets, which are called quarter-bathrooms in Lakeland. She decorated enthusiastically here, but she selected good stuff, beyond our means, which could be used without shame in a twenty-six five hundred house. She connived and politicked and was appointed to the Lakeland Residents Council. Our friends were conservative and selected with care. We had nothing to do with the jet set. There is one in Lakeland, you know."

"Is there?" Garnet said hopelessly.

"Oh, yes. But my wife thoroughly enjoyed faculty teas, meetings of the Council, supporting the local police, voting against liberal city officials, joining groups opposed to further property taxes and extensions of freeways, and those awkward hours when I put on a cap and gown and helped confer honorary degrees on ignorant tradesmen, who made long speeches, and shoved our graduates out into filling stations and wards of state institutions and typing bureaus. Miss Brennan, presently I lost it."

"Yes . . . Long ago. I realize that now."

"Good for you. My first aberration was to stop feeding the lawn and to let it die for lack of water. Then I dug it up and planted ivy. A terrible outcry arose. I resisted the demands made upon me, and nobody knew exactly what to do. Mrs. Wyitt, as a member of the Council, was placed in an untenable position. In the middle of this, I put in the cypresses and made the situation even hairier. My wife expostulated with me, resorted to harsh words, and started crying. In fact, in words I didn't know she had at her command, she called me an egotistical prick and the worst shitheel in Lakeland. I was astonished at the colorful vocabulary apparently imparted to female undergraduates at San Francisco U. Yet somehow I couldn't compel myself to withdraw. A madness had seized me, the Lakeland *cafard*. And worse is coming, Miss Brennan."

"I have no doubt."

"Negroes are quietly, almost politely turned away from our frightful enclave here," Wyitt said, "where seldom is heard an encouraging word to the underdog and the sky is smoggy all day. But a Japanese was insistent—he wasn't black, but still he was too many degrees off white, and he had no right to intrude. The guy next door—over there—a mean young man eager to get his money out, sold to Mr. Yashihara. In the view of the Council, it was treason. They endeavored to get rid of Mr. Yashihara by every means at their command, and although he's made of stern stuff, they might have succeeded if I had not left my treasured ivy and cypresses and taken up his fight. Mrs. Wyitt resigned from the Council, and also offered me her resignation. I retained my dignity and quoted Lovelace, telling her I could not love her less loved I not honor more."

"You would."

"Yes, that's true. It wasn't particularly original. And my honor was not really involved. I was just attaining my ends by indirection. I got a Jewish lawyer to help me, and we proceeded to secure Mr. Yashihara's tenancy for him. *The Lakeland Observer,* a local throwaway paper, referred to me as a 'community malcontent, beatnik inspired, and probably a Communist sympathizer.' My mouthpiece and I sued the editor for libel; the trial is pending, and I don't believe I'll go through with it. I'm tired, Miss Brennan, and you and your father haven't helped my *weltschmerz.* I accepted Mrs. Wyitt's resignation and she bugged out for San Francisco with all of the good pieces she had bought. The Board of Regents at Laguna Seca decided my conduct was deleterious to the reputation of a hitherto perfectly innocuous academic circle and asked me to go away quietly. Naturally they hated the thought of further unfortunate publicity and feared me and my galvanic, righteous attorney, but I was content with my ground cover and trees and Mr. Yashihara and let them off the hook . . . Any questions?"

"You're not a real liberal," Garnet said. "You don't actually belong with people who come in the wrong shades or are downtrodden. You haven't got enough money, power or assurance to afford the cold-turkey, meaningful gestures. I laughed at you the night at dinner when I expressed my affection for Al Washington. You turned red and bristled instinctively—you're faking these assumptions of equality."

"Yes, I thought about that afterwards. An agonizing reappraisal, I presume you could call it. The reaction was honest and involuntary, but you're mistaken as to the cause. I was jealous. He's better looking than I am, surer of himself because of you and Cham, and probably much more intelligent. I resented your preference for him . . . I'm over that now. It was just a passing fancy."

Garnet's morale improved. "Are you positive you're over the jealousy?"

"I swear it by all that's good and holy," he said, and turned quickly from her.

The front door was unlocked. Inside waited two youthful married couples, and last names were not in order—Garnet never was sure of them, or which wife, both streamlined and volatile and smiling, belonged to which vigorous, sport-shirted and slack-clad man. There was Sim (he wore glasses and had a leather holder containing pens and pencils clipped to the breast pocket of his shirt), an engineer; Bart, jocular and an accomplished dancer, district sales manager for a business machines company; Patsy, with dark hair and some preposterous costume jewelry and skintight stretch pants and an equally tight jersey top and an agreeable little bulldog face; and Jody, who had long honey-colored locks and a flawless complexion and was exceedingly pretty, in a short bolerolike shirt insecurely fastened over her firm, unconfined, upstanding bosom and hip-slung jeans of a pale yellow material which exposed her smooth abdomen and lotus navel. Wyitt instantly was hailed as "Abie" and Garnet became "Garnie," and everybody shouted odds and ends of unfinished sentences above the clamor of the music. Producing glasses of a pale liquid, Bart said to Garnie, "Just Beefeaters on the rocks. We've abandoned coloring gin with vermouth out here—it wastes time. I hope your drinking lamp is lit."

"Oh, yes, thank you," Garnie said, and swallowed and choked.

Abie apologized for his unkempt condition and went in a bathroom to shower and change his clothing. At Patsy's invitation, Garnie sat down in the cramped living room, divided from the miniscule dining room by an accordion-pleated plastic sliding curtain that would have provoked Junior's wrath, and stole glances at the eccentric furnishings which ran from a Victorian rocker to Swedish free-form and seemed to have come out of a junk shop. On the walls were numerous hooks and the remains of plate holders, and darker squares where pictures must have hung. The rear of the house was glassed and the curtains were open, disclosing a patio roofed-in with a corrugated transparent material; beyond was a lighted area of scabby lawn, a grapestake fence with portions missing, and the back of a dwelling on the next street where another gathering was in progress. The whole scene was curiously reduced in size, as if the builders had intended to make a playhouse for children, reconsidered, and not enlarged the dimensions sufficiently. On the patio, cluttered with canvas and metal chairs, was a round glass-topped table set for dinner, and a glowing, smoking hibachi. Patsy noted Garnie's inspection, and said, "It looks a little ticky-tacky at the moment. When Dottie and Abie broke up, she had a moving van come and take away the valuable stuff. These are only things the rest of us wanted to get rid of or he bought at secondhand stores. You should have seen the place when Dottie was here. Her taste is good, and she loves collecting. She had a wonderful bunch of Delft china and prints by Picasso and Degas and Chirico and everybody."

"It must have been lovely . . ." Garnie said.

The Lakelanders talked politely to her until ennui set in. Their conversation was of folk she didn't know, civic events she'd never heard of, community problems that seemed trifling, washer-dryers, schools, cars, the P.T.A., and children. The latter were particularly baffling to Garnie. They represented a separate race, evidently, and caused frightful difficulties. Patsy, Jody, Sim and Bart were all engaged in raising not only their own progeny, but participating communally in the care, feeding, education, entertaining and discipline of the whole horde of infants springing up around them. Their parenthood was the prime element in their lives, and a badge of honor. Yet, in spite of their burdens, they were offhand, amused and even resigned. A new generation didn't prevent them from living it up. Garnie learned that Jody had become mother of three in a span of four years, and Patsy had established her fruitfulness by bearing two babies in twenty-one months. "I only had one period after I got back from the hospital," she said. "Ye gods!"

"For purposes of convenience," Sim said, "I simply leave my motor running at all times."

"Me too," Bart added. "It's the only way to keep their heads in the washtubs."

"I think that angle might have contributed to Abie and Dottie blowing their biscuits," Jody commented. "She had a miscarriage, you know, a messy one, and started running like a deer. I don't believe Abie ever caught her again. The patter of little feet helps people settle in."

Presently Sim eased off to tend the fire in the hibachi, and Bart, exhibiting signs of tedium, arose to pour more drinks. Garnie declined his ministrations; the cold gin was lethal. "You'd better reload, Garnie," he admonished. "We may have to fire and fall back, and what will your dinner have to splash on?" Then he and Jody dipped their noses in the new potion, changed the tape cartridge on Abie's stereo machine with the widely detached speakers, and began dancing the jerk.

"I have the makings of a dip in the kitchen," Patsy said to Garnie. "Why not come out and help me?"

Garnie followed her to where the appliances were electric and built-in and enamelled a stylish shade of burnt umber, and watched as Patsy put canned clams and juice in a bowl, poured on sour cream and various condiments, and whipped the mixture. They tasted it with the aid of potato chips. "It's delightful," Garnie said. She was feeling a bit queasy, and shook her head when Patsy had more ice and Beefeaters.

"Have you been in California long?" Patsy asked.

"Quite a while."

"I can tell you are from the east. You have the accent. You're un-married—working?"

"Well, yes. I'm—a sort of accountant."

Patsy smiled. "Do you mind my questioning you, Garnie? You're the first girl Abie's had around since Dottie went up in smoke."

"Oh, no . . ."

"Naturally we're curious. Are you interested in him?"

"He seems nice. I don't know him very well—"

Tapping her arm for emphasis, Patsy said, "Don't be fooled by that academic jazz. Abie is a swinger. He has that quiet, insidious, helpless approach, but he's habit-forming. Watch out for him."

"I suppose I'd better."

"A swinger, Garnie. Even old Jody had a kind of a crush on him for a while, and Dottie reacted badly. Oh, it was nothing serious—at least on his part. He just isn't serious, Garnie, and he's always hurling himself once more into the breach. We have some lousy breaches here in Lakeland. He's broken his pick, and he ought to get out. I think he's going to."

"I guess he is."

"He has a job now he's mysterious about," Patsy said, "but I under-stand it's coming to an end. Do you know what it is?"

"Something in connection with civic planning, I believe."

"He should get back in a school. That suits him better. Recently he's been saucing a lot, and he didn't use to drink. If he hangs out here much longer he'll be in the jet set."

Garnie wanted to question her on that branch of Lakeland society, but quelled the impulse.

"Well," Patsy said, "I suppose we'd better serve this gook. It'll keep them from getting totaled too early . . . Garnie, do you object to my giving you a tip? That is, if you like Abie."

"Not at all."

"I see you got dressed up for tonight. I wouldn't in the future. Re-member he had Dottie, who was our leading clotheshorse and always freshly bathed and painted and dreamy—he must be tired of that and looking for something more natural. Dottie was a living knockout. I don't mean to say you're not, but—"

"I know."

"Well, there you are," Patsy said. "A word to the wise is—"

Abie entered the kitchen, in a fresh shirt and suit, his hair still damp from the shower, a drink in his hand. "Ah, Miss Brennan," he said. "I've been hunting all over for you . . . Patsy, you appear crocked. Pull yourself together. Get the steaks out of the freezer; Sim has the fire ready, and Bart is mixing the salad. I have to take Miss Brennan next door to visit my child. She's the mother."

"Oh, that bare-behinded cat," Patsy said. "He is a child to you!"

"She," Abie said. "Come, Miss Brennan."

They left by the back door and crossed the yard behind the patio. Sim and Bart were busy, and Bart called, "We have the broads, but where is the booze? I'm drying out in this Santa Ana."

"Take it easy," Abie replied. "We're having an exquisite Chilean still wine with dinner. You'll find the bottles in the kitchen closet."

He led Garnie to the back door of the next house, and they were welcomed by Yoshio Yashihara, a small, sturdy, bronzed man in slacks and a flowered sport shirt not tucked in his belt. He was a statistical analyzer at Astronautics Development Corporation (an AAC subsidiary), he mentioned, and from Hawaii. He poured more gin in Abie's glass and seemed disappointed at Garnie's refusal. Abie borrowed a spare bottle of Beefeaters from him. His kitchen was spotless. Circe lived there, in a padded teakwood box, and looked to be flourishing; she had grown, her coat was oily and shining, and she purred when Abie kissed her brick-red nose. He handed her to Garnie. "I wish Mary was here," Yoshio said. "She'll be unhappy at missing you. She's out attending a Democratic fund-raising meeting."

"Yoshio and Mary are caring for Circe until I can devote full time to her," Abie explained. "How do you find our girl, mother?"

"She's in good shape," Garnie replied. "You may yet win permanent possession of her, Professor. And Yoshio must have a way with cats."

"In the Orient," Yoshio said, "all cats are tailless. Circe makes me feel at home. Mary and I are trying to figure out how we can steal her."

Garnie returned Circe to the teakwood box and scratched her saffron belly, and Circe closed her eyes and flexed her paws; Abie said, "Well, back to the drawing board. Love to Mary, Yoshio. Why don't you come over to the rout when she gets home?"

"Alas, we have to go to bed," Yoshio said. "We can't live like Caucasians, we haven't the strength. Another time, Abie. Please bring Garnie by again."

When they were outside, Abie paused to take a deep breath and swallow gin. "The Yashiharas don't often participate in our crowd scenes," he remarked. "I can't make out whether they feel isolated and strange and the leveling processes of our democracy are not working, or only if they are decent, abstemious folk and plan to live to a ripe old age. I wish I was more extroverted for their sakes."

"Patsy says you're a swinger and may end up in the jet set."

"She should keep her fat mouth shut."

"She says you're saucing a lot and have broken your pick here," Garnie said.

"The drinking is Cham's fault," he said. "He led me into evil doing. Look, stop complaining. You want to settle down in Lakeland, don't you?"

"No," she said.

The dinner on the patio, held in a warm gritty wind, was loud and gay, matching its counterpart at the rear of the house on the next street. Everyone was on what they called their "fivesies" of gin and ice, and the bottles of wine circulated. Only Garnie toyed with her glass and was cold sober and laughed obediently and watched these peculiar outsiders wide-eyed. The talk was inevitably Lakeland oriented, and the others tended to forget her. Occasionally Abie, joining enthusiastically in the fun and tending to be flushed, took time out to regard Garnie and raise his brows in ironic interrogation. He reflected an air of satisfaction that she resented. Hope and expectation, which had sustained her during the freeway drive, was ebbing. She realized that Lakeland was quite impossible, together with its inhabitants. The odds inherent in random selection could drop dead. Her falling morale was complicated by digestive vagaries, for the steaks, hurried from the freezer onto the fire, were mushy and tasteless, and Bart's salad was too peppery. Frozen vegetables always repelled her. And she was accustomed to choice wines, not the watery, pale red, innocuous vintage that reposed in Abie's kitchen closet. But the hardy, raucous Lakelanders were high in praise of the food and fell on it voraciously. They were unflagging in their attentions to the ice cream cake that followed, and swigged coffee that Chambers would have cursed and chased down the weak stuff with raw brandy and draughts of Drambuie and a sweet Mexican liqueur fortified by cream. Garnie felt gas rising in her throat. When Jody leaned forward, which she did frequently to talk to Abie, her breasts were revealed to the nipples. Sometimes Abie would look away from them to Garnie, a hint of apology in his eyes. She could not avoid glaring at him.

The music played continuously, and Bart rose at regular intervals to choose a partner and dance. With Garnie in his arms, he abandoned the latest measures and placed one hand down on her hips and contrived to bring the other far enough around to touch her bosom; her body was crushed into his, and his groin pushed on her pelvis insistently. But the queer position didn't inhibit his dancing, and aside from the fact that he was in the process of an erection, she almost enjoyed his smooth, intricate grace. More to take her mind off his priapian advances than

467

out of curiosity, she inquired about the jet set. "They could be called the café society of Lakeland, Garnie," he said. "They're having the full life, if you know what I mean. No holds barred, constant yellow alert, and the squadrons scrambling all the time. You know what I mean? It's fun, but a little dicey, and expensive. Are you getting a trifle hot under the collar, baby? I am."

"No," Garnie said. "It's expensive, you say?"

"In more ways than one. There are divorces and fights and select drunken orgies at the country club, and whatnot. Some of the kids are hard to identify and have two or three homes in the course of getting through grade school. Naturally, talk of the jetters is out of all proportion to their true numbers. I imagine everybody feels a certain amount of envy of them. I know I do. But the sensible, staid, careful managerial class you're meeting here tonight at Abie's comprises the larger population of Lakeland. Living with us has that slow, Spanish siesta rhythm. You know? And we have an old group, too—people of forty, et cetera —they're more of a minority than the jetting types. Baby, don't you feel anything? Dancing is just another form of America's oldest indoor sport."

"No, Bart. Relax. Your motor's racing . . . Patsy says Abie might join the jet set."

"Well, he's a swinger," Bart said. "Underneath, I mean. You know? He could fit in, if he doesn't teach again. Believe me, if you don't like it, don't knock it. Those cats have their laughs. One guy has a Polaroid and takes flash pictures of the girls naked. They all carry them—call 'em their identity cards. There're no secrets in that group. Everybody can compare the fine points of the camp followers. Listen, have you heard of their latest game?"

"No."

"Darken a room. This is at the end of the evening, you know, with the boys and girls feeling playful. The husbands toss their car keys into a pile and the wives scramble for them. Whoever comes up with the keys goes home with the owner of the car. The big joke is when husbands and wives find themselves paired off."

"I see," Garnie said.

"However, sweetie," Bart said, "the odds favor the brave. They let in stags also, like old Abie. You can count on getting a change of pace sooner or later." He stopped their movements suddenly and smiled without malice, reaching for a handkerchief to mop his face. "Say, there's no use three of us standing here. Shall we sit the next one out?"

Jody danced mostly with Abie, and she was extremely willowy and bent to him with a fine ingenuity, employing the span above her long slim legs as a fulcrum. Conversing with Sim or Patsy, Garnet had to strain to avoid watching them. Bart crossed to the Yashiharas and borrowed ice, broke out the fresh gin bottle, and "sixies" and "sevensies" were commenced. Weary and impatient, Garnie surreptitiously consulted her watch. It was far earlier than she had thought. These people crowded a tremendous amount into short runs. As she settled down to wait out a chain reaction in the brave new Lakeland world, the party ended as casually as it had begun. Everyone had to go to work in the morning, minding intricate electronic devices and selling calculators and monitoring complicated, late-model children. Sim, Jody, Bart and Patsy floated hilariously away, saying what a ball it had been, embracing Garnie and Abie, telling them to play it cool, suggesting parties at their houses soon. Abie turned off lights and gathered up dishes, and Garnie peeked out a front window attempting to determine which woman went with which man; she could not be certain because of the poor quality of Lakeland street illumination and the abrupt, screeching departures of the cars. The festivities at the house behind lasted only ten minutes later, and those lights were extinguished. "This is an orderly encampment," Abie said, as Garnie helped him scrape plates and put them in the dishwasher. "The citizens keep the same hours, wear the same clothes, conceive the same babies, parrot the same thoughts, buy the same automobiles, smoke the same filter cigarettes, and go to hell in the same fashion. There's a certain sameness, as it were."

"Hurry up," she said. "I'd like to get home to my quiet asylum."

They made short work of tidying the kitchen and the patio. Just prior to darkening the house, Abie remembered to silence the tape machine. Again the wind could be heard, and the sound was comforting. Locking the front door, he said: "Hopeless, isn't it? What would you do here? You give up, don't you?"

"Almost."

"Don't be too hard on them. They're young and full of vigor. No footholds exist for them anymore. All they have is the machinery and sex and a deadening complex that may not be civilization, and they have to fight against the universal sausage factory. They're in a terrible hurry. The entire structure might end in five minutes, lit by a minor sun they've helped put together. Copulating and drinking and turning out babies helps to reassure them. Perhaps it's solider than they suspect."

"Yes, I understand. And you're less foolish than I thought."

"Thanks. I regret having to teach you this lesson, but you were just too simple. Members of the royalty don't leave their castles to dwell with the peasantry. You could never acquire a common touch. Accept your golden lot."

"All right."

"Garnie, I'm smashed once more. Do you object to driving home to the Xanadu?"

"No," said Garnet grimly. "But let's have one item settled between us. Henceforth I am not Garnie and you are not Abie. That I cannot abide."

"Yes, Miss Brennan," Wyitt said, and made unsteadily for the Cadillac and the back seat.

Junior was waiting for them in the penthouse foyer, pacing up and down, her coiffure disordered, tending to wring her hands. "Thank God you didn't stay out all night," she said. "We've had a flap, Garnet, in your absence. Chambers received a telephone call from Albert and went rushing out with Lagonda—they wouldn't tell me where they were going. I had to get them a cab. When they returned, your father was complaining of a heart attack and Lagonda was in tears and actually deserted him. She went to her room." She was compelled to pause and rein in her emotions. "I had to cope. Chambers struck me as being a victim of gas again, and not in extremis. I called Dr. Rommer. He feels nothing is wrong; he's in the recreation room with Chambers now."

"Oh, dear . . ." Garnet said, and removed the hand she had put to her breast. "That's a relief." She looked at Wyitt. Recently awakened from a sound sleep, he appeared barely able to follow the conversation. But he exhibited genuine alarm, and she was moved and relieved by that.

"Let's go see him," he said. "Doctors are always making wrong diagnoses—"

"One moment, please," Junior said. "Larry Smith is here. I have him out on the terrace studying the view. He arrived shortly after Chambers came home, and he is also in a peculiar state." She summoned more breath to get her through the crisis. "Garnet, he's demanding an explanation from you for your ignoring him these last weeks. He insists on talking to Chambers, despite my telling him Chambers is ill—"

"Father comes first," Garnet said.

She hurried into Chambers's lair, Wyitt and Junior at her heels. Her father was seated, coat and glasses off and wrinkled shirt open at the chest, glaring at Dr. Erich Rommer, an undersized, fat, imperturbable man with the half-smiling full lips and ageless rounded countenance of a Thailand deity. Music was playing loudly. Struck by the conviction that she never cared to hear any more recorded popular tunes, Garnet cut off the machine. Swiveling, Chambers shifted his glare to Junior.

470

"Why do you bring in a stupid head-shrinker when I think I'm dying?" he demanded. "Why isn't my internist here, or the heart specialist? This bastard hasn't seen a patient with his clothes off since he set up his couch. Psychosomatic, psychosomatic! Functional! He can't say anything else. He hasn't even got a stethoscope, and he thinks oxygen is for welding."

"I felt your chest," Junior replied. "Your—"

"You might as well have felt my balls," Chambers said.

"Pardon me, your grace," Junior said, with dignity. "No doubt what you mentioned are in poor condition, but your heart was steady and you were only belching. You weren't turning blue—"

"What the hell do you know about it?" Chambers said. "Since when did you become a physician? Where is Lagonda? She ran out on me!"

"She was very upset," Junior said. "I'll go get her."

"No you won't," Garnet said. "Father, stop orbiting. The more you indulge your temper, the worse you'll feel. Pay attention to me, please!"

"Okay, okay," Chambers said. Notwithstanding his discomfort and display of anger, he conveyed an impression of overriding, superior good humor. "Who cares what happens to me?"

"What do you think, Erich?" Garnet asked.

The doctor grimaced. "The usual, my dear. Self-pity, hypochondria, overindulgence in food and drink, and the same old personality lesions. His ulcer is kicking up. When I massaged his abdomen and he had voided gas, the cardiac failure was ended."

"That's all you have to do for him," Chambers said, with new bitterness. "Fart! Then you're cured. If you can't break wind, he can't handle you. The son of a bitch ought to have been a veterinary."

"I'm not going to tolerate much more of this," Garnet said.

"I want a glass of milk," Chambers said, "with a stick of bourbon in it. Will you join me, A.B.?"

"Oh, no, thank you," Wyitt said. "I—"

"I'll get it," Junior said.

"Without the bourbon," Garnet commanded.

"Nine times out of ten," Chambers said, "they pronounce it stomach trouble, and then the patient dies of heart failure. The doctor is so sorry. But not Erich. He calls it a sibling rivalry with my sister and an intensive guilt trauma. That's good enough for me to die with. Meanwhile I need therapy at fifty bucks an hour."

"You enjoy talking," Rommer said, and smiled. "In the talking, you relive those ancient woes and put them to rest. I help you to forget."

"If you weren't so Goddamned omniscient," Chambers told him, "maybe I could stand you."

"I give reassurance," Rommer said. "In my confessional you are forgiven your sins. Who could ask for more?"

"Listen to the son of a bitch!" Chambers roared.

"That's all," said Garnet, in flat accents. "Absolutely all. You are not suffering, Father, you are enjoying something now. What is it? Where did you go with Lagonda? What happened?"

Junior came in, bringing a glass of milk. Sipping it, burping luxuriously, Chambers gazed around at his auditors with reddened eyes. "Precisely what I wanted," he said. "Everything I want is going to happen if my luck holds a little longer . . . Ferris Washington, Junior, is overscrewed and overalcoholed. The old black bastard collapsed tonight. Al and I had to put him in a hospital, and he realizes the mistake he's made. As soon as he's better, we're going to have him back."

Garnet felt tears coming. "Well, that's a relief. The poor old guy—"

Her father looked at her and softened; he said, "We can't pour it on him. The prodigal's returning, so to speak. He's got to have a little dignity after this, see? And we have to work on Lagonda to accept everything. She doesn't know exactly how she feels at the moment . . . You get me?"

"Yes," Garnet said.

Junior nodded her head.

"That's what I hate most about Cham," Wyitt said sadly. "His baffling magnanimity. It's too damned much!"

"But don't worry," Chambers said, his attention still on Garnet. "About anything. Let me handle it. You follow me?"

"Yes," she said. Their glances locked. They were of the same breed, different from anybody else in the world, and tasted their kinship. She moved up and kissed him on the nose, and his Adam's apple bobbed painfully in his stringy neck and for an instant he touched her forearm. It was complete.

"Sir," Wyitt said, "I would like to go home and go to bed and have a good cry. I'm pooped. I'll be happy to check in with you tomorrow—"

"No," Chambers said. "I've got to talk to you. Stick around."

"Oh, God," Wyitt said.

"I have to see poor Larry," Garnet said. "Junior, make Father behave."

She started for the terrace, and Wyitt stopped her with an outstretched hand. "Miss Brennan," he said, "this is your opportunity. Don't blow it. Poor Larry is worried. Sympathize with him, apologize, humble yourself—if that is at all possible. Tell him I have died—I think I'm going to die—and play down the less palatable aspects—"

"Shut up," she said.

"Yes, Miss Brennan," he said, and put a palm over his eyes.

"This is a madhouse," Rommer said.

Garnet walked out on the terrace. The warm wind was blowing from the direction of Lakeland. In her thorax was an irregular thumping, and she became aware of a gaseous column ascending her throat; apparently this ran in the family. Larry Smith rose from a deck chair beside the pool and strode to her. She said, "Hello, Larry . . ." as he took both her hands. He was good-sized, and squash rackets at the Athletic Club and golf and sailing on weekends had given him solidity. He was tanned, neat and sober in attire, with crisp hair and a friendly, open face and a very low private-school voice. He never swore, he had stopped smoking cigarettes, he limited himself to two cocktails a day, and he detested untoward exhibitions of feelings and loud conversations. His idol was John Cabot Lodge, and he had worked hard for him in the preliminaries to the last Republican Convention.

"Hi," he said, and bent to kiss her forehead. "You've been avoiding me, haven't you?"

"Why, no, Larry—"

"Yes, you have. But I don't propose to embarrass you by asking why. Descending on you unannounced at this hour is bad enough. I won't be a pest, Garnet, dear. I'll be brief and businesslike. May I speak to your father? I know he isn't available except in the middle of the night."

"Well," she said, "I'm not sure you should. He's in a bad mood and claims to have had a heart attack."

"I won't trouble him much. I've just a few words to say to him—a question to put, really."

"Larry, may I inquire—"

"Of course," he said. "I want his leave to ask you to marry me."

"Oh." Garnet had to stifle and silence the hot surge in her mouth; to have belched at such a moment, even with a father like hers, would have been unforgivable. "I—I must say this is awfully sudden . . . to coin a phrase. What brought on your haste?"

"I'm afraid of losing you. It's that simple. Don't misunderstand me, though—there aren't going to be any recriminations. Whatever I've got I deserve in taking you for granted." He released her hands and she stepped back apprehensively. "Or shall we reverse the procedure, darling? Will you give me an answer right now? I put Mr. Brennan first because I appreciate and approve of how close you are, and how necessary his assent is to you."

The inspection of the San Cristobal and the dancing in Lakeland had caused Garnet's feet to hurt. They were aching miserably. In a gesture of universal defiance—and perhaps in tribute to Chambers's strange practices—she kicked off her slippers and stood on one leg and then the other and rubbed her sore insteps, which was scarcely in the romantic vein. It unnerved her to realize nobody had ever asked her before to marry him. She did the asking, and was refused . . . "I'm sorry," she said. "My feet are in awful shape. I had a date tonight and danced a lot."

"Yes, I know," he said. "Junior told me."

"There is another man, Larry—I met him not long ago. I don't quite know how to put it—"

"Don't explain. Just tell me if I have a chance."

What's more, she perceived, she had no conception of how to impart the fact that she had been sleeping with the other man. To say it outright to Larry would be like kicking an amiable dog. Yet he certainly deserved better than a fallen woman. Or the shock of having to accept a poor creature who had stooped to folly and would go on sinning if given half a chance. With an access of relief, she saw that she could not possibly accept his impulsive offer. A pure, demented happiness pervaded her. "Not a chance, Larry," she said. "You haven't got a prayer. And my father doesn't like you. He likes the other man . . . I feel badly about this. I suppose I've swindled you. If there's any way I can apologize—"

He raised a hand to his face, rubbed it across his mouth, smoothed his hair. "You can't. I'm grateful for your being frank. Goodbye, Garnet."

Turning from her, he headed into the living room, and she followed disconsolately, forgetting her slippers. The vast carpet was comforting to her soles. The marble of the foyer brought returning pains that extended up her calves. Larry pushed the button, entered the elevator through the opening doors, swung around, pushed a button inside, nodded curtly to her as the doors slid shut, and sank from her sight presumably forever. She leaned against the wall and closed her eyes. She heard footsteps, and Junior saying, "Oh, here you are, love. Where's Larry?" and opened her eyes.

"He's gone." Dr. Rommer was with Junior, and reaching for the elevator button.

"Erich says Chambers is a squalid ruin mentally," Junior said, "but otherwise in passable condition."

"I'm glad to hear it," Garnet replied.

"Garnet, is there anything I should know?" Junior said. "You seem strange—"

"No stranger than the other Brennans, by God," Garnet said, in ringing tones that brought Rommer popping back out of the elevator.

474

"Larry wanted to marry me, and I turned him down. I'm going all to pieces. I've been sleeping almost every night with Professor Wyitt, a man I have known three weeks. I think I am obsessed by sex. I proposed to him, but he won't marry me. I have lost my pride, my modesty, any sense of shame, and probably my mind."

"I'm aware of that, dear," Junior said.

Garnet gaped at her. "Oh?"

"We are all aware of it," Junior said. "Lagonda and I have been discussing the situation, and your father has taken a ribald attitude we both abhor. Albert is very concerned but calm. Erich stands ready to help. Unfortunately, Lagonda is less worldly than the rest of us, and you have given her a good deal of worry and sleepless nights." She smiled. "But your heart has been touched, eh? That will do."

"It will?" Garnet said.

Rommer put an arm about her shoulders. "It is nothing, young lady. You cannot allow this to inhibit your actions or afflict your conscience. Reaching out for contacts and satisfactions is as inevitable as the sun's rising. Perhaps the closest one can come to ultimate rapport with another being is in the sexual joining. Mores and customs alter rapidly in an expanding and profoundly changing civilization. Don't be fettered by outworn customs in realizing yourself. An act which was once bound up in foolish mysteries and tribal taboos is now scarcely more than a gesture of friendship, a momentary generosity that is exploratory, life-giving and healing. Dismiss the absurdly exaggerated significance from your thoughts. You have been friendly and honest, and you owed the adventure to yourself. The consequences, if any, are unimportant. I presume you have taken the usual precautions?"

"Well," Garnet said, "I started swallowing pills after the first night."

"Excellent," Rommer said. "But you strike me as overstimulated at the moment. We must put you to bed, dear."

He and Junior accompanied Garnet to her room, and Rommer prescribed a sodium amytal from Chambers's store. Still exuding infallibility, he disappeared. Junior helped Garnet undress, and persuaded her to swallow the capsule. "I'll tell you something silly," Garnet said. "I love him madly. I can't live without him. What am I going to do?"

"Go to sleep. We'll deal with that tomorrow."

"Somebody ought to tell this to my father. I hate to. It's a confession of weakness. But Wyitt should be made to marry me. Doesn't being betrayed mean anything anymore?"

"Don't ask me," Junior said. "It's your generation."

"It's a fine thing, that's all I can say. My father—"

"He knows, my dear. Let him cope."

"Couldn't you talk to A.B.? Appeal to his better side, if any—"

"I'll try," Junior said resignedly. "Possibly your rejection of poor old Larry will count in your favor. Or we might have Albert threaten him with something or other in the legal line. These days, though, a woman's virtue seems rather unimportant and not recoverable in court. And A.B. and Chambers are thick as thieves—you'll have a hard time infringing on that love feast—and you started it, you remember."

"Please don't harp on that."

"Another element worries me. Miss Calvert was entrancing. What if he's still in love with—"

"Oh, go away!" Garnet said.

When she was alone she cried, wondering if she wasn't in the middle of a nightmare, and the tears made the mascara run and sting her eyes. She struggled from the covers and walked blindly into the bathroom to wash her face—which in the mirror reminded her of an African mask—and returned to bed utterly spent. As she sank into a creeping, dizzying unconsciousness, Lagonda appeared, cradled Garnet's head in her arms, and whispered comforting words in her ear. Having a nurse again dispelled her fears; it was a safe regression to childhood, and she drifted off to sleep.

And she distinctly heard Lagonda say Chambers would make it all right. He was her father, and she depended on him.

A tapping on the door disturbed Garnet. She shifted and mumbled. The tapping was repeated, and she managed to sit up. Ascertaining the time on the radio clock was impossible, and she could not find the switch for the lamp. A. B. Wyitt materialized at her bedside. "I'm bagged again, Miss Brennan," he said. "For the second time in twelve hours. Your father is drinking more and enjoying it more—the milk and bourbon is now flavored with cinnamon and a dash of Pernod."

"Leave me alone," she said.

"I have to discuss an important matter with you."

"I've taken a pill. I can't think . . ."

"Try hard," he said. "I've recommended to Cham that he give the ranch to Los Angeles County for a park. Heaven knows the megalopolis needs a few of them. It's a magnificent, princely *beau geste,* worthy of a nut like your father. We've been discussing the move for two weeks. Today at lunch I attempted to give you the details and you wouldn't listen. You were only interested in your tawdry romance."

Her spine had stiffened and she was looking at him wildly.

"I have been to the Regional Planning Commission and the County Parks and Recreation Commission," he continued. "The final approval would be up to the Board of Supervisors. But there's no doubt of any-body's decision—except yours. One woman official cried, and the mayor hugged me. Cham's name is now mentioned in the same breath with those of our Savior and General Eisenhower. There are people who say it will put the Music Center and the new Art Museum in the shade and ennoble the Brennans forever. This is their town, you know, and the time may have come to pay the Queen in full. The blessings of future generations, starved for a place to picnic and make love and simply be alone, could ring in the ears of your progeny forever. It should be a reasonably wild park, a real Spanish rancho, unchanged and unchang-ing. It—"

"Wh-why my decision?" she asked.

"Let me finish. Cham promised Grandpa to keep the San Cristobal. Grandma was also set on its remaining in the family. It is the good luck charm of the Brennans. If it goes to the city and county, perhaps Cham has kept his oath. After all, he is giving it away, not selling it. And it becomes the possession of everybody and remains intact. Grandpa could gather his ashes from the city and go see it as it was, and Grandma could come back and never know the Villanuevas had been dispos-sessed. Cham thinks that might preserve his good fortune and the suc-cession of his line. That expert in divination, Lagonda, is positive he can't do anything else and still appease the gods. Albert wants a bit of country where Negroes can shake off the grime of housing developments and slums. Junior feels the Brennans can acquire the stature of eastern seaboard potentates by this; it satisfies her deepest intimations of ele-gant snobbery. The Baltims, Junior and Senior, were at first shocked and then full of mounting approbation, mostly for the reason that the second Baltim was devoted to your mother and believes it would constitute a worthy memorial to her. Old Mr. Burton Lely, who has been searching for a sign of common decency in your breed for going on a century, suspects he has at last seen the light. I talked to Irving Shapiro at the Hillcrest Country Club, and to begin with he nearly choked on his her-ring in sour cream; but gradually the idea of enlightened munificence seized him, and he came over to my side with his tribe. He says the conception of public service is sweeping a city which has finally arrived; he thinks the Queen can become a modern Athens."

"You're very efficient in an underhanded way."

"My idealism is generally admired. I'm a new breed of outsider, giving rather than taking. Aaron Eindhoven said as much when I talked on the phone to him in New York. He supports the proposition. It's only money, he said, and everyone should fluff out his own nest; the town and the park will be here when the money's gone. Harry Sego lost his temper, regained it, remembered what Cham and the Queen had done for him, and decided Cham's instincts were always right. Tom Sego was delighted and offered to work gratis on plans for beautifying the San Cristobal . . . Have I taken care of everybody?"

"Everybody but me. I'm the last to hear. Why is my vote important?"

"Because Cham won't give away your inheritance without your consent," he said. "If you are determined to have the ranch for your own purpose, then you may have it. I'm his emissary. What's your answer?"

There was a long silence. Garnet rubbed her burning eyes, which watered profusely. She sighed. "All right," she said.

He cleared his throat. "No stipulations? I'm referring to my own fair white body—"

"Well, don't. There are no stipulations."

"You're not a real Brennan. I could tell that all along."

"Don't be fooled," she said. "I'm a real one."

"Junior says you discarded Larry Smith."

"Yes."

"Why?"

"Why do you suppose?"

"Try not to be irritable in your hour of triumph," he said. "Cham tells me I have no right to lay you and then just take flight. It makes you out a bad lay. He has not himself had a lay in years, but he may attempt one soon . . . Don't ask me to untangle his reasoning for you. The dirty old bastard put his arms around me and wept and said he wished I could be his son—or that he could have a son of mine. You can count on him."

"Good Lord . . ."

He groaned. "Well, the chances of escape were infinitesimal anyhow, from the first day. I might have evaded you, but not him . . ."

She lay down and turned over. A great happiness filled her. "What are you doing?"

"Taking off my clothes. Surprised?"

"No. But glad."

Afterward, when he had snuggled in beside her and had an arm around her middle, he said, "I hope you'll be terribly happy. I don't know about me . . . lodged among the Brennans . . ."

"I'll do all I can to—"

"No sentiment, please. I'll do my best, too."

Garnet seemed to acquire a spectral size and authority, and an ancestral note invaded her voice. "You've cost me fifty million," she said, "and you damned well better do your best!"